I've been fascinated by the paranormal for as long as I can remember. And I've been an animal lover for just as long, with a particular interest in canines. Put those two together, and perhaps it's not surprising that werewolves are my favorite supernatural creature.

Still, *Bitten* came to me in a roundabout way. I was watching the first season of *The X-Files*. It was their werewolf episode, with your typical hairy man-eating monster. While I enjoyed it, I thought, "That's not how I'd do werewolves." There was nothing wrong with the interpretation—it certainly fits a lot of the folklore—but it didn't speak to my own interest in werewolves. What fascinated me was the idea of being not part-monster, but part-wolf. What would it be like to carry those wolf instincts inside you, even in human form? How would it change your behavior? Your way of seeing the world?

I decided to write a story that would let me explore the "wolf" in "werewolf." Rather than crazed two-legged beasts driven by the full moon, these characters could change into actual wolves. They would be people for whom "the animal within" was a very real part of their daily lives. That story is *Bitten*, which gave rise to the Women of the Otherworld series, including subsequent werewolf stories, *Stolen* and *Beginnings*, which are included in this omnibus. Enjoy!

Kelley Armstrong

Books by Kelley Armstrong

WEREWOLVES

KELLEY ARMSTRONG

VINTAGE CANADA

For Jeff

VINTAGE CANADA EDITION, 2012

Author's note copyright © 2012 K.L.A. Fricke Inc.
Bitten copyright © 2001 K.L.A. Fricke Inc.
Stolen copyright © 2002 K.L.A. Fricke Inc.
Beginnings copyright © 2010 K.L.A. Fricke Inc.

Published in Canada by Vintage Canada, a division of Random House of Canada Limited, Toronto, in 2012. *Bitten* was originally published in hardcover in Canada by Random House Canada, a division of Random House of Canada Limited, in 2001. *Stolen* was originally published in hardcover in Canada by Random House Canada in 2002. *Beginnings* was first published in *Tales of the Otherworld* in Canada by Random House Canada in 2010. Distributed by Random House of Canada Limited.

Vintage Canada with colophon is a registered trademark.

www.randomhouse.ca

LIBRARY AND ARCHIVES CANADA CATALOGUING IN PUBLICATION

Armstrong, Kelley
Werewolves : Bitten, Stolen and Beginnings / Kelley Armstrong.

(Women of the otherworld)
Contents: Bitten—Stolen—Beginnings.
Also issued in electronic format.

ISBN 978-0-307-36290-2 (bk. 1)

I. Title. II. Series: Armstrong, Kelley. Women of the Otherworld.

PS8551.R7637W47 2012   C813'.6   C2012-901864-3

Text and cover design by Terri Nimmo
Cover image: © William Attard Mccarthy | Dreamstime.com

Printed and bound in the United States of America

2 4 6 8 9 7 5 3 1

Contents

Bitten

PROLOGUE

I have to.

I've been fighting it all night. I'm going to lose. My battle is as futile as a woman feeling the first pangs of labor and deciding it's an inconvenient time to give birth. Nature wins out. It always does.

It's nearly two A.M., too late for this foolishness and I need my sleep. Four nights spent cramming to meet a deadline have left me exhausted. It doesn't matter. Patches of skin behind my knees and elbows have been tingling and now begin to burn. My heart beats so fast I have to gulp air. I clench my eyes shut, willing the sensations to stop but they don't.

Philip is sleeping beside me. He's another reason why I shouldn't leave, sneaking out in the middle of the night again and returning with a torrent of lame excuses. He's working late tomorrow. If I can just wait one more day. My temples begin to throb. The burning sensation in my skin spreads down my arms and legs. The rage forms a tight ball in my gut and threatens to explode.

I've got to get out of here—I don't have a lot of time left.

Philip doesn't stir when I slip from the bed. There's a pile of clothing tucked underneath my dresser so I won't risk the squeaks and groans of opening drawers and closets. I pick up my keys, clasping my fist around them so they don't jangle, ease open the door, and creep into the hallway.

Everything's quiet. The lights seem dimmed, as if overpowered by the emptiness. When I push the elevator button, it creaks out a complaint at being disturbed at so ungodly an hour. The first floor and lobby are equally empty. People who can afford the rent this close to downtown Toronto are comfortably asleep by this time.

My legs itch as well as hurt and I curl my toes to see if the itching stops. It doesn't. I look down at the car keys in my hand. It's too late to drive to a safe place—the itching has crystallized into a sharp burn. Keys in my pocket, I stride onto the streets, looking for a quiet place to Change. As I walk, I monitor the sensation in my legs, tracing its passage to my arms

3

and the back of my neck. Soon. Soon. When my scalp starts to tingle, I know I have walked as far as I can so I search for an alley. The first one I find has been claimed by two men squeezed together inside a tattered big-screen TV box. The next alley is empty. I hurry to the end and undress quickly behind a barricade of trash bins, hide the clothes under an old newspaper. Then I start the Change.

My skin stretches. The sensation deepens and I try to block the pain. Pain. What a trivial word—agony is better. One doesn't call the sensation of being flayed alive "painful." I inhale deeply and focus my attention on the Change, dropping to the ground before I'm doubled over and forced down. It's never easy—perhaps I'm still too human. In the struggle to keep my thoughts straight, I try to anticipate each phase and move my body into position—head down, on all fours, arms and legs straight, feet and hands flexed, and back arched. My leg muscles knot and convulse. I gasp and strain to relax. Sweat breaks out, pouring off me in streams, but the muscles finally relent and untwist themselves. Next comes the ten seconds of hell that used to make me swear I'd rather die than endure this again. Then it's over.

Changed.

I stretch and blink. When I look around, the world has mutated to an array of colors unknown to the human eye, blacks and browns and grays with subtle shadings that my brain still converts to blues and greens and reds. I lift my nose and inhale. With the Change, my already keen senses sharpen even more. I pick up scents of fresh asphalt and rotting tomatoes and window-pot mums and day-old sweat and a million other things, mixing together in an odor so overwhelming I cough and shake my head. As I turn, I catch distorted fragments of my reflection in a dented trash can. My eyes stare back at me. I curl my lips back and snarl at myself. White fangs flash in the metal.

I am a wolf, a 130-pound wolf with pale blond fur. The only part of me that remains are my eyes, sparking with a cold intelligence and a simmering ferocity that could never be mistaken for anything but human.

I look around, inhaling the scents of the city again. I'm nervous here. It's too close, too confined; it reeks of human spoor. I must be careful. If I'm seen, I'll be mistaken for a dog, a large mixed breed, perhaps a husky and yellow Labrador mix. But even a dog my size is cause for alarm when it's running loose. I head for the back of the laneway and seek a path through the underbelly of the city.

My brain is dulled, disoriented not by my change of form but by the unnaturalness of my surroundings. I can't get my bearings and the first alley I go down turns out to be the one I'd encountered in human form, the one with the two men in the faded Sony box. One of them is awake now. He's tugging the remnants of a filth-encrusted blanket between his fingers as if he can stretch it large enough to cover himself against the cold October night. He looks up and sees me. His eyes widen. He starts to shrink back, then stops himself. He says something. His voice is crooning, the musical, exaggerated tones people use with infants and animals. If I concentrated, I could make out the words, but there's no point. I know what he's saying, some variation of "nice doggy," repeated over and over in a variety of inflections. His hands are outstretched, palms out to ward me off, the physical language contradicting the vocal. Stay back—nice doggy—stay back. And people wonder why animals don't understand them.

I can smell the neglect and waste rising from his body. It smells like weakness, like an aged deer driven to the fringe of the herd, prime pickings for predators. If I were hungry, he'd smell like dinner. Fortunately, I'm not hungry yet, so I don't have to deal with the temptation, the conflict, the revulsion. I snort, condensation trumpeting from my nostrils, then turn and lope back up the alley.

Ahead is a Vietnamese restaurant. The smell of food is embedded in the very wood frame of the building. On a rear addition, an exhaust fan turns slowly, clicking with each revolution as one blade catches the metal screen casing. Below the fan a window is open. Faded sunflower-print curtains billow out in the night breeze. I can hear people inside, a room full of people, grunting and whistling in sleep. I want to see them. I want to stick my muzzle in the open window and look inside. A werewolf can have a lot of fun with a roomful of unprotected people.

I start to creep forward but a sudden crackle and hiss stops me. The hiss softens, then is drowned out by a man's voice, sharp, his words snapped off like icicles. I turn my head each way, radar searching for the source. He's farther down the street. I abandon the restaurant and go to him. We are curious by nature.

He's standing in a three-car parking lot wedged at the end of a narrow passage between buildings. He holds a walkie-talkie to his ear and leans one elbow against a brick wall, casual but not resting. His shoulders are relaxed. His gaze goes nowhere. He is confident in his place, that he has a right to be here and little to fear from the night. The gun dangling from his belt probably helps. He stops talking, jabs a button, and slams the walkie-talkie into its holster. His eyes scan the parking lot once, taking inventory and seeing nothing requiring his attention. Then he heads deeper into the alley maze. This could be amusing. I follow.

My nails click against the pavement. He doesn't notice. I pick up speed, darting around trash bags and empty boxes. Finally, I'm close enough. He hears the steady clicking behind him and stops. I duck behind a Dumpster, peer around the corner. He turns and squints into the darkness. After a second he starts forward. I let him get a few steps away, then resume the pursuit. This time when he stops, I wait one extra second before diving for cover. He lets out a muffled oath. He's seen something—a flash of motion, a shadow flickering, something. His right hand slips to his gun, caressing the metal, then pulling back, as if the reassurance is enough. He hesitates, then looks up and down the alley, realizing he is alone and uncertain what to do about it. He mutters something, then continues walking, quicker this time.

As he walks, his eyes flick from side to side, wariness treading the border of alarm. I inhale deeply, picking up only wisps of fear, enough to make my heart pound, but not enough to send my brain spinning out of control. He's safe quarry for a stalking game. He won't run. I can suppress most of my instincts. I can stalk him without killing him. I can suffer the first pangs of hunger without killing him. I can watch him pull his gun without killing him. Yet if he runs, I won't be able to stop myself. That's a temptation I can't fight. If he runs, I *will* chase. If I chase, either he'll kill me or I'll kill him.

As he turns the corner down a connecting alley, he relaxes. All has been silent behind him. I creep from my hiding place, shifting my weight to the back of my foot pads to muffle the sound of my nails. Soon I am only a few feet behind him. I can smell his aftershave, almost masking the natural scent of a long day's work. I can see his white socks appearing and disappearing between his shoes and pant legs. I can hear his breathing, the slight elevation in tempo betraying the fact that he's walking faster than usual. I ease forward, coming close enough that I could lunge if I wanted to and knock him to the ground before he even thought to reach for his gun. His head jerks up. He knows I'm there. He knows *something* is there. I wonder if he will turn. Does he dare to look, to face something he can't see or hear, but can only sense? His hand slides to his gun, but he doesn't turn. He walks faster. Then he swings back to the safety of the street.

I follow him to the end and observe from the darkness. He strides forward, keys in hand, to a parked cruiser, unlocks it, and hops inside. The car roars and squeals from the curb. I watch the receding taillights and sigh. Game over. I won.

That was nice but it wasn't nearly enough to satisfy me. These city backstreets are too confining. My heart is thudding with unspent excitement. My legs are aching with built-up energy. I must *run*.

A wind gusts from the south, bringing the sharp tang of Lake Ontario with it. I think of heading to the beach, imagine running along the stretch of sand, feeling the icy water slapping against my paws, but it's not safe. If I want to run, I must go to the ravine. It's a long way, but I have little choice unless I plan to skulk around human-smelling alleyways for the rest of the night. I swing to the northwest and begin the journey.

Nearly a half hour later, I'm standing at the crest of a hill. My nose twitches, picking up the vestiges of an illegal leaf fire smoldering in a nearby yard. The wind bristles through my fur, chill, nearly cold, invigorating. Above me, traffic thunders across the overpass. Below is sanctuary, a perfect oasis in the middle of the city. I leap forward, throwing myself off. At last I'm running.

My legs pick up the rhythm before I'm halfway down the ravine. I close my eyes for a second and feel the wind slice across my muzzle. As my paws thump against the hard earth, tiny darts of pain shoot up my legs, but they make me feel alive, like jolting awake after an overlong sleep. The muscles contract and extend in perfect harmony. With each stretch comes an ache and a burst of physical joy. My body is thanking me for the exercise, rewarding me with jolts of near-narcotic adrenaline. The more I run, the lighter I feel, the pain falling free as if my paws are no longer striking the ground. Even as I race along the bottom of the ravine, I feel like I'm still running downhill, gaining energy instead of expending it. I want to run until all the tension in my body flies away, leaving nothing but the sensations of the moment. I couldn't stop if I wanted to. And I don't want to.

Dead leaves crackle under my paws. Somewhere in the forest an owl hoots softly. It has finished its hunting and rests contented, not caring who knows it's around. A rabbit bolts out of a thicket and halfway across my path, then realizes its mistake and zooms back into the undergrowth. I keep running. My heart pounds. Against my rising body heat, the air feels ice-cold, stinging as it storms through my nostrils and into my lungs. I inhale, savoring the shock of it hitting my insides. I'm running too fast to smell anything. Bits of scents flutter through my brain in a jumbled montage that smells of freedom. Unable to resist, I finally skid to a halt, throw my head back, and howl. The music pours up from my chest in a tangible evocation of pure joy. It echoes through the ravine and soars to the moonless sky, letting them all know I'm here. I own this place! When I'm done, I drop my head, panting with exertion. I'm standing there, staring down into a scattering of yellow and red maple leaves, when a sound pierces my self-absorption. It's a growl, a soft, menacing growl. There's a pretender to my throne.

I look up to see a brownish yellow dog standing a few meters away. No, not a dog. My brain takes a second, but it finally recognizes the animal. A coyote. The recognition takes a second because it's unexpected. I've heard there are coyotes in the city, but have never encountered one. The coyote is equally confused. Animals don't know what to make of me. They smell human, but see wolf and, just when they decide their nose is tricking them, they look into my eyes and see human. When I encounter dogs, they either attack or turn tail and run. The coyote does neither. It lifts its muzzle and sniffs the air, then bristles and pulls its lips back in a drawn-out growl. It's half my size, scarcely worth my notice. I let it know this with a lazy "get lost" growl and a shake of my head. The coyote doesn't move. I stare at it. The coyote breaks the gaze-lock first.

I snort, toss my head again, and slowly turn away. I'm halfway turned when a flash of brown fur leaps at my shoulder. Diving to the side, I roll out of the way, then scramble to my feet. The coyote snarls. I give a serious growl, a canine "now you're pissing me off." The coyote stands its ground. It wants a fight. Good.

My fur rises on end, my tail bushing out behind me. I lower my head between my shoulder bones and lay my ears flat. My lips pull back and I feel the snarl tickling up through my throat then reverberating into the night. The coyote doesn't back down. I crouch and I'm about to lunge when something hits me hard in the shoulder, throwing me off balance. I stumble, then twist to face my attacker. A second coyote, gray-brown, hangs from my shoulder, fangs sunk to the bone. With a roar of rage and pain, I buck up and throw my weight to the side.

As the second coyote flies free, the first launches itself at my face. Ducking my head, I catch it in the throat, but my teeth clamp down on fur instead of flesh and it squirms away. It tries to back off for a second lunge, but I leap at it, backing it into a tree. It rears up, trying to get out of my way. I slash for its throat. This time I get my grip. Blood spurts in my mouth, salty and thick. The coyote's mate lands on my back. My legs buckle. Teeth sink into the loose skin beneath my skull. Fresh pain arcs through me. Concentrating hard, I keep my grip on the first coyote's throat. I steady myself, then release it for a split second, just long enough to make the fatal slash and tear. As I pull back, blood sprays into my eyes, blinding me. I swing my head hard, ripping out the coyote's throat. Once I feel it go limp, I toss it aside, then throw myself on the ground and roll over. The coyote on my back yips in surprise and releases its hold. I jump up and turn in the same motion, ready to take this other animal out of the game, but it scrambles up and dives into the brush. With a flash of wire-brush tail, it's gone. I look at the dead coyote.

Blood streams from its throat, eagerly lapped up by the dry earth below. A tremor runs through me, like the final shudder of sated lust. I close my eyes and shiver. Not my fault. They attacked me first. The ravine has gone quiet, echoing the calm that floods through me. Not so much as a cricket chirps. The world is dark and silent and sleeping.

I try to examine and clean my wounds, but they are out of reach. I stretch and assess the pain. Two deep cuts, both bleeding only enough to mat my fur. I'll live. I turn and start the trip out of the ravine.

In the alley I Change then yank my clothes on and scurry to the sidewalk like a junkie caught shooting up in the shadows. Frustration fills me. It shouldn't end like this, dirty and furtive, amidst the garbage and filth of the city. It should end in a clearing in the forest, clothes abandoned in some thicket, stretched out naked, feeling the coolness of the earth beneath me and the night breeze tickling my bare skin. I should be falling asleep in the grass, exhausted beyond all thought, with only the miasma of contentedness floating through my mind. And I shouldn't be alone. In my mind, I can see the others, lying around me in the grass. I can hear the familiar snores, the occasional whisper and laugh. I can feel warm skin against mine, a bare foot hooked over my calf, twitching in a dream of running. I can smell them: their sweat, their breath, mingling with the scent of blood, smears from a deer killed in the chase. The image shatters and I am staring into a shopwindow, seeing nothing but myself reflected back. My chest tightens in a loneliness so deep and so complete I can't breathe.

I turn quickly and lash out at the nearest object. A streetlamp quavers and rings with the blow. Pain sears down my arm. Welcome to reality— changing in alleyways and creeping back to my apartment. I am cursed to live between worlds. On the one side there is normalcy. On the other, there is a place where I can be what I am with no fear of reprisals, where I can commit murder itself and scarcely raise the eyebrows of those around me, where I am even encouraged to do so to protect the sanctity of that world. But I left and I can't return. I won't return.

As I walk to the apartment, my anger blisters the pavement with every step. A woman curled up under a pile of dirty blankets peers out as I pass and instinctively shrinks back into her nest. As I round the corner, two men step out and size up my prospects as prey. I resist the urge to snarl at them, but just barely. I walk faster and they seem to decide I'm not worth chasing. I shouldn't be here. I should be home in bed, not prowling downtown Toronto at four A.M. A normal woman wouldn't be here. It's yet another reminder that I'm not normal. Not normal. I look down the darkened street and I can read a billet on a telephone post fifty feet off. Not normal. I catch a whiff of fresh bread from a bakery starting production miles away. Not normal. I stop by a storefront, grab a bar over the windows, and flex my biceps. The metal groans in my hand. Not normal. Not normal. I chant the words in my head, flagellating myself with them. The anger only grows.

Outside my apartment door, I stop and inhale deeply. I mustn't wake Philip. And if I do, I mustn't let him see me like this. I don't need a mirror to know what I look like: skin taut, color high, eyes incandescent with the rage that always seems to follow a Change now. Definitely not normal.

When I finally enter the apartment, I hear his measured breathing from the bedroom. Still asleep. I'm nearly to the bathroom when his breathing catches.

"Elena?" His voice is a sleep-stuffed croak.

"Just going to the washroom."

I try to slip past the doorway, but he's sitting up, peering nearsightedly at me. He frowns.

"Fully dressed?" he says.

"I went out."

A moment of silence. He runs a hand through his dark hair and sighs. "It's not safe. Damn it, Elena. We've discussed this. Wake me up and I'll go with you."

"I need to be alone. To think."

"It's not safe."

"I know. I'm sorry."

I creep into the bathroom, spending longer than necessary. I pretend to use the toilet, wash my hands with enough water to fill a Jacuzzi, then find a fingernail that needs elaborate filing attention. When I finally decide Philip has fallen back asleep, I head for the bedroom. The bedside lamp is on. He's propped on his pillow, glasses in place. I hesitate in the doorway. I can't bring myself to cross the threshold, to go and crawl into bed with him. I hate myself for it, but I can't do it. The memory of the night lingers and I feel out of place here.

When I don't move, Philip shifts his legs over the side of the bed and sits up.

"I didn't mean to snap," he says. "I worry. I know you need your freedom and I'm trying—"

He stops and rubs his hand across his mouth. His words slice through me. I know he doesn't mean them as a reprimand, but they are a reminder that I'm screwing this up, that I'm fortunate to have found someone as patient and understanding as Philip, but I'm wearing through that patience at breakneck speed and all I seem capable of doing is standing back and waiting for the final crash.

"I know you need your freedom," he says again. "But there has to be some other way. Maybe you could go out in the morning, early. If you prefer night, we could drive down to the lake. You could walk around. I could sit in the car and keep an eye on you. Maybe I could walk with you. Stay twenty paces behind or something." He manages a wry smile. "Or maybe not. I'd probably get picked up by the cops, the middle-aged guy stalking the beautiful young blond."

He pauses, then leans forward. "That's your cue, Elena. You're supposed to remind me that forty-one is far from middle-aged."

"We'll work something out," I say.

We can't, of course. I have to run under the cover of night and I have to do it alone. There is no compromise.

As he sits on the edge of the bed, watching me, I know we're doomed. My only hope is to make this relationship so otherwise perfect that Philip might come to overlook our one insurmountable problem. To do that, my first step should be to go to him, crawl in bed, kiss him, and tell him I love him. But I can't. Not tonight. Tonight I'm something else, something he doesn't know and couldn't understand. I don't want to go to him like this.

"I'm not tired," I say. "I might as well stay up. Do you want breakfast?"

He looks at me. Something in his expression falters and I know I've failed—again. But he doesn't say anything. He pulls his smile back in place. "Let's go out. Someplace in this city has to be open this early. We'll drive around until we find it. Drink five cups of coffee and watch the sun come up. Okay?"

I nod, not trusting myself to speak.

"Shower first?" he says. "Or flip for it?"

"You go ahead."

He kisses my cheek as he passes. I wait until I hear the shower running, then head for the kitchen.

Sometimes I get so hungry.

Chapter 1

Human

I stood at the door before ringing the bell. It was Mother's Day and I was standing at a door holding a present, which would have been quite normal if it was a present for my mother. But my mother was long dead and I didn't keep in touch with any of my foster mothers, let alone bring them gifts. The present was for Philip's mother. Again, this would have been very normal if Philip had been there with me. He wasn't. He'd called from his office an hour ago to say he couldn't get away. Did I want to go alone? Or would I rather wait for him? I'd opted to go and now stood there wondering if that was the right decision. Did a woman visit her boyfriend's mother on Mother's Day without said boyfriend? Maybe I was trying too hard. It wouldn't be the first time.

Human rules confounded me. It wasn't as if I'd been raised in a cave. Before I became a werewolf, I'd already learned the basic mechanics: how to hail a taxi, operate an elevator, apply for a bank account, all the minutiae of human life. The problem came with human interactions. My childhood had been pretty screwed up. Then, when I'd been on the cusp of becoming an adult, I'd been bitten and spent the next nine years of my life with other werewolves. Even during those years, I hadn't been locked away from the human world. I'd gone back to university, traveled with the others, even taken on jobs. But they'd always been there, for support and protection and companionship. I hadn't needed to make it on my own. I hadn't needed to make friends or take lovers or go to lunch with coworkers. So, I hadn't. Last year, when I broke with the others and came back to Toronto alone, I thought fitting in would be the least of my concerns. How tough could it be? I'd just take the basics I'd learned from childhood, mix in the adult conversational skills I'd learned with the others, toss in a dash of caution and voilà, I'd be making friends and chatting up new acquaintances in no time. Hah!

Was it too late to leave? I didn't want to leave. Taking a deep breath, I rang the doorbell. Moments later, a flurry of footsteps erupted inside. Then a round-faced woman with graying brown hair answered.

"Elena!" Diane said, throwing the door open. "Mom, Elena's here. Is Philip parking the car? I can't believe how packed the street is. Everyone out visiting."

"Actually, Philip's not—uh—with me. He had to work, but he'll be along soon."

"Working? On a Sunday? Have a talk with him, girl." Diane braced the door open. "Come in, come in. Everyone's here."

Philip's mother, Anne, appeared from behind his sister. She was tiny, not even reaching my chin, with a sleek iron gray pageboy.

"Still ringing the doorbell, dear?" she said, reaching up to hug me. "Only salesmen ring the bell. Family walks right in."

"Philip will be late," Diane said. "He's working."

Anne made a noise in her throat and ushered me inside. Philip's father, Larry, was in the kitchen pilfering pastries from a tray.

"Those are for dessert, Larry," Anne said, shooing him away.

Larry greeted me with a one-armed hug, the other hand still clutching a brownie. "So where's—"

"Late," Diane said. "Working. Come into the living room, Elena. Mom invited the neighbors, Sally and Juan, for lunch." Her voice lowered to a whisper. "Their kids are all out west." She pushed open the French doors. "Before you got here, Mom was showing them your last few articles in *Focus Toronto*."

"Uh-oh. Is that good or bad?"

"Don't worry. They're staunch Liberals. They loved your stuff. Oh, here we are. Sally, Juan, this is Elena Michaels, Philip's girlfriend."

Philip's girlfriend. That always sounded odd, not because I objected to being called a "girlfriend" instead of "partner" or anything as ridiculously politically correct. It struck me because it'd been years since I'd been anyone's girlfriend. I didn't do relationships. For me, if it lasted the weekend, it was getting too serious. My one and only lengthy relationship had been a disaster. More than a disaster. Catastrophic.

Philip was different.

I'd met Philip a few weeks after I'd moved back to Toronto. He'd been living in an apartment a few blocks away. Since our buildings shared a property manager, tenants in his complex had access to the health club in mine. He'd come to the pool one day after midnight and, finding me alone swimming laps, he'd asked if I minded if he did some, as if I had the right to kick him out. Over the next month, we'd often found ourselves alone in the health club late at night. Each time, he'd checked to make sure I was comfortable being alone there with him. Finally, I'd said that the reason I was working out in the health club was to ensure I didn't need to worry about being attacked by strange men and I'd be defeating the whole purpose if I was nervous about having him there. That had made him laugh and he'd lingered after his workout and bought me a juice from the vending machine. Once the postworkout juice break became a habit, he worked his way up the meal chain with invitations to coffee, then lunch, then dinner. By the time we got around to breakfast, it was nearly six months from the day we'd met in the pool. That might have been part of the reason I let myself fall for him, flattered that anyone would put that amount of time and effort into getting to know me. Philip wooed me with all the patience of someone trying to coax a half-wild animal into the house and, like many a stray, I found myself domesticated before I thought to resist.

All had gone well until he'd suggested we move in together. I should have said no. But I hadn't. Part of me couldn't resist the challenge of seeing whether I could pull it off. Another part of me had been afraid of losing him if I refused. The first month had been a disaster. Then, just when I'd been sure the bubble was ready to burst, the pressure eased. I forced myself to postpone my Changes longer, allowing me to run when Philip was away on overnight business trips or working late. Of course, I can't take all the credit for saving the relationship. Hell, I'd be pushing it if I took half. Even after we moved in together, Philip was as patient as he'd been when we were dating. When I did something that would raise most human eyebrows, Philip brushed it off with a joke. When I was overwhelmed by the stress of fitting in, he took me to dinner or a show, getting my mind off my problems, letting me know he was there if I wanted to talk, and understanding if I didn't. At first I thought it was too good to be true. Every day I'd come home from work, pause outside the apartment door, and brace myself to open it and find him gone. But he didn't leave. A few weeks ago he'd begun talking about finding us a bigger place when my lease was up, even hinting that a condo might be a wise investment. A condo. Wow. That was almost semi-permanent, wasn't it? A week later and I was still in shock—but it was a good sort of shock.

It was mid-afternoon. The neighbors were gone. Diane's husband, Ken, had left early to take their youngest to work. Philip's other sister, Judith, lived in the U.K. and had to settle for a Mother's Day phone call, phoning after lunch and speaking to everyone, including me. Like all of Philip's family, she treated me as if I were a sister-in-law instead of her brother's girlfriend-of-the-hour. They were all so friendly, so ready to accept me that I had a hard time believing they weren't just being polite. It was possible they really did like me but, having had rotten luck with families, I was reluctant to believe it. I wanted it too much.

As we were washing dishes, the telephone rang. Anne answered it in the living room. A few minutes later, she came and got me. It was Philip.

"I am so sorry, hon," he said when I answered. "Is Mom mad?"

"I don't think so."

"Good. I promised to take her to dinner another time to make up for it."

"So are you coming over?"

He sighed. "I'm not going to make it. Diane'll give you a ride home."

"Oh, that's not necessary. I can take a cab or the—"

"Too late," he said. "I already told Mom to ask Diane. They won't let you out of that house without an escort now." He paused. "I really didn't mean to abandon you. Are you surviving?"

"Very well. Everyone's great, as always."

"Good. I'll be home by seven. Don't make anything. I'll pick up. Caribbean?"

"You hate Caribbean."

"I'm doing penance. See you at seven, then. Love you."

He hung up before I could argue.

"You should have seen the dresses," Diane was saying as she drove to my apartment. "God-awful. Like bags with armholes. Designers must figure by the time women need a mother-of-the-bride dress they don't give a damn what they look like. I found this one gorgeous navy number, probably meant for the father-of-the-bride's new young wife, but the middle was tight. I thought about crash dieting to fit, but I won't do it. It's a matter of principle. I've had three kids, I earned this belly."

"There's got to be better stuff out there," I said. "Have you tried the non-bridal shops?"

"That's my next step. I was actually leading up to asking if you'd come with me. Most of my friends think bags with armholes are great. Middle-age camouflage. Then there's my daughters, who won't look at anything that doesn't show off their belly-rings. Would you mind? I'll throw in a free lunch. A three-martini lunch."

I laughed. "After three martinis, any dress will look good."

Diane grinned. "My plan exactly. Is that a yes?"

"Sure."

"Great. I'll give you a call and we'll set it up."

She drove into the roundabout in front of my apartment. I opened the door, then remembered my manners.

"Would you like to come up for a coffee?"

I was sure she'd offer some polite refusal, but instead she said, "Sure. Another hour of peace before reentering the trenches. Plus a chance to give my little brother proper hell for tossing you to the sharks today."

I laughed and directed her to visitor parking.

CHAPTER 2

SUMMONS

Maybe I've given the wrong impression by making such a big deal out of my quest to live in the human world, as if all werewolves cut themselves off from human life. They don't. By necessity, most werewolves live in the human world. Short of teaming up and creating a commune in New Mexico, they don't have much choice. The human world provides them with food, shelter, sex, and other necessities. Yet, although they may live in that world, they don't consider themselves part of it. They view human interaction as a necessary evil, with attitudes ranging from contempt to barely concealed amusement. They are actors playing a role, sometimes enjoying their turn on the stage, but usually relieved to get off it. I didn't want to be like that. I wanted to live in the human world and, as much as possible, be myself doing it. I didn't choose this life and I damn well wasn't about to give in to it, surrendering every dream of my future, ordinary, mediocre dreams of a home, a family, a career, and above all, stability. None of that was possible living as a werewolf.

I grew up in foster homes. Bad foster homes. Not having had a family as a child, I became determined to create one for myself. Becoming a werewolf pretty much knocked those plans into the dumper. Still, even if a husband and children were out of the question, that didn't mean I couldn't pursue some part of that dream. I was making a career for myself in journalism. I was making a home in Toronto. And I was making a family, albeit not the traditional family, with Philip. We'd been together long enough that I'd begun to believe some stability in my life was possible. I couldn't believe my luck in finding someone as normal and decent as Philip. I knew what I was. I was difficult, temperamental, argumentative, not the sort of woman someone like Philip would fall for. Of course, I wasn't like that around Philip. I kept that part of me—the werewolf part—hidden, hoping I'd eventually slough it off like dead skin. With Philip, I had the chance to reinvent myself, to become the kind of person he thought I was. Which, of course, was exactly the kind of person I wanted to be.

The Pack didn't understand why I chose to live among humans. They couldn't understand because they weren't like me. First, I wasn't born a werewolf. Most werewolves are, or at least they're born carrying the blood in their veins and will experience their first Change when they reach adulthood. The other way to become a werewolf is to be bitten by one. Very few people survive a werewolf's bite. Werewolves are neither stupid nor altruistic. If they bite, they intend to kill. If they bite and fail to kill, they'll stalk their victim and finish the job. It's a simple matter of survival. If you're a werewolf who has comfortably assimilated into a town or city, the last thing you want is some half-crazed new werewolf lurching around your territory, slaughtering people and calling attention to himself. Even if someone is bitten and escapes, the chances of surviving are minimal. The first few Changes are hell, on the body and the sanity. Hereditary werewolves grow up knowing their lot in life and having their fathers to guide them. Bitten werewolves are on their own. If they don't die from the physical stress, the mental stress drives them either to kill themselves or raise a big enough ruckus that another werewolf finds them and ends their suffering before they cause trouble. So there aren't many bitten werewolves running around. At last count, there were approximately thirty-five werewolves in the world. Exactly three were nonhereditary, including me.

Me. The only female werewolf in existence. The werewolf gene is passed only through the male line, father to son, so the only way for a woman to become a werewolf is to be bitten and survive, which, as I've said, is rare. Given the odds, it's not surprising I'm the only female. Bitten on purpose, turned into a werewolf on purpose. Amazing, really, that I survived. After all, when you've got a species with three dozen males and one female, that one female becomes something of a prize. And werewolves do not settle their battles over a nice game of chess. Nor do they have a history of respect for women. Women serve two functions in the werewolf world: sex and dinner, or if they're feeling lazy, sex followed by dinner. Although I doubt any werewolf would dine on me, I'm an irresistible object for satisfying the other primal urge. Left on my own, I wouldn't have survived. Fortunately, I wasn't left on my own. Since I'd been bitten, I'd been under the protection of the Pack. Every society has its ruling class. In the werewolf world, it was the Pack. For reasons that had nothing to do with me and everything to do with the status of the werewolf who'd bitten me, I'd been part of the Pack from the time I was turned. A year ago I'd left. I'd cut myself off and I wasn't going back. Given the choice between human and werewolf, I'd chosen to be human.

✣

Philip had to work late the next day. Tuesday evening, I was waiting for his "I'll be late" phone call when he walked into the apartment carrying dinner.

"Hope you're hungry," he said, swinging a bag of Indian takeout onto the table.

I was, though I'd grabbed two sausages from a vendor on the way home from work. The predinner meal had taken the edge off, so a normal dinner would now suffice. Yet another of the million tricks I'd learned to accommodate to human life.

Philip chatted about work as he took the cartons from the bag and set the table. I graciously shifted my papers to the side to let him lay out my place setting. I can be so helpful sometimes. Even after the food was on my plate, I managed to resist eating while I jotted down the final line of the article I was working on. Then I pushed the pad of paper aside and dug in.

"Mom called me at work," Philip said. "She forgot to ask on Sunday whether you could help her plan Becky's wedding shower."

"Really?"

I heard the delight in my voice and wondered at it. Throwing a shower wasn't exactly cause for high excitement. Still, no one had ever asked me to help at one before. Hell, no one had even invited me to one, excluding Sarah from work, but she'd invited all her coworkers.

Philip smiled. "I take it that's a yes. Good. Mom will be happy. She loves that kind of stuff, all the fussing around and planning."

"I don't have much experience with throwing showers."

"No problem. Becky's bridesmaids are giving her the main shower, so this will just be a little family one. Well, not exactly little. I think Mom plans to invite every relative in Ontario. You'll get to meet the whole bunch. I'm sure Mom's told them all about you. Hope it's not too overwhelming."

"No," I said. "I'll be looking forward to it."

"Sure, you can say that now. You haven't met them."

After dinner, Philip went downstairs to the fitness center for some weight-training. When he worked normal hours, he liked to get his workout in early and get to bed early, wryly admitting that he was getting too old to survive on five hours of sleep per night. For the first month we'd lived together, I'd joined him in his early workouts. It wasn't easy pretending to struggle bench-pressing a hundred pounds when I could do five times that. Then came the day when I was so engrossed in conversation with one of our neighbors that I didn't realize I was doing a sixty-pound lat pulldown one-handed and chatting away as casually as if I were pulling down a window blind. When I noticed the neighbor double-checking my weights, I realized my goof and covered it up with some bullshit about an incorrectly adjusted machine. After that, I restricted my workouts to between midnight and six, when the weight room was empty. I'd told Philip some story about taking advantage of a late-night second wind. He bought that, as he'd readily accepted so many other of my quirks. When he worked late, I went down to the health club afterward with him and did my swimming and running workouts as I'd done when we first met. Otherwise, he went alone.

That evening after Philip left, I switched on the TV. I didn't watch it much, but when I did, I wallowed in the dregs of the broadcasting barrel, flicking past educational shows and high-grade dramas to tabloids and talk shows. Why? Because it reassured me that there were people in the world who were worse off than I was. No matter what went wrong with my day, I could turn on the TV, watch some moron telling his wife and the rest of the world that he's sleeping with her daughter, and say to myself, Well, at least I'm better than that. Trash television as reaffirmation therapy. You gotta love it.

Today *Inside Scoop* was following up on some psycho who'd escaped from a North Carolina jail several months ago. Pure sensationalism. This guy had broken into the apartment of a total stranger, tied the man up, and shot him because he—quote—wanted to know what it felt like. The show's writers had peppered the piece with words like "savage," "wild," and "animalistic." What bullshit. Show me the animal that kills for the thrill of watching something die. Why does the stereotype of the animalistic killer persist? Because humans like it. It neatly explains things for them, moving humans to the top of the evolutionary ladder and putting killers down among mythological man-beast monsters like werewolves.

The truth is, if a werewolf behaved like this psychopath it wouldn't be because he was part animal, but because he was still too human. Only humans kill for sport.

The show was almost over when Philip returned.

"Good workout?" I asked.

"Never good," he said, making a face. "I'm still waiting for the day when they invent a pill to replace exercise. What are you watching?" He leaned over my head. "Any good fights breaking out?"

"That's Jerry Springer. I can't watch Springer. I tried once. Watched for ten minutes, trying to get past the profanity to figure out what they were saying. Finally figured out the profanity was all they were saying—a break between wrestling bouts. The WWF of daytime TV. No, strike that. At least WWF has a story line."

Philip laughed and rumpled my hair. "How about a walk? I'll grab a shower while you finish your show."

"Sounds good."

Philip headed to the bathroom. I sneaked to the fridge and grabbed a hunk of provolone that I'd hidden amongst the vegetables. When the phone rang, I ignored it. Eating was more important, and since Philip already had the water running, he wouldn't hear the ringing, so he wouldn't know I wasn't answering it. Or so I thought. As I heard the water shut off, I shoved the cheese behind the lettuce and jogged for the phone. Philip was the sort who'd answer the phone during dinner rather than subject someone to the answering machine. I tried to live up to his example—at least when he was around. I was halfway across the apartment when the machine clicked on. My recorded voice sang out a nauseatingly cheery greeting and invited the caller to leave a message. This one did.

"Elena? It's Jeremy." I stopped in midstride. "Please call me. It's important."

His voice trailed off. The phone hissed with a sharp intake of breath. I knew he was tempted to say more, to issue a call-me-or-else ultimatum, but he couldn't. We had an agreement. He couldn't come here or send any of the others here. I resisted the urge to stick out my tongue at the answering machine. Nyah-nyah-nyah, you can't get me. Maturity is highly overrated.

"It's urgent, Elena," Jeremy continued. "You know I wouldn't call if it wasn't."

Philip reached for the phone, but Jeremy had already hung up. He lifted the receiver and held it out to me. I averted my gaze and walked to the couch.

"Aren't you going to call back?" he said.

"He didn't leave a number."

"He sounded as if he expected you to have it. Who was it anyway?"

"A—uh—second cousin."

"So my mysterious orphan has family? I'll have to meet this cousin someday."

"You wouldn't want to."

He laughed. "Turnabout's fair play. I inflicted my family on you. Now's your chance for revenge. After Becky's shower you'll want to sic your worst on me. Dig up the mad cousins who've been locked in attics for years. Though, actually, crazy attic-dwelling cousins would probably be the best kind. Definite dinner party interest. Better than the great-aunts who've told you the same story since childhood and fall asleep over dessert."

I rolled my eyes. "Ready for that walk yet?"

"Let me finish my shower. How about giving 411 a call?"

"And get dinged with a service charge whether they find the number or not?"

"It's less than a buck. We can afford it. Call. If you can't find his number, maybe you can get someone else who can give you his number. There must be more of these cousins, right?"

"You think they have phone service in those attics? They're lucky if they get electric lighting."

"Call, Elena," he said, giving a mock growl as he disappeared into the bathroom.

Once he was out of the room, I stared at the phone. Philip may have joked about it, but I knew he expected me to call Jeremy back. Why wouldn't he? It was what any decent human being would do. Philip had heard the message, heard the urgency in Jeremy's voice. By refusing to return what seemed to be a very important call, I'd appear callous, uncaring. A human would call back. The kind of woman I wanted to be would call back.

I could pretend I'd made the call. It was tempting, but it wouldn't stop Jeremy from phoning again . . . and again . . . and again. This wasn't the first time he'd tried communicating with me in the past few days. Werewolves share some degree of telepathy. Most werewolves ignored it, preferring less mystical ways of communication. Jeremy had refined the ability to an art, mainly because it gave him one more way to get under our skin and harass us until we did his bidding. While he'd been trying to contact me, I'd been blocking him. So he'd resorted to the phone. Not quite as effective as bombarding someone's brain, but after a few days of filled message tapes, I'd cave in, if only to get rid of him.

I stood next to the phone, closed my eyes, and inhaled. I could do this. I could make the call, find out what Jeremy wanted, politely thank him for letting me know, and refuse to do whatever it was he demanded, knowing full well he was going to demand something of me. Even if Jeremy was the Pack Alpha and I'd been conditioned to obey him, I didn't have to do it anymore. I wasn't Pack. He had no control over me.

I lifted the receiver and punched in the numbers from memory. It rang four times, then the machine picked up. A recorded voice started, not Jeremy's deep tones, but a Southern drawl that made me fumble to hang up before I heard the entire message. Sweat broke out along my forehead. The air in the apartment seemed to have shot up ten degrees and lost half its oxygen. I wiped my hands over my face, gave my head a sharp shake, and went to find my shoes for my walk with Philip.

Before breakfast the next morning, Philip asked what Jeremy had wanted. I admitted that I hadn't been able to get in touch with him, but promised to keep trying. After we ate, Philip went downstairs to get the newspaper. I called Jeremy and once more got the answering machine.

As much as I hated to admit it, I was starting to worry. It wasn't my fault, really. Being concerned about my former Pack brothers was instinctive, something I couldn't control. Or, at least, that's what I told myself when my heart pounded on the third unanswered call.

Jeremy should have been there. He rarely went far from Stonehaven, preferring to rule from his throne of power and sending his minions to do his dirty work. Okay, that wasn't a fair assessment of Jeremy's leadership style, but I was in no mood to be complimentary. He'd told me to call and, goddamn it, he should have been there when I did.

When Philip came back, I was hovering over the phone, glaring down at it as if I could mentally force Jeremy to pick up.

"Still no answer?" Philip said.

I shook my head. He studied my face more closely than I liked. As I turned away, he crossed the room and put his hand on my shoulder.

"You're worried."

"Not really. I just—"

"It's okay, hon. If it were my family, I'd be worried. Maybe you should go there. See what's wrong. It sounded urgent."

I pulled away. "No, that's ridiculous. I'll keep calling—"

"It's family, hon," he said, as if that answered any argument I could come up with. For him, it did. That was one thing I couldn't argue with. When Philip and I first became serious, the lease on his apartment came up and he'd made it clear he wanted to move in with me, but I'd resisted. Then he'd taken me to his family reunion. I'd met his mother and his father and his sister and seen how he interacted with them, how integral they were to his life. The next day I'd told him not to extend his lease.

Now Philip expected me to go to the aid of someone he thought was my family. If I refused, would he think I wasn't the kind of person he wanted? I wouldn't take that chance. I promised to keep trying. I promised if I didn't get hold of Jeremy by noon, I'd fly to New York State to see what was wrong.

Each time I called over the next few hours, I prayed for an answer. The only reply I got was the click of the answering machine.

Philip drove me to the airport after lunch.

CHAPTER 3

PRODIGAL

The plane landed at Syracuse-Hancock at seven P.M. I tried Jeremy's number, but only got the answering machine. Again. By now I was more annoyed than worried. As the distance between us lessened, my memory improved and I remembered what it was like to live at Stonehaven, Jeremy's country estate. In particular, I recalled the resident phone-answering habits, or lack thereof. Two people lived at Stonehaven, Jeremy and his foster-son-turned-bodyguard, Clayton. There were two phones in the five-bedroom house. The one in Clay's room was connected to the answering machine, but the phone itself had lost the ability to ring four years ago, when Clay whipped it across the room after it dared disturb his sleep two nights in a row. There was also a phone in the study, but if Clay needed to use the line for his laptop, he often neglected to plug the phone back in, sometimes for days. Even if, by chance, there was an operating telephone in the house, both men had been known to sit five feet away and not bother picking it up. And Philip thought my phone habits were bad.

The more I thought about it, the more I fumed. The more I fumed, the more determined I was not to leave the airport until someone answered the damned phone. If they summoned me, they should pick me up. At least, this was my excuse. The truth was that I was loath to leave the bustle of the airport. Yes, that sounds crazy. Most people judge the success of a plane flight by how little time they have to spend in the airport. Normally, I would have felt the same way, but as I sat there, taking in the sights and smells of the nearly empty terminal, I reveled in the humanness of it. Here in the airport I was an anonymous face in a sea of equally anonymous faces. There was comfort in that, the feeling of being part of something larger, but not at the center of it. Things would change the minute I walked out of here and into Stonehaven.

Two hours later, I decided I couldn't put it off any longer. I made my last call to Stonehaven and left a message. Two words. "I'm coming." It would do.

Getting to Stonehaven wasn't easy. It was in remote upstate New York near a small town called Bear Valley. As my cab pulled away from the airport, it was already night. Syracuse glowed somewhere to the south, but the cab turned north once it reached highway 81. The lights of North Syracuse appeared to my left, faded fast, then vanished into the night. A dozen miles later the driver turned off the highway and the darkness was complete. In the quiet of the country night, I relaxed. Werewolves weren't meant for urban life. There was no place to run, and the sheer crush of people often provided more temptation than anonymity. Sometimes I think I chose to live in downtown Toronto simply because it was against my nature, one more instinct for me to defeat.

As I looked out the window, I ticked off the time with the landmarks. With each passing mark, my stomach danced faster. Trepidation, I told myself. Not anticipation. Even if I'd spent the better part of ten years at Stonehaven, I didn't consider it my home. The concept of home was difficult for me, an ethereal construct emerging from dreams and stories rather than actual experience. Of course, I did have a home once, a good home and a good family, but it didn't last long enough to leave more than the most fleeting impression.

My parents died when I was five. We'd been coming home from the fair, taking a back road because my mother wanted to show me a miniature pony foal she'd seen at a farm along there. I could hear my father laughing, asking my mother how she expected me to see anything in a field at midnight. I remember him turning to look over the seat, grinning at me while he teased my mother beside me. I don't remember what happened next, no squealing tires, no screams, no careering out of control. Just blackness.

I don't know how I got on the side of the road. I'd been seat belted in, but must have crawled out after the accident. All I remember is sitting in the gravel beside my father's bloodied body, shaking him, talking to him, pleading with him to answer and not understanding why he didn't, knowing only that my father always answered, never ignored me, but all he did now was stare at me, eyes wide and unblinking. I remember hearing myself start to whimper, a five-year-old, crouched by the side of the road, staring into my father's eyes, whimpering because it was so dark and there was no one coming to help, whimpering because my mother was back in the crushed car, not moving, and my father was lying here in the dirt, not answering me, not holding me, not comforting me, not helping my mother get out of the car, and there was blood, so much blood, and broken glass everywhere, and it was so dark and so cold and no one was coming to help.

If I had any extended family, I never heard of them. After my parents died, the only person who tried to claim me was my mother's best friend and she was refused on the grounds that she was unmarried. However, I only spent a couple of weeks in the children's home before I was snatched up by the first couple who saw me. I can still see them, kneeling before me, cooing and ahhhing about what a beautiful child I was. So tiny, so perfect with my white-blond hair and my blue eyes. A porcelain doll, they called me. They took their doll home and started their perfect life. But it didn't work out quite that way. Their precious doll sat in a chair all day and never opened her mouth, then at night—every night—she screamed until dawn. After three weeks they returned me. So I went from one foster family to the next, always taken by the ones utterly charmed by my face and utterly incapable of handling my scarred psyche.

As I grew into adolescence, the couples who picked me from the home changed. It was no longer the wife who chose me but the husband, picking up on my childish beauty and my fear. I became the favored choice of male predators who were looking for a very special kind of child. Ironically, it was through these monsters that I first found my strength. As I grew older, I began to see them for what they were, not all-powerful bogeymen who slipped into my room at night, but weak creatures terrified of rejection and exposure. With that realization, the fear slipped away. They could touch me, but they couldn't touch *me,* not the me who lay beyond my body. As the fear subsided, so did the rage. I despised them and their equally weak, blind wives, but they weren't worthy of my anger. I wouldn't let myself be angry at them, wouldn't let myself waste time and effort better spent elsewhere. If I wanted to escape this life, I had to do it myself. That didn't mean running away. It meant staying and surviving. It meant studying hard and making the honors list even if I rarely went a full year without switching schools. Succeeding at school would mean acceptance into university, which would mean a degree, which would mean a career, which would mean the kind of life my social workers and foster families assumed was beyond me. At the same time, I discovered another source of power—the strength of my own body. I grew tall and rangy. A teacher signed me up for track-and-field, hoping it would help me get close to other children. Instead I learned to run, discovering the absolute bliss, the unparalleled pleasure of the physical, feeling my strength and my speed for the first time. By the time I was midway through high school I was lifting weights and working out daily. My foster father wasn't touching me by then. I wasn't anyone's idea of a victim by then.

"Is this it, miss?" the driver asked.

I hadn't felt the car stop, but when I looked out the window I could see we were at the front gates of Stonehaven. A figure sat on the grass, ankles crossed as he leaned against the stone wall. Clayton.

The driver squinted, trying to make out the house in the dark, as blind to the brass nameplate as to the man waiting by the gate. The moon had gone behind a cloud and the coach lamps at the end of drive were unlit.

"I'll get out here," I said.

"Uh-uh. No can do, miss. It's not safe. There's something out there."

I thought he was referring to Clay. "Something" was an apt description. I was about to say, unfortunately, that I knew that "something" when the driver continued.

"We've been having ourselves some trouble in these woods, miss. Wild dogs by the looks of it. One of our girls from town was found not too far from here. Butchered by these dogs. Buddy of mine found her and he said—well, it wasn't nice, miss. You just sit back and I'll unlatch that gate and drive you up."

"Wild dogs?" I repeated, certain I'd heard wrong.

"That's right. My buddy found tracks. Huge ones. Some guy from some college said all the tracks came from one animal, but that can't be right. It's gotta be a pack. You don't see—" The driver's eyes went to the side window and he jumped in his seat. "Jesus!"

Clay had left his post at the gate and materialized at my window. He stood there, watching me, a slow grin lighting his eyes. He reached for the door handle. The driver put the car in gear.

"It's okay," I said, with deep regret. "He's with me."

The door opened. Clay ducked his head inside.

"You getting out or just thinking about it?" he asked.

"She's not getting out here," the driver said, twisting back to look over the seat. "If you're fool enough to be wandering around these woods at night, that's your problem, but I'm not letting this young lady walk god-knows-how-far to that house back there. If you want a ride up, unlock the gate for me and get in. Otherwise, close my door."

Clay turned to the driver, as if noticing him for the first time. His lip curled and his mouth opened. Whatever he planned to say, it wasn't going to be nice. Before Clay could cause a scene, I opened the opposite door and slid out. As the cab driver rolled down his window to stop me, I dropped a fifty on his lap and skirted around the back of the cab. Clay slammed the other door and headed for the front walk. The driver hesitated, then sped off, kicking up a hail of gravel as a parting shot of disgust at our youthful foolishness.

As I approached, Clay stepped back to watch me. Despite the cold night air, he wore only faded jeans and a black T-shirt, displaying slim hips, a broad chest, and sculpted biceps. In the decade I'd known him, he hadn't changed. I was always hoping for a difference—a few wrinkles, a scar, anything that would mar his model-perfect looks and bring him down to mortality with the rest of us, but I was always disappointed.

As I walked toward him, he tilted his head, his eyes never leaving mine. White teeth flashed as he grinned.

"Welcome home, darling." His Deep South drawl mangled the endearment into a "*dah*-lin" straight out of a country-and-western song. I hated country music.

"Are you the welcoming committee? Or has Jeremy finally chained you up to the front gate where you belong?"

"I missed you, too."

He reached out for me, but I sidestepped back onto the road, then started down the quarter-mile lane to the house. Clay followed. A breeze of cool, dry night air lifted a tendril of hair from my neck, and with it came a dusting of scents—the sharp tang of cedar, the faint perfume of apple blossoms, and the teasing smell of long-devoured dinner. Each smell loosened my tense muscles. I shook myself, throwing off the feeling and forced myself to keep my eyes on the road, concentrating on doing nothing, not talking to Clay, not smelling anything, not looking left or right. I didn't dare ask Clay what was going on. That would mean engaging him in conversation, which would imply that I wanted to talk to him. With Clay, even the simplest overtures were dangerous. As much as I wanted to know what was happening, I'd have to hear it from Jeremy.

When I reached the house, I paused at the door and looked up. The two-story stone house seemed not to loom over me, but to lean back, expectant. The welcome was there, but muted, waiting for me to make the first move. So very much like its owner. I touched one of the cool stones and felt a rush of memory leap out to greet me. Pulling away, I flung open the door, threw my overnight bag to the floor, and headed for the study, expecting to find Jeremy reading by the fireplace. He was always there when I came home, not waiting at the gate like Clay, but waiting nonetheless.

The room was empty. A folded copy of Milan's daily paper *Corriere della Sera* lay beside Jeremy's chair. Stacks of Clay's anthropology magazines and research publications covered the couch and desk. The main phone rested on the desk and appeared to be intact and plugged in.

"I called," I said. "Why wasn't anyone here?"

"We were here," Clay said. "Around, anyway. You should have left a message."

"I did. Two hours ago."

"Well, that explains it. I've been out by the gate all day waiting for you, and you know Jer never checks the machine."

I didn't ask how Clay knew I was coming back today when I hadn't left a message. Nor did I question why he'd spent the entire day sitting at the gate. Clay's behavior couldn't be measured by human standards of normalcy . . . or by any standards of normalcy at all.

"So where is he?" I asked.

"Dunno. I haven't seen him since he brought out my dinner a few hours ago. He must have gone out."

I didn't need to check the garage for Jeremy's car to know Clay didn't mean he'd gone out in the usual sense. Common human phrases took on new meanings at Stonehaven. Going out meant he'd gone for a run—and that didn't mean he'd gone jogging.

Did Jeremy expect me to fly all the way here, then wait on his convenience? Of course he did. Was it punishment for ignoring his summons? Part of me wished I could accuse him of that, but Jeremy was never petty. If he'd planned a run for tonight, he'd have gone, regardless of whether I was coming or not. A sliver of hurt ran through my anger, but I tried to disown it. Did I expect Jeremy to be waiting for me like Clay? Of course not. Didn't expect it and didn't care about it. Really. I was pissed off, nothing more. Two could play this game. Jeremy valued his privacy when he ran. So what was I going to do? Invade that privacy, of course. Jeremy may never be petty, but I sure as hell could be.

"Out?" I said. "Well then, I'll just have to find him."

I swerved to pass Clay, heading for the door. He stepped in front of me.

"He'll be back soon. Sit down and we'll—"

I sidestepped Clay on my way to the rear hall and the half-open back door. Clay followed at my heels, keeping pace a step behind. I walked through the walled garden to the path leading into the forest. The wood-chip path crunched underfoot. From beyond, the night smells began to sift in: burning leaves, distant cattle, wet soil—myriad inviting scents. Somewhere in the distance a mouse shrieked as an owl snatched it from the forest floor.

I kept walking. Within fifty feet the trail dwindled to a thin path of trodden grass, then disappeared into the undergrowth. I paused and sniffed the air. Nothing. No scent, no sound, no sign of Jeremy. At that moment, I realized I heard no sound at all, not even the clomp of Clay's footsteps behind me. I turned and saw only trees.

"Clayton!" I shouted.

A moment later the reply came back in a crashing of distant bushes. He was off to warn Jeremy. I slammed my hand into the nearest tree trunk. Had I really expected Clay to let me intrude on Jeremy's privacy that easily? If so, I'd forgotten a few things in the past year.

I pushed through the trees. Twigs lashed at my face and vines grabbed my feet. I stumbled forward, feeling huge, clumsy, and most unwelcome out here. The path wasn't made for people. I didn't stand a chance of heading off Clay like this, so I found a clearing and prepared for the Change.

My Change was rushed, making it awkward and torturous and afterward I had to rest, panting on the ground. As I got to my feet, I closed my eyes and inhaled the smell of Stonehaven. A shiver of elation started in my paws, raced up my legs, and quivered through my entire body. In its wake, it left an indescribable blend of excitement and calm that made me want to tear through the forest and collapse in blissful peace at the same time. I was home. As a human, I could deny that Stonehaven was my home, that the people here were my Pack, that the woods here were anything more than a patch of someone else's land. But as a wolf in Stonehaven's forest, one chorus trumpeted through my head. This forest was mine. It was Pack territory and therefore it was mine. Mine to run in and hunt in and play in without fear of partying teenagers, overeager hunters, or rabid foxes and raccoons. No discarded sofas to block my path, no rusty cans to slice open my paws, no stinking garbage bags to foul the air I breathed, or dumped chemicals to pollute the water I drank. This wasn't some patch of woods claimed for an hour or two. This was five hundred acres of forest, every acre crisscrossed with familiar paths and stocked with rabbits and deer, a smorgasbord supplied for my pleasure. *My* pleasure. I downed huge gulps of air. Mine. I darted out of the thicket to the well-worn path. Mine. I rubbed against an oak tree, feeling the bark scratch and pull away tickling clumps of dead fur. Mine. The ground shuddered in three low vibrations—a rabbit thumping somewhere to my left. Mine. My legs ached to run, to rediscover the intricate world of my forest. Somewhere deep in my brain, a tiny human voice shouted No, no, no! This isn't yours. You gave it up. You don't want it! I ignored it.

There was only one thing missing, one last thing that differentiated these woods from the lonely ravines of Toronto. Even as I was thinking this, a howl pierced the night; not musical night singing, but the urgent cry of a lone wolf, blood calling to blood. I closed my eyes and felt the sound vibrate through me. Then I threw back my head and responded. The small warning voice stopped yelling invective, anger taken over by something closer to dread. No, it whispered. Not that. Claim the forest. Claim the air and the paths and the trees and the animals. But don't claim that.

The bushes crackled behind me and I whirled around to see Clay in midair. He caught my forequarters and knocked me flying onto my back, then stood over me and nipped at the loose skin around my neck. When I snapped at him, he pulled back. Standing over me, he whined and prodded my neck with his nose, begging me to come play with him, telling me how lonely he'd been. I could feel the resistance somewhere within me, but it was too deeply buried. I grabbed his foreleg between my jaws and yanked him off balance. As he fell, I leapt atop him. We tumbled into the thick undergrowth, nipping and kicking and fighting for the top position. Just as he was about to pin me, I wriggled free and leapt away. We circled each other. Clay's tail lashed against my side, running along it like a caressing hand. He inched closer and rubbed his flank against mine. As we circled the next round, he put a leg in front of mine to stop me and buried his nose against my neck. I could feel his hot breath against my skin as he inhaled my scent. Then he grabbed me by the throat and threw me over backward, giving a yip of triumph as I fell for it—literally. He didn't hold the victory spot for more than a couple of seconds before I dethroned him. We wrestled a while longer, then I leapt free. Clay stepped back and crouched, leaving his hindquarters high. His mouth hung open, tongue out and ears forward. I hunkered down as if preparing to meet his attack. When he pounced, I sprang to the side and started to run.

Clay tore after me. We raced through the forest, crossing acre after acre of ground. Then, just as I was circling back toward the front of the property, a shot exploded the peace of the forest. I skidded to a stop.

A shot? Had I really heard a shot? Of course I'd encountered guns before, guns and hunters were an expected danger when you roamed strange forests. But this was Stonehaven. It was safe.

Another shot rang out. I swiveled my ears. The blasts had come from the north. There were orchards far to the north. Was the farmer using one of those devices that mimicked shotgun blasts to scare off birds? It had to be. Either that or someone was hunting in the neighboring fields. Stonehaven's forests were clearly marked with fences and signs. The locals respected the boundaries. They always had. Jeremy's reputation with the locals was peerless. He may not have been the most sociable landowner, but he was respected.

I headed north to solve the mystery. I'd barely gone three yards when

Clay leapt in front of me. He growled. It wasn't a playful growl. I stared at him, wondering if I'd misinterpreted his meaning. He growled again and I was certain. He was warning me off. I put my ears back and snarled. He blocked my path. I narrowed my eyes and glared at him. Obviously I'd been away too long if he thought he could boss me around like he did the others. If he'd forgotten who I was, I'd be willing to give him a refresher lesson. I curled my lips back and growled one last warning. He didn't back down. I threw myself at him. He met me in midleap, knocking the wind from me. When I regained my senses, I was lying on the ground with Clay's teeth locked in the loose skin behind my head. I was out of practice.

Clay growled and gave me a rough shake, as if I were a misbehaving pup. After a few rounds of this, he pulled back and stood up. I got to my feet with as much dignity as I could muster. Before I was even fully standing, Clay butted my backside with his muzzle. I turned to give him an indignant glare. He butted me again, driving me in the opposite direction. I went along with it for nearly a quarter mile, then swerved to the side and tried an end run around him. Seconds after I flew past him, a two-hundred-pound weight dropped on my back and I skidded into the dirt. Clay's teeth sunk into my shoulder, deep enough to draw blood and send a stab of pain and shock through me. This time he didn't even let me get to my feet before he started herding me back to the house, nipping at my back legs if I showed signs of slowing.

Clay drove me to the clearing where I'd Changed and made his own Change on the other side of the thicket. My Change back to human was even more hurried than my Change to a wolf. This time, though, I didn't need to rest afterward. Fury gave me energy. I yanked on my clothes, ripping the sleeve of my shirt. Then I strode out from the clearing. Clay was there, arms crossed, waiting. He was naked, of course, his clothing abandoned in a clearing deeper in the forest. Naked, Clay was even more perfect than when he was dressed, a Greek sculptor's dream come to life. Seeing him, a slow flush of heat ran through me, bringing to mind memories of other runs and their inevitable aftermath. I cursed my body's betrayal and strode toward him.

"What the hell were you doing?" I shouted.

"Me? Me? I wasn't the idiot running toward men with guns. Where the hell was your head at, Elena?"

"Don't give me that crap. I wouldn't leave the property and you know it. I was just curious. I'm back an hour and you're already testing the waters. How far can you push me, how much can you control—"

"Those hunters were on the property, Elena." Clay's voice was low, his eyes locked on to mine.

"Oh, that's a load of—" I stopped and studied his face. "You're serious, aren't you? Hunters? On Jeremy's land? Are you getting soft in your old age?"

The barb struck deeper than I hoped. Clay's mouth tightened. His eyes went hard. Rage simmered there, mere degrees from explosion. The anger wasn't directed at me, but at those who had dared invade his sanctuary. Every fiber in Clay would rebel at the thought of allowing armed men on the property. Only one thing would keep him from hunting them down— Jeremy. So Jeremy must have forbidden him to take care of these trespassers, forbidden him not only to kill them, but even to use his infamous scare techniques, Clay's usual method of dealing with human trespassers. Two generations of local teenagers in search of party sites had grown up passing along the story that Stonehaven's backwoods were haunted. So long as the tales involved spooks and phantasms, with no mention of werewolves, Jeremy allowed it, even encouraged it. After all, letting Clay scare the locals was safer and far less messy than the alternative. So why wasn't Jeremy letting him do it now? What had changed?

"He should be inside now," Clay said. "Go talk to him."

He turned and headed into the woods to find his clothing.

As I walked to the house, I thought about what the cab driver had said. Wild dogs. There were no wild dogs here. Dogs wouldn't set foot anywhere near werewolf territory. Nor did dogs run around slaughtering healthy young women. Huge canine tracks found around the body could only mean one thing. A werewolf. Yet who would be killing that close to Stonehaven? The question itself was so unfathomable it could have no answer. A non-Pack werewolf would have to be suicidal to cross the New York State border. Clay's methods for dealing with trespassers were so renowned that one hadn't come within a hundred miles of Stonehaven in over twenty years. The story goes that Clay had dismembered the last trespassing werewolf finger by finger, limb by limb, keeping him alive until the last possible moment, when he'd ripped off his head. Clay had been seventeen at the time.

The idea that either Clay or Jeremy could be responsible for the woman's death was equally ludicrous. Jeremy didn't kill. That wasn't to say he couldn't kill or even that he never felt the urge, but simply that he realized his energy was better channeled elsewhere, as an army general must forgo the heat of the battle and devote himself to matters of strategy and leadership. If someone had to be killed, Jeremy ordered it done. Even that was done only in extreme cases and rarely involved humans. No matter what the threat,

Jeremy would never order the killing of a human on his own territory. As for Clay, whatever his legion of faults, sport-killing humans wasn't one of them. Killing them would involve touching them, which meant lowering himself to physical contact with them, which he didn't do unless absolutely necessary.

When I reentered the house, it was still silent. I went back to the study, the heart of Stonehaven. Jeremy wasn't there. I decided to wait. If he was in the house, he'd hear me. For once, he could come to me.

Jeremy ruled the Pack with absolute authority. That's the law of wild wolves, though it hadn't always been the law of the Pack. At times, the history of the Pack Alphas made Roman imperial succession look downright civilized. A Pack werewolf would scramble to the top of the heap, hold the Alpha position for a few months, maybe even a few years, then get assassinated or executed by one of his more ambitious Pack brothers, who would then take over until he met his own—almost certainly unnatural—demise. Pack Alpha-hood had nothing to do with leadership and everything to do with power.

By the second half of the twentieth century, the Pack was falling apart. The postindustrial world wasn't kind to werewolves. Urban sprawl swallowed deep forests and wide open spaces. People in modern society were far less likely than those in feudal England to respect the privacy of their wealthy, reclusive neighbors. Radio, television, and newspapers could spread stories of werewolf sightings across the globe within hours. New methods of police work meant a strange canine-like killing in Tallahassee could be swiftly linked to similar ones in Miami and Key West. The world began to close in on the Pack. Instead of banding together, they'd begun fighting one another for every last vestige of security, even going so far as to steal prime territory from their own Pack brothers.

Jeremy changed that.

Although Jeremy could never be considered the best fighter in the Pack, he possessed a strength that was even more important for the survival and success of the modern Pack. Jeremy had absolute self-control. Being able to master his own instincts and urges meant he could see the problems the Pack was facing and deal with them rationally, making decisions untainted by impulse. As suburbs consumed the land surrounding cities, he moved the Pack farther into the countryside. He taught them how to deal with humans, how to be part of the world and outside of the world at the same time. As stories of werewolves travelled faster and more easily, he exerted his control over not just the Pack, but the non-Pack werewolves. In the past, non-Pack werewolves—known as mutts—were seen as second-class citizens, beneath the notice of the Pack. Under Jeremy's rule, mutts didn't gain any status, but the Pack learned that they couldn't afford to ignore them. If a mutt caused enough trouble in Cairo, it could resonate all the way to New York. The Pack started keeping dossiers on mutts, learning their habits and tracing their movements. When a werewolf caused trouble anywhere in the world, the Pack responded quickly and decisively. The penalty for endangering the security of the Pack ranged anywhere from a rousting to a beating to a swift execution. Under Jeremy's rule, the Pack was stronger and more stable than ever, and no one contested it. They were smart enough to know when they had a good thing.

I shook off my thoughts and walked to the desk, looking at the nest of papers piled there. "Excavation Reveals New Insights on the Chavín Phenomenon" read the title of one article. Peeking out from under it was another about ancient Chavín de Huántar jaguar cults. Fascinating stuff. Yawn. Though it came as a shock to most who met him, Clay had a brain, actually a brilliant brain, one that had earned him a Ph.D. in anthropology. He specialized in anthropomorphic religions. In other words, he studied man-beast symbolism in ancient cultures. His reputation was built on his research, since he didn't like to deal directly with the human world, but when he deemed it necessary to make a foray into the live world of academics he'd take on brief teaching stints. That was how I'd met him.

Again, I shook off my thoughts, harder this time. Turning from the mess of Clay's papers, I sank onto the couch. As I glanced around, I realized that the room looked exactly as I'd left it fourteen months ago. I pulled up a picture of the study from memory, compared it with what I was seeing, and found not a single difference. That couldn't be right. Jeremy redecorated this room—and most of the house—so often it was a running gag that we could blink and see something different. Clay said once that the changes had to do with bad memories, but he wouldn't elaborate. Soon after Clay brought me here, Jeremy had recruited me as his decorating assistant. I could remember entire nights spent poring over catalogues, dragging around furniture, and holding up paint chips. When I looked up at the ceiling by the fireplace, I could see hardened lumps of wallpaper paste, still there from a four A.M. wallpapering spree that had turned the study into a battleground, Jeremy and I too exhausted to do anything more than lob clumps of paste at each other.

I remembered staring at those hardened lumps the last time I'd been in this room. Jeremy had been there, standing before the fireplace, his back to me. As I'd told him what I'd done, I'd ached for him to turn around, to tell me that it wasn't wrong. But I knew it was wrong. So completely wrong. Still, I'd wanted him to say something, anything, to make me feel better. When he hadn't, I'd left, promising myself that I wouldn't return. I looked up at the paste clumps. Another battle lost.

"So you've come back . . . finally."

The deep voice made me jump. Jeremy stood in the doorway. Since I'd last seen him, he'd grown a close-clipped beard, something that usually happened when he got too distracted to shave, then couldn't be bothered undoing the damage. It made him look older, though still nowhere near his true age of fifty-one. We age slowly. Jeremy could pass for mid-thirties: his hairstyle furthering the illusion of youth, shoulder-length and tied at the nape of his neck. It was a style adopted not out of fashion but because it meant fewer haircuts. Trips to a public barber were intolerable for Jeremy, so Clay or I cut his hair, which wasn't an experience to be endured more than a few times a year. When he stepped into the room, his bangs fell into his eyes, shattering the austerity of his face. He shoved them back, a gesture so familiar it made my throat ache.

He looked around. "Where's Clay?"

Typical. First, he gets after me for being late. Then he asks about Clay. A twinge of hurt darted through me, but I pushed it away. It wasn't like I expected him to welcome me back with hugs and kisses. That wasn't Jeremy's way, though a "good to see you" or "how was your flight?" would have been nice.

"We heard shots in the back forest," I said. "He mumbled something about shallow graves and took off."

"I've been trying to contact you for three days."

"I was busy."

His cheek twitched. With Jeremy, this was the equivalent of an emotional outburst. "When I call, you call me back," he said, his voice deceptively soft. "I wouldn't call you if it wasn't important. If I do call, you answer. That was the arrangement."

"Correct, that *was* the arrangement. Past tense. Our arrangement ended when I left the Pack."

"When you left the Pack? And when did this happen? Forgive me if I missed something, but I don't recall any such conversation, Elena."

"I thought it was understood."

Clay walked in the room carrying a tray of cold cuts and cheese. He laid it on the desk and looked from me to Jeremy.

Jeremy continued. "So you're no longer part of the Pack now?"

"Correct."

"Then you're one of them—a mutt?"

"Of course not, Jer," Clay said, thumping down beside me on the couch. I moved to the fireplace.

"Well, which is it?" Jeremy asked, his gaze skewering mine. "Pack or not?"

"Come on, Jer," Clay said. "You know she doesn't mean it."

"We had an arrangement, Elena. I wouldn't contact you unless I needed you. Well, I need you and now you're sulking and fuming because I had the gall to remind you of your responsibilities."

"You need me for what? To take care of a trespassing mutt? That's Clay's job."

Jeremy shook his head. "You don't use a wrecking ball to exterminate one mouse. Clay has his strengths. Subtlety is not one of them."

Clay grinned at me and shrugged. I looked away.

"So what's going on that's so damned important you need me?" I asked.

Jeremy turned and headed for the door. "It's late. I've called a Meet for tomorrow. I'll tell you everything then. Hopefully you'll feel less confrontational after a good sleep."

"Whoa!" I said, stepping out to block his path. "I dropped everything to come here. I skipped out of work, paid for an airline ticket, and raced here as fast as I could because no one was answering the damned phone. I want to know why I'm here and I want to know now. If you walk out that door, I'm not going to promise you'll still find me here in the morning."

"So be it," Jeremy said, his voice so cool I shivered in the draft. "If you decide to leave, have Clay drive you to Syracuse."

"Yeah, right," I said. "I'd be more likely to get to the airport by thumbing a ride with the local psychopath."

Clay grinned. "You forget, darling. I am the local psychopath."

I muttered my complete and heartfelt agreement. Jeremy said nothing, just stood there and waited for me to step aside. I did. Old habits are hard to break. Jeremy left the room. A minute later, his bedroom door closed upstairs.

"Arrogant son-of-a-bitch," I muttered.

Clay only shrugged. He was leaning back in his seat, eyes watching me, lips curved in a pensive smile that set my teeth on edge.

"What the hell do you want?" I said.

His smile turned to a grin, white teeth flashing. "You. What else?"

"Where? Right here? On the floor?"

"Nah. Not that. Not yet. Just the same old thing I always want. You. Here. For good."

I wished he'd stuck with my interpretation. He caught my eye.

"I'm glad you're home, darling. I missed you."

I nearly tripped over my feet running from the room.

CHAPTER 4

MEET

No matter what Jeremy had said, I knew better than to leave. He might pretend not to care what I did, but he'd stop me if I tried to leave before he'd told me whatever he'd wanted to tell me. I had three choices. First, I could call him on it and walk out. Second, I could storm to his room and demand he tell me what was going on. Third, I could go to my old bedroom, sleep, and find out what he wanted in the morning. I weighed the options. Getting a cab back to Syracuse would be impossible now, since the local taxi service shut down over an hour ago. I could take one of the cars and ditch it at the airport, but my chances of catching a flight to Toronto at three A.M. were next to none and I didn't relish sleeping in the airport. Nor did I relish the idea of fighting with Jeremy. One didn't fight with Jeremy Danvers; one shouted and raged and cursed him while he stood there with an inscrutable look on his face, waited until you'd exhausted yourself, then calmly refused to discuss the matter. I'd learned ways of getting under his skin, but I was out of practice. No, tonight I'd fight back by refusing to play their games. I'd go to bed, get a good sleep, settle this in the morning, and leave. Simple as that.

I grabbed my overnight bag and went upstairs to my old room, ignoring the fact that—although supposedly no one knew I was coming—the bedroom was aired out, window cracked open, fresh bedding on, and covers turned back. I took the cell phone from my bag and called Philip. With each unanswered ring, I felt a stab of disappointment. He was probably in bed already. When the machine clicked on, I thought of hanging up, calling back, and hoping the additional ringing would wake him, but I knew I was being selfish, wanting to talk to him to reestablish my link with the outside world. So I settled for leaving a brief message to let him know I'd arrived safely and I'd call again before I left the next day.

The silence of the house woke me the next morning. I'd become accustomed to waking in the city, cursing the sounds of traffic. When nothing conspired to get me up this morning, I bolted awake at ten, half expecting to see the world had ended. Then I realized I was at Stonehaven. I can't say I was relieved.

I struggled up from the embroidered bedsheets and thick feather pillows and pushed back the curtains from my canopy bed. Waking up in my room at Stonehaven was like awakening into a Victorian romance nightmare. The canopied bed alone was bad enough, something straight out of "The Princess and the Pea," and it only got worse. A Hepplewhite cedar chest at the foot of my bed held wood-scented down comforters, just in case the two Egyptian cotton duvets on my bed weren't enough. Layers of opulent lace billowed around the window, streaming over a satin-covered window seat. The walls were pale pink, adorned with watercolors of flowers and sunsets. Across the room was a huge carved oak vanity, with a floor-length gilt mirror and silver vanity set. Even the top of the dresser was cluttered with Dresden figurines. Scarlett would have felt right at home.

The window seat was the reason Jeremy had picked this room for me, that and the cherry trees that had been blossoming just below the window. It had seemed appropriately pretty and feminine. The truth is, Jeremy had known squat about women and expecting me to go gaga over cherry blossoms had been the first of many mistakes. In Jeremy's defense, he couldn't be expected to know any better. Women played the most insignificant of roles in the world of werewolves. A werewolf's only reason for delving into the mind of a woman is to find the best way to get her in bed. Most of them can't even be bothered learning that. If you're ten times stronger than the gorgeous redhead standing at the bar, why waste your money buying her a drink? At least, that's the mutt point of view. Pack werewolves have developed more finesse. If a werewolf wants to live in one place, he can't make a habit of raping a woman every time the urge strikes. Pack werewolves even have mistresses and girlfriends, although they never form what humans would call close relationships. They certainly never marry. Nor do they let women raise their sons. As I've said, only sons inherit the werewolf gene. So, while daughters were ignored, it was a law of the Pack that all male children must be taken from their mothers in infancy and all ties with the mother must be severed. Jeremy couldn't be expected to know much about the opposite sex, having grown up in a world where mothers, sisters, and aunts were only words in a dictionary. And there were no female werewolves. Except me, of course. When I'd been bitten, Jeremy had expected a docile childlike creature who would meekly accept her fate and be happy with a pretty room and nice clothes. If he'd foreseen the future, he might have tossed me out the door . . . or worse.

The person who bit me had betrayed me in the worst possible way. I'd loved him, trusted him, and he'd turned me into a monster then left me with Jeremy. To say I reacted badly is an understatement. The bedroom arrangement didn't last. Within a week, Jeremy had to lock me in the cage. My Changes became as uncontrolled as my rages, and nothing Jeremy could say would make me listen. I despised him. He was my captor, the only one around upon whom I could heap the blame for every torment, physical and emotional, I was undergoing. If the cage was my hell, Jeremy was my Satan.

Finally, I'd escaped. I'd hitched rides back to Toronto, trading in the only commodity I had—my body. But within days of my arrival, I'd realized my assessment of the cage had been horribly inaccurate. It was not hell. It was only a way station on the voyage. Living unrestrained and being unable to control my Changes was the ninth circle of the inferno.

I started by killing animals to stay alive, rabbits, raccoons, dogs, and even rats. Before long I lost all illusion of control and sank into madness. Unable to reason, barely able to think, I'd been driven entirely by the needs of my stomach. The rabbits and raccoons weren't enough. I killed people. After the second one, Jeremy found me, took me home, and trained me. I never tried to escape again. I'd learned my lesson. There were worse things than Stonehaven.

After struggling out of bed, I trotted across the cold hardwood floor to the throw rug. The dresser and closet were stuffed with clothing I'd accumulated over the years. I found jeans and a shirt and yanked them on. Too lazy to comb my hair, I raked my fingers though it and tied it into a loose braid.

Once semi-presentable I opened the bedroom door and glanced across the hall. As Clay's deep snores reverberated from his bedroom, some tension eased out of my shoulders. That was one problem I could avoid this morning.

I slipped out into the hall and past his closed door. With an uncanny abruptness, the snoring stopped. Cursing under my breath I hurried down the first few stairs. Clay's door creaked open, followed by the padding of bare feet on hardwood. Don't stop, I warned myself, and don't turn around. Then I stopped and, of course, turned around.

He stood at the top of the stairs looking exhausted enough to tumble down them at the slightest touch. His close-cropped gold curls were an unruly mess, rumpled and plastered down by sweaty sleep. Sandy blond beard shadow covered his cheeks and square chin. His eyes were half-lidded, struggling to focus. He was dressed only in the white boxer shorts with black paw prints that I'd bought him as a joke during one of our better periods. With a yawn, he stretched and rolled his shoulders, rippling muscles down his chest.

"Rough night guarding my escape routes?" I asked.

He shrugged. Whenever I had a bad day at Stonehaven, Clay spent the night staking out my possible escape venues. Like I'd ever be so cowardly as to sneak off in the night. Well, okay, I'd done it before, but that wasn't the point.

"How 'bout some company for breakfast?" he asked.

"No."

Another drowsy shrug of his shoulders. Let a few more hours pass and he'd never take the rebuff without a fight. Hell, in a few hours, he wouldn't bother *asking* if he could join me. I started back down the stairs. I got exactly three steps when he jolted awake, trotted down the stairs after me, and grabbed my elbow.

"Let me get your breakfast," he said. "I'll meet you in the sunroom. I want to talk to you."

"I don't have anything to say to you, Clayton."

"Give me five minutes."

Before I could answer, he'd jogged up the stairs and vanished into his room. I could have gone after him, but that would have meant following him into his bedroom. Definitely not a good idea.

At the bottom of the stairs, a smell stopped me in my tracks. Honeyed ham and pancakes, my favorite breakfast. I stepped into the sunroom and checked the table. Yes, stacks of ham and pancakes were waiting on a steaming platter. They hadn't materialized on their own, but I might have been less surprised to find that they had. The only person who could have made them was Jeremy, but Jeremy didn't cook. Not couldn't—didn't. That isn't to say he expected Clay or me to serve him, but when he did fix breakfast for us the only thing that steamed was the coffee. The rest was always a hodgepodge of breads, cheeses, cold meats, fruits, and anything else requiring minimal preparation.

Jeremy walked behind me into the sunroom. "It's getting cold. Sit and eat."

I said nothing about the breakfast. When Jeremy made a gesture he didn't like it recognized, much less thanked. For a moment I was sure this was Jeremy's way of welcoming me back. Then the old doubts resurfaced. Maybe he'd only fixed breakfast to placate me. With Jeremy, I could never read his intentions, even after all these years. Sometimes I was certain he wanted me at Stonehaven. Other times I was convinced he only accepted me because he had no choice, because I'd been thrust into his life and keeping me calm and under control was in the best interests of his Pack. I knew I spent too much time dwelling on this, struggling to interpret his every gesture, far too eager to see some sign of approval. Maybe I was still stuck in the old patterns of childhood, wanting a father more than I'd admit. I hoped not. Needy waif wasn't exactly an image I cared to project.

I sat down and dug in. The pancakes came from a mix, but I wasn't complaining. They were hot and filling, and came with butter and maple syrup—the real stuff, not the imitation junk I always bought to save a few bucks. I gulped down the first stack and reached for a second. Jeremy didn't so much as raise his eyebrows. One good thing about Stonehaven: I could eat as much as I wanted without anyone commenting or even noticing.

While Clay had staked out my bedroom window last night, it looked like Jeremy had been lying in wait for me here this morning. His easel was set up between his chair and the window. On it was a fresh sheet of paper with a few unconnected lines. He hadn't got far on the new sketch. The few lines he had drawn had obviously been erased and redrawn several times. One spot of paper was threatening to break through to the easel behind.

"Are you going to tell me what's going on?" I asked.

"Are you going to listen? Or are you trying to pick another fight?"

He drew a new line over the ghost of the last, then erased it. The brown of the easel peeked through the hole.

"It hasn't gone away, has it?" I said. "The reason I left. You're still angry."

He didn't look up from his sketch. Damn it, why didn't he look up?

"I was never angry with you, Elena. You were angry with yourself. That's why you left. You didn't like what you did. It frightened you, and you thought you could make it go away by leaving. Has it gone away?"

I said nothing.

Sixteen months ago, I'd gone to investigate a report of someone selling werewolf information. Now, the Pack doesn't chase down every joe who says he has proof of werewolves. That would be a full-time job for every living werewolf in and out of the Pack. We do keep an eye on stories that sound legitimate, excluding anything with keywords like silver bullet, baby killing, and ravaging half man–half beast creatures. What's left is a part-time job for two people: Clay and me. If an outside werewolf was causing trouble and Jeremy wanted to make an example of him, he sent Clay. If the trouble had gone beyond the point of a quick fix—or if it involved a human—then it needed caution and finesse. For those, he sent me. The case of Jose Carter required my brand of troubleshooting.

Jose Carter was a small-time con man who specialized in paranormal phenomena. He'd spent his life bilking the gullible and vulnerable with tales of loved ones trying to make contact from the beyond. Then, two years ago, while working in South America, he came across a small town that claimed a werewolf was preying on their village. Never one to miss an opportunity, Carter moved in and started gathering what he assumed would be phony evidence that he could sell in the United States. Trouble was, it wasn't phony. One of the mutts had been touring across Ecuador, hitting village after village and leaving a trail of dead bodies. The mutt thought he had the perfect gig, raiding villages so remote that no one would see the pattern. He hadn't counted on Jose Carter. And Carter hadn't counted on ever finding the real thing, but he was quick to recognize it when he did. He left Ecuador with eyewitness reports, hair samples, plaster paw-print casts, and photographs. Returning to the United States, he'd contacted several paranormal societies and tried to sell the information. He'd been so certain of his find that he'd offered to accompany the highest bidder back to South America to track the beast.

I'd caught up with Jose Carter at his "information auction" in Dallas. I'd tried to discredit him. I'd tried to steal the evidence. When nothing worked, I'd taken the only route left. I'd killed him. I did it on my own, without orders from Jeremy and without even contacting Jeremy. Afterward, I'd gone back to my hotel, cleaned up, and enjoyed a good sleep. When I awoke, the full impact of what I'd done hit me. No, not so much *what* I'd done, but how I'd done it, how easily I'd done it. I'd killed a man with as much moral compunction as I would have swatted a fly.

On the way back to New York, I'd prepared my argument for Jeremy, to explain why I'd acted without consulting him. Carter had been a clear threat. I'd done everything I could to stop him. Time had been running out. Had I called Jeremy, he would have wanted me to do the same thing, so I'd saved a step and taken care of matters myself. Before I'd reached Stonehaven, I'd realized the truth. It wasn't Jeremy I was trying to convince. It was myself. I'd crossed the line. I'd acted with the single-minded purpose of protecting my Pack, devoid of even a drop of compassion or mercy. I'd acted like Clay. That scared me, scared me so bad I'd run and sworn I'd never go back to that life again.

Had it gone away? Did I once again feel in complete control of my instincts and impulses? I didn't know. For over a year, I hadn't done anything so blatantly wrong, but nor had I been in a position where the opportunity arose. One more reason why I hadn't wanted to come back to Stonehaven. I didn't know if it was gone and I wasn't sure I wanted to find out.

A commotion at the front door snapped me out of my memories. As I glanced up, a tall, dark-haired figure burst into the sunroom. Nick caught sight of me, covered the room in three running steps, and swung me up off my seat. My heel caught the edge of my chair and toppled it over. He gave a mock growl as he squeezed me.

"You were gone too long, little sister. Much too long."

Lifting me up, Nick kissed me. Whatever his greeting, the kiss was definitely not fraternal, but a deep kiss that left me gasping. Anyone else would have gotten smacked for it, but anyone else wouldn't have kissed with half of Nick's expertise, so I overlooked the indiscretion.

"Well, just make yourself at home," Clay drawled from the doorway.

Nick turned to Clay and grinned. Still holding me captive in one arm, he strode across the floor and thumped Clay on the back. Clay's arm flew up and grabbed Nick in a headlock. He pulled me free and shoved Nick away. Nick regained his balance and his grin, and bounced back to us.

"When did you get in?" he asked me, then poked Clay in the ribs. "And why didn't you tell me she was coming?"

From behind, someone grabbed me in a bear hug and lifted me off the ground.

"The prodigal has returned."

I twisted to see a face as familiar as Nick's. "You're as bad as your son," I said, wriggling out of his grasp. "Can't you guys just shake hands?"

Antonio laughed and let me down. "I should squeeze harder. Maybe that would teach you to stay home for a while."

Antonio Sorrentino shared his son's wavy dark hair and heart-stopping brown eyes. They usually passed themselves off as brothers. Antonio was fifty-three and looked half that, which owed as much to his passion for healthy living as to being a werewolf. He was shorter and sturdier than his son, with broad shoulders and bulging biceps that made Clay look like a featherweight.

"Has Peter arrived yet?" Antonio said, pulling out the chair beside Jeremy, who was sipping his second cup of coffee, undisturbed by the uproar.

Jeremy shook his head.

"So everyone's coming?" I asked.

"Finish your breakfast," Jeremy said, giving me the critical once-over. "You've lost weight. You can't do that. If you don't get enough energy, your control will start to slip. I've warned you before."

Finally pushing his easel aside, Jeremy turned to talk to Antonio. Clay reached over my shoulder, snatched a hunk of ham, and downed it in one gulp. When I glared at him, he gave me a disarming "just trying to help" shrug.

"Keep your fingers off her plate," Jeremy said without turning around. "Yours is in the kitchen. There's enough for everyone."

Antonio was first out the door. When Nick went to follow, Clay grabbed his arm. He didn't say a word. He didn't need to. Nick nodded and bounded off to fill two plates while Clay took the seat beside me.

"Bully," I muttered.

Clay lifted his eyebrows, blue eyes flashing innocently. His fingers darted out to snag another piece of ham off my plate. Grabbing my fork, I stabbed the back of his hand hard enough to make him yelp. Jeremy sipped his coffee and ignored us.

Antonio came back into the sunroom, plate piled so high I expected the pancakes to slide to the floor at any second, especially since he was holding the plate with only one hand. His other hand was busy forking a pancake toward his mouth. Nick followed his father and dropped Clay's plate in front of him, then pulled up a fifth chair, turned it backward, and straddled it. For a few minutes, there was blessed silence. Werewolves weren't much for mealtime conversation. The task of filling their stomachs demanded full concentration.

The quiet might have lasted even longer if the doorbell hadn't shattered the silence. Nick went to answer it and came back with Peter Myers. Peter was short and wiry with an easy grin and wild red hair that always looked as if he'd forgotten to comb it. Once again, we went through the rituals of bear hugging, back-thumping, and mock punching. Greetings amongst the Pack were as exuberant as they were physical, often leaving as many bruises as a few rounds of roughhousing.

"When's Logan coming?" I asked as everyone settled back to the business of eating.

"He's not," Jeremy said. "He had to fly to Los Angeles for a court case. Last-minute legal substitution. I contacted him last night and let him know what's going on."

"Which reminds me," Clay said, turning to me. "Last time I talked to Logan, he let something slip about speaking to you. 'Course, that's not possible, since you cut off all contact with the Pack, right?"

I looked at Clay, but didn't answer. I didn't need to. He could see my reply in my eyes. His face flushed with anger and he stabbed a slice of ham hard enough to rock the table. I'd spoken to Logan at least once a week since I'd left, telling myself that so long as I didn't go see him, I wasn't exactly breaking my vow. Besides, Logan was more than my Pack brother; he was my friend, maybe the only true friend I'd ever had. Although we were the same age, we shared more in common than being able to name both members of WHAM! . . . Logan understood the allure of the outside world. He enjoyed the protection and companionship the Pack offered, but he was equally at home in the human world, where he had an apartment in Albany, a long-term girlfriend, and a flourishing legal career. As soon as I realized that Jeremy had called a Meet, my first thought had been, Great, Logan's coming. Now I wouldn't even have that compensation for this unwanted visit.

A few minutes later, Jeremy and Antonio went out to the back porch to talk. As Jeremy's closest and oldest friend, Antonio often served as a sounding board for Jeremy's ideas and plans, a court adviser of sorts. Antonio and Jeremy had grown up together, sons of the Pack's two most distinguished families. Antonio's father had been Pack Alpha before Jeremy. When Dominic died, many in the Pack had assumed Antonio would take over the role, even though Pack leadership was not hereditary. As with real wolves, the Alpha of the Pack was traditionally the best fighter. Before Clay grew up, Antonio was the Pack's top warrior. Moreover, he had brains and more common sense than a dozen normal werewolves. Yet, on his father's death, Antonio had backed Jeremy, recognizing in him strengths that would save the Pack. With Antonio's help, Jeremy had been able to squash any objection to his succession. No one had challenged him since. The only werewolf with the power to contest Jeremy's position was Clay, and Clay would sooner cut off his right arm than challenge the man who had rescued and raised him.

When Jeremy was twenty-one, his father had returned from a trip with a strange story. He'd been passing through Louisiana when he'd scented a werewolf. He'd tracked it and discovered a preadolescent werewolf living like an animal in the swamps. To Malcolm Danvers, this had been nothing more than an intriguing dinner tale, since no one had ever heard of a child werewolf. While hereditary werewolves didn't experience their first Change until adulthood, usually between the ages of eighteen and twenty-one, a human bitten by a werewolf was a werewolf immediately, regardless of his age. The youngest person known to have become a werewolf was fifteen. It was assumed that if a child was bitten, he would die, if not of the bite, then surely from the shock. Even if he miraculously survived the attack, a child couldn't have the fortitude to survive the first Change. This boy in Louisiana looked no more than seven or eight, but Malcolm had seen him in both forms, so he was clearly a full-fledged bitten werewolf. The Pack chalked up his survival to sheer luck, a fluke of nature having nothing to do with strength or willpower. The wolf-child may have lived this long, but he certainly couldn't survive much longer. The next time Malcolm visited Louisiana, he expected to find the boy long dead. He even laid a few hefty wagers on this with his Pack brothers.

The next day, Jeremy caught a flight to Baton Rouge where he'd found the boy, who had no idea what had happened to him or how long he'd been a werewolf. He'd been living in the swamps and tenements, eking out an existence killing rats and dogs and children. At such an early age his Changes were uncontrollable and he vacillated continually between forms, reason having almost given way to madness. The boy had looked like an animal even in human form, naked with matted hair and nails like talons.

Jeremy had brought the boy home and tried to civilize him. As it turned out, the task was as impossible as civilizing a wild animal. The best you can hope for is to tame it. Clay had lived on his own as a werewolf for so long that he no longer remembered being human. He had become a wolf, more of a true wolf than any normal werewolf could be, governed by the simplest of instincts, the need to hunt for food, to defend his territory, and to protect his family. If Jeremy had questioned this, Clay's first encounter with Nicholas had banished any doubts.

As a boy, Clay would have nothing to do with human children, so Jeremy decided he should meet one of the Pack sons, thinking Clay might be more willing to accept a playmate, who, while not a werewolf yet, at least had the blood in his veins. As I've said, sons of the Pack were taken from their mothers and raised by their fathers. More than that, they were raised by the Pack itself. The boys were indulged and cherished by the whole Pack, maybe to compensate for a difficult life to come, more likely to foster the bonds necessary for a strong Pack. The children would often pass their summer holidays moving from one house to another, spending as much time as possible with the "uncles" and "cousins" who would become their Pack brothers. Since the Pack was never large, there were usually no more than two boys of a similar age. When Clay came to live with Jeremy there were only two Pack sons under ten: Nick, who'd been eight and Daniel Santos, who'd been almost seven—the age Jeremy decided Clay would officially be. Of the two, Nick would be Clay's first playmate. Maybe Jeremy picked Nick because he was the son of his best friend. Or maybe he already saw something in Daniel that made him decide he'd make an unsuitable playmate. Whatever the reason, Jeremy's choice was one that would resonate throughout the lives of the three boys. But that's another story.

At their first meeting, Antonio brought Nick to Stonehaven and introduced him to Clay, fully expecting the two boys to run off and play a good old-fashioned game of cops and robbers. As Antonio tells the story, Clay stood there for a moment, sized up the older and taller boy, then sprang, pinning Nick to the ground with his arm on his throat, whereupon Nick promptly pissed his pants. Disgusted at his adversary's lack of worthiness, Clay decided to let him live and soon found Nick had his uses . . . as a wrestling dummy, an errand boy, and a devoted follower. Which isn't to say the two never engaged in a good old-fashioned game of cops and robbers, but whenever they did, no matter which role Nick was given, he always ended up being the one gagged, bound to a tree, and sometimes abandoned.

Clay eventually learned better instinct control, but even now it was a struggle against his nature. For Clay, instinct ruled. He'd learned tricks he could employ if he had advance notice, such as hearing hunters on the property in the distance. But without such warning, his temper took over and he'd explode, sometimes endangering the Pack. No matter how smart he was—his IQ was once measured at 160—he couldn't control his instincts. Sometimes I thought this made it harder, having the brains to know he was screwing up and being unable to stop himself. Other times I figured if he was so smart, he should be able to control it. Maybe he just didn't try hard enough. I liked that explanation better.

Jeremy and Antonio returned from their talk and we all moved to the study, where Jeremy explained the situation. There was a werewolf in Bear Valley. The wild dog story was a plausible explanation devised by locals desperate for an answer. There had been canine tracks around the body. The kill itself was canine, throat ripped out and body partly devoured. Of course, no one could explain how the young woman had come to be wandering around the forest at night in the first place, particularly in a skirt and high heels. It looked like a dog kill, so the locals had decided it was. We knew better.

The killer was a werewolf. All the signs were there. The surprise was that he was still in Bear Valley, even that he'd arrived there at all. How had one of the mutts gotten so close to Stonehaven? How had he killed a local woman before Jeremy and Clay had even figured out he was there? The answer was simple: complacency. After twenty years of not seeing a werewolf set foot north of New York City, Clay had relaxed his guard. Jeremy had continued to monitor the papers, but he'd paid more attention to events in other parts of the Pack territory. If he expected trouble, he expected it elsewhere, maybe in Toronto, or Albany where Logan kept an apartment, or the Catskills, where the Sorrentinos' estate was, or across the border in Vermont where Peter lived. But not near Stonehaven. Never near Stonehaven.

When the dead woman had disappeared Jeremy knew about it but paid little attention. Humans went missing all the time. There had been no suggestion that the disappearance had anything to do with a werewolf. Three days ago the woman's body had been found, but by then it was too late. The window of opportunity for quickly and safely dispatching the trespasser had passed. The townsfolk were up in arms over the killing. Within hours hunters were combing the woods looking for predators, human or canine. As much as Jeremy was respected in the community, he was still an outsider—someone who lived there but held himself apart from the community. For years people in and around Bear Valley had granted the Danvers their privacy, prompted in part by the large checks that came from Stonehaven each Christmas earmarked for school improvements or a new library or whatever else city council was struggling to pay for. When danger came calling, though, it was human nature to look to the outsider. It wouldn't be long before someone looked toward Stonehaven and its generous yet mysterious inhabitants and said, "You know, we don't really know them, do we?"

"What we need to do first is find this mutt," Jeremy said. "Elena has the best sense of smell, so she'll be—"

"I'm not staying," I said.

The room went silent. Everyone turned to look at me, Jeremy's expression inscrutable, Clay's jaw setting for a fight, Antonio and Peter looking shocked, and Nick staring at me in confusion. I cursed myself for having let things get this far. The middle of a meeting was not the time to assert my independence from the Pack. I'd tried to tell Jeremy the night before, but he'd obviously chosen to ignore it and hope it went away with a good night's sleep. I should have taken him aside this morning and explained it, instead of sitting down for breakfast and letting the others think everything was back to normal. But that's the way Stonehaven worked. I came back, got caught up in it—running with Clay, arguing with Jeremy, sleeping in my room, reuniting with the others—and I forgot everything else. Now, as Jeremy began to make plans for me, my memory improved.

"I thought you came back," Nick said, breaking the silence. "You're here. I don't understand."

"I'm here because Jeremy left me an urgent message to call him. I tried calling, but no one answered, so I came out to see what was wrong."

I realized this sounded lame even as the words left my mouth.

"I called," I said. "And called and called and called. I was worried, okay? So I came to find out what Jeremy wanted. I asked him last night, but he wouldn't tell me."

"So now that you know, you're leaving. Again," Clay said, his voice low but hard.

I turned on him. "I told you last night—"

"Jeremy called you for a reason, Elena," Antonio said, stepping between Clay and me. "We need to find out who this mutt is. You keep the dossiers. You know them. That's your job."

"That *was* my job."

Nick straightened up, confusion now mixed with alarm. "What does that mean?"

Clay started getting to his feet.

"It means Elena and I have something to discuss in private," Jeremy said. "We'll continue this meeting later."

CHAPTER 5

LEGACY

Peter and Antonio cleared the room quickly. Nick lingered, trying to catch my eye. When I looked away, he hesitated, then followed his father. Clay thumped back into his seat.

"Clayton," Jeremy said.

"I'm staying. This has as much to do with me as it does you. Probably more. If Elena thinks she can show up, then walk right back out, after I've been waiting for over a year—"

"You'll do what?" I said, stepping toward him. "Kidnap me and lock me in a hotel room again?"

"That was six years ago. And I was only trying to convince you to talk to me before you left."

"Convince? Hah. I'd probably still be there if I hadn't convinced you to set me free by hanging you off the balcony by your ankles. If I'd had any sense, I'd have let go while I had the chance."

"Wouldn't have done any good, darling. I bounce. You can't get rid of me that easily."

"I'm getting rid of you now," Jeremy said. "Out. That's an order."

Clay paused, then sighed, hauled himself to his feet, left the room, and closed the door. That didn't mean he was gone, though. No footsteps receded down the hall. The floor thudded as he dropped down to sit outside and eavesdrop. Jeremy chose to ignore it.

"We need your help," Jeremy said, turning back to me. "You've researched the mutts. You took that on as a job. You know more about them than any of us."

"I took on the job when I was part of the Pack. I told you—"

"We need your nose to find him and your knowledge to identify him. Then we need your help to get rid of him. It's a tricky situation, Elena. Clay's not the one to handle this. We need to proceed with absolute caution. This mutt has killed on our territory and he's insinuated himself into our town. We need to lure him out without calling attention to ourselves or making him panic. You can do that. Only you."

"I'm sorry, Jer, but this isn't my problem. I don't live here anymore. I'm not supposed to be looking for mutts. It's not my job."

"It's my job, I know. This should never have happened. I wasn't paying enough attention. But that doesn't change the fact that it's happened and we're all in danger because of it—even you. If this mutt continues making trouble, he runs the risk of being caught. If he's caught, what will prevent him from telling the authorities about us?"

"But I—"

"All I want is your help dealing with this problem. Once it's cleared up, you can do as you wish."

"And if I wish to leave the Pack? Did you mean what you said last night? That the choice is mine?"

Something flitted across Jeremy's face. He brushed his bangs back and the expression was gone. "I was angry last night. There's no reason to be in such a rush to make this decision, Elena. I said I'd let you go and live your own life and I'd only call you back if it was urgent. This is urgent. I haven't phoned you for anything else. I haven't let Clay contact you. I haven't summoned you back for the other Meets. I haven't expected you to maintain the dossiers or anything else you normally do for us. No one else would get that kind of treatment. You get it because I want to give you all the freedom you need to make the right decision."

"You're hoping I'll grow out of it."

"Adjusting to this has been more difficult for you than anyone else. You didn't grow up knowing you'd become a werewolf. Being bitten would have been bad enough, but the way it happened, the circumstances under which it happened, make it ten times harder. It's in your nature to fight something you didn't choose. When you make your choice, I want it to be because you've spent enough time out there to know that it's what you want, not because you're stubborn and want to assert your right to self-determination here and now."

"In other words, you're hoping I'll grow out of it."

"I'm asking for your help, Elena. Asking, not demanding. Help me solve this problem and you can go back to Toronto. No one will stop you." He glanced toward the door, listening for Clay's protest, but only silence returned. "I'll give you some time to think about it. Come see me when you're ready."

I stayed in the study for over an hour. Part of me cursed myself for coming back, cursed Jeremy for putting this on me, cursed Clay for . . . well, for everything else. I wanted to stomp my feet in a two-year-old's tantrum and shout that it wasn't fair. But it was fair. Jeremy was being perfectly reasonable. That was the worst of it.

I owed the Pack a debt I hadn't finished paying. I owed Antonio and Peter and Nick and Logan for their friendship and their protection and, even if they were inclined to treat me like a kid sister, someone to pet and coddle and tease, they'd accepted me and looked after me when I couldn't look after myself. Most of all, though, I owed Jeremy. As much as I railed at his demands and tyrannical authority, I never forgot how much I owed him.

When I'd been bitten, Jeremy had taken me in, sheltered me, fed me, and taught me how to control my Changes, rein in my impulses, and fit into the outside world. The Pack often jokes that raising Clay was Jeremy's greatest challenge, the seven labors of Hercules all rolled into one. If they knew what Jeremy had gone through with me they might change their minds. I put him through hell for one solid year. When he'd brought food, I'd thrown it at him. When he'd talked to me, I'd cursed and spat at him. When he'd come near me, I'd attacked him. Later, when I'd escaped, I'd put the entire Pack at risk. Any other werewolf would have given up, hunted me down, and killed me. Jeremy hunted me down, brought me back to Stonehaven, and started all over again.

When I was well again he'd encouraged me to finish my university degree, footing the bill for tuition, an apartment, and anything else I needed. When I'd finished school and started doing freelance journalism he'd encouraged and supported me. When I'd announced I wanted to try living on my own he'd disagreed, but he'd let me go and watched over me. It didn't matter whether he did these things because he was fond of me or, as I feared, only because it was in the best interests of the Pack to keep me safe and under their control. It only mattered that he'd done it. Now I cursed him for interfering with my new life. The truth was that without Jeremy's help I wouldn't have a new life. If I'd survived at all, I'd be like the mutts, barely able to control my Changes, completely unable to control my impulses, killing humans, moving from place to place one step ahead of suspicions, no job, no apartment, no friends, no lover, no future.

Now he asked something of me. One favor, not even phrased as such. Just a request for help.

I couldn't refuse.

I told Jeremy I'd stay long enough to help them find and kill this mutt on the condition that, when it was over, I could leave without him or Clay trying to stop me. Jeremy agreed. Then he went to tell the others, taking Clay out back for an extended explanation. When Clay returned, he was in high spirits, joking with Peter, mock-wrestling with Nick, chatting with Antonio, and offering me the couch when we went back to the study to resume the meeting. Since Jeremy wouldn't have sugarcoated my arrangement, Clay had obviously reinterpreted the facts through his own filter of logic, a logic as indecipherable as his code of behavior and ethics. I'd straighten him out soon enough.

As expected, the plan was to hunt down and kill the mutt. Given the dicey nature of the affair, this would take place in one or two phases. Tonight, the five of us, excluding Jeremy, would go into town to track the mutt down. We'd split into two groups, Antonio and Peter in one, the rest of us in the other. If we found the mutt's lair, Antonio or I would determine whether or not the mutt could be killed safely. If it wasn't a safe kill, we'd gather information to plot the killing for another night. After the Jose Carter fiasco I was surprised Jeremy was willing to give me the responsibility of making such a decision, but no one else questioned it, so I kept quiet.

Before lunch I went to my room and called Philip. Downstairs, Peter and Antonio were loudly debating some fine point of high finance. Drawers in the kitchen banged open and shut and the smell of roasting lamb wafted up to me as Clay and Nick made lunch. Although I couldn't hear Jeremy I knew he was still where we'd left him, in the study poring over maps of Bear Valley to determine the best areas of town for our search that night.

Once in my room I walked to my bed, pushing back the canopy, crawled inside with my cell phone, and let the curtain swing closed, cutting off the outside view. When Philip didn't answer his office number, I tried his cell phone. He picked up on the third ring. As his voice crackled down the line, all noise from downstairs seemed to stop and I was transported to another world, where planning to hunt down a werewolf was only a B movie plotline.

"It's me," I said. "Are you busy?"

"Heading off for lunch with a client. Potential client. I got your message. I went downstairs for a thirty-minute workout and missed your call. Can I get your number there? Hold on while I find some paper."

"I've got my cell phone."

"Okay, I'm an idiot. Of course you do. So if I need you, I can call your cell, right?"

"I can't take it in the hospital. Against the rules. I'll check for messages though."

"Hospital? Damn it. I'm sorry. Five minutes into the conversation and I haven't even asked what happened to your cousin. An accident?"

"His wife actually. I used to come down here in the summers and a bunch of us hung out together, Jeremy, his brothers, Celia—that's his wife." Philip knew my parents were dead but I'd told him none of the gory details, such as how young I was when it happened, so I was free to improvise. "Anyway, Celia was in a car accident. Touch-and-go for a while, when Jeremy called me. She's off the critical list now."

"Thank God. Geez, that's awful. How's everyone holding up?"

"Okay. The problem is the kids. Three of them. Jeremy's really at loose ends here, trying to look after the little ones and worrying about Celia. I offered to stay for a few days, at least until Celia's parents get back from Europe. Everyone's pretty shaken up right now."

"I can imagine. Hold on." Static buzzed down the line. "Good. I'm off the expressway. Sorry about that. So you're staying to help out?"

"Until after the weekend. Is that okay?"

"Sure. Absolutely. If I wasn't so tied up with work this week I'd come down to help out myself. Do you need anything?"

"Got my credit card."

He chuckled. "That's all anyone needs these days. If you max out, give me a shout and I'll transfer some money from my account. Damn—passed my turn."

"I'll let you go."

"Sorry. Call me tonight if you get a chance, though I expect you'll be pretty busy. Three kids. How old?"

"All under five."

"Ouch. You will be busy. I'll miss you."

"It'll only be a couple days."

"Good. Talk to you soon. Love you."

"You too. Bye."

As I hung up, I closed my eyes and exhaled. See? Not so bad. Philip was still Philip. Nothing had changed. Philip and my new life were out there, waiting for me to return. Only a few more days and I could go back to them.

After lunch, I went to the study to check my dossiers, hoping to find something that might help me figure out which mutt was causing trouble in Bear Valley. One of my jobs with the Pack was to keep tabs on non-Pack werewolves. I'd built a dossier of them, complete with photos and behavioral sketches. I could recite over two dozen names and last known locations, and separate the list into the good, the bad, and the ugly—those who could suppress the urge to kill, those who couldn't, and those who didn't bother trying. Judging by this mutt's behavior, he fell into the last category. That narrowed it down from twenty-seven to about twenty.

I turned to the cupboards below the bookshelf. Opening the second one, I cleared a path through the brandy glasses and felt around the back panel for an exposed wooden nail. When I found it, I twisted the nail and the rear panel sprang open. Inside the secret compartment we kept the only two condemning articles in Stonehaven, the only things that could link us to what we were. One was my book of dossiers. When I looked, though, it wasn't there. I sighed. Only Jeremy would have taken it out and he'd left for a walk an hour ago. Though I could always go looking for him, I knew he wasn't just taking in exercise but was finalizing the plans for our mutt hunt that night. Interruptions were not appreciated.

As I was closing the compartment I saw the second book lying there and, on a whim, pulled it out and opened it, though I'd read it so many times before I could recite most of it from memory. When Jeremy first told me about the Legacy I expected some musty, stinking, half-rotted tome. But the centuries-old book was in better shape than my college texts. Naturally the pages were yellowed and fragile, but each Pack Alpha had kept it in a special compartment, free from dust, mildew, light, and any of the other elements that could kill a book.

The Legacy purported to tell the history of werewolves, particularly of the Pack, yet it wasn't a straightforward account of dates and events. Instead, every Pack Alpha had added what he considered important, making it a mishmash of history, genealogy, and lore.

One section dealt entirely with scientific experimentation on the nature and boundaries of the werewolf condition. A Pack Alpha during the Renaissance had been particularly fascinated with legends of werewolf immortality. He'd detailed every one, from the stories of werewolves becoming immortal by drinking the blood of infants to the tales of werewolves becoming vampires after death. Then he'd proceeded with well-controlled experiments, all involving mutts that he'd capture, work on, then kill and wait for their resurrection. None of his experiments worked, but he'd been remarkably successful at decreasing the European mutt population.

A century later, a Pack Alpha became obsessed with the pursuit of better sex—the only surprising part of this being that it took several hundred years for someone to do it. He'd started with the hypothesis that human-werewolf sex was inherently dissatisfying because it involved two different species. So he bit a few women. When they didn't survive, he concluded that rumors of female werewolves throughout the ages were false and such a thing was biologically impossible. Moving right along, he tried variations on sex in both forms—as a wolf and as a human with both normal wolves and humans. None approached being in good old-fashioned human form having human sex, so he went back to women and started experimenting with variations on positions, acts, locales, et cetera. Finally, he found the ultimate act of sexual satisfaction—waiting until the first notes of climax struck, then slashing his partner's throat. He described his formula in vivid detail, with all the flowery emoting of a new religious convert. Fortunately, his practice never gained popularity among the Pack, probably because the Alpha was burned at the stake a few months later, after having depleted his village's entire supply of eligible young women.

On the less factual side, the Legacy contained countless stories of were-wolves through the ages. Most of these were "my father told me this when I was a child" sort of yarns, many dating back to before the first edition of the Legacy was written. There were tales of werewolves who'd lived their lives in reverse, staying wolves most of the time and changing to humans only when the physical need demanded. There were stories of knights and soldiers and bandits and marauders who'd supposedly been werewolves. Most of these names had vanished from history, but one was still known, even by those who'd never cracked open a history book in their lives. Human history tells of the legend that Genghis Khan's family tree started with a wolf and a doe. According to the Legacy, that was more truth than allegory, the wolf being a werewolf and the doe being a symbol for a human mother. According to that line of reasoning, Genghis Khan himself would have been a werewolf, which explained his lust for blood and his near-supernatural abilities in war. It likely wasn't any truer than the count-less human genealogies that include Napoleon and Cleopatra in their family tree. Still, it made a good story.

An equally good tale is one that was also found in human werewolf mythology. A newlywed nobleman's village was plagued by a werewolf. One night, while staking out the beast, the nobleman hears a noise in the bushes and sees a monstrous wolf. He jumps from his saddle and gives chase through the woods on foot. The beast flees from him. At one point, he gets close enough to swing his sword and lops off one of the wolf's front paws. The creature escapes, but when the nobleman goes back to retrieve the paw, it's turned into a woman's hand. Exhausted, he returns to his home to tell his wife what happened. He finds his wife hiding in the back rooms, binding the bloody stump where her hand used to be. Realizing the truth, he kills her. Now, the human version of the story ends there, but the Legacy goes further, giving the ending a pro-werewolf twist. In the Legacy tale, the nobleman kills his new wife by slicing open her stomach. When he does so, out tumbles a litter of wolf pups, his own children. The sight drives the nobleman mad and he kills himself with his sword. Now, as a female werewolf, I'm not particularly keen on the thought of a bellyful of puppies. I prefer to interpret the pups as an allegorical symbol of the nobleman's guilt. When he realizes he's killed his wife without giving her a chance to explain, he goes mad and kills himself. A much more fitting end.

In addition to these stories and musings, each Alpha chronicled the genealogy of the Pack during his reign. This included not only family trees, but brief descriptions of each person's history and life story. Most family trees were long and convoluted. In the current Pack, though, there were three blips, one name with no others before or after it. Clay and I were two. Logan was the third. Unlike Clay and me, Logan was a hereditary werewolf. No one knew who Logan's father was. He'd been put up for adoption as an infant. The only thing that came with him was an envelope to be opened on his sixteenth birthday. Inside the envelope was a slip of paper with two surnames and two addresses, that of the Danvers at Stonehaven and the Sorrentinos at their estate outside New York City. It was unlikely that Logan's father was Pack, since no Pack member would put a son up for adoption. Yet his father had known that the Pack wouldn't turn a sixteen-year-old werewolf away, whatever his parentage, so he'd directed his son to them, ensuring Logan would find out what he was before his first Change and, in doing so, have the chance to start his new life with training and protection. Maybe this proved that not all mutts were lousy fathers, or maybe only that anomalies were possible anywhere in life.

Most other Pack family trees had plenty of branches. Like the Danvers, the Sorrentino family could trace its roots to the beginning of the Legacy. Antonio's father, Dominic, had been Alpha until his death. He'd had three sons, Gregory, who was dead, Benedict, who'd left the Pack before I arrived, and Antonio, the youngest. Antonio's only son was Nick. In the Legacy, the annotation LKB was marked in parentheses beside Nick's initials. Nick didn't know what it meant. As far as I knew, he'd never asked. If he'd even read the Legacy, which I doubted, he'd have figured that if no one had explained the notation to him it must not be important. Nick was like that, totally accepting. The letters were important, but there was no sense telling Nick what they stood for, stirring up questions that couldn't be answered and emotions that couldn't be satisfied. LKB were Nick's mother's initials. It was the only place in the Legacy where a mother was memorialized. Jeremy had added it. Neither Jeremy nor Antonio had explained this to me. It was Peter who'd told me the story years ago.

When Antonio was sixteen, attending a posh private school outside New York City, he'd fallen in love with a local girl. He'd known better than to tell his father, but had let his best friend, fourteen-year-old Jeremy, in on the secret and the two had conspired to keep the relationship hidden from the Pack. It worked for a year. Then the girl became pregnant. On Jeremy's advice, Antonio told his father. Apparently, Jeremy had thought Dominic would see that his son was in love and break Pack law to help him. I guess everyone is young once. Young, romantic, and very naive. Even Jeremy. Things didn't exactly work as Jeremy had envisioned. Big surprise there. Dominic yanked Antonio out of school and put him under house arrest while the Pack waited for the baby to be born.

With Jeremy's help, Antonio had escaped, gone back to the girl, and declared his independence from the Pack. From there, things got really ugly. Peter glossed over the details, saying only that Antonio and his girlfriend had gone into hiding while Jeremy ran interference between father and son, desperate for a reconciliation. Somewhere in the midst of this, Nick was born.

Three months later, Antonio had his first Change. Over the next six months, he'd realized that his father was right. No matter how much he loved Nick's mother, it wouldn't work. Not only would he ruin her life, but he'd ruin his son's, sentencing him to a life as a mutt. One night he took Nick, left an envelope of money on the table, and walked out. He delivered Nick to Jeremy and told him to take the child to Dominic. Then he vanished. For three months, Antonio was gone, not even Jeremy knew where. Just as abruptly, he returned. He took Nick to raise and never mentioned the girl again. Everyone thought that was the end of it. Years later, though, Peter came to visit Antonio and tracked him to a suburb, where he'd found Antonio sitting in his car outside a playground, watching a young woman playing with a toddler. I wondered how often he'd done that, wondered if he ever did it now, checking up on Nick's mother, maybe watching her playing with her grandchildren. When I look at Antonio—boisterous, loud, self-assured Antonio—I can't imagine him holding a torch for a lost love, but in all the years I've known him, I've never heard him mention any woman in his life. Oh, there are women in his life, but they come and go, never staying long enough to make it into even the most idle conversation.

At the time, I wondered why Peter told me that story, a chapter of Pack history that would never make it into the Legacy. Later I came to realize that he'd thought letting me in on a harmless Pack secret might make me feel more a part of the Pack, might help me better understand my Pack brothers. Peter did a lot of that. Not to say that the others shut me out or made me feel unwelcome. Nothing of the sort. The only person whose acceptance I'd ever doubted was Jeremy's and maybe that was more my problem than his. I'd met Logan and Nick, through Clay, before I became a werewolf. After I was bitten, they'd both been there and, when I was ready to accept their help, they'd done whatever they could to cheer me up—as much as you could cheer up someone who's just learned that life as she's known it is over. When I met Antonio at my first Pack meeting, he'd flattered and teased and engaged me in conversation as easily as if he'd known me for years. But Peter had been different. Acceptance wasn't enough. He always went that extra step. He'd been the first to tell me his background, like a newfound uncle filling me in on family history.

Peter had been raised in the Pack but, at twenty-two, decided to leave. No major argument or rebellion precipitated his departure. He'd simply decided to try life from the other side, more an experiment in alternate lifestyles than a revolt against the Pack. As Peter put it, Dominic saw him neither as a dangerous non-Pack liability nor as a necessary Pack asset, so he let him leave. With a college degree in audiovisual technology Peter had gone after the most glamorous work he could imagine, as a sound technician for rock bands. He'd started with bar bands and, within five years, had worked his way up to big concert venues. That was when his thirst for new experiences got dangerous, as he'd lapped up the whole rock band lifestyle—drugs, booze, and parties past dawn. Then something happened. Something bad. Peter didn't elaborate, but said it was bad enough to warrant the death sentence if the Pack found out. He could have run, hid, and hoped. But he didn't. Instead, he'd looked at his life and what he'd done and realized it wouldn't get any better if he ran. He'd only screw up again. He decided to throw himself on the mercy of the Pack. If Dominic ordered his execution, at least his first mistake would be his last. He hoped, though, that Dominic would grant him absolution and let him return to the Pack, where he could get help regaining control over his life. To improve his chances, he appealed to the one Pack brother he trusted to plead his case with Dominic. He'd called Jeremy. Instead of going to Dominic, Jeremy flew to Los Angeles, bringing ten-year-old Clay. While Peter babysat Clay,

Jeremy spent a week erasing all traces of Peter's mistake. Then he took Peter back to New York and orchestrated his return to the Pack with nary a word about his misstep in California. Today no one would guess Peter had ever made such a mistake or had ever left the Pack. He was as devoted to Jeremy as Clay and Antonio, though in his own way, quiet and accepting, never arguing or offering so much as a dissenting opinion. The only trace of Peter's wild years was his job. He still worked as a sound technician, one of the best in the business. He routinely took off on long tours, but Jeremy never worried about him or doubted that he was anything but absolutely circumspect in his outside life. Jeremy had even let me take off with Peter for a few weeks back when I was still getting my bearings as a werewolf. Peter had invited me along on the Canadian leg of a U2 tour. It had been the experience of a lifetime, making me forget all the problems of my new life, which was exactly what Peter had intended.

As I was thinking this, a pair of hands grabbed me under the armpits and hoisted me off my chair.

"Wake up!" Antonio said, tickling me, then dropping me back onto the chair. He leaned over my shoulder and picked up the Legacy. "Just in time, Pete. Five more minutes of reading this and she'd have been in a coma."

Peter walked in front of me, took the book from Antonio, and made a face. "Are we such bad company that you'd rather hide out in here reading that old thing?"

Antonio grinned. "I'd guess it's not us she's avoiding, but a certain blond-haired tornado. Jeremy sent him to the store with Nicky, so you can come out of hiding now."

"We came to ask if you felt like taking a walk," Peter said. "Stretch our legs, get caught up."

"Actually, I was—" I began.

Antonio lifted me by the armpits again, this time putting me on my feet. "Actually, she was just going to come find us and tell us how much she missed us and is dying to get caught up."

"I was—"

Peter grabbed my wrists and tugged me toward the door. I dug in my heels.

"I'll go," I said. "I was just going to say that I came in here to read the dossiers, but Jeremy must have them. I was hoping maybe they'd help me figure out who could be behind this. Do you guys have any ideas?"

"Plenty," Antonio said. "Now come for a walk and we'll tell you."

When we'd left the backyard and headed into the forest, Antonio began.

"My money's on Daniel," he said

"Daniel?" Peter frowned. "How'd you figure that?"

Antonio lifted a hand and started counting off reasons on his fingers. "One, he used to be Pack so he knows how dangerous this kind of killing on our territory is, that we can't—and won't—leave town. Two, he hates Clay. Three, he hates Jeremy. Four, he hates all of us—with the exception of our dear Elena, who, conveniently, wasn't at Stonehaven to be affected by the mess, which I'm sure Daniel knew. Five, he really hates Clay. Six— oh, wait, other hand—six, he's a murderous cannibalizing bastard. Seven, did I mention he chose to strike when Elena wasn't around? Eight, if he caused enough havoc, Elena might be in the market for a new partner. Nine, he really, really, REALLY hates Clay. Ten, he's sworn undying revenge against the entire Pack, particularly those two members who happen to be currently living at Stonehaven. I'm out of fingers here, buddy. How many more reasons do you need?"

"How about one that involves utter suicidal stupidity. Daniel doesn't meet that qualification. No offense, Tonio, but I think you're seeing Daniel in this because you want to see him in it. He makes a convenient fall guy— not that I wouldn't like to help him with that final fall. But if you're placing wagers—small wagers, please, I don't have your capital to blow—I'd go with Zachary Cain. Definitely dumb enough. Big brute probably woke up one morning, thought, Hey, why don't I kill some girl on Pack territory for a kick. Probably wondered why he hadn't thought of it before. Because it's stupid, stupid."

"It could be someone minor," I said. "One of the bit players tired of being banished to the wings. Any mutts been making a ruckus lately?"

"Petty stuff," Antonio said. "None of the minor leagues making any major plays. Of the big four, Daniel, Cain, and Jimmy Koenig have been quiet. Karl Marsten killed a mutt in Miami last winter, but I don't think this Bear Valley problem could be him. Not his M.O., unless he's taken up not only killing humans but eating them. Unlikely."

"Who'd he kill?" I asked.

"Ethan Ritter," Peter said. "Range dispute. Clean kill. Thorough disposal. Typical Marsten stuff. We only know about it because I was passing through Florida earlier this spring on a tour. Marsten caught up with me, took me to dinner, told me he'd offed Ritter so you could strike his name from your dossiers. Had a nice little chat, rang up an astronomic bill, which he paid for in cash. He asked if we'd heard from you, sent his regards to everyone."

"I'm surprised he doesn't send Christmas cards," Antonio said. "I can see them now. Tasteful, embossed vellum cards, the best he can steal. Little notes in perfect penmanship, 'Happy holidays. Hope everyone is well. I sliced up Ethan Ritter in Miami and scattered his remains in the Atlantic. Best wishes for the New Year. Karl.'"

Peter laughed. "That guy has never figured out which side of our fence he's on."

"Oh, he's figured it out," I said. "That's exactly why he takes us out to fancy dinners and updates us on his mutt kills. He's hoping *we'll* forget which side of the fence he's on."

"Not likely," Antonio said. "A mutt is a mutt and Karl Marsten is definitely a mutt. A dangerous mutt."

I nodded. "But, as you said, not likely to be eating humans in Bear Valley. I'm as biased as you, but I really like the idea of Daniel. Do we have his last known whereabouts?"

There was a moment of silence. More than a moment. Much more.

"No one's been keeping track," Peter said at last.

"Not a big deal," Antonio said, breaking into a grin, grabbing me and swinging me in the air. "Forget Pack business. Tell us what you've been up to. We missed you."

It was a big deal. I knew why they were making light of it. Because the big deal was my fault. Tracking mutts was my job. If I'd told Jeremy I was leaving the Pack last year, he'd have found someone else to do it. If I'd called at any point and said I wasn't coming back, he'd have found someone else to do it. But I'd left my departure open-ended. I always did. I'd left Stonehaven before, getting into a fight with Clay and storming out for a much-needed rest. Days, maybe weeks later, I'd return. This time, the weeks had turned to months, then to a year. I thought they'd figure it out, know I wasn't coming back, but maybe they hadn't, maybe they'd still been waiting, like Clay waiting all day at the front gate, confident that I'd eventually return because I always did and because I hadn't said I wouldn't. I wondered how long they would have waited.

After dinner, I was heading to my room when Nicholas pounced out of Clay's room, grabbed me around the waist, and dragged me inside. Clay's bedroom was opposite mine, both in location and decor. The color scheme was black and white. The thick carpet was snow white. Jeremy had painted the walls white with bold, geometric black shapes. Clay's bed was king-size and brass, covered with a black-and-white bedspread embroidered with symbols from some obscure religion. Along the west wall was a top-of-the-line entertainment system, complete with the only stereo, VCR, and television in the house. The far wall was covered with pictures of me—a montage of photographs and sketches that reminded me of the "altars" found in the homes of obsessed psychopaths, which, all things considered, wasn't such a bad description of Clay.

Nick threw me onto the bed and jumped on top of me, pulling my shirt from my jeans to tickle my stomach. He grinned suggestively, white teeth glinting beneath his dark mustache.

"Looking forward to tonight?" he asked, running his fingers from my belly button farther under my shirt. I slapped his hand back down to my stomach.

"We aren't supposed to have fun," I said. "This is a serious matter, requiring a serious attitude."

A whoop of laughter exploded from the bathroom. Clay came out, wiping his hands on a towel. "You can almost say that with a straight face, darling. I'm impressed."

I rolled my eyes and said nothing.

Clay thudded down beside me, making the bedsprings groan. "Come on. Admit it. You're looking forward to it."

I shrugged.

"Liar. You are. How often do we get to run in town? An officially sanctioned mutt hunt."

Clay's eyes glinted. He reached down to stroke the inside of my forearm and I shivered. Nervous anticipation twirled in my stomach. Turning his head to the side, Clay looked out the window at the gathering dusk. His fingertips tickled against the inside of my elbow. My gaze swept over his face, taking in the line of his jaw, the tendons on his neck, the dark blond shadow on his chin, and the curve of his lips. Heat started in the pit of my stomach and radiated down. He swiveled back to face me. His pupils were dilated and I could smell his excitement. He gave a hoarse chuckle, leaned toward me, and whispered those three magical little words.

"Time to hunt."

CHAPTER 6

Hunt

B ear Valley was a blue-collar town of eight thousand that had got its start
in the heyday of industrialization and boomed during the forties and
fifties. But three recessions and downsizing had taken their toll. There was a
tractor factory to the east and a paper plant to the north and most people
worked in one of these two behemoths. Bear Valley was a place that prided
itself on hometown values, where people worked hard, played hard, and
filled the baseball stadium regardless of whether the local team was first or
last in the league. In Bear Valley, the bars closed at midnight on weekdays,
the annual PTA jumble sale was a major social event, and gun control meant
not letting your kids shoot with anything bigger than a twenty-gauge. At
night, young women walked the streets of Bear Valley fearing little more
than catcalls whistled from passing pickups by guys they'd known since
childhood. They did not get murdered by strangers and they certainly did
not get dragged off, slaughtered, and eaten by mad dogs.

We split up for the drive. Antonio and Peter headed for the west side
of town, where there were a couple of three-story walk-ups and two
highway-side motels. This meant that they had the better sector, since the
mutt was more likely to be found in less permanent housing, but the down-
side was that Jeremy had decided they'd have to search in human form,
since they couldn't exactly roam an apartment complex as wolves.

Clay, Nick, and I were to canvass the east end, where we hoped to find
the mutt renting or boarding. We took my car, an old Camaro that I always
found some excuse for leaving at Stonehaven. Clay was driving. It was my
fault, really—he'd challenged me in a race to the garage. My ego accepted
and my feet lost. We arrived in the city just past nine-thirty. Clay dropped
me off behind a medical clinic that had closed at five. I Changed between
two Dumpsters that reeked of disinfectant.

Changing forms is much like any other bodily function in that it comes
most easily when the body needs to do it. An uncontrolled werewolf under-
goes the transformation under two circumstances: when he is threatened

and when his internal cycle dictates the need. The need is roughly lunar based, though it has little to do with the full moon. Our natural cycles are usually weekly. As the time approached, we could feel the symptoms: the restlessness, the itchy skin, the internal cramps and pangs, the overwhelming sensation that something needed to be done and the body and mind wouldn't rest until that need had been satisfied. The signals became as recognizable as the signs of hunger, and like hunger, we could put off dealing with it, but before long the body would take over and force a Change. Also like hunger, we could anticipate the symptoms and satisfy the need beforehand. Or we could forgo the natural cycle completely and learn how to transform ourselves as often as we liked. That is what the Pack taught us to do, to Change more often to improve our control and ensure we didn't wait too long, since waiting could lead to nasty side effects like our hands turning to paws in the middle of grocery shopping, or, once a wolf, being overcome by frustrated rage and bloodlust. In Toronto I'd ignored Jeremy's teachings and given in to my need only when necessary, partly to distance myself from my "curse" and partly because in the city it was a major production requiring so much planning and caution that I was left too exhausted to repeat the experience more than once a week. So once again, I was out of practice. I'd Changed only yesterday and I knew doing it again less than twenty-four hours later would be hell. Like having sex without foreplay, it was either going to be extremely painful or I wasn't going to be able to perform at all. I should have told Jeremy this when he said we had to become wolves for the hunt, but I couldn't. I was, well, I was embarrassed. In Toronto, I'd done it as little as possible because I was ashamed. Two days later I was at Stonehaven refusing to admit that I couldn't do it as often as the others because I was ashamed. One more thing to send my brain spinning into permanent confusion.

It took over a half hour to complete the process, triple the normal amount of time. Did it hurt? Well, I don't have a lot of experience with non-shapechanging pain, but I feel safe in saying that being drawn and quartered might have hurt a bit less. When it was over, I rested for another twenty minutes, thankful I'd been able to do it at all. Given the choice between the agony of the Change and admitting to Clay and the others that I could no longer do it on demand, I'd pick drawing and quartering any day. Physical pain fades faster than wounded pride.

I started in a subdivision of old row houses that hadn't been converted to condos and probably never would be. It was past ten o'clock, but the streets were already deserted. Children had been yanked from the playground hours ago by anxious parents. Even adults had taken cover when the sun went down. Despite the warm May night, no one sat on their porches or shot hoops in their driveway. The wavering blue light of television flashed against drawn curtains. Sitcom laugh tracks screeched through the still night, offering escapism for the nervous. Bear Valley was afraid.

I stole along the front of the town houses, hidden between the brickwork and foundation shrubbery. At each doorway, I stuck my muzzle out and sniffed, then scampered across to the safety of the next string of bushes. Every flash of car lights made me freeze. My heart thudded, tripping with nervous excitement. There was little fun in this, but the danger added an element I hadn't experienced in years. If I was seen, even for a second, I was in trouble. I was a wolf skulking around a town in the throes of a collective nightmare about wild dogs. A flash of my shape silhouetted against a drawn blind would bring out the shotguns.

Over an hour later, I was midway through my fourth lane of row houses when a click-clicking stopped me cold. I pressed myself against the cool brick of the house and listened. Someone was coming down the sidewalk, clicking with each step. Clay? He'd better not. Even if hunting together might be more fun, Jeremy had instructed us to work separately to cover more ground. I stopped between the boughs of a cedar, peered out, and saw a woman hurrying up the sidewalk, heels clacking against the concrete. She wore a uniform of some kind, polyester skirt barely covering ample hips. Clutching an imitation leather handbag, she was moving as fast as her two-inch heels would allow. With every few steps she glanced over her shoulder. I sniffed the air and caught a faint whiff of Obsession cologne overladen with the stink of grease and cigarette smoke. A diner waitress coming home after her shift, not expecting darkness to have fallen so completely. As she drew closer, I smelled something else. Fear. Untainted, unmistakable fear. I prayed she wouldn't run. She didn't. With one final, fearful glance back at the street she scurried into her house and locked the door. I went back to work.

A few minutes later, a howl rang out. Clay. He didn't use the distinctive wolf howl, which would have certainly roused attention, but instead mimicked the cry of a lonely dog. He'd found something. I waited. When a second howl came, I used it to pinpoint his location, then started to run. I kept to the gutters, but didn't worry so much about staying out of sight. At this pace, anyone spotting me would see only a flash of pale fur.

I ran into an obstacle when I hit the main road and realized I had to cross it. While not many locals were still out, the main road was also a state highway meaning truckers sped through every few minutes. I waited for a big enough gap between semis and darted across. On the other side was Clay's assigned district, a subdivision of aging wartime houses and duplexes. As I tried to find his scent, I caught another, one that made me skid to a halt, my rear legs sliding forward and tumbling me backward. I shook myself, cursing my clumsiness, then retraced my steps. There, at the junction of two streets, I smelled a werewolf, someone I didn't recognize. The trail was old, but clear. He'd passed this way more than once. I gazed down the street. It was still in the general direction of where I'd heard Clay, so I changed course and followed the mutt's trail.

The scent led to a single-level brick house with aluminum-sided additions on the back. The yard was small and freshly cut, but creeping weeds competed for space with the grass. Garbage was piled next to a gatepost and the odor made me wince. Judging by the three mailboxes out front, there were three apartments. The house was dark. I snuffled along the sidewalk. It was inundated with werewolf scent and I couldn't tell where one trail ended and the next began. The distinguishing factor was age. He'd been past here regularly for several days.

In my excitement at finding the mutt's apartment, I didn't see a shadow slip beside me. I swung my head up to see Clay, in human form. He reached down and ran his hand through the fur behind my head. I snapped at him and dove into the bushes. After Changing to human form, I stepped out.

"You know I hate that," I muttered, raking my fingers through my tangled hair. "When I'm Changed, either you stay Changed or you respect my privacy. Petting me doesn't help."

"I wasn't 'petting' you, Elena. Christ, even the smallest gesture—" He stopped himself, inhaled, and started again. "This is the mutt's place, the rear apartment, but he isn't here."

"You've been inside?"

"I was checking things out and waiting for you."

I looked down at his naked body, then at my own. "I don't suppose you thought to get clothing while you were standing around."

"You expect me to find something on a clothesline at this hour? Sorry, darling. Anyway, this has its advantages. If someone comes out, I'm sure you can convince him not to call the cops on us."

I snorted and walked around to the rear apartment door. It was secured only with a key lock. A sharp twist on the handle broke that. I'd barely pushed the door open a crack when the fetid odor of rotting meat hit me. I gagged and swallowed back the urge to cough. The place smelled like a charnel house. At least, it did to me. A human probably wouldn't have smelled a thing.

The door opened into a living room that looked like a stereotypical bachelor's place: unwashed clothing strewn across the threadbare sofa set and empty beer cans stacked like a house of cards in the corner. Boxes with pizza crusts littered the corner table. But that wasn't the source of the stink. The mutt had killed here. There was no sign of a body, but the overpowering smell of blood and rotted flesh gave it away. He'd brought someone back to his apartment, killed her, and kept her around a day or two before dumping the remains.

I started in the main room, checking in closets and under furniture for any clue to the mutt's identity. Although I didn't recognize his scent, I might be able to figure out who he was with a few hints. When I didn't find anything, I went into the bedroom where Clay was on the floor, looking under the bed. As I walked in, he pulled out a hank of hair with the scalp still attached, tossed it aside, and kept searching for something more interesting. I stared at the bloody clump, feeling my gorge rise. Clay paid as much attention to it as he'd pay to a dirty tissue, more concerned with soiling his hands than anything else. As brilliant as Clay was, he couldn't understand why killing humans was taboo. He didn't slaughter innocent people, any more than the average person would swerve his car to intentionally hit an animal. But if a human posed a threat, his instincts told him to take whatever action was necessary. Jeremy forbade him to kill humans, so he avoided it for that reason and no other.

"Nothing," he said, his voice muffled. He backed out. "How about you?"

"Same. He knows enough to keep his place clear of ID."

"But not enough to keep his hands off the locals."

"Hereditary, but young," I said. "He smells new, but no new bitten werewolf could have that kind of experience so he must be young. Young and cocky. Daddy's taught him the basics, but he hasn't got enough experience to keep his nose clean or stay off Pack territory."

"Well, he's not going to live long enough to gain that experience. His first screwup was his last."

We were doing a last sweep of the apartment when Nick swung though the door, panting.

"I heard you call," he said. "You found his apartment? Is he here?"

"No," I said.

"Can we wait?" Nick asked, eyes hopeful.

I hesitated, then shook my head. "He'd smell us before he even got to the door. Jeremy said to kill only if we can do it safely. We can't. Unless he's a complete novice, he'll pick up our scents when he gets back. With any luck, he'll take a hint and get out of town. If so, we can hunt him later and kill him off Pack territory. Definitely safer."

Clay reached over to the nightstand, where he'd put things that he'd pulled from under the bed. He handed me two matchbooks.

"Bet I can guess where the mutt spends his evenings," Clay said. "If he's too dumb to blow town before we come after him tomorrow night, we can probably find him scouting for dinner at the local meat markets."

I looked at the matchbooks. The first was for Rick's Tavern, one of only three licensed establishments in the area. The second was a cheap brown matchbook with an address rubber-stamped on the back. I memorized the address, since we couldn't take anything with us, being a bit short of pocket space at the time.

"Back to get our clothes," Clay said. "Nick and I left ours across Main near where we dropped you off, so we can run together most of the way. You want to Change in the bedroom? We'll stay in here."

My heart started to hammer. "Change?"

"Yeah, Change. You planning to jog back to the car naked, darling? Not that I mind, so long as no one else gets an eyeful. But it might get a bit tricky, streaking across the highway."

"There's clothing here."

Clay snorted. "I'd rather be caught naked than wearing some mutt's clothes." When I didn't reply, he frowned. "Something wrong, darling?"

"No, I just— No. Nothing's wrong."

I walked into the bedroom, shutting the door all but a crack, so I could get out when—or if—my Change was successful. Thankfully, no one thought it odd that I wanted privacy. As close as the Pack was, most liked to make their transformations in private. As always, Clay was the exception. He didn't care who saw him Change. To him, it was a natural state and therefore nothing to be ashamed of, even if the midpoint of a Change turned you into something fit only for a freak show. For Clay, vanity was yet another bizarre and foreign human concept. Nothing natural should need to be hidden. The bathroom locks at Stonehaven had been broken for over twenty years. No one bothered to fix them. Some things weren't worth the effort of fighting Clay's nature. We drew the line, though, when it came to Changing together.

I crossed to the other side of the bed so Clay and Nick couldn't see me through the door. Then I sank to all fours, concentrated, and hoped. For five long minutes, nothing happened. I started to sweat and tried harder. Several more minutes passed. I thought I felt my hands changing into claws, but when I looked down, it was only my very human fingers digging into the carpet.

Out of the corner of my eye, I saw the door move. A black nose poked into the room. A golden muzzle followed. Jumping forward, I slammed the door shut before Clay saw me. He gave a questioning whine. I grunted, hoping the noise sounded sufficiently canine. Clay grunted back and padded away from the door. A respite, but a brief one. In less than five minutes he'd try again. Clay wasn't known for his patience.

Creeping across the carpet, I eased the door back open a crack so I could prod it open if—when, please when—I Changed. Just in case, I thought of backup plans. Grab some clothing and break out the window? As I was sizing up the tiny window, my skin started to tingle and stretch. I glanced down to see my fingernails thickening, my fingers shortening. Giving a deep sigh of relief, I closed my eyes and let the transformation take over.

We crept through the yard behind the house and came out on the north side of Bear Valley's fast-food strip, a gauntlet of every known chain restaurant with a drive-through. After sneaking through the rear parking lots, we headed into a maze of alleys wending through a block of storage units. Finally out from under the floodlights, we began to run.

Before long, Clay and I started to race. It was more of an obstacle course than a flat-out race, slipping in the puddles and stumbling over garbage bags. I'd taken the lead when a garbage can crashed at the end of the alley. All three of us skidded to a halt.

"What the fuck are you doing?" said a young male voice. "Watch where you're going and get your ass in gear. If my old man finds I snuck out, he'll nail my hide to the woodshed door."

Another male voice only gave a drunken giggle in reply. The garbage can scraped along the gravel, then two heads came into view, moving into the alley. I inched into the shadows until my rump hit the brick wall. I was sandwiched between a pile of garbage and a stack of boxes. Across from me, Clay and Nick retreated into a doorway and disappeared into the darkness, leaving only Clay's glowing blue eyes. He looked from me to the approaching boys, telling me that the shadows weren't doing their job and I was exposed. It was too late to move. I could only hope the boys were too drunk to pay attention as they stumbled past.

The boys were chattering about something, but the words passed through my ears as white noise. To understand human speech in this form, I had to concentrate, much like I would to understand someone speaking

French. I couldn't bother with that now. I was too busy watching their feet as they drew closer.

As they came alongside the garbage pile, I crouched, flattening myself to the ground. Their boots took three more steps, propelling them just past my hiding spot. I forced myself not to listen, instead looking up at their faces and taking my cue from there. They were no more than seventeen years old. One was tall, dark haired, wearing a leather jacket, ripped jeans, and combat boots, with a tattoo around his neck, and studs through his lips and nose. His red-haired companion wore a similar outfit, but without the tattoo and piercings, lacking the courage—or the idiocy—to turn a fashion statement into permanent disfigurement.

They continued to jabber as they walked away. Then the dark-haired kid tripped. Falling, he twisted, grabbed the side of a garbage bin, and saw me. He blinked once. Then he tugged his friend's jacket sleeve and pointed. Instinct goaded me to counter threat with attack. Reason forced me to wait. Ten years ago, I'd have killed the boys the moment they entered the alley. Five years ago, I'd have leapt as soon as one noticed me. Even today I could feel the struggle deep in my gut, a twisting fear that made my muscles twitch in readiness for the attack. It was this—the battle for control of my body—that I hated more than anything else.

A low rumble echoed through the alley. Feeling the vibrations in my throat, I realized I was growling. My ears were plastered against my head. For one second, my brain tried to override instinct, then saw the advantage in surrendering, in letting the boys see how close they stood to death.

I curled back my lips and snarled. Both boys jumped backward. The redhead turned and ran down the alley, tripping and stumbling through the trash. The other boy's eyes followed his friend. Then, instead of bolting after him, his hand shot out into the garbage pile. When he pulled back, the moonlight glinted off something in his hand. He turned to me, holding a broken bottle, the fear on his face replaced by a grin of power. Motion blurred behind him and I glanced up to see Clay in a crouch. The muscles in his shoulders bunched. I looked back at the boy, then sprang. Clay leapt. In midair, I twisted away from the boy and caught Clay full in the chest. We tumbled through the air together and hit the ground running, Nick at our heels. We ran the rest of the way back to our clothes.

We got to Stonehaven after two. Antonio and Peter were still out. There hadn't been any safe way to find them and tell them we'd already discovered where the mutt was staying. The house was silent and dark. Jeremy hadn't waited up. He knew if anything had happened, we'd wake him. Clay and I raced for the steps, jostling to be the first one up, bickering as we ran. Behind us, Nick mimicked our fight, but kept on our heels. We hit the top of the stairs and raced for Jeremy's room at the end of the hall. Before we could get there, the door creaked open.

"Did you find him?" Jeremy asked, a disembodied voice from the darkness.

"We found where he's staying," I said. "He's—"

"Did you kill him?"

"Nah," Clay said. "Too risky. But we'll—"

"Good. Tell me the rest in the morning."

The door closed. Clay and I looked at each other. Then I shrugged and headed back down the hall.

"I'll just have to beat you to it tomorrow," I said.

Clay pounced, knocking me onto the hardwood floor. He stayed on top of me, pinning my arms to the floor and grinning down, the excitement of the hunt still shining in his eyes. "You think so? How about we play for it? You name the game."

"Poker," Nick said.

Clay twisted to look up at him. "And what stakes are you playing for?"

Nick grinned. "The usual. It's been a long time."

Clay laughed, got up, and lifted me into his arms. When we got to his room, he tossed me onto the bed, then headed to the bar to mix drinks. Nick jumped on top of me. I threw him off and struggled up.

"What makes you think I'm going to play at all?" I asked.

"You missed us," Nick said.

He made a show of unbuttoning his shirt and shrugging it off, making sure I saw a good display of his muscles. Undressing was like some damned mating ritual with these guys. They seemed to think that the sight of a handsome face, muscular biceps, and a flat stomach would turn me into a helpless mass of hormones, willing to play their juvenile games. It usually worked, but that wasn't the point.

"Whiskey and soda?" Clay called from across the room.

"Perfect," Nick said.

Clay didn't ask what I wanted. Nick took the clip from my hair and nibbled my ear, warm breath smelling faintly of dinner. I relaxed on the bed. As his lips moved down my neck, I twisted my face, nuzzling his neck and inhaling the musky smell of him. I moved to the hollow in his collarbone and felt his heartbeat leap.

Nick jumped. I looked up to see Clay pressing a cold glass against Nick's back. He grabbed Nick's shoulder and yanked him off me.

"Go find the cards," he said.

"Where are they?" Nick asked.

"Look. That'll keep you busy for a while."

Clay sat down next to my head and handed me a drink. I took a sip. Rum and Coke. He gulped his own, then leaned over me.

"Perfect night, wasn't it?"

"It could have been." I smiled up at him. "But you were there."

"Which means it was only the beginning of a perfect night."

As he leaned over me, his fingers brushed against my thigh and slid over my hip. The thick, almost palpable smell of him sent a slow burn radiating down from my stomach.

"You had fun," he said. "Admit it."

"Maybe."

Nick jumped back onto the bed. "Playtime. Are you guys sticking to your stakes? Winner tells Jeremy what happened tonight?"

Clay's lips curved in a slow smile. "Nah. I'm going for something else. If I win, Elena comes outside with me, to the woods."

"For what?" I asked.

The smile widened to show perfect white teeth. "Does it matter?"

"And if I win, what do I get?" I asked.

"Whatever you want. If you win, you choose your prize. You can tell Jeremy what happened, or you can take the kill tomorrow, or anything else you'd like."

"I can take the kill?"

He threw his head back and laughed. "I knew you'd like that one. Sure, darling. You win and the mutt is yours."

That was an offer I couldn't resist. So we played.

Clay won.

Chapter 7

BLAME

I followed Clay to the woods. Nick had tried to come with us, but at one look from Clay, he'd stayed in the bedroom. When we got to a clearing, Clay stopped, turned around, and looked at me, saying nothing.

"We can't," I shivered in the night air.

He didn't answer. How many times had we replayed this scene? Didn't I ever learn? I knew how this would end when I picked up the cards—I'd been thinking of nothing else throughout the game.

He kissed me. I could feel the heat from his body, so familiar I could drown in it. The rich scent of him wafted through my brain, as intoxicating as peyote smoke. I felt myself succumbing to the smell, but a part of my brain that could still think sounded the alarm. Been here. Done this. Remember how it turns out?

I moved back, more testing his reaction than seriously resisting. He pushed me against a tree, hands sliding to my hips and gripping hard. His lips went back to mine, kisses deepening. I started to struggle in earnest. He pinned me between his body and the tree. I kicked out at him and he pulled back, shaking his head. I scrambled to catch my breath and looked around. The clearing was empty. Clay was gone. As my fogged brain struggled to process this, my arms were yanked behind my head, toppling me to my knees.

"What the—"

"Hold still," Clay said from behind me. "I'm helping."

"Helping? Helping what?"

I tried to pull my arms down, but he held them tight. Something soft slipped around my wrists. A sapling swayed overhead. Then Clay let go. I jerked my arms but only moved a couple of inches before the cloth around my wrists snapped tight. Once I was secured, he walked around and knelt over me, obviously far too pleased with what he was seeing.

"This isn't funny," I said. "Untie me. Now."

Still grinning, he took hold of the top of my T-shirt and ripped it down the middle. Then he undid my bra. I started to say something, then stopped, inhaling sharply. He'd taken my breast in his mouth and was teasing the nipple with his teeth. He flicked his tongue and it sprang up, hard. A dart of lust fogged my brain. I gasped. He chuckled and the vibration sent a shivering tickle through me.

"Is that better?" he whispered. "Since you can't fight me, you can't be expected to stop me. It's out of your control."

His hand moved from my breast and stroked my stomach, moving lower with frustrating slowness. I had an unbidden image of his naked body over me. The lust flared. He shifted around. I could feel his erection slide up my thigh. I spread my legs a bit and felt the roughness of his jeans brush against me. Then he pulled back.

"Can you still feel tonight?" he whispered, bending to my ear. "The hunt. The chase. Running through the city."

I shivered.

"Where do you feel it?" Clay asked, his voice deepening, eyes burning phosphorescent blue.

His hands slid to my jeans, unbuttoning them and sliding them over my hips. He touched the inside of my thigh, holding his fingers there just long enough to make my heart skip.

"Do you feel it here?"

He slid his hand down to the inside of my knees, tracing the path of the chills coursing through me. I closed my eyes and let the images of the night flow through my brain, the locked doors, the silent streets, the scent of fear. I remembered Clay's hand running through my fur, the spark of hunger in his eyes as he entered the apartment, the joy of racing through the city. I remembered the danger in the alley, watching the two boys, waiting, hearing Clay's roar as he lunged at them. The excitement was still there, pulsing through every part of my body.

"Can you feel it?" he asked, face coming to mine.

I started to close my eyes.

"Don't," he whispered. "Watch me."

His fingers traced up my thigh, slowly. He toyed with the edge of my panties for a moment, then plunged his fingers into me. I let out a gasp. His fingers moved inside of me, finding the center of my excitement. I bit my lip to keep from crying out. Just as I could feel the waves of climax building, my brain kicked in and I realized what I was doing. I struggled to pull back from his hand, but he kept it tight against me, fingers moving in me. The climax started to crest again, but I fought it, not wanting to give him that. I closed my eyes tight against him and jerked my arms hard against their bindings. The tree groaned, but the bindings held. Suddenly, his hand stopped and moved away. The metallic whir of a zipper cut through the night air.

My eyes flew open to see him pulling his jeans down over his hips. As I saw the hunger in his eyes and his body, my hips moved up unbidden to meet him. I shook my head sharply, trying to clear it. I twisted away. Clay bent down, his face coming to mine.

"I won't force you, Elena. You like to pretend I would, but you know I won't. All you have to do is tell me no. Tell me to stop. Tell me to untie you. I will."

His hand slipped between my thighs, parting them before I could clench them shut. Heat and wetness rushed out to meet him, my body betraying me. I felt the tip of him brush against me, but he didn't go any further.

"Tell me to stop," he whispered. "Just tell me."

I glared at him, but the words wouldn't come to my lips. We lay there a moment, eyes locked. Then he grabbed me under the arms and pushed into me. My body convulsed. For one long second, he didn't move. I could feel him inside me, his hips pressed against mine. He pulled back slowly and my body protested, moving involuntarily against him, trying to keep him. I felt his arms go over my head. My bindings jerked once, then broke in his hands. He thrust into me and my resistance snapped. I grabbed him, hands entwining in his hair, legs wrapping around him. He released my arms and kissed me, deep kisses that devoured me as he moved inside me. So long. It had been so long and I'd missed him so much.

When it was over we collapsed on the grass, panting as if we'd run a marathon. We lay there still entwined around each other. Clay buried his face in my hair, told me that he loved me, and nodded off. I lay in a drowsy haze. Finally I turned my head and looked down at him. My demon lover. Eleven years ago, I'd given him everything. But it hadn't been enough.

"You bit me," I whispered.

Clay bit me in the study at Stonehaven. I'd been alone with Jeremy, who'd been trying to figure out a way to get rid of me, though I didn't know that at the time. He seemed to be asking simple, benign questions, the sort a concerned father might ask of the young woman his son planned to marry. Clay and I were engaged. He'd already introduced me to his best friends, Nicholas and Logan. Now he'd brought me to Stonehaven to introduce me to Jeremy.

While Jeremy was interrogating me, I thought I heard Clay's footsteps, but they'd stopped. Either I'd imagined it or he'd gone someplace else.

Jeremy was standing by the window, quarter profile toward me. He looked out over the backyard.

"By the time you marry, Clayton's term at the university will have ended," Jeremy said. "What if he finds work elsewhere? Are you prepared to abandon your studies?"

Before I could formulate a reply, the door opened. I wish I could say it creaked open or something equally ominous. But it didn't. It simply opened. Seeing it move, I turned. A dog slipped in, head low as if expecting a reprimand for being in the wrong part of the house. It was huge, nearly as tall as a Great Dane, but as solid as a well-muscled shepherd. The gold of its fur sparkled. As it came in the room, it turned to look at me with eyes of the brightest blue. The dog looked up at me, mouth falling open. I smiled back. Despite its size, I knew I had nothing to fear. I felt that clearly.

"Wow," I said. "He's gorgeous. Or is it a she?"

Jeremy turned. His eyes widened and he blanched. He stepped forward, then stopped and shouted for Clay.

"Did Clay let him out?" I said. "It's okay. I don't mind."

I dangled my fingers, enticing the dog over.

"Don't move," Jeremy said, his voice low. "Take your hand away."

"It's okay. I'm letting him smell me. You're supposed to do that with a strange dog before you pet them. I had some dogs growing up. Well, my foster families did, at least. See his posture? Ears forward, mouth open, tail wagging? That means he's calm and curious."

"Pull your hand back now."

I glanced over at Jeremy. He was tensed, as if ready to jump at the dog if it attacked me. He called for Clay again.

"Really, it's okay," I said, getting annoyed now. "If he's skittish, you're only going to scare him by yelling. Trust me. I was bitten by a dog once. Yappy little Chihuahua, but it hurt like hell. I've still got the scar. This guy's a big brute, but he's friendly enough. Big dogs usually are. It's the little buggers you have to watch."

The dog had crept closer. One eye was on Jeremy, wary, watching his body language as if expecting a beating. Anger surged through me. Was the dog abused? Jeremy didn't seem the type, but I'd barely met him. I turned from Jeremy and reached out farther.

"Hey, boy," I whispered. "You're a pretty one, aren't you?"

The dog stepped toward me, moving slowly and carefully, as if we were both afraid of startling each other. Its muzzle came toward my hand. As it lifted its nose to sniff my fingers, it suddenly jerked up, grabbing my hand and nipping. I yelped, more in surprise than in pain. The dog began to lick my hand. Jeremy sprang across the room. The dog ducked and bolted out the door. Jeremy started after him.

"Don't," I said, leaping to my feet. "He didn't mean it. He was just playing."

Jeremy strode over to me and grabbed my hand, inspecting the bite. Two teeth had broken through the skin, leaving tiny puncture wounds that only trickled a few drops of blood.

"He barely broke the skin," I said. "A love bite. See?"

Several minutes passed while Jeremy examined my wound. Then there was a commotion at the door. I looked up, expecting to see the dog again. Instead, Clay swung through. I couldn't see his expression. Jeremy was between us, obstructing my view.

"The dog nipped me," I said. "No big deal."

Jeremy turned on Clay. "Get out," he said, his voice so low I barely heard it.

Clay stood frozen in the doorway.

"Get out!" Jeremy shouted.

"It's not *his* fault," I said. "Maybe he let the dog in, but—"

I stopped. My hand started to burn. The twin punctures had turned an angry red. I gave my hand a sharp shake and looked over at Jeremy.

"I should clean this," I said. "Do you have Bactine or something?"

As I stepped forward, my legs gave out. The last thing I saw was Jeremy and Clay both grabbing for me. Then everything went black.

After Clay bit me, I didn't regain consciousness for two days, though at the time I thought only hours had passed. I awoke in one of the guest rooms, the one that would later become my bedroom. Opening my eyes required major effort. The lids felt hot and swollen. My throat ached, my ears ached, my head ached. Hell, even my teeth hurt. I blinked a few times. The room dipped and swayed, then came into focus. Jeremy was sitting in a chair by the bed. I lifted my head. Pain exploded behind my eyes. My head fell back to the pillow and I groaned. I heard Jeremy stand, then saw him looking down at me.

"Where's Clay?" I asked. It sounded more like "whaaaclaaa," as if I were speaking through a mouthful of marshmallows. I swallowed, wincing at the pain. "Where's Clay?"

"You're sick," Jeremy said.

"Really? I couldn't tell." The retort cost me too much. I had to close my eyes and swallow again before continuing. "What happened?"

"He bit you."

The memory flashed back. I could feel my hand throbbing now. I struggled to lift it. The two puncture wounds had swollen to the size of robin's eggs. Heat radiated off them. There was no sign of pus or infection, but something was definitely wrong. A lick of fear raced through me. Was the dog rabid? What were the symptoms of rabies? What else could you contract from a dog bite? Distemper?

"Hospital," I croaked. "I should go to the hospital."

"Drink this."

A glass appeared. It looked like water. Jeremy slid his hand behind my neck and lifted my head so I could drink. I jerked away, striking the glass with my chin and toppling it onto the bed. Jeremy swore and pulled the soaked coverlet back.

"Where's Clay?"

"You have to drink," he said.

He lifted a fresh coverlet from the foot of the bed, shook it, and laid it over me. I squirmed from under it.

"Where's Clay?"

"He bit you."

"I know the damned dog bit me." I jerked back as Jeremy put his hand on my forehead. "Answer my question. Where's Clay?"

"He bit you. Clay bit you."

I stopped struggling and blinked. I thought I'd heard wrong.

"Clay bit me?" I said slowly.

Jeremy didn't correct me. He stood there, looking down at me, waiting.

"The dog bit me," I said.

"It wasn't a dog. It was Clay. He . . . he Changed form."

"Changed form," I repeated.

I stared at Jeremy, then twisted from side to side, trying to get up. Jeremy grabbed my shoulders and held me down. Panic ignited in me. I fought with more strength than I thought I had, flailing and kicking. He pinned me to the bed with as much effort as he might use to restrain a two-year-old.

"Stop it, Elena." My name came off his tongue awkwardly, like a foreign word.

"Where's Clay?" I shouted, ignoring the pain searing down my throat. "Where's Clay?"

"He's gone. I made him leave after he . . . bit you."

Jeremy seized both my arms and held them fast, pinning me so securely I couldn't move. He inhaled and started again.

"He's a . . ." He faltered, then shook his head. "I don't need to tell you what he is, Elena. You saw him Change forms. You saw him become a wolf."

"No!" I kicked up, my legs striking only air. "You're crazy. Fucking crazy. I saw a dog. Let me go! Clay!"

"He bit you, Elena. That means . . . it means you're the same thing. You're becoming the same thing. That's why you're sick. You need to let me help you."

I closed my eyes and screamed, drowning his words. Where was Clay? Why had he left me with this madman? Why had he abandoned me? He loved me. I knew he loved me.

"I know you don't believe it, Elena. But watch me. Just watch."

I wrenched my head sideways, so I wasn't looking at him. I could see only his arm holding mine to the bed. After a moment, his forearm seemed to shimmer and contract. I shook my head sharply, feeling the pain inside it bounce around like a red-hot coal. My vision blurred, then cleared. Jeremy's arm convulsed, the wrist narrowing, the hand twisting and contorting into a knot. I wanted to close my eyes, but I couldn't. I was transfixed by the sight before me. The black hairs on his arm thickened. More hairs sprouted, shooting out from his skin and growing longer and longer. The pressure of his fingers relaxed. I looked down. There were no fingers there. A black paw rested on my arm. I shut my eyes then and screamed until the world went dark.

It took over a year for me to truly comprehend what I'd become, that it wasn't a nightmare or a delusion, and that it would never end, that there was no cure. Jeremy allowed Clay back eighteen months later, but it would never be the same between us again. It couldn't be. There are some things you cannot forgive.

I awoke several hours later, feeling Clay's arms around me, my back pressed against him. A slow wave of peace started lulling me back to sleep. Then I jerked awake. Clay's arms around me. My back pressed against him. Lying together in the grass. Naked. Oh, shit.

I extricated myself from his grasp without waking him, then slipped from the clearing and hurried to the house. Jeremy was on the back porch, reading the *New York Times* in the first blush of sunrise. When I saw him I stopped, but it was too late. He'd seen me. Yes, I was naked, but that wasn't why I would have rather avoided Jeremy. Years of Pack life had stripped me of my modesty—no pun intended. Whenever we ran, we finished naked and often far from our clothing. Disconcerting at first, waking from a post-run sleep to find yourself lying in a grotto with three or four naked guys. Disconcerting, though not an altogether unpleasant experience, given that these guys were all werewolves, hence in excellent physical condition and didn't look too shabby au naturale. But I digress. The point is that Jeremy had been seeing my naked body for years. When I stepped from the trees sans clothing, he didn't even notice the lack.

He folded the paper, got up from his lounge chair, and waited. Lifting my chin, I made the journey to the porch. He would smell Clay on me. There was no way I could escape that.

"I'm tired," I said, trying to brush past him. "It's been a long night. I'm going back to bed."

"I'd like to hear what you found last night."

His voice was soft. A request, not a command. It would've been easier to ignore a direct order. As I stood there, the thought of going to bed, being alone with my thoughts, was suddenly too much. Jeremy was offering a distraction. I decided to take it. Sinking onto a chair, I told him the whole story. Okay, it wasn't the whole story, but I told him about finding the mutt's apartment, leaving out the aftermath with the boys in the alley and definitely excluding anything that happened after we got back. Jeremy listened and said little. As I finished, I caught a flicker of movement in the backyard. Clay strode from out of the forest, shoulders rigid, mouth set in a hard line.

"Go inside," Jeremy said. "Get some sleep. I'll look after him."

I escaped into the house.

Up in my room, I took my cell phone from my bag and called Toronto. I didn't call Philip, but it wasn't because I felt guilty. I didn't call him because I knew I should feel guilty and, since I couldn't, it didn't seem right to call. Does that make sense? Probably not.

If I'd had sex with anyone other than Clay, I would have felt guilty. On the other hand, the chances of me cheating on Philip with anyone other than Clay were so infinitesimal that the point was moot. I was loyal by nature, whether I wanted to be or not. Yet what I had with Clay was so old, so complex, that sleeping with him couldn't be compared to normal sex. It was giving in to something I felt so deeply that all the anger and hurt and hate in the world couldn't stop me from going back to him.

Being a werewolf, being at Stonehaven, and being with Clay were so tightly interwoven that I couldn't separate the strands. Surrender to one meant surrender to all. Giving myself to Clay wasn't betraying Philip, it was betraying myself. That terrified me. Even as I sat on my bed, clutching the phone in one hand, I felt myself slipping. The barrier between my worlds was solidifying and I was trapped on the wrong side.

I sat there, staring at the phone, trying to decide who to call, what contact in my human life had the power to pull me back. For a second, I thought of calling Anne or Diane. I rejected the idea immediately then wondered why I'd thought of it at all. If talking to Philip wouldn't help me, why would I ever consider calling his mother or sister? I chased the thought a moment, but something in it scared me off. After a brief pause, my fingers hit buttons of their own accord. As the phone rang, I numbly wondered who I'd called. Then the voice mail clicked on. "Hi, you've reached Elena Michaels at *Focus Toronto*. I'm not in the office right now, but if you'll leave your name and number at the sound of the tone, I'll return your call as soon as possible." I hung up, pulled back the covers, crawled into bed, then reached for the phone and hit redial.

By the fifth call, I was asleep.

It was nearly noon by the time I awoke. As I dressed, footsteps in the hallway stopped me cold.

"Elena?"

Clay rattled the door handle. It was locked. The only lock in the house Clay didn't dare break.

"I heard you get up," he said. "Let me in. I want to talk to you."

I finished tugging on my jeans.

"Elena? Come on." The door rattled harder. "Let me in. We need to talk."

Pulling my hair back, I clipped it at the nape of my neck. Then I walked across the room, opened the window, and swung out, hitting the ground below with a thud. Pricks of shock raced up my calves, but I wasn't hurt. A two-story jump wasn't dangerous for a werewolf.

Above me, Clay pounded at my door. I headed around the house and went in the front. Jeremy and Antonio were walking down the hall when I stepped in. Jeremy stopped and raised one eyebrow.

"The stairs aren't challenging enough anymore?" he asked.

Antonio laughed. "Challenge has nothing to do with it, Jer. I'd say it's the big bad wolf huffing and puffing at her door up there." He leaned around the corner and shouted up the stairs. "You can stop shaking the house apart now, Clayton. You've been outmaneuvered. She's down here."

Jeremy shook his head and steered me toward the kitchen. By the time Clay came down, I was halfway through breakfast. Jeremy directed him to a seat at the opposite end of the table. He grumbled, but obeyed. Nick and Peter arrived shortly after and, in the ensuing chaos of breakfast, I relaxed and was able to ignore Clay. When we were done eating, I told the others what we'd found the night before. As I talked, Jeremy scanned the newspapers. I was wrapping up when Jeremy put down the paper and looked at me.

"Is that everything?" he asked.

Something in his voice dared me to say it was. I hesitated, then nodded.

"Are you quite certain?" he asked.

"Uh—yes. I think so."

He folded the paper with maximum bustle and delay, then laid it in front of me. Front page of the *Bear Valley Post*. Top headline. Wild Dogs Spotted in City.

"Oh," I said. "Whoops."

Jeremy made a noise in his throat that could have been interpreted as a growl. I read the article. The two boys we'd seen in the alley had woken their parents with the story, who'd in turn woken the newspaper editor. The boys claimed to have seen the killers. Two, maybe three, huge shepherd-like dogs lurking within the very heart of town.

"Three," Jeremy said, his voice low. "All three of you. Together."

Peter and Antonio slipped from the table. Clay looked at Nick and jerked his chin, telling Nick he was free to leave, too. No one would blame Nick for this. Jeremy knew the instigators from the followers. Nick shook his head and stayed put. He'd take his share.

"We were returning from the mutt's apartment," I said. "The kids walked into the alley. They saw me."

"Elena didn't have enough room to hide," Clay interjected. "One of them grabbed a broken bottle. I lost it. I leapt at them. Elena stopped me and we took off. No one got hurt."

"We all got hurt," Jeremy said. "I told you to split up."

"We did," I said. "Like I said, this was after we found the apartment."

"I told you to Change to human after you found him."

"And do what? Walk to the car butt-naked?"

Jeremy's mouth twitched. A full minute of silence followed. Then Jeremy got to his feet, motioned for me to follow, and walked from the room. Clay and Nick looked at me, but I shook my head. This was a

private invitation, as much as I'd love to share it. I followed Jeremy out of
the house.

Jeremy led me into the woods, taking the walking paths. We'd gone nearly
a half mile before he said anything. Even then, he didn't turn around, just
kept walking in front of me.

"You know we're in danger," he said.

"We all know—"

"I'm not sure you do. Maybe you've been away from the Pack too
long, Elena. Or maybe you think because you've moved to Toronto this
doesn't affect you."

"Are you suggesting I'd purposely sabotage—"

"Of course not. I'm saying that maybe you need to be reminded how
important this is to all of us, no matter where we live. People in Bear
Valley are looking for a killer, Elena. That killer is a werewolf. We are
werewolves. If he's caught, how long do you think it'll be before the town
comes knocking at our door? If they find this mutt alive and figure out
what he is, he'll talk. He's not in Bear Valley by accident, Elena. Any mutt
with a father knows we live around here. If this one is discovered, he'll
lead the authorities here, to Clayton and me and, through us, to the rest
of the Pack, and eventually, to every werewolf, including any who are
trying to deny any connection with the Pack."

"Do you think I don't realize that?"

"I trusted you to set the tone last night, Elena."

Ouch. That hurt. More than I liked to admit, so I hid it in my usual way.

"Then that was your mistake," I snapped. "I didn't ask for your trust.
Look what happened with Carter. You trusted me with that, didn't you?
Once burned . . ."

"As far as I'm concerned, your only mistake with Carter was not contacting me before you acted. I know it has more meaning for you, but
that's exactly why you're supposed to contact me, so I give the order. I
take the responsibility for the decision. For the death. I know you—"

"I don't want to talk about it."

"Of course not."

We walked in silence. I felt the words jammed up in my throat, desperate for release, for the chance to talk about what I'd done and what I'd
felt. As I walked, a smell hit me and, with it, the words dissolved.

"Do you smell that?" I asked.

Jeremy sighed. "Elena. I wish you would—"

"There. Sorry. I didn't mean to interrupt, but"—my nose twitched, picking up the smell in the breeze—"that scent. Do you smell it?"

Jeremy's nostrils flared. He sniffed the breeze impatiently as if he didn't expect to find anything. Then he blinked. That smallest, most benign reaction was enough. He'd smelled it, too. Blood. Human blood.

CHAPTER 8

TRESPASS

I tracked the scent of blood to the east fence line. As we got closer, something else overpowered the smell of blood. Something worse. Decomposing flesh.

We came to a low wooden bridge that crossed a stream. Once on the other side, I stopped. The smell was gone. I sniffed the east wind again. There were traces of rot in the air, but the overwhelming stench had vanished. I turned and looked down at the stream. Something pale protruded from under the bridge. It was a bare foot, bloated, gray toes pointing at the sky. I jogged down the incline and waded into the stream. Jeremy leaned over the bridge, saw the foot, then pulled back and waited for me to investigate.

Grabbing the side of the bridge, I knelt in the icy water of the stream, drenching my jeans from ankle to knee. The bare foot was attached to a slender calf. The stench was overwhelming. As I switched to breathing through my mouth, my stomach lurched. Now I could taste the rot as well as smell it. I went back to breathing through my nose. The calf led to a knee, then fell away into shredded skin and muscle with bone shining through, leaving the femur looking like a big ham bone gnawed by a dog with more appetite for destruction than dinner. The other thigh was a maggot-infested stump, the bone snapped by powerful jaws. When I peered under the bridge, I saw the rest of the second leg, or pieces of it, strewn around, like someone shaking the last bits of garbage from the bag. Above the thighs, the torso was an indistinguishable mass of mangled flesh. If the arms were still attached, I didn't see them. Likely they were some of the bits scattered farther back. The head was twisted backward, the neck almost bitten through. I didn't want to look at the face. It's easier if you don't see the face, if you can dismiss a rotting corpse as a prop from a B horror movie. Still, easier isn't always better. This wasn't a movie prop and she didn't deserve to be dismissed as one. I assumed it was a she because of the size and slenderness but, as I shifted the head, I realized my mistake. It was a young man, little more than a boy. His eyes were wide, crusted with dirt, as dull as scuffed marbles. Otherwise, his face was unmarred: smooth-skinned, well fed, and very, very young.

It was another werewolf kill. Even if I couldn't smell the mutt through the rot and the blood, I knew it by the rough tearing of the throat, the gaping chew marks on the torso. The mutt had brought the body here. To Stonehaven. He hadn't killed the boy here. There was no sign of blood, but the caked dirt indicated he'd been buried and dug up. Last night, while we were ransacking the mutt's apartment, he'd been taking the body to Stonehaven, where we would find it. The insult sent tremors of fury through me.

"We'll have to dispose of it," Jeremy said. "Leave it for now. We'll go back to the house—"

A crash in the bushes stopped him short. I yanked my head from under the bridge. Someone was trampling through the undergrowth like a bull rhino. Humans. I quickly bent, rinsed my hands in the stream, and scrambled up the bank. I was barely at the top when two men in bright orange hunting vests burst from the forest.

"This is private property," Jeremy said, his quiet voice cutting through the silence of the clearing.

The two men jumped and spun around. Jeremy stayed on the bridge and reached one hand behind his back, pulling me to him.

"I said, this is private property," he repeated.

One man, a stout kid in his late teens, stepped forward. "Yeah, then what are you doing here, buddy?"

The older man grabbed the kid's elbow and pulled him back. "Excuse my son's manners, sir. I'm assuming you're . . . " He trailed off, searching for a name and coming up blank.

"I own the property, yes," Jeremy said, voice still soft.

A man and a woman came up behind the two, nearly bowling them over. They stopped short and looked at us as if seeing apparitions. The older man whispered something to them, then turned back to Jeremy and cleared his throat.

"Yes, sir. I understand you own this land, but you see, we've got ourselves a bit of a situation. I'm sure you heard about that girl that got killed a few days ago. Well, it's dogs, sir. Wild dogs. Big ones. Two of our boys from town saw them last night. Then we got a call this morning, saying something had been spotted on the far side of the woods out here around midnight."

"So you're conducting a search."

The man straightened. "Right, sir. So, if you don't mind—"

"I do mind."

The man blinked. "Yes, but you see, we've got to check things out and—"

"Did you stop at the house to ask permission?"

"No, but—"

"Did you phone the house to ask permission?"

"No, but—"

The man's voice had gone up an octave and the boy behind him was fidgeting and mumbling. Jeremy continued in the same unruffled tone.

"Then I'd suggest you go back the way you came and wait for me at the house. If you want to search these woods, you need permission. Under the circumstances, I certainly don't mind granting that permission, but I don't want to worry about running into armed men when I'm taking a walk on my own property."

"We're looking for wild dogs," the woman said. "Not people."

"In the excitement of the hunt, any mistake is possible. Since this is my land, I choose not to take that chance. I use these woods. My family and my guests use these woods. That's why I don't allow hunters up here. Now, if you'll go around to the house, I'll finish my walk and meet you there. I can provide you with maps of the property and warn my guests to stay out of the forest while you're here. Does that sound reasonable?"

The couple had joined the boy in his grumbling, but the older man seemed to be considering it, weighing inconvenience with propriety. Just as he appeared ready to relent, a voice rang out from behind them.

"What the hell is going on here?!"

Clay barreled out from the forest. I winced and thought I saw Jeremy do the same, although it might have been a trick of the sunlight through the trees. Clay stopped at the edge of the clearing and looked from the search party to us and back again.

"What the hell are you doing here?" he said, stepping up to the group of searchers.

"They're looking for wild dogs," Jeremy said softly.

Clay's hands clenched at his sides. The heat of his fury scorched all the way across the clearing. The other day when we'd heard the hunters on the property, Clay had been furious. His territory had been invaded. Yet he'd been able to control it because he hadn't seen the trespassers, had been forbidden to get close enough to them to see them and smell them and react as his instincts demanded. Even if he'd come upon them, he would have had enough advance warning to get his temper under control.

This was different. He'd come looking for us and hadn't smelled them until it was too late to prepare. The trespassers were no longer unseen guns firing in the dark, but actual humans, standing right in front of him, live targets for his rage.

"Did you miss the fucking signs on the way in?" he snarled, turning on the younger man, the strongest of the group. "Or is trespassing too god-damned many syllables for you?"

"Clayton," Jeremy warned.

Clay didn't hear him. I knew that. All he could hear was the blood pounding in his ears, the need to defend his territory screaming through his brain. He stepped closer to the young man. The boy inched back against a tree.

"This is private property," Clay said. "Do you understand what that means?"

Jeremy started down from the bridge with me at his heels. We were halfway across the clearing when a sound trumpeted from the woods. A baying hound. A dog on a scent. I looked from Jeremy to Clay. They'd both stopped and were listening, trying to pinpoint the direction of the noise. I stepped back toward the bridge. With every second, the hound's song drew closer, the tempo rising, infused with the joy of triumph. It smelled the body under the bridge.

I took another step backward. Before I could think, the dog flew from the forest. It was heading straight for me, eyes unseeing, brain bound up with the smell. It got within a yard of me, then skidded to a halt. Now it smelled something else. Me.

The dog looked at me. It was a big crossbreed, something between a shepherd and a redbone hound. It dipped its muzzle and blinked in confusion. Then it lifted its head and pulled back its lips in a deep growl. It didn't know what I was, but it sure as hell didn't like me. One of the men shouted. The dog ignored it. It growled another warning. The older man ran at the dog. Seeing my window of opportunity evaporating, I met the dog's eyes and bared my teeth. Come and get me. It did.

The dog leapt. Its teeth clamped around my forearm. I fell to the ground, lifting my arms over my face as if protecting myself. The dog held on tight. As its teeth sank into my arm, I let out a wail of pain and fear. I kicked feebly at the beast, my blows barely connecting with its stomach. Over my head, I heard an uproar. Someone tore the dog away, jerking my arm with it. Then the dog went limp. Its teeth fell from my arm. I looked up to see Clay standing over me, hands still wrapped around the dead dog's throat. He threw the corpse aside and dropped to his knees. I buried my head in my arms and started to sob.

"There, there," he said, pulling me close and stroking my hair. "It's all over."

He was trying hard not to laugh, his body shaking with the effort. I resisted the urge to pinch him and continued wailing. Jeremy demanded to know who owned the dog and whether its shots were up to date. The searchers' voices drowned out one another as they babbled apologies. Someone tore off to find the dog's owner. Clay and I stayed on the ground as I sobbed and he comforted me. He was enjoying this far too much, but I didn't dare stand for fear the searchers would notice that my eyes were dry and I looked remarkably composed for a woman savaged by a vicious beast.

After a few minutes, the dog's owner arrived and was none too pleased to find his prized hound lying dead in the grass. He shut up when he found out what had happened and started promising to pay for medical bills, probably fearing a lawsuit. Jeremy gave him a dressing-down over letting his dog run unleashed on private property. When Jeremy finished, the man assured him that the dog had all its shots, then quietly hauled away the carcass with the help of the younger man. This time, when Jeremy asked them all to leave the property, no one argued. When the chaos finally fell to silence, I shoved Clay off me and got to my feet.

"How's the arm?" Jeremy asked, walking toward me.

I examined the injury. There were four deep puncture wounds, still seeping blood, but the tearing was minimal. I clenched and unclenched my fist. It hurt like hell, but everything appeared to be in working order. I wasn't too concerned. Werewolves heal quickly, which is probably the reason we inflict injury on one another with such abandon.

"The first war wound," I said.

"Hopefully the last," Jeremy said dryly, taking my arm to examine the damage. "It could have been worse, I suppose."

"She did a great job," Clay said.

I glared at him. "I wouldn't have had to if you hadn't charged in ranting and raving like a lunatic. Jeremy had almost got rid of them when you showed up."

Jeremy shifted to the left, blocking my view of Clay, as if we were Siamese fighting fish that wouldn't attack if we couldn't see each other. "Come with me to the house and we'll get your arm cleaned up. Clay, there's a body under the bridge. Put it in the shed and we'll dispose of it in town tonight."

"A body?"

"A boy. Probably a runaway."

"You mean that mutt brought a body—"

"Just get it out of here before they decide to come back."

Jeremy took my good arm and led me away before Clay could argue.

On the way back to the house, we talked. Or, I should say, Jeremy talked, I listened. The danger seemed to be escalating with each passing hour. First we'd been spotted in the city. Next we'd found a body on the property. Then we'd had a confrontation with the locals, calling attention to ourselves and probably raising suspicion. All in twelve hours. The mutt had to die. Tonight.

When Clay came back to the house, he wanted to talk to Jeremy and me. I found an excuse and hightailed it up to my room. I knew what he wanted to say, to apologize for screwing up, for confronting the searchers and causing trouble. Let Jeremy absolve him. That was his job, not mine.

After Jeremy and Clay had finished their talk, Jeremy took the others into the study to explain what had happened. Since I didn't need the instant replay, I stayed in my room and called Philip. He talked about an ad campaign he was trying to snag, something about lakefront condos. I admit I wasn't paying much attention to his words. Instead, I listened to his voice, closing my eyes and imagining I was there beside him, in a place where dead bodies in the backyard would have been cause for indescribable horror, not quick cleanup plans. I tried to think as Philip would, to feel compassion and grief for that dead boy, a life as full as my own cut short.

As Philip talked, my thoughts wandered to my night with Clay. I didn't have to work very hard to guess how Philip would feel about that. What the hell had I been thinking? I hadn't been thinking—that was the trouble. If I hadn't felt guilt a few hours ago, I felt it now, listening to Philip and picturing how he would react if he knew where I'd spent the night. I was a fool. Here I had a wonderful man who cared for me and I was screwing around with a self-absorbed, conniving monster who'd betrayed me in the worst possible way. It was a mistake I swore not to repeat.

After a late lunch, Jeremy took Clay for a walk to give him instructions for that night. I'd already received mine. Clay and I were going after the mutt together—I didn't have a choice in the matter, but I'd still argued. I would find the mutt and lure him out to a safe place where Clay would finish him off. It was an old routine and, as much as I hated to admit it, one that worked.

While the others were cleaning up the dishes, I slipped away. I wandered through the house and ended up in Jeremy's studio. The mid-afternoon sun danced through the leaves of the chestnut tree outside, casting pirouetting shadows on the floor.

I thumbed through a stack of canvases leaning against the wall, scenes of wolves playing and singing and sleeping together, curled up in heaps of intertwining limbs and varicolored fur. Juxtaposed with these were pictures of wolves in city alleys, watching passersby, wolves allowing children to touch them while mothers looked the other way. When Jeremy did agree to sell one of his paintings, it was the second style that earned him the big bucks. The scenes were enigmatic and surreal, painted in reds, greens, and purples so dark they looked like shades of black. Bold splashes of yellows and oranges electrified the darkness in incongruous places, like the reflection of the moon in a puddle. A dangerous subject, but Jeremy was careful, selling them under an assumed name and never making public appearances. No one outside the Pack ever came to Stonehaven, except chaperoned service people, so his paintings were safe displayed here in his studio.

Jeremy painted human models too, though only members of the Pack. One of his favorites was on the wall by the window. In it, I was standing on the edge of a cliff, naked, with my back to the viewer. Clay was sitting on the ground beside me, his arm wrapped around my leg. Below the cliff, a pack of wolves played in a forest clearing. The title was scrawled in the bottom corner: *Eden*.

On the opposite wall hung two portraits. The first showed Clay in his late teens. He was sitting out back in a white wicker chair, with a wistful half smile on his face as his gaze focused on something above the painter. He looked like Michelangelo's *David* come to life, youthful perfection all innocence and dreaminess. On a good day, I saw the portrait as Jeremy's wishful thinking. On a bad day, it smacked of outright delusion.

The portrait that hung next to it was equally unsettling. It was me. I was sitting with my back to the painter, twisting to give a view of my full face and upper body. My hair was loose, falling in tangled curls and hiding my breasts. Like Clay's picture, though, the expression was the focal point. My dark blue eyes looked clearer and sharper than normal, giving them an animal-like glint. I was smiling with my lips parted and teeth showing. The impact was one of feral sensuality, with a dangerous edge that I didn't see when I looked in the mirror.

"Ah-ha," Nick called from the doorway. "So this is where you're hiding. Phone call for you. It's Logan."

I was out the door so fast I nearly knocked over a pile of paintings. Nick followed and pointed me to the phone in the study. As I was heading down the hall, Clay walked through the back door. He didn't see me. I slipped into the study and shut the door as I heard Clay asking Nick where I was. Nick made some noncommittal answer, not daring to risk Clay's anger by admitting the truth. Clay was still pissed off over me contacting Logan during my absence. He didn't suspect I was screwing around with Logan or anything so banal. He knew the truth—that Logan and I were friends, very good friends, but that was enough to ignite his jealousy, not of my body, but of my time and my attention.

I picked up the phone and said hello.

"Ellie!" Logan's voice boomed through a blanket of static. "I can't believe you're actually there. How's it going? Still alive?"

"So far, but it's only been two days." The line buzzed, went silent for a second, then hissed back to life. "Either L.A. has worse phone service than Tibet or you're on a cell phone. Where are you?"

"Driving to the courthouse. Listen, things here are wrapping up fast. We got a settlement. That's why I called."

"You're coming back?"

His laugh sizzled across the line. "Eager to see me? I'd be flattered if I didn't suspect you just want a buffer against Clayton. Yes, I'm coming back. I'm not sure exactly when, but it should be tonight or tomorrow morning. We've got to finish up work here and I'll catch the next plane out."

"Great. I can't wait to see you."

"Likewise, though I'm still miffed you wouldn't let me come to Toronto at Christmas. I was looking forward to burnt gingerbread. Another great holiday tradition lost."

"Maybe this year."

"Definitely this year." The phone crackled and went silent, then clicked back. "—lo?"

"I'm still here."

"I'd better sign off before I lose you. Don't wait up for me. I'll see you tomorrow and I'll whisk you away to lunch so you can relax for a while, catch your breath. Okay?"

"Definitely okay. I'll see you then."

He said good-bye and hung up. As I put the receiver back in the cradle, I could hear Nick in the hall, rounding up players for a game of touch football. He stopped outside the study door and tapped.

"I'm in," I said. "I'll meet you out there."

I looked back at the phone. Logan was coming. That was enough to make me forget all the problems and annoyances of the day. I smiled to myself and hurried out the door, suddenly eager for a good rough-housing before the excitement of the mutt hunt.

CHAPTER 9

PREDATOR

After dinner, I prepared for the evening. The choice of clothing posed a problem. If I was going to hook this mutt, I needed to pull on the mask that worked best with werewolves: Elena the sexual predator. This didn't mean miniskirts, fishnets, and see-through blouses, namely because I didn't own any. And I didn't own any because they looked ridiculous on me. Skimpy tops, stiletto heels, and barely there bottoms made me look like a coltish fourteen-year-old playing dress up. Nature didn't bless me with curves and my lifestyle didn't let me develop extra padding. I was too tall, too thin, and too athletic to be any guy's idea of centerfold fodder.

When I'd started living at Stonehaven, my wardrobe was strictly thrift-shop casual, no matter how much money Jeremy gave me for shopping. I didn't know what else to buy. When Antonio had bought us seats to a Broadway opening, I'd panicked. There were no women around to ask for help in choosing a dress and I didn't dare ask Jeremy for fear I'd end up in some taffeta and lace monstrosity fit only for a high school prom. I'd gone to a row of upscale shops in New York, but I got lost, literally and figuratively. My savior had appeared in a most unlikely form: Nicholas. Nick spent more time around women, particularly beautiful, rich young women, than any man outside of a James Bond film. His taste was impeccable, favoring classic designs, simple fabrics, and smooth lines that somehow turned my height and lack of curves into assets. All of my dress-up clothes had been bought with Nick in tow. Not only didn't he mind spending an entire day touring Fifth Avenue, but he'd have his credit card on the counter before I could fish mine from my wallet. Little wonder he was so popular with the ladies.

I picked out a dress for that night, one that Nick had actually bought me for my birthday two years ago. It was gorgeous indigo silk, knee length with no fancy trim or other adornment. Simple, yet elegant. To keep it casual, I decided to forgo nylons and wear sandals.

As I was putting on my makeup, Clay walked in and gave my outfit the once-over. "Looks good," he said. Then he glanced around at my princess bedroom and grinned. "'Course, it doesn't really suit the setting. It needs a little something. Maybe a lace shawl from the curtains. Or a sprig of cherry blossoms."

I snarled at him through the mirror and went back to my makeup, studying a jar of pink stuff and trying to remember whether it was for my lips or my cheeks. Behind me, Clay bounced on the bed, fluffing the over-stuffed pillows and laughing. He'd changed into baggy Dockers, a white T-shirt, and a loose linen jacket. The outfit hid his build and gave him a collegiate, clean-cut look, the message here being as non-threatening as possible. Nick must have helped him pick his clothes. Clay didn't know the meaning of non-threatening.

At nine we left, taking Jeremy's Explorer. Clay loathed the bulky SUV, but we needed the cargo space if we managed to capture and kill this mutt. Later that night, Antonio and Nicholas would dispose of the young boy's body at the local dump. We could have saved them a trip and taken it ourselves, but eau de decomposing flesh wasn't a good perfume choice when mingling with humans.

Although I hated the idea of spending the evening with Clay after what had happened between us, I soon relaxed. He didn't mention the previous night or say anything about Logan's call. By the time we got to town, we were carrying on a perfectly normal conversation about South American jaguar cults. If I didn't know him better, I'd almost think he was making a conscious effort to play nice. But I knew him better. Whatever his motivation, I went along with it. We had a job to do and we had to be together all evening to do it. Duty came first.

Our first stop was the mutt's apartment. I parked at the McDonald's behind the house, then we circled the block. The apartment was dark. The mutt was out. We could only hope he was at one of the bars.

All three bars were a bust. The fourth place on our list was the one without a name, only the address I'd memorized from the matchbook. The address led us behind the paper plant to an abandoned warehouse. Judging by the music booming from within, it wasn't "abandoned" tonight.

"What's up with this?" Clay asked.

"It's a rave. Not quite a bar, not quite a private party."

"Huh. Can you get in?"

"Probably."

"Go on then. I'll take up my post at a window."

I went around to the back of the building. The entrance was a basement door down a flight of steps. A sliver of light illuminated the edges. When I knocked, a bald man opened the door. A tilt of my head and a promise in my smile and I was in with a handful of free drink tickets. I'd hoped it would be more of a challenge.

The hallway led to a massive open room, roughly rectangular. A second-story catwalk had been converted into a narrow balcony with a makeshift set of stairs and no second-level railing. With no railing to stop them, people were sitting on the edge of the balcony, tossing beer caps onto the crowd below. Dusty warehouse boxes and old boards served as a bar along the left wall. Scattered in front of the bar were rusty tables and chairs, the sort of folding furniture you'd find in yard sales and pass over if your tetanus shots weren't up to date.

I'd been worried this would be like a Toronto rave, where the average patron spent more time worrying about midterms than mortgage payments. Definitely not a party where I could pass unnoticed. I looked young, but I was definitely past the zit cream and orthodontics stage of life. I needn't have worried. Bear Valley wasn't the big city. There were some underage kids here at this rave, but they were outnumbered by young and not-so-young adults, most sticking to Millers and marijuana but a few shooting heroin as openly as they downed their drinks. This was the side of Bear Valley the town councillors liked to ignore. If a local politician had wandered in here, he would have convinced himself they were all out-of-towners, probably from Syracuse.

The right side of the room was the dance floor, A.K.A. an unfurnished expanse of space where people were either dancing or suffering in the throes of a mass epileptic fit. The music was deafening, which I wouldn't have minded so much if the tunes didn't sound like something the bouncers had recorded in the back room. The smell of cheap booze and cheaper perfume pirouetted in my stomach. I stifled my nausea and began to search.

The mutt was there.

I picked up his scent on my second tour of the room. Weaving in and out of the crowd, I followed the smell until it led to a person. When I saw the person that the trail led to, I doubted my nose and circled back to double check. Yes, the guy at the table was definitely our mutt. And a less prepossessing werewolf, I had yet to meet. Even *I* looked scarier than this guy. He had acorn brown hair, a slender build, and a scrubbed, wholesome face—the quintessential college kid, right down to the Doc Martens and chinos. He looked familiar, but I hadn't committed all the photos in the Pack's dossiers to memory. It didn't matter who he was. It only mattered that he was here. A flash of rage burst inside me. This was the mutt causing all the trouble? This baby-faced brat had the Pack all in a panic, looking over our shoulders for guns and racing around Bear Valley to find him? I had to stop myself from marching over, grabbing him by the collar, and tossing him outside to Clay.

I resisted the urge even to go to him. Let him find me. He'd pick up my scent soon enough and he'd know who I was. All mutts knew who I was. Remember, I was the only one of my kind. From my scent, a mutt could tell that I was both werewolf and female. Not exactly a Sherlockian feat of deduction to figure out who I was. I passed twenty feet from this mutt's table and he didn't pick up my scent. Either the smells in the room were too overpowering or he was too dumb to use his nose. Probably the latter.

Knowing he'd smell me eventually, I turned in a drink ticket for a rum and Coke, found a table near the dance floor, and waited. As I scanned the crowd, I found the mutt again easily. With his short hair, polo shirt, and clean-shaven face, he stuck out like a Yanni fan at an Iron Maiden concert. He was sitting by himself, scanning the crowd with a hunger that stole the innocence from his eyes.

I took a few sips of my drink, then glanced back at the mutt's table. He was gone.

"Elena."

Not turning, I inhaled his scent. It was the mutt. I settled into my chair, took another sip of my drink, and continued watching the dance floor. He moved around the table, looked at me, and smiled. Then he pulled out a chair.

"May I sit?" he asked.

"No."

He started to sit.

I looked up at him. "I said no, didn't I?"

He hesitated, grinning as he waited for some sign that I was kidding. I hooked the chair with my foot and yanked it into the table. He stopped grinning.

"I'm Scott," he said. "Scott Brandon."

The name tickled the back of my mind. I mentally tried to pull forward his page from the Pack's dossier, but couldn't. It had been too long. I should have done my homework before I left.

He stepped toward me. When I glared, he backed off. I sipped my drink again, then looked at him over the rim.

"Do you have any idea what happens to mutts who trespass on Pack territory?" I asked.

"Should I?"

I snorted and shook my head. Young and cocky. A bad combination, but more annoying than dangerous. Obviously this mutt's daddy hadn't told him bedtime stories about Clay. A serious educational oversight, but one that would soon be resolved. I almost smiled at the thought.

"So, what brings you to Bear Valley?" I said, feigning bored interest. "The paper mill hasn't been hiring in years, so I hope you're not looking for work."

"Work?" A nasty smile lit his eyes. "Nah, I'm not much for work. I'm looking for fun. Our kind of fun."

I stared at him for a long minute, then got to my feet and walked away. Brandon came after me. I made it to the far wall before Brandon grabbed my elbow. His fingers dug into the bone. I yanked away and whirled to face him. The smile was gone from his face, replaced by a hard edge mingled with the petulant ill-humor of a spoiled child. Good. Very good. Now all I had to do was break away and let him follow me outside. By then he'd be in enough of a temper that he wouldn't see Clay until it was too late.

"I was talking to you, Elena."

"So?"

He grabbed me by both arms and slammed me back against the wall. My arms flew up to throw him off, but I stopped myself. I couldn't afford a scene, and somehow the sight of a woman brawling with a man is always an attention-grabber, particularly if she can pitch him across the room.

As Brandon leaned toward me, an ugly smile contorted his features. He reached up and stroked one finger down my cheek.

"You are so beautiful, Elena. And do you know what you smell like to me?" He inhaled and closed his eyes. "A bitch in heat." He pressed into me, letting me feel his erection. "You and I could have a lot of fun together."

"I don't think you'd like my kind of fun."

His smile turned predatory. "I've heard you don't get a lot of fun in your life. You've got this Pack breathing down your neck, smothering you with all their stupid rules and laws. A woman like you deserves better. You need someone to teach you what it's like to kill, really kill, not bring down some mindless rabbit or deer, but a human. A thinking, breathing, conscious human."

He paused, then continued, "Have you ever seen someone's eyes when they know they are about to die, at that moment when they realize you *are* death?" He inhaled, then exhaled slowly, the tip of his tongue showing through his teeth, eyes flooded with lust. "That's power, Elena. True power. I can show you that tonight."

Keeping hold of my arms, he moved aside to show me the crowd. "Pick someone, Elena. Pick anyone. Tonight they die. Tonight they're yours. How does that make you feel?"

I said nothing.

Brandon continued, "Pick someone and imagine it. Close your eyes. See yourself leading them out, taking them into the woods, and ripping out their throat." A shudder ran through him. "Can you see their eyes? Can you smell their blood? Can you feel the blood, everywhere, soaking you, the power of life flowing out at your feet? It won't be enough. It never is. But I'll be there. I'll make it enough. I'll fuck you right there, in the pool of their blood. Can you imagine that?"

I smiled up at him and said nothing. Instead, I slid a finger down his chest and over his stomach. For a moment, I toyed with the button on his fly, then slowly slid my hand under his shirt and stroked his stomach, tracing circles around his belly button. As I concentrated, I could feel my hand thickening, the nails lengthening. This was something Clay had taught me, a trick few other werewolves could do, changing only part of the body. When my nails became claws, I scraped them over Brandon's stomach.

"Can you feel that?" I whispered in his ear, pressing myself against him. "If you don't step away right now, I'm going to rip out your guts and feed them to you. That's my kind of fun."

Brandon jerked back. I held him tight with my free hand. He slammed me against the wall. I dug my half-formed talons into his stomach, feeling them pop through skin. His eyes widened and he yelped, but the roaring music swallowed his cry. I looked around, making sure no one was paying attention to the young couple embracing in the corner. When I turned back to Brandon, I realized I'd let the game stretch one period too long. His face contorted, jaw stiffening as the veins in his neck bulged. His face shimmered and rippled like a reflection in a barely flowing stream. His brow thickened and his cheeks sloped upward to meet his nose. The classic fear reflex of an untrained werewolf: Change.

I grabbed Brandon by the arm and dragged him into the nearest corridor. As I searched for an exit, I could feel his arm changing beneath my grip, his shirtsleeve ripping, his forearm pulsing and contracting. I was almost at the end of the hallway when I realized there wasn't an exit, only two bathroom doors. The men's room door opened and a man belched loudly. Another man laughed. I glanced back at Brandon, hoping his Change hadn't progressed beyond the point where it could be fluffed off as a physical deformity. No such luck—unless the bar's patrons were drunk enough to overlook someone whose face looked as if giant maggots were squirming under his skin. A man stepped from the bathroom. I spun Brandon around and saw a storage room door a few feet away. Shoving him ahead of me, I sprinted to the door, then snapped the lock, opened the door, and thrust Brandon inside.

As I leaned against the door, my mind raced for a solution. Could I get him out? Oh, sure, just slap a collar and leash on a 150-pound wolf and lead him to the door. No one would notice. I cursed myself. How had I let this happen? I'd had him. At the moment where he'd offered to show me how to kill a human, I'd had him. All I had to do was say yes. Pick some guy leaving the bar and tail him into the street. Brandon would have followed me and Clay would have been waiting outside. Game over. But no, that hadn't been enough. I had to push it, to see how far I could go.

"Shit, shit, shit," I muttered.

From behind the closed door, there was a deafening roar of pain, one that even the music down the hall couldn't drown out. Two passing women turned and stared.

"My boyfriend," I said, trying to smile. "He's sick. A bad batch. New dealer."

One of the women looked at the closed door. "Maybe you should get him to a hospital," she said, but continued walking, advice dispensed, duty done.

"Clayton," I whispered. "Where are you?"

I wasn't surprised that Clay hadn't busted down any doors when Brandon cornered me. Clay never underestimated my ability to defend myself. He'd only come to my rescue when I was in real danger. I wasn't in danger now, but I needed his help. Unfortunately, wherever he was hiding, he couldn't possibly see me in this hallway.

A crash echoed from inside the storage room. Brandon was done with his Change and was trying to get out. I had to stop him. And to stop him, I almost certainly had to kill him. Could I do that without causing a scene? Another crash resounded from the room, followed by the sound of splintering wood. Then silence.

I yanked open the door. Tattered scraps of clothing covered the floor. On the south wall was a second door leading back into the warehouse. In the middle of the cheap plywood was a gaping hole.

Chapter 10

Chaos

I raced into the main room. There wasn't any screaming. Not right away. The first sounds I heard were voices, more annoyed than alarmed. "What the—" "Did you—" "Watch it—" When I rounded the corner, I saw a path of toppled chairs and tables looping a tipsy half circle from the storage room to the dance floor. People milled around the overturned tables, collecting coats and purses and broken drink glasses. A boy well under legal drinking age sat cross-legged on the floor, cradling a broken arm. A woman stood on a chair, thrusting an empty glass toward the swath Brandon had cut across the dance floor and demanding that the "damn bastard" pay for her spilled drink, having somehow failed to notice that the "damn bastard" had fangs, fur, and no obvious place to carry a wallet.

I was still making my way toward the dance floor when Brandon roared. Then came the first scream. Then the thunder of a hundred people stampeding for the exit.

The stampede really didn't help matters, especially when my goal lay in the exact opposite direction of the human flow. At first, I was polite. Really. I said "excuse me," tried to squeeze through gaps, even apologized for stepping on some toes. What can I say, I'm Canadian. After a few elbows to the chest and more than a few obscenities shouted in my ear, I gave up and cut my own path. When one hefty bruiser tried to shove me back, I grabbed him by the collar and showed him the express route to the door. Things got a bit better after that.

Although I was no longer in danger of being trampled, I was still progressing by inches. I couldn't see anything. I'm not short—five foot ten to be precise—but even an NBA superstar couldn't have seen over that seething mass of humanity. If there was a back door or emergency exit, no one knew about it. They were all heading for the main entrance and getting jammed in the narrow front corridor.

Not only couldn't I see, I couldn't hear anything but the sound of the crowd, curses and shouts and cries melding into a Babel's tower of noise, nothing clear except the universal language of panic. People shoved and hammered at one another, as if being one step closer to the door meant the difference between life and death. Others weren't moving of their own volition at all, but were carried along by the tide of the mob. I looked into faces and saw nothing there. They were as white and expressionless as plaster masks. Only the eyes held the truth, rolling and wild, the instinct for survival taking over. Most didn't even know what they were running from. It didn't matter. They could smell the fear rising from the crowd as well as any werewolf could and the scent of it seeped into their brains, infecting them with its power. They smelled it, they felt it, and they ran from it. They were giving Brandon exactly what he craved.

I was midway across the dance floor when I stumbled over a woman lying in a pool of blood. Blood still jetted from her neck in a fountain, spraying anyone who came close. People tripped over her and slid in her blood. Not one of them even looked down. I shouldn't have looked down either. But I did. Her eyes rolled, meeting mine for a second. Bloody froth trickled and bubbled from her lips. Her hand convulsed off the floor as if trying to reach up. Then it stopped in midair, paused, and fluttered down into the pool of blood. Her eyes died. The blood had stopped spurting and was now streaming. A man tripped over her, looked down, swore, and kicked her out of his way. I tore my gaze away and kept moving.

As I stepped over the body, glass shattered overhead. I looked up to see Clay's feet shooting through a high window near the bar. He swung in and dropped to the floor. It was a good twenty-foot fall, not something Jeremy encouraged us to do in front of a crowd, but considering no one was paying any attention to a dead body beneath their feet, surely no one was going to notice a man vaulting through a window behind them. Clay climbed onto the bar and surveyed the crowd. When he saw me, he waved me over. I pointed deeper into the throng, where I assumed Brandon was. Clay shook his head and motioned again. I picked an angle roughly in line with the crowd flow and made my way toward him.

"Love that entrance," I shouted over the din as I climbed onto the bar.

"Have you seen the front door, darling? I'd need a blowtorch to cut through the crowd. The only other exit is bricked over."

I looked above the crowd. "So Brandon's not back in that corner?"

"Who?"

"The mutt. Is he there?"

"Oh, he's there all right. But you're wasting your energy trying to get to him."

I spotted Brandon. As I suspected, he'd fully changed into a wolf. He seemed to be bouncing between the corner walls, leaping and pouncing and slashing at nothing. I was about to say that it looked as if the mutt had snapped. Then the crowd parted enough for me to see that he was attacking more than air. A man lay in crash position on the floor, back up, knees to his chest, head down, hands linked to protect the back of his neck. His clothing was shredded and drenched with blood. He was motionless, obviously dead, but Brandon wasn't leaving him alone. He leapt at the man, grabbed his foot, and spun him in a circle. Then he danced back, tail high. He crouched and mock-lunged, then feinted to the side. The man now lay twisted half on his side, letting me see more of his injuries than I wanted. His shirt was ripped open. His torso was streaked with blood, his stomach solid red. The end of his belt dangled to the floor. Then I realized it wasn't his belt, but a loop of intestine. As I was turning away, the body moved. The man rocked, as if trying to flip back on his stomach to protect himself.

"Oh God," I whispered. "He's not dead."

Brandon leapt at his prey again and sank his teeth into the man's scalp. He yanked him up, tossed him aside, and pranced away again.

"He's not even trying to kill him," I said.

"Why would he?" Clay said, curling back his lip. "He's having fun."

Disgust dripped from every word. This wasn't killing for food or killing for survival. That Clay could understand. This was, to him, a display of another incomprehensible human trait—killing for pleasure.

"While he's busy, I'll do some scouting," Clay continued. "Give me five minutes. When the crowd clears, make your move. Drive him toward that side hall. I'll be waiting."

Clay jumped off the bar and vanished into the mob. I looked back at Brandon torturing his prey. Again, I didn't want to look, didn't want to think about what was going on below me, that a man was dying horribly but was still alive and I wasn't doing a damned thing about it. I reminded myself that it was almost certainly too late to save him and, even if he did survive, he'd have to go to the hospital, which we couldn't allow because, having been bitten by Brandon, the man was now a werewolf himself. Although rationally I knew I couldn't risk going to him, I felt compelled to, if only to end his suffering. Sometimes I think it would be better if I could be like Clay, to acknowledge that what Brandon was doing was wrong but equally acknowledge that it wasn't in my power to right that wrong and to walk away without regret. But I don't ever want to be like that, that hard, that tough. Clay had an excuse. I didn't.

I tore my gaze away from Brandon and his prey. Sick bastard. No animal would do something like that. As I thought this, something clicked in my brain, a piece falling into place so hard the resonance made me jump. The room went suddenly silent, the drumming in my ears drowning out the crowd, giving me one moment of perfect clarity amidst the chaos.

I knew where I'd seen Brandon's face, heard his name, and it wasn't in the Pack's werewolf dossiers. Television. *Inside Scoop*. The piece on the killer in North Carolina. The tape of the police interview flipped through my head again, the grainy image sparking to life. "I wanted to watch someone die." Scott Brandon. I shook my head sharply. No, that couldn't be. That didn't make sense. A werewolf couldn't survive in prison without being discovered. Then I remembered Brandon's scent again, a nuance I'd picked up that night in his apartment. "He's new," I'd told Clay. I could smell it in his scent and I'd assumed it meant he was a hereditary were-wolf recently come of age. But he wasn't. He'd been bitten.

Again, my brain rejected the idea. Brandon had only escaped from jail a few months ago. It took longer than that for a werewolf to recover from the shock of being turned. Or did it? Was it impossible that he'd recovered so quickly? I had to admit that it wasn't. My own recovery had been hampered by my refusal to accept what had happened to me. What if it wasn't like that? What if someone *wanted* to become a werewolf, was prepared for it, embraced it? That could make all the difference.

Yet there was still more that didn't make sense. What was Brandon doing here? If he was a hereditary werewolf, that would explain how he knew about Bear Valley, the Pack, and Stonehaven. How would a newly turned werewolf know that? But Brandon knew. He'd called me by name. He'd talked about the Pack, said he'd heard things about me. From who? Another werewolf, of course. An experienced werewolf. But mutts didn't do that. They didn't allow bitten werewolves to live, let alone help them. It was impossible. No, I corrected. Not impossible. Just so incredibly unlikely that my brain refused to consider the implications.

I couldn't deal with this now. We had a more serious problem on our hands than sorting out the whys and wherefores of Brandon's existence. The fact of his existence was enough. Ending that existence wouldn't be as simple as I'd thought. He wasn't a careless punk kid, but something far more dangerous: a true killer. I looked for Clay, wanting to warn him. Then I realized it wouldn't do any good. Brandon was a killer from the human world. I could tell Clay that Brandon was a chartered accountant and it would have the same impact. He wouldn't understand.

I hopped from the bar and eased through the last scattering of the crowd. In the back corner, Brandon was still playing with his food, which gave the occasional twitch of life. The crowd was almost out of the main room, now jammed in the hallway. I kept moving. Brandon skirted his prey, then leapt in for a pounce and grab. He had his fangs around the man's forearm and was shaking it like a chew toy when he noticed me. He growled uncertainly, his blood-fogged brain taking time to recognize me.

I stopped. We stared at each other. I thought about how dangerous it was to face him down in this form. I thought of Brandon's eyes gleaming with near-carnal bloodlust as he talked about killing. I thought of what he could do to me before Clay could come to my aid. It worked. Fear seeped from me like sweat. That got Brandon's attention. He dropped his prey and lunged at me. I waited until he was in mid-jump, then I turned and ran. Of course he followed. Fleeing prey is so much more fun than the near-comatose variety.

I circled toward the back wall to keep Brandon away from the clogged exit. Running behind the bar, I headed for the balcony stairs. As I stepped onto the first tread, I veered and dashed toward the bathroom hall. Clay was there. I passed him and slid to a stop. Behind me, Brandon did the same, nails careering over the linoleum. He stopped in front of Clay. His nostrils flared, again uncertain. His nose told him Clay was a werewolf and some dimly functioning part of his brain realized this was cause for concern. He growled experimentally. Clay's foot shot out, caught him under the muzzle, and knocked him flying onto his backside. Brandon scrambled to his feet, wheeled, and bolted. Clay ran after him. They disappeared into the main room. By the time I got there, Clay had driven Brandon onto the balcony.

I was almost to the top of the balcony stairs when Brandon leapt over the edge, followed by Clay's resounding "Fuck!" Before I could turn, Clay was jumping to the floor. I rushed down the stairs and ran to the exit to head Brandon off if he tried to escape. The front half of the hall was still clogged with people. No one was getting in or out.

Brandon didn't head for the door. Instead, he circled back to the rear corner of the room. Clay was right behind him. I staked out my post by the exit. Brandon ran for the corner, maybe because it held some vague sense of familiarity. When he got there, he nearly collided with the wall. He turned sharply and veered in a tight circle, tripping over the body on the floor. This time, the man didn't move. His dead eyes stared up at the ceiling. Recovering from his stumble, Brandon headed back toward the corner as if expecting a door to materialize there. Finally, he realized he was trapped and turned to face Clay.

For several long seconds, Clay and Brandon stared at each other. The first flicker of real anxiety sparked in me. Not even Clay was safe against a werewolf in wolf form. As I watched them, I could feel the tension thrumming through me, instinct telling me to protect Clay while common sense told me to guard the exit.

Brandon broke the standoff. He growled and hunkered down, hackles rising. Clay didn't move. Brandon growled again as if giving fair warning. Then he leapt. Clay dropped and rolled to the side. Brandon crashed and slid on the linoleum. Before Brandon could recover, Clay was on him. He grabbed Brandon by the loose skin at the back of his neck and threw his leg over Brandon's back. Then he shoved Brandon's head to the floor, pinning him.

Brandon struggled wildly. His claws skittered along the floor, unable to get a grip. He snarled and growled, snapping from side to side, trying to bite Clay's hands. Clay put his left knee on Brandon's back and wrapped his hands around Brandon's throat. As Clay squeezed, Brandon gave one last tremendous buck. Clay's right foot bounced off the ground just enough to make him shift position. As his foot came back down, it headed for a puddle of the dead man's blood.

"Clay!" I shouted.

Too late. His shoe hit the blood and his ankle twisted, shooting out from under him. Brandon threw himself forward at exactly the right second. Clay tumbled off his back. The second Brandon was free, he saw the exit and made a beeline for it.

I didn't bother blocking the hallway. He could have plowed through me as if I weren't there. Instead, as he passed, I dove at him and grabbed two handfuls of fur. We toppled over together. As we rolled, he snapped at my arm. I twisted it away, but not quite fast enough. One of his canines caught the skin under my forearm, ripping a path to my elbow and tearing through my injuries from that morning. I gasped. I didn't let go, but I did loosen my grip. It was enough. Brandon wrenched free. Clay arrived one second too late. Brandon was already tearing down the hall. The far end of it was still congested with people, but they somehow found a way to clear out when they saw Brandon coming.

Clay started going after Brandon, but I grabbed the back of his shirt.

"We shouldn't go out together," I said.

"Right. You follow him. I'll go back through the window."

I wasn't sure how this was possible, unless he'd developed the ability to scale walls, but there wasn't time to debate the matter. I nodded and ran down the rest of the hallway. I burst through the door to find myself in the midst of a chaos twice as bad as that inside the warehouse earlier. The crowd had got itself outside the door and stopped. Some people looked like they were in shock. The rest weren't moving because they didn't want to miss anything. Added to that, the entire Bear Valley police force and a battalion of state troopers had arrived. Most of the police were still half asleep, milling around in dazed confusion. Sirens howled. Cops barked orders. Nobody listened. Brandon was gone.

I paused to get my bearings. Finally, I was able to filter out the garbage and zero in on the clues. To my left, a barricade had been toppled over. One of the partygoers was waving toward the road. Three cops were jogging over to him. I followed. When I slipped past the fallen barricade, I found that another group of cops was in pursuit, fanned across the roadway, shouting instructions and motioning at an alleyway. When two officers started to run forward, someone stopped them, yelling that there was no need to rush, it was a blind alley. Brandon was trapped.

I scouted the area, trying to determine the likelihood of getting to Brandon before the cops did, and preferably without intercepting any stray bullets. As I stepped off the curb, someone grabbed my arm. I turned to see a middle-aged state trooper.

"Back behind the line, miss. There's nothing to see."

As he tugged me onto the curb, he looked down. The blood from my cut arm trickled over his fingers.

"Thank God," I gasped. "I've been trying to find someone. No one's paying attention—everyone's—" I stopped and gulped air. "Inside. There's people. They're still in there. There was this dog, this huge dog— They're hurt. My boyfriend—"

The officer swore and dropped my arm. He turned to a group of cops heading out onto the roadway.

"There's still people in there!" he yelled. "Has anyone checked inside?"

One of the cops said something I didn't catch. I inched backward as the two officers yelled and gestured. Apparently, neither one knew who was in charge or whether ambulances had been summoned or whether anyone had gone inside yet. Several ran off toward the warehouse. More decided their time and energy was better spent arguing. I slipped across the street. No one noticed.

There were still enough cops guarding the alleyway that I couldn't waltz down there and confront Brandon. I looked for a back way. As I creeped down a nearby alley, garbage cans clanged ahead. In the distance, something flashed against the moonlight. A four-legged figure appeared atop a brick wall. It crouched, then jumped. Obviously the alley wasn't as well blocked as the cops thought—although, to their credit, they wouldn't expect an animal to leap onto an eight-foot wall.

I ran toward the wall, then realized Brandon was making his escape in the opposite direction and heading straight for me. So I waited. He raced straight at me, too panicked to take in his surroundings. As he approached, I broke into a running leap and vaulted over his back, dropping to the ground behind him, rolling in a somersault, and landing in a runner's crouch. It was an absolutely perfect move, one that I couldn't duplicate for a million bucks. Of course, no one was there to appreciate it. I started to run. I'd calculated correctly. Brandon's love of the chase outweighed his instinct for survival. When I turned a corner, he followed. I weaved through the alleys, leading him away from the blockaded street and the police. Once or twice, I caught Clay's scent. He was close by, waiting for the ambush, but the location wasn't right. Finally, I glanced down a connecting alley and saw the highway. On the other side, the industrial section gave way to wooded parkland. Perfect. A place for us to Change and safely ambush Brandon, then smuggle his body out.

I sprinted for the road. Unfortunately, I forgot that most basic of kindergarten rules: I didn't look both ways before crossing. I ran in front of a semi, so close that the draft knocked me off my feet. I rolled to the roadside and leapt to my feet. As I spun around, a gunshot shattered the night air. Brandon was running across the road when the shot struck him. The top of his head burst in an explosion of blood and brain. The force of the blast knocked him sideways into a path of an oncoming pickup. The truck hit him with a sickening splat, then careered out of control. It spun past me, Brandon's body on the front grill, most of his head gone, other assorted body bits flying free as the truck did a three-sixty. With the force of the spin, Brandon's body flew free and jettisoned across the roadway. Most of his body, at least. As the driver got the truck under control and stopped, I could see swaths of fur, blood, and skin still embedded in the grill. It was enough to make me wish the legends were true, that ordinary methods couldn't kill a werewolf, and somewhere in that mangled heap of blood and gore on the roadway Scott Brandon was still alive, conscious and unable to scream. A fitting end for a sadist. Unfortunately, he'd been dead as soon as the first shot hit him. Silver bullets made a nice gothic touch, but they weren't necessary for killing a werewolf. Anything that could kill a human or a wolf could polish us off just as neatly.

A crowd was gathering around Brandon's remains. All they would see was a very large, very dead, brown canine. He wouldn't change back into a human. That was another falsehood about werewolves. According to myth, werewolves are supposed to turn back into humans when wounded. There's a zillion legends where a farmer or hunter shoots a wolf, but when he goes to track the wounded beast he finds—egad!—bloody human foot-prints instead. Nice trick, but it didn't work that way. Which was really good for us, or we'd be changing shape every time a Pack brother nipped us too hard. Damned inconvenient, really. Truth is, die a wolf and you'd better forget those plans for an open-casket funeral. Brandon's remains would be hauled off to the Bear Valley Humane Society and disposed of without ceremony or autopsy. Scott Brandon, the escaped killer from North Carolina, would never be found.

"Damn, I do hope he gets a proper burial," a voice drawled behind me. "Poor misguided bastard deserves one, don't you think?"

I turned to Clay and shook my head. "I screwed up."

"Nah. He's dead. That was the point of the evening. You did just fine, darling."

He put his arm around my waist and leaned down to kiss me. I squirmed out of his grasp.

"We should go," I said. "Jeremy wouldn't like us hanging around."

Clay reached for me again, mouth opening to say something. I turned away fast and headed down the street. After a few steps he jogged up beside me. The walk back to the parking lot was a quiet one.

We rounded the corner beside the grocery, where I'd left the Explorer. The parking lot was dark, the overhead lights turned out when the store closed for the night, Bear Valley being the kind of place where lighting was still used for customer convenience rather than security. We'd left the Explorer at the rear of the lot, beside a chain-link fence. There had been a few other cars when we'd arrived, but they were gone now, the legal bars having closed long ago. I took the car keys from my purse. They jangled harshly in the silence.

"Son of a bitch," Clay muttered.

I turned, thinking the sound of the keys had startled him, but he was staring at the Explorer. He slowed and shook his head.

"Looks like someone caught a flight tonight after all," he said.

I followed his gaze. A fair-haired, bearded man sat on the asphalt, lean-ing back against the Explorer's front tire, ankles crossed. An overnight bag lay by his side. Logan. I grinned and started to run. Behind me, Clay shouted. I ignored him. I'd been waiting a year to see Logan. Clay could stick his jealousy up his ass. Better yet, he could rant and rave to himself as he walked all the way back to Stonehaven. After all, I was the one with the keys.

"Hey!" I called. "You're an hour too late. You missed all the excitement."

Clay was running now, still calling my name. I stopped in front of Logan and grinned down at him.

"Are you just going to sit there or—"

I stopped. Logan's eyes stared out across the parking lot. Blank. Unseeing. Dead.

"No," I whispered. "No."

Dimly, I heard Clay run up behind me, felt his arms going around me, catching me as I stumbled back. A deafening howl split open the quiet of the night. Someone howling. Me.

Chapter 11

Grief

I don't remember how I got back to Stonehaven. I assume Clay bundled me into the Explorer, then got Logan's body into the rear compartment and drove us home. I vaguely recall walking through the garage door into the house, Jeremy appearing in the hall and starting to ask what happened with the mutt. He must have seen my face because he didn't finish the question. I brushed past him. Behind me, I heard Clay say something, heard Jeremy's oath, heard running footsteps as the others overheard and appeared from wherever they'd been waiting for us. I kept walking to the stairs. No one tried to stop me. Or maybe they did and I just don't remember it. I went to my room, closed the door behind me, pulled back the canopy from my bed, and crawled into its sanctuary.

I don't know how long passed. Maybe hours. Probably minutes, just long enough for Clay to explain things to the others. Then I heard his footfalls on the stairs. He stopped outside my door and rapped on it. When I didn't answer, he knocked louder.

"Elena?" he called.

"Go away."

The door groaned, as if he were leaning against it. "I want to see you."

"No."

"Let me come in and talk to you. I know how much you're hurting—"

I scrambled up and snarled toward the door, "You don't have any idea how much I'm hurting. Why should you? You're probably glad he's gone. One less obstacle to my attention."

He inhaled sharply. "That's not true. You know it isn't. He was my brother." The door groaned again. "Let me in, darling. I want to be with you."

"No."

"Elena, please. I want to—"

"No!"

He was quiet for a moment. I listened to his breathing, heard it catch as he swallowed. Then he made a low noise of anguish that crescendoed in a growl of grief. His shoes squealed as he turned suddenly, then slammed his fist against the far wall. A shower of plaster chunks pattered to the floor. His bedroom door slammed. Then another crash, something larger this time—a nightstand or a lamp hurling into the wall. In my head, I followed the path of his rampage, seeing each piece of furniture smash into bits and wishing I could do the same. I wanted to throw things, destroy things, feel the pain of my hand striking the wall, lash out at everything around me until my grief and rage were swallowed by exhaustion. But I couldn't do it. Some rational part of my brain stopped me, reminded me that there would be consequences. When I recovered my senses, I'd be ashamed of myself for losing control and leaving a swath of destruction that Jeremy would have to pay for. I looked up at the Dresden shepherdesses on my dresser and imagined smashing them on the hardwood, seeing their insipid faces shatter into razor-sharp shards of glass. It would feel wonderful, but I'd never do it. I'd remember how much time Jeremy had put into picking them out for me, how it would hurt him if I destroyed his gift. However much I wanted to explode, I couldn't bring myself to do it. I couldn't afford the luxury. And because Clay could, I hated him for it.

Having no way to vent my pain, I spent the next few hours curled atop my bedcovers, not moving even when my leg muscles seized up and begged me to shift position. I stared at the canopy curtains, my mind as blank as I could make it, afraid to think anything or feel anything. Hours later I was still lying like that when Jeremy tapped at my door. I didn't answer. The door opened, then closed, jamb clicking as it slid back in place. The canopy curtains whispered, then the mattress dipped as Jeremy sat behind me. His hand went to my shoulder, resting there. I closed my eyes as the warmth of his fingers seeped through my shirt. For several minutes, he said nothing. Then he reached over, pulled a strand of hair from my face, and tucked it behind my ear.

I didn't deserve Jeremy's kindness. I knew that. I suppose that was why I always questioned his motivation. In the beginning, every time he'd done something nice for me, I'd searched for a glimpse of evil behind the kindness, some nefarious motivation. After all, he was a monster. He had to be evil. When I'd realized there was nothing bad in Jeremy, I'd latched on to another excuse: that he was good to me because he was stuck with me, because he was a decent guy and maybe even because he felt some responsibility for what his ward had done to me. If he took me to Broadway plays and expensive dinners for two, it was because he wanted to keep me quiet and happy, not because he enjoyed my company. I wanted him to enjoy my company, but couldn't believe in it because I didn't see much in myself to warrant it. Not that I thought I was unworthy of love and attention, but not from someone of Jeremy's moral caliber. I'd failed to win the affection of a dozen foster fathers, so I couldn't believe I'd won it now, from someone worth more than those men combined. Still, there were times when I let myself believe Jeremy truly cared for me, when I was hurting too much to deny myself the fantasy. Now was one of those times. I closed my eyes, felt his presence, and let myself believe.

For a while, we sat in silence, then he said softly, "We've buried him. Is there anything you'd like to do?"

I knew what he was asking: was there any human rite of burial that would make me feel better? I wished there was. I wished I could reach inside myself and find some reassuring ritual of death, but my early religious experiences hadn't allowed for reassurance or trust in the power of an almighty being. My most vivid memory of church was sitting in a pew between one set of foster parents, my foster mother leaning forward, straining to hear the pastor and to ignore the fact that her husband's hand was exploring the spiritual mysteries shrouded beneath my skirt. The only thing I'd ever prayed for was deliverance. God must have had more important things on his mind. He'd ignored me and I'd learned to return the snub.

Still, whatever my beliefs, I felt I should do something to mark Logan's passing, at least go to the burial site to pay my respects. When I told Jeremy this, he offered to accompany me, which I accepted with a nod. He helped me get up and put his hand under my elbow, gently guiding me down the stairs. Had it been anyone else or any other time, I would have shrugged off the assistance. But right then I was grateful for it. The floor swayed and dipped under my feet. I walked cautiously down the steps and into the back hall. The study door opened and Antonio looked out, a half-full brandy glass in his hand. He glanced at Jeremy. When Jeremy shook his head, Antonio nodded, then retreated into the room. As we passed the door, it opened again. Without looking I knew who was coming out. Jeremy glanced over his shoulder and held up a hand. I didn't hear the door close, nor did I hear Clay's footsteps following us. I imagined him in the hallway, watching us leave, and I walked a little faster.

They'd buried Logan in a grove just inside the woods behind the house. It was a pretty spot where the midday sun danced through the leaves onto the wildflowers below. I thought of this, then realized the absurdity of picking a pleasant place to bury the dead. Logan couldn't see it. He didn't care where he lay. The carefully chosen spot was only a comfort to the living. It didn't comfort me.

I bent to pick some tiny white flowers to lay on the overturned earth. Again, I didn't know why I was doing it. Logan wouldn't care. Another meaningless gesture intended to offer some small degree of comfort, the comfort of a ritual enacted over the bodies of the dead since humans first began to mourn their dead. As I stood over the grave, clutching my pathetic bunch of flowers, I remembered the last and only funeral I'd been to. My parents'. My mother's best friend—the one who had tried to adopt me— had arranged a small funeral. Later I'd learned that my parents didn't have life insurance, so I'm sure my mother's friend must have paid for it. She took me to the funeral, stood beside me, and held my hand. It would be the last time I ever saw her. The foster system believed in clean breaks.

That day, I'd stood there, looking down at the graves and waiting. My parents were coming back. I knew that. Sure, I'd seen the coffins and had been allowed a glimpse of my mother's body inside one. I'd seen the men lower the boxes into the ground and cover them with dirt. That didn't matter. They were coming back. I had no experience with real death, only the loud, garish renderings of it on Saturday morning cartoons, where the coyote died and died again but always returned in time to plot one last silly scheme before the credits rolled. That was the way it worked. Death was temporary, lasting only long enough to provoke a laugh from kids in pajamas sitting cross-legged in front of the TV set, gorging themselves on handfuls of Froot Loops. I'd even seen this trick performed with real people when my father had taken me to a magic show at his office Christmas party. They'd put a woman in a box, cut her in half, and spun the box around. When they reopened the door, she'd jumped up, smiling and whole, to the cheers and laughs of the crowd. So too would my parents leap from their boxes, smiling and whole. It was a joke. A wonderful, terrifying joke. All I had to do was wait for it to be over. As I'd stood there, over my parents' graves, I'd started to giggle. The pastor turned on me then, fixing me with a glare that condemned me as an unfeeling brat. I didn't care. He wasn't in on the joke. I stood there, smiling to myself as I waited . . . and waited.

As I stared down at Logan's grave, I ached for that fantasy to return, to allow myself to pretend he was coming back, that death was only temporary. But I knew better now. Dead was dead. Buried was buried. Gone was gone. I fell to my knees, crushing the flowers in my fist. Something inside me snapped. I fell forward and started to sob. Once I started, I couldn't stop, the tears flowing until my eyes throbbed and my throat ached. Finally, a voice pierced my grief. Not Jeremy, who'd stood silently behind me, knowing not to interfere. This was the one who dared interfere.

"—now!" Clay was yelling. "I can't listen to her and not—"

Jeremy's voice, words muffled in a soft whisper.

"No!" Clay shouted. "They can't do this. Not to Logan. Not to her. I will not stand by—"

Another interrupting murmur.

"Christ! How can you—" Clay's voice choked off in rage.

I heard something, a rustling of branches, Jeremy pulling Clay off into the woods to talk to him, leaving me to my grief. As I knelt there, I listened. Clay wanted to go after Logan's killer—not tomorrow or even tonight, but right now. They'd picked up the scent of an unfamiliar werewolf on Logan's body. While we'd been chasing Brandon, another mutt had killed Logan. Jeremy was trying to dissuade Clay, telling him that it was still daytime, he was too angry, they needed to plan. It didn't matter what Jeremy said or how much sense he made. The storm of Clay's fury drowned all logic. I waited for Jeremy to forbid Clay to go after the mutt. I listened for the words. But they didn't come. Distracted by his own grief, Jeremy argued and tried to reason with Clay, but didn't expressly forbid him to take revenge. A fatal oversight. As I rubbed my dirt-streaked hands over my wet face, my grief was swallowed by fear. While they argued, I crept from the grove, and hurried to the house.

Ten minutes later, Clay yanked open the door of his Boxster and thumped onto the driver's seat.

"Where are we going?" I asked, my sore throat barely allowing me a whisper.

He jumped and turned to see me huddled in the passenger seat.

"You're going after him," I said before he could say anything. "I want to be there. I need to be there."

That was partly true. I did need some way to exorcise my grief and, like Clay, I only knew one way to do it. Revenge. When I thought of some mutt killing Logan, the rage that filled me was terrifying. It whipped through my body like some demonic snake, inciting every part of me to anger, moving so fast and out of control that I had to physically clench my fists and hold them rigid to keep from striking out. I'd known rages like this since childhood. Back then, I'd been frustrated at my inability to use them, to lash out in any meaningful way. Today I could use the anger more than I ever imagined possible. That only made the rages more frightening. Even I didn't know what would happen if I ever gave in to them. Knowing I was taking concrete action by going after the killer helped me rein in my fury.

There was another reason why I was going with Clay. I was afraid to let him leave by himself, afraid that if I wasn't there to watch over him something would happen to him and there would be another grave in the wildflower grove. The thought of that made me feel things I couldn't even admit to myself.

"Are you sure?" he asked, twisting to face me. "You don't need to come along."

"Yes, I do. Don't try to stop me or I'll tell Jeremy that you've gone. I'll make him forbid you to do this. If you're already gone, I'll lead him to you."

Clay reached to touch me, but I turned to look out the window. After a moment of silence, the automatic garage door squealed open and the car's engine roared to life. He backed down the driveway at neck-snapping speed and we were off to Bear Valley.

On the road to Bear Valley, the fog of grief and anger whirling through my brain parted with the prospect of action—clear, definitive action. I focused on that instead. Any impulse to fly into Bear Valley and madly search for Logan's killer dissipated under the cold weight of reality. If I wanted revenge, we needed a plan.

As we entered Bear Valley, we got caught in rush hour traffic and had to wait through an entire light change before making a left turn from Main onto Elm. As the second light turned red, Clay tore through anyway, ignoring the horn blasts around him.

"Do you know where you're going?" I asked.

"To park."

"And then . . . ?"

"To find the bastard who killed Logan."

"Great idea. Precision planning." I grabbed the door handle as Clay spun into the downtown core's only public parking lot. "We can't hunt for him now. It's still daytime. Even if we found the mutt, we couldn't do anything."

"So what do you suggest? Enjoy a leisurely dinner while Logan's killer runs free?"

Although I hadn't eaten since the previous evening, my stomach lurched at the thought of food. I wanted to start hunting Logan's killer as much as Clay did, but reason dictated caution. No matter how I hated the thought of anything distracting us from avenging Logan, we had to do exactly that. Distract ourselves for a few hours.

"We should find out what happened last night."

Clay slammed into a parking space. "What?"

"Find out how the town is reacting to what happened at the rave last night. Assess the damage. Are they looking for more wild dogs? Are they doing anything with Brandon's body? Did anyone see you jumping through a second-story window? Did anyone see me leading the mutt away?"

"For Christ's sake, who gives a damn what they saw or what they think?"

"You don't? If they decide to submit what's left of Scott Brandon for testing and they find something a wee bit strange, you aren't concerned? This is your backyard, Clay. Your home. You can't afford not to care."

Clay made a noise between a sigh and a frustrated snarl. "Fine. What do you suggest?"

I paused, not having thought this far ahead yet. Thoughts of Logan still filled my numbed mind. I forced them aside and concentrated on our next steps. After a few minutes, I said, "We buy the paper, go to the coffee shop, and read it while we listen to what people are talking about. Then we plan how we'll stalk this mutt. After dark, we do it."

"Reading a damn paper isn't going to help us find Logan's killer. We'd be better off having dinner."

"Are you hungry?"

He turned off the ignition and was quiet. "No, I'm not."

"Then unless you have a more productive way to kill a couple of hours, that's the plan."

CHAPTER 12

TRAIL

After buying a paper, I stopped at a pay phone to call Jeremy. Peter answered, so I didn't need to actually speak to Jeremy. I asked Peter to tell Jeremy that I was with Clay and I'd convinced him that now wasn't the time to go after Logan's killer. Instead, we were taking inventory of the damage from the night before. Of course, I didn't mention that we'd be tracking down Logan's killer *later*. It was all a matter of interpretation. I wasn't actually lying. Really.

Bear Valley had three coffee shops, but The Donut Hole was the only one that counted. The other two were reserved for out-of-towners, truckers, and anyone else pulling off the highway for a caffeine-and-sugar jolt. As we walked into the Hole, the cowbell over the door jangled. Everyone turned. A few people at the counter smiled, one lifted a hand in greeting. I may have looked vaguely familiar, but it was Clay they recognized. In a town of eight thousand, a guy who looked like Clay stood as much chance of going unnoticed as his Porsche Boxster did in the local parking lot. Clay hated the attention. To him, his curse was his face, not his werewolf blood. Clay wanted nothing more than to fade into the background of human life. I think he would even have gotten rid of the Boxster if he could, but like my bedroom, it was a gift from Jeremy, the latest in a string of sports cars bought to indulge Clay's love of fast driving and sharp curves.

Still, Clay was lucky in Bear Valley. Even if his sports car and good looks turned heads, no one bothered him as they would have in the city. He was exempted from undue female attention by the gold band he wore on the fourth finger of his left hand, Bear Valley being the kind of place where a wedding ring still meant you were off-limits to the opposite sex. The ring wasn't a ruse, either. Clay wouldn't lower himself to such a petty deception. His ring was one of a matching pair we'd bought ten years ago, before the small matter of a bite on my hand kiboshed the whole wedding bliss and happily ever after thing. The fact that no marriage took place didn't matter to Clay. The ceremony itself was irrelevant, a meaningless human ritual he'd been willing to undergo for my sake. The underlying commitment was what mattered to him—the idea of a life partner, something the wolf in him recognized, call it marriage or mating or what you will. So he wore the ring. *That* I could live with, dismissing it as another fantasy of his delusion-plagued brain. It was when he'd introduce me as his wife that things could get a bit ugly.

The Donut Hole was a typical, one-on-every-corner coffee shop, down to the cracked red vinyl booth seats and the lingering smell of burnt chicory. The smoking section was inescapable—even if you managed to find a booth without an ashtray, the smoke from nearby booths found you within seconds, ignoring the upward path to the undersized ventilation system. The staff were all middle-aged women who'd raised a family, decided to spend their empty-nest years earning some cash, and discovered this was the only job for which the world considered them qualified. At this time of day, most of the patrons were working people, grabbing a last cup of coffee before heading home or lingering here to avoid going home sooner than necessary.

While I picked a booth, Clay went to the counter and returned with two coffees and two slices of homemade apple pie. I pushed the food aside and spread the *Bear Valley Post* across the Formica tabletop. The incident at the rave party had made the front page. Of course, the paper didn't call it a rave, since most of their readership—and probably most of their staff—wouldn't have a clue about what a rave was. Instead, they described it as a large private party rife with "illicit activity," which made it sound a whole lot more fun than the real thing. Although the paper didn't say so explicitly, it implied that the majority of partygoers had come from outside Bear Valley. Naturally.

The details of the "incident" were sparse, due to a combination of mitigating factors, namely that most of the witnesses had been drunk or stoned and the perpetrator was a dead dog, making him doubly difficult to interview. What facts there were could be reduced to this: a large canine had slaughtered two people at a party before being killed by police. Not exactly a story to fill the front page, so the reporter had bulked it up with enough speculation to earn him a job with the tabloids. It was assumed the dead canine was a dog and everyone seemed content with that explanation, meaning the authorities had no intention of calling in wildlife experts or sending the remains off to an expensive city laboratory. What was left of Brandon had already been disposed of, read: incinerated at the local humane society. They'd even forgone rabies testing, probably deciding that anyone who'd been at the rave deserved a round of rabies shots.

Further, the reporter assumed the dead dog was involved with the killing of the young woman the previous week, although police hadn't ruled out the possibility of more wild dogs roaming the forests, especially since those teenage boys had spotted at least two canines the night before. Finally, despite all the speculation, there was no mention of anyone spotting a blond man or woman who'd seemed unusually involved in the incident. As I'd hoped, Clay and I had been just two more bystanders lost amidst the chaos.

"Waste of time," Clay grumbled. He'd been scanning the article upside down as I'd read it. "There's nothing there."

"Good. That's what we hoped for, so it was hardly a waste of time making sure."

He snorted and jabbed his fork into his untouched pie, sending up an explosion of crust, then shoved it away without taking a bite.

"You're sure whoever you smelled on—on—" I inhaled against the surge of pain—"on Logan was someone you didn't recognize."

"Yeah." Clay's eyes clouded, then sparked with anger. "A mutt. A fucking mutt. Two in Bear Valley. Of all the—"

"We can't think about that now. Forget how and why. Focus on who."

"I didn't recognize the scent. Neither did anyone else. Meaning it's a mutt we haven't run into often enough to recognize the scent."

"Or he's new. Like Brandon."

Clay frowned. "Two new mutts? One's odd enough, but—"

"Skip it. You didn't recognize him. Let's leave it at that for now. See if you can hear anyone talking about last night."

Clay grumbled. Ignoring him, I leaned back in my seat to listen to the conversations around us while I pretended to sip my coffee. The experience was a depressing one, not because no one was discussing the "incident," but because what most of them *were* discussing didn't exactly provide an uplifting glimpse into ordinary human life. Complaints of unfair bosses, backstabbing coworkers, ungrateful kids, meddling neighbors, boring jobs and even more boring marriages ricocheted from every corner of the room. No one was happy. Maybe it wasn't as bad as it seemed. Maybe the impersonal relationships formed in coffee shops were perfect for venting the trivial frustrations of life that city folks would take to a therapist—and spend a lot more than a buck for coffee to unload.

As I listened, an old anger and resentment started to surface. Why did people always complain about jobs and spouses and children and extended family? Didn't they realize how lucky they were to have these things? Even as a child, I'd hated hearing kids complain about their parents and siblings. I wanted to shout at them: if you don't like your family, give it to me—I'll take it and I'll never whine about an early bedtime or an annoying little sister. Growing up, I'd been surrounded by images of family. All children are. It seems to be the focus of every book, every television show, every movie, every damned commercial. Mother, father, brother, sister, grandparents, pets, and home. Words so familiar to every two-year-old that any other sort of life would be unthinkable. Unthinkable and wrong, just wrong. When I grew out of the self-pity stage, I realized that missing these things in my childhood didn't mean I had to miss them forever. I could give myself a family when I grew up. It didn't even have to be the traditional husband, three kids, a dog, and a cute little bungalow. Any variation would do. As an adult, I could provide myself with everything life had cheated me of. Then, on the very cusp of adulthood, I became a werewolf.

My plans for the future vanished in that moment. I could make a life for myself in the human world, but it would never be what I had imagined. No husband. Living with someone was risky enough, sharing my life with someone was impossible—there was too much of it that could never be shared. No children. There was no record of a female werewolf giving birth, but even if I was willing to take the risk, I could never subject a child to the possibility of life as a werewolf. No husband, no children, and without either, no hope for a family or a home. All of that stripped away, as far beyond my reach as they'd been when I was a child.

Clay was watching me, eyes troubled. "You okay?"

He reached out for me, not with a sympathetic hand or a pat on the knee or anything so obvious. Instead, he slid his leg forward, touching mine, and continued to study my face. I turned to look at him. As I met his eyes, I wanted to shout at him, say that I was not okay, that I'd never be okay, that he had made sure I would never be okay again. He'd stolen all my dreams and hopes of a family in one act of unforgivable selfishness. I yanked my leg from his and looked away.

"Elena?" he said, leaning over the table. "Are you okay?"

"No. I'm not okay."

I stopped myself. What good would it do to say more? We were here to hunt Logan's killer, not to hash out our personal problems. It wasn't the time. Part of me knew it would never be the time. If we talked about it, we might work it out. That was a risk I wasn't willing to take. I never wanted to forget and I never wanted to forgive. I wouldn't let myself.

Mending fences with Clay would mean surrender. It would mean he'd won, that biting me had been worth the trouble. He'd have his mate, the life partner of his choice, the realization of his own domestic dreams.

Well, I had my own dreams, and Clay had no role in them. Werewolf or not, I couldn't bear to give them up, especially now when I'd finally caught a glimpse of the possibilities in my life with Philip. I had a good, decent man, someone who saw and encouraged my potential for good-ness and normalcy, things Clay never saw, didn't care about, and certainly never encouraged. Maybe marriage, kids, and a house in the suburbs weren't in our future but, as I said, any variation would do. With Philip, I could envision a satisfying variation, with a partner, a home, and an extended family. My brass ring had come into sight. All I had to do was muddle through this mess with the Pack, get back to Toronto, and wait for the chance to grab it.

"No," I repeated. "I'm not okay. Logan's dead and his killer is out there and I'm stuck sitting in some stupid coffee shop with—" I bit back the rest. "We're supposed to be listening for rumors, remember? Be quiet and listen."

I forced my attention back to the conversations around us. People were still bitching about their lives, but I ignored that and concentrated on listen-ing for what I wanted to hear. Adding to the general despair, customers here and there discussed the events of last night in the weary "what is the world coming to" tone that people have probably used since early man saw his neighbors starting to walk upright. While most people were just rehashing the newspaper article, a few were giving birth to rumors that would be buzzing about town by nightfall. A woman in the back corner said that she'd heard the dog wasn't a wild dog at all, but an escaped guard dog owned by some relative of the mayor, the police force having been bribed or threatened by the mayor into circulating the wild dog story. Some people even thought the dog hadn't been involved at all, that the drug-crazed party-goers had killed the two people themselves in some kind of mass hysteria, then the cops shot an innocent dog outside. People can be damned creative sometimes. One thing was for sure, no one was talking about impossibly big wolves or demanding an inquest to know why the beast had acted as it had. Everyone assumed that it was perfectly natural for a dog to go berserk and slaughter people in a crowded warehouse. As I'd been eavesdropping, Clay had been pretending to read the paper. I say pretending because he didn't give a shit about current affairs in Bear Valley or anyplace else in the world. Like me, he'd been listening for rumors, though he'd never admit it.

"Can we go now?" he asked finally.

I sipped my cold coffee. The mug was still three-quarters full. Clay hadn't even started his. Neither of us touched our pie. For once, hunger was a distant concern.

"I suppose," I said, glancing out the window. "It's far from dark, but we probably won't find the trail for a while. Should we start at the parking lot?"

I couldn't bring myself to say "the parking lot where we found Logan," but Clay knew which one I meant. He nodded, got up, and ushered me out the door without another word.

As we approached the grocery store, I stopped before rounding the corner so I wouldn't see the spot where we'd found Logan. My heart was tripping so fast I had to concentrate to breathe.

"I can do it," Clay said, putting his hand against my back. "Stay here. I'll pick up the trail and see which way it leads."

I moved away from his hand. "You can't. The scent was faint last night. It'll be worse now. You need my nose."

"I can try."

"No."

I stepped around the corner, hesitated, almost stopping, then propelled myself forward. When I saw the spot where the Explorer had been parked, I jerked my gaze away, but it was too late. My mind was already replaying the scene from the night before, me rushing forward, Clay calling my name and running after me. He'd realized what had happened before I had. That's why he'd been trying to stop me. I understood that now—not that his motive mattered at this moment. It was just a meaningless distraction that ran through my brain, preventing me from thinking of what had happened here last night.

During the day, the parking lot looked like a different place. People bustled from car to store and back again. Like the coffee shop, the lot was filled with working people, most in jeans, a few in suits, toting single grocery bags with tonight's dinner or extra milk or bread grabbed on the way home. No one paid attention to us as we crossed the lot to the back fence. The spot where we'd parked last night was empty, being too far from the store to get used on any but the busiest shopping days.

I stood on the right side, where the passenger door of the Explorer had been. Closing my eyes, I inhaled. The scent of Logan filled my head. My knees buckled. Clay grabbed my elbow. I steadied myself, then sniffed again, trying to block Logan's scent. It didn't work. His lingering odor shoved aside all less familiar scents. With my eyes closed, I could imagine him standing in front of me, close enough to touch. I opened my eyes. The bright light of day chased the fantasy back to the shadows of my brain.

"I'm—" I started. "I'm having some trouble."

"It's here," Clay said. "Faint, but I'm picking up something. Hold on a sec and I'll see if I can grab it."

He paced to the left, shook his head, then came back and started again in another direction. On his second round of the compass points, he turned to me.

"Got it," he said. "Entrance trail is east, but the mutt exited here."

There was nothing in a scent that could tell even the best tracker whether someone was coming or going. Clay knew the difference because the approaching trail would also carry traces of Logan's smell, though he didn't mention this.

"Come over here and try," he said.

Once I got away from the parking spot, I relaxed. Clay stood near a minivan. I walked to him and sniffed the air. Yes, the scent was there. An unfamiliar werewolf. The trail led across the parking lot, away from the grocery store and toward Jack's Hunting and Hardware. From there, it ran along the sidewalk heading west, then circled back toward the main street, where we followed it to the downtown core. If that sounds quick and easy, it wasn't. A straight walk from point A to point B would have taken fifteen minutes. We spent over an hour, constantly missing the trail, looping back, finding where the mutt had turned a corner, and starting again. Once or twice I lost the scent completely. Trailing as humans made it even more difficult, not only because I couldn't smell as well, but because I couldn't exactly put my nose to the ground and sniff the mutt out. Well, I *could*, but such actions are frowned upon in polite society and often lead to a complimentary ride to the nearest psychiatric ward. Even the sight of someone on a street corner twitching her nose or pacing in a circle raised eyebrows. So I had to be discreet. Even if I could convince Clay to wait until nightfall, we couldn't change into wolves. After everything that had happened in Bear Valley, that wouldn't be a challenge, it'd be suicide.

Downtown Bear Valley closed at five, allowing employees to make it home for dinner and ignoring the fact that the average person worked until five and needed to shop afterward. This oversight may have explained the vacancy rate that had spread through the core like a cancer, affecting one shop, then its neighbors, and their neighbors, until the block looked like a massive advertisement for Bear Valley Realty. By the time we got back downtown, it was past seven and even the most dedicated shelf stockers had left for the evening. The streets were bare. The town seemed to have shut down for a collective dinner hour. I was able to be less cautious with my sniffing and we covered the next half mile in twenty minutes. The trail stopped at a Burger King that had been ostracized from its fast-food buddies on the other side of town. Here the mutt had presumably stopped to refuel. After another twenty minutes of circling and retracing my steps, I picked up the trail again. Ten minutes later we were standing in the parking lot of the Big Bear Motor Lodge.

"Well, this was a no-brainer," I muttered as we looked out over the collection of pickup trucks and ten-year-old sedans. "Two hotels in town. He's staying at one. Duh."

"Hey, you're the one who insisted we start from the grocery store."

"I didn't hear you suggesting anything else."

"It's called survival, darling. I know when to keep my mouth shut."

"Since when have—" I stopped, noticing a woman standing in her hotel room doorway, making no effort to hide her eavesdropping. It's always nice to know you can provide entertainment when the afternoon soaps are over.

I walked behind a pickup truck and squinted up at the two-story building. "How many rooms by your count?"

"Thirty-eight," Clay said without missing a beat. "Nineteen each up and down. A main-floor entry for the bottom. A lobby entrance and emergency exit for the second floor."

"If it were me, I'd take a room on the first floor," I said. "Direct room access. Easier to come and go at all hours."

"But the second floor has balconies, darling. And a hell of a view."

I looked across the road into a vacant lot filled with overgrown weeds, crumbling concrete blocks, and enough litter to keep a Scout troop busy for an entire Earth Day.

"First floor," I said. "I'll start. Go hide somewhere."

"Uh-uh. We've played this game before. I hide. You never seek. I'm a bit slow on the uptake, but I'm beginning to sense a pattern."

"Go."

Clay grinned, grabbed me around the waist, and kissed me, then ducked out of the way before I could retaliate. While it was nice to see his mood had improved, it would be even nicer if it didn't take the prospect of murder and mayhem to improve it. Over the past couple hours of tracking, the old resentment that had resurfaced in the coffee shop had faded into my subconscious, where it would wait, like a wound that never healed over, only needing a bump or prod to reignite the pain. We had work to do and I had to deal with Clay to do it. For Logan's sake, I couldn't afford to be distracted by my own problems. If I dwelled on my anger with Clay every second I was forced to spend in his company, I'd have turned into a bitter, waspish harpy long ago. Of course, some might argue that I'd crossed that threshold years ago, but that wasn't the point.

While Clay went off to find a suitable waiting place, I scanned the area for props. Near a corrosion-encrusted Chevy Impala I spotted a sheet of paper. It was a receipt for a new car stereo, which I hoped hadn't gone into the Impala, or the owner had spent more money on the sound system than on the car. I brushed a wet leaf from the corner of the sheet, flattened it, then folded it in half and headed for the sidewalk connecting the doors of the main-floor rooms. Starting by the emergency exit, I walked slowly down the sidewalk, pretending to study the sheet of paper and allowing for generous sniffing pauses in front of each door. The eavesdropping woman had gone back into her room. Two people came out of a room near the end, but they ignored the young woman having such difficulty finding the room number written on her scrap of paper. People make special allowances for the mental capacity of blonds.

When I got to the end, I picked up the scent of the werewolf, heading not into a room, but into the lobby. The trail was thick here, indicating he'd gone this way several times. A second-floor room, accessible only through the lobby. Maybe he liked waking up to the sunrise over a vacant lot. I looped back through the parking lot. Clay came out from behind the building before I could look for him.

"Upstairs," I said.

"See, darling? No one ever claimed mutts have brains."

I tossed the stereo receipt into the bushes and we headed for the front door. As we went into the lobby, Clay put his arm around my waist and started complaining about an imaginary dinner at a local restaurant. As he prattled, I saw the stairs to the left of the check-in desk and steered us there, nodding as he bitched about waiting twenty minutes for the dinner check. The show wasn't necessary. The desk clerk didn't even look up as we went by.

Upstairs, the trail stopped at the third door on the left. Clay grabbed the handle, twisted, and broke it with a muffled snap. As I kept an eye out for other motel guests, Clay waited to see if anyone inside the room responded to the sound of the lock breaking. When he heard nothing, he eased the door open. The curtains were drawn and the room was dark. A door down the hall opened. I pushed Clay forward and we slipped inside.

Clay checked the bathroom to make sure the mutt was gone, then pulled a quarter from his pocket. "Heads we lie in wait, tails we give chase."

"We should stay here," I said. "Check the place out, search for clues while we wait."

Clay rolled his eyes.

"Oh fine," I said. "Just flip the damned thing."

When it came up heads, I stuck my tongue out at him. His hand darted out to grab it, but I pulled it back in time.

"Next time you won't be so fast," he said, then looked around the room. "So what do you hope to find?"

"Anything to explain why we had two mutts in Bear Valley within a week. Aren't you the least bit concerned about that?"

"'Course I am, darling. But I'm sticking concern and curiosity on the back burner. Plenty of time to examine them both when the mutt's dead. I'm not waiting around for this bastard to go after you or the others while I try to find out what he's doing here."

"You think I'm stalling?"

"No, I think you're trying to make efficient use of time. That's fine. I'm just saying don't expect me to be too eager to riffle through dresser drawers while that mutt's roaming our streets."

"Then go watch out on the balcony or something while I search."

Clay didn't do this, of course. He helped me look, having simply made it clear that his heart wasn't in it. Mine wasn't either, but I know better than to pass up an opportunity. Besides, looking through this mutt's junk kept my hands and mind busy, leaving me little time to dwell on *why* we were tracking him.

Clay started in the bathroom. He was gone maybe ten minutes before he called out, "Here's the scoop. The guy uses hotel shampoo and hotel soap. He hasn't broken the seal on the conditioner. There's a Bic razor and no sign of a toothbrush, toothpaste, or mouthwash. So we're looking for a guy with split ends and a serious breath problem. Any of this helping, darling?"

I gritted my teeth against a reply. The walls were too thin for arguing. Besides, my own search of the main room hadn't turned up much more. I'd found two pairs of jeans, three shirts, and assorted socks and underwear, all of it previously worn and dumped on a chair for reuse. The Gideon Bible in the nightstand had been defaced with pentagrams and inverted crosses. Lovely. Also terribly unoriginal. I mean, if you feel compelled to scribble Satanic symbols on a Bible, the least you can do is draw stuff not found in every edition of *Weekly World News*. A very uncreative and obviously uninformed werewolf. He'd be in for a disappointment when he discovered werewolves were more likely to know a good recipe for beef Wellington than the recipe for a Satanic rite. In ten years, the devil had never contacted me with special instructions or even to say hello.

Then again, neither had God. Maybe that meant they didn't exist. More likely, it meant neither was willing to take responsibility for me.

"Christ, you should see the stuff in there, darling," Clay said as he walked from the bathroom. "Aftershave, cologne, and musk deodorant. If we couldn't tell the mutt was new by the way he smells, we'd know it by the *way* he smells."

No experienced werewolf would be caught dead wearing cologne, at least not if he had a functioning olfactory system. The very smell of himself would drown out all other scents, making his nose useless. I don't even use scented hand soap. Finding unscented women's toiletry products wasn't easy. The cosmetics industry seemed obsessed with making women smell like anything but themselves. And we piled the stuff on with no regard for achieving a uniform masking smell, layering herbal shampoo on baby powder deodorant on lilac soap on the latest fragrance from Calvin Klein. When I had the misfortune to get stuck in a full elevator early in the morning, the overpowering clash of scents could leave me with a headache until noon.

After checking out the window, Clay walked to where I was sifting through the bedside trash can.

"I'd offer to help," he said. "But you seem to have things under control."

"Thanks."

"Have you checked under the bed?"

"Can't. The frame's solid to the floor." I used the hotel pen to push aside a used Kleenex. I won't say what it had been used for, but werewolves don't contract cold and flu viruses.

"I'll check under the mattress," Clay said.

I'd forgotten that. Werewolves often carry fake ID and stash the real stuff someplace like under their mattress.

"No ID," Clay said. "Just this scrapbook. I don't suppose you want that."

I jumped up so fast I conked my head on the giraffe-neck lamp. Clay grinned and held a blue book out of my reach.

"Mine," he said, grin broadening. Holding it out of my range, he leafed through a few pages, then curled his lip and tossed the book on the bed. "On second thought, it's all yours. Happy reading, darling. I'll stand guard by the window. Give me a synopsis later."

I took the book and sat on the edge of the bed. It was a photo album, the type with plastic film you can pull back from the pages and stick pictures underneath. Instead of photos, the mutt had filled this album with newspaper clippings. Not random clippings, but ones following a specific theme: serial killers. I flipped past page after page of articles, seeing some faces that were familiar—Berkowitz, Dahmer, Bundy—and others I didn't know. Not only were all the clippings about serial killers, but they all contained one key element, something the mutt had highlighted—a number: the number of people murdered. He'd even color-coded the stats, yellow highlighter for the number of people the killer claimed to have killed, blue for the number of bodies found, and pink for the number the authorities believed he was responsible for. In the margins, the mutt had written notes, tallying and comparing numbers like a fan compiling stats for some macabre sporting event.

About halfway through the book, the articles stopped. I was about to close it when I realized there were more clippings near the back. I flipped through the blank pages and came to another article. Unlike the others, this one didn't deal with statistics. In fact, it didn't even name the killer. The article, dated November 18, 1995, from the *Chicago Tribune*, simply stated that the body of a young woman had been found. The next article gave more details, telling how she'd been missing for over a week and appeared to have been held captive during the intervening time, before being strangled and dumped behind an elementary school. I flipped through the next few pages. Three more women found, all following the same pattern. Then one escaped, telling a horrifying story of a weeklong ordeal of rape and torture, held captive in the basement of an abandoned house. The police had traced the house to Thomas LeBlanc, a thirty-three-year-old medical lab technician. However, when it came time for the woman to identify LeBlanc, she couldn't. Her attacker had only come to her in the dark and had never spoken. Furthermore, LeBlanc had been out of town on business the week the third woman went missing. In a newspaper photo, LeBlanc could have passed for Scott Brandon's older brother, not in any real physical resemblance but in the complete banality of his face, well-groomed, blandly handsome, and completely unprepossessing, your quintessential Wall Street WASP, features stripped of any ethnicity or interest. The face of the serial killer next door.

Despite an extensive investigation, the police were unable to come up with enough evidence to charge LeBlanc. In the last *Tribune* article, LeBlanc had packed his bags and left Chicago. Even if the justice system hadn't been able to convict LeBlanc, the people of Illinois had. Although that was the last article from Chicago, the scrapbook didn't end there. I counted six more clippings from the past few years, tracing a path of missing women through the Midwest to California and looping back up the East Coast. Thomas LeBlanc had been on the move. The last clipping was dated eight months ago, from Boston.

"Shit," Clay said, making me jump. "No way. No fucking way. Drop the book, darling. You've got to see this."

I hurried to the window. Clay held the heavy curtain back just enough for me to look out. An Acura had pulled into a spot near the lobby doors. Three men were walking away from it. When I saw the man heading from the driver's side, I wasn't shocked to see the face that had stared out from the *Tribune* article—Thomas LeBlanc, looking not nearly as well-groomed as he had in his photo. Of course, Clay didn't recognize him or even know from this distance that he was a werewolf. It was the other men who'd caught his attention. Karl Marsten and Zachary Cain, two mutts we both knew very well.

"Marsten and Cain? What the hell are they doing together?" Clay said. "And who's the other guy? He must be the one."

"Logan's killer," I said. "Thomas LeBlanc. We have to get out of here."

"Whoa," Clay said, holding his ground as I tugged him toward the door. "We're not going anywhere. This is what we came for, darling."

"We came to kill one mutt. One inexperienced mutt. Three against two is bad enough but—"

"We can handle it."

"With no sleep or food in twenty-four hours?"

"We could—"

"I can't."

Clay stopped there. He was quiet for a moment.

"If you stay," I continued, "then I stay. But I'm in no shape for a fight. I'm exhausted and hungry and my arm is screwed up from the dog bite and Brandon."

I was hitting below the belt, but I didn't care. I'd say whatever it took to get us out of that room. Clay's expression changed, first uncertain, then resolute.

"Okay," he said. "We bolt. Is there still time . . . ?"

"The balcony. We'll have to lower ourselves down. No jumping."

"Your arm?" He looked down at the scabbed-over wound. We heal fast and it felt fine, but I wasn't about to admit that. Not now.

"I'll live," I said.

Clay strode to the balcony, shoved the drapes aside, and slid the door open. "I'll go first and catch you if your arm gives out."

He was over the railing before I got out the door. I swung one leg over the ledge, then looked back into the room and saw the photo album on the bed. I should have grabbed it. There would be more clues there, more to help me get to know Thomas LeBlanc. Rule one of hunting: know your prey.

"Be right back," I called to Clay over the railing.

"No!"

I grabbed the book from the bed just as a card key slid into the door lock.

"It's not working," an unfamiliar voice said through the door. "The green light should come on."

I lunged from the bed to the balcony, tripping over a pair of underwear and nearly flying headfirst out the sliding door. As I was swinging over the railing, someone tried the door, found it open, and gave it a shove. I dropped to the ground. Clay wasn't there to catch me. When I turned, I saw him racing to the lobby door. I started to shout his name, thought better of it, ran and tackled him instead. We tumbled to the concrete just outside the first-room door. The photo album flew from my hands, knocking him hard under the chin.

"Whoops," I said. "Sorry."

"You almost sound like you mean it," he growled, holding the book aloft in one hand. "You went back for this? For this?"

"I needed it."

He muttered something under his breath. I couldn't hear what he said and probably didn't want to. We were still lying on the sidewalk, me atop him. I lifted my head to listen. Someone walked out onto the balcony in LeBlanc's room. I heard the railing groan as the person leaned over it, looking out across the parking lot. We were hidden beneath the balcony.

"Shhh," I whispered.

"I know," he mouthed.

He shifted under me, hands moving to rest on my rear. It wasn't an uncomfortable position to be in—not that I wanted to be there, given the choice, but . . . Oh, never mind.

"You gave me a scare," he whispered.

He moved one hand to the back of my head, pulled me down, and started to kiss me. I closed my eyes and kissed him back. After all, if we had to lie on the sidewalk outside a hotel, we should at least be doing something that might explain why we were lying on the sidewalk, right? After a moment, Clay's eyes flickered to the right and narrowed. As I pulled back, he slid from under me and focused his glare on something behind us. The woman who'd been watching us argue earlier was back in her doorway, this time drinking a Diet Coke as she took in the show.

"Would you like some popcorn with that?" Clay said, getting to his feet and brushing himself off.

"It's a free country," the woman replied.

Now, if Clay had little patience with humans in general, he had even less with humans who invaded his privacy and could only manage the lamest of comebacks. His jaw hardened and he stepped past me. He stopped, back to me, facing the woman. It only took a second. Her eyes widened, she stumbled back, and the door slammed, locks clicking into place. Clay hadn't said anything. He'd just given her "the look"—a stare of pure malevolence that never failed to send humans scurrying. I tried to perfect the look once. When I thought I had it down pat, I'd tested it on some jerk who'd been coming on to me in a bar. Instead of scaring him off, it'd only set his engines revving at full throttle. I learned my lesson. Women can't do malevolence.

By now, whoever had been on LeBlanc's balcony was gone. Their next step might be to come outside for a closer look, since Marsten and Cain would be able to smell that Clay and I had been in LeBlanc's room and would probably assume we hadn't been gone long. I prodded Clay forward. As we skirted along the sidewalk, staying close to the building, I crossed my fingers and hoped the mutts didn't come outside. Not that we couldn't get away. We could. But Clay wouldn't. If they came out and saw him, he wouldn't run.

We got around the building and slipped away without being seen. The walk to the car was a quick one. Less than twenty minutes later we were on our way back to Stonehaven for reinforcements.

Chapter 13

Synchronous

"Absolutely not," Jeremy said, getting up from his chair to walk to the fireplace.

We were all in the study. The others had been waiting for us. Clay and I sat on the couch, Clay perched on the edge ready to bolt the second Jeremy said we could go after the mutts. Nick stood beside Clay, fingers tapping against the sofa back, equally anxious, but taking his cues from Clay. Peter and Antonio sat across the room. Both looked angry at the news, but they remained composed, awaiting Jeremy's decision with the greater control of age and experience.

"I can't believe you're asking," Jeremy continued. "I made it clear that I didn't want this, but you took off anyway. Then Elena calls to say you're just scouting out news about last night and somehow you end up—"

"It wasn't intentional," I said. "We came across his trail. We couldn't pass up the opportunity."

Jeremy gave me a look that advised me to shut my mouth before I dug myself in deeper. I shut it.

Jeremy walked back to his chair, but didn't sit. "No one is going after these three tonight. We are all exhausted and upset after last night, especially you two. If I hadn't trusted Elena's word when she called, I would have been down there this afternoon hauling the two of you back here."

"But we didn't *do* anything," Clay said.

"Only for lack of opportunity."

"But—"

"Yesterday we had one mutt in town. Today, he's dead and three more have shown up. Not only that, but of those four, we have Karl Marsten and Zachary Cain, two mutts who would be enough of a problem individually."

"Are you absolutely sure it was Marsten and Cain?" Antonio asked. "Of any two mutts I could imagine ever teaming up, those two rank right at the bottom of the list. What could they possibly have in common?"

"They're both mutts," Clay said.

"My guess would be that they haven't teamed up," I said. "Marsten must have something over Cain. A definite leader-follower relationship. Karl wants territory. Has for years."

"If he wants territory, he has to join the Pack," Jeremy said.

"Fuck that," Clay spat. "Karl Marsten is a thieving, conniving son-of-a-whore who'd stab his father in the back to get what he wanted."

"Don't forget the new recruits," I said. "Brandon and LeBlanc are both killers. Human killers. Someone—probably Marsten—found them, bit them, and trained them. He's creating an army of mutts. Not just any mutts, but ones who already know how to hunt, to kill. Know it and like it."

Antonio shook his head. "I still can't picture Marsten behind this. Parts of it, yes. But this thing about creating new mutts, it lacks . . . finesse. And recruiting Cain? The man's an idiot. A first-rate heavy hitter, but an idiot. The chances of him screwing up are too high. Marsten would know that."

"Who the fuck cares!" Clay said, exploding from his seat. "We've got three mutts in town. One of them killed Logan. How can you sit around discussing motivation and—"

"Sit down, Clayton," Jeremy said, his voice low.

Clay started to sit, then stopped. For a moment, he hung there, twin instincts battling within him. Then his hands clenched at his sides. He straightened up, turned on his heel, and strode to the study door.

"If you go, don't come back." Jeremy's voice was barely above a whisper, but it stopped Clay cold. "If you can't control the urge, Clayton, then go downstairs to the cage. I'll lock you in until it passes. But if the problem is that you *won't* control it, and you leave, then you're not welcome back."

Jeremy didn't mean it. Well, yes, he meant it, but not as it sounded. If Clay took off and Jeremy had threatened banishment, he'd have to follow through with it. But he wouldn't let Clay go without a fight. The threat was the best way to prevent that. Clay stood there, jaw working as if chewing his anger, his hands clenched at his sides. But he didn't move. He wouldn't. Banishment for Clay would be death—not from outside forces, but from within, the slow death of severing himself from what he believed in most. He'd never leave Jeremy or the Pack. It was his life. Jeremy might as well threaten to kill him if he went after the mutts.

Slowly, deliberately, Clay turned to Jeremy. Their eyes locked. There was a long pause, the mantel clock ticking off seconds like a time bomb, then Clay turned and walked out the door, veering not toward the garage or front door but heading for the rear of the house. The back door opened and slammed shut. I looked at Jeremy, then went after Clay.

I followed Clay into the woods. He walked until we were out of sight and hearing of the house. Then he slammed his fist into the nearest tree, making it rock and groan in protest. Flecks of blood flew.

"We can't let Cain and Marsten get away with this," he said. "We can't let them think we're backing down. We have to act. Now."

I said nothing.

He whirled to face me. "He's wrong. I'm so sure he's wrong."

He closed his eyes and inhaled deeply, face spasming as if the words cut him. The very notion of questioning Jeremy pierced him like the worst possible betrayal.

"He's right," Clay continued after a moment. "We're not ready for this. But I can't stand around while Logan's killer is out there, knowing the next one those mutts might go after could be you or Jeremy. I can't do it. He's got to know that."

Still I said nothing, knowing he wasn't looking for an answer, that he was only trying to work things out in his own mind.

"Fuck!" he yelled into the forest. "Fuck! Fuck! Fuck!"

He slammed his fist into the tree again, then raked his hand through his curls, crimson scattering through the gold leaving a red smear on his forehead. His eyes closed, chest heaving as he inhaled deeply. Then he exhaled, shuddered, and looked at me. Frustrated rage shone from his eyes, mingled with touches of dread.

"I'm trying here, darling. You know how hard I'm trying. Everything in me screams to go after them, hunt them down, tear out their goddamned throats. But I can't disobey him. I can't do it."

"I know."

He stepped toward me, arms going around me, mouth coming down to mine. His lips touched mine lightly, tentatively, waiting to be shoved away. I could taste his panic, his fight to control the dueling instincts that raged stronger than anything I could imagine. I put my arms around him, hands going up and entwining in his hair, pulling him closer. A moan of relief shuddered through him. He let the mantle of control slide free and grabbed me, pushing me back against a tree trunk.

He ripped at my clothes, nails scraping against my skin as he tore my shirt and pants free. I fumbled with his jeans, fingers clumsy as the heat of his desperation caught me like a brushfire. He pushed his jeans down and flung them off.

His lips came back to mine, bruisingly rough. I twisted my hands in his hair, pulling him closer. He moaned hoarsely. His hands ran over my naked body, kneading, grabbing my hips, my waist, my breasts. The bark of the tree bit into my back. As his fingers came up to my face, I smelled the blood on his hand, felt it running fresh and streaking across my cheeks as he caressed my face. The blood dripped onto our lips and I tasted it, metallic and familiar.

Without warning, his hands dropped to my rear, jolting me off the ground onto him. He growled as he slid inside me. My feet were off the ground, leaving me dangling and putting him in control. He slammed against me. His eyes stayed locked with mine. From deep in his chest came a rhythmic growl of desperate lust. His teeth were clenched. As his fingers dug into my hips, I felt the edge of his wedding band cut into me. Then his eyes clouded. His focus wavered and his body shuddered convulsively. He gave a low, panting moan, then slowed, face burrowing into my collarbone and hands moving up to protect my battered back from the tree. He moved slowly in me, still hard. He hadn't climaxed yet. It was a release of another sort, a sudden abatement of the violence that had ripped through him.

His hands stroked my back and pulled me against him. Face still nuzzled against me, he whispered, "I love you, Elena. I love you so much."

I wrapped my hands around him, nuzzling his ear and murmuring wordless noises. Still moving in me, he eased me away from the tree and stepped back and lowered us down to the ground with me on top of him. I wrapped my legs around his hips, then rose into the air, picking up the pace again. I tilted my head back, closing my eyes and feeling the cool night air on my face. I could hear Clay's voice, as if from a great distance, repeating my name. I heard myself answer, my voice calling his name into the silent forest. The climax came slow, almost languid, each wave passing through me with glorious singularity. I felt his climax, equally slow and decadent, and groaned with sympathetic release.

He put his arms up and pulled me down onto his chest, tucking my head under his chin. For a long time, we didn't move. I stayed there, listening to his heartbeat and waiting for the dread moment when reality would return. It would happen. The fog of lovemaking would part and he'd say something, do something, demand something to send us snarling at each other's throats. I felt him swallow, knew words were coming, and wished I could stop up my ears against them.

"I'd like to run," he said softly.

I was quiet for a moment, not sure if I'd heard right, waiting for the punch line.

"Run?" I repeated.

"If you're not too tired."

"You still need to work it off?"

"No. I just want to run. To do something. Something with you."

I hesitated, then nodded. We lay there for a few minutes longer before getting up to find a place to Change.

I took my time and my Change came surprisingly easy. Afterward I stood in the clearing and stretched—turning my head, flicking my ears, stretching my hind legs, and moving my tail. It felt gloriously good, as if I hadn't Changed in weeks. I blinked, adjusting to the darkness. The air smelled delicious and I inhaled greedily, filling my lungs, then snorting it out and seeing the barest wisps of condensation trumpet from my nostrils.

I was about to go back to the clearing when a lead weight barreled into my side and sent me flying. I caught a flash of golden fur, then found myself alone again with only traces of Clay's scent for company. Getting to my feet, I took a few wary steps forward. Nothing happened. I cocked my head, sniffing. Still nothing. I took three more steps and got torpedoed again, this time crashing sideways into a bush and not seeing so much as a hair of my attacker.

I waited, got my breath back, then leapt to my feet and started to run. Behind me, Clay burst into the clearing again and yipped on finding his quarry vanished. I ran faster. Bushes crashed somewhere behind me. Rounding a corner, I dove headfirst into a patch of underbrush and dropped to the ground. A blur of gold raced by. I sprang to my feet and backtracked. It took Clay a few seconds to realize the trick, but soon I heard the pounding of running paws behind me.

The next time I leapt to the side of the path, I must have been a split second too slow, giving him a flash of my hind legs or tail. I'd just crouched behind a bush when two hundred pounds of muscle vaulted it and dropped onto me. We tusseled for a few minutes, yelping and growling, nipping and kicking. I managed to get my muzzle under his throat and heaved him over backward, then scrambled to my feet. Sharp teeth clamped on my hind leg and twisted, flipping me over. Clay pounced and pinned me. He stood over me for a minute, blue eyes gloating. Then, without warning, he leapt off and ran back into the forest. Now I was "it."

I chased Clay for about a half mile. He veered off the path at one point and tried to lose me in the thick brush. The trick gave him a twenty-foot advantage, but no more. I was expecting another ruse when a small shadow bolted across the clearing ahead. The smell of rabbit drifted over on the breeze. Clay slowed, twisting to do a double take at the fleeing rabbit. I picked up speed, tensed, and sprang at his back, but I was too late. He was gone.

As I was regaining my balance, a high-pitched squeal sliced through the forest. Within seconds, Clay bounded back through the bushes, the dead rabbit dangling from his jaws. He looked at me and waggled the rabbit, his eyes conveying the message with his actions: "Want it?" As he shook the rabbit, blood splattered to the ground. The smell wafted up, mingling with the scent of warm meat. I stepped forward, sniffing. My stomach rumbled. Clay made a noise low in his throat, a half growl that almost sounded like a laugh, and yanked the rabbit out of my reach. "Tease," I glared. He feigned tossing the rabbit toward me, but didn't release it. With a growl, I lunged. He danced backward, holding the rabbit just close enough that the smell of it filled my brain and made my stomach twist. I gave him a baleful stare, then looked out at the forest. There was plenty more dinner where that rabbit came from.

As I was turning to leave, Clay tossed the rabbit at my feet. I looked from it to him, expecting another trick. Instead, he sat back on his haunches and waited. I gave him one final glance, then ripped into the rabbit, gulping the warm meat in mouthfuls. Clay walked over and rubbed against me, licking flecks of splattered blood from my muzzle and neck. I stopped eating long enough to thank him with a nuzzle. When I went back to feeding, he loped into the woods to catch his own meal.

When I awoke the next morning, I was lying alone in the dew-damp grass. I scrambled up and looked around for Clay. The last thing I remembered, we'd Changed back, curled up, and gone to sleep. I put out my hand and touched the dry spot beside me where he'd been. As I glanced around the empty clearing, a sliver of anxiety ran through me. Clay didn't take off on me like that. Getting rid of him was the problem. As I was looking, a sprinkle of cold water hit my head. I jumped to see Clay standing over me, grinning. Water dripped from his hands and glistened from his forearms. He was still naked; we hadn't bothered going back for our clothes the night before, not quite sure where we'd left them and even less certain they'd be in any condition to be worn again.

"Looking for me?" he asked, dropping down beside me.

"I thought that pack of wild dogs might have got you."

"You looked worried."

"I was. God knows what kind of indigestion you'd give the poor things."

He laughed and knelt on all fours, pushing me back down to the ground and kissing me. I kissed him back, entwining my legs around his, then jerking back as my feet touched his, ice-cold and wet.

"I was checking the pond," Clay said before I could ask. "I thought we might go for a swim. First of the season. It would definitely wake us up."

"Any food there?"

He chuckled. "That rabbit last night didn't quite do it?"

"Not by half."

"Okay then. Here's the deal. If you can't wait, we'll eat breakfast, then swim. Otherwise, come swimming with me now and I'll make you breakfast afterward, anything and everything you want."

I didn't hesitate long before agreeing to option two. Not because I wanted someone to prepare my breakfast, but because I knew if we went to the house first, we'd never come back out to go swimming. Something would happen. We'd remember that Logan was dead and there were three mutts in Bear Valley. Real life would destroy the fantasy world we'd built so carefully over the past night. I didn't want it to end. Just a few more hours, a little more time to pretend that it could really be like this, with no past or future to intrude on our utopia.

When I said yes to the swim first, Clay grinned and kissed me, then jumped to his feet.

"Race?" he asked. "Last one there gets thrown in?"

I pretended to think it over, then jumped to my feet and took off. Five seconds too late, I realized I'd picked the wrong route. As I raced into the clearing beside the pond, Clay stood on the north bank, grinning.

"Lose your way, darling?" he called.

I limped over to him, dragging my right foot.

"Damned vines," I muttered. "I think I twisted my ankle."

After all these years, you'd think he'd know better. You really would. But no, as I hopped onto the bank, he came forward to meet me, blue eyes clouding with concern. I waited until he bent down to check my ankle, then knocked him flying into the pond.

We stumbled back to the house later, still naked and not noticing or caring. After our swim, we'd made love on the edge of the pond, leaving us looking like we'd been mud wrestling, which wasn't entirely inaccurate. We'd done a quick washup in the pond, but Clay still had a smear of dirt across one cheek. He looked about twelve years old, eyes glowing with mischief, lips settled in a lingering grin that turned to a laugh every time we tripped over something in our path.

"Pancakes, right?" he said as he helped me up from a tumble over a hidden root.

"From scratch. No shortcuts."

"And ham, I assume. What else?"

"Steak."

He laughed and put his arm around my waist as the path widened enough for two. "For breakfast?"

"You said I could have whatever I wanted."

"Can I get you some fruit to balance that meal?"

"No, but you can dig up some bacon. Bacon and eggs."

"Dare I ask for a little help?"

"I'll make coffee."

He laughed again. "Thanks a hell of a—"

He stopped. We'd come to the forest's edge and stepped through to the backyard. There, on the back patio, less than fifty feet away, stood Jeremy . . . surrounded by five or six unfamiliar human faces, all of which turned the second we walked from the woods. Clay growled an oath and stepped in front of me, covering my nakedness. Jeremy wheeled around and ushered the group off to the side. It took a few seconds for them to move, and a few more for them to stop staring.

When the visitors had vanished around the side of the garage, I grabbed Clay's arm and made a run for the back door, not stopping until we were upstairs. Before he could say anything, I shoved him into his room and went to my own. I'd only put on panties and a bra before I heard Clay's door open. Expecting him to head downstairs to confront the trespassers, I hurried to my door and yanked it open, only to find him holding the handle.

"Hey," he said, grinning as he recovered his balance. "If you're that eager to let me into your bedroom, I should offer to make breakfast more often."

"I was— You're not— You're okay?"

"I'm fine, darling. Just coming to round you up for breakfast while Jeremy gets rid of our uninvited guests." He leaned forward, put a hand against my back, and kissed me. "And no, I'm not going out to help him. I'm in too good a mood to let a bunch of humans spoil it. Jeremy can handle them."

"Good," I said, putting my arms around his neck.

"Glad you approve. So let's get breakfast going, then we can dream up a few ways to distract ourselves until Jeremy's ready to tell us how he plans to deal with Marsten and Cain."

As he leaned forward to kiss me again, someone cleared his throat in the doorway. I peeked over Clay's shoulder to see Jeremy there, arms crossed, a slight smile on his lips.

"Sorry to interrupt," he said. "But I need Elena downstairs. Fully dressed if we ever intend to get rid of these men."

"Yes, sir," I said, disentangling myself from Clay. "I'll be right there."

"Hold up," Clay said as Jeremy turned to leave the room. "I need to talk to you."

They left. I could hear Clay apologizing for his behavior the night before, but quickly tuned them out, not wanting to intrude. I finished dressing, ran a brush through my hair, checked in the mirror, then went into the hall. Jeremy and Clay were still there.

"I'll start breakfast," Clay said, heading off down the stairs. "Have fun, darling."

"I'm sure I will," I said. As we went down the steps, I glanced over my shoulder at Jeremy. "Sorry about that. The walking naked from the woods thing. We didn't expect visitors."

"Nor should you," he said, steering me toward the back door. "There's no need to apologize. You should be able to come and go as you like here. It's these damned intrusions that . . ." He shook his head and didn't finish.

"What is it this time?"

"Another missing person."

"The boy from the other day?"

Jeremy shook his head as he held open the back door for me. "This time they're looking for one of the men who came on the property Friday. The middle-aged one. The leader."

"He's missing?"

"Not just missing, but missing after having left a message for a friend saying he was coming here last night to check things again. Something about this place was bothering him. He wanted another look around."

"Oh, shit."

"In a nutshell—exactly."

CHAPTER 14

Mistrust

There were six people in the search party, three local cops and three
civilians. Jeremy, Peter, Nick, and I went out to help them look while
Antonio returned to the house to keep an eye on Clay, in case his commitment to non-interference didn't last. The four of us played the role of
good and concerned citizens, scouring the bushes while keeping our noses
on alert for anything we didn't want the searchers to find. One thing I
would have rather they hadn't found turned up early in the quest.

"Got something!" one of the men yelled.

"Is it Mike?" another called, rushing from our sides.

As everyone converged on the scene, Nick's voice rang out, choked with
barely contained laughter. "Forget it. It's—uh—nothing important."

"What the hell do you mean?" the first man said. "Maybe this is all a
joke to you, son, but . . ."

The rest of the sentence trailed off as we burst into the clearing to find
one of the searchers bending over a ripped shirt. Torn clothing littered the
ground, more hung from bushes. Nick held up half a pair of white panties
and grinned at me.

"Wild dogs? Or just Clayton?"

"Oh God," I muttered under my breath.

I walked over to snatch the underwear from him, but he held it over his
head, grinning like a schoolboy.

"I see Paris, I see France, I see Elena's underpants," he chanted.

"Everyone's already seen much more than that," Jeremy said. "I think
we can safely resume the search."

Peter plucked Clay's shirt from a low-hanging branch and held it up,
peering through a hole in the middle. "You guys can really do some
damage. Where's the hidden video when you need it?"

"So this—uh—wasn't done by wild dogs?" one of the searchers said.

Peter grinned and tossed the shirt to the ground. "Nope. Just wild
hormones."

The other men, who'd finally stopped casting sidelong glances at me after the "naked in the yard" incident, now looked me over with renewed interest. I smiled, trying hard not to bare my teeth, then hurried back into the woods.

Jeremy, two of the searchers, and I were beating the bushes in the northeast quadrant of the woods when we heard another shout, this time infused with enough urgency to make us run. When we got there, Nick and two searchers were standing over a body. Nick looked up, caught my eye, and gave me a look that said he'd tried unsuccessfully to distract the men's attention. Jeremy and I walked to the body and looked down. It was the missing man. His shirt collar was torn and drenched with blood. Above the collar his throat was shredded, flaps of flesh hanging from the wound. Empty eye sockets stared up at us. Crows or turkey vultures had found him first, lying exposed in the clearing. Besides taking his eyes, they'd pecked at his face, leaving bloody holes where white bone peeked through. Bits of scattered flesh covered his shirtfront and surrounded his head, as if the searchers had scared the scavengers mid-meal.

"Like the others," one man said, then turned away from the sight.

"One difference," another said. "He wasn't eaten. Not by the dogs at least. Birds got to him though. Buggers don't waste any time."

A younger man bolted for the woods. Seconds later, the sound of retching filled the air. Two of the men shook their heads in sympathy, both looking a little green themselves. My stomach wasn't feeling so great either, though it had nothing to do with seeing a dead body. When the younger man stopped throwing up, he was quiet a moment, then ran from the thicket.

"Come here! You guys have to see this!"

I knew what he'd found. I knew it and I dreaded stepping into that thicket to confirm my suspicions, but Jeremy prodded me on. When I stepped into the woods, the sickly sweet smell of vomit made my gorge rise. Then I looked down at the ground, following the path of the young man's finger. There, in the damp earth, were paw prints.

"Can you believe the size of those things?" the young man said. "Christ, they're as big as saucers. Just like those kids said. These dogs are huge!"

As I surveyed the thicket, my eyes caught sight of something snagged on a thornbush. A tuft of fur, shining golden even in the shadows. While everyone stared at the paw prints, I slipped over to the bush, stood in front of it, reached behind my back, and slid the fur into my pocket. Then I looked around for more. When I didn't see any, I glanced back at the paw prints, as recognizable as footprints from a familiar pair of shoes. As I stared at them, I felt sick. Then the disappointment turned to something else. Anger.

"I have to go," I muttered, turning from the thicket.

No one tried to stop me, the humans assuming it was a delayed reaction to the sight of the dead man, and the Pack not wanting to make a scene.

"Clayton!" I shouted as the back door slammed behind me.

Clay appeared in the kitchen doorway, wooden spoon in hand. "That didn't take long. Come in and get the coffee going."

I didn't move. "Aren't you going to ask if they found the missing man?"

"That would imply I give a damn."

"They found him."

"Good, so I presume they're leaving. All the better. Now come in and—"

"I found this by the body," I said, pulling the tuft of fur from my pocket.

"Huh. Looks like mine."

"It is yours. Your prints were there, too."

Clay leaned against the doorpost. "My fur and my prints in my forest? Fancy that. I hope you're not implying what I think you're implying, darling, 'cause if you recall, I was with you all last night, which is when Tonio says this guy went missing."

"You weren't with me this morning when I woke up."

Clay sputtered, nearly dropping the spoon. "I was gone five minutes! Five minutes to track and kill a guy? I'm good, but I'm not that good."

"I have no idea how long you were gone."

"Yes, you do, because I'm telling you. Come on, you know I didn't do it. Use your head, Elena. If I lost control and killed this guy, I'd have told you about it. I'd have asked for your help getting rid of the body and deciding what to tell Jeremy. I wouldn't have been frolicking in the pond while some dead human is lying in our forest waiting for another group of hunters to trip over him."

"You didn't expect an immediate search party, so you thought you had more time. You planned to hide the body later, after you got me out of the way."

"That's bullshit and you know it. I don't hide things from you. I don't lie to you. I don't deceive you. Not ever."

I stepped forward, lifting my face to his. "Oh, really? Somehow, I forget the discussion we had before you bit me, when you told me what you were planning to do. Convenient amnesia, I guess."

"I did not plan that," Clay said, looming over me. The wooden spoon snapped in two as he clenched his fist. "We've been through this before. I panicked and—"

"I don't want to hear your excuses."

"You never do, do you? You'd rather talk about things I *didn't* do, then toss that in for good measure when the opportunity arises. Why do I bother defending myself? You've made up your mind about everything I do and don't do, and the reasons I do them. Nothing I can ever say will change that."

He spun on his heel and stalked back to the kitchen. I turned the opposite way, strode into the study, and slammed the door.

As I sat in the study, I realized with some surprise that I had no urge to bolt. My fight with Clay hadn't left me with the usual overwhelming impulse to get free of Stonehaven. Yes, last night had been a mistake, but an instructive one. I'd let down my guard, given in to my most subconscious desire to be with Clay again, and what had happened? Within hours he was lying to me. Even while we'd been together in the woods, while I'd been sleeping, he was off indulging the darkest side of his nature. He wouldn't change. I couldn't change him. He was violent, selfish, and completely untrustworthy. If it took one regrettable night to remind me of that, it'd been worth it.

About twenty minutes later, the study door opened and Nick peeked around. I'd been curled up in Jeremy's armchair. When Nick opened the door, I unfolded myself and straightened up.

"Can I come in?" he asked.

"I smell food. If you can share, you're more than welcome."

He slipped into the room and put a plate of pancakes and ham on the footstool. The pancakes were plain, finger food without butter and syrup. I picked up one and gulped it too fast to taste it, not wanting to remember who'd made them and why.

"All done outside?" I asked.

Nick lowered himself onto the sofa and stretched out. "Pretty much. A couple more cops showed up. Jeremy sent Peter and me in."

Antonio walked through the door. "Are they investigating the scene?" he asked, pushing his son's legs off the sofa and sitting down.

Nick shrugged. "I guess so. They brought cameras and a bag of stuff. Someone from the morgue is on the way to pick up the body."

"Do you think they'll find anything?" Antonio asked me.

"Hopefully nothing that doesn't link this killing to a wild dog," I said. "If it seems clear-cut, they should wrap up the investigation pretty fast and devote their efforts to finding the dogs. No sense wasting time gathering evidence when the presumed killers will never see a courtroom."

"Just the business end of a shotgun," Antonio said. "If they see so much as a flash of fur in the woods, they'll shoot. When we need to run, we're going to have to find someplace far from here and Bear Valley."

"Damn," Nick said, shaking his head. "When we find out who's responsible, they're going to pay for this."

"Oh, I have a good idea who's responsible," I said.

I took the tuft of fur from my pocket and tossed it on the footrest. Nick stared at it a moment, confused. Then his eyes widened and he looked at me. I avoided his gaze, not wanting to see the disbelief I knew would be there. Antonio took one look at the fur, then sat back in his seat, and said nothing.

An hour or so later, I was alone again in the study, the others having drifted off to find less sedentary pursuits or more amiable companionship. As I sat there, my gaze wandered to the desk across the room. The top was still scattered with the piles of papers and anthropology journals Clay hadn't got around to reading yet. They reminded me of how I'd met Clay, how I'd come to be in this mess in the first place. While I was a student at the University of Toronto, I'd had a peripheral interest in anthropology. In my sophomore year I'd done a term paper on anthropomorphic religions, which was Clay's specialty, and I'd referenced enough of his work to recognize his name when I saw a notice on his lecture series in the student paper. His public appearances were so rare that the lecture series had been full and I'd needed to sneak in. Biggest mistake of my life.

I don't know what Clay saw in me to make him overlook his contempt for humans. He says it was a mirroring of something he recognized in himself. That's bullshit, of course. I was nothing like him or, if I was, I became that way after he bit me. Left on my own, I would have grown up, assimilated into the human world, and been a perfectly happy, well-adjusted person, leaving all my childhood baggage and anger behind. I'm sure of it.

"Blood," Clay said, swinging open the study door so hard it smacked against the wall and added to a decade's accumulation of dents. "Where was the blood?"

"What blood?"

"If I killed that guy, I would have had blood on me."

"You washed it off in the pond. That's why you made up the story about checking the water temperature, to explain why you were wet."

"Made up? Why the—" He stopped, inhaled, and started again. "Okay, assuming I cleaned up in the pond and decided it would be easier to invent some excuse for being wet instead of just drying off, you still would have smelled blood on me. The scent wouldn't wash off that easily."

"The smell would be weak. I'd have to be sniffing for it."

"Well, then sniff for it now. Come on." He locked my gaze and held it. "I dare you."

"You've had plenty of time to wash it off."

"Then check my shower. See if it's wet. Check my towels. See if they're damp."

"You'd have covered your tracks by now. You're not stupid."

"No, just stupid enough to leave a body in the woods with my prints and fur scattered all around. Why do I bother? Nothing I can say will change your mind. Do you know why? Because you want to believe I did it. That way, you can hole up in here and dwell on how wrong you were to come to me last night, curse yourself for having given in to me again, for forgetting what a monster I am."

"That's not what I'm—"

"It's not?" He stepped forward. "Look me in the eye and tell me that's not what you've been doing for the last hour."

I glared at him and said nothing. Clay stood there for at least a full minute, then threw up his hands and stormed out.

A while later, Jeremy came in. Without saying anything, he walked to the footrest, picked up the tuft of Clay's hair and looked at it, then put it down and sat in his chair.

"You don't think he did it, do you?" I said.

"If I say no, you'll try to convince me otherwise. If I say yes, you'll use that as ammunition against him. It's not important what I think. What's important is what you think."

"I once went to a therapist who talked like that. I canned him after two sessions."

"I'm sure you did."

I didn't know how to answer that, so I didn't. Instead, I feigned great interest in the patterns of the Turkish floor rug. Jeremy leaned back in his chair and watched me for a while before continuing.

"Have you called him?"

"Who?" I said, though I had a good idea who he meant.

"The man in Toronto."

"He has a name, though I'm sure you already know it."

"Have you called him?"

"I called the day before last. Yesterday was a bit hellish, if you recall, and I've been understandably preoccupied this morning."

"You have to call him every day, Elena. Make sure he knows you're okay. Don't give him any excuse for calling here or showing up."

"He only has my cell phone number."

"I don't care. You can't take any chances. Clay knows he exists, though he's trying to forget. Don't give him any reason to be reminded of it. And don't start accusing me of protecting Clay's feelings. I'm protecting the Pack. We can't afford to have Clay distracted now. And we certainly can't afford to have this man show up on our doorstep. We've had quite enough visitors as it is."

"I'll go call."

"Not yet. I've sent Nick to round up the others for a meeting."

"You can fill me in later."

"A meeting implies a group meeting," Jeremy said. "A group meeting implies that all the members of the group are expected to be there."

"What if I'm not a member of the group?"

"You are as long as you're here."

"I could remedy that."

Jeremy lifted his feet onto the footstool and leaned his head back against the headrest. "Beautiful weather we're having, isn't it?"

"Do you ever discuss anything you don't want to discuss?"

"It's the privilege of age."

I snorted. "It's the privilege of position."

"That, too."

Jeremy's lips curved in the barest of smiles and his black eyes flashed. I recognized the look, but it took me a few minutes to place it. Challenge. He was waiting for me to re-engage in a debate we'd been grappling with since I first came to the Pack. As someone who'd once been a human in a democratic society, the idea of an all-powerful, unquestionable leader rankled. How many nights had Jeremy and I spent debating it, here in this room, drinking brandy until I was too tired and drunk to walk up to my room and fell asleep here, only to awaken later in my bed?

I'd missed him. Even now, living in the same house with him for almost five days, I missed him. Everyone else in the Pack had welcomed me back, no questions asked, no grudges held. Not Jeremy. He hadn't been unfriendly or even distant, but he hadn't been himself. He was keeping me at a distance, as if unwilling to recommit himself until he was certain I wasn't going to bolt again. The problem was that I wasn't all that certain of it myself.

I tried to think of a comeback, my brain rusty to the old argument, struggling to remember how it went. As I thought, Jeremy's eyes shuttered and his smile faded. I saw my opportunity skittering past and dove to catch it. As I opened my mouth, ready to say the next thing that came to mind, the door opened. The others came in and my moment alone with Jeremy evaporated.

The first issue of business at the meeting was that Jeremy forbade us to run on the property until this mess with the police had been settled. When the time came for a run we'd all go on a field trip to the northern forests. Now, I have nothing against group runs and, under normal circumstances, I love running as a Pack, but there's something about turning a Pack run into an organized and scheduled event that sucked the pleasure out of it. Next thing you know, we'd be renting a bus, taking bagged lunches, and singing "On Top of Old Smokey" on the way.

Issue two involved Jeremy's next plan of action. Once again, it didn't go over well with Clay. It didn't sit too nicely with me either, but I wasn't the one jumping to my feet and flipping out before Jeremy even finished.

"You can't leave me here," Clay shouted.

Jeremy's eyebrows went up the barest fraction. "I can't?"

"You shouldn't. It's stup— It doesn't make sense."

"It makes perfect sense. And you're not the only one being left behind."

I grumbled, but calmly and quietly and to myself, although Jeremy's eyes did flicker my way as I did it.

Jeremy continued, "I won't have you and Elena coming along when you're at each other like this."

"But I didn't do anything!" Clay said. "You haven't even accused me of killing that guy. You know I didn't do it. So why should I be punished—"

"It's not a punishment. Whether you did it or not doesn't matter. So long as you two are fighting, I want you here, where the only damage you can cause is to each other . . . and assorted pieces of furniture."

"Why leave us both?" I asked.

"Because I don't *need* either of you. I'm not intending to track or fight

anyone. It's simple information gathering. Even if you two weren't arguing, I wouldn't take you. It's an unnecessary risk. I want to learn more
about these mutts. I don't want to rely on secondhand information, so I'm
going myself and I'm taking Tonio and Peter as backup. Nick isn't coming
either and I don't hear him complaining."

"It doesn't sound like much fun," Nick said.

Jeremy smiled. "Exactly."

"But—" I said.

"It's past lunchtime," Jeremy said, getting to his feet. "We should eat
before we leave."

He left before we could argue, which was probably the point. When he
was gone, I got to my feet.

"I guess I'll make myself useful and fix something for lunch."

Nick offered to help. For once, Clay didn't. He didn't even follow us
into the kitchen to supervise.

After lunch Jeremy, Antonio, and Peter left for reconnaissance duty. This
was Jeremy's way of handling the curveball the mutts had thrown. The
Pack was accustomed to dealing with only one mutt at a time. As I've
said, mutts didn't team up. Not ever. This meant the Pack was ill-equipped
to deal with the threat. Since Jeremy didn't have any experience handling
a multiple-mutt onslaught, he was taking his time, gathering information
before plotting a course of action. Logically, this made sense. Emotionally,
it was infuriating. If I were in charge, I'd have been planning direct and
immediate action against the mutts, risks be damned. That was why
Jeremy was the Alpha and I was the lowly foot soldier.

Once they were gone, I retreated again, this time to my room, where
I called Philip. I told him that I'd be a few days longer.

He inhaled. "Okay." A moment of silence. "I miss you."

"I—"

"I don't mean it as a guilt trip, hon. It's just— I miss you. I know you're
doing the right thing and I wouldn't ask you to abandon your cousins.
I just—didn't expect it to be this long." He paused, then clicked his
tongue. "Got it. Brainstorm. I'll pop out there. How about tomorrow?"

My hands tightened around the receiver, brain shouting, Oh shit! I clamped
my mouth shut until I'd forced the panic down. "And lose a vacation day?"
I said as lightly as I could. "You promised me a week in the Caribbean. All-
inclusive resort. Remember? As much as I'd love to see you, if it means
giving up a week of all-you-can-drink booze and sun . . . "

He chuckled. "A day helping you babysit three kids is a poor substitute, eh? I can see that. Maybe I can swing something with James, work next Saturday instead . . . though it already looked like I'd be working Saturday, and probably Sunday."

"Uh-uh. Don't go making any deals or I may not see you for weeks even after I get home."

"Point taken. I'll survive a few more lonely days. But if it gets longer than that . . ."

"It won't."

We talked for a few more minutes, then signed off. A few more days. No longer. This time, I didn't have a choice. If I didn't get my butt back to Toronto in a few days, Philip might find a way to get that day off and show up in New York. That would be . . . well, it was more than I cared to contemplate.

After talking to Philip, I stretched back in bed and rested, dozing to catch up on two nights of minimal sleep. It didn't work. I worried about the possibility of Philip showing up at Stonehaven and my stress level jumped a half-dozen notches. Then I remembered why I was still at Stonehaven and thought about Logan, feeling the grief ooze back, filling my brain until I could think of nothing else, especially sleep. Finally, Nick came to my rescue, walking into my room unannounced.

"Do you ever knock?" I said, sitting up in bed.

"Never. I'd miss everything if I did that." Pulling back the canopy, he grinned wickedly. "Did I miss anything?"

"Everything."

"Guess I'll have to start something myself then," he said, thumping down beside me on the bed and letting the canopy swing shut. "It's nice in here. Nice and quiet and very private."

"Perfect for sleeping."

"It's too early to sleep. I have something better in mind."

"I'm sure you do."

He grinned and leaned over to kiss me, then ducked out of swatting range. "Actually, I was thinking of something else for a change. Since we're not allowed to run on the property, I thought maybe the three of us could drive somewhere for a run tonight."

"I ran last night."

"But I didn't and I'm going to need to Change soon."

"Then go with Clay. There's no reason all three of us have to go."

"I've already talked to him. He'll only go if you will. He doesn't want anyone staying here alone, in case the mutts make a surprise visit."

"I'm sure they wouldn't—" I stopped myself, realizing I wasn't so sure. The thought sent a chill through me. "Do you have to go tonight? It's been a long day and—"

"I was thinking of a hunt."

"I'm not sure I—"

"A deer hunt."

"Deer?"

He laughed. "Now her ears perk up. How long has it been since you hunted anything bigger than a rabbit? Not on your own, I'll bet."

"He's right." Clay's voice came from the other side of the curtains, startling us both. When I turned, I could see his silhouette, but he didn't pull the canopy back.

"A hunt would be a good idea," Clay continued. "Keep us busy while we're waiting for Jeremy. Nick needs to Change and he can't do that here. I'm not leaving you behind by yourself, Elena. I'm sure you can stomach my company for an hour or two."

I opened my mouth to reply, but he'd already left. I hesitated for a moment, then turned to Nick and nodded. He grinned and bounced from the room, leaving me to follow.

CHAPTER 15

STALKING

We took my car. Nick drove, and Clay sat up front with him. I took the backseat and dozed so I wouldn't be expected to join in the conversation. I needn't have worried; Clay wasn't about to engage me in idle discussion, and Nick filled the void by chattering to anyone who would listen.

Nick was talking about his latest business venture, something to do with E-commerce and a new company he was backing. The question wasn't whether Nick's new venture would succeed, but how much it would lose. Exact dollar figures weren't important, since the Sorrentinos were wealthy enough to make Jeremy look middle-class. Antonio ran three multinational businesses. Nick had inherited none of his father's Midas touch. In fact, he'd been banned from all Antonio's business ventures. Nick was a playboy, plain and simple. He dabbled in an unending series of attempts at starting his own company, all of which succeeded in winning him nothing but friends and lovers, which was all he really wanted from life. How did Antonio react to this, watching his son squander his fortune? He encouraged it. Antonio recognized this lifestyle was the only thing Nick was truly qualified for, and if it made him happy and they could afford it, why not? Having scrimped and saved pennies for most of my life, I couldn't understand that philosophy. I envied it; not the idea of having so much money that you could throw it away, but the thought of growing up in a world where someone cared so much about your happiness and so little about what you accomplished in life.

Nick drove to the outskirts of a forest we'd used before. He took my car past a barricade and down an abandoned logging road, grounding out the bottom more times than I cared to count. My car wasn't in the greatest of shape and I suspected the undercarriage was more rust than steel, though I'd never worked up the nerve to test my theory. Jeremy kept offering to restore it for me or, better yet, buy me something else. I put up enough of a fuss that he was never tempted to surprise me with a new or newly restored car. Not that I'd mind getting my Camaro fixed up, if only to prolong its usefulness, but I was terrified that if I let Jeremy near it, it would come back a lovely shade of Mary Kay pink.

Farther into the forest, Nick stopped the car and put it in park. The engine died with a very unhealthy thunk. I tried not to think about that, namely because it might imply that it wouldn't start up again and that would definitely be a bad thing, stuck in backwoods New York, out of cell phone range, with a dead car and two guys who didn't know motor oil from antifreeze.

As we walked into the woods, Nick continued to talk.

"After this mess is cleaned up, we should do something. Go somewhere. Like a vacation. Maybe Europe. Clayton was supposed to go skiing with me in Switzerland this winter, but he backed out."

"I didn't back out," Clay said. He was walking ahead of us, cutting a path through the overgrown brush, maybe being helpful, more likely so he wasn't walking with me. "I never said I'd go."

"Yes, you did. At Christmas. I had to hunt you down to ask you." Nick turned to me. "He barely showed his face the whole week the Pack was at Stonehaven. He was holed up with his books and papers. He kept expecting you to show up and when you didn't—" At a look from Clay, Nick stopped. "Anyway, you did say you'd come skiing. I asked you and you grunted something that sure sounded like a yes."

"Huh."

"Exactly. Just like that. Okay, it wasn't really a yes, but it wasn't a no either. So you owe me a trip. The three of us will go. Where do you want to go when this is all over, Elena?"

"Toronto" was on the tip of my tongue, but I didn't say it. Squashing Nick's plans when he was trying so hard to smooth things over was like telling your kid there was no Santa Claus just because you had a bad day at work. It wasn't fair and he didn't deserve it.

"We'll see," I said.

Clay looked sharply over his shoulder and met my eyes. He knew exactly what I meant. With a scowl, he shoved a branch out of the way, then stalked off to find a place for his Change.

"I'm not sure this is such a good idea," I said to Nick after Clay was gone. "Maybe I should wait in the car."

"Come on. Don't do that. You can blow off some steam. Just ignore him."

I agreed. Well, I didn't actually agree, but Nick took off before I could argue and he had my car keys.

Just ignore Clay. Good advice. Really, really good advice. For practicality, though, it ranked up there with telling an acrophobic "just don't look down."

When I stepped from the thicket after my Change, Clay was there. He stood back, nose twitching. Then his mouth fell open, tongue lolling out in a wolf-grin as if we'd never argued. I searched for my own anger, knowing it should be there, but unable to find it, as if I'd left it in the thicket beside my discarded clothes.

I eyed Clay for a moment, then cautiously started to skirt around him. I was almost past him when he twisted and lunged sideways, grabbing my hind leg and yanking it out from under me. As I tumbled down, he jumped on top of me. We rolled through the underbrush, knocking into a sapling and sending a squirrel scampering for a steadier perch, chattering its annoyance as it ran. When I finally got out from under him, I leapt to my feet and ran. Behind me, Clay crashed through the brush. After no more than ten yards, I heard a yelp, then felt the ground shudder as Clay fell. I glanced over my shoulder to see him snapping and tugging at a vine caught around his forepaw. I slowed to turn around and go back for him, then saw him break free and lunge into a run. Realizing I was losing my lead, I turned forward and plowed into something solid, somersaulting over it and into a patch of nettles.

I looked up from my crash landing to see Nick standing over me. With a growl and as much dignity as I could muster, I got to my feet. Nick stood back and watched, eyes laughing as I disentangled myself from the nettles. Out of the corner of my eye, I saw Clay sneak up behind Nick. He crouched, forequarters down, rear end in the air. Then he pounced, knocking Nick flying into the nettles. As Nick was struggling to stand, I walked by him with a "serves you right" snort. He grabbed my foreleg and yanked me down. We tussled for a minute before I managed to get free and dart behind Clay.

While Nick extricated himself from the nettles, Clay rubbed his muzzle against mine, hot breath ruffling the fur around my neck. Nick walked around us, rubbing and sniffing a greeting. When he lingered too long sniffing near my tail, Clay growled a warning and he backed off.

After a couple of minutes, we pulled apart and began to run, Clay and I jostling for the lead, Nick content to stay at our heels. The forest was rife with smells, including the musky scent of deer, but most of it was old trails and long-dried spoor. We'd gone about a half mile before I caught the scent we wanted. Fresh deer. With a spurt of energy, I raced forward. Behind me, Nick and Clay ran through the woods in near silence. Only the rustle of dead undergrowth beneath their feet betrayed them. Then the wind changed and drove the scent of deer full in our faces. Nick yelped and raced up beside me, trying to take the lead. I snapped at him, catching a chunk of dark fur as he scrambled out of my way.

As I dealt with Nick, I realized Clay wasn't right behind us. I slowed, then turned and went back. He was standing about twenty feet away, nose twitching as he sniffed the air. As I loped over, he caught my eye and I knew why he'd stopped. We were close enough. It was time to plan. It might seem silly to think of deer as dangerous, but we're not human hunters who never get within a hundred feet of their prey. A slash of antlers can lay a wolf open. A well-aimed hoof can split a skull. There was a twelve-inch scar on Clay's thigh where he'd had his flank sliced by a hoof. Even real wolves know that a deer hunt requires caution and planning.

Planning obviously didn't mean discussing the matter, since such high-level communication was impossible as wolves. Unlike humans, though, we had something better: instinct and a brain ingrained with patterns that had proven successful for thousands of generations. We could assess the situation, recall a plan, and communicate it with a look. Or, at least, Clay and I could. Like many werewolves, Nick either wasn't in tune with the messages his wolf brain sent or his human brain didn't trust them. It didn't matter. Clay and I were the Alpha pair there, so Nick would follow orders without needing an explanation.

I walked to the east, sniffed the air, and caught the deer's scent again. A lone stag. That meant we didn't have to worry about cutting a deer from a herd. Still, a stag was more dangerous than a doe, especially one with a full set of antlers. Clay moved up beside me and sniffed for the deer, then caught my eye with a look that said "what the hell, you only live once." I snorted my agreement and walked back to Nick. Clay didn't follow. He slipped into the forest again and vanished. The plan was set.

Nick and I circled through the woods, getting downwind before following the scent again. We found the stag grazing in a thicket. As Nick waited for the signal, he nudged me and rubbed against me, whining too low for the buck to hear. I growled low in my throat and he stopped. The stag lifted its head and looked around. When it returned to its feeding, I crouched and sprang. The deer paused only a millisecond before leaping over the bushes and breaking into a gallop. Nick and I tore after it, but the gap between us and the deer grew. Wolves are distance runners, not sprinters, and our only chance to catch a running deer from behind is to wear it down.

As often happened, the deer made the fatal error of throwing his energy into the opening spurt. We hadn't gone far when he started to slow, wheezing and snorting for breath, too frightened to pace himself. I was getting winded, too, having already expended a fair amount of energy finding and chasing the stag. What kept me going was the smell of the buck, the musky, tantalizing odor that made my stomach rumble.

I found Clay's scent in the air, and ran the deer toward him by veering out one way with a short burst of speed that sent it flying in the opposite direction. As we ran, the stag's fear escalated into panic. It galloped full-out, vaulting fallen trees and careering through undergrowth. The trees and bushes tore at its hide and the scent of blood seeped into the air. As we rounded a corner, Clay lunged from the bushes and caught the deer by the nose.

The stag slid to a halt and shook its head wildly, trying to dislodge Clay. Meanwhile, we caught up. I darted under the deer and sank my teeth into its stomach. I tasted the hot blood under a layer of fat and my mouth began to water. Nick attacked the deer's side, lunging and biting and skittering out of the way before the deer could aim a hoof or antler in his direction. Clay was being tossed from side to side, but he hung on. This was a ploy dredged up from deepest memory: bite the face of your prey and it'll be too busy trying to free itself from the most obvious danger to bother with the other attackers.

As I clung to the stag's underbelly, I ripped and sliced, dancing on my hind legs to keep out of hoofs' reach. When I'd torn a gaping hole, I released my grip and clamped down farther up. Entrails began to slide from the first hole and the smell nearly drove me mad. Blood was also dripping from Nick's lightning attacks, making the stag's coat slick and difficult to grasp. I bit harder, feeling my teeth slide through the skin into vital organs. At last the deer's front legs slid forward. Clay released his grip on its nose and tore into its throat. The deer thudded to the ground.

Once the deer was down, Nick backed off and found a place nearby to lie down. Clay lowered his head and looked at me. His muzzle was stained with blood. I licked it and rubbed against him, feeling the shudders of spent adrenaline coursing through him. Below us, the stag's limbs were still quivering, but its eyes stared forward, all life gone. As we tore into its side, steam swirled into the cool evening air. We began to feast, tearing off chunks of meat and gulping them whole.

When we'd eaten our fill, Nick approached and began to feed. Clay walked to a clearing and looked over his shoulder at me. I followed and dropped down beside him. Clay shifted closer, put one paw around my neck, and started to lick my muzzle. I closed my eyes as he worked. When he'd cleaned the blood from my neck and shoulders, I worked on him. Once Nick finished eating, he curled up with us and we drifted off to sleep in a huddle of intertwined limbs and varicolored fur.

We hadn't been napping long when Clay jumped up, spilling Nick and me to the ground. I snapped awake when my head struck a rock. I scrambled to my feet, tense and looking for danger. We were alone in the clearing. Night had fallen, bringing with it only nocturnal sounds of nature, the calls of the hunters and the shrieks of the hunted. I growled at Clay and started settling back down to my nap. He knocked me in the ribs with his muzzle and made a show of sniffing the air. I glared at him, but did as he asked. At first, I smelled nothing. Then the wind shifted and I knew what had made him jump up. Someone was here. Another werewolf. Zachary Cain.

Clay was gone as soon as he knew that I understood. Behind me, Nick was still shaking off the groggy haze of interrupted sleep. I glanced back at him, then started to run, knowing he'd follow even if he wasn't sure why. At the edge of the clearing, Cain's smell grew stronger. I followed my nose to a thicket nearby. The trampled and flattened grass reeked of Cain's scent. He'd been lying here, close enough to us that he could stick his muzzle through the brambles and watch us sleep. Something about that scenario jarred, but I wasn't sure why. The human part of me wanted to sit back and contemplate the problem, but the wolf instinct shut my brain down and propelled my feet to action. There was an intruder to be dealt with.

Even if I hesitated near the thicket, Nick didn't. He stuck his nose in, took a deep breath, backed out, and raced after Clay. For once, I was left bringing up the rear. The other two were so far gone, I couldn't see or hear them and had to follow Clay's trail. It wove deeper into the woods, through trees so dense that they snuffed out the moon and stars. As good as my night vision was, I needed some light, even reflected light, with which to work. Here there was nothing. I could make out only the looming shapes of tree trunks and bushes, dark shadows against a darker canvas. Slowing, I put my nose to the ground and relied on Clay's trail instead.

On the other side of the dense hollow, the trees opened up to let in some moonlight. As I picked up speed, bushes crackled to the north, something big breaking through the undergrowth. It wasn't Clay or Nick. Even Nick moved through the woods with more finesse than that. Leaving

Clay's trail, I veered north. I'd run about a quarter mile when I felt the vibration of running paws hitting the ground somewhere behind me. That was Clay and Nick. I recognized them without looking, so I didn't slow down. Since I was cutting the trail, though, I wasn't running as fast as they were, and before long, I heard Clay's rhythmic breathing at my heels. We skirted a large outcropping of rock. Branches snapped somewhere behind us. Twisting around, I saw a huge reddish brown shadow burst from behind the rock and run in the opposite direction.

I dug my claws into the soft ground to stop, then pivoted and raced after Cain. Only one pair of footfalls followed: Nick. Clay was gone, taking another route in hopes of cutting Cain off like he had the stag. Cain followed the trail I'd cut, looping back the way he'd come. After a quarter mile, he swerved to the east. He was heading for the road, hoping to escape. I shot forward and got close enough for his tail hairs to brush my muzzle. Then my paw caught on an indentation in the ground, not a hole or anything large enough to make me trip, just the barest change in elevation that slowed me down enough for Cain to get that extra foot ahead. Nick raced up from behind me. As he started to overtake me, I eased back to conserve my energy. Ahead, the forest opened up as we approached the road. I swung to the left, hoping to gain a few feet by anticipating Cain's route. He didn't turn, though. He kept running, back into the forest.

Seeing what Cain was doing, I looked ahead and saw a clearer patch of land to the northwest. When Cain didn't head that way, I did. Nick stayed on Cain's tail, not so much trying to catch him as hoping to run him into the ground. My path led to a rocky hill. As I climbed it, I picked up traces of Clay's scent. The terrain got rougher as I ran, slowing me and making me curse my choice of shortcuts. Halfway up the hill, my forepaw slipped on some stones, one of them sharp enough to slice through my foot pads. I grunted, but kept moving. Once I was at the top of the hill, my effort seemed worthwhile. From here I could look down and see the whole terrain. To the east, I caught a flash of gold as Clay weaved through the trees. As a nearly black wolf, Nick wasn't so easy to spot at night, but after a moment, I saw some trees shake below me. I followed the path of the rustling trees and bushes. They were coming this way. I traced the line of their route and moved to the spot where I guessed they'd come out. I was rewarded by the crashing of undergrowth directly in front of me. Seconds later, a massive shape shot through the brush.

Seeing me in his path, Cain stopped. He growled and dropped his head. His green eyes blazed and his dark blond fur stood on end, adding a couple inches to his size. The extra size was superfluous; Cain didn't need it to look imposing. As a human, he stood over six-five, with the shoulders and sheer bulk of an all-star quarterback. As a wolf, he was literally more than twice my size. I pulled back my lips and snarled, but felt about as threatening as a Pomeranian facing down a pit bull. One part of my brain, soaring on adrenaline, insisted I could take Cain, whatever the size difference. Another part wondered where the hell Nick and Clay were. The loudest part just shouted: Run, you idiot, run!

As I was thinking this, Cain suddenly turned and . . . ran. For a moment, I couldn't move, unable to believe my eyes. Cain was running? From me? No matter how much my ego liked to think he was afraid of me, common sense told me otherwise. So why did he bolt? Again, my wolf instincts wouldn't let my brain ponder the question. As Cain disappeared down the hill, my instincts kicked in and I started after him.

I'd gone maybe a dozen feet when something landed on my back, knocking my legs from under me. I twisted to see Clay standing over me. I tried scrambling to my feet, but he held me down. Was he crazy? Cain was getting away. I snapped at him, catching his foreleg in my jaws and clamping down, growling. He grabbed me under the throat and pinned me. With each second, I pictured Cain getting farther away. I struggled, but Clay fought back and kept me down. Finally, I knew it was too late. Cain was gone. For a second, Clay hesitated. Then he bounded off, not after Cain, but in the opposite direction. When I was back on my feet, I raced after him. I followed his scent fifty feet to a clearing where I could smell his clothing. This was where we'd first Changed. I poked my muzzle through the undergrowth to see Clay in the midst of his Change, his back arched, his skin throbbing and pulsing, too immersed in the transformation to notice me. I paused, uncertain. Then I found my own clothes and Changed back.

When I stormed from the clearing, Clay was already there.

"Where's Nick?" Clay said before I could say anything. "Goddamn it! He's got the keys. Wasn't he right behind you?"

"What are you talking about?"

Clay strode into the bushes, looking around. "Don't you get it? He was distracting us, keeping us busy."

"Nick?"

"Cain." Clay was out of sight now, only his voice echoing from the forest. "We were asleep and he didn't attack us. We chased him and he didn't fight or try to escape. He just kept us going in circles. Nicholas!"

"But why—"

"Jeremy. They've gone after Jeremy. Goddamn it! They've probably been watching the house and we didn't even— There you are!"

"Hold on," Nick's voice emerged from the darkness. "Can I have a second to do up my pants?"

Clay crashed from the bush, dragging Nick by one arm. "To the car. Both of you. Move!"

We moved.

Chapter 16

Ambush

O n the way to Bear Valley, Clay drove, Nick took the backseat, and I sat up front where the safety restraints were better. As I'd feared, the Camaro wasn't eager to restart. When it hesitated, Clay rammed the gas pedal to the floor, revved the engine into the red zone, then slammed the gearshift into reverse, ignoring the clanking sounds coming from under the hood. Forced into a battle of wills, the car surrendered and meekly let him drive the shit out of it all the way to Bear Valley.

"No, take the next exit," I said as Clay started turning off the first road to Bear Valley. "Head for the east end. To the hotel."

"Hotel?"

"There's no sense chasing our tails all over Bear Valley if the mutts haven't even left their hotel room. If they are gone, maybe I can track them from there."

Clay's hands tightened on the steering wheel. I knew he was certain the mutts had gone after Jeremy and checking the hotel only meant precious minutes lost. Still, it made sense. Instead of answering me, he veered back onto the highway, darting in front of a fully loaded logging truck. I closed my eyes for the rest of the ride.

When we got to the motor lodge, Clay whipped the car into the handi-capped spot beside the lobby and was flying out of his seat before the engine died. I grabbed the car keys from the ignition and went after him. This time, he made no effort to fool the desk clerk. Luckily, there wasn't anyone behind the desk. Clay ran up the stairs two at a time. At LeBlanc's room, he snapped the freshly repaired lock and barreled through the door without waiting to see if anyone was on the other side. I was mounting the last steps when he came out.

"Gone," he said, pushing past me back down the stairs. About halfway down, he realized I was still going up and turned around. "I said, they're gone."

"This isn't the only room," I said. "Marsten wouldn't be caught dead camping out on anyone's floor."

Clay growled something, but I was already heading down the hall, pausing at each door and trying to pick up Cain's or Marsten's scent. Clay came back up the stairs and strode down the hall toward me.

"We don't have time—"

"Then go," I said. "Just go."

He didn't. Three rooms past LeBlanc's, I stopped.

"Cain," I said, reaching for the door handle.

"Got it. Keep moving and find Marsten's."

Marsten had the next room down. While Clay was still checking Cain's room, I broke open Marsten's door and walked inside. Except for the Italian leather suitcase in the corner, the room looked uninhabited. The bed was made, the tables were spotless, and the towels were all neatly hung on the rack. Definitely Karl Marsten's room. If he had to stoop to taking a room in the Big Bear Motor Lodge, he wouldn't spend any more time there than necessary. I was about to leave the room when I caught another familiar scent.

"Jeremy," Clay said from behind me as he stepped into the room.

"He's gone," I said. "He must have been here checking things out."

Clay nodded and brushed past me on his way out the door. We went back to the car. Next, Clay cruised the parking lots looking for the Mercedes or the Acura. Actually, "cruise" is misleading; I should say he ripped into the lots, circled around sharp enough to induce whiplash, and tore out again. In the parking lot behind Drake's Family Wear, we found Marsten's Acura.

I was only guessing that the Acura belonged to Marsten, but it was a pretty safe bet. LeBlanc may have had a steady income while he was living in Chicago, but by the looks of his hotel room, he wasn't shelling out the big bucks on luxury cars these days. Marsten, on the other hand, was very successful at his career . . . if you call thievery a career. Stealing was the number one occupation among mutts. Their lifestyle didn't encourage them to stay in one town long enough to settle into a job. Even if they were inclined to lay down roots, it wouldn't last. The Pack routinely rousted mutts who seemed to be settling into a non-nomadic lifestyle. Making a home for oneself meant claiming territory and only the Pack could claim territory. So most mutts wandered from city to city, stealing enough to stay alive. Some did better than that. Marsten specialized in jewels, namely jewels from the necks and bedrooms of lonely middle-aged dowagers. He had money and he considered himself a cut above other werewolves. It didn't matter to the Pack that he could speak five languages and didn't touch wine younger than he was. A mutt was a mutt.

Clay slowed down behind the Acura, then hit the gas and swung from the parking lot.

"We aren't tracking them?" Nick asked, leaning over the seat.

"I don't care where *they* are. I care where Jeremy is."

We found Antonio's Mercedes a couple blocks away in the paper-mill parking lot. This trail was easy for me to follow, the scents being so familiar that I could let my brain process on autopilot while I concentrated on looking ahead for clues.

The trail looped past the local newspaper office, The Donut Hole, the warehouse where the rave had been held, and a country-and-western bar just off the main street. I could follow Jeremy's logic as we passed each point: the paper for late-breaking news, the coffee shop for gossip, and the warehouse for any overlooked clues. The tavern was a bit trickier, until I picked up the acrid scent of stale urine where Cain had pissed on the rear wall, presumably after a round of drinking the night before. From there, the trail headed back toward the paper mill where Antonio's car was parked.

"They're heading back," Nick said. "I bet we just missed them."

We went about five steps when a cat hissed at us from a pile of garbage. Nick hissed back. The cat's eyes narrowed, tail shooting up into an affronted exclamation mark.

"Leave the kitty alone," I said. "He's too skinny to be more than a mouthful and a stringy one at that."

As I turned, I saw something sticking out from under the bags of garbage. At first it looked like a row of four pale pebbles peeking out from between two bags. The sight was so out of place that I stepped toward it, ignoring the reek of garbage that overpowered everything else. As I drew closer, I realized what I was really seeing: fingertips.

"Shit," I muttered. "Look at this. Either those mutts are getting careless with their kills or they're leaving them lying around on purpose."

"Twenty bucks on the latter," Clay said.

He stepped forward and nudged the top bag back for a better view. The fingertips were attached to a hand, which was attached to an arm. As Clay heaved the bag up, the lower bag slid out and the body tumbled to the ground. It rolled onto its back. The man's head lolled to the side at an impossible angle, neck broken. Unruly red hair glittered even in the dark.

"Peter," I whispered.

"No," Clay said. "Jeremy. No!"

Clay shot off into the darkness, running footsteps echoing down the alley. Nick's eyes widened and met mine. Then something behind them clicked as he remembered that Jeremy hadn't been the only one with Peter.

He raced after Clay. I paused to hide Peter's body, then ran after them, my heart pounding so hard I couldn't breathe, gasping and choking for air as I ran. Twenty feet away, I saw a pool of thick red glimmering under the sick light of a half-dead light. From it, trails of blood tentacled out, then converged in a single thread leading into the distance. I followed the trail. Ahead, Nick's white shirt bobbed against the blackness. I could hear Clay's footfalls, but couldn't see him. The blood trail wove around two corners. As I wheeled around the second, I saw Clay and Nick just ahead, both stopping and circling back. They'd run past the trail, which ended in a puddle of blood just past the corner.

I bent, put a finger to the blood, then lifted it to my nose.

"Is it?" Clay asked.

"Jeremy's," I whispered.

"And there's plenty more here if you'd like a closer look," a deep voice said.

Clay's head shot up. We looked around, then saw a loading dock to our right. Clay hopped onto the three-foot-high ledge and disappeared into the darkness of the opening. Nick and I followed. At the back of the loading dock, Jeremy sat in the corner, propping his right leg on a broken crate as Antonio tore strips from his shirt. As we approached, Jeremy lifted his left arm to push his bangs back from his face, then winced and used his right hand instead, letting the left fall awkwardly to his side.

"Are you okay?" I asked.

"Peter's dead," Jeremy said. "We were ambushed."

"We were heading back to the car," Antonio said as he added another layer of bindings to Jeremy's leg. "I took off to find a bathroom. Five minutes. I must have barely turned the corner and—" He kept his eyes on his task, but self-reproach leached from every word. "Less than five minutes. While I'm taking a damned piss-break—"

"They were waiting for an opportunity," Jeremy said. "Any of us could have turned our back for a moment and they would have attacked the other two."

Antonio glanced over his shoulder as he worked. "The new one, the mutt that killed Logan, attacked Jeremy with a knife."

"A knife?" Clay glanced at Jeremy for affirmation, as disbelieving as if Antonio had said Jeremy was attacked with an antique Howitzer. "A knife?"

Jeremy nodded.

Antonio continued, "They jumped Peter and Jeremy. No one had time to react. When I showed up they took off. I'd have gone after them, but Jeremy was bleeding pretty badly."

"Not that I would have let you go after them anyway," Jeremy said. "We don't have time to rehash events now. We need to get things cleaned up and go."

He started getting to his feet. Clay hopped over a crate and helped him up.

"We left Peter at the scene," Jeremy said.

"I know," I said. "We found him."

"In the garbage," Antonio said, wiping a hand over his face. "That wasn't right. I'm sorry, but Jeremy was bleeding and I—"

"You needed to find a quick hiding spot," Jeremy finished. "No one's blaming you for that. We'll get him now and take him home."

Clay helped Jeremy down from the dock. I moved up on his left side to take his other arm, then remembered it was injured and settled for walking beside him, ready to catch him if his leg gave out. I gave Nick my car keys and he ran ahead to back up the Camaro to the end of the alley. When we got to the garbage heap, Antonio uncovered Peter and cleaned him off.

"Marsten's going to pay for this," Clay said, looking at Peter's body, hands clenching and unclenching at his sides. "He's really going to pay."

"Marsten didn't kill Peter. Daniel did."

"Dan—" Clay choked on the rest of the name. "Ah, shit."

I rode back to Stonehaven in Antonio's Mercedes, sitting in the backseat with Jeremy, in case the bleeding worsened. Antonio drove in silence. Jeremy stared out the window while holding the bindings tight on his leg. I tried to concentrate on something other than watching my car through the windshield and thinking about Peter's body in my trunk. Instead, I thought about the mutts.

So it was Daniel after all. That meant trouble. Big trouble. More than Marsten or Cain, Daniel knew how the Pack operated, how everyone in it operated. He'd been Pack, having grown up with Nick and Clay . . . or, more accurately, he grew up around them, "with them" sounding as if the three had been buddies, a definite misconception. Now, before Clay's arrival, Nick and Daniel had been semi-playmates, thrown together by their closeness in age, like two cousins who play with each other at family reunions because there's no one else to hang around with. Then came Clay. I was a bit fuzzy on the details, but I'd been told that Clay and Daniel loathed each other from the beginning. The precipitating event seemed to have occurred when Daniel eavesdropped on Nick and Clay's conversation and raced off to regale the Pack with the story of Clay's expulsion from kindergarten, which had something to do with dissecting the classroom guinea pig to see how it worked, but like I said, I was fuzzy on the details—when I asked Clay about it, all he'd say was "it was already dead," which was apparently supposed to explain everything. Whatever the story, it embarrassed Jeremy, who'd been fudging the details when explaining to the others why Clay's school career had lasted only a month. By upsetting Jeremy, Daniel had earned Clay's eternal rancor.

In the years to follow, the relationship between the two only grew more acrimonious as Daniel and Clay fought for supreme position among the younger generation. Or, I should say, Daniel fought for it. Clay simply assumed it was his and squashed Daniel's aspirations with the lazy contempt of someone batting away a mosquito. When the three were in their early twenties, Jeremy became Alpha. I may have given the impression that this was a bloodless ascension. It wasn't. Seven members of the Pack backed Jeremy and four didn't, including Daniel and his brother Stephen. The dissension crescendoed when Stephen tried to assassinate Jeremy. Clay killed him. Daniel insisted his brother had been innocent and that Clay had murdered him to quell opposition to Jeremy's leadership. When Jeremy was confirmed Alpha, Daniel decided there wasn't a place for him in the new Pack.

Unfortunately for all, that wasn't the end of the story. Even if they were no longer Pack brothers, Daniel and Clay had had plenty of run-ins since that time. After I came along, things got even worse. Daniel decided he absolutely had to have me, if only because I "belonged" to his archrival. When Daniel first approached me, I even thought he was a decent guy. I believed his stories about being mistreated and maligned by Clay—at the time I was quite happy to believe anything bad about Clay. One day I was in San Diego with Antonio delivering a warning to another mutt and, knowing Daniel had been living there a few months, I slipped away from Antonio to say hello to Daniel. When I got to his apartment, I caught him trying to hide a woman in the closet. It wouldn't have been so bad if the woman was still alive. Apparently, she had been, right up until I rang the doorbell, upon which Daniel snapped her neck and tried to stuff her into a closet so I wouldn't find him with someone. After that, I'd put a lot more credence in Clay's warnings about Daniel.

The woman in the closet wasn't the first of Daniel's kills. When he'd left the Pack, he'd abandoned its teachings and become a man-killer. Like all successful—and long-lived—man-killing mutts, Daniel learned the trick to killing humans, the same trick a wolf uses when confronted with a large herd of prey: cull from the edges. If you stick with the marginalized—the drug users, the teenage runaways, the prostitutes, the homeless—you stand a good chance of getting away with it. Why? Because nobody gives a damn. Oh sure, they say they do, the police and the politicians and everyone who's supposed to uphold justice, but they really don't. People can vanish and, so long as they stay gone, nobody will care. I'm not talking about third-world dictatorships or even American metropolises infamous for their crime rates. Vancouver had over twenty prostitutes disappear from a single neighborhood before authorities began to suspect a problem. Trust me, if these women had been students at the University of British Columbia, people would have perked up a whole lot quicker. That's where Thomas LeBlanc went wrong, picking the daughters and wives of middle-class families as his prey. If he'd stuck to hookers and runaways, he'd still be doing a booming business in Chicago. In all my arguments with Jeremy over the unfairness of the Pack's hierarchical system, I'd upheld the human democratic model for comparison, where everyone was supposedly equally important. It was bullshit, of course. Even though the Pack had a strict hierarchy, it would never let even the death of its Omega member go unavenged.

Back at the house, Jeremy asked me to help dress his wounds. Maybe he assumed I'd be a gentler, more tolerable nurse than the men. Right. Jeremy may not have known much about women, but he'd learned enough about this particular one never to mistake me for Betty Crocker, Martha Stewart, or Florence Nightingale. More likely he thought that, given the choice between nursing and gravedigging, I'd be much happier donning a cute little white hat and dress. My last graveside episode wasn't one I cared to repeat any sooner than necessary. At least if I was looking after Jeremy, I could block out what was going on in the back field.

Normally, Jeremy would be the one doing the nursing. He was the Pack doctor. No, that wasn't a time-honored role passed down through generations of werewolves. It was something Jeremy took on when, as a child, Clay jumped five stories down a department-store elevator shaft (don't ask) and fractured his arm in several places. Not wanting to risk Clay's future mobility on a makeshift splint, Jeremy took him to a doctor. Although he was careful, citing religious reasons for not wanting blood work and other routine lab tests done, the doctor did them anyway. The results might have gone ignored, having little to do with a broken arm, but a bored lab technician on the night shift spotted something peculiar in the workups and called Jeremy at two A.M. Werewolf blood is screwed up. Don't ask me for the exact details—I barely passed tenth-grade biology.

All I know is that we aren't supposed to let anyone draw and analyze our blood. Whatever the technician saw in Clay's workup made him think Clay had some life-threatening condition and he ordered Jeremy to bring Clay to the hospital immediately. The upshot of the whole mess was that both the technician and Clay's file were missing when the day shift arrived. After that, Jeremy bought and studied a shelf full of medical books. A few years ago I made the mistake of giving him a copy of the *St. John Ambulance Official Wilderness First Aid Guide.* He'd liked it so much he had me buy copies for all of us so we could keep them in our glove boxes and fix our own emergency amputations. Call me a wimp, but if I ever lose a limb and there's no one around, I'm a goner, even if the guide does have wonderful instructions (complete with helpful illustrations) for tying off the injury with a stick and a plastic garbage bag.

"Leg first?" I asked Jeremy as he took his box of medical supplies from the bathroom closet.

"Arm. I'll get the bone in place. You splint it."

That didn't sound too bad. Jeremy sat on the toilet seat and I crouched beside him as we worked. It was a clean break, not an open fracture, so there wasn't any of that nasty pulling the bone back under the skin stuff required. The break was just below his elbow. After he got it realigned, I placed the padded splint under his arm. Then I got the bandage roll out. Following Jeremy's instructions, I bound it first below his elbow, then above his wrist. Then I fashioned a sling to keep his arm elevated. It took a while, but it was fairly easy . . . compared to what he wanted me to do next.

"You'll need to stitch up my leg," he said.

"Stitch . . . ?"

"I can't do it with one hand." He stood and leaned against the vanity, undoing his jeans with his good hand, then struggling to get them off. "I could use some help with this, too, if it's not too much to ask."

"Sure," I said. "Undressing men, I'm good at. Sewing people up, though, is questionable. Maybe the cut isn't that bad."

I unwound the blood-soaked strips of Antonio's shirt from Jeremy's thigh. The skin and muscle parted like the Red Sea, an even more apt analogy considering the gush of blood that streamed out. I had no problem seeing Jeremy with his pants off, but this internal view was more than I wanted to see of anyone.

"Grab the facecloth," he said, sitting quickly and shoving a towel against the gash.

I wet the cloth, cleaned the wound, then applied antiseptic. I didn't work as fast as I should have, and by the time I was finishing, blood was gushing over my fingers.

"Get the tape," Jeremy said. "No, not that tape. The other—right."

Using the tape and some fancy maneuvering, we got the blood flow stopped before Jeremy passed out. He took something that looked remarkably like a needle and thread from the kit and handed it to me.

"Stop backing away, Elena. It's not going to bite. Take the needle and start. Don't think about it. Just try to make a reasonably straight line."

"Sounds easy, but you never saw my home economics projects."

"No, but I've had the privilege of experiencing your haircuts. As I said, *try* to make a straight line."

"I always cut your hair straight."

"If I hold my head on a certain angle, it's perfectly straight."

"Watch it. I've got a needle."

"And maybe if I get you mad enough, you'll actually jab me with it and get to work before I bleed out."

I took the hint. Despite what Jeremy said, it was not like sewing fabric nor could I pretend that it was. Cloth doesn't bleed. I concentrated on doing a good job, knowing that if I didn't, I'd be razzed about Jeremy's crooked scar for the rest of my life. It was nearly done when I felt a rush of anger that some mutt had dared do this to Jeremy, which made me think about how it had happened, which made me remember that Peter was dead. First Logan. Now Peter. Of all the Pack, they deserved it least. Jeremy never sent them to roust or kill any mutts, not even to deliver warnings. Their deaths weren't about revenge. They weren't about taking out the Pack's strongest fighters. Logan and Peter had been killed to make us sit up and take notice. Nothing more. My hands started to clench. The old serpent of rage started moving through me. I stopped, inhaled, and started again, but couldn't steady my fingers.

"So we're up against three experienced mutts," Jeremy said, breaking into my thoughts.

I swallowed back the clot in my throat and played along with the distraction. "Plus at least one new one."

"I haven't forgotten, though I'm more concerned about the experienced ones. Yes, they're good—my arm and leg prove that—but they're not on the same playing field as Daniel."

I broke off the thread. "That's because you know Daniel. And even if you don't know Marsten and Cain equally well, you know what to expect from them because they're like you. They think like you, they react like you, they kill like you. These new ones don't. Werewolves don't strangle people. That's how LeBlanc killed Logan and he succeeded because it's the last thing Logan would have expected. Then he pulled a knife on you. You'd expect that as much as a samurai would expect a kick in the balls. That's why LeBlanc is still alive. He threw you off balance. If—"

"We've dug the grave," Antonio said, coming into the bathroom. "I'm sorry. Did I interrupt something?"

"Nothing that can't be finished later," Jeremy said, getting to his feet and testing the stitches. When they didn't burst apart or gush blood, he nodded. "Perfect. I'll get dressed and we'll go out."

Conviction

I went to Peter's burial site with Jeremy. It wasn't something I particularly wanted to do, with my last graveside breakdown less than thirty-six hours old. Nor did Jeremy need my help making sure the grave was well concealed. He did, however, need my help in another way, though he'd never have admitted it or asked for it. With his leg freshly stitched, he was in no shape for walking without a supporting arm. So I helped him out to the backyard, though to an onlooker it would have appeared that Jeremy was the one helping me. That wasn't unintentional. The Pack Alpha could not show weakness, even if he was fresh from a fight for his life. Not that any of us would ever seize an opportunity to challenge Jeremy for leadership. Yet because the Pack placed its Alpha in total control, the idea that he might not be up to the task, even temporarily, would throw the whole Pack off balance.

Although Jeremy had to be in tremendous pain, he never showed it. He accepted my arm going to and from the grave site, but never put more than the minimum amount of weight on it. Only when we were heading back to the house did he pause for a second, presumably to catch his breath, though he pretended to be checking a crumbling stone in the garden wall.

"I guess we should grab some sleep now," I said, feigning a yawn. "I know I could use it."

"Go on," Jeremy said. "You've had a rough couple of days. I want to discuss what we found in Bear Valley before we were ambushed, but I can fill you in tomorrow."

"Everyone's probably exhausted. We can meet in the morning, can't we? I wouldn't want to miss anything."

"I'd like to get through it tonight. If you want to be there, claim the couch and you can doze while we talk."

Okay, forget subtlety. Full-frontal-assault time. "*You* need to sleep. Your leg has to be killing you, not to mention your arm. No one's going to think anything's wrong if you delay the meeting until tomorrow."

"I can handle it. Don't grind your teeth like that, Elena; I'm not qualified to do dental work. If you want to help, you can round up the others and get them into the study, if they're not already there."

"If you'd like me to really help, I can knock you unconscious until morning."

He gave me a wry half smile that said my suggestion sounded more tempting than he cared to admit. "How about a compromise? You can help by rounding up the others and fixing me a drink, preferably a double."

Before the ambush, Jeremy's information-gathering had confirmed what Clay and I knew, that we had three mutts in Bear Valley. He'd also learned a few additional bits of information. Marsten had actually been the first of the three to arrive, before Cain and LeBlanc. He'd checked into the Big Bear three days ago, meaning he'd been in town before Brandon's death. After a few twenties loosened the desk clerk's powers of recall, he'd remembered a young man matching Brandon's description visiting Marsten at the hotel several times. Any doubt that Brandon had been involved with the others was now gone. I wondered if Marsten had been at the rave that night, enjoying a whiskey and soda as he watched Brandon and me, his scent and form hidden away in a dark, smoky corner. Yes, I was sure he'd been there. He'd seen Brandon start his Change, realized what was about to happen, and slipped out before the chaos erupted, abandoning his protégé to his fate. Mutts may have been able to form relationships with each other, but they lasted only so long as proved advantageous to both parties. Once Marsten saw Brandon was in trouble, his only thought would be to get the hell out of there before he got sucked into the mess.

Cain and LeBlanc had checked into the Big Bear the night Brandon died. Presumably they'd either followed Logan from Los Angeles or met him at the airport. Waylaying him in Bear Valley would have been next to impossible. While we'd been chasing Brandon, Logan had already been dead, probably in the back of some rented car on his way to Bear Valley. Somewhere along the way, they must have found out from Marsten that Clay and I were in town and the prank of staging Logan's body near our car was born. I guessed that was LeBlanc's idea. Cain didn't have the wits to think of it and Marsten would consider such crude humor beneath him.

It wasn't quite seven when the doorbell rang. We all looked up, startled by the sound. The doorbell at Stonehaven rarely rang, the house being too remote for salesmen and Jehovah's Witnesses. Deliveries went to a post office box in Bear Valley. Even the Pack didn't ring the bell—except for Peter. I think we all remembered this as it rang. No one moved until the second buzz, then Jeremy got to his feet and left the room. I followed. From the dining room window we could see a police cruiser parked in the driveway.

"We don't need this," I said. "We really don't need this."

Jeremy shrugged off his arm sling and tucked it into the hall stand, then grabbed Clay's sweatshirt from the hooks. I helped him into it. The bulky shirt hid his splint and his pants covered his leg bandages. His clothes were clean and unwrinkled, since he'd changed only a few hours ago. That was more than I could say for the rest of us. One glance in the hall mirror told me that I looked like hell, clothes covered in dirt and blood, face blotchy, hair knotted from lying on the sofa.

"Get the others upstairs to dress," Jeremy said. "Tell Clay, Antonio, and Nick to stay up there. You can join me on the back porch."

"It's going to look suspicious if you usher them around the house for a second time."

"I know."

"Invite them in and offer them coffee. There's nothing here for them to see."

"I know."

"I'll meet you in the study, then?"

Jeremy hesitated. Knowing he should invite the police into the house was one thing, doing it was another. The only humans who came into Stonehaven were repairmen, and even that was done only when necessary. There was nothing at Stonehaven that would make anyone suspicious, no body parts in the freezer or pentagrams etched into the hardwood. The scariest thing in Stonehaven was my bedroom and I had no intention of inviting any cop up there, no matter how cute he looked in uniform.

"The living room," he said as the doorbell rang a third time. "We'll be in the living room."

"I'll make coffee," I said, and left before he could change his mind.

When I got back to the living room, there were two police officers with Jeremy. The older one was the town police chief, a burly, balding man named Morgan. I'd seen him around town, though he hadn't been with the search party the day before. With Morgan's arrival, things were obviously heating up, though in a town as small as Bear Valley, having the police chief show up at your house was a cause for concern but not panic. The other officer was young and bland-faced, the kind of guy you could see twenty times before you remembered him. According to his badge, his name was O'Neil. Neither the face nor the name triggered any recollection from yesterday, but he'd likely been there. The look he gave me indicated he remembered me, though he seemed disappointed to find me fully dressed. At least I came bearing coffee.

Jeremy and Morgan were discussing some local native land claim. Jeremy leaned back in a chair, feet on the ottoman, broken arm resting so casually against his leg no one would guess it was splinted. His face was relaxed, eyes alert and interested, as if he had policemen in his home every day and not only knew about the land claim, but was deeply concerned over it, mirroring the police chief's opinions with the ease of a consummate con artist. The younger officer, O'Neil, was unabashedly gawking around the room, taking in all the details to relate later to curious friends.

Conversation stopped when I entered. I set up the tray on an end table and started pouring coffee like a perfect hostess.

"Oh, I don't drink tea," Morgan said, eyeing the silver coffeepot as if it might bite.

"It's coffee," Jeremy said with a self-effacing smile. "You'll have to excuse us. We don't have many guests, so Elena has to use the teapot."

O'Neil leaned forward to take his coffee from me. "Elena. That's a pretty name."

"It's Russian, isn't it?" Morgan said, eyes narrowing.

"Could be," I said, smiling brightly. "Cream and sugar?"

"Three sugars. I didn't see your husband around. Is he sleeping in?"

I spilled scalding coffee on my hand and bit back a yelp. So Clay's marital fabrication had worked its way up the rumor chain to the police chief. Wonderful. Just wonderful. Common sense told me I should play along. After all, Bear Valley wasn't the kind of place that tolerated a woman romping naked in the woods with a man other than her husband. Actually, they probably didn't tolerate naked-forest-romping much at all, but that wasn't the point. The point was that this "placating the locals" was going too far. It was one thing to let them into our house, to tolerate their gawking, and to let them think we couldn't tell a teapot from a coffeepot, but to officially confirm the rumor that I was married to Clay? Branding me forever in Bear Valley as Clay's wife? Uh-uh. A girl's got to have limits.

"Yes, he's sleeping in," Jeremy said before I could speak. "Elena's always up early to get his breakfast ready."

I shot him a glare to say he'd pay for that. He pretended not to notice, but I could see the glimmer of laughter in his eyes. I dumped five sugars in his coffee. He'd have to drink it. After all, it would be impolite not to partake of social beverages with his visitors.

"Like I said," Morgan began. "I apologize for coming to see you folks so early in the morning, but I thought you'd want to know. Mike Braxton wasn't killed on your property. Coroner's one hundred percent certain on that. Somebody killed him elsewhere and dumped him on your land."

"Somebody?" Jeremy said. "Do you mean a person, not an animal?"

"Well, I'd still say it was an animal, but one of the human variety. Doesn't make a hell of a lot of sense to us. The other two were definitely animal kills, but the coroner says Mike's throat was slashed with a knife, not teeth."

"What about the paw prints?" I hated to ask, but we had to know what the police were thinking.

"We figure they're fake. Whoever planted the body stamped them into the ground to make it look like another dog kill. Guy made a mistake, though. They were too big. That was the tip-off. Dogs don't get that big. Well, my son says there's some kind of dog, a mastiff or something, that might leave a print like that, but we don't have any of those around here. Our hounds and shepherds don't grow that big, no matter how much we feed them. You'll recall I said yesterday that Mike left a message with someone saying he was coming here. Turns out, he left it with the fellow's wife, who now says she thought Mike sounded 'funny,' not like himself, but she figured maybe it was a bad phone connection. Seems fair to assume Mike didn't leave the message at all. Whoever killed him must have left it to make sure we hightailed it out to your place and found the body. Put all that together and I'm damned— sorry, ma'am—darned sure we've got a human killer."

"So we don't have wild dogs in our forest," Jeremy said. "That's a relief, though I can't say I prefer the idea of a human killer on the loose. Do you have any leads?"

"We're working on it. Likely someone Mike knew. Mike was a great guy and all but—" Morgan paused, as if thinking twice before speaking ill of the dead. "We've all got our problems, don't we? Enemies and such." Another pause. A slow sip of coffee. "How about you folks? Any idea why someone would dump Mike's body on your property?"

"No," Jeremy said, his voice unruffled but firm. "I was wondering about that myself."

"You haven't made any enemies in town? Maybe had a falling out with someone?"

Jeremy gave a small smile. "As I'm sure you're aware, we aren't the most sociable bunch in Granton County. We don't have enough contact with any of our neighbors to have a falling out with them. Either the killer thought blaming it on the 'outsiders' would divert attention from himself or he had no intention of involving us at all and simply thought this was a good place to dump the body."

"You're sure there's no one you folks have pissed off?" Morgan said, leaning forward. "Maybe someone who thinks you owe him money? Maybe a jealous husband"—Morgan shot a look at me—"or wife?"

"No and no. We don't gamble or do any business in credit. As for the other, I'm certain no one has ever seen me prowling the local singles bars, and Elena and Clayton have neither the inclination nor the energy to seek extramarital excitement. Bear Valley is a small town. If there were any rumors about us, you'd be asking more pointed questions."

Morgan didn't answer. Instead, he stared at Jeremy for two full minutes. Maybe this tactic worked on sixteen-year-old vandalism suspects, but it wasn't about to break down a fifty-one-year-old Pack Alpha. Jeremy just stared back, his expression calm and open.

After a few minutes, Jeremy said, "I'm sorry you had to make the drive out here two days in a row, but I appreciate you coming this morning to tell us."

Jeremy laid aside his mug and shifted to the edge of his seat. When Morgan and O'Neil didn't take the hint, he stood and said, "If that's everything . . ."

"We'll want to search the property some more," Morgan said at last.

"By all means."

"We may want to question your guests."

Morgan conducted another minute-long stare down. When Jeremy didn't so much as blink, he heaved himself to his feet.

"A killer dumped that body on your property," he said. "If I were you, I'd be trying damned hard to think of who might have done it and I'd be calling us if you come up with any answers."

"I wouldn't hesitate," Jeremy said. "I hope whoever dumped Mr. Braxton's body here hadn't any grudge against us, but if he did, I wouldn't want to ignore it and wait for his next move. No one here has any desire to tangle with a killer. We're more than happy to let the police do that."

Morgan grunted and swigged the last of his coffee.

"Anything else?" Jeremy asked.

"I wouldn't be hiking in those woods for a while."

"We've already stopped," Jeremy said. "But thank you for the warning. Elena, would you see our guests to the door?"

I did. Neither cop said a word to me, beyond Morgan's gruff good-bye. Obviously, as a female, I wasn't worth questioning.

After the police left, we realized Clay, Nick, and Antonio were gone. Had it been just Clay, or even Clay and Nick, we would have worried. Since Antonio had gone with them, though, we knew they weren't planning any impromptu revenge in Bear Valley.

The police had been gone barely ten minutes when the Mercedes turned into the drive. Nick hopped out from the passenger side. I didn't notice who was driving, my attention being consumed by the sight of the large paper bag in Nick's hand. Breakfast. Not exactly hot and steaming after the drive from the highway diner, but I was too hungry to care.

Fifteen minutes later, the bag was empty, its contents reduced to the ghosts of crumbs and grease marks on plates scattered across the sunroom table. After the meal, Jeremy explained what the police had said. I kept expecting Clay to say something, proclaim his proven innocence and wait for me to apologize. He didn't. He listened to Jeremy, then helped Antonio clear the kitchen table while I escaped to the study, ostensibly to read the newspaper they'd brought back from town.

It took exactly three minutes for Clay to hunt me down. He walked into the study and closed the door behind him, then stood there, watching me read, for two minutes more. When I couldn't stand it any longer, I folded the paper noisily and tossed it aside.

"Okay, you didn't kill the man," I said. "For once, you were innocent. But if you expect me to apologize for thinking you were capable of doing it—"

"I don't."

I shot him a look.

Clay continued, "I don't expect you to apologize for thinking I could do it. Of course I could do it. If the guy saw us running or Changing or threatened us, I would have killed him. But I would have told you. That's what I'm pissed off about. That you'd think I'd sneak behind your back, hide the evidence, and lie about it."

"No, I guess it wouldn't occur to you that I might not *want* to know you did it. The thought of sparing me wouldn't enter your head."

"Sparing you?" Clay gave a harsh laugh. "You know what I am, Elena. If I pretended otherwise, you'd accuse me of trying to deceive you. I don't want you to come back to me because you think I've changed. I want you to come back because you accept what I am. If I could change, don't you think I'd have done it for you by now? I want you back. Not for a night or a few weeks or even a couple of months. I want you back for good. I'm miserable when you're not here—"

"You're miserable because you don't have what you want. Not because you want *me*."

"Goddamn it!" Clay swung his fist out, knocking a brass penholder off the desk. "You won't listen! You won't listen and you won't see. You know I love you, that I want *you*. Damn it, Elena, if I just wanted a partner, any partner, do you think I'd have spent ten years trying to get you back? Why haven't I just given up and found someone else?"

"Because you're stubborn."

"Oh, no. I'm not the stubborn one. You're the one who can't get past what I did no matter how much—"

"I don't want to talk about it."

"Of course you don't. God forbid any truth should complicate your convictions."

Clay turned and strode from the room, slamming the door behind him.

After Clay left, I decided to stay in the study—or hide out there, depending on the interpretation. I perused the selection on the bookshelves. It hadn't changed in the past year. Actually, it hadn't changed in the past decade. A motley collection of literature and reference books filled the shelves. Only a few of the reference books belonged to Clay. He bought every book and magazine related to his career, then trashed them as soon as he finished the last word. He didn't have a photographic memory, just the uncanny ability to absorb everything he read, making it pointless to save any form of the written word. Almost all of the books belonged to Jeremy. Over half of them weren't even in English, a throwback to Jeremy's early career as a translator.

Jeremy hadn't always been able to lavish sports cars and antique beds on his adopted family. When Clay first came to Stonehaven, Jeremy had been struggling to pay the heating bills, a situation deriving entirely from his father's spending habits and refusal to dirty his hands with any work that might generate income. Throughout Jeremy's twenties, he'd worked as a translator, an ideal occupation for someone with a gift for languages and a tendency toward reclusion. Later, the financial situation at Stonehaven took a drastic upswing, owing to twin circumstances of fortune: Malcolm Danvers's death and the launch of Jeremy's painting career. These days Jeremy sold very few paintings, but when he did, they brought in enough cash to keep Stonehaven running for several years.

While I was looking for something to read, Jeremy popped in to remind me to call Philip. I hadn't forgotten. I'd intended to do it before dinner and didn't appreciate the reminder, as if Jeremy thought I needed one. I didn't know how much Jeremy knew about Philip and I didn't want to know. I preferred the idea that when I left Stonehaven, I escaped to a foreign place the Pack knew nothing about. Okay, I was delusional, but it was a nice fantasy. I suspected Jeremy had investigated Philip, but I didn't bother to call him on it. If I did, he'd only claim he was protecting me from getting involved with some guy who had three wives or a history of battering his girlfriends. Of course Jeremy would never do anything simply to interfere with my life. Perish the thought.

No matter how much Jeremy knew about Philip, he didn't know how I felt about him. Again, I had no plans to enlighten him. I knew what he'd say. He'd sit back, watch me for a minute, then start talking about how difficult my circumstances were, with Clay and being the only female werewolf and all, and how he didn't blame me for being confused and wanting to explore my choices in life. Though he'd never say it outright, he'd imply that he was certain if he gave me enough latitude to make my own mistakes, I'd eventually see that I belonged with the Pack. Through the whole conversation, he'd be completely calm and understanding, never raising his voice or taking offense at anything I said. Sometimes I think I preferred Clay's rages.

The truth was that I cared about Philip more than Jeremy could imagine. I wanted to go back to him. I hadn't forgotten about him. I'd been planning to call him . . . later.

Now seemed like the perfect time for Jeremy to update us on his plans. When he didn't, no one else appeared to notice. More likely, they didn't care. Werewolves raised in the Pack are brought up with a certain set of expectations. One of those expectations was that their Alpha would look after them. Asking Jeremy what his plans were would imply that they didn't think he had any. Even Clay, as anxious as he was to take action, would give Jeremy plenty of plotting time before hinting about his plans. Such a trusting attitude drove me crazy. Not that I didn't think Jeremy was making plans. I knew he was. But I wanted in on them. I wanted to help. When I finally dreamed up a subtle way to ask, I found him outside with a pair of revolvers. No, he wasn't going after the mutts armed like Billy the Kid. Nor was he contemplating a quick end to his pain. He was target shooting, something he often did while he was deep in thought—not exactly the safest method of achieving mental focus, but who am I to judge? The revolvers were a gorgeous antique pair given to him by Antonio many years ago. Along with the guns, Antonio had given Jeremy a silver bullet inscribed with Malcolm Danvers's initials, a half-joking suggestion, which, of course, Jeremy never took. More seriously, Antonio intended the guns for their current purpose—marksmanship. By that time Jeremy had already mastered the longbow and crossbow and was looking for a new challenge. Don't ask me why he chose marksmanship for a hobby. He certainly never used the bows or guns off the target range. You might as well ask me why he painted. Neither was what you'd call a typical werewolf hobby. Then again, no one had ever accused Jeremy of being a typical werewolf. Anyway, when I went outside and saw him shooting, I decided it was an inopportune time to bug him about his plans. Urban survival rule twenty-two: never annoy an armed man.

Leaving Jeremy, I'd gone upstairs for a nap. A couple of hours later, I awoke and headed downstairs for lunch. The house was silent, all the upstairs doors closed as if everyone else was catching up on sleep, too. As I headed for the kitchen, Clay walked out from the study. His eyes were bloodshot and dark. Though he was exhausted, he wouldn't sleep. Not now, with two Pack brothers dead, his Alpha wounded, and none avenged. Once Jeremy gave us his plans, Clay would rest, if only to prepare.

He stepped in front of me. When I tried to squeeze past him, he braced his hands on either side of the corridor.

"Truce?" he said.

"Whatever."

"Love those definitive answers. I'll take that as a yes. Not that we're done with our little discussion, but I'll let it ride for now. Tell me when you want to pick it up again."

"Tell me when Satan starts a snowball fight."

"I'll do that. Lunch?"

When I finally nodded, he stepped back and motioned for me to go into the kitchen. I could feel him simmering, but he'd plastered on a happy face, so I decided to ignore it. In a crisis, we were both capable of summoning enough maturity to know that we couldn't afford to threaten the stability of the Pack with our fighting. Or, at least, we could fake it temporarily.

We gathered a cold meal from the kitchen, filling platters with meats and breads and fruits, knowing the others would wake up hungry. Then I sat down in the sunroom and loaded a plate. Clay did the same. Neither of us spoke as we ate. Although this wasn't unusual, the silence had a dead quality that made me eat a little faster, anxious to be done and out of the room. When I glanced over at Clay, he was dispatching his food just as quickly and with as little enjoyment. We were halfway through our meal when Jeremy and Antonio walked in.

"We need groceries," I said. "I'm sure that's the last thing on everyone's mind, but it won't be when we run out. I'll run into town and grab some."

"I'll call in an order," Jeremy said. "Assuming this mess with the police hasn't changed that arrangement. You'd best pick up cash, in case my checks aren't as welcome these days. Someone will have to go with you, of course. No one's leaving the house alone or staying here alone anymore."

"I'll go," Clay said around a mouthful of cantaloupe. "I've got a package waiting at the post office."

"I'm sure you do," I said.

"He does," Jeremy said. "The postman left a card the other day."

"Books I ordered from the U.K.," Clay said.

"Which you need right now," I said. "For a little light reading between maiming and killing."

"They shouldn't sit at the post office," Clay said. "Someone might get suspicious."

"Of anthropology texts?"

Antonio leaned over the table and grabbed a handful of grapes. "I've got a couple things to fax. I'll go with the two of you and run interference."

I pushed back my chair. "Well, then there's no need for me to go, is there? I'm sure you guys can handle the groceries."

"But you're the one who wanted to go," Clay said.

"I changed my mind."

"You're going," Jeremy said. "All three of you. You could use the diversion."

Antonio grinned. "And Jeremy could use a couple hours of peace and quiet."

When I glanced up, I swore Jeremy rolled his eyes, but the movement was so fast, I couldn't be sure. Antonio laughed and sat down to lunch. Just as I was about to start arguing again, Antonio launched into an anecdote about meeting a mutt in San Francisco last time he was there on business. By the time he finished, I'd forgotten what I'd meant to say, which was probably the point of the story.

An hour later, when Antonio and Clay were calling me to the car, I remembered that I didn't want to go and had been trying to find a way out of it when Antonio had interrupted. By then, it was too late. Jeremy was nowhere to be found, Antonio was waiting in the Mercedes, and Nick was ransacking the kitchen for his lunch, cleaning out what little food remained. Someone had to get the groceries, and if I didn't do it, I'd be cursing my stubbornness by dinnertime. So I went.

The bank was right across from the post office. Since Antonio was able to get a parking spot right in front of the bank, I convinced them that it was safe for me to go to the bank alone while Clay went to the post office alone. From his spot out front, Antonio would be able to see both Clay and me at all times. And it shaved a few minutes from the total amount of time I had to spend running errands with Clay.

Jeremy's bank account was also in my name and Clay's, allowing any of us to withdraw money for household needs. I used to have an ATM card for the account, but I'd trashed it last year when I left Stonehaven. Now I wished I hadn't. Bear Valley was the kind of town where people still used the tellers. As I stood in line for fifteen minutes, listening to an elderly man talking to the teller about his grandchildren, I gazed longingly at the shiny, unused ATM. When he started pulling out photographs, I began to wonder how long it would take to get a new bank machine card. With a sigh, I abandoned the idea. It would probably require filling out two forms in triplicate and waiting until the bank manager returned from his hour-long coffee break. Anyway, since I would be leaving Stonehaven in a couple of days, I wouldn't need it again.

Finally, I got up to the teller and had to produce three pieces of signed photo ID before she'd let me withdraw a couple hundred dollars from the account. I shoved the money into my pocket, headed for the door, and saw a brown pickup in the front parking spot. Thinking I must have been mistaken about where Antonio parked, I walked outside and looked around. The spot behind the pickup was empty. In front of it was a Buick. I searched up and down the road. There was no sign of the Mercedes.

CHAPTER 18

PRISONER

There were as many Mercedeses in Bear Valley as there were Porsches, so I didn't need to spend much time surveying the street to know Antonio's car wasn't there. I could imagine only two reasons for them abandoning me. One, the meter maid had been making her rounds and neither had a nickel for the meter. Two, they hadn't been able to see me in the bank, and when I'd been gone so long, they thought I bolted. There was a third possibility: Clay was *really* pissed off at me, knocked Antonio unconscious, and drove off, abandoning me to my fate. A nice dramatic twist, but not terribly likely.

There was a tiny dirt parking lot behind the bank for the employees and any customers unwilling to spend the dime-per-hour at the meters out front. I checked the lot and saw only a minivan and another pickup. I cocked my head to listen. Even these few feet from the road, quiet had fallen, as if the buildings lining Main Street were constructed to block all sound and limit it to the shopping district. In the distance, I heard the soft chugging of a well-tuned diesel engine. Definitely not a pickup. I closed my eyes and tuned out everything else. The Mercedes was less than a few blocks away, the sound of its engine fading, then growing, then fading as it seemed to be moving in slow circles. Where? Logically, another parking lot, where Antonio was circling, waiting for me. Had I missed some instruction? Was I supposed to meet them someplace else? That didn't make sense, since Clay hadn't even wanted to let me go into the bank alone. Well, whatever the reason, there wasn't any sense standing here thinking about it.

Narrow car tracks traced a path down an alley heading in the direction of the circling car. The passage was muddy and barely wide enough for the compact Mercedes to traverse without scraping the side mirrors, yet I knew Antonio wouldn't be worried about dirt or scratches. Clay and Antonio liked their expensive cars, but they were purely utility pieces, designed to get them from point A to point B with speed and comfort. Looking good wasn't a concern.

I started down the alley, sidestepping the puddles and deep muddy ruts. At one point, the alley branched right. I didn't need to follow the car's tracks to know that it kept going straight. Navigating a turn in these tight quarters would have taken off more than a few layers of paint. As I got farther and farther from the main road, the alley widened and rose up on a slight incline, turning from mud to gravel. Garbage Dumpsters lined the right side of the passage, but still left enough room for the Mercedes to pass. The drier ground only served to emphasize the amount of muddy water that had seeped into my shoes. With each step, my sneakers squelched and my mood sank. I was getting ready to storm back to the bank and call Jeremy for Antonio's cell number when I saw a glimmer of silver ahead. I stopped. Over a hundred feet away, the alley ended in a weedy vacant lot. As I watched, the Mercedes drifted past the alley opening. I waved my arms, but the car vanished behind the brick walls.

"Come on, guys," I muttered. "What's with the hide-and-seek?"

I tromped along in my soaked shoes, waving each time the Mercedes passed the alley and muttering increasingly nasty epithets each time it didn't stop. As I went by another branching alleyway, I heard a soft noise, but ignored it, being in no mood for idle curiosity. About ten feet later, gravel crunched behind me and the edge of a large shadow encroached on the left of my vision field. Clay. He was downwind, but I didn't need to smell him to recognize his flavor of practical joke.

As I whirled around, a hand grabbed the back of my shirt and sent me sailing face first to the ground. Okay. Not Clay.

"Get up," a voice said as a huge shape passed over me.

I lifted my head, spitting gravel and blood. "What? No witty riposte? No clever throwaway line?"

"Get up."

Cain grabbed my collar again and heaved me to my feet, setting me down so hard my ankle twisted beneath me. I made a show of wiping the dirt from my face and running my fingers through my hair.

"That's no way to greet a girl, Zack," I said. "No wonder you have to pay for it."

Cain stood there with his arms crossed, saying nothing. His shoulders spanned half the passage between buildings. Dark blond hair topped a face with bulldog features.

"Waiting for me to run?" I asked. "Or still trying to think up a comeback?"

He started forward. I wheeled and sprinted for the end of the alley. A mutt always stands his ground and fights. A Pack werewolf knows when to run like hell. I wasn't a match for Zachary Cain on my best days and today certainly wasn't one of those. I was half Cain's size, but twice his speed. If I could get to the end of the alley, I was safe. The Pack's two best fighters were there, and I wasn't stubborn or stupid enough to refuse help. Halfway there, the Mercedes passed the alley opening again. I lifted both arms to wave and my left foot hit the gravel wrong. As I fell, the silver car slowly vanished from sight.

I scrambled to my feet, but it was too late. Again, Cain reached out and caught me by the back of the shirt. This time, he swung me off the ground. My left foot smacked into a metal Dumpster and I swallowed a yelp. With his free hand, Cain grabbed me beneath the chin and smashed me backward into the wall. My head hit the brick, sending lightning bolts through my skull. He held me there, feet suspended off the ground. Then he reached up and tore my shirtfront open.

"Not much to see, is there?" I said, struggling to talk with a crushed windpipe. "I know, I know, they can fix things like that these days. Call me a feminist, but I think a woman's worth should be defined not by the size of her bust, but—"

I rammed my fist up into his Adam's apple. He grunted and stumbled back.

"—by the strength of her right hook," I said, throwing myself against his chest before he regained his balance.

Cain toppled to the ground. As he fell, I stayed on him, slamming my open hand against his neck and pinning him by the throat.

"Yes, I can talk and think at the same time," I said. "Most people can, though I suppose you wouldn't know that from personal experience."

With a roar, Cain swung one arm up toward me. In midair, a shoe shot down and stomped his hand to the ground.

"Uh-uh," Clay drawled above me. "Elena's played with you long enough. It's my turn."

I waited until Clay moved his foot to Cain's throat, then backed off. Antonio was standing to the side.

"Trap?" I asked.

Antonio nodded. "Clay saw him lurking in the alley. We figured you'd come looking for us."

"So you left a trail and circled that vacant lot waiting for me to take the bait, and Cain to take me as bait."

"Something like that."

Clay hauled Cain to his feet. The redness and dark circles had vanished from Clay's eyes. He was fully awake now. This was what he'd been waiting for.

Cain towered a good six inches over Clay and outweighed him by at least seventy pounds. It was a fair fight.

The two stepped back and looked at each other. Then Cain took a step left toward Clay. Clay mirrored the maneuver, but moved forward to the right. They repeated the dance steps, gazes locked, each watching the other for the lunge. The pattern for the ritual was ingrained in our brains. Step, circle, watch. To win, you either had to lunge without warning or catch the other about to lunge and sidestep. It went on for several minutes. Then Cain lost patience and dove. Clay dodged out of the way, grabbed him by the waistband, and flung him into the wall. Cain recovered in a heartbeat and slammed into Clay's chest, knocking him to the ground.

I won't detail the fight, partly because it would be a boring recitation of hit, jab, grunt, stumble, recover, and partly because I wasn't watching it that closely. I wasn't *not* watching because I wasn't interested, but because I was too interested. Standing back and seeing Clay get pummeled and kicked and slammed into walls was a bit more than I could bear. Not that I didn't occasionally want to do the same to him myself, but this was different. I would have felt the same about watching any of my Pack brothers fight. It wasn't just Clay. Really.

Although I wasn't watching the fight, that didn't keep me from smelling it. I smelled Cain's blood first, but Clay's followed shortly. When I looked up, blood was streaming from Clay's nose and mouth, making him cough and sputter.

Antonio and I had to stand back and watch. This was how we fought. One-on-one, no weapons, no tricks. It was the wolf in us that dictated the rules of battle; the human side would goad us into winning at all costs. That wasn't to say we'd stand back and watch Clay get killed. If that seemed possible, loyalty to one's Pack brother overrode all codes of conduct. Still, there was a lot of blood and broken bones between life and death, and until that line was crossed, we couldn't interfere.

It finally ended with Cain sprawled facedown in the gravel. When he didn't get up, I thought he was dead. Than I saw his back rising and falling as he breathed.

"Unconscious," Clay wheezed, wiping his shirt over his bloody nose. "You can look now."

"I was watching," I said. "I turned away because I thought I heard something down the alley."

Clay grinned and blood gushed from his split upper lip.

"Don't start," Antonio said. "We need to get this mutt back to Stonehaven so Jeremy can question him. Elena, could you go down the alley to the car?

Make sure no one's around? Clay, take the keys and open the trunk. I'll get this one."

As I'd thought, the alley ended in a vacant lot. Once there'd been road access to the north, but now it was barricaded with Dumpsters, leaving the long trip down the south alley as the only way in or out. The blocking Dumpsters left enough room for someone to walk through, so I went and stood by them to watch for passersby. Behind me, Antonio and Clay loaded Cain into the trunk. Then Clay walked over to where I was standing watch.

"You okay?" he asked.

"Other than a scraped cheek, a twisted ankle, a possible concussion, soaked sneakers, and a ruined shirt? I'm peachy. Feel free to use me for bait anytime."

"Glad you feel that way."

"Watch it or you'll have more than a bloody nose and split lip." I gave him a quick once-over. "Is that it?"

"Maybe a few bruised ribs. Nothing permanent."

He coughed and fresh blood spurted from his nose. He ripped off his shirt and wadded it up against the flow.

When we got back to the car, Antonio was closing the trunk. Cain's unconscious body took up every square inch of space.

"No groceries on this run, I assume," I said.

"Doesn't look like it," Antonio said. "I'll have to come back for them. We'll grab a snack on the way to tide us over."

I thought he was kidding. I should have known better. Before we left town, Antonio pulled into a strip mall and went in to get submarines and salads, leaving Clay and me half naked and bleeding in the car and Cain unconscious in the trunk. No wonder I was anxious to get back to Toronto. Spend too much time around these guys and you become a little too nonchalant about blood-soaked clothes and bodies in the trunk.

At Stonehaven, Antonio and Nick loaded the still-unconscious Cain into the basement cage while Jeremy inspected Clay's and my injuries. I got two aspirins for my head and iodine and sympathy for my scrapes and bruises. Clay got a plaster for his lip, binding for his ribs, and a few stiff words on the dangers of using me as bait. In spite of what I'd said to Clay, I wasn't upset about the bait thing. Getting Cain was worth a ripped shirt and a sore head. Clay knew I could handle it, and in a way, I was glad of that. I'd be more pissed off if he thought I was too fragile to play with the big boys. Of course, I didn't forgive or defend him. Not out loud at least.

If I had, Jeremy would have started worrying a lot more about that bump to my head.

After Cain was secured and Jeremy finished nursing, we had our snack. Then Nick and Antonio went back to town for the groceries while Jeremy, Clay, and I talked about what information we wanted from Cain. Around six o'clock, shouts and clangs from the basement told us that our prisoner was awake. Jeremy and Clay went down to the cage.

I stayed upstairs. I was welcome to go down and help, but I knew what was coming, so I stayed in the study, where I could hear what Cain said without seeing what made him say it. I'm squeamish about torture. Maybe that seems silly, considering how much violence I'd witnessed and participated in during my life. But there was something about being brutalized and unable to defend yourself that sent chills down my spine and nightmares to my sleep. Maybe it was vestiges of long-buried victim pathology from my childhood. Years ago, I went to see *Reservoir Dogs* with Clay. When it came to the infamous "Stuck in the Middle with You" scene, I covered my eyes and Clay picked up pointers. While I didn't think he'd tied anyone up and doused them with gasoline yet, he'd done things just as bad. I knew because I'd been there. I'd seen him do it, and what frightened me the most was the look in his eyes. They didn't burn with excitement or anticipation, like when he chased his prey. Instead, they were blue ice, frozen and impenetrable. When he tortured a mutt, he was completely methodical, showing no emotion at all. Of course, I'd be a whole lot more worried if he approached his work with glee, but there was something equally chilling about someone who could do things like that with such single-minded detachment. Most people torture for information. Clay did it for instruction. For every mutt he'd maimed and let live, five more would see and take a lesson from it. For every one he'd killed, a score heard the story. Those who thought of attacking a Pack member only had to recall these stories to change their minds. Most werewolves weren't afraid of dying, but there were worse fates than death and Clay made sure they knew it.

As I sat in the study and listened to the scene taking place below, I had to admit that there was another advantage to Clay's methods. The more his reputation spread, the less he had to do to uphold it. No bloodcurdling shrieks rent the air as Jeremy interrogated Cain. In the four long hours of questioning that followed, I heard exactly three pained grunts as Clay presumably hit Cain when he wasn't forthcoming with an answer. Just having Clay standing there and knowing what he *could* do was enough to make Cain talk.

Of the three experienced mutts in Bear Valley, Zachary Cain was the worst choice for an informant. Any plans Daniel and Marsten had deigned to share with him had since become lost in the empty wasteland of his brain. According to Cain, Jimmy Koenig was also part of the "revolution," but he hadn't shown up yet.

Cain had joined them because he was seeking "release from tyranny," a phrase doubtless assimilated through one too many viewings of *Braveheart*. As Cain so eloquently put it, he was "sick of having to watch my fucking back every time I piss the wrong way." Since the Pack has never taken any interest in the urinary habits of mutts, I assumed he meant that he was fighting for his right to kill humans without fear of reprisal, something I was sure was covered under the werewolf subclauses of the American constitution. According to Cain, Koenig wanted the same thing—the extermination of the Pack, much the way criminals dream of eliminating the police. Somehow the two of them were convinced that if the Pack was gone they'd be free to indulge their worst natures without fear of reprisal. Daniel had more grandiose plans, as always. He wanted to wipe out the Pack and start his own, probably envisioning some kind of werewolf Mafia. Cain wasn't clear on the details and wasn't interested in them. As for Marsten, Cain had no idea why he'd joined the fight. Again, he didn't really care.

Daniel had masterminded the new-recruit plan. He'd done the research, found the subjects, and played the psychopath's version of the Godfather—approaching them with an offer they couldn't refuse. If they helped him eliminate a few old enemies, he'd grant them the ultimate killer's body. None had refused. From there, Daniel had assigned a recruit to each of his comrades. Daniel had bitten and trained Thomas LeBlanc. Marsten had taken Scott Brandon. We hadn't met Cain's protégé yet. Apparently, he was a man named Victor Olson who'd been waiting in the car the day Cain led us on a chase through the forest. Jeremy asked Cain what Olson had done in his human life. That was my question and I think Jeremy only asked it to humor me . . . and because he knew I was listening. Cain wasn't clear on the details, being as uninterested in Olson's past as he was in anything that didn't directly concern him. All he knew was that Olson had been in jail for "screwing around with a couple girls" and killing one of them. That sounded like a rapist moving up the ladder to a Thomas LeBlanc–type killer. Not exactly an experienced murderer, but Daniel must have seen some potential in him, since he'd sent Cain all the way to Arizona to break Olson out of jail.

So with Cain out of the way, we were down to two experienced and two new mutts. Right? I wish. As I said, Koenig hadn't arrived yet. His recruit was still recovering from being turned, but they'd be in Bear Valley soon. Fighting these guys was like battling a Hydra. Each time we lopped off a head, a few more appeared in its place. Clay tried to get more out of Cain, but didn't push it. So far, Cain hadn't tried to hold anything back, so it was unlikely he was starting now. His neck was on the line. He'd say anything to save himself from torture, even if it meant condemning his co-conspirators to death. The loyalty of a mutt was an inspiring thing to behold.

It was past ten when Jeremy came upstairs. He stepped into the study where I was curled up in his chair.

"Anything else?" he asked.

I shook my head and he went back downstairs. There was a shout, a muffled sound, half anger, half pleading. Then silence. Seconds later, the basement door opened and I heard Jeremy's footsteps headed to the back patio. I knew to leave him alone for a while. When the door opened a second time, I peeked out from the study. Clay was rubbing a hand over his face. Specks of blood dotted his shirt. He looked exhausted, as if he'd been beating on Cain for the past four hours instead of playing silent enforcer. When he saw me, he managed a wan smile.

"Hey."

"Done?" I asked.

"Yeah. He's dead. We'll take him out tomorrow. He's in the cubbyhole for now." He rubbed the back of his neck. "Have you eaten?"

I shook my head. "Tonio made stew earlier. Do you want a bowl?"

"Right now, I want a shower, but if you'll heat up some, I'll be down before it's ready. Jeremy won't be hungry, so you'll be stuck with me. Okay?"

I nodded and he headed upstairs.

An hour later, Clay and I went into the study to find Jeremy already there, leaning back in his chair, eyes closed. He half-opened one eye as we walked in.

"Sorry," I said. "Should we leave?"

He motioned us in with his good hand, then closed his eyes again. I sat on the couch while Clay fixed drinks. He laid one by Jeremy's elbow, but Jeremy made no move to take it.

"So we have four in town," I said to Clay as he sat beside me. "Plus two more on the way. The question is, what to do about it."

"Kill 'em all."

"Good plan," Jeremy murmured, not opening his eyes. "Very succinct."

"Hey, if you don't want to hear my ideas, don't be eavesdropping."

"I was here first."

"We thought you were sleeping," I said.

Jeremy raised one eyebrow, then fell silent, eyes still closed. Clay reached across me for his drink, took a sip, then left his arm behind my head, fingers dangling against my shoulder.

"We should take out Daniel first," he said. "He's the ringleader. No one else knows shit about organizing into a pack. Rip out the center and the whole thing falls apart."

"Right," I said. "That'll be easy. Daniel's such a pushover. The only reason you haven't killed him before now is that you still have a soft spot for your childhood playmate, right?"

Clay snorted.

"Exactly," I said. "He's still alive because he knows how you operate and he's not about to walk into a trap like Cain. I say we go after the two new ones first. They're the wild cards. Get rid of them and we know exactly what we're dealing with."

"I'm not wasting my time on a couple of brand-new mutts."

"Then I will. Without you."

"Ah, shit." He banged his head against the top of the sofa. "Jer, are you listening to this?"

"Now I'm asleep," Jeremy said.

He was silent for a moment. When we didn't resume our conversation, he sighed and opened his eyes.

"Clay is right to target Daniel," Jeremy said. "But killing him isn't that easy. I'll settle for talking to him."

"Talking to him?" Clay said. "Why?"

"Because I know what he's like and it might be easier to appease him than to risk more lives fighting him. With Daniel out of the picture, the others will break apart, as you said. Then we strike individually and destroy any future threat. I've put up with a lot from Daniel because he was Pack and his father was a good man. No more. We make him happy this once, then we keep our eyes on him. If he so much as kills a human in Australia, he dies."

"What makes you think Daniel will bargain?" I said. "Cain seemed to think he wants the Pack eliminated."

"Maybe so, but more than that, he wants revenge," Jeremy said. "He wants us on our knees. By offering to bargain with him, he'll see that he's succeeded. When he realizes Zachary Cain is dead, he'll start to worry. Jimmy Koenig hasn't shown up yet. All he has is Karl Marsten."

"And the two new mutts."

"They have no stake in this battle," Jeremy said, "They've been recruited for a war that doesn't concern them. They're only fighting because they made a deal with Daniel. They've got what they want from him. Once they see things falling apart, they'll leave. What motivation do they have to stay? They haven't had enough dealings with the Pack to want revenge. They haven't been werewolves long enough to develop a need for territory. Why would they fight?"

"For fun." I turned to Clay. "You saw Brandon in that bar. You saw how he killed that man, how much pleasure he took in it. Have you ever seen a werewolf act like that?"

"I'm not dismissing them, darling," Clay said. "LeBlanc dies for what he did to Logan and Jeremy. I won't forget that."

Clay's hand fell from the back of the sofa onto my shoulder and toyed with my hair. I leaned against him, feeling the effects of a stiff drink and sleepless nights. When Jeremy closed his eyes again, I did the same, letting my head fall on Clay's shoulder. He twisted toward me and reached his other hand over to rest on my leg. I could feel the warmth of it through my jeans. The smell of scotch wafted from his breath. I was drifting off to sleep when the door slammed open.

"What's this?" Nick said. "Bedtime?"

No one answered him. I kept my eyes closed.

"You look positively content, Clayton," Nick continued, thumping down on the floor. "That wouldn't have anything to do with the fact that Elena is cuddled up with you, would it?"

"It's cold in here," I murmured.

"Doesn't feel cold."

"It's cold," Clay growled.

"I could start a fire."

"I could start one, too," Clay said. "With your clothes. Before you get them off."

"That's a hint, Nicky," Antonio said from the doorway. "Take it. I have no desire to spend my waning years a childless old man."

I heard Antonio move across the room. Glasses clinked as he fixed two drinks. Then he settled into the other chair. Nick stayed on the floor, stretching out and leaning back against our legs. After a few minutes, quiet fell again, punctuated only by occasional murmurs of conversation. Soon the drowsiness that affected me spread its soft tentacles across the others. Voices turned to murmurs, conversation became sparse, then evaporated into silence. I spread my fingers across Clay's chest, feeling his heartbeat, and fell asleep.

CHAPTER 19

DETOUR

When I awoke, I dimly remembered having fallen asleep on the sofa and began to adjust myself accordingly, putting my arms out and legs down to avoid sliding to the floor as I got up. Then I realized none of my limbs were where I expected them. My arms were folded under a pillow and my legs were entwined in sheets. The powdery scent of fabric softener filled my nostrils. I opened one eye to see the silhouette of dancing tree branches against my bed canopy. Surprise and surprise again. Not only was I in bed, but I was in my own. Usually if I fell asleep downstairs with Clay, he carted me off to his room like a caveman dragging his mate to his lair. Waking in my own room was a surprise close to a shock . . . until I roused enough to feel an arm over my waist and hear soft snoring against my back. As I moved, the snoring stopped and Clay shifted closer.

"Nice to see you remember how to make yourself at home in my bed," I said.

"I was with you when you fell asleep," he murmured drowsily. "Didn't see that it made much difference to stay with you."

I glanced down at my naked body. "As I recall, I was still dressed when I fell asleep."

"Just making sure you were comfortable."

"And making yourself equally comfortable, I see," I said, moving my legs and feeling his bare skin against mine.

"If you want to *see,* you need to turn over."

I snorted. "Not likely."

He snuggled against my back. His hand slid from my hip to my stomach. I closed my eyes again, my brain still adrift in the fog of near-sleep. Clay was warm against me, his body heat fighting off the chill of early morning. The canopy kept the bed dark and invited lingering. Outside the room, the house was silent. There wasn't any reason to get up yet and no need to invent a reason. It was comfortable here. We needed the rest. The thought and feel of Clay's naked body against mine sparked a few unbidden images and ideas, but he wasn't doing anything to provoke the need to fight them. His breathing was slow and deep, as if he was drifting back to sleep. His legs were entangled with mine, but they were staying still, as were his hands. After a couple minutes, he started to kiss the back of my neck. Still no cause for alarm. The back of my neck was hardly an erogenous zone, although it did feel good. Really good, actually. Especially when he moved his hand up to brush the hair from my shoulder and ran his fingertips across my jawline to my lips.

I parted my lips, flicking my tongue out to taste his finger, then ran my tongue across the roughness of his fingernail. As my lips parted, he moved his fingertip between my teeth. I nibbled at it, teeth grazing over the ridges of skin. He moved his lips down the back of my neck. His breath tickled the tiny hairs there and sent a shiver through me. As I nibbled on his finger, his lips and other hand moved over my back, raising goosebumps in their path. His hand slipped to the dip between my rib cage and hipbone and stroked the curve there. When his fingers slid down to my stomach, I turned toward him. He pulled me onto my side, facing him, then started to kiss me. The kisses were gentle and slow, their pace matching his hands as they explored my body, gliding across my sides, my back, my arms, my shoulders, along the backs of my thighs and over my hips. I kept my eyes closed, floating between sleep and waking. Moving against him, I luxuriated in the heat of his skin and the smooth planes and sinews of his body. When I felt the hardness of him against my stomach, there was no question of what to do next. My body responded without instructions, shifting my torso up, easing my legs apart and . . .

"Did you call him yesterday?" Jeremy asked.

"Huh?" I was emptying the dishwasher. My mind was still in bed with Clay.

"Your . . . friend called before you woke up. You left your cell phone in the front hall."

My brain snapped out of the bedroom. "You answered it?"

"Would you have rather I waited until Clay answered it? You didn't call, did you?" He didn't wait for an answer. "Don't worry, I didn't say anything, so whatever story you're telling him is safe. It seems he was expecting you back today."

"I'll handle it."

"Elena . . ."

"I said I'd handle it."

I put away the last plate and headed for the door.

I hadn't called Philip because I forgot him. It sounded awful, but it was the plain truth. I loved this man, I knew I did, and that only made it worse. At least if I could say I wasn't in love with . . . In love? Was I in love with Philip? Damn it, that was such a trite, overworked cop-out. I loved him. There was no "in love." There was "in lust," "infatuated," and "in heat," three ultimately destructive emotions that had nothing to do with real, lasting love. I forgot Philip because that was how I was coping with this mess, splitting my life into two compartments, human and Pack. Philip belonged in the human world and to even think about him while I was in the Pack world somehow tainted what we had. Or at least, that was how I explained the oversight to myself.

As I was about to get my cell phone from the front hall, Clay showed up. Naturally, I couldn't excuse myself and run upstairs with my phone. So I left the phone where it was and went for a walk with Clay. I meant to call Philip when I got back. He'd left a message on my cell phone, but as we got in the door, Jeremy reminded us that we needed to dispose of Cain's body. From there, things got complicated, and in light of what happened that day, I think I could be forgiven if I forgot to call Philip . . . again.

Back in the good ol' days of lawlessness and circuit judges, the Pack could dump bodies wherever it pleased. As humans became more concerned with dead and missing people, the Pack had to start burying the mutts it killed. Today, with postmortems and computer-linked detective units, and DNA testing, disposing of a body was a full-blown event requiring a good half day of preparation and work. Every member of the Pack had been drilled in the procedures until we could dispose of a body better than the most forensics-savvy human killer.

We drove the Explorer an hour north, avoiding any dumping grounds used in the previous few decades. Another hour was spent navigating down a logging road and 4×4'ing deeper into the forest, then removing and dragging Cain's body to a suitable site where we stripped, washed, and examined it for injuries. The only marks on the body were two splotches under Cain's throat, bruises from Clay's thumbs when he'd snapped Cain's neck. To be safe, Clay excised the bruises with a penknife. Finally, we buried Cain. Then I replaced the sod while Clay rounded up two rocks too heavy to be lifted by a human, and placed them over the grave. We backtracked to the Explorer, covering our trail, then drove to site number two.

Site two was chosen with as much caution as site one, but it was over an hour away. Here we dug a pit, threw in Cain's clothing, ID, and the bags and cloths we'd used for transporting and cleaning his body. These were doused with kerosene and burned, keeping the smoke to a minimum. Once everything was reduced to ashes, Clay buried the remains and we declared the job complete. It wasn't foolproof, but no one would ever look for Zachary Cain. Mutts didn't leave mourners.

We were less than twenty minutes from Stonehaven when blue lights flashed in the rearview mirror. I looked up and down the road, certain the lights were meant for someone else. I knew I wasn't breaking any laws. The dumbest thing you could do after dumping a body is to break a few highway traffic laws making your escape, which is why I was driving instead of Clay. The cruise control was set to two miles over the speed limit—driving exactly on the speed limit always struck me as just as suspicious as speeding. I'd been traveling down a straight highway road for the past thirty miles, with no chance of making an illegal turn or missing a stop sign. I checked for other cars ahead and behind, but we were alone on the road. Clay glanced over his shoulder at the police car.

"Did the speed limit change here?" I asked.

"Speed limit?"

"Never mind. I'm pulling over."

"No big deal. Everything's clean."

I pulled onto the shoulder and hoped the cops would zoom past in pursuit of some emergency ahead. As the police car eased onto the gravel behind me, I swore under my breath.

"Everything's clean," Clay said. "Stop worrying."

One of the officers walked over to the passenger side and tapped on the window. Clay waited long enough to express annoyance, but not so long as to be disrespectful, then hit the button to roll down the window.

"Clayton Danvers?" the officer said.

Clay looked at the man, but said nothing.

The young officer continued, "My partner recognized the vehicle. We were hoping you were in it. Saves us a trip up to your place."

Clay continued to stare at the man.

"Could you step out of the car please, Mr. Danvers?"

Again, Clay hesitated the longest acceptable length of time before opening the door. I took off my seat belt and got out too, staying on my side. Panic nudged my memory for answers. The rear compartment was clean, right? We'd scrubbed our hands and inspected our clothes, right? We'd disposed of all the supplies, right? Check, check, and check. At least, as far as I knew. What if we'd missed something? Was there an overlooked scrap of fabric snagged in the back of the Explorer? Did our clothes smell as strongly of smoke to human noses as they did to mine?

The other officer, a solidly built man in his late thirties, wandered around the Explorer, looking in the back window, then putting his face close to the tinted glass and shielding his eyes so he could see inside.

"Lots of storage space," he said. "How much stuff can you fit in these things?"

"Stuff?" I blinked. "Oh, like baggage? Enough luggage for a week's vacation, I'd guess."

He laughed. "If you pack like my wife, that's saying a lot." He squinted inside. "Sure is nice and clean. You folks don't have kids, do you?" He laughed again and dropped to his knees, checking the tires and the undercarriage. "This is one of those new suburban assault vehicles, isn't it? A four-by-four that's not meant for four-by-four-ing."

"It'll go off-road," I said, struggling to stay calm as he continued to check under the Explorer. "But it's too bulky for serious 4×4'ing. Comes in handy in the middle of a New York winter, though."

"I bet it does." He looked over at Clay. "What's the towing capacity on one of these?"

"No idea," Clay said. He'd been standing to the side, letting me handle the niceties. One of his tricks for keeping his temper under control. Avoid confrontation.

"We've never towed with it," I said.

The older cop kept looking under the Explorer, maybe checking the suspension, maybe looking for something else. I waited as long as I could, then asked, "Was I speeding?"

"We had a tip," the younger officer said. He turned to Clay. "An anonymous tip telling us you know something about Mike Braxton's murder. We need you to come to the station to answer some questions."

Clay's jaw tensed. "You expect me to drop whatever I'm doing—"

He stopped. I didn't say anything, but he knew what I was thinking. Antagonizing the cops wasn't going to help. Taking the defensive might make them back off if they didn't have any reason to arrest him, but it was too risky. Piss them off and they might decide to search the Explorer and Clay himself. Small-town cops have a reputation for not always following proper procedure. Legally, they couldn't force Clay to talk to them, but at least they weren't likely to uncover any evidence of our morning's activities through simple conversation.

Clay allowed that he'd spare them an hour. He went to the station in the back of the police car. I followed in the Explorer. The anonymous caller had to be one of the mutts, making this a good bet for a trap. With me following in a separate car, the mutts wouldn't dare try an ambush. Once we were at the station, we'd be safe. They wouldn't attack in a building full of armed humans.

The police station waiting room was smaller than my bedroom at Stonehaven and had probably cost less than my silver vanity set to furnish. It was roughly ten feet square with one door and two windows. Actually, the south window was one-way glass looking into an even smaller room. The one-way glass didn't make much sense until you considered that the entire police station was originally a Depression-era home. Most rooms had to serve double duty. In the unlikely event that the police needed to watch a suspect or an important interview, they probably used the waiting area as an observation room. Clay didn't warrant that treatment; he'd been ushered off to a private interview room as soon as we'd arrived.

The second window was a barred opening into a cage where a twenty-something receptionist covered the phone, the front desk, and the waiting room, while fielding nonstop requests from the officers for typing, filing, and fresh coffee. Don't ask me why the window was barred. Maybe they were afraid she'd escape. The three chairs in the waiting room were upholstered with moth-eaten harvest gold velour and peeling duct tape. I picked the best one and sat down carefully, not letting any exposed skin touch the fabric and reminding myself to wash my clothes as soon as I got home. I sifted though the pile of magazines on a pressed-wood table. The word "Canada" on a copy of *Time* caught my eye. I picked it up, realized the article was about the Quebec referendum, and put the magazine back. Not only was it a subject guaranteed to cure insomnia in ninety percent of Canadians but, unless something drastic had happened at home in the past week, it made the magazine over five years old. Very timely indeed.

I glanced up to see the receptionist watching me with the wary look people normally reserve for beggars and rabid dogs. Through the window, I could see the young officer who'd come out to Stonehaven leaning over the counter, talking to the receptionist. Since they were both staring at me, I assumed I was the topic of the conversation. Something told me they weren't discussing the disgraceful condition of my scuffed and graying Reeboks. Doubtless, he was retelling the story of my escapade in the forest. Just what I needed. Ten years of building a decent reputation in Bear Valley and I'd blown it all in a day, running around naked in the woods on a cold spring morning and having my clothing found shredded from some bizarre S/M ritual. Towns like Bear Valley had a special spot for women like me—as guest of honor at the annual summer picnic and bonfire.

As I was leafing through the magazines, the door to the waiting room opened. I looked up to see Karl Marsten walk through, followed by Thomas LeBlanc. Marsten was wearing chinos, thousand-dollar leather shoes, and a designer golf shirt. I didn't notice what LeBlanc was wearing. Beside Marsten, no one would notice. Marsten sauntered in with the casual, unstudied air of a man who'd spent years studying how to look that way. His hands were in his pockets, just enough to look relaxed, not enough to make his pants pull or sag unbecomingly. The half smile on his lips was the perfect mixture of interest, boredom, and amusement. When he turned that smile on the receptionist, she sat up straighter, hands straightening her blouse. He murmured a few words to her. She blushed and squirmed in her seat. Marsten leaned into the bars and said something more. Then he turned to me and rolled his eyes. I shook my head. Karl Marsten's sole redeeming feature was that he knew exactly how much of a fake he was.

"Elena," he said, taking the seat beside me. He kept his voice low, not whispering, but quiet enough that the receptionist couldn't eavesdrop from her cage across the room. "You're looking good."

"Don't practice on me, Karl."

He laughed. "I meant that you look surprisingly good for someone who had a run-in with Zachary Cain. I'm assuming that's where you got the scrape on your cheek. I'm also assuming he's no longer in the game."

"Something like that."

Marsten leaned back and crossed his ankles, obviously very concerned about his partner's passing. "I haven't seen you in a while. What's it been, two years? Too long. Don't give me that look. I'm not practicing on you and I'm not hitting on you. God gave me a few ounces of brain. I simply meant that I've missed talking to you. If nothing else, you're always intriguing company."

LeBlanc had taken a seat on my other side. I was ignoring him. Given the choice, I'd much rather speak to Marsten than the man who had killed Logan.

"I read a couple magazine articles you wrote," Marsten continued. "Very well done. You've got quite a successful career, it would seem."

"Not as successful as some," I said, eyeing his Rolex. "Bought or stolen?"

His eyes glittered. "Guess."

I thought about it. "Bought. It would be easier—and cheaper—to steal it but you wouldn't wear someone else's jewelry. Though you wouldn't object to buying it with the money you made stealing someone else's jewelry."

"Dead-on, as always."

"Business must be good."

Marsten laughed again. "I do well enough, thank you, considering I'm damned useless at everything else. And on that topic, I picked up something a few months ago that made me think of you. A platinum necklace with a wolf's head pendant. Gorgeous craftsmanship. The head is actually woven platinum filigree with emerald chips for eyes. Very elegant. I thought of sending it to you, but I figured it would end up in the nearest trash can."

"Excellent foresight."

"I haven't given it up, though. If you want it, it's yours. No strings attached. It would suit you, a nice twist of irony I'm sure you'd appreciate."

"You know, I'm surprised you're involved in this," I said. "I thought you didn't like Daniel."

Marsten sighed theatrically. "Must we talk shop?"

"I just never pictured you as the anarchist type."

"Anarchist?" He laughed. "Hardly. The others have their reasons for wanting the Pack dead, most of which have to do with allowing them to indulge some rather nasty, antisocial habits. The Pack has never given me any trouble. Of course, they've never done anything for me either. So, in a gesture of reciprocity, I don't care what happens to the Pack one way or the other. I only want my territory."

"If you had that, you'd back out of the fight?"

"And abandon my fellow anarchists? That would be the act of a despicable, unconscionable rogue, someone completely absorbed in furthering his own fortunes at the expense of others. Does that sound like me?"

LeBlanc made a noise of impatience beside me. Before I could resume the conversation with Marsten, he waved his hand at the other man.

"This one wanted to meet you," Marsten said. "When we saw you following the police into town, he decided he wanted to speak to you. I came along to provide the introduction. If he starts to bore you, scream. I'll be reading a magazine." Marsten pulled one from the pile. "*Hunter's Digest.* Hmmm. Maybe I can pick up a few tips."

Marsten settled into his chair and opened the magazine. LeBlanc shot him a look of pure contempt. He'd obviously decided before now that

Marsten was a third-rate werewolf, barely deserving of the name. He was wrong. If I had to pick the most dangerous mutt in the country, it would be a toss-up between Marsten and Daniel. How did Marsten gain that reputation? By killing more humans than anyone else? By tormenting the Pack or causing trouble for us? No and no. Marsten was one of the few mutts who didn't kill humans. Like so many things, that was beneath him. As for the Pack, when he met us, he was as civil and personable as he'd been to me right now. Yet we kept a closer eye on him than on any mutt besides Daniel. Why? Because he possessed a single-minded strength of purpose that rivaled Clay's. When Marsten moved into a new town, he met with any werewolves in the area, took them out to an expensive dinner, chatted them up, gave them one warning to clear out of town, then killed them if they weren't gone by midnight. What Marsten wanted, Marsten took . . . with no compunction and no rancor. What he wanted now was territory. For several years, he'd been making noises about settling in one place, joking that he was hitting retirement age. The Pack had ignored him. Now Marsten was tired of waiting. Today he'd sit beside me, compliment me on my writing, and offer me jewelry. Tomorrow, if I got in his way, he'd take me out of the game. Nothing personal, that was just the way it worked.

CHAPTER 20

Impressions

For at least ten minutes LeBlanc studied me like an entomologist examining some new kind of insect. I wanted to leave. Maybe that was the plan. Let this scumbag gawk at me long enough and I'd bolt to the bathroom to scrub my hands, where he and Marsten could corner me. I tried only to remember that LeBlanc had killed Logan and attacked Jeremy, but I couldn't. I kept thinking of the women he'd killed, the details I'd read in his scrapbook. For Logan, I wanted to kill him. For the others, I wanted him dead, but didn't want to do it myself, since that would require physical contact.

I forced myself to forget these things and concentrate on sizing him up. Life hadn't been good to Thomas LeBlanc in the past few years. He'd fallen a long way from the well-groomed man in his arrest photo. That wasn't to say he was greasy or unshaven, any of the things the average person expects of a serial killer psychopath. He looked like a thirty-something laborer wearing no-name jeans, a faded T-shirt, and sneakers from Wal-Mart. He'd put on weight since his photo. Unfortunately, it was muscle, not fat.

"You wanted to talk to me?" I said finally.

"I was wondering what all the fuss was about," he said, giving me a look that said he was still wondering.

He fell into silent bug-gazing mode again. It took all my strength to stay beside him. I fought to keep things in perspective: he was a new were-wolf; I was an experienced werewolf. No sweat. But my frame of reference kept shifting. He preyed on women; I was a woman. No matter how much I rationalized, no matter how tough I tried to be, this man scared me. Scared me deep in my gut, where logic and reason couldn't intrude.

After a few minutes, a shadow of movement passed the one-way glass. Anxious for the distraction, I got up and walked over. Clay was in the other room. Alone. He sat at the table and leaned back in his chair, tipping the front legs off the ground. He wasn't cuffed or guarded or bruised and battered. Good. So far.

"That's him?" LeBlanc said from behind me. "The infamous Clayton Danvers? Say it isn't so."

I kept watching Clay.

"Jesus fucking Christ," LeBlanc muttered. "Where the hell did the Pack find you two? At a beach volleyball tournament? Great tan. Love those curls." LeBlanc shook his head. "He's not even as big as I am. He's what, six foot nothing? Two hundred pounds in steel-toed boots? Christ. I'm expecting some ugly bruiser bigger than Cain and what do I find? The next *Baywatch* star. Looks like his IQ would be low enough. Can he chew gum and tie his shoes at the same time?"

Clay stopped playing with his chair and turned to face the mirror. He got up, crossed the room, and stood in front of me. I was leaning forward, one hand pressed against the glass. Clay touched his fingertips to mine and smiled. LeBlanc jumped back.

"Fuck," he said. "I thought that was one-way glass."

"It is."

Clay turned his head toward LeBlanc and mouthed three words. Then the door to his room opened and one of the officers called him out. Clay grinned at me, then sauntered out with the officer. As he left, a surge of renewed confidence ran through me.

"What did he say?" LeBlanc asked.

"'Wait for me.'"

"What?"

"It's a challenge," Marsten murmured from across the room. He didn't look up from his magazine. "He's inviting you to stick around and get to know him better."

"Are *you* going to?" LeBlanc said.

Marsten's lips curved in a smile. "He didn't invite me."

LeBlanc snorted. "For a bunch of killer monsters, the whole lot of you are nothing but hot air. All your rules and challenges and false bravado." He waved a hand at me. "Like you. Standing there so nonchalantly, pretending you aren't the least bit concerned about having the two of us in the room."

"I'm not."

"You should be. Do you know how fast I could kill you? You're standing two feet away from me. If I had a gun or knife in my pocket, you'd be dead before you had time to scream."

"Really? Huh."

LeBlanc's cheek twitched. "You don't believe me, do you? How do you know I'm not packing a gun? There's no metal detector at the door. I could pull one out now, kill you, and escape in thirty seconds."

"Then do it. I know, you don't like our little games, but humor me. If you have a gun or a knife, pull it out. If not, pretend to. Prove you could do it."

"I don't need to prove anything. Certainly not to a smart-mouthed—"

He whipped his hand up in mid-sentence. I grabbed it and snapped his wrist. The sound cracked through the room. The receptionist glanced over, but LeBlanc had his back to her. I smiled at her and she turned away.

"You—fucking—bitch," LeBlanc gasped, cradling his arm. "You broke my wrist."

"So I win."

His face purpled. "You smug—"

"Nobody likes a sore loser," I said. "Grit your teeth and bear it. There's no crying in werewolf games. Didn't Daniel teach you that?"

"I think you've outworn your welcome," Marsten said, getting to his feet and tossing the magazine back on the stack.

When LeBlanc didn't move, Marsten stepped toward him and reached for his arm. LeBlanc sidestepped before Marsten could touch him, glared once at me, then strode from the room.

"The joys of babysitting," Marsten said. "I'll be off then. Say hello to Clayton for me." Marsten left.

I stood there, heart pounding. I'd pulled it off, hidden my fear with false bravado and LeBlanc hadn't noticed the difference. Piece of cake. I could beat this mutt no problem. So why was my heart still jumping around like a rabbit in a trap?

Twenty minutes later, I was still in the waiting room, trying very hard to find something to read. A survey in *Cosmo* caught my eye. It was entitled: "Constructive Arguing: Are You Strengthening Your Relationship with Your Lover or Driving Him Away?" Intriguing, especially the part about driving him away, but I forced myself to put the magazine down. *Cosmo* never speaks to my life. Its surveys always ask questions like "How would you react if your lover announced he was taking a job in Alaska?" and jumping for joy is never one of the options. Move to Alaska? Hell, my lover was thirty-seven and hadn't moved away from home yet. Where were the questions relevant to my life? What about "How would you react if your lover's hair and footprints were found beside a dead man?" Show me that in *Cosmo* and you have a subscriber.

I was searching for something else to read when Clay walked into the room. Again the receptionist perked up. She smiled and murmured something I couldn't catch. All she got in return was a level stare and a dismissive twist of the lip. As she deflated back into her typing, I almost felt sorry for her. Clay could be such a charmer.

"Death penalty?" I asked as he walked over to me.

"In your dreams. It was bullshit, darling. Pure bullshit and I missed lunch because of it."

"You should sue."

"I might do that." He walked back to the door and held it open for me. "So you had visitors?"

"Marsten and LeBlanc."

"What did Marsten want?"

"He offered me a necklace."

"In return for?"

"Nothing. Just Karl being Karl. As personable as ever, totally disregarding the small matter of being on opposite sides of a bloody battle to the death. Speaking of death, LeBlanc boasted he could kill me in the waiting room. I broke his wrist. He wasn't impressed."

"Good. What did he tag along for?"

"To stare at me, I think. Didn't seem too impressed with what he saw, either."

Clay snorted and we headed into the parking lot.

We parked in the drive at Stonehaven. Jeremy met us at the front door.

"You missed lunch," he said. "Did something go wrong?"

"Nah," Clay said. "I got hauled down to the police station for questioning."

"*After* we took care of Cain," I said, before Jeremy experienced any major chest pains. "I'd have called from the station, but the phone was too public. The police pulled us over on the way back from dumping the body. Looks like Daniel tipped them off that Clay might know something about Mike Braxton's death. Seems he hoped they'd catch us before we disposed of Cain's body. No such luck, though."

"How much did the police seem to know?"

"Not much," Clay said. "The questions were pretty general. A fishing expedition."

"Did they search the car?"

"Hard to say," I said. "One of them took a really good look through the windows and checked out the undercarriage. He acted like he was only interested in the Explorer in general, how much can it store, how does it do off-road, stuff like that. On the other hand, it may have been his way of doing a subtle plain-view search."

"Wonderful," Jeremy said, shaking his head. "Come inside and eat quickly. We need to leave."

"Have you figured out how to get a message to Daniel?" I asked.

Jeremy waved his hand. "That wasn't a problem. I've already conveyed my message."

"Did he reply?"

"Yes, but it doesn't concern what we're doing right now. Hurry up. We haven't much time."

"Where're we going?" Clay asked, but Jeremy was already in the house.

Less than an hour later, the five of us were in the Explorer. It was the first time the Pack didn't need to take multiple vehicles to travel together. There were only five of us left. Of course, I'd noticed that before, but I hadn't actually *realized* it until we were driving down the highway in one car. Five left. Four men and one woman who wasn't sure she even counted herself as part of the group. If I left, would there be a Pack? Could two fathers and two sons be considered a Pack? I shook off the thought. With or without me, the Pack would survive. It always had. Besides, there was no urgent need for me to declare my independence now or even in the near future. I planned to return to Toronto when this was over, but as Jeremy had said, there was no need to make a hasty decision on my Pack status.

We were going to the airport to meet Jimmy Koenig. Call it a surprise welcoming committee. Jeremy had found out that Koenig was arriving in New York City today on the seven-ten flight from Seattle. Don't ask me how he knew. I guessed the information came as the result of several phone calls, a few lies, and a heap of good manners. That was Jeremy's usual method. It was amazing what you could learn from airline clerks, motel reservation staff, credit card phone reps, and other customer service employees simply by telling a good story and being exceedingly polite doing it. Like I said, I assumed this was what Jeremy did. He didn't mention the how when parlaying the information. He never did. If it was anyone else, I'd suspect him of showing off, like a magician pulling the rabbit from the hat without revealing the trick. With Jeremy, I knew he had no such motive. He'd consider it showing off to give an explanation, as if expecting us to be wowed by his cleverness.

The plan was to meet Koenig at the gate, help him with his luggage, and escort him back to Bear Valley in high style after getting re-acquainted over a few drinks at 21. Really.

Okay. That wasn't the plan.

The plan was to terminate the sorry mutt before he got his first look at the Empire State Building. The time for carefully exploring the problem was over. At last, we were taking action.

Chapter 21

Vengeance

The flight from Seattle was forty minutes late, which was a good thing, considering that we didn't get there until twenty minutes after the plane was due to arrive. A jackknifed tractor trailer on the highway put us nearly an hour behind schedule. Antonio squealed into the airport at seven-thirty, weaved through traffic like a New York cabbie, and dropped us off at the front doors a couple minutes later. By the time he found a parking spot and joined us in the terminal, Koenig's flight was touching down. We'd made it, but barely. I wasn't sure whether to interpret that as a good omen or bad.

We stood well back from the crowd of welcoming friends and relatives, and watched the passengers disembark. Jimmy Koenig was easy to spot. He was tall and scrawny with a face that could be mistaken for Keith Richards on a bad day. He looked every day of his sixty-two years, his body's revenge for fifty years of being subjected to every stress test known to man. Too much booze, too many drugs, and way too many mornings waking up in strange hotel rooms beside even stranger women. The people who script Just Say No campaign ads should hire guys like Jimmy Koenig. Flash his face on television and any kid with an ounce of vanity would swear off booze and dope for life. Trust me.

Koenig wasn't traveling alone. He got off the plane with a guy who looked like his FBI escort—thirty-something, clean-shaven, and well-groomed, wearing a dark suit and dark sunglasses. Though his eyes were hidden behind the shades, his head turned from side to side as if constantly scanning his surroundings. I almost expected to see handcuffs linking him to Koenig. When they got to the bottom of the Jetway, they stopped. The two exchanged a brief flurry of words. FBI guy looked pissed, but Koenig wasn't backing down. After a few minutes, FBI guy stalked off toward the baggage claim area. Koenig headed for the waiting room and plopped into the nearest chair.

"Clay, Elena, take Koenig," Jeremy said. "Tonio and I'll go after his friend. Nick?"

"I'll stick with Clay," Nick said.

Jeremy nodded and he and Antonio started for the baggage area. After Clay and I discussed tactics, Clay and Nick headed off into the crowd. I waited until they were out of sight, then looped around a loud family reunion and walked behind Koenig. When I got to his seat, I stood in back of his chair and waited. It took a couple of minutes before his head jerked up. He sniffed the air, then slowly turned.

"Boo," I said.

He reacted as all mutts react when I confront them. He leapt from his chair and dove for the nearest exit, shaking in terror. In my dreams. He glanced at me and started looking for Clay. It never failed. Mutts only quaked when I appeared because it usually meant Clayton wasn't far behind. I was nothing but a harbinger of doom.

"Where is he?" Koenig asked, narrowing his eyes and surveying the crowds.

"It's only me," I said.

"Yeah, right."

I circled around the row of chairs and sat down beside Koenig. There was only the barest whiff of scotch on his breath, meaning he'd only imbibed a single drink on the plane. Again, I wasn't sure if this was a good sign or not. When sober, he was like a toothless lion, nasty but with little bite. It also meant, though, that his brain and reflexes were in perfect working order.

"Clay's gone to take care of your buddy with the shades," I said.

"Budd—" Koenig stopped and grunted.

"He figured I could handle you on my own."

Koenig's dark eyes snapped, obviously insulted. He muttered something. I was about to ask him to repeat himself when I saw Nick approaching from the other side. I watched him and swore under my breath. Koenig jerked his head around to look. When he saw Nick, his first reaction was relief. He started to relax, then tensed again. Nick might not be as bad as Clay but, as far as Koenig was concerned, he was definitely more cause for concern than me.

"Son-of-a-bitch," I muttered. "He wasn't supposed to interfere."

Nick grinned, not a friendly smile, but the predatory grin of a hunter scenting prey. His strides lengthened as he walked toward us. His gaze was fixed on Koenig.

"Nicholas . . . " I warned beneath my breath as I got to my feet.

Koenig fell for it. Thinking I was preoccupied getting ready to confront Nick, he bolted. Nick flashed a victory grin at me and we took off in pursuit. Although Koenig was running, he wasn't getting very far. It was like racing through a dense forest. He kept weaving to circumvent people and chairs and only succeeded in avoiding one to crash into the next. Nick and I pursued at a quick walk. Not only was it easier to dodge obstacles, but it wouldn't look as if we were chasing Koenig. Considering Koenig's appearance, no one seemed to think it was odd that he was tearing through the airport running from invisible pursuers. People probably figured he was drunk, stoned, or having one hell of a sixties flashback. They cursed when he mowed them down, but no one got involved.

Nick and I kept on opposite sides of Koenig. It was the same technique we'd used with the deer. Keep him running and steer him toward the finish line. And guess who was waiting at the finish line? I was almost surprised that Koenig fell for it. I say "almost," because I knew better than to be completely shocked that he'd fall for such an old ruse. Mutts didn't hunt deer. The pattern for the trick may have been in Koenig's brain, but he'd never bothered to use it so he didn't recognize it when it was being played on him.

I followed Clay's scent and we herded Koenig out of the crowded lobby, down a deserted hall, and behind a narrow stairwell. Clay jumped out from the stairwell, grabbed Koenig by the throat, and broke his neck. Anticlimactic, really, but we couldn't afford the risk of questioning him in a busy airport. Jeremy said to kill him, so that was what Clay did, with absolute efficiency. Before Koenig's body even went limp, Clay was stuffing him into the shadows under the stairwell.

"Are we leaving him here?" I asked.

"Nah. There's an exit door over there. I saw Dumpsters outside. If you guys stand guard, I'll move him."

"Do you need both of us?" I asked. "Tonio and Jeremy might need help."

"Good idea. Go on then. Nick can handle guard duty."

I took off.

By the time I got to the baggage claim area, most of the people from Koenig's flight had come and gone. All that was left were the inevitable stragglers standing by the conveyer belt, staring at it, transfixed. With each pile of luggage that passed, they perked up and checked it over, hoping against hope that their baggage was somehow there, hidden from sight, refusing to believe it had been devoured by the demon god of lost luggage. FBI guy was not amongst the believers. Nor were Jeremy and Antonio. I took one last look around, then headed back the way I'd come.

By the washrooms, I caught sight of FBI guy. I tried to pick up the were-wolf scent, but it was lost amidst the stink of strangers. I also didn't smell Jeremy or Antonio, but that wasn't surprising. First, with all the human traffic that went up and down that hall every hour, I was lucky I could pick out any scent at all. Second, Jeremy was probably approaching from another angle, being far less inclined to childish stunts like walking up to his target and saying boo.

I followed the new werewolf's trail, staying well enough back that I wouldn't bump into him and screw up Jeremy's plan—whatever that was. I expected the mutt to walk back into the terminal where Koenig had been waiting. He didn't. Instead, he went out a side exit. I followed him onto some kind of laneway that looked like a loading zone. From there, he headed toward the parking lot.

Again his route didn't meet my expectations. Instead of going into the parking lot, he turned down another lane. As I started down it, a high-pitched bleating shattered the silence and I jerked around to see a forklift motoring up behind me. I jumped out of the way. As the machine scooted past, the driver stabbed a finger toward the parking lot, but didn't slow down, obviously too busy to worry about tourists wandering into what was probably a restricted area. After that, I kept close to the wall, ready to hightail it to a hiding spot if someone else appeared.

I raced to the end of the alley, but the mutt had vanished. I searched for his scent. It was still lost, now hidden by the smells of machinery and exhaust. I began to suspect that Jeremy and Antonio were nowhere nearby. The air was dense with oil and diesel fumes. They'd probably given up long ago. I was about to turn back when I rounded a corner and saw the mutt less than twenty feet away. I quickly stepped back out of sight, stopped, listened, and considered my options. If I was so certain Jeremy and Antonio weren't around, I should back off. Jeremy would tear a strip out of my hide if I went after the mutt alone, even if I succeeded in bring-ing him down. I knew this, but the temptation was too great. Telling myself I only wanted a better look, I crept forward.

When I got around the corner again, the mutt was gone. Keeping close to the building on my left, I slipped along the roadway and found him. We walked another fifteen or twenty feet. Then he stopped and looked around, as if getting his bearings. I flattened myself against the wall and waited. When he resumed walking, I stayed in my hiding place, letting him get farther ahead. I was so busy concentrating on my prey that I didn't hear footsteps behind me. Too late, I turned. An arm grabbed me by the throat and shoved me against the wall.

"Elena," LeBlanc said. "Fancy meeting you here."

I jerked my head to look down the alley, expecting FBI guy to be circling back. He was gone.

"Friend of yours?" LeBlanc asked.

"Yours, not mine."

LeBlanc's eyebrows went up, then he laughed. "Ah, I see. You were tracking him because you saw him talking to Koenig, so you figured he was one of us. Faulty deduction, girlie. Very faulty. Koenig's protégé didn't make it. Couldn't handle the Change. Died yesterday. Too bad, so sad. Daniel sent me to pick the old coot up. I saw your bunch lurking around, so I stood back and took in the show. Then I saw you take off and thought, huh, maybe this errand could be fun after all."

As he spoke, I tensed for attack, but before I could strike, he pulled something from his pocket. A gun. LeBlanc lifted the pistol and rested it against the middle of my forehead. The ground swayed beneath me, my knees threatening to give way. Stop it, I told myself. He's playing a game. Not the sort of game you're used to, but a game nonetheless. Sure, there was a gun at my forehead, but I'd find a way out of this. Mutts were predictable beasts. LeBlanc wouldn't kill me because I was a prize too valuable to waste on a few seconds of murderous pleasure. I was the only female werewolf. He might try to rape me or kidnap me or rough me up a bit, but he wouldn't kill me.

I swallowed my fear. False bravado had worked last time. Stick with the tried-and-true.

"Werewolves don't use guns," I said. "Weapons are for wimps. You guys realize that, right?"

"Shut up," LeBlanc said, tilting his gun up.

"Guess you were right about us not being too bright," I said. "If I was smart, I'd have broken your right wrist. How is it anyway? Giving you any trouble?"

"Shut up."

"Just making small talk."

"If you want to talk," LeBlanc said, "I'd suggest you start with an apology."

"For what?"

His face went deep red, eyes suffusing with an emotion it took me a moment to recognize. Hate. Pure hate, ten times stronger than what I'd seen at the police station that morning. Was he that angry with me for breaking his wrist? The thought came as something of a shock. Of course, most people would get a bit pissed about stuff like that, but mutts didn't normally make a big deal of it, especially if I was the one doing the damage. In fact, they usually laughed it off, as if in some perverse way they were pleased with me for having the guts to do it. Years ago, I'd bit off one of Daniel's ears. He didn't hold a grudge. If anything, he was proud of that missing ear, and would tell any mutt who asked exactly how he'd come to lose it, as if it proved we had some kind of close, personal relationship. Nothing says lovin' like permanent mutilation.

"Is it the wrist?" I asked. "You're the one who wanted to prove you could knife me. I was only proving I could defend myself."

"Bullshit. You thought it was funny. Humiliate the new guy. We got back to the house, what do you think Marsten does? Tells Daniel and Olson. Gave them a good laugh." He cocked the gun. "I want an apology."

I thought about this. Apologizing wasn't a big deal. Of course, I wasn't sorry I'd done it, but he didn't need to know that. The words stuck in my craw, though. Why should I apologize? Well, stupid, because the guy has a gun to your head. But if I was sure he wasn't going to use it. . . It didn't matter. There was no sense escalating the matter.

"I'm sorry," I said. "I didn't mean to embarrass you."

"On your knees."

"What?"

"Apologize on your knees."

"The hell I—"

LeBlanc rammed the gun into my mouth. I clamped down involuntarily. Needles of pain ran though my jaw as my teeth hit metal. I tried to jerk away, but he had me backed against the wall. LeBlanc shoved the gun in until I gagged.

The taste of metal was sharp and foul. I tried to pull my tongue back, but the barrel was in too far. My heart was tripping, but I wasn't panicking. Whatever LeBlanc said, I knew he wouldn't kill me. He expected that the threat of death would be enough to make me do whatever he wanted. He'd realize his mistake soon enough. As soon as I figured out how to get his gun out of my mouth. Even as I thought this, I realized the answer was simple. I hated to do it, but it was the easiest way.

I lifted one leg, making a motion to show that I was ready to kneel. LeBlanc's lips twisted in an ugly smile and he pulled the gun from my mouth.

"Good girl," LeBlanc said. "Werewolf or not, I see you're still a woman. When push comes to shove, you know your place."

I gritted my teeth and kept my eyes down, which he seemed to take as proof that I'd been properly cowed.

"Well?" he said.

I tilted my head forward, letting my hair fall in a curtain around my face. Then I started to sniffle.

LeBlanc laughed. "Not nearly so cocky now, are you?"

Triumph rang from his voice. I sniffled some more and lifted a hand to wipe at my eyes. Through the blindfold of my hair, I could only see LeBlanc's lower half. It was enough. After a couple seconds of my crying, his arm dropped, letting the gun fall to his side. I lifted both hands to my face, covering it. Then, I pulled my hands down again, wrapped my left hand over my right fist, and brought both hands slamming upward into LeBlanc's crotch. As he stumbled back, I lunged. I knocked him down and started running. Halfway down the alley, I heard the first shot. Instinctively, I flung myself forward to the ground. Something stung my left shoulder. I hit the pavement in an awkward half flip, managed to get back to my feet, and kept going. Two shots rang out in quick succession, but I was already rounding the corner.

As I ran, blood trickled down my shoulder, but the pain was minimal, no more than a nasty scrape. Left shoulder, I thought. And six inches or so below the left shoulder, my heart. He'd been aiming for my heart. I shook the thought and impending panic from my head. Behind me, I could hear his running footfalls. I took the first corner, then the next and the next, keeping my straight-out runs short so he wouldn't have a chance at another shot. It worked for about five minutes, then I ended up in a long alley with no exit except at the end. I leaned forward and sprinted like hell. It wasn't fast enough. LeBlanc rounded the corner before I got to the end of the alley. Another shot. Another dive. This time either the shot wasn't accurate or I'd moved faster. The bullet whammed into the side of a Dumpster. I veered left and made a headlong dash forward. A car was directly in front of me, and another one beside it, and another and another. Parking lot. A spark of joy zinged through me. A public place. Safety.

I raced around the corner, getting out of shooting range. As I ran, I tried to find the largest concentration of human activity. That was the key. Get near enough people that LeBlanc would be forced to hide his gun. If he didn't, I'd attract attention by screaming—a feminine ploy almost as universally effective as crying. In my first glimpse around, I didn't see anyone, but it was hard to take a good look while running full out. I swerved down a line of cars and slowed behind the shield of a minivan. I looked around. There was no one on the east side of the parking lot. I peeked over the passenger door and squinted through the window to check the west side. There was no one around. Absolutely no one. I was either in an employee parking lot or in long-term parking.

LeBlanc's scent floated over on the breeze.

I dropped to my hands and knees. Taking a deep breath, I controlled the returning panic and lowered my head to survey the lot from ground level. About fifty feet to my right were a pair of sneakers. LeBlanc. I rolled under the minivan and craned my neck to get a better look around. The rows of tires seemed to stretch to infinity in every direction. After a moment, I decided that the line of tires to my right seemed the shortest. Creeping on my stomach, I moved to the front of the minivan, stuck my head out and looked left. Beyond the parking lot, I couldn't see anything. As I watched, a car went by the end of the row. Then another. Some kind of road. Maybe only a service route, but where there were moving cars there had to be people. I eased out from under the minivan and started forward, staying doubled over behind the cars.

"Come out, come out, wherever you are," LeBlanc chanted.

A brief pause, then: "I don't like games, Elena. You make me look for you and you'll regret it. I can make you regret it. You took my scrapbook. You know what I can do."

I moved along the rear of a sedan and peered around the other side, checking before I dashed across an empty parking spot. A flash of motion caught my eye and I yanked my head back. Looking under the car, I saw LeBlanc's shoes. I froze and checked the wind direction. Southeast. I was upwind. I stopped breathing, but knew it wouldn't matter if I didn't make any noise. He'd smell me. He had to. The sneakers passed the other end of the sedan and kept moving. LeBlanc didn't even pause. I closed my eyes and exhaled slowly. He wasn't using his nose. One less concern. I waited until his shoes vanished, then kept moving down the narrow passage between the two rows of parked cars. Each time I came to an empty space, I checked before crossing it. More than once there wasn't room to pass between the cars, the driver having pulled up within inches of the car in the opposite row. This was trickier than dashing across the empty spaces. I could go over or under. The first time, I tried to go over and set the car rocking. I spent a few breathless minutes standing there before I was sure LeBlanc hadn't noticed. After that, when cars abutted each other, I went under. Slower but safer.

I'd gone past fifteen cars and estimated another ten to go when I heard footsteps to my left. I dropped down, stopped moving, and listened. I knew LeBlanc was to my left, but at last check, he was left and rear. These footsteps came from left and front. They didn't sound like sneakers either. Hard-soled footsteps clacked across the pavement moving fast and coming almost straight for me. I fell to my stomach and looked out under the row of cars. Brown pumps were moving fast down the row immediately to my left. A woman hurrying to her car. I thought about standing up, waving my arms, calling attention to myself. Would one witness be enough to keep LeBlanc from firing?

"Aha," LeBlanc sang out.

My head jolted up and hit the undercarriage of the car with a thunderous bang. LeBlanc cursed and started running. I looked about wildly, trying to see his feet to figure out which way to escape. The woman. I had to take the chance and bolt toward her. But I couldn't hear her footsteps anymore. Was she already in her car?

"Fuck!" LeBlanc shouted. "I don't fucking believe it. Elena!"

I stopped moving. Why was he calling me? He knew where I was, didn't he? Even if he hadn't been calling out to me, he must have heard my head strike the car's underside. The sound had been so loud it had reverberated through the parking lot. LeBlanc was still cursing. I followed the sound and saw LeBlanc's sneakers about twenty feet away. And beside his shoes, the body of a woman, lying on the pavement, open eyes staring at me beneath a bloody crater in the middle of her forehead. When LeBlanc had shouted, it wasn't because he'd seen me. The bang I'd heard hadn't been my head hitting the car. He'd seen a motion, a woman moving fast, caught a glimpse of light-colored hair and fired. As I stared at the dead woman I started to shake. I told myself that my horror was for her, an innocent, gunned down in a parking lot. It wasn't true. The tightness in my throat and the pounding in my chest wasn't for her. It was for me. I looked at her body, staring sightless into eternity, and I saw myself lying there. It was supposed to be me. Killed in a second. One brief second. Alive and running. Then dead. Over. Everything. Would I have heard the shot? Would I have felt it? I could have died here, today, in this parking lot. I could still die. This morning could have been my last time waking up. Lunch my last meal. Thirty minutes ago in the airport, the last time I saw Antonio, Nick, Jeremy . . . Clay. The shaking got worse. I could die. Really die. Despite all my battles, I'd never thought of that before. Never really contemplated what it meant. The end could come in one impossibly short second. Now, thinking of it, I was afraid. More afraid than I'd ever been.

I felt stabs of pain in my clenched fists. I unclenched them and the pain lessened into a stretching, a pulsating as if something was moving under the skin. I ignored it. I had more important things to think about. Yet the sensation didn't go away. It got worse. I glanced down and saw my fingers retracting into my hands, hair sprouting from the backs. I hadn't done anything to precipitate a Change, hadn't even thought about it. I shook my hands sharply and flexed them, willing the transformation to stop. As I moved my fingers, fresh pain shot down my arms. Then my feet started to tingle. I closed my eyes and ordered my body to stop. My back arched. My shirt started to rip. No! my brain shouted. Not now! Stop! It didn't stop. My legs jerked and spasmed, wanting to pull under my body, but there wasn't room. I was jammed under a new VW Beetle with barely inches to spare. I couldn't get up on all fours. I couldn't move my legs and arms into position. I clenched my eyes shut and concentrated. Nothing happened. The first licks of alarm darted through me. As they came, the Change sped up, my clothing tearing and my body intent on moving itself into impossible contortions. The fear was doing it. Fear of being trapped in this parking lot with a killer had started the Change and now the fear of being trapped under the car was making it worse. I knew what I had to do. I had to get out. A fresh spark of fear made my torso jerk up, crashing my back into the underside of the car. This time I knew the resulting bang was real. Dimly I heard LeBlanc's shoes squeak against the pavement. Heard him say something. Heard him laugh . . .

I vaulted from under the Beetle. My nails scraped against the pavement. Halfway out my legs seized up and I fell face first to the ground. Every muscle in my arms and legs seemed to spasm at once. A howl of agony broke from my throat. I clamped my jaw shut. My eyes bugged out with the pain. It was too late to reverse the Change. I'd passed the midway mark; going back would take longer than going forward. I focused my energy on finishing, feeding it with fear. At last, the final phase hit with a shuddering wave of agony so blinding that I passed out. I came to as soon as my muzzle hit the pavement, then lay on my stomach, panting and gulping air. I didn't want to move. I could hear footsteps getting closer. He'd heard me. He knew approximately where I was and was narrowing his search, closing in. For a moment, I was too exhausted to care. Then I turned my head and saw the dead woman. Heaving myself to my feet, I started to run.

Any thoughts of a cautious, stealthy escape had fled from my brain, overpowered by the need to get away as quickly as possible. I tore out from between the cars, got onto the laneway, and ran full-out. I didn't listen for sounds of pursuit. I couldn't waste the energy. I poured everything I had into running. A shout rang out behind me. Then a shot. It whizzed over my head. I didn't slow or veer from my course. I blocked out everything and kept going. Finally the row of cars came to an end. I was on a through road. A horn blared. A gust of air from a passing truck sliced through my fur. Still, I didn't slow down. On the other side of the road were two buildings. I ran toward them, no longer knowing where I was going, just that I had to get away.

As I was emerging from between the buildings, I heard a shout. Someone calling my name. The sound came from beside me. I hunkered down and ran faster. A brick wall suddenly popped up in my path. I tried to stop, but it was too late. My legs slid out from under me and I skidded into the wall with a bone-jarring thud. Behind me, LeBlanc was still running, shouting my name. I got to my feet and twisted around to see the shape of my pursuer at my back. There wasn't time to escape. Even as I was still turning, I launched myself at him. As I flew through the air, his arm went up, blocking his throat. I hit him full in the chest and we toppled over backward. I curled my lips. As I slashed down, the red fog of panic that blinded me cleared and I saw who lay beneath me. Not LeBlanc. Clay.

I yanked my head back just in time. The momentum of the sudden change in direction sent me tumbling sideways. When I tried scrambling up, Clay grabbed me and held me still. He whispered something, but I couldn't make it out. Not seeing any comprehension in my eyes, he waited a second, then spoke again, enunciating slowly.

"He's gone," he said. "Don't worry. He's gone."

I hesitated and looked back between the two buildings, certain LeBlanc would appear at any moment, gun in hand. Clay shook his head.

"He's gone, darling. When you crossed the road, he backed off. Too public."

I still waited, shaking. Clay buried his hands in my fur and tried to pull me against him, but I resisted. We had to be ready to run. He started saying something when footsteps echoed from somewhere nearby. I leapt to my feet, but Clay restrained me. Jeremy, Antonio, and Nick emerged from around the building. I stood there a moment, legs trembling, sniffing the air to make sure my eyes weren't betraying me. Yes, they were here. They were all here. I was safe. I paused for a second, then sank to the ground.

CHAPTER 22

PROMISE

Clay sat beside me on the way back to Stonehaven. I was still shaky, maybe even in shock, but he didn't try to pull me against him or comfort me. He knew better. Instead, he held my hand and glanced over from time to time, checking whether I wanted to talk about it. I didn't.

We were almost home when Clay broke the silence, leaning forward to catch Jeremy's attention in the front passenger seat. "You didn't tell us what Daniel demanded," he said. "It was Elena, wasn't it?"

"Yes," Jeremy said softly, not turning.

Antonio turned off the highway. "It's like an airplane hijacker asking for ten billion dollars. He knows we wouldn't consider it, so it's another way of saying he's not dealing."

"It's not just that," Clay said. "He's giving us a warning. He knows we would never give Elena up. He's telling us his next move. He's going to take her."

Jeremy nodded. "I should have realized that. We could have saved ourselves a very close call. I thought as Tonio did—that by asking for Elena, Daniel was saying he wouldn't bargain."

Nick asked, "So that mutt at the airport was trying to kidnap Elena?"

"No," I said. "He was trying to kill me."

"A mutt wouldn't do that, Elena," Jeremy began. "You're too valuable to them alive. It may have seemed—"

"You weren't there. A woman was hurrying through the parking lot. LeBlanc mistook her for me and blew a hole through her head. That's not an incapacitating shot. That's an execution."

Clay's hand tightened around mine. Jeremy pulled back into his seat. No one spoke for at least five minutes.

"Why would he do that?" Nick asked. "If Daniel wants you, he'd want you alive."

"LeBlanc doesn't give a damn what Daniel wants," I said. "Maybe it's because he's new or because he's been killing on his own for so long, but he doesn't seem to have the instinct to obey a stronger werewolf."

"But why kill you at all?" Nick said. "Like Jeremy says, these new mutts have no stake in this fight, other than some promise to Daniel. If Daniel doesn't want you dead, why go through all that trouble trying to kill you?"

"Thomas LeBlanc preys on women. He tortures them and rapes them and kills them. Men like that hate women and they're easily threatened by them. I forgot that. After all my talk about not treating these men like other mutts, I did exactly that. I humiliated him at the police station, taunted him, insulted him, and broke his wrist in front of Marsten. Now he wants to overpower me. He needs to."

Clay's thumb rubbed against my wrist, but he said nothing. Neither did anyone else.

When we got to Stonehaven, I went up to my room. As I climbed the stairs, I could hear Clay behind me, but I didn't say anything. I walked into my room, leaving the door open. He closed it behind him. I got partway to my bed and stopped. I stood there, Clay still silent behind me. A cold worm of fear wound up through my body and I started to shake. I gulped air and closed my eyes. I was okay. I was home and I was safe. And I'd almost been killed. The fear shot through me, mingling with anger and outrage, melding into something white-hot. I wanted to dive into my bed and hide under the covers. I wanted to throw something against the wall and watch it shatter. I wanted to storm back to those mutts and scream "How dare you!"

When I looked at Clay, I saw my emotions mirrored in his face, the anger and the outrage and something so rare I barely recognized it, a haunted look half hidden behind his eyes. Fear. He reached out and pulled me to him. I turned my face to his, found his lips and kissed him. His lips parted against mine. I kissed him harder, closing my eyes and pressing myself into him. Some spark of life penetrated the dead shock in my brain. I chased it, kissing him harder still, deeper, moving my body against his. The spark fanned into a flame, and all my senses jumped to life again. The world shrank and all I could experience, all I wanted to experience was him. I tasted him, smelled him, saw him, heard him, felt him, and reveled in the sensations like someone rising from a coma.

Moving backward toward the bed, our feet tangled and we tumbled onto the carpet. Once on the floor, I grabbed Clay's shirt and yanked it up, but his arms were still around me and I couldn't bear to make him pull back, as if that one second of broken contact would send me sliding back into fear and shock. I wrapped my fists in the back of his shirt and tore. As the material ripped, I stopped pulling. It was too much bother, too much wasted time. I moved my hands to his jeans, tore open the fly, and shoved them down over his hips. Still kissing me, he kicked them off, then fumbled with mine. I pushed his hands away and took off my pants myself. As I was pushing them down, Clay ripped my underwear and threw it aside. His hand moved from my rear to my inner thigh. He slid his fingers inside me.

"No," I said, twisting away from his hand.

I reached down and pulled him inside me. His eyes widened. I moved against him. When he drew back and thrust, I grabbed his hips and held him still.

"Don't," I panted. "Let me."

He shifted up and held himself motionless over me. I arched my hips to his and rubbed against him. Above me, Clay gasped. A shudder ran through him and I pushed his shoulders up off me so I could watch him. As I moved, he kept his eyes on mine, the tip of his tongue showing between his teeth as he fought to keep still. I thrust up against him and held myself there, relishing the control, the feeling of taking control after I'd lost it so completely a few hours ago. I moved one hand to his chest and held it against his heart. I could feel life there, tripping under my fingers.

"Okay," I whispered.

Clay buried himself in me and moaned. I arched up to meet him. We moved together. When climax threatened, I pulled back, not willing to give him up yet.

"Wait," I gasped. "Just wait."

I closed my eyes and inhaled. The smell of him was overwhelming, almost enough in itself to make me peak. I pressed my face against the hollow of his collarbone and inhaled greedily. As I breathed him in, the world seemed to stop and the jumble of sensations came apart, letting me experience each one untainted by the others. I could feel it all: the twitching of Clay's biceps under my hands as he held himself over me, the sweat trickling from his chest to mine, the scratchy pressure of his sock resting against my calf, the throbbing of him inside me. I wanted to hold everything right there until I'd committed it to memory. This was what it felt like to be alive.

I tightened myself around him, heard his answering groan, and felt my own response shudder through me. The perfection of the moment faded in a sudden need to attain another kind of perfection, another perfect image of life.

"Now," I said. "Please."

Clay bent his face to mine and kissed me hard as he moved inside me. I felt the waves of climax building, tasted it in his kiss. I wrapped myself around him, legs twisting with his, arms pulling him against me. Just as I was about to lose myself in him, he broke the kiss and reached up, entwining his hands in my hair. He didn't pull his head back, but kept his face above mine, eyes so close I could see nothing but blue.

"Don't ever scare me like that again," he rasped. "If I lost you . . . I can't lose you."

I moved my hands to his hair and kissed him. Again he stopped in mid-kiss.

"Promise," he said. "Promise me you'll never take a risk like that again."

I promised and he bent his face to mine as we let all remaining vestiges of control slide away.

Jeremy rapped on the door before dawn penetrated the trees outside my window. Clay opened his eyes, but made no move to get up or even respond.

"I need you two downstairs," Jeremy said through the closed door.

I glanced over at Clay and waited for him to answer. He didn't.

"Now," Jeremy said.

Clay was quiet for another thirty seconds, then grunted "Why?" in a tone I'd never heard him use with Jeremy. It threw Jeremy off balance too, and for a few long seconds, he didn't answer.

"Downstairs," he said finally. "Now."

Jeremy's footsteps receded down the hall.

"I'm sick of it," Clay said, throwing the covers off and shoving them aside. "We're not getting anywhere. All we've done so far is chase our tails. Chase, run away, chase, run away. And where has it gotten us? It's killed Logan, killed Peter, it almost killed Jeremy, and almost killed you. Now you're in danger and he'd better be planning to do something about it."

"I am," Jeremy's voice floated up from the stairway. "That's why I'm asking you to come downstairs."

Spots of red flared in Clay's cheeks. He'd forgotten Jeremy could hear him as well from the bottom of the stairs as from the bedroom door. He mumbled something that sounded apologetic and got out of bed.

Antonio and Nick were already in the study, grazing from a plate of cold meats and cheeses. As we walked in the door, Jeremy was laying out coffees by the sofa for us.

"I know you're worried about Elena, Clayton," Jeremy said as we settled in. "We all are. That's why I'm sending her away. Today."

"What?" I sat up sharply. "Wait a minute. Just because last night gave me a bit of a scare, it doesn't mean—"

"You weren't the only one given a scare last night, Elena. Daniel has targeted you and now it seems this LeBlanc has done the same. One wants to capture you. The other wants to kill you. Do you honestly think I'm going to sit back and wait to see which one succeeds? I've lost Logan and I've lost Peter. I won't take the remotest chance of losing anyone else. I made a mistake yesterday in letting you go with us after I knew Daniel wanted you. I'm not making another mistake by letting you stay one day longer."

I glanced at Clay, expecting him to protest as well, but he was holding his mug of coffee halfway to his lips, staring into its dark depths like a fortune-teller searching for answers in the bottom of a teacup. After a moment, he put the mug down, untasted. Even Jeremy looked over at him and paused, waiting for an argument that didn't come.

"Great," I said. "One panic attack and I'm a liability to be stashed away for safekeeping. Do I get to know where you're going to hide me? Or can't I be trusted with the information?"

Jeremy continued in the same even tone. "You're going to the last place the mutts would expect to find you. Back to Toronto."

"And what the hell am I supposed to do there? Hole up someplace by myself while the men fight the battle?"

"You won't be by yourself. Clay's going with you."

"Whoa!" I leapt to my feet. "You're kidding, right?" I turned to Clay. He hadn't moved. "Didn't you hear that? Say something, damn it."

Clay said nothing.

"What are we supposed to do in Toronto?" I asked. "Hide in a hotel room?"

"No, you'll do exactly what you normally do. You'll go back to your apartment, resume your job if you like, pick up the old routines. That's what will keep you safe. Familiarity. You know your apartment building, the routes you walk, the restaurants and stores you frequent. You'll be better able to spot potential danger than you would in an unfamiliar setting. And you'll be comfortable."

"Comfortable?" I sputtered. "I can't take Clay back to my apartment. You damn well know I can't."

Clay's head jerked up, as if snapped out of a deep sleep. "Why can't you?"

As I met his eyes, I realized he didn't know I was living with Philip. I opened my mouth to say something, but the look on his face froze the words in my throat.

"You'll have to get rid of him," Jeremy said. "Call him and tell him to leave."

"Get rid of who? Call—" Clay stopped. A sick look passed over his face. He stared at me for one long moment. Then he got to his feet and walked from the room.

Now, Jeremy had more talents than any person I knew and he was better at each of them than any person I knew. He could speak and translate in over a dozen languages, he could splint a broken bone so it healed as good as new, he could paint scenes I couldn't even imagine, and he could stop a two-hundred-pound charging wolf with a look. But he didn't know shit about romantic relationships.

"Thank you," I said after Nicholas and Antonio slipped out. "Thank you very much."

"He knows about this man," Jeremy said. "I assumed he knew about your living arrangement."

"And in case he didn't? You decided to humiliate him in front of Nick and Tonio?"

"I said, I thought he knew."

"Well, he does now, and you'll have to deal with it. He's not coming to Toronto with me, if I go at all."

"You are and he is. As for this man, he moved in with you, didn't he? It was your apartment first."

I didn't ask how Jeremy knew this. Nor did I answer.

"Then you can ask him to leave," Jeremy said.

"Just pick up the phone, call him, and tell him I'll be home later today and I want him gone by then?"

"I don't see why not."

I gave a harsh laugh. "You don't dump someone you've been living with by phone. You don't sever all ties at a moment's notice. You don't give him a few hours to clear out of the apartment, not without damn good reason."

"You have a good reason."

"That's not—" I stopped and shook my head. "Let me put this in a way you'll understand. If I call him and tell him it's over, he won't leave. He'll want an explanation, and he'll stay until he's satisfied with it. In other words, he'll cause trouble. Is that a good enough reason?"

"Then don't break up with him. Move back in."

"With Clay?! Not in this lifetime. If you have to send a babysitter, send Nick. He'll behave himself."

"Clay knows Toronto. And nothing will distract him from protecting you." Jeremy walked toward the door. "I have you booked on an early afternoon flight."

"I'm not—"

Jeremy was already gone.

Clay was next in line to argue with Jeremy. I didn't eavesdrop, but I would have had to leave the house not to hear them. And since the conversation concerned my future, I didn't see any point in trying *not* to listen. Clay didn't like this arrangement any more than I did. His strongest instinct was to protect his Alpha and he couldn't do that from hundreds of miles away. Unfortunately, the instinct to obey Jeremy was almost equally strong. As I listened to them battle it out—Clay protesting loudly enough to drown out Jeremy's quiet insistence—I prayed Clay would win and we'd be allowed to stay. Jeremy stood firm. I was going and, since Clay had been responsible for bringing me into this life, he was responsible for ensuring I survived it.

I stood in the study and fumed. Then I made up my mind. I wasn't going back to Toronto and I wasn't taking Clay anywhere with me. No one could make me do it.

I walked into the empty hall, grabbed my keys and wallet from the hall table, and headed out the garage door. I started walking to my car, then stopped. Where was I going? Where could I go? If I left, I couldn't go back to Toronto and I couldn't come back to Stonehaven. Instead of choosing between two lives, I'd be abandoning both. My fingers clenched around my keys, digging the metal into my palm hard enough to draw blood. I inhaled and closed my eyes. I couldn't leave, but if I stayed, I'd have to obey Jeremy. No one could have that kind of power over me. I wouldn't let them.

As I walked around the car, I heard the squeak of shoe rubber on concrete and looked up to see Jeremy standing at the passenger door, holding the handle.

"Where are we going?" he asked calmly.

"I'm leaving."

"So I see. As I asked, where are we going?"

"We're not—" I stopped and glanced around the garage.

"Clay's car is right there," Jeremy said, his voice still even and unruffled. "You have the keys, but not the alarm remote. The Explorer's outside. No alarm, but it's about fifty feet away. The Mercedes is closer, but you don't have the keys. Shall we race to the Explorer? Or would you rather bolt down the drive and see if you can outrun me?"

"You can't—"

"Yes, I can. You're not leaving. The cage is downstairs. I won't hesitate to use it."

"This isn't—"

"Yes, it's terribly unfair. I know. No one would do this to you in the human world, would they? They'd understand that you have a right to kill yourself."

"I'm not—"

"If you leave here alone, you're committing suicide. I won't let you do that. Either you go to Toronto with Clay or I'll lock you up here until you agree."

I whipped the keys to the cement floor and turned my back on Jeremy. After a minute of silence, I said, "Don't make me take him. You know how hard I've worked to create a life there. You've always said you'd support that, even if you don't agree with it. Send me someplace else or send someone else with me. Don't make me take Clay. He'll destroy everything."

"No, I won't."

Clay's voice was as soft as Jeremy's, so much so that I hesitated, thinking I'd mistaken Jeremy for Clay. The door to the house clicked shut as Jeremy went inside. I didn't turn to look at Clay.

"Protecting you is the most important thing to me right now," Clay said. "No matter how angry I am, that doesn't change. I am capable of fitting in out there, Elena. Just because I don't do it, doesn't mean I can't. I've studied and practiced fitting in since I was eight years old. For fifteen years, I did nothing but study human behavior. Once I figured it out and knew I could fit in, I stopped trying. Why? Because it's not necessary. So long as I can modify my behavior in public enough that I don't have to worry about being attacked by mobs with silver bullets, that's good enough for Jeremy and the rest of the Pack. If I did more, I'd be betraying myself. I won't do that without reason. But protecting you is reason enough. This man may not think I'm the most pleasant person in the world, but he'll have no reason to think anything worse of me. I won't destroy anything."

"I don't want you there."

"And I don't want to be there. But neither of us has much say in the matter, do we?"

Again, the door clicked. When I turned, Clay was gone. Jeremy was back, holding the door open for me. I glared at him, then averted my gaze and walked into the house without another word.

That afternoon, Clay and I were on a plane to Toronto.

CHAPTER 23

DESCENT

This was going to be a catastrophe.

As the plane gained altitude, my mood plummeted. Why had I let Jeremy do this to me? Did he know he was about to ruin my life? Did he care? How could I bring Clay to the apartment I shared with Philip? I was about to bring the man I'd been sleeping with into the home of the man I'd made a commitment to. I could never believe stories I heard about people sneaking their lover into their homes as a housekeeper, a nanny, a gardener. Anyone who did something like that was morally bankrupt bottom-feeding trash . . . which was a pretty good description of what I thought about myself right then.

I'd called Philip that morning and told him I was bringing a guest home. I'd explained that Clay was my cousin, Jeremy's brother, and he was inter- ested in moving to Toronto, so I'd agreed to put him up for a week or so while he looked for work. Philip was perfectly gracious about the whole thing, though when he'd said he'd like to meet my cousins, I suspected he meant inviting them to dinner, not sharing our tiny apartment.

And what about Clay? Jeremy had to know how much this would hurt him. Again, didn't he care? How were Clay and I supposed to get along under these circumstances? We had to live together in a one-bedroom apartment with none of the Pack to act as a buffer. So far, we hadn't spoken a word to each other since Clay came out to the garage that morning. Thirty minutes from Toronto and we were sitting side by side like strangers.

"Where do you live?" Clay said.

I jumped at the sound of his voice. I glanced over, but he was looking straight ahead, as if talking to the headrest in front of him.

"Where do you live?" he repeated.

"Uh—near the lake," I said. "South of Front Street."

"And work?"

"Bay-Bloor district."

It sounded like idle conversation, but I knew it wasn't. Behind Clay's eyes, his brain ticked, working out the geography and distances.

"Security?" he asked.

"Pretty good. The apartment building has a secured entrance. Nothing fancy. Just keys and a buzz-in system. Dead bolt and chain on my door."

Clay snorted. If a mutt could get past the front door, all the locks in the world wouldn't keep him out of my apartment. I'd once mentioned a security system to Philip, but he thought the only reliable home protection was a good insurance policy. I couldn't tell him I was worried about being attacked. That hardly fit the persona of a woman who took solitary walks at two o'clock in the morning.

"At work there's a first-floor security guard," I said. "You need an ID card to get into my office. Plus it's a busy place. If I stick to regular working hours, no one's going to target me there. I don't even have to go back to work, really . . ."

"Stick to regular routines, like Jeremy said." Clay looked out the window. "So who am I supposed to be?"

"My second cousin. In town looking for work."

"Is that necessary?"

"It sounded good. If you're my cousin, then I'd be obligated to put you up—"

"I meant the looking for work part. I'm not going to be looking for work, Elena, and I don't want some elaborate script to follow. Say I'm in town doing work at the university—my normal work. I'll contact a few people there, stop by the department, maybe do a bit of research. Keep it real."

"Sure, but it would seem easier just to say—"

"I'm not playing a role, Elena. Not any more than I have to."

He faced the window and didn't say anything else for the rest of the flight.

No matter how much I'd brooded during the flight, the full impact of what we were doing didn't hit me until we were in the airport. We'd picked up our luggage and were heading to the taxi stand when I realized I was about to take Clay to the apartment I shared with Philip. My chest constricted, my heart pounded, and by the time we were at the entrance, I was in the middle of a full-blown panic attack.

Clay was a full pace ahead of me. I reached forward and grabbed his arm.

"You don't have to do this," I said.

He didn't look at me. "It's what Jeremy wants."

"But that doesn't mean you *have* to do it. He wants me safe, right? There's got to be another way."

Clay kept his back to me. "I said I'd stay with you. That's what I'm going to do."

"You can do that without going to my apartment."

He stopped and turned just enough so I could see his quarter profile. "How am I supposed to do that? Sleep in the alley outside your building?"

"No, I mean *we* don't have to go to my apartment. We'll go someplace else. A hotel room or something."

"And you'll go with me?"

"Sure. Of course."

"And you'll stay with me?"

"Exactly. Whatever you want."

I could hear the desperation in my voice and despised it, but I couldn't stop myself. My hands were shaking so badly that people around us were starting to stare.

"Whatever you want," I repeated. "Jeremy won't know. He said he won't contact us by phone, so he won't know whether we're staying at the apartment. I'll be safe and you'll be with me. That's what's important, right?"

For nearly a minute, Clay didn't move. Then he slowly turned toward me. As he did, I caught a glint of something like hope in his eyes, but it vanished as soon as he saw my expression. His jaw tightened and he locked my gaze.

"Fine," he said. "Anything I want?" He wheeled toward a bank of pay phones and grabbed the nearest receiver. "Call him."

"He said we can't call him. No phone contact."

"Not Jeremy. This man. Call him and tell him it's over. The apartment's his. You'll pick up your stuff later."

"That's not—"

"Not what you meant, right? I didn't think so. What's the plan then? You run back and forth between us until you've made up your mind?"

"I've made up my mind. Anything that happened at Stonehaven was a mistake, like it's always been a mistake. I never misled you. You knew there was someone else. It was the same damned thing that happens every time I go back to that place. I get caught up in it. I lose myself."

"In what? The house? A pile of bricks and mortar?"

"In that place," I said, gritting my teeth. "That world and everything about it, including you. I don't want it, but when I'm there, I can't resist. It takes over."

He gave a harsh laugh. "Bullshit. There is nothing in this world or that world or any world that you couldn't fight, Elena. Do you know what magical spell 'that place' has you under? It makes you happy. But you won't admit that because, to you, the only acceptable happiness comes in the 'normal' world, with 'normal' friends and a 'normal' man. You're bound and determined to make yourself happy with that kind of life, even if it kills you."

People were openly staring now. Alarm bells should have been going off in my head, telling me I was acting improperly for the human world. But they weren't. I didn't give a damn. I turned on my heel and glared at two elderly women tut-tutting behind me. They fell back, eyes widening. I strode toward the exit.

"When's the last time you called him?" Clay called after me.

I stopped.

Clay walked up behind me and lowered his voice so no one else could hear. "Not counting this morning when you called to tell him we were coming. When did you last call?"

I said nothing.

"Sunday," he said. "Three days ago."

"I've been busy," I said.

"Bullshit. You forgot him. You think he makes you happy? You think this life makes you happy? Well, then here's your chance. Take me there. Show me how happy it makes you. Prove it."

"Screw you," I snarled and strode to the door.

Clay came after me, but he was too late. I was out of the airport and in a cab before he caught up. I slammed the cab door, narrowly missing Clay's fingers, then gave the driver my address. As we pulled away, I allowed myself the small satisfaction of looking in the side mirror and seeing Clay standing on the sidewalk.

Too bad I hadn't been more specific when I told him where I lived. "Near" the lake covered a lot of real estate . . . with a lot of apartment buildings.

When I got to my building, I buzzed up to my apartment. Philip answered, sounding surprised when I announced myself. I hadn't lost my key. Don't ask why I buzzed to be let in. I only hoped Philip wouldn't ask either.

When I got upstairs, Philip was in the hall outside the elevator. He reached out and embraced me. I instinctively stiffened, then hugged him back.

"You should have called from the airport," he said. "I was waiting to pick you up'." He looked over my shoulder. "Where's our guest?"

"Delayed. Maybe indefinitely."

"He's not coming."

I shrugged and feigned a yawn. "Rough flight. Lots of turbulence. You have no idea how glad I am to be home."

"Not as glad as I am to have you home, hon." Philip escorted me into the apartment. "Go sit down. I picked up roast chicken at the deli for dinner. I'll reheat it."

"Thanks."

I didn't even have my shoes off when someone pounded at the door. I thought of ignoring it, but it wouldn't do any good. Philip may not have had my sense of hearing, but he wasn't deaf.

I yanked open the door. Clay stood there holding our luggage.

"How did you—" I started.

He held up my overnight bag. Dangling from the handle was the tag with my name and address neatly printed on it.

"Pizza delivery kid held open the front door for me," he said. "Great security."

He walked in and threw our luggage by the coat rack. Behind me, the kitchen door opened. I tensed and listened to Philip's footsteps as he approached. The introduction jammed in my throat. What if Clay didn't go along with it? Was it too late to change my story? Was it too late to shove him out the door?

"You must be Elena's cousin," Philip said, walking up and extending a hand.

"Clay," I managed to get out. "Clayton."

Philip smiled. "Nice to meet you. Which do you prefer? Clayton or Clay?"

Clay said nothing. He didn't even glance at Philip, hadn't looked at him since he'd entered the room. Instead, he kept his eyes on mine. I could see the anger simmering there with the outrage and the humiliation. I braced for the outburst. It didn't come. Instead, he settled for unconscionable rudeness, ignoring Philip, his greeting, his question, and his outstretched hand, and striding into the living room.

Philip's smile faltered only a second, then he turned to Clay, who stood at the window with his back to us. "The sofa bed's right there," he said, waving at the couch, where he'd left a pile of bedding. "I hope it's not too uncomfortable. It's never been used, has it, hon?"

Clay's jaw tightened, but he kept looking out the window.

"No," I said. I struggled to think of something to add, some elaboration or change of subject, but nothing came.

"We're *supposed* to have a lake view," Philip said with a forced chuckle. "I think if you stand three paces to the left of the window between one and two in the afternoon, turn right, and squint a certain way, you can see a sliver of Lake Ontario. At least, that's the theory."

Still Clay said nothing. Neither did I. Silence deadened the room, as if Philip were talking into a vacuum, his words leaving no echo or impression.

Philip continued, "The other side of the building has a better view of Toronto. It's a great city, really. World-class amenities with a decent cost of living, low crime rate, clean streets. Maybe I can get off work a few hours early tomorrow and take you for a driving tour before Elena gets home."

"Not necessary," Clay said. The words came out so tightly clipped that his accent was lost, making him sound like a stranger.

"Clay used to live in Toronto," I said. "For a while. A—uh—few years ago."

"How'd you like it?" Philip asked. When Clay didn't answer, he forced another chuckle. "You came back, so I guess it wasn't a totally bad experience."

Clay turned and looked at me. "It has good memories."

He held my gaze for a moment, then broke eye contact and stalked into the bathroom. Within seconds, I heard the shower running.

"Just help yourself to the shower," I muttered, rolling my eyes. "Mr. Congeniality, eh?"

Philip smiled. "So it's not jet lag?"

"I wish. I should have warned you. Undiagnosed antisocial personality disorder. Don't take that crap from him while he's here. Either ignore him or tell him where to shove it."

Philip's eyebrows went up. At first I thought it was because of my description of Clay, but as Philip stared at me, I replayed what I'd said and heard the sarcasm and bite. Not the Elena Philip was used to. Damn Clay.

"Just kidding," I said. "It was a long flight with him. By the time we got to the airport, I lost my temper and we had a bit of a falling out."

"Lost your temper?" Philip said, walking over to kiss my forehead. "I didn't think you had one."

"Clayton brings out the worst in me. With any luck, he won't be here long. He's family, though, so I have to put up with it until then." I turned toward the kitchen and made a show of sniffing the air. "Smells like that chicken's done."

"Should we wait for your cousin?"

"He wouldn't wait for us," I said and headed to the kitchen.

The only good thing I can say about that evening was that it was short. Clay came out of the shower (dressed, thankfully), walked into the living room, and pulled one of my books from the shelf. We were still eating. I went into the living room and told him so. He grunted that he'd eat later and I left it at that. By the time we'd eaten and cleaned up, it was late enough for me to claim exhaustion and head off to bed. Philip followed and I quickly realized I'd forgotten one small thing about the living arrangement. Sex.

I was putting on my nightgown when Philip walked in. Now, I wasn't big on nighttime fashion, having slept in my underwear since I left my last foster family, but when Philip moved in and I noticed he wore pajama bottoms to bed, I figured maybe I was expected to wear something, too. I tried lingerie, all those sexy, skimpy things the women's magazines rave over. But the damned lace itched in places I'd never itched before and the elastic pinched and the shoulder straps twisted, and I decided maybe such nightwear was only meant to be worn before sex and discarded for something more comfortable afterward. Since Philip didn't get excited by black lace and red satin, anyway, I'd pitched the stuff and settled for oversized T-shirts. Then, for Christmas, Philip had bought me a white knee-length nightgown. It was very feminine and old-fashioned and a tad too virginal for my taste, but Philip liked it, so I wore it.

Philip waited until I started brushing my hair, then walked up behind me, leaned over, and kissed the side of my neck.

"I missed you," he murmured against my skin. "I didn't want to complain, but it was a longer separation than I expected. A few days more and you'd have had a guest in New York."

I covered a choking fit with an awkward wheezing laugh. Philip in Bear Valley. That was a scenario even more hellish than the one I was enduring now.

Philip's lips moved to the back of my neck. He pressed against me. One hand slipped under my nightgown and pushed it up to my hip. I stiffened. Without thinking I glanced at the bedroom door. Philip's gaze followed mine through the mirror.

"Ah," he said with a chuckle. "I forgot about our guest. We could keep it quiet, but if you'd rather wait for a more private moment . . ."

I nodded. Philip kissed my neck again, gave a mock sigh, and headed for the bed. I knew I should curl up in bed with him, cuddle, talk. But I couldn't.

I just couldn't.

This was going to be a catastrophe.

CHAPTER 24

SETTLING

The next morning I awoke to the smell of French toast and bacon. I checked the clock. Nearly nine. Philip was normally gone by seven. He must have stayed late to make breakfast. A very pleasant surprise.

I padded out of the bedroom and into the kitchen. Clay stood at the stove, ramming a spatula under a mountain of bacon. He turned as I walked in. His eyes traveled over my nightgown.

"What the hell is that?" he asked.

"A nightgown."

"You sleep in it?"

"If I didn't, it would be a day-gown, wouldn't it?" I snapped.

Clay's lips quivered as if choking back a laugh. "It's very . . . sweet, darling. It looks like something Jeremy would buy you. Oh, by the way. He sent flowers."

"Jeremy?"

Clay shook his head. "They're by the front door."

I walked into the hall to find a dozen red roses in a silver-plated vase. The card read: "Thought I'd let you sleep in. Welcome home. Missed you. Philip."

See? Nothing had changed. Philip was as thoughtful as ever. Smiling, I picked up the vase and looked for a place to put it. The living room table? No, the flowers were too tall. Leave it on the hall table? Too crowded. The kitchen? I opened the door. No room.

"Bedroom," I murmured and backed out.

"Water," Clay called after me.

"What?"

"They need water."

"I knew that."

"And sunlight," he added.

I didn't answer. I'd have remembered water and sun . . . eventually. I must admit, I'd never quite understood the custom of sending flowers.

Sure, they looked nice, but they didn't *do* anything. That's not to say I didn't appreciate them. I did. Jeremy always cut fresh flowers from the garden and put them in my room and I enjoyed them. Of course, if he didn't place them in the sunlight and keep them watered, I wouldn't have enjoyed them for long. I was far better at killing things than keeping them alive. Good thing I never planned to have children.

After watering and placing the roses, I went back into the kitchen. Clay put two pieces of French toast on my plate and lifted a third.

"That's good," I said, pulling my plate back.

He arched both eyebrows.

"I mean, that's good for now," I said. "Of course, I'll have more after I finish these."

"Is that all you eat when he's here? I'm surprised you make it to work without fainting. You can't eat like that, Elena. Your metabolism needs—"

I pushed my chair back. Clay stopped talking and dished out my bacon, then fixed his own plate and sat down.

"What time do you start work?" he asked.

"I called last night and said I'd be there by ten-thirty."

"We'd better move then. How long a walk is it? Thirty minutes?"

"I take the subway."

"Subway? You hate the subway. All those people stuffed in that tiny car, getting jostled around by strangers, and the smell—"

"I've gotten used to it."

"Why bother? It's an easy walk, over to Bloor and straight up."

"People don't walk to work," I said. "They bicycle, they Rollerblade, they jog. I don't own a bike or blades and I can't jog in a skirt."

"You wear skirts to work? You hate skirts."

I shoved my plate aside and left the table.

I tried to convince Clay that he could walk to my office and let me take the subway alone. He wouldn't have it. For the sake of my safety and in accordance with the express will of his leader, he would suffer through the torture of the underground train. I must admit I took a bit too much pleasure in watching him squirm throughout the excruciating seven-minute ride. Not that he literally squirmed. Anyone watching him would have seen a man standing in the crowded car, impatiently tracking our progress on the overhead map. But deep in his gaze, I could see the look of a caged animal, claustrophobia tinged with equal parts revulsion and impending panic. Every time someone brushed against him, he clenched the pole a bit tighter. He breathed through his mouth and kept his eyes on the map, looking away only to check the name of each station as the train slowed to a stop. Once he glanced at me. I smiled and made a show of relaxing in my seat. With a glare, he turned away and ignored me for the rest of the trip.

I had lunch with coworkers. As we were returning, I saw a familiar figure sitting on a bench outside my office building. I made some excuse for not going inside and circled back to Clay.

"What's wrong?" I asked as I came up behind him.

He turned and smiled. "Hey, darling. Good lunch?"

"What are you doing here?"

"Guarding you, remember?"

I paused. "Please don't tell me you've been sitting here all morning."

"'Course. I didn't figure I'd be welcome in your office."

"You can't just sit here."

"Why not? Oh, let me guess. Normal people don't sit on street benches. Don't worry, darling. If I see any cops, I'll switch to the bench across the road."

I glanced toward the building, making sure no one I knew was coming out. "I don't work in my office all day, you know. I'm covering a rally at Queen's Park this afternoon."

"So I'll come along. At a safe distance, making sure you don't have to endure the horror of publicly associating with me."

"You mean you'll stalk me."

Clay grinned. "A skill that can always use improvement."

"You can't just sit here."

"Back around we go . . ."

"At least *do* something. Read a book, a newspaper, a magazine."

"Sure, and let some mutt sneak past while I'm doing the daily crossword."

I threw up my hands and stalked into the building. Five minutes later, I returned to his bench.

"Miss me already?" he asked.

I dropped a magazine over his shoulder and onto his lap. He picked it up, glanced at the cover, and frowned.

"*Rod World?*"

"It's about cars. A good guy kinda magazine. At least pretend to read it."

He flipped through the pages, stopping on a photo of a bikini-clad redhead sprawled over the hood of a Corvette Stingray. He scanned the text, then examined the picture.

"What's the woman doing there?" he asked.

"Covering a scratch on the hood. She was cheaper than a new paint job."

He flipped through a few more pages of barely dressed women and classic cars. "Nick used to have magazines like this when we were kids. But without the cars." He rotated a photo sideways. "Or the bathing suits."

"Just pretend you're reading it, okay?" I said, turning back toward the doors. "You never know. Maybe I'll get lucky and you'll find something you like."

"I thought you liked my car."

I started walking away. "I wasn't talking about the cars."

After dinner, Clay and I hung out at the apartment and played cards. By the time Philip got home, I was ahead thirty dollars and fifty cents. I'd just won my fourth game in a row and was most immaturely crowing over it when Philip walked in. As soon as Philip asked to join us, Clay decided it was shower time again. At this rate, he was going to be the cleanest guy in Toronto. Philip and I played a few rounds together, but it wasn't the same. Philip didn't play for money. Worse yet, he expected me to abide by the rules.

That night, Jeremy contacted me to see if we were okay. Although he'd forbidden phone calls, that didn't mean we were out of touch. As I've said before, Jeremy had his own way of contacting us through a sort of nighttime psychic connection. All werewolves have some degree of psychic power. Most of them ignore it, finding it far too mystical for creatures accustomed to communicating with fists and fangs.

Clay and I shared a type of mental bond, maybe because he bit me. Not that we could read each other's minds or anything so earth-shattering. It was more like the heightened awareness of each other that twins often claim to experience, little things like feeling a twinge when he was injured or knowing when he was nearby even if I couldn't see, hear, or smell him. The whole thing made me uncomfortable, though, so it wasn't a skill I cultivated or even admitted to.

Jeremy's ability was different. He could communicate with us while we were sleeping. It wasn't like hearing voices in my head or anything so dramatic. I'd be sleeping and I'd have a dream about talking to him, but I'd subconsciously sense it was more than a dream, and I could listen and respond rationally. Quite cool, actually, though I'd never say so to Jeremy.

I awoke to the smell of pancakes. This time, I knew exactly who was making breakfast and I didn't mind. Food was food. For me, nothing beat a ready-made breakfast. I couldn't cook in the morning. By the time I got up, I was too hungry to mess with stoves and frying pans—sometimes even the toaster took too long. Even better than having someone cook breakfast for me was being able to crawl out of bed and go straight to the table, skipping shower, clothes, hair and teeth brushing, all those things necessary to make me a suitable eating companion. With Clay, it didn't matter. He'd seen worse. I buried myself under the covers. When breakfast was ready, Clay would bring me a coffee. All I had to do was wait.

"This is really great. We don't get pancakes very often. Elena's not much of a breakfast person. Cold cereal and toast usually. I'm not sure she'll eat this, but I know I will."

I bolted upright. That was not Clay's voice.

"What do they call these in the South?" Philip continued. "Flapjacks? Johnnycakes? I can never keep it straight. That is where you're from, right? Originally, I mean. With that accent, I'm guessing Georgia, maybe Tennessee."

Clay grunted. I leapt out of bed and ran for the door. Then I caught a glimpse of my nightgown in the mirror. A housecoat. I needed a housecoat.

"Your brother Jeremy doesn't have an accent," Philip said. "At least, I didn't notice it when I spoke to him on the phone."

Shit! I rummaged through the closet. Where was that housecoat? Did I own a housecoat?

"My stepbrother," Clay said.

"Oh? Oh, I see. That makes sense."

I grabbed clothing and yanked it on, wheeling out of the bedroom and through the kitchen door. I skidded to a halt between Clay and Philip.

"Hungry?" Clay asked, still facing the stove.

Philip leaned over, kissed my cheek, and tried to smooth my tangled hair. "Make sure you call Mom this morning, hon. She didn't want to go ahead with Becky's shower plans without you." He looked over at Clay. "My family is crazy about Elena. If I don't marry her soon, they're liable to adopt her."

His gaze lingered on Clay. Clay flipped three pancakes onto a growing stack, turned, and carried them to the table, face expressionless. A frown flickered across Philip's lips. Probably tired of making small talk and not getting any response.

"The butter's in the—" Philip started, but Clay already had the fridge open. "Oh, and the syrup is over the stove in the cup—"

Clay pulled from the refrigerator a fancy glass bottle of maple syrup, the kind sold in tourist shops for the price of liquid gold.

"That's new," I said, smiling over at Philip. "When did you pick it up?"

"I—uh—didn't."

I glanced at Clay.

"Grabbed it yesterday," he said.

"Oh, I'm not sure Elena likes—" Philip stopped, eyes going from me to Clay and back again. "Yes, well, that was very nice."

The phone rang, rescuing me from a fruitless struggle for something to say.

"I'll get it," Philip said, and vanished into the living room.

"Thank you," I hissed at Clay, keeping my voice low. "You just had to do that, didn't you? First breakfast, then the syrup. Make a big deal out of knowing what I like and embarrass him."

"Make a big deal? I didn't say a word. You brought up the syrup."

"You wouldn't have?"

"'Course not. Why would I? I'm not competing here, Elena. I noticed when I made French toast yesterday that you didn't have real syrup. I know how you complain about the fake stuff, so I figured you were out and bought you some."

"And breakfast? Tell me you weren't saying something by making me breakfast."

"Sure, I was saying something. I was saying that I'm concerned you're not eating right and wanted to make sure you got at least one decent meal. As your guest, I'm sure he only thinks I was trying to be helpful. I made enough for him."

"You made enough for the whole build—" I stopped, looking around and realizing there was only enough food out to feed three normal people.

"The rest is in the oven," Clay said. "I hid it when I heard him wake up. I'll pack it for you to take to work. If anyone comments, you can say you missed breakfast."

I struggled for something to say and, again, was saved by an interruption, this time by Philip coming back into the kitchen.

"Work," he said, pulling a face. "What else? Plan to come in late one morning and they call looking for me. Don't worry, hon. I said I'm having breakfast with you and I'll be in afterward." He pulled out a chair, sat down, and turned to Clay. "So, how's that job search going?"

I'd agreed to meet Clay for lunch. He bought a picnic box from a nearby deli and we went to the university grounds to eat. Going to the university wasn't my choice. I didn't even realize that was where we were headed until we got there. Although I worked only a few blocks away from the U of T, I hadn't visited the campus in all the months I'd been at the magazine. Nor had I gone there in all the times I'd visited Toronto in the past ten years. The university was where I'd met Clay, where I'd fallen in love. It was also the place where I'd been deceived, lied to, and ultimately betrayed. When I realized where Clay was headed for lunch that day, I balked. I thought up a dozen excuses and a dozen alternate places to eat. But none of them reached my mouth. Remembering what he'd said about Stonehaven, I was too embarrassed to admit I didn't want to go to the university. It was only a place, a "pile of bricks and mortar." Maybe there was more to it than embarrassment, though. Maybe I didn't want to admit how much emotional resonance that particular brick and mortar pile held for me. Maybe I didn't want him to know how much I remembered and how much I cared. So I said nothing.

We sat on benches beside University College. Exams were finishing up and only a handful of students sauntered around King's College Circle, the rush of classes a fading memory. A group of young men played touch football inside the circle, spring jackets and knapsacks abandoned in a heap near the goalpost. As we ate, Clay talked about his paper on jaguar cults in South America and my mind floated backward, remembering past conversations under these trees, between these buildings. I could picture Clay all those years before, sitting at a picnic table across the road in Queen's Park, eating lunch and talking, his focus so completely on the two of us that Frisbees could whiz over his head and he'd never notice. He always sat in the same pose, legs stretched out until his feet hooked behind mine beneath the table, hands moving constantly, flexing and emphasizing, as if some part of him always had to be moving. His voice sounded the same, now so familiar that I could follow the beat in my head, predicting each change of tone, each note of accentuation.

Even back then, he'd wanted to know my thoughts and opinions on everything. No flitting of my young mind was too trivial or boring for him. In time, I'd told him about my past, my aspirations, my fears, my hopes, and my insecurities, all the things I'd never imagined sharing with anyone.

I'd always been afraid of opening up to anyone. I'd wanted to be a strong, independent woman, not some damaged waif with a background straight out of the worst Dickensian melodrama. I hid my background or, if some-one found out, pretended it hadn't made a difference, hadn't affected me. With Clay, all that had changed. I'd wanted him to know everything about me, so I could be sure he knew what I was and that he loved me anyway. He'd listened and he'd stayed. More than that, he'd reciprocated. He'd told me about his childhood, losing his parents in some trauma he couldn't remember, being adopted, not fitting in at school, being ridiculed and shunned, getting into trouble and being expelled so often he seemed to go through schools the way I'd gone through foster parents. He'd told me so much that I'd been sure I knew him completely. Then I'd found out how wrong I'd been. Sometimes that deception hurt worse than being bitten.

CHAPTER 25

TURBULENCE

When Philip returned from work it was past midnight. Clay and I were watching a late movie. I was stretched out on the couch. Clay was on the recliner, hogging the popcorn. Philip walked in, stood behind the sofa, and watched the screen for a few minutes.

"Horror?" he said. "You know, I haven't seen a horror flick since I was in university." He walked around the couch and sat beside me. "What's this one?"

"*Evil Dead II,*" I said, reaching for the remote. "I'm sure there's something else on."

"No, no. Leave it." He looked at Clay. "You like horror films?"

Clay was silent a moment, then grunted something noncommittal.

"Clay's not keen on horror," I said. "Too much violence. He's very squeamish. I have to switch channels if things get gory."

Clay snorted.

"This one's pure camp," I said to Philip. "It's a sequel. Horror sequels suck."

"*Scream 2,*" Clay said.

"That's an exception only because the writers knew that sequels suck and played it up."

"Uh-uh," Clay said. "The idea—" He stopped, glanced at Philip who was following our conversation like a Ping-Pong tournament, and stuffed a handful of popcorn into his mouth.

"Pass it over," I said.

"I bought it."

"And cooked it in my microwave. Pass it."

"There's two more bags in the kitchen."

"I want that one. Pass it over."

He tossed the bowl onto the table and booted it toward me with his foot.

"It's empty!" I said.

Philip laughed. "I can tell you two knew each other as kids."

Silence ticked by. Then Clay heaved himself to his feet.

"I'll be in the shower," he said.

The next day was Saturday. Philip went golfing, leaving before I woke up. Golf was one sport I avoided. It demanded too little of me physically and too much behaviorally. Last fall, I'd agreed to try it, so Philip gave me two lists of course rules. One was on how to play the sport. The other was on how to dress and behave while playing the sport. Now, I was well aware that certain sports required certain modes of dress for protection, but I failed to see how wearing a sleeveless blouse on the course qualified as a safety hazard. God forbid the sight of my bare shoulders should send male golfers into a tizzy, knocking balls everywhere. I had enough to worry about in life without measuring the length of my shorts to see if they complied to course standards. Besides, after a couple rounds with Philip, I discovered golf really wasn't my thing. Whacking the hell out of a ball was great for working off aggression, but apparently it wasn't the point of the game. So Philip golfed. I didn't.

After golf, the three of us went out for lunch, undoubtedly marking the first time in ten years that I haven't enjoyed a meal. For twenty excruciating minutes, Philip tried to engage Clay in conversation. He'd have had better luck addressing his salad. To save him, I started a running monologue, which I then had to sustain until the bill arrived, thirty-eight minutes and twenty seconds later. At that point, Clay miraculously regained his voice, suggesting that we walk back to the apartment, knowing full well that we'd brought Philip's car, which meant Philip would have to drive back alone. Before I could argue, Philip suddenly remembered he had some work to do at the office, so if we didn't mind walking back, he'd drive straight there. This agreed, both men bolted for the exit like escaping convicts, leaving me to scrounge up the tip.

Sunday morning, while Philip golfed, Clay and I did the boring weekly chores like cleaning, laundry, and grocery shopping. When we returned from getting groceries, there was a message from Philip on the machine. I called him back.

"How was your game?" I asked when he answered.

"Not good. I was calling about dinner."

"You're not going to make it?"

"Actually, I wanted to ask you out for dinner. Something nice." He paused. "Just the two of us."

"Great."

"That's not a problem?"

"Not at all. Clay can fend for himself. He hates fancy meals. Besides, he didn't bring any dress-up clothes."

"What does he wear for interviews?"

Whoops. "It's academic," I said. "Very laid-back."

"Good." Another pause. "After dinner I thought we could take in a show. Maybe find half-price same-day tickets to something."

"Might not be easy on a holiday weekend, but we can manage something."

"I thought we'd"—throat clear—"go alone. The two of us."

"That's what I figured. Do you want me to make reservations? Get the tickets?"

"No, I'll handle it. I should be there by six. You might want to tell Clayton we'll be late getting in tonight. Dinner, a show, drinks or coffee afterward."

"Sounds great."

Philip was silent a moment, as if expecting me to say more. When I didn't he said good-bye and we signed off.

Dinner was another nightmare meal. Not that anything went wrong. I almost wished it had. If our reservations had been given away or if our food had arrived cold, at least we'd have had something to talk about. Instead, we sat for over an hour acting like two people on a first date after it became clear there wouldn't be a second. We didn't seem to know what to say to each other. Oh, we talked. Philip told me about the lakeside condo campaign he was working on. I told an amusing little story about a gaffe the premier had made at the latest scrum. We discussed Toronto's ideas for rejuvenating the harbor front. We complained about the latest talk of TTC fare increases. We discussed the Jays' early chances for the pennant race. In short, we talked about everything two near-strangers would discuss over dinner. Worse yet, we discussed these topics with the desperation of near-strangers terrified of dead silence. By dessert, we'd run out of subjects. Behind us, three men barely past acne were trumpeting their success with dot-com stocks loud enough that people on the street would know about their good fortune. I was about to make some eye-rolling comment to Philip, then stopped myself. I wasn't sure how he'd react. Would my remark sound overly negative? Snide? It was the sort of observation Clay would appreciate. But Philip? I wasn't sure, so I kept quiet.

As the server refilled our coffees, Philip cleared his throat.

"So," he said. "How much longer do you expect your cousin will be with us?"

"A few days probably. Is that a problem? I know he can be a jerk—"

"No, no. That's not it." He managed a wan smile. "I must say, he's not the most pleasant company, but I'll survive. It's just been . . . strange."

"Strange?"

Philip shrugged. "I guess it's because you two have known each other so long. There's a real . . . I don't know. I sense . . ." He shook his head. "It's just me, hon. I'm feeling a bit left out. Not the most mature response in the world. I don't know . . ." He tapped his fingers against his coffee cup, then met my eyes. "Was there something . . . ?" He trailed off.

"What?"

"Never mind." A sip of coffee. "Is he having any luck finding work?"

"He's setting some things in motion at U of T. Once that's a go, he'll move out."

"So he's staying in Toronto?"

"For a while."

Philip opened his mouth, hesitated, then took another swig of coffee.

"So," he said. "Did you hear Mayor Mel's latest pronouncement?"

We hadn't been able to get last-minute tickets for any decent shows, so we ended up seeing a movie instead, then going to a jazz bar for drinks. By the time we returned to the apartment, it was almost two. Clay wasn't there. While Philip went into the bedroom to get his cell phone and retrieve messages, Clay wheeled in the door, cheeks flushed.

"Hey," he said, gaze darting past me to look for Philip.

"He's in the bedroom," I said. "Did you go for a run?"

"Without you?"

Clay walked into the kitchen. Seconds later he returned with a bottle of water, uncapped it, gulped half, and held the rest out to me. I shook my head.

"Please tell me you were exercising downstairs in the gym," I said.

Clay took another drink of water.

"Damn you," I muttered, dropping onto the sofa. "You promised you wouldn't follow me tonight."

"No, you told me not to follow you. I didn't answer. My job here is to protect you. That's what I'm gonna do, darling."

"I don't need—"

Philip reappeared from the bedroom. "Bad news." He looked from Clay to me. "Oh, am I interrupting something?"

Clay guzzled his water and headed for the kitchen.

"What's the bad news?" I asked.

"Emergency meeting tomorrow." He sighed. "Yes, it's Victoria Day. I know. I'm really sorry, hon. But I called Blake and bumped our golf game up to eight o'clock, so I'll have time to play and take you out to lunch before the meeting. I'd really hoped to spend more time with you this weekend."

I shrugged. "No big deal. Clay and I can keep ourselves amused."

Philip hesitated, seemed ready to say something, then glanced toward the kitchen and shut his mouth.

At noon Monday, as I waited for Philip to pick me up, he called to say there'd been a mix-up at the golf course and his party had been over an hour late teeing off. They'd just finished their game. So, no lunch date.

After Philip called, Clay and I decided to hike to Chinatown for lunch. We spent the rest of the day slacking off, discovering unexplored neighborhoods, looping down residential streets, then jogging along the beach before returning to the apartment with supplies for a steak dinner. Around seven someone buzzed the apartment. I was in the washroom, so I yelled for Clay to get it. When I came out, he was holding another vase of flowers, this time a mix of irises in an earthenware jar.

"He's sorry for missing lunch," Clay said. "You want them in the bedroom with the others?"

I stopped, watching him hold the flowers and waiting.

"Say it," I said.

"Say what?"

I snatched the flowers from his hand. "I know what you're thinking. If he really regretted it, he'd have cut his golf game short."

"I wasn't going to say that."

"You were thinking it."

"No, you were. You said it."

I marched toward the bedroom.

"Water," he called after me.

With a growl, I veered into the bathroom. I sloshed water into the pot, dislodging a bunch of green marbles. Three plinked into the sink, more onto the floor. I scooped the ones from the sink, gave a cursory look for the others, and decided to leave them for cleaning day.

"Unlike some people," I said as I strode back into the hall, "Philip doesn't feel the necessity for a couple to lead their lives joined at the hip. That's fine with me. At least he sends flowers."

Silence returned from the living room. I plunked the vase on my night-stand, beside the roses, and stalked back to Clay. He was perched on the sofa back, reading the rough notes I'd brought home from work Friday.

"Say it," I said.

He glanced up from the notes. "Say what?"

"You've been waiting all week to tell me what you think of Philip. Go ahead. Get it out."

"My honest opinion?"

I gritted my teeth. "Yes."

"You sure?"

I ground my teeth. "Yes."

"I think he's a decent guy."

My teeth were starting to hurt. "What's that supposed to mean?"

"Exactly what I said, darling. I think he's a decent guy. Not perfect, but who is? He obviously cares for you. He tries to be considerate. He's very patient. If I were him, I'd have kicked my ass out of here days ago. He's been nothing but polite. A nice guy."

"But what?"

"But it's not going to work." He held up a hand against my protest. "Come on, Elena. You do know why you've picked this guy, right? I don't mean because you're looking for a home and a family and all that. You think I don't know that's what you want? I do. And I'd tell you it's right under your nose, but you wouldn't listen. The question is: why have you picked this particular guy to fulfill those fantasies? You do know, don't you, darling?"

"Because he's a good man. He's—"

"Good and patient and caring. Doesn't that remind you of someone?"

"Not you."

Clay slid off the couch back, laughing. "Definitely not me." He laid my portfolio on the table and studied my face. "You really don't get it, do you, darling? Well, when you do, you'll know why it can't work. You can care for this guy, but it'll never be what we have. It can't be. As decent as he is, you've picked him for all the wrong reasons."

"You're wrong."

He shrugged. "Always a first time. How about those steaks? The barbeque should be ready. Pass them to me and you can get the veggies cooking."

We went for a long walk after dinner. When we got back to the apartment, Philip had stopped by and left a note on the table saying the partners had invited him to a meeting in Montreal the next morning. He'd stopped by to pack an overnight bag and was already on a train to Quebec.

"So he'll be gone all night?" Clay asked, leaning over my shoulder to read the note.

"Looks that way."

"Damn shame. Guess we'll have to find something else to do." He walked over to the calendar. "Let's see. Six days since you Changed. Eight for me. You know what that means."

Time for a run.

CHAPTER 26

FIREWORKS

We debated whether to drive or walk to the ravine. Although it was a long hike, neither of us minded walking there—it was walking back after an exhausting run that wasn't nearly so appealing. We'd almost agreed to drive when I made the mistake of mentioning that the car belonged to Philip, and Clay decided it was such a beautiful night it would be a crime not to walk. I didn't argue. Taking Philip's car was often more bother than it was worth. Finding an overnight parking spot near the ravine was tough and I was always worried I'd get ticketed or towed and would have to explain to Philip what I was doing in that part of town in the middle of the night.

It was midnight when we got to the ravine. We split up. I found a thicket and undressed. As I crouched to start my Change, I was struck by something I'd never felt before, at least not in Toronto. I was getting ready for my Change with all the mental preparation that I'd use brushing my teeth. While my brain was occupied with other thoughts, my body was moving into position as if what I was doing was the most natural thing in the world. Now after ten years the routine should've become pretty automatic and it did . . . when I was with the Pack or at Stonehaven. Not that it hurt any less, but mentally, the transition was smooth. One minute I was human, the next I was a wolf. No big deal— I'm a werewolf, right? Yet Changing here in Toronto was another matter. Ninety-five percent of the time I lived like any normal human. I got up, went to work, took the subway home, ate dinner, spent the evening with my boyfriend, and went to bed. A perfectly normal routine interrupted by the occasional need to change into a wolf, run through the woods, hunt down a rabbit, and bay at the moon. The juxtaposition was so jarring that I often got to the ravine, took off my clothes, and stood naked thinking I'm supposed to be doing *what*? I half expected to get down on my knees, concentrate on Changing, and have nothing happen . . . except maybe to wake up wearing a straitjacket with a nice doctor telling me for the millionth time that people cannot change into wolves.

When I started getting into position that night, it felt perfectly natural. That probably had a lot to do with Clay being there. He was like a bridge between the worlds. If he was there, I couldn't forget what I was. Not that this was a big surprise. The shock was that I didn't mind, even that I felt good about it. For so long, I'd been trying to suppress that side of my nature, certain that I had to become someone else to fit into the human world. Now I was seeing the possibility of another option. Maybe Clay was right. Maybe I was trying too hard, making things more difficult for myself than necessary. With Clay around, it was nearly impossible to maintain the "human" Elena persona for long. I'd been my usual self—snappish, willful, argumentative. And the earth hadn't crashed and burned around me. Maybe I didn't have to be the "good" Elena, nice and demure and quiet. Not that I should start flying into a rage when Philip left the toilet seat up or sucker punching strangers who stepped on my feet in the subway, but maybe I didn't have to back down every time a confrontation threatened. If I let some aspects of my normal personality slip into my "human" persona, living in the human world might be easier, might even come to feel natural. Perhaps that was the key.

The bushes rustled, snapping me back to reality. I caught a glimpse of Clay's fur passing by the thicket. He gave a low growl of impatience. I laughed and dropped back into position to start my Change, thinking how odd it was that the person who most loathed the human world might be the one who most helped me live in it. Clay growled again and poked his muzzle into the clearing.

"Hold on," I said.

I shook my head, clearing it, then prepared for the Change.

After our run, we Changed back and lay in a grassy clearing, resting and talking. It was the darkest and quietest part of the night, long after evening had passed and still long before dawn arrived. Despite the chill in the air, neither of us had dressed. The run had pumped our blood so hot we could probably lie in a snowdrift until sunrise and not notice. I lay on my back, luxuriating in the sensation of the cool wind against my skin. Overhead, the trees blocked out the stars and moon. Only enough light filtered in to keep total darkness at bay.

"Got something for you," Clay said after we'd rested a while. He reached behind him into the darkness, pulled two long wire rods from his discarded jacket, and flourished them over his head.

I sat up. "You brought sparklers?"

"This is a fireworks weekend up here, isn't it? Did you think I'd forget your sparklers?"

I loved sparklers. Okay, I was probably the only thirty-year-old in the world who got giddy over sulfur-coated sticks, but I didn't care. At least, I didn't care when Clay was around. He didn't know that grown people didn't normally play with sparklers and I didn't care to enlighten him. One of my few memories of my parents was of a Canada Day party. I only knew that it was Canada Day because, in my memory, I could see a cake in the shape of the flag. I also saw fireworks, lots of fireworks. I heard music and laughter. I smelled sulfur and old camp blankets. I remembered my father handing me a sparkler, my first. I remembered my mother and me dancing barefoot on wet grass, waving the sparklers like magic wands, giggling and spinning around, watching the trail of fairy light we left behind.

Clay pulled a book of matches from his jacket and lit the first sparkler. I scrambled to my feet and took it. Sparks of orange shot out in a star, sizzling and sputtering. Lifting it, I drew an experimental line through the air. Too slow. I did it quicker and the image stayed for a few seconds, a line of fire in the darkness. I spun it in a circle, watching the sparks flash and spin. I wrote my name in the sky, the first E vanishing before I finished the A. I tried it again, faster. This time my name hung there for an eye-blink.

"Almost done," Clay called after me. "Throw it and make a wish."

"That's birthday candles," I said. "Only you blow them out, you don't throw them."

"You threw them once. Cake and all."

"I threw them at you. And the only wish I made can't be repeated."

Clay laughed. "Well, you always throw the sparklers, so you might as well make a wish. A new werewolf superstition."

As I drew my arm back, the sparkler winked out. Clay lit the other one and handed it to me. I lifted it over my head and spun a figure eight, then brought my arm down and twirled around so fast I nearly tripped over Clay. He laughed and put a hand on the back of my calf to steady me. When I recovered, he didn't take his hand away. I looked down at him, lying on his back beneath me.

"I love you," he said.

I blinked and froze.

"Bad timing?" he said with a small smile. He took his hand off my leg. "Better?"

"I—" I started, then stopped. I didn't know what I'd been going to say, didn't know what I wanted to say.

"I'm not trying to seduce you, Elena. The run, the sparklers, they're not leading up to anything. The last few days, I've been trying to keep things easy for you. No tricks. No pressure. I want you to see things clearly. When you do, you'll be able to make your choice. The right choice."

"Which would be you."

He waved a hand at my sparkler. "Better hurry up. It's almost gone. That's the last one until next fireworks day."

I looked down to see that the glow had almost reached the end of the sparkler. I looked up into the trees above, then pulled back my arm and threw it high. The glowing ember shot into the sky, arced, then came tumbling down, end over end like a falling star. I glanced down at Clay. He was watching the sparkler and grinning with as much childlike joy as I'd felt, dancing around the grove with my fairy wand. I looked back up at the light, closed my eyes, and made my wish.

I wished I knew what I wanted.

CHAPTER 27

POSSIBILITIES

We slept in the forest until dawn, then dressed and headed out before morning hikers and joggers intruded on our domain. We found a tiny bistro near Yonge and had breakfast on the front patio. Business was brisk, but it was all takeout, commuters stopping to grab a double espresso and biscotti on the way to the office. No one had time to stop and sit. We had the patio to ourselves and the staff left us alone even when we'd been there more than an hour. I was leaning back in my chair, eyes closed, fingers against my warm coffee cup, listening to Clay's running commentary on the morning traffic of cars and people rushing by.

"You look happy," he said suddenly.

"I am," I said, not opening my eyes. I tilted my head back and felt the heat of the sun on my face. "You know, I couldn't imagine living somewhere without seasons."

"Yeah?"

"Real seasons, I mean. I'd miss the changes, the variety. Especially spring. I couldn't live without spring. Days like today are worth every snowstorm and slush puddle. By March, it seems like winter will never end. All that snow and ice that seemed so wonderful in December is driving you crazy. But you know spring's coming. Every year, you wait for that first warm day, then the next and the next, each better than the last. You can't help but be happy. You forget winter and get the chance to start over. Fresh possibilities."

"A fresh start."

"Exactly."

Clay hesitated, then leaned forward as if to say something, but then stopped, pulled back, and said nothing.

We got back to the apartment after nine. I was late for work, but I was in too good a mood to care. I could always work through lunch or stay late. No big deal.

As we headed up the elevator, Clay told me how some street punks had tried to steal his car on a trip to New York City last winter. By the time I got to the apartment, I was laughing so hard I nearly fell inside as we walked into the apartment.

"Seriously?" I said as I closed the door.

Clay didn't answer. When I glanced at him, he wasn't laughing. He wasn't even looking at me. His gaze was trained somewhere over my shoulder. I turned to see Philip sitting on the recliner, arms crossed, looking like a parent who'd been waiting up all night for an errant child. I opened my mouth, but nothing came out. My brain raced, wondering how long he'd been home, what excuse would be appropriate. Had he come back that morning? If so, I could say we'd gone out for breakfast. As we stepped farther inside, Philip stood.

"I'd like to talk to Elena," he said.

Clay headed for the bathroom. Philip stepped in his path. Clay halted, shoulders tightening. He started turning his gaze toward Philip, then stopped, looking somewhere past him. He tried stepping around, as if he didn't see anyone there.

"I said, I want to talk to Elena," Philip said. "I'd like you to leave."

Clay turned and headed for the sofa. Again, Philip stepped in front of him and again Clay tensed. His hands clenched once at his sides, then relaxed. Philip was challenging him and it cost every ounce of self-control to ignore it. I was about to step in when Clay turned and looked at me.

"Please," I said.

He nodded and headed for the door, murmuring, "I'll be downstairs," as he passed me. When the door closed, I turned to Philip.

"When did you get back?" I asked.

"I didn't go."

"So you—"

"I was here all night."

I stalled as I struggled to think up an excuse. "The meeting was canceled?"

"There was no meeting."

I looked up sharply.

"Yes, I lied, Elena," he said. "I had to prove to myself that my suspicions were wrong."

"You think Clay and I are—"

"No. I wondered, but you wouldn't have needed to leave the apartment for that. Something's going on, it's just not the obvious." Philip paused. "You know he's in love with you, don't you?"

As I opened my mouth, he held up his hand.

"Don't," he continued. "It doesn't matter whether you know or not, or agree or not. He is. It's there for anyone to see, every time he looks at you, the way he talks to you. I don't know how you feel about him. I can't tell. Whenever I walk into the room, you two are arguing or laughing or doing both at the same time. I don't understand it. I don't understand a lot of things since you got back."

"He'll be leaving soon."

"Not soon. Now. Today."

He turned and walked into the bedroom. As I debated going after him, he returned with a handful of papers. He handed them to me. I looked at the top one. It was a real estate listing sheet for a house in Mississauga. I leafed through the papers and found three more listings for houses in the suburbs.

"I didn't go golfing Sunday," he said. "I was looking at houses. For us."

"You want to move into a house?"

"No, I— Yes, I do want to move into a house but—" He paused, crossed then uncrossed his arms. "I mean that I want to get married. That's what a house means to me. Commitment, marriage, children some-day. The whole nine yards. That's what I want."

I stared at him. Philip stepped toward me, then stopped, crossing and uncrossing his arms again, as if he couldn't figure out what to do with them.

"Is it such a surprise?" he asked softly.

I shook my head. "It's just . . . sudden. Clay and I were drinking last night and I'm still a bit . . . I'm not sure I can . . ."

"Don't answer, then. Give me time to buy a ring and do things right."

He shoved his hands in his pockets and stood there looking, despite his words, as if he still expected a reply. I said nothing.

"Go to work," he said. "Think about it."

We stood there for another awkward moment, then I broke away. I headed for the door, then hesitated, went back and embraced Philip. He hugged me back, holding on for a second or two after I let go. I kissed him, mumbled something about being home by seven, and made my getaway.

I went to work in a such a daze I was amazed I got off the subway at the right stop. I was sitting at my desk when I remembered Clay. He hadn't been outside the apartment when I'd left and I hadn't looked for him. It wouldn't take long before he figured out I'd gone to work and followed.

What would I do when he showed up? What would I say? I shook the questions from my head. I didn't want to think about Clay now.

Philip had proposed.

Marriage.

The thought resuscitated hopes and dreams I thought had died ten years ago. I knew I couldn't get married, but the point had been moot for so long that I'd forgotten how much I'd wanted it. Did I still want it? The ache in my chest answered my question. I told myself I was being silly, old-fashioned. Marriage was for women who wanted someone to take care of them. I didn't need that. I didn't want it. But there were things I did want. Stability. Normalcy. Family. A permanent place in the human world. Marriage could give me that. Philip could give me that. But I couldn't get married. Or could I? I'd lived this long with Philip. Was it possible to sustain it forever? A small voice in my head asked if I wanted to be with Philip forever, but I stifled it. I loved Philip. Right now, the question wasn't whether I wanted to marry him, but whether it was a possibility.

Was it possible?

Perhaps.

I could adapt better if we had a house. I could make sure we bought one near a forest or maybe a place in the country with some acreage. I could work from home and Change during the day so I'd never need to disappear from our bed in the middle of the night. The voice surfaced again, this time asking if I could imagine a life Changing by daylight, sneaking out and hurrying through it, not daring to run or hunt or anything else that would be too dangerous in the day. Again, I silenced the voice. I was considering my options, not making decisions.

Maybe I could continue hiding my secret from Philip, but would I want to? While I'd never felt the urge to tell him the truth before, maybe someday the deception would weigh so heavily on me that I couldn't bear it any longer. I remembered Clay when we were dating, painstakingly revising his history, in hindsight so obviously uncomfortable with it. How would I have reacted if Clay had told me the truth? I would have accepted it. I'd loved him enough that I wouldn't have cared. Philip said he loved me, but did he love me that much? Even if he accepted what I was, would he resent all the lies between us? I jumped to my own defense, insisting that there had been no other way. As much as I cared for Philip, it would have been impossible to tell him the truth. Then why did I still blame Clay for his lies? I pushed past that question. This was about Philip, not Clay. It wasn't the same. I'd never bite Philip. The thought was unfathomable. But what if he wanted that, wanted to join me? A cold shiver went through me. No.

Never. Not even if he wanted it. That was a part of my life I'd never bring Philip into.

My desk phone rang. As I lifted the receiver, I knew who was on the other end. I knew and I answered it anyway.

"Where are you?" Clay said in greeting.

"At work."

Pause. "Dumb question, right? If I call you at work and you answer, it should be pretty apparent where you are. I'm surprised you didn't pick up on that one."

I said nothing.

"What's wrong?" he asked.

"Nothing."

"Darling, anytime you miss a chance to slam me, there's something wrong."

"It's nothing."

Another pause. "It's those papers. For the houses. I saw them on the table when I went up looking for you. I'd hoped . . . That's it, isn't it?"

I didn't answer. Clay pulled the phone away from his mouth and swore. The line hissed and twittered as if the receiver was being jerked. I heard a thump and crackle. Then silence. I started to hang up when Clay's voice came back, muffled, then clear.

"Okay," he said. "Okay." He inhaled, the sound echoing down the line. "We need to talk. I'll be right there and we'll talk."

Again, I didn't answer.

"We need to talk," he repeated. "No tricks. I promised and I'm sticking to it, Elena. No tricks. I don't want to win that way anymore. We'll go someplace public, wherever you're comfortable, and we'll talk. Hear me out, then you can leave whenever you want."

"Okay."

"I mean it. I know—" He stopped. "Okay?"

"That's what I said."

He hesitated, then hurried on. "Give me ten minutes, fifteen tops. I'll take the subway and meet you in front of your office."

He hung up without waiting for a reply.

As soon as I got off the phone, I went downstairs. I wondered what I was doing. Why had I agreed to meet Clay? What did I expect him to say: "Philip asked you to marry him?—that's great, darling, I'm so happy for you"? Still, I didn't turn around and go back inside. It wouldn't do any good. I couldn't hide. I didn't want to hide. I shouldn't need to hide.

My stomach began to churn. Anxiety. I closed my eyes and tried to relax, but the nausea got worse. The ground beneath me grew rubbery, unstable. I stumbled to one side, then righted myself, glancing around to make sure no one had noticed. My body jerked up, suddenly tense, alarmed. I looked around, but saw nothing out of the ordinary. As I turned to look behind me, I felt a brief moment of light-headedness. Everything went black.

A middle-aged man grabbed me as I fell. At least, that's what I assume. One second I was standing on the sidewalk feeling light-headed, the next I was reclining backward looking up into the worried face of a stranger. My rescuer and his wife led me to a bench and sat me down. I mumbled something about skipping breakfast. They made sure I was okay, secured my promise to eat something and get out of the sun, then reluctantly moved on.

I went into the building, stood inside the doors, and checked my watch. Fifteen minutes had passed since Clay had called. He should be here any moment. My stomach was still churning. It was definitely anxiety, but I couldn't pin it down to a cause. Sure, my mind was spinning after Philip's proposal and I didn't really want to talk to Clay, yet for some reason the anxiety didn't seem linked to either of these stressors. It floated there, oddly disconnected and distant.

I focused back on Clay. He'd promised not to trick me. That vow would last only as long as he got his way. If I decided to marry Philip or even to stay with him, Clay would go ballistic, all bets off, all promises forgotten. I knew that but, to my surprise, I wasn't afraid of what he'd do. After all these years, I knew his tricks so well that they were no longer tricks. Whatever he tried, I could anticipate it. I would be ready for it. He'd said last night that I needed to make a choice. He was right. *I* needed to make that choice. I wasn't going to let him do it for me.

A clock somewhere sounded eleven chimes. I double-checked my watch. Yes, it was eleven. Clay had called at ten thirty-five. The anxiety pushed to the surface. Don't be silly, I told myself. Twenty-five minutes wasn't unreasonable. Maybe he couldn't face the subway after all and had decided to walk. Something's wrong, the voice from earlier whispered inside me. No, I told it. Nothing's wrong.

I waited ten minutes longer. The anxiety was worse, my stomach roiling now. I had to go. Back to the apartment.

CHAPTER 28

DISCOVERY

As I swung open the apartment door, it struck something and bounced back toward me. I pushed it again. It opened a few inches, then stopped. I pushed harder. Whatever was in the way was heavy, but it moved, making a swishing sound against the carpet. Looking down, I saw a leg stretched across the floor. I squeezed through the narrow opening, nearly tripping over the leg in my haste to get inside.

It was Philip. He was sprawled behind the door. As I looked at him, my brain refused to register what I was seeing. I stood there, staring down, perversely thinking not, Oh, my God but, How did he get there? Even as I saw the blood pooled at his side, dripping from his mouth, smeared in a bloody trail across the carpet, my brain would only accept simple and ridiculous explanations. Had he passed out? Fainted? Heart attack? Stroke? Seizure? Still numb, I dropped to his side and started going through the motions for basic first aid. Conscious? No. Breathing? Yes. Pulse? Neither strong nor weak. I lifted his eyelids, but didn't know what I was checking for. As I pulled back his shirt, my fingers grazed across his side and slipped into a gaping wound. I pulled my hand back and stared at my bloodied fingers.

Clay.

I gagged, yanking back from Philip as if afraid of soiling him, and vomited a thin string of bile onto the carpet. The shock passed in a second and I started to shake, alternating between fear and rage. Clay did this. No, he couldn't have. Yes, he *could* have, but he wouldn't. Wouldn't he? Why wouldn't he? What would stop him? I hadn't been here to stop him. But no, he wouldn't do something like this. Why not? Because he'd been sweet and even-tempered for a few days? Had I forgotten what he was capable of? Not this. Never this. Clay didn't attack humans. Unless they were a threat. But Philip didn't know what we were, so he wasn't dangerous, wasn't a threat to the Pack, to our way of life. Maybe not to the Pack's way of life, but to Clay's . . . ?

Philip stirred. I jumped to my feet, suddenly remembering the most basic first aid response. I ran to the phone, lifted it, and dialed 911. It took a few seconds to realize I wasn't hearing anything on the other end. I jammed the plunger up and down and dialed again. Still nothing. I looked down. The phone cord snaked around the table leg. The end lay a foot away, colored wires sticking out. Cut. Someone had deliberately cut the phone cord. I knew then that Clay hadn't done this to Philip. He wouldn't leave him alive, bleeding to death, then cut off the phone. Whatever else Clay was, he wasn't a sadist.

I raced to the hall closet and flung it open. Philip's briefcase was on its usual hook and his cell phone was inside its usual spot. I punched in 911, then told the operator that my boyfriend was wounded and unconscious, that I'd come home to find him like that and had no idea how badly he was hurt or how it had happened. I didn't know if she believed me and I didn't care. She took the address and promised an ambulance. That was good enough.

After turning off the phone, I ran to the closet, grabbed a sheet, and ripped it into strips. As I bound Philip's side, I bent close enough to smell who had touched him, who'd done this to him. The scent that wafted up from his clothes wasn't Clay's, but it was someone I knew, someone whose smell registered without a moment of surprise. Thomas LeBlanc. In the back of my brain, I wondered how he'd found me, where he was now, whether he'd return, but I didn't waste time pondering the questions. First priority was Philip. Second priority was finding Clay and warning him.

I checked Philip's breathing and pulse again. Still the same. I leaned over him, braced his neck with one hand, and lifted him to check for any hidden wounds. As I shifted myself upward to kneel, I caught a glimpse of something under the hall table. A hypodermic needle. Fresh alarm surged through me. Had LeBlanc injected Philip with something? Poisoned him? Easing Philip down, I scrambled to the table. I was about to bend over to pick up the needle when I saw the ring on the tabletop. A gold band so familiar that I knew what it was without a closer look. Clay's wedding band. Beneath it was a sheet of torn paper with a scribbled note. For a brief second, I thought Clay had taken off his ring, that he'd come up here before LeBlanc had arrived, removed the ring, written the note, then left—left me. Some emotion surged through me, but before I could analyze it, I realized the writing wasn't Clay's. My hands started to shake. I lifted the note. The ring slipped off and fell, tumbling toward the carpet. I lunged to grab it, my hand closing around the cool metal before it struck the floor. I turned back to the note.

Elena,
Big Bear Motor Lodge. Rm. 211. Tomorrow. 10 A.M.
—D.

A sick feeling settled in my gut. Even as I bent to pick up the syringe, I knew what I'd smell on it. Daniel's scent on the plunger. Clay's on the needle.

"No," I whispered.

I yanked out the plunger and sniffed inside. A strong medicinal smell clung to the empty casing, but I couldn't place it. Not poison, I told myself. Daniel wouldn't use poison. LeBlanc might, but not Daniel. If it was poison, they would have left Clay, not just his ring. The ring and note were a sign. Clay was still alive. Still alive? The thought went through me like an icy knife, not that he was alive but that I would even need to consider the alternative.

"Oh, God," I whispered and swayed, grabbing the table to steady myself.

Get a grip, I told myself. Clay was okay. Daniel gave him something to knock him out. That's why I'd fainted earlier, a manifestation of the sympathetic bond between us. Daniel drugged Clay and took him away but he was okay. I'd know if he wasn't. Oh, God, I hoped I'd know. I looked at the note again. A meeting. Daniel had Clay and he wanted me to meet him tomorrow at ten in Bear Valley. And if I didn't show up . . .

I dropped the paper and turned to run out the door. Philip's body was still blocking the way.

"I'm sorry," I whispered. "Very, very sorry."

I bent to move him out of the way. As I touched him, his eyes flew open and his hand clasped around my wrist.

"Elena?" he said, looking around in confusion, eyes not focusing.

"You're okay," I said. "I've called an ambulance."

"There was a man . . . Two men . . ."

"I know. You're hurt but you'll be okay. An ambulance is coming."

"Asking where you were . . . Didn't tell them . . . Then Clayton . . . Fighting . . ."

"I know." Panic was edging into my voice. I had to go. Now. "Wait here. I'm going down to wait for the ambulance."

"No . . . Could still be there . . . Looking for you . . ."

"I'll be careful."

I tried to pry Philip's fingers from my wrist but he tightened his grip. As gently as possible, I wriggled free, then got to my feet. He lifted himself a couple inches and fell back again, blocking the door. He put a hand on my leg.

"No," he said again. "You can't go."

"I have to."

"No!"

His eyes blazed with fever and pain. A pang of anguish went through me. I'd done this. I'd brought this to him. I had to stay and help. If he got upset, he might make himself worse. A few more minutes wouldn't make any difference. My hands clenched at my sides. Clay's ring jabbed into my palm and I jerked upright.

Ten o'clock. I had to be there by ten o'clock.

Philip said something, but I didn't hear it. Panic flooded through me.

I had to leave. I had to leave now.

I tried to reason with myself, calm myself down, but it was too late. My body was already responding to the fear. A sudden jolt of agony doubled me in half. I was dimly aware of Clay's ring falling to the floor, of Philip saying something. My head shot down, pulling back into my chest. A wail split the air, leaving my throat raw. I gasped, choking, sputtering for air. As I toppled forward, my arms went out to break my fall. I tried to pull into myself, keeping my head down, but my legs spasmed and my head jerked back. Through the fog of pain I saw Philip's face in front of mine, saw his eyes, saw the revulsion and horror there. I fell to all fours, hunching into myself. My back went up. My shirt split. I wailed again, this time an unearthly howl. The Change was coming so fast and so strong I couldn't even think of stopping it. My brain went blank, filled with nothing but fear and agony. My body convulsed once, then again, seizures so powerful that I felt I'd be ripped in half and I didn't care, aware only that it would stop the pain. Then it ended.

I lifted my head and knew that I was a wolf. There was one moment of total exhaustion that vanished as quickly as it came. Panic and terror instantly took its place. I looked up. Philip lay on the floor a few feet away. All I could see were his eyes, staring at me in helpless horror.

I turned, ran across the room, closed my eyes, and plunged through the balcony doors. The glass exploded. Shards of glass sliced through my fur and skin, but I barely felt them. Without pausing or even thinking, I vaulted up and over the railing. For a moment, I was airborne. Then I hit the grass four stories below. My left front paw twisted. Pain shot through my leg. Someone shouted. I ran.

I tore around the building and into the underground parking garage. Ducking behind the first car, I listened for following footsteps. When none came, I shook myself and tried to relax and concentrate. Even if no one came after me, I was stuck. So long as I was anxious and panicked,

I couldn't Change back. Even if I did, I'd be naked in a parking garage. I might be able to find clothes, but then what? My wallet, with money, credit cards, and ID, was in the apartment. Without them, I couldn't get out of Toronto. Not only would I need to find clothing, but I'd need to go back up to the apartment. I couldn't do that. Philip had seen me and the ambulance would be here any minute. Maybe if I waited . . . For how long? When, if ever, would it be safe to go back? Daniel's note flashed in my brain. Ten A.M. tomorrow. The deadline. Anxiety surged again, shoving all rational thought from my brain.

Go.

Go now.

I hesitated only a moment, then obeyed.

I took the back alleys where I could and side roads where I couldn't. People saw me. I didn't care. I kept running. When I got out of Toronto, I raced across fields and forests and open pastures. Logically, my flight made no sense. I would have been better off waiting in the parking garage, sneaking back up to the apartment after an hour or so, and catching a plane. Yet this never occurred to me. Every fiber in me rebelled at the thought of waiting. My gut told me to act and I did.

My brain shut off as I ran, letting instinct control my muscles. Hours later I arrived at an obstacle that my instincts alone couldn't handle: the Niagara Falls border crossing. I spent nearly an hour pacing behind a warehouse, my thoughts slipping and sliding like a car on ice, whirring uselessly. Finally, I regained enough control to contemplate the problem and come up with a solution. There was a huge line of trucks backed up across the bridge, slowed down in customs by some new U.S. entry regulation. Thanks to bureaucratic red tape, I had time to pick out a truck with a canvas-covered trailer and sneak on board. Thankfully the cargo wasn't checked at the border and the truck continued unhindered from Niagara Falls, Ontario, to Niagara Falls, New York. The truck left the city and headed south toward Buffalo. My gut screamed, Wrong Way! and I found myself flying off the back of the truck before my brain had time to protest. I hit the curb hard and rolled into a ditch. As I got to my feet, the paw that I'd hurt leaping from the balcony buckled under me. My stomach growled, reminding me I'd missed lunch and dinner. I thought of slowing down, finding a patch of woods and hunting for dinner, but the panic switch in my head went on, shutting down all higher reasoning. Run, it said. So I did.

By nightfall I was moving on pure fear and momentum. No matter how hungry I was, I was certain that if I stopped, I'd never get started again. Ten o'clock, my gut screamed each time I thought of pausing to rest or eat. Ten o'clock. Stop even for a second and you'll never make it. And if you don't make it . . . I refused to think of that. It was easier to keep running.

It must have been nearly midnight when a thunderous roar in my head sent me pitching forward into the grass. As I got back up, the boom came again. I whined, lowered my head and shook it, scratching at my right ear with my forepaw. Got to run. Can't stop. I lurched forward.

"Elena!" The boom in my head took on a voice and words. Jeremy. His voice roared again, splitting my skull with its intensity. "Elena! Where are you?!"

I lowered my head again and whimpered. Go away, Jeremy. Go away. You're making me stop. I can't stop.

"Where are you, Elena? I can't contact Clay! Where the hell are you?"

I tried to answer, if only to shut him up, but my brain wouldn't form words, only images. Jeremy went silent and I stood there, dazed and wondering if I'd heard him at all. Was I hallucinating? I was awake, wasn't I? Jeremy couldn't contact us when we were awake. Was I sleeping or losing my mind? It didn't matter. Ten o'clock, ten o'clock, ten o'clock. You'll never make it. Run.

I stumbled forward and ran. Soon I started blacking out. I was still moving, but everything kept fading in and out. My legs were numb. I could smell the blood trailing from my torn pads. One minute the ground was like a bed of nails beneath my paws, the next it was like cotton and I was floating above it, racing faster than the wind. It was suddenly day, then night again. I was running through a town. No, I was running through Toronto, the CN Tower beckoning in the distance. I heard voices. A shout. A laugh. Clay's laugh. I strained to see through the night. Fog had rolled in from Lake Ontario, but I could hear him laughing. The concrete turned to grass. The fog wasn't from the lake, but from a pond. Our pond. I was at Stonehaven, bounding through the back acres. Clay was running ahead of me. I could see snatches of gold fur bobbing through the trees. I dug my claws in and ran faster. Suddenly, the ground ended. I was running through the air. Then I was falling. I scrambled for a foothold, but there was nothing around me but inky blackness. Then there was nothing at all.

CHAPTER 29

CAGED

I awoke to the sensation of cold. As I shivered, I felt wet grass beneath my bare skin. I opened one eye. Trees. Long grass. A meadow. I tried lifting my head but couldn't. Clay. That was my first thought, but I didn't know why. Had I been running with him? I couldn't smell him. Why couldn't I raise my head? There was nothing holding me down. My muscles just refused to respond. Was I dead? Dead. Clay. I remembered and my head shot up. Blinding pain pierced my skull.

Something warm and soft fell around my shoulders. I jerked up, crying out in pain as I moved. A jacket lay over my bare torso, the smell of it so familiar, yet so impossible. Was I dreaming? Hallucinating? I felt hands slipping under me to lift me up, the touch as familiar as the scent on the coat.

"Elena?"

A face bent over mine. Jeremy, dark hair falling over his forehead, shoved back with an impatient hand. Not possible. Not here. I closed my eyes.

"Elena?" Sharper now, worried.

I tried to move, but it hurt too much. Deciding to abandon myself to the hallucination, I lifted one eyelid.

"H—" I croaked, wanting to ask how he'd got there. "H—" Nothing more would come.

"Don't try to talk," he said. "And don't try to move. I'm going to carry you to the truck. It's right over there."

"C—Cl—"

"They have him, don't they?" His arms tightened around me.

"T—ten—o'clock," I managed to get out, then everything went dark again.

This time I woke to warmth, artificial heat blowing across my face. I heard the humming of a motor, felt the vibration and small bumps of a car moving over a smooth road. I smelled old leather and shifted beneath the jacket slung around me. I stretched my legs, but the pain made me whimper and pull back.

"Is that too hot?" Nick's voice. I felt his arm move over me and reach for the vent. He tilted it away from my face.

"Is she awake?" Jeremy somewhere nearby. In front of me. The front seat.

"I'm not sure," Nick said. "Her eyes are closed. You can probably turn down the heat. She's got her color back."

The click of a dial. The harsh blowing fell to a quiet drone. I opened one eye, then the other. I was propped half-reclining in the back seat of the Explorer, my head resting near the side window, legs curled beside me on the seat. Scenery and cars sped past. Antonio was in front of me, in the driver's seat. His eyes flickered toward me through the rearview mirror.

"She's awake," he said.

A seat belt clicked open. Then the whir of denim on the cloth seats. Nick bent over me.

"Is it warm enough?" he asked. "Can I get you anything?"

"T—ti—"

"Don't talk, Elena," Jeremy said. "Grab the water bottle from the cooler, Nick. She's dehydrated. Let her sip it, but not too much."

Nick rummaged around in the cooler. Then a cold plastic straw touched my lips. I pulled back and gave a small shake of my head that sent lightning bolts through my skull.

"Ti—" I croaked. "Ti—me. Wha—ti—me."

"What time?" Nick lowered his face to mine. "What time is it?"

I nodded, sending a shower of burning sparks through my head this time. Nick still looked confused, but he checked his watch.

"Eleven-twenty . . . almost eleven-thirty."

"No!" I shot upright. "No!"

Nick jerked back. The Explorer swerved and Antonio swore, then yanked the steering wheel back on track. I fought to get out from under Jeremy's jacket.

"Elena." Jeremy's voice came from the front seat, calm and firm. "It's okay, Elena. Calm her down, Nick, before she gives your father a heart attack."

"She just surprised me," Antonio said. "Nicky, make sure—"

I didn't hear the rest. I struggled free of the jacket and flung it aside, then fumbled to undo the seat belt. Every movement ripped through me. My hands were bruised and torn. I didn't care. I was late. I had to go. I had to get there. Now.

Nick grabbed the seat belt fastener away from me, but I already had it open and was squirming out of the restraining strap. Nick grabbed my shoulders.

"No!" I shouted and flung his hands off.

He grabbed me again, harder this time. I fought, baring my teeth and scratching any part of him I could reach.

"Stop the car," I shouted.

The Explorer slowed to half speed, but no more, as if Antonio was deciding what to do.

"Keep going," Jeremy said. "She's delirious. *Keep going.*"

Nick struggled to keep me in my seat, his face hardening with resolve. I heard a sound in the front. Over Nick's shoulder, I saw Jeremy getting up from his seat, reaching back to restrain me. I gathered all my strength and control, drew back my fist, and punched Jeremy in the stomach. His eyes went wide and he doubled over. Some deep part of me was horrified, but I didn't care. The fever in my brain incinerated any pangs of conscience. I had to get out. I was late. Nothing else mattered.

I shoved Nick away and flung myself past him toward the opposite door. Grabbing the handle, I thrust it open and looked down. Gravel flew by in a gray blur. Nick shouted. The brakes squealed. The Explorer veered right. I tensed to jump. Two sets of hands grabbed me, one by the back, the other by the shoulders, and yanked me inside. I felt Jeremy's hands go around my neck, then pressure on the side of my throat, then blackness again.

I awoke in a memory. Every part of my body ached. I'd Changed last night. The recollection was dim, a montage of images—pain, fear, rage, disbelief. Yet I hadn't been running through New York State. I'd Changed in an eight by six cell, manacled hand and foot. My seventh Change. Seven weeks since I'd come to this place. I had no idea what day it was, but I knew how many times I'd gone through hell and marked the time by that. When I awoke, I was still in the cage. I'd been in it for five weeks now, five Changes since the man gave up trying to keep me in a bedroom upstairs. I knew his name: Jeremy, but I never used it, not to his face, not even when I thought of him. To his face, I called him nothing. I refused to speak to him. In my mind, he was simply "he" or "the man," a designation devoid of thought and emotion.

I awoke feeling the scratchy fabric of a mattress beneath me. There had been sheets once, soft flannel sheets and a comforter. Then he caught me tearing them into strips and thought I was planning to hang myself. I wasn't. I wouldn't give him the satisfaction of seeing me dead. I'd torn up the sheets for the same reason I'd destroyed the magazines and clothing he'd brought for me, and the pretty pictures he'd affixed to the stone cage walls. I wanted nothing from him. I would accept nothing meant to make this cage seem like anything other than the hellhole it was. The only offering I accepted was food and I ate that only because I had to keep my strength up for when I escaped. That was what kept me going, the thought of escape. Soon I would get away, back to the city, to people who could help me, heal me.

I opened my eyes to see a figure on the chair outside the cage. At first I thought it was him. He sat there most of the day, watching me and talking to me, trying to brainwash me with the insanity that spilled from his lips. When my eyes focused, the figure became clearer, bent over, elbows on knees, gold curls shining in the artificial light. The one person I hated more than the man. Quickly, I closed my eyes and feigned sleep, but it was too late. He'd seen me. He got to his feet and started to talk. I wanted to stop up my ears, but it would do no good. I could hear too well now. Even if I could block his words, I knew what he'd be saying. He said the same things every time he came, sneaking in when the man was out. He tried to explain what he'd done, why he'd done it. He apologized. He pleaded with me to obey the man so that I could get out of the cage. He wanted me to talk to the man, to ask that his banishment be revoked so he could come back and help me. But there was only one way he could help me. Each time he came, each time he swore he'd do anything to make it up to me, I told him the same thing. The only words I'd speak to him. Fix me. Undo what you did.

"Clay."

The sound of my voice woke me from my memories. I was on my back, staring up at a naked lightbulb on a whitewashed cement ceiling. I turned my head and saw solid stone walls. No windows. No ornaments. Beneath me, I felt the scratchy twin-size mattress. The cage.

"No," I whispered. "No."

I turned my head and saw the bars. Beyond them, someone was sitting on the chair. My heart leapt. Then the figure stood, black eyes meeting mine.

"No," I whispered again, sitting up. "Damn you, no."

"I had to, Elena," Jeremy said. "I was afraid you'd hurt yourself. Now, if you're feeling better—"

I threw myself at the bars. Jeremy stepped out of arm's reach, cautious but not surprised.

"Let me out of here!" I shouted.

"Elena, if you'd—"

"You don't understand!"

"Yes, I do. Daniel has Clay. He took him in Toronto. He wanted you to show up at the hotel at ten today. You were talking in your sleep on the way back."

"You—" I stopped and swallowed. "You know?"

"Yes, I—"

"You know and you're keeping me in here? How could you?!" I grabbed the bars and strained against them. "You knew Clay's life was in danger and you put me in here?"

"What do you think Daniel planned to do, Elena? Take you and let Clay go? Of course not. If you went there, we'd lose you both."

"I don't care!"

Jeremy rubbed a hand over his face. "You do care, Elena. You're just too upset to think about this logically—"

"Logically? Logically? Are you really that cold? You raised him. You mean the world to him. He's spent his life protecting you. He's risked his life protecting you, risks it constantly for you. You'd sit back, logically assess the situation, and decide it's not worth the gamble to save him?"

"Elena—"

"If he's dead, it's your fault."

"Elena!"

"It's my fault. If he's dead because I didn't get there on time—"

Jeremy grabbed my arm through the bars, fingers cutting to the bone. "Stop it, Elena! He's not dead. I know you're upset, but if you'd calm down—"

"Calm down? Are you saying I'm hysterical?"

"—calm down and think about it, you'll know Clay isn't dead. Think about it. Daniel knows how important Clayton is to the Pack. To you. To me. He's too valuable as a hostage."

"But Daniel doesn't know why I didn't show up. Maybe he thinks we don't care, that we've abandoned Clay, given him up for dead."

"Daniel would know better. To be sure, I've sent him a note. Last week he gave me a post office box to contact him through. Antonio and Nick dropped off a letter saying that we weren't letting you make that appointment, but that I'm willing to negotiate so long as Clay's not harmed. I'm sure Daniel already knows that, but I wanted to make it clear. I'm not taking any chances with Clay's life, Elena."

On some level I knew Jeremy was right. It didn't help. I kept thinking, What if he's wrong? What if Clay had never even made it back to New

York? What if he'd woken up and they'd fought and he was lying in a Dumpster in Toronto? What if Daniel couldn't resist the opportunity to destroy his lifelong enemy while he was drugged and powerless? Even if Daniel managed to keep it together, what about LeBlanc? He'd already proven he didn't give a damn what Daniel wanted. If Clay angered LeBlanc, he'd kill him. Even if Clay didn't do anything to LeBlanc, he might kill him just because he could. As all the possibilities ran through my mind, my aching legs surrendered and I slumped to the floor, still clutching the bars.

"You didn't warn me," I said.

Jeremy crouched down, putting one hand over mine. "I didn't warn you about what, sweetheart?" he asked softly.

"I didn't think. I should have known."

"Known what?"

"That he was in danger, too. He was looking after me. But I wasn't looking after him."

I dropped my head to my knees and felt the first prick of tears behind my eyes.

Jeremy left me in the cage overnight. As much as I wanted to believe otherwise, I knew he wasn't being heartless or unfeeling. After my crying jag, one might have expected me to give up the fight and meekly accept Jeremy's will. At least, anyone who didn't know me very well might expect that. Jeremy knew me better. When I was sobbing on the floor, he'd reached through the bars to comfort me, but didn't unlock the door. After I'd had a good cry and wiped away the tears, I flew into a rage. I broke the bed, it being the only breakable thing in the cell. I kicked the toilet, but that didn't break anything except maybe a couple of my toes. I flung my dinner on the floor. I cursed Jeremy at the top of my lungs. And once it was all over, I should have felt better, right? I didn't. I felt stupid. I felt like I'd had a fit of hysterics and made a fool of myself. I needed to get a grip and take control. Throwing tantrums wouldn't help Clay.

Of course, just because I was ready to leave the cage didn't mean Jeremy was prepared to let me out. He left me in there all morning, stopping by periodically to make sure I hadn't resumed my *Exorcist* imitation. When he came down with my lunch, he brought a letter-size manila envelope. Before giving me the food tray, he wordlessly passed me the envelope.

Inside was a Polaroid shot of Clay. He was sitting on the floor, knees pulled up, feet bound together, and arms behind him. His hands were out of sight, but judging by his position they must have been tied or manacled. His eyes were half closed and so clouded by drugs they looked gray instead of blue. Though I couldn't see any sign of bars, I knew he was in a cage. No werewolf would capture Clay without making damn sure he couldn't Change and break out. Keeping him secure would mean drugs, bindings, and/or a cage. Daniel would use all three. He'd fought Clay before and he wouldn't take any chance on an accidental rematch.

I looked at the picture again. Bruises covered Clay's arms and bare torso, an ugly slice bisected his left cheek, his lips were swollen and split, and he had one blackened eye. Despite his condition, he stared into the camera with a look of bored annoyance, like a supermodel who's had one too many photographers in her face that day. Showing defiance would have only set Daniel off. Clay knew better.

I reached inside the envelope again and found it empty. I looked up at Jeremy. For the first time since he'd brought me back, I really looked at him. His eyes were underscored with purple and his bangs fell lankly against his forehead, as if he hadn't slept or showered in days. Tiny lines had appeared around his eyes and mouth. He almost looked his age.

"Where's the letter?" I asked, more gently than I'd intended. "I know Daniel must have sent a letter. Can I see it?"

"It says they have Clay, which is obvious, and that he's not in great shape, but he's alive, both equally obvious. If you check the background of the photo, you'll see a newspaper hanging on the wall. It's today's *New York Times,* presumably to prove the picture was taken today."

"What does Daniel want?"

"Clay's in no immediate danger."

"Are you going to give me a direct answer to any of my questions?"

"I've sent a note back. I'm demanding daily pictures while we negotiate."

I scowled and stomped to the other side of the cell, reminding myself that I had to play nice. Another tantrum wouldn't get me out of the cage anytime soon.

"I know I lost it yesterday," I said. "But I'm fine now. I want to help. Can I come out?"

"Eat your lunch. I'll be back in a while to see if you're still hungry."

Jeremy slipped the tray through the slot near the floor and went upstairs. I bit my tongue to keep from calling him anything I might regret . . . at least until he was out of earshot.

Chapter 30

Plans

Jeremy let me out later that afternoon. Before we were even up the stairs, I asked about his plans. He made me wait until after dinner, probably testing how far he could stretch my patience before I snapped. I'll admit, by mealtime I was getting close, but I managed to hold it together. While Antonio and Nick cleaned up the dinner mess, Jeremy took me into the study for our talk. The *Reader's Digest* condensed version of our hour-long talk was this: Jeremy had a plan for getting Clay back and I wasn't allowed to know anything about it or allowed to help him carry it out. As one might expect, I accepted this news with grace and understanding.

"That is the stupidest idea I've ever heard!" I snarled for the dozenth time that hour. "I won't just sit here and do nothing."

"Would you prefer to sit in the cage and do nothing?"

"Don't threaten me."

"Then don't threaten me."

Something in Jeremy's voice made me clamp my mouth shut and settle for pacing.

"I can help," I said, keeping my voice low and, I hoped, calm. "Please, Jer, don't shut me out. Maybe you blame me for what happened in Toronto, but don't punish me like this."

"You didn't do anything wrong in Toronto. If it's anyone's fault, it's mine. I thought Toronto was safe. I didn't realize Daniel was gone until Tuesday morning, when he was already there. I'm not going to tell you how I plan to get Clay back because then you'll want to help and if I don't let you, you'll go ahead and try anyway."

"But—"

He leaned forward. "I'm being honest with you, Elena. More honest than I'd dare be with anyone else. Everything is falling apart. I wasn't prepared to handle this. If I've been a good Alpha all these years it's because I've never been tested. Not like this. I started slow, feeling things out, gathering information. Peter and Logan got killed. I changed course and took off again, going after Jimmy Koenig. You almost got killed. I sent you two away where I thought you'd be safe. Less than a week later, Daniel found you. Now he has Clay."

"But—"

Jeremy stood and smiled down at me, a crooked half smile, and brushed a lock of hair off my shoulder. "I'm sorry, sweetheart. I really am. But this is how it has to be."

Before I could respond, he was gone.

Despite Jeremy's orders, I had no intention of sitting on my hands and doing nothing. After all, he hadn't specifically forbidden me to do anything. So I started to plan.

Step one: find an ally. This was easy. Well, there wasn't a lot of selection, but even if there had been, Nick would be the obvious choice. Not only was he Clay's best friend, but he'd been shut out of the rescue plan as well, and was as unhappy about it as I. Jeremy claimed he needed Nick to guard me, but even Nick was smart enough to know that Jeremy wasn't telling him anything for fear he'd take it back to me. I persuaded Nick by saying I only wanted to gather information, so we could prove our value to Jeremy. Not that this was a lie. I had every intention of sharing any information I uncovered with Jeremy. And if he still refused to let me help? I didn't worry about that. I could always renegotiate my arrangement with Nick later.

Step two: plot a course of action. Jeremy would be trying to find where the mutts were keeping Clay. It didn't take a genius to figure this out. Bargaining with Daniel would only be a cover to keep him busy while Jeremy figured out where they were staying. Nick confirmed this. Yesterday, before he was cut out of the plan, Jeremy had sent him and Antonio to the Big Bear Motor Lodge. Everyone except Daniel had checked out of the motel on Monday. Daniel had checked out Wednesday. So the conclusion I'd drawn, and likely the same one Jeremy had drawn, was that the mutts had found another hiding place and had taken Clay there upon his return from Toronto. Since I didn't want to interfere with Jeremy's plans—or, more realistically, I didn't want to get caught interfering—I'd have to leave the mutt-tracking to him and find another way to discover where they were hiding Clay.

Step three: divert attention from my activities. Had it been anyone but Jeremy, I'd have played the role of the cowed subordinate. To Jeremy, though, that would be a sure sign that I was up to something. So, I bitched and complained and made his life hell. He expected nothing less. Every chance I got, I demanded, begged, or wheedled to be let in on his plans. Finally, after an evening and morning of being in his face at every possible opportunity, I gave him an ultimatum. If he didn't find Clay in three days, I was going after him with or without Jeremy's permission. He therefore assumed that he had three days before I started raising hell again, so he relaxed. An ingenious ruse if I do say so myself.

Although Nick had agreed to help me, he refused to disobey Jeremy's order of house arrest, so I couldn't actually go anywhere. Well, I could knock Nick over the head and make a run for it, but I wouldn't do that to him. Besides, Jeremy would only find me and bring me back and Nick wouldn't be too enthusiastic about helping me again if he was suffering from a concussion.

The first thing I did was call the hospital. No, I didn't call the local hospital on some premonition that they might have Clay or know where he was. I called St. Michael's Hospital in Toronto. I hadn't forgotten that I'd left Philip bleeding on the floor of our apartment. I'll admit I might not have spent as much time dwelling on it as I should have, but I knew his injuries weren't life threatening, at least not after I'd stopped the bleeding and called for help, and Clay's situation was far more dire, so I think I can be excused if my attentions weren't evenly divided between the two. Philip wasn't at St. Mike's. The emergency room had been closed to new arrivals last Tuesday afternoon, not an uncommon occurrence after years of health care budget cuts. Philip had been taken to Toronto East General and was still there. I spoke to the nurse on his floor, introducing myself as his sister, and learned that he'd suffered some internal injuries and had required surgery, but he was recovering and was expected to leave on Monday, which meant he'd actually be feeling better by next Wednesday or Thursday— budget cuts again. She offered to put me through to his room to speak to him, but I declined, claiming I didn't want to disturb his rest. The truth was I was too much of a coward to speak to him. Even if he forgave me for abandoning him, there was the small matter of having watched me Change into a wolf. I settled for sending him flowers with a note saying I'd see him soon, and hoped that didn't scare him back into intensive care.

The next thing I did was call the local real estate office. No, not because I was planning to move out and needed a place to stay. Tempting idea, but I knew I wouldn't get far. If Jeremy had tracked me to a field in upstate New York—and he still wouldn't tell me how he'd accomplished that—then he could certainly find me living in Bear Valley, either before or after the mutts found me. Either way, I wasn't suicidal. I called the real estate office to check for homes rented or purchased in the past couple of weeks, particularly houses in the rural area. Only three homes had been sold in the Bear Valley district recently. Two were bought by young families and the third by a retirement-age couple. There were more rentals, but all to longtime Bear Valley residents.

When the house idea didn't pan out, I looked for a possible cottage rental. The bad news was that we lived in cottage country. The good news was that it was still early in the season and the Bear Valley area itself wasn't prime cottage land, having too many trees and too few lakes and waterways. I called the Bear Valley Cottage Association. With a little ingenuity, a lot of lying, and even more politeness—Jeremy had taught me well—I discovered that only four local cottages were being rented, three to honeymooning couples and the fourth to a bunch of middle-aged men from New York who came up every May for some kind of male-bonding-in-the-wilderness therapeutic retreat. Another dead end. I'd have to try another tack. I just wasn't sure yet what that might be.

Purposeful action made the hours fly past, leaving little time to brood over Clay's situation. By evening though, I was left alone with my thoughts. I was tending the fire in the study. It didn't need tending. It didn't even need to be lit, the temperature outside still hovering in the mid-seventies. But there was comfort sitting on the hearth, poking at the logs and watching the fire dance and spark. Unnecessary action was better than no action. Besides, staring at the flames had a mesmerizing effect, giving me something to concentrate on other than the thoughts and fears that kept slipping past the mental barriers I'd carefully erected in the past twenty-four hours.

I wasn't alone in the study. Nick was there, half dozing on the couch. Every so often he'd open his eyes and say something. We'd talk for a few minutes, then the conversation would begin moving dangerously close to Clay and we'd both fall silent. As the clock on the mantel chimed midnight, Nick woke again. He tilted his head backward over the arm of the sofa and looked at the window.

"Full moon coming," he said. "Two, three days?"

"Two."

"I'll need to run. How about you?"

I managed a small smile. "You know perfectly well that I don't need to run, since I did more than enough of that three days ago. What you really want to know is: will I run with you and save you from the horrifying prospect of having to run alone."

"I don't know how you did it in Toronto all those months," he said with a shudder. "I had to do it a couple times last winter. Tonio took off on business and Logan was wrapped up in some court case and Clay— Anyway, I had to Change by myself."

"Poor baby."

"It was awful. It was, like, walk out to the woods, Change, stand there until enough time passed, Change back. It was about as much fun as taking a shit."

"Nice analogy."

"I'm serious. Come on, Elena. Admit it. That's what it's like if you're by yourself. I remember when I was a kid, before my first Change, and Clay used to—"

He stopped. This time, he didn't pick up again. Silence fell and I turned back toward the fire, poking it and watching the sparks cascade from the logs. The door opened. I heard Jeremy come in, but didn't turn around. A moment later, the sofa springs groaned as Nick got up. He walked across the room and the door closed again. Jeremy sat beside me on the hearth. His hand touched the back of my head, hesitated, then stroked my hair.

"I know how difficult this is for you, Elena. I know how scared you are, how afraid you are of losing him."

"It's not that. I mean, of course I'm afraid of losing him. But if you think it's because I've suddenly realized how much I love him and that if—when we get him back, I'll come home and everything will be fine, then you're wrong. I'm sorry. I know you want that, that it would be easier for you and everyone else, but it's not going to happen. Yes, I care about him. Very much. And yes, I want him back. I want him back for you and for Nick and for the Pack. I'm upset because I hold myself responsible."

Jeremy said nothing.

I looked over my shoulder at him. "So you hold me responsible, too?"

"No, not at all. I didn't answer because I thought it best to hold my tongue about the rest. If you think that's why you're upset—"

"It is."

He was quiet for a moment, then reached over to rub my back, fingers moving to the tight ball between my shoulders. "Whatever the reason for your worry, I don't hold you responsible for what happened. We've been through this before. I should have sent you two someplace else. I thought I was being clever, but I didn't even realize something happened until I tried contacting Clay that night—"

"Have you done it since?" I asked, straightening up and turning to face him. "Have you contacted Clay since he's been captured? You've tried, haven't you? What did he say? Is he—"

Jeremy put his fingers to my lips. "Yes, I've tried. Tried and tried again. But I can't get through to him. It's the drugs."

There was another possible reason why Jeremy couldn't get in touch with Clay, but I didn't dare speak it. Jeremy seemed to read it in my face, though, and shook his head.

"Don't think that. You saw today's picture. He doesn't look good, but he's alive."

He sounded so tired. The Pack was under siege, and the mutts were ripping down the defenses as fast as Jeremy could erect them. It was wearing him out. I wished I didn't see that. I wished I could believe, as Antonio and Nick did, that the Pack Alpha was indestructible. That's the way Pack werewolves were raised, secure in the knowledge that no matter what happens, their Alpha will protect them. That was wrong. Plain wrong. It worked great under normal circumstances, when the Pack was never troubled by more than one mutt at a time and the Alpha's job was more focused on settling internal dissent and presenting a united front against the mutts. Faced with a problem of this size, though, the Alpha needed help, not just in fighting the threat, but in deciding how to fight it. Such collaboration was unthinkable. Jeremy might bounce his ideas off Antonio, but he'd never think of asking for advice, nor would any Pack member dream of offering it. I did. I wanted to tell Jeremy what I thought and try to help him, but I knew I couldn't. If he felt overwhelmed now, having me second-guess his plans would only make things worse. Like Antonio and Nick, Jeremy was bound by the same misconception of leadership. The responsibility of saving the Pack fell squarely on his shoulders. The only way I could help was to plot strategies on my own.

CHAPTER 31

AWAKENING

The next morning, Jeremy and Antonio took off again. I went to work. Or, at least, I prepared to go back to work. I called the hospital to check on Philip, then sat at the desk in the study, fired up Clay's laptop, and sat there, looking from the phone to the laptop and back again. These were my only tools for finding Clay and I had no idea what to do now with either one. I pulled out a pad of paper and reviewed what I knew, hoping some new avenue of exploration would leap out at me.

We had two experienced mutts left, half of the original number. This was reassuring, until I reminded myself that we'd eliminated the lesser mutts, leaving the more dangerous ones alive. Not so good. We also had two new mutts. LeBlanc, I knew, and understood how he worked. Again, I felt a momentary burst of complacency before remembering that I hadn't even met Cain's protégé, Victor Olson. So there it was, the next step: find out more about Olson. Of course, deciding *what* I was going to do wasn't the same as determining *how* I was going to do it. Of the two tools I had available, the Internet seemed the best bet, namely because I wasn't sure where to even begin with the telephone.

Cain had said that his protégé's name was Victor Olson and that he'd broken him out of jail in Arizona where he'd been imprisoned for sex crimes. Since Daniel had found Olson, his crimes must have been big enough to warrant media attention. A simple search on the name and city brought up seven complete matches. The first one was for some long-dead city father named Victor Olson. The next four matches were for Vic "Mad Dog" Olson, which sounded promising, until I clicked on one site and found an advertisement for a personal injury lawyer. On the last two I hit pay dirt. Victor Olson had escaped from jail four months ago, cutting short a life sentence for raping and killing a ten-year-old-girl. I reread his victim's age several times. Cain said Olson had been in jail for "screwing around with a couple girls." I'd assumed by "girls" he really meant women. Obviously not. Suppressing my revulsion, I read the article. Olson was a lifetime pedophile who'd been charged several times with acts of indecency, but the charges had always been dismissed when the judge ruled his victims' testimony "unreliable." With the last victim, the judge had to admit the testimony provided by her dead body was reasonably reliable. I skipped to the news article on the other site and discovered why Daniel had chosen Olson. He was a stalker. He chose his victims with care and trailed them for weeks before making his move. One detective said he'd never seen someone so skilled at "the hunt"—his choice of words, not mine.

I spent another hour going over what I knew. When that led nowhere, I tracked down Nick in the exercise room and repeated everything to him, hoping either he'd think of something or the very act of verbalizing it would help me think of something. Nick listened, but didn't have any ideas. Nick wasn't used to having ideas. That sounded worse than I intended. What I meant was that he was accustomed to following the plans of others. He was an enthusiastic lieutenant and a loyal friend, but he wasn't exactly— how do I put this nicely—not exactly a deep thinker. Talking to him didn't help me think of anything either. So I put aside my papers, turned off the laptop, and did the most mind-numbing, menial chore I could imagine. I did the laundry.

No one had done laundry since we'd gone to Toronto, probably because it was the last thing on anyone's mind. I didn't realize the full implications of that until I was folding the first load and came across one of Clay's shirts. I stood there in the laundry room holding the shirt. Clay had worn it the day before we left. I don't know why I remembered that. It was a dark green golf shirt, one of the few departures from Clay's plethora of plain white and black cotton T-shirts. It must have been a gift from Logan, who'd considered it his thankless job to add some fashion to Clay's wardrobe. I stared at the shirt, thinking about Logan and the grief surged fresh. Then I thought about Peter, remembered him ribbing Clay about his monochromatic wardrobe, threatening to give him a stack of the most garish concert T-shirts he could find. Blinking hard, I tucked the shirt under a stack of Nick's pants and kept going.

After I'd folded the first load, I took it upstairs to put the clothes away. I left Clay's pile for last. For several minutes, I stood outside his closed bedroom door and screwed up the courage to go inside. I rushed through the job, stuffing shirts, underwear, and socks into his drawers. His jeans went in the closet. Yes, he hung up his jeans, probably because if he didn't, there wouldn't be anything in there. I was putting the jeans on hangers when I saw the pile of wrapped presents on the closet floor. Without even checking the tags, I knew what they were. Part of me wanted to slam the door shut and run. I didn't want to see them. Yet I couldn't resist. I reached down and picked up the top gift. It was wrapped in Christmas paper, bright candy canes and bows. On the tag, one name scrawled across, obliterating the TO: and FROM: label. Elena.

Nick had said Clay expected me back. I'd half expected to come back last Christmas myself, not through my own volition, but magically, as if I could fall asleep in Toronto on Christmas Eve and wake up in Stonehaven the next morning. Easter, Thanksgiving, birthdays, they'd all passed unnoticed, untainted by the urge of return. Christmas was different.

Growing up, I'd hated Christmas. Of all the holidays, it was the one that most glorified the family, all those movies and TV specials and advertisements and magazine covers showing happy families going through the rites of the season. That's not to say I was deprived of the normal trappings of Christmas. My foster families weren't complete ogres. I got presents and turkey dinners. I went to parties and midnight mass. I sat on Santa's knee and learned to sing "Up on the Rooftop" for the school concert. But without real family bonds, all the rituals of the season were as phony as sprayed-on snow. So when I moved out on my own at eighteen, I stopped celebrating. Then I met Clay. That first year together, I finally felt that a true Christmas was possible. Sure, I wasn't surrounded by parents and grandparents and aunts and uncles, but I had someone. I had the first link to everything else I wanted so bad.

I should say that Clay had no idea how to celebrate Christmas. It wasn't an official werewolf holiday. Okay, there were no official werewolf holidays, but that wasn't the point. The Pack recognized Christmas only as a time to get together as they did umpteen other times a year. They exchanged presents, the same as they did on birthdays, but that was the extent of the celebration. So what did Clay do when I hinted that I wanted a full-blown Christmas? He gave me one.

Although I didn't know it at the time, Clay spent weeks researching the holiday. Then he gave me Christmas with all the trimmings. We went out and cut down a tree—then realized the impossibility of getting it back to his apartment on his motorcycle. We had the tree delivered and decorated it. We made shortbread, gingerbread, and sugar cookies, and discovered how hard it is to form gingerbread men without a cookie cutter. We made a fruitcake, which was probably still on the balcony of his old apartment, where we'd eventually used it to hold open the door. We bought lights for the balcony, then had to go back to the hardware store for an extension cord, then had to go back for wire cutters to snip a hole in the screen to slip the cord through. We listened to Christmas music, watched *How the Grinch Stole Christmas* and rented *It's a Wonderful Life,* though Clay fell asleep during the latter—okay, we both fell asleep during the latter. We drank eggnog by the fire, or by a magazine photo of a fire that Clay stuck on the wall. No tradition went unobserved. It was the perfect Christmas. We didn't make it to Easter.

There was no Christmas the next year. I assume Christmas still occurred in the outside world, but at Stonehaven, it passed unnoticed. I'd barely got out of the cage by winter. Clay was still banished. Logan came to see me, but I drove him away, as I'd driven him away the half-dozen other times he tried to visit. Nick sent a gift. I threw it out unopened. Before Clay bit me, I'd met both Logan and Nick, had even started considering them friends. Afterward, I blamed them for not warning me. So, Christmas came and went and I barely realized it.

The next year, Clay was still banished. I was well on the road to recovery by then. I'd forgiven Logan and Nick and even Jeremy. I'd started getting to know Antonio and Peter. I was coming to accept life as a werewolf. Then came Christmas. I expected it would pass again with little fanfare, like the year before. Instead, we had a full-blown Christmas, complete with presents under the tree, colored lights sparkling against the snow, and a turkey on the table. The whole Pack came to Stonehaven for a week, and for the first time, I knew how hectic, stressful, loud, and wonderful a family Christmas could be. I thought this was how the Pack normally celebrated Christmas, when they didn't have an angry new female werewolf to contend with. It wasn't until January that I learned the truth. Clay had contacted Jeremy and asked him to do this for me. That was his gift to me. My gift to him was to ask Jeremy to repeal his banishment.

For every year after that, we had a full Christmas at Stonehaven. The Pack indulged my fantasy completely, without ever making me feel that they were only doing it to humor me. I can't say that every Christmas was a good one. Sometimes Clay and I were getting along, more often we weren't, but we were always together. If this last Christmas away from Clay had been hard, one thing had made it bearable: knowing he was out there, somewhere. As I stared at the pile of presents in his closet, I realized this applied to my life every day of the year, not just at Christmas. Somehow, knowing Clay was there, waiting for me should I ever return, gave me a cushion of comfort in my life. In a perverse way, he was the most stable thing in my life. No matter what I did, he'd be there. What if he wasn't? The thought filled me with something so icy cold that my breath seemed to freeze in my lungs and I had to gasp for air. I hadn't lied to Jeremy the night before. This wasn't one of those fairy-tale romances where the heroine realizes her undying love for the hero after he's placed in mortal danger. There were no heroes or heroines in this story and there would be no happily ever after ending, even if we got Clay back. I still couldn't imagine living with him, nor could I envision my world without him. I needed him. Maybe that was unspeakably selfish. It almost certainly was. But it was honest. I needed Clay and I had to get him back. I looked at the gifts again and I knew I wasn't doing enough.

"I'm going to Bear Valley," I said.

It was the next day. Nick and I were on the back patio, lying on lounge chairs, luncheon plates on our laps. Jeremy and Antonio had left an hour ago. Since then, I'd been trying to figure out how to tell Nick what I'd planned. After a half-dozen false starts, I went with the blurt-it-out approach.

"I told Daniel I wanted to see him," I said.

"Is that what was in the note?"

When Antonio and Nick had gone to deliver Jeremy's latest missive to Daniel's post office box, I'd slipped Nick a note to add to Jeremy's. Nick hadn't asked what the note said, probably because he didn't want to know.

"Yes," I said. "I'm meeting him at two o'clock."

"How'd he get back to you?"

"He didn't. I said I was meeting him at two. He'll be there."

"And Jeremy's okay with this?"

I could tell by Nick's tone that he knew perfectly well I hadn't mentioned it to Jeremy. The question was his way of prudently broaching the topic. Or maybe he was just hoping against hope that this was something I'd already planned with Jeremy and we'd both somehow forgotten to mention it to him.

"I'm not sitting around anymore," I said. "I can't do it. I tried, but I can't."

Nick swung his legs over and sat on the edge of his lounge chair. "I know how hard this is for you, Elena. I know how much you love him—"

"That's not it. Look, I've already been through this with Jeremy. We need Clay back. Whether or not you want to help is up to you."

"I want to help get him back, but I'm not going to help you get yourself killed doing it."

"What's that supposed to mean?"

"Just what it sounds like. I saw the way you were a few days ago—"

"Is that what this is about? Because I flipped out three days ago? Look at me now. Do I seem flipped out?"

"No, and that probably scares me more than if you were."

"I am going," I said.

"Not without me."

"Fine."

"But I'm not going. So neither are you."

I got up and started for the back door. Nick leapt to his feet and blocked my path.

"What are you going to do?" I asked. "Knock me out and lock me in the cage?"

He looked away, but he didn't move. I knew he wouldn't do anything. If it came down to it, Nick wouldn't use physical force to stop me. It wasn't in his nature.

"Where's this meeting?" he asked at last. "Is it in a public place? Because if it's not—"

"It's in The Donut Hole. As public as I can make it. No matter what you might think, I'm not doing anything that might endanger myself. I wouldn't do anything to endanger *you*. The only risk I'm taking is in breaking Jeremy's orders. And I'm only doing that because he's wrong to exclude me."

"So you'll meet Daniel in the coffee shop and I'll be there. We'll park right out front. We won't go anyplace with him, even for a walk down the street."

"Exactly."

Nick turned and walked to the house. He wasn't happy, but he'd do it. I'd make it up to him someday.

As I pulled into a parking spot in front of the coffee shop, I could see Daniel through the window. He was sitting in a booth. His shoulder-length auburn hair was pushed back behind his left ear—his only ear, actually, after that little biting mishap a few years ago. His profile was sharp, high cheekbones, pointed chin, and thin nose, not unhandsome in a feral way, but his looks were more fox than wolf, which better complemented his personality.

As I got out of the car, his green eyes followed me, but he didn't acknowledge me in any other way, having learned long ago that I didn't respond well to fawning. His body was lean and compact. Standing, we'd be on perfect eye level, making him no more than five feet ten. Once, when I'd needed to meet Daniel to deliver a warning from Jeremy, I'd worn two-inch heels and had quite enjoyed the sensation of talking down to Daniel, until he told me how sexy I looked. Since then he'd never seen me in anything but my oldest, grubbiest sneakers.

Today Daniel was wearing a plain black T-shirt and blue jeans, which was pretty much what he wore all the time. He copied Clay's monochromatic, construction-worker-casual wardrobe as if it would lend him a certain cachet. It didn't.

Marsten sat across from Daniel. As usual, he was groomed and dressed like he'd stepped from the pages of *GQ*, which only made Daniel look like a slob in comparison. Okay, Karl Marsten made everyone look like a slob.

As Nick and I walked in, Marsten stood and strolled to the door to meet us.

"You came," he said to me. "I'm surprised Jeremy let you. Or does he know?"

I mentally kicked myself. I hadn't thought how it would look if I showed up against Jeremy's wishes. Dissension in the Pack. Wonderful. Trust Marsten to pick up on it in five seconds flat.

"You look good, Elena," Marsten continued, not waiting for me to answer. "Tired, but that's to be expected. Hopefully all this will be over soon."

"That depends on you," I said.

"In part." He turned to the server behind the counter. "Two coffees. Black for the lady and—" He looked over at Nick. "One cream, two sugars, correct?"

Nick only glared at him.

"One black. The other with one cream, two sugars," Marsten repeated to the server. "Put it on my tab." He paused, then turned to me with a wry smile. "I can't believe I just said that in a doughnut shop. I have to get out of this town."

I looked away.

"It's been a long time, Nicholas," Marsten continued. "How's your father? I invested in one of his companies last year. Thirty percent return. He certainly hasn't lost his touch."

Ignoring him, Nick sat on a stool at the counter and studied the doughnut display. Marsten took the stool beside him and waved me toward Daniel.

"I'll keep Nicholas company," he said.

Daniel didn't look up as I walked over. He stirred his coffee and acknowledged me only with the barest nod. The server delivered my coffee. I pushed it aside and sat on the bench across the table from Daniel. He kept stirring. For a few seconds, I sat there. Under any other circumstances, I would have waited to see how long he could stretch this coffee-stirring feigned indifference before he cracked and looked at me. But the time for games was over.

"What do you want?" I asked.

Still stirring, eyes on the mug as if it might skitter away if he stopped watching it. "What do I usually want?"

"Revenge."

He glanced up and met my gaze, then broke eye contact to give me the usual slow once-over. I gritted my teeth and waited. After a few seconds I was tempted to snap my fingers in front of his face and tell him there wasn't *that* much of me to look at.

"You want revenge," I repeated to get his brain back on track.

Daniel leaned back in his seat, pulling one leg up to look oh-so-cool and relaxed. "No, I don't. I've never wanted that. Whatever the Pack did to me, I'm over it. They're not worth my time. But you are."

"Here we go," I muttered.

Daniel ignored me. "I know why you're with them, Elena. Because you're afraid to leave, afraid of what they'll do, and afraid of what will happen to you without their protection. I'm trying to show you that they can't hurt you and they can't protect you. If you want a partner, a true partner, you deserve better than some freak who has to turn around three times before he lies down. I can give you better."

"So this is all about winning me? Bullshit."

"You don't think you're worth it? I thought your self-esteem was higher than that."

"My IQ is higher than that. This isn't about me. It never has been. It's about you and Clay. You think he has me, so you want me. Your motivation is as complex as that of a two-year-old seeing another kid with a shiny toy. You want it."

"You underestimate yourself."

"No, I don't underestimate how much you hate him. What happened? Did he always get the bigger slice of birthday cake?"

"He made my life hell. Him and Tonto over there." Daniel glared toward Nick. "Poor little Clay. He has problems. He's had a tough life. You should be nice to him. You should make friends with him. That's all I ever heard. All they saw was a cute little runt of a wolf cub. He bared his teeth and they thought it was cute. He ordered us around like a miniature Napoleon and they thought it was cute. Well, it wasn't cute from where I was standing. It was—"

I held up my hand. "You're ranting."

"What?"

"Just wanted to let you know. You're ranting. It's kinda ugly. Next thing you know, you'll be laying out your plans for world domination. That's what all villains do after they rant about their motivation. I was hoping you'd be different."

Daniel took a swig of coffee, then shook his head and gave a small laugh. "Well, you've put me in my place. You've always been good at that. You say bark and I say how loud."

"I say let Clay go . . ."

Daniel made a face. "And I say why bother? Okay, there's a limit to my obedience training. I won't let him go just because you want it, Elena. You could pout and bat your eyes and plead and, while I'd find that damned arousing, it wouldn't make me release him. I'll make you the same exchange offer I made to Jeremy. You for Clay."

"Why?"

"I already told you."

"Because I'm so damned irresistible. Uh-huh. Give me a better explanation or I'm out of here."

Daniel was silent for a moment, then leaned forward. "Have you ever thought of starting your own Pack? Not recruiting a bunch of half-wit mutts, but creating a dynasty? We aren't immortal, Elena, but there is a way to ensure our immortality."

"I really hope you're not implying what I think you're implying."

"Children, Elena. A new breed of werewolves. Not half-werewolf, half-human, but complete werewolves, inheriting the genes from both parents. Perfect werewolves."

"Wow. You really do want to rule the world."

"I'm serious."

"Seriously crazy. Sorry, but this womb isn't for sale or rent."

"Not even for the price of a life? Clay's life?"

I pulled back and pretended to think about it. Time to call his bluff.

"So I agree to go with you and you'll release him?"

"Right. Only, I'm not just going to trust you to come with me and stay with me, so let's get that straight right off. I've got a place I plan to take you, someplace suitably remote and secure. You'll be confined. Something like the cage at Stonehaven, but far more luxurious. You give me what I want, everything I want, and you won't be in there very long. Once I've convinced you that I'm the better choice, I'll let you out. If you try to run, I'll put you back in."

"Gee, doesn't that sound tempting."

"I'm being honest, Elena. It's an exchange. His captivity for yours."

I pretended to think about it, staring out the window. Then I turned back to Daniel. "Here's my condition. I want to see him released. You'll do it in broad daylight and in a public place. I'll be there with you to watch it happen. Once he's free, I'm yours."

"That's not how it works. Once you're mine, he's free."

"You have no intention of letting him go," I said. "That's what I thought."

I got to my feet, turned, and walked out of the coffee shop. Both Nick and Daniel hurried after me. When I got to the car, Daniel's hand shot out and held the door shut.

"You've seen the photos, haven't you?" he asked.

I stopped, but didn't turn around.

"I know you've seen the photos," Daniel continued. "You've seen what kind of shape he's in. You've seen that it's getting worse. How much longer do you think he can hold out?"

I turned around slowly. I turned and I saw Daniel's face and I saw the satisfaction in his eyes and I lost it. For the past half hour, I'd been struggling not to think about Clay. As I'd talked to Daniel, I'd fought not to remember that he was the one holding Clay captive, that he'd drugged him and beaten him until there was scarcely an inch of skin left unmarked. I'd concentrated on talking to Daniel as I'd talked to him a hundred times before, as it if was just another message I was conveying from Jeremy telling him to shape up or face punishment. I'd really, really, really tried to forget what was actually happening. But when he stood there and threatened Clay, I couldn't pretend anymore. The rage inside me bubbled over before I could rein it back.

I grabbed him by the shirtfront and threw him against my car so hard the driver's window shattered into a million bits of safety glass.

"You sniveling hyena." I pressed myself against him until our faces were only inches apart. "You kidnap him with a hypodermic needle. You chain him up so you can beat him. But that's not good enough. You have to drug him first. You have to make absolutely certain he can't even summon the strength to spit in your face. Then you beat him. Did it feel good? Did it make you feel like a man, beating your enemy to a pulp when he can't lift a finger to fight back? You're not a man and you're not a wolf. You're a hyena, a bottom-feeding coward. If you lay another hand on him, I'll do something to you that will make that ear bite look like a paper cut. And if you kill him, I swear to God and the devil and anyone who will listen, if you kill him, I will hunt you down. I will find you and I will inflict on you every torture I can imagine. I'll blind you and I'll castrate you and I'll burn you. But I won't kill you. I won't let you die. I'll put you in hell and I'll make you live there for the rest of your life."

I threw Daniel aside. He stumbled, recovered, and turned to face me. His mouth opened, closed, opened again, but he couldn't seem to think of a suitable reply, so he settled for turning on his heel and stamping back into the coffee shop, where it looked as if every one of the dozen customers had suddenly taken a window seat. As I looked away I heard a low whistle and turned to see Marsten leaning against the back of the car.

"The bitch is back," Marsten said. "Well, well. This might get interesting."

"Go to hell," I snarled.

I threw open the car door, got in, and started it up as Nick jumped into the passenger side. The Camaro roared from the parking spot, tires squealing. I didn't look at the speedometer the whole way back to Stonehaven.

I'd been right about one thing. The time for games was over.

CHAPTER 32

REGRESSION

I left Stonehaven after everyone had gone to bed. I dressed in the dark, jumped out my window, then rolled my car a half mile down the road before starting it. I hadn't told Nick my plans. He was better off not knowing.

I'd gone to my room early and spent the evening in bed, thinking. My meeting with Daniel had been a mistake. By refusing his offer, I'd only made things worse. Jeremy had been buying time for Clay. I'd stolen it away. To fix things, I had to act now.

For several hours that evening, I'd tried mentally contacting Clay. Of course it didn't work. I wasn't even sure how to do it, but I'd held out some small hope that our connection might be enough. Maybe it would have been, but it was like demanding special effort from a muscle I'd ignored for too long. Nothing happened. When I couldn't get into Clay's mind, I decided to work on getting into the minds of the mutts who held him captive. Get into their minds figuratively, I mean. If I put myself in their position and tried to imagine what they'd be feeling or thinking, maybe I could find a weakness. Daniel and Marsten were easy to understand. I knew what they wanted and I knew how they operated. Marsten wouldn't leave any openings for me to slip through. Daniel's weakness was his obsession with Clay and with me. I could work on that, contact him again and try reeling him in with lies and smiles, but it would take time and I didn't have time. That left the new mutts. Here I was on unfamiliar ground. They weren't werewolves, I reminded myself. Not real ones. So how could I get inside their heads?

For the longest time, I lay in bed, staring at the ceiling, overwhelmed by the impossibility of understanding these two. Then it came to me. They weren't werewolves, but they were human. I'd been human. I was still trying to be human. Why couldn't I get into their heads? All I had to do was strip away my wolf side, something I'd been trying to do for years already. Yet there was more to understanding these killers than that. I couldn't be the sort of human I'd been trying to be—even-tempered, passive, and caring. I had to be what I had been before.

Every defense mechanism in my brain threw up barriers at the thought. Be what I'd been before Clay bit me? But I'd been even-tempered, passive, caring. Clay had changed that. Before him, I was different. I wasn't like *this*. That's what I wanted to believe, but I knew it wasn't true. I'd always had the capacity for violence. Clay had seen that. The child-werewolf looked at the child victim and saw a soul mate, someone who understood what it was like to grow up alienated, our odd behavior scrutinized by adults and mocked by children. By the age of seven Clay was a full were-wolf with an inherent capacity for violence and a temper to match. By the same age my foster families had taught me how to hate, developing my own capacity for violence, though I'd been better at hiding it, turning it inward and struggling to show the world the passive little girl it expected to see. It was time I confronted that. Clay didn't make me the way I was. He only gave me an outlet for the anger and the hate. I had to go back there, back to the mistrust and the hatred and the impotence and the rage, most of all the rage, against everyone who had wronged me. There I'd find the mind of a killer, a human killer.

LeBlanc hated women. Maybe he'd been mistreated by his mother or laughed at by girls in school or maybe he had such low self-esteem that he needed to feel superior to some group of people and chose women instead of blacks or Jews. If it was self-esteem, I could use that. But to find the truth, I'd need to research his life, looking for some road sign to his psychopathology. Again, I didn't have time.

What about Victor Olson? I started to dismiss the idea without a second thought. After all, I'd never even met the man. But did I need to? I pulled the two Internet article printouts from my dresser drawer and studied them. What did they tell me about Olson? He was a stalker. A compulsive stalker. In one article, he'd admitted to going out every night to watch his victims sleep, said that seeing their peaceful sleeping faces relaxed him and helped his insomnia. Would becoming a werewolf cure that compulsion or that insomnia? Of course not. Which meant there was a very good chance Olson hadn't abandoned his old patterns, that he was still watching young girls sleep, here in Bear Valley.

I'd left Stonehaven to find Olson. The articles said he targeted girls from middle-class homes. I assumed he'd be looking for single-story homes, so he could peek through a first-floor window. There were only two such subdivisions in Bear Valley. All I had to do was cruise the streets and sniff him out.

After driving around Bear Valley for over an hour, I began to realize how big a task this was. Sure, there were only two subdivisions, but each contained a dozen or more streets with at least a hundred homes. I only had several hours before dawn. To cover as much ground as possible, I drove slowly with all the windows down—except the smashed driver's window, which was now permanently down. Sometimes the wind favored me. Mostly it didn't and the only thing I smelled was the musty interior of my little-used car. Making matters worse, the police were out in full force, still looking for a killer. They were pulling over every car out that late that night, so I spent as much time avoiding them as looking for Olson. After two hours, I finished both subdivisions. No sign of Olson. For all I knew, he wasn't even out that night.

I was circling the second subdivision one last time when I saw a lone car in the parking lot of a convenience store, now conveniently closed for the night. As I passed, I noticed the rental sticker on the car's back bumper. Of course. If the mutts weren't hiding in town, Olson would need transportation to Bear Valley. I swung my car down a side road, parked, and got out. I didn't even make it halfway to the convenience store when I caught the scent of an unfamiliar werewolf.

I jogged around the corner and stopped short. A heavyset, middle-aged man in a windbreaker walked along the sidewalk, less than twenty feet from the corner. Fortunately, Olson had his back to me. He was heading toward his car. I hurried back around the corner and ran for my car. He drove by as I was turning the car around in a driveway. Keeping my headlights out, I followed.

As we drove out of Bear Valley, my heart pounded. I was right. They were staying in the countryside. Olson would lead me right to them. We'd been heading northwest for almost twenty minutes when Olson turned into an overgrown drive carved into deep forest. He stopped the car past the edge of the woods. I was about to enact part two of my plan when I realized Olson wasn't getting out of his car. Staying well back, I killed the engine and waited. Ten minutes passed. I could see the outline of his head in the car. I leaned over, carefully opened my passenger door, and slipped into a ditch.

I crept to the end of the drive. The forest was black. Even when my eyes adjusted, I could see no sign of a house. As I turned back toward Olson's car, I saw that the driveway went nowhere. It was only a turnaround or a one-car parking spot for a nature trail beyond. I moved into the woods and snuck closer to the car. When I was parallel to the driver's side, I stopped and squinted through the darkness. Olson's head was resting against the headrest. His eyes were closed. Asleep. I briefly wondered why, but the question was irrelevant. Maybe he couldn't sleep near the others. Or maybe he liked to be alone after his spying trips. It didn't matter. Victor Olson wasn't leading me back to Clay. At least not tonight. But I couldn't wait until morning. Come morning, Jeremy would know I was gone. The Pack would be looking for me. Even if I managed to elude them for another day, that would be another twenty-four hours for Daniel to kill Clay. And what if Olson wasn't just taking a break from the mutts? What if he wasn't ever going back to them? He knew where Clay was. I had to know—tonight.

A plan formed in my head as I watched Olson sleep. Even as I contemplated it, I rebelled at the thought. I hesitated, then forced myself forward out of the trees before I could change my mind. I crept to the side of the car, then pulled my fist back and smashed the driver's side window. Even as Olson was bolting awake, I was reaching through the window. I jerked the seat belt. It slid through my fingers as it tightened around him. He snapped his head back, away from my hand, but I was already reaching past him. Leaning into the car, I grabbed the seat belt buckle, twisting the metal and breaking the plastic, jamming the buckle closed. Then I pulled my head out of the car.

Olson whipped his head around, following my hand as it moved past him. He looked up at me. For a moment, he just stared, fixing me with the wide eyes of a coward bracing for the first blow. Even as I stepped away, he flinched. When he realized I was backing off, his brow furrowed, then his eyes lit up with a flash of malevolent cunning and he started to smile. Keeping his eyes on me, he lowered his right hand to the seat belt lock. He pushed the release button, but nothing happened. Realizing what I'd done, he grabbed the seat belt strap and yanked, but it was locked tight against his chest.

I knew what I had to do, but again I hesitated. Could I do it? Thoughts of Jose Carter flashed in my brain. This was different, I told myself. This wasn't some human con man, but a killer. Still, what I was about to do was beyond what I'd done to Carter. Way beyond. This was Clay's territory. Could I do it? Detach myself from my feelings and do it? Olson's a killer, I told myself. More than a killer. A sick pervert who'd preyed on little girls, little girls like the one I'd been so many lifetimes ago. I closed my eyes and concentrated, feeling the serpent of anger whiplashing through my body.

Olson struggled against the seat belt, but it held, the fabric made to withstand more punishment than even a werewolf could deal out. I ignored him and focused all my energy into my left hand. It started to throb, then twist, the pain shooting up my arm. I opened my eyes and watched.

When my hand was half changed, I stopped. With my right hand, I reached into the car and grabbed Olson's right wrist. I slashed it with the claws on my left. He screamed, a high-pitched rabbity squeal. A red line opened on the underside of his wrist. Blood gushed. I grabbed his left hand and did the same. He screamed again and squirmed wildly. Blood sprayed the steering wheel and dashboard.

"Moving will only make it worse," I said, keeping my voice calm and willing my hand back to normal. "If you want the bleeding to slow down, hold your hands up."

"Wh—wh—?"

"Why? Why am I doing this? Or why am I telling you how to slow it down? I shouldn't need to answer the first. Obviously you know who I am. That's answer enough. As for the second, I'm not trying to kill you. I just want information. If you give it to me, I'll undo the seat belt. You can bind your wrists and probably have time to get to the hospital. If you don't tell me what I want to know, you'll be killing yourself."

"Wh—" Olson gulped. "What do you wa—want to know?"

"Again, I shouldn't have to answer that. But since you might be going into shock and not thinking too clearly, I'll humor you. Where's Clayton?"

I won't report the rest of the conversation. Olson was in no shape to bargain or argue and he knew it. As I expected, he didn't give a damn about the others. Only his own life mattered. He told me everything I needed to know and more, babbling madly as if every word he spoke would improve his chance of survival.

When he was done, I left him sitting in his car. I thought about undoing the seat belt and giving him a fighting chance to escape. After all, I'd promised him that. I'd never reneged on a deal before. Then I thought of all the girls he'd victimized and imagined all the times he'd made promises to them, promising not to hurt them, promising never to do it again. He hadn't kept his promises. Why should I?

I walked away and left Victor Olson to bleed to death in the forest.

Chapter 33

Confrontation

I stopped at a gas station and called Stonehaven. The first two times, the machine picked up. On the third round, Nick answered. He was half asleep and I had to repeat myself twice before he clued in that I wasn't somewhere in the house. No one had noticed my disappearing act yet. I gave him instructions and had him write them down then read them back to me. By then, he had finally realized what I was saying and what I planned to do. I hung up when he started yelling.

Ten minutes later, I was knocking on the front door of the mutts' hideaway. It was a rundown cottage set so far back in the woods that no light penetrated the canopy of trees. As I stood on the front step, I listened for the rustle of the wind or the chirping of crickets, but heard nothing. The silence and the dark were complete.

Several minutes passed without a response. I knocked again. More minutes ticked by, but I didn't doubt Olson's directions. This was the right place. I could feel Clay here.

I pounded on the door. Finally the barest shimmer of light shone from between heavy front drapes. Footsteps sounded on a wooden plank floor. I looked down at the door handle and saw it was broken. Above it was a hole and fresh splinters where a dead bolt had been. Did I really expect the mutts to buy or rent a cottage when they could break into one? How stupid I'd been. How much time I'd wasted.

The door opened. I glanced up. It took a second to recognize the man standing there was Karl Marsten, partly because of the dim lighting and partly because of his attire. He wore only pajama bottoms, his bare chest showing muscles and battle scars normally hidden by expensive shirts. He squinted and blinked at me, then swore under his breath and quickstepped out the door, closing it behind him.

"What the hell are you doing here?" he said in a whispery growl.

I looked around him at the closed door. "Afraid I'll wake up your wife?"

"My—?" He glanced over his shoulder at the door, then turned back to me, his scowl smoothed over, studied nonchalance firmly back in place. "I'm sure this is a wonderful plan, Elena, but I really must advise against it. If you go in there, you'll leave in chains or a body bag. Neither would suit you."

"So you came out here to warn me? Wow, chivalry isn't dead after all."

"You know me better than that. I see an opportunity, I take advantage of it."

"So you'll let me leave in return for . . . ?"

"What I came for." His eyes glittered, something hard piercing the sangfroid. "Territory. Promise me that and I'll let you go. I'll leave, too. One less 'mutt' for the Pack to worry about."

"To hell with the others?"

"Daniel would do the same to me. I didn't hear my name being bandied about in that deal he offered you at the coffee shop."

I shook my head. "It doesn't matter. I'm not leaving."

I reached around him for the door handle. Marsten grabbed my wrist, squeezing hard enough to bruise.

"Don't be stupid, Elena. You're not getting him out that way."

"What way?" Daniel's voice was smooth and cool as he swung open the door. He met Marsten's eyes. "What way, Karl?"

"Sleeping soundly enough, Danny-boy? Christ, the whole Pack could be howling on your doorstep before you woke up." Marsten threw Daniel a contemptuous look and pushed me into the cabin. "It's an ambush, you moron. Elena wouldn't show up alone. Get your flunky out there searching the woods. Make himself useful for once."

I don't know if Daniel argued. I was too busy picking myself up off the floor after a shove from Marsten that sent me flying across the room. Before I could recover, Marsten had a knee on my back and had pinned me to the floor. I expected to be tied up. I wasn't. Maybe Marsten didn't think I posed enough of a threat. Moments later, footsteps sounded behind me. I smelled LeBlanc join Daniel and Marsten.

"Olson's gone," Daniel said.

"Gone for good, I would assume," Marsten said. "How else did you think she found us? It's a great loss for the cause, though. One never knows when a kiddie raper would come in handy."

"He had other—" Daniel began, then snapped his mouth shut. "Thomas, outside. Look for the others."

The front door slammed behind LeBlanc.

"That's one loyal pup you've got there," I said, lifting my mouth from the floor. "You know he tried to kill me at the airport. Before I left for Toronto."

A moment of silence. Then Daniel laughed. "Nice try, Elena. Sowing dissension?"

"Doesn't seem like I need to."

"Now, now, Elena," Marsten said, knee pressing me further into the floor. "As much as we all admire that tongue of yours, this is not the time to use it."

"Don't forget who's downstairs," Daniel said. "You're in no position to defend him now."

I shut my mouth and calculated how long it would take Jeremy, Antonio, and Nick to arrive. At least fifteen minutes to wake up, dress, and get into the car, another thirty to drive here. When LeBlanc came in after ten minutes, I knew he hadn't found anyone. The others wouldn't have arrived yet.

"No one out there," he said, knocking dirt off his boots.

"Take the car," Daniel said. "Drive around and make sure. Look for a vehicle by the side of the road. They would have driven."

For a moment, LeBlanc didn't move. I thought he was going to tell Daniel where to stuff it. Instead, he grabbed a ring of keys and tramped out the door. This time he was gone at least twenty minutes, during which neither Daniel nor Marsten said a word. When LeBlanc finally returned, I managed to turn my head to the side and saw him grinning.

"What?" Daniel said.

"Oh, you're gonna love this. The cavalry has been detained." He turned his shark's grin on me. "They're on Pinecrest, just off the highway, enjoying the hospitality of the local P.D. Cops nailed them. Don't know what for, but they're taking the car apart bolt by bolt. What do you think of that?"

"I think it's bullshit," I said.

His grin broadened. "Green Ford Explorer? Three guys? All dark-haired. Two over six foot, thin? Oldest shorter than me, quarterback shoulders? When I drove by, the young guy was trying to slip into the woods. Cops grabbed him and had him spread-eagled when I circled back."

"Bullshit," I said.

LeBlanc laughed. "Not quite the same air of certainty that time."

"Enough," Marsten said, yanking me to my feet. "They won't be detained forever." He jerked my wrists behind my back and clamped one hand around them. "Tommy, bring our other guest upstairs. Time to move."

LeBlanc turned to stare at him. "Move? This is what you guys wanted, isn't it? To take down this 'pack'? We've got two here. The last three on the way. Three against three and we've already been forewarned. We have the upper hand."

"Bring Clayton upstairs," Daniel said.

"What the fuck?" LeBlanc looked from Marsten to Daniel. "This is it. Showdown at the OK Corral. Killing time. Don't tell me you guys don't have the balls—"

"We have more brains than balls," Marsten said. "That's why we're still alive. Now get Clayton. We have him and we have Elena. That guarantees you'll get your fight soon, with odds of our making, not theirs."

LeBlanc shot a glare of pure contempt at Marsten, marched into a side hall, and vanished.

I gritted my teeth and focused on my plan. Were the others really detained by the cops? I didn't believe it. I couldn't. But I'd seen the police presence out here. If they'd come roaring down the highway, driving the very vehicle that the police had expressed such interest in the other day . . . ? Why hadn't I warned Nick?

Okay. Relax. Time to switch to plan B. If only I had a plan B.

As I was frantically working on an alternate plot, Marsten swung me around. Daniel sat on the arm of an overstuffed recliner that stank of mildew. Two figures emerged from another room. One stumbled forward and tripped. A flash of gold curls glinted in the dim light.

"Clay!"

Without thinking, I dove toward him. Still holding my wrists, Marsten swung me backward, jolting my arms so hard I gasped. Clay was on his knees, hands bound behind him. He struggled to lift his head. He met my eyes. For a second, he stared, his eyes struggling to focus. Then recognition broke through the drugged haze.

"No," he whispered, his voice paper-thin. "No."

He made a move, so slight I barely saw it. Behind him, LeBlanc's foot came up and kicked him square in the back, sending him sprawling face first to the floor.

"No!" I shouted.

I lunged at LeBlanc. Again, Marsten yanked me back, nearly dislocating my shoulders. I didn't care. I kept pulling. LeBlanc grabbed Clay by the handcuffs and dragged him to his feet.

"Leave him there," Marsten said. As LeBlanc sauntered by, Marsten whipped out his free hand and snagged something from LeBlanc's waistband. His gun. "Aren't you ever going to outgrow your security blanket?"

LeBlanc grabbed for the pistol. Marsten held it out of reach.

"A werewolf with a handgun?" Marsten said. "This is a sorry day. Brilliant idea, Daniel. Turn a bunch of human killers into werewolves. Now why didn't I think of that? Maybe because . . . it's stupid. You're never going to wean him off his weapons, Danny-boy."

To my left, I could hear Clay breathing. I forced myself not to look at him. While Marsten and Daniel discussed their next move, I cast a surreptitious glance at my watch. Five-fifty. If the cops had stopped Jeremy, how long would they hold him? How much longer did I have to wait? Was that all I could come up with for a backup plan? Wait it out until help arrived? Not good enough. For all I knew, they could be taken to the precinct and kept there for hours. Jeremy would be frantic, but the only alternative would be to kill the police and he wouldn't do that unless absolutely necessary. He'd know Daniel would hold Clay and me as hostages, not kill us—at least not right away. Since the danger wasn't immediate, Jeremy would wait out the police procedures. Yet by the time he arrived, we might be gone. No, strike that. We would be gone. Daniel was already gathering his wallet and car keys.

I looked at Clay. He was still lying facedown on the floor. His back was a quilt-work of purple, yellow, and black bruises with red welts and cuts sewing the pieces together. His left leg buckled awkwardly to the side, as if it was broken and he'd been forced to walk on it. His back rose and fell with shallow breaths. I looked at him and I knew what I had to do.

"We had a deal," I said, turning to Daniel. "I'm here. Let him go."

No one answered. Marsten and Daniel stared at me as if I'd lost my mind. An hour ago, this was exactly the reaction I'd anticipated. I'd planned to show up at the front door and turn myself over to Daniel. They'd be shocked, of course. Somewhere between the surprise and the eventual self-congratulations, the Pack would arrive. My version of the old Trojan horse trick. Only the warriors weren't coming. The gift was in the enemy camp and there was no taking it back now.

"Don't. You. Dare." Clay's whisper floated up from the floor.

He raised his head enough to glare at me. I looked away. Everyone else ignored him. For the first time in Clay's life, he was with a group of mutts and no one was paying the least attention to him. They'd stolen not only his strength, but his dignity. It was my fault. I was supposed to stay with him in Toronto, but I hadn't. What had distracted me so much that I'd gone to work and left Clay behind? A marriage proposal from another man. My stomach clenched at the memory.

I turned back to Daniel. "You wanted me, you have me. You wanted Clay on his knees. You have that. Now live up to your end of the bargain. Let him go and I'll go with you willingly. Right now." I twisted to look over my shoulder at Marsten. "Make sure he leaves Clay here and you'll get your territory. When Jeremy shows up, Clay will tell him that I made the deal. He'll honor it."

More silence. Marsten and Daniel were thinking. I was offering exactly what they wanted—territory for Marsten and my willing self for Daniel, sealing his revenge against Clay and the Pack. Was it enough? They didn't want a showdown. Time was already ticking past, each second increasing the likelihood that Jeremy, Antonio, and Nick would arrive. I'd fight before I let them take me out of here. They knew that. They'd have to subdue and restrain me, then haul both Clay and me into the car.

"No deal."

I jerked my head up. The answer had come from Daniel's direction, but it hadn't sounded like him. From behind Daniel, LeBlanc stepped forward, hands in his pockets.

"No deal," he repeated. His voice was soft, but it sliced through the silence.

Marsten gave a low chuckle. "Ah, the peasants revolt. I suppose—"

Before he could finish, LeBlanc's hand darted from his pocket. Silver winked in the lamplight. His hand shot in front of Daniel's throat and sliced sideways. For a millisecond, it appeared as if nothing had happened. Daniel stood there, looking slightly confused. Then his throat split open in a slash of crimson. Blood spurted. Daniel's hands flew to his neck. His eyes bugged disbelieving. The blood gushed over his fingers and streamed down his arms. His mouth opened. He blew a bubble of pink, like some macabre bubblegum, then slid to the floor.

I stared at Daniel, blinking, as unable to believe his death as he. Daniel was dying. The mutt who'd plagued the Pack for over a decade, who'd outwitted plots by both Clay and me to make him screw up enough to deserve execution. Dead. Not killed in some long, dangerous fight. Not killed by Clay. Not even killed by me. Killed by a new mutt with a knife. Killed in an instant. In a trick so cowardly and so completely human that all Marsten and I could do was gape.

As Daniel lay gasping and dying on the floor, LeBlanc stepped over him as if he were a fallen log. He held up the switchblade. It was almost clean, discolored only by specks of crimson.

"No deal," he said, advancing on Marsten.

Marsten snatched the gun from the table and pointed it at LeBlanc.

"Yes, I know. I said real werewolves don't use weapons. But you'll find I'm quite adaptable, particularly when it comes to saving my own hide." Marsten smiled, lips curving, eyes ice-cold. "Is this your 'showdown at the OK Corral'? Knife versus gun? Any bets on the outcome?"

LeBlanc jiggled the knife, as if contemplating throwing it. Then he stopped.

"Smart man," Marsten said. "What do you say we save ourselves some bloodshed and make a deal? An even split. I get Clayton. You get Elena. We go our separate ways from here."

When LeBlanc didn't respond, Marsten continued, "That's what you want, isn't it? That's why you killed Daniel, because Elena humiliated you and you want revenge."

From the look that flashed across LeBlanc's face, I knew he hadn't killed Daniel to get me. He hadn't killed him to get anything at all. LeBlanc had joined this battle because he liked to kill. Now as a cease-fire had been nearing, he'd turned on his comrades, not out of anger or greed, but simply because they were there, more lives to take before the fun came to an end. Now he was weighing his options. Should he take me and be satisfied? Or could he get Marsten and Clay in the bargain?

"You don't want her?" LeBlanc asked. "I thought all you guys wanted her."

"I've never been one for following the crowd," Marsten said. "While Elena certainly has her attractions, she wouldn't suit my lifestyle. I want territory. Clayton is the better bargaining chip. And I'm sure you'll have more fun with Elena."

"You son-of-a-bitch," I snarled.

I whipped around, yanking my arms free from Marsten's grasp. I aimed a fist at his stomach, but he twisted at the last moment and my knuckles only grazed his abs. His foot shot out and hooked mine, flipping me to the floor. My head struck the corner of an empty gun rack. I blacked out for a moment. When I came to, Marsten's gray eyes were boring into mine. I blinked and tried to get up, but he held me down. He pushed my chin forward so I faced the wall.

"She's unconscious," he said, getting to his knees. "All the better. We're getting low on sedatives."

Unconscious? I blinked again, slowly, feeling my eyes close, then reopen. I was staring at a line of mouse turds along the bottom of the wall. I was definitely awake. Hadn't Marsten seen me open my eyes? I began to lift my head, then thought better of it and lay still. Let them think I was unconscious. I needed all the advantages I could get.

Marsten stood. I heard him move a few feet away.

"What are you doing?" LeBlanc asked sharply.

"Taking my booty and getting the hell out of here, which is what I suggest you do as well. If Elena isn't enough of a reward, you're more than welcome to take any money you can find in Daniel's and Vic's belongings."

"Stop untying him," LeBlanc said.

Marsten sighed. "Don't tell me Daniel made you paranoid, too. Clayton is barely breathing. He wouldn't be a threat to a Chihuahua. I'm in a hurry. If he can walk, I want him walking."

"I haven't agreed to the deal yet."

Eyes closed, I inched my chin down, then peeked. Marsten was bent over Clay. He'd pulled him onto his knees. Clay swayed. Only a hint of blue showed from narrowed eyes. The gun lay ten feet away, abandoned. I doubted Marsten would know how to use it anyway.

"I said, stop untying him," LeBlanc said.

"Oh, for Christ's sake," Marsten muttered. "Fine."

He straightened up. Then, before Marsten was even fully standing, he lunged at LeBlanc. Marsten and LeBlanc fell to the floor. While the two fought, I got to my hands and knees and crept toward Clay. As I took hold of his handcuffs, his head jolted up. He looked over his shoulder at me.

"Go," he rasped.

I grabbed the two cuffs and yanked hard on the chain. The links stretched, but didn't break.

"No time," he said, trying to twist toward me. "Go."

As I met his eyes, I knew how wrong I'd been. I didn't come here to get him back for Jeremy or the Pack. I came to get him back for me. Because I loved him, loved him so much I'd risk everything for the faintest hope of saving him. Even now, as I realized he was right, that there wasn't time to get him out, I knew I wouldn't leave him here. I'd rather die.

I looked around wildly for a weapon, then suddenly stopped. Weapon? I was looking for a weapon? Had I lost my mind? I already had the best possible weapon. If only I had time to get it ready.

I dropped to my hands and knees and concentrated. Dimly, I heard Clay growl my name. I moved away. The Change started at its normal pace. Not good enough. Not enough time! My thoughts flitted in panic for a moment. I started trying to rein them in, then realized my Change was gaining speed. Throwing control aside, I let my fears run wild. If I failed, I was dead. If I failed, Clay was dead. I'd screwed up so badly, so completely. Fear and pain twisted through me. I doubled over and surrendered to it. A blinding flash of agony. Then victory.

I stood. Ahead, I saw LeBlanc bent over Marsten's prone form. He lifted his hand. The switchblade flashed. I growled. LeBlanc stopped in mid-strike and looked back at me. I flew at him. He dropped the knife and rolled out of the way. I'd put too much into the leap and hit the floor crooked, somersaulting into the wall. By the time I recovered, LeBlanc was gone.

I heard a voice and jerked my head toward it. Marsten was sitting up, wheezing. He pointed to the open back door and coughed blood. More blood trickled from slashes on his arms and chest. I glanced at the rear door. I couldn't let LeBlanc escape. A woman had made him turn tail and run. He wouldn't rest until he'd had his revenge. Marsten said something, but I couldn't understand him. Blood pounded in my ears, urging me to go after LeBlanc. I started for the door. Behind me, Clay grunted and I heard scuffling as he tried to stand. Remembering him, I turned back to Marsten. I wasn't leaving him with Clay. Lowering my head between my shoulder blades, I snarled. Marsten froze. His lips moved. Only a jumble of meaningless sound reached my ears. I crouched.

"Elena!" Clay said.

I could understand him. I stopped. Clay was on his feet now.

"Don't. Waste. Time," he said.

I looked at Marsten. He said one word. I still couldn't understand him, but I could read his lips. Territory. It was all he wanted. All he cared about. He'd known perfectly well that I was conscious on that floor. I'd played right into his plans. He was a single-minded, treacherous bastard, but he wouldn't hurt Clay. Killing Clay wouldn't get Marsten his territory. Keeping him alive and safe would.

I growled once more at Marsten, then tore out the door after LeBlanc.

LeBlanc's trail was easy to find. I didn't even have to track his scent. I could hear him thundering through the thick brush. Fool. I dove into the forest and started to run. Branches snagged in my fur and whipped against my face. I closed my eyes to slits to protect them and kept running. LeBlanc had trampled a path through the undergrowth. I stuck to it. Minutes later, the woods turned silent. LeBlanc had stopped. He must have realized that his only hope was to Change. I lifted my nose and sampled the breezes. The east wind held traces of his scent, but when a draft from the southeast hit me, it was full of him. I lifted one forepaw and brought it down on a pile of dead undergrowth. It was damp with the morning dew and barely whispered under my weight. Good. I turned southeast and crept forward.

Night had passed. Dawn lightened the thick blanket of trees overhead, sending shards of sun through to the forest floor. As I stepped in one pool of light, I could feel it warm my back with the promise of a sultry late spring day. Mist rose from the long grass and shrubs, the cool night earth rising to meet the warm morning. I inhaled the fog, closing my eyes to enjoy the clean nothingness of the smell. An eastern bluebird started singing somewhere to my left. A beautiful morning. I inhaled again, drinking it in, feeling the fear of the night give way to the anticipation of the hunt. It would end here. It would all end here, on this most beautiful of mornings.

When I heard LeBlanc's breathing, I stopped. I tilted my head and listened. He was crouching behind a thicket, breathing hard as he worked at his Change. I inched forward until I was outside the edge of his thicket and peeked through a fringe of fern. As I'd guessed by the height of his breathing sounds, he was crouching. But I'd been wrong about one thing. He wasn't Changing. He hadn't even undressed. A tremor of excitement raced through me. He was afraid, but instead of giving into the fear, he was fighting the Change. I pushed my muzzle through the fern and drank in the mead of his fear. It warmed me, fanning the spark of excitement into near-lust. LeBlanc might have scared me in the airport parking lot, but this was my arena.

LeBlanc shifted his weight and leaned forward to peer from the thicket. Use your nose, I thought. One sniff and you'd know the truth. But he didn't. He eased one leg back. His knee cracked and he froze, breath coming in shallow spurts. His head moved from side to side, listening and looking. Lifting the switchblade, he snapped it open, then waited for the sound to bring me to him. Something padded through the undergrowth beyond, a cat or a fox or something equally small and silent. LeBlanc tensed, raising the knife. Fool, fool, fool. I was growing tired of this. I wanted to run. I wanted to chase. I crept backward a dozen feet. Then I lifted my muzzle to the trees and howled. LeBlanc broke from the thicket and ran. I pursued.

LeBlanc had a head start. I let him keep it. We wove through the bushes and trees, jumping logs, trampling wildflowers, and sending two pheasants into the sky. He kept going deeper and deeper into the forest. Finally, he stopped running. As I realized I couldn't hear him any longer, I was bursting through into a clearing. Something slashed across my hind leg. I tumbled forward into the long grass. As I fell, I twisted around to see LeBlanc standing behind me, legs apart, switchblade raised, poised like a fighter waiting for the next round. He sneered and said something. I didn't need to hear the words to know what he said. Come and get me. A shudder of pleasure ran through me. He really was a fool.

I crouched and leapt at him. I didn't bother trying to figure out how to avoid the switchblade. It didn't matter. I felt the blade nick the side of my neck and slide across my shoulder. Blood welled up, hot against my skin. But there was no gushing, no pain worse than an irritating tingle. My fur was too thick. The knife had only scratched me. LeBlanc's arm went back to stab again, but it was too late. I was already on him. He flew backward, the blade arcing from his hand and vanishing in the trees. As my face came down to his, his eyes widened. Shock. Disbelief. Fear. I allowed myself one long moment to drink in his defeat. Then I ripped out his throat.

CHAPTER 34

READY

Jeremy, Antonio, and Nick did eventually show up at the cabin. They came through the door as I was using Clay's bindings to tie up Marsten. Naturally, Jeremy was incredibly impressed by how well I'd handled things on my own and vowed never to shut me out of anything ever again. Yeah, right. His first words were nonrepeatable. Then he said that if I ever, ever did anything so stupid again, he'd—well, that part was unrepeatable, too, though Clay, Antonio, and Nick were quick to repeat it, each adding their own threats. So, the brave soul who saved the day was forced to slink from her victory site and ride home in the backseat of her own car. It could have been worse. They could have put me in the trunk. Actually, Nick suggested that, but he was kidding . . . I think.

Jeremy gave Marsten his territory. Wyoming, to be exact. When Marsten complained, Jeremy offered to switch it to Utah. Marsten left muttering something about ten-gallon hats and rhinestone pants. Of course, he wouldn't settle for retiring on a dude ranch. He'd be back in search of territory more amenable to his lifestyle, but for now he knew when to shut his mouth and take what was offered.

Clay took a while to heal. A long while, actually. He had a broken leg, four broken ribs, and a dislocated shoulder. He was so bruised and battered that he was in pain lying down, sitting, standing—basically every moment he was awake. He was exhausted, starved, dehydrated, and pumped full of enough drugs to fell a rhino for days. I spent a week living in a chair by his bed before I was convinced he was going to make it. Even then, I only left his room to make meals and only because I decided Jeremy's cooking was doing Clay more harm than good.

I had to go back to Toronto. I'd known it since that day in the cabin, but I postponed it, telling myself Clay was too sick, Jeremy needed my help around the house, the Camaro was low on gas, pretty much any excuse I could come up with. But I had to go back. Philip was waiting. I had to confront him with what he'd seen, find out how he planned to handle it. Once that was done, I'd come back to Stonehaven. There was no longer any question of which home I'd choose. Maybe there never had been.

I belonged at Stonehaven. The idea still rankled. Maybe I'd never be entirely at peace with this life because I hadn't chosen it and I was too stubborn to ever completely accept something that had been forced on me. But Clay was right. I was happy here. There would always be a human part of me that would see fault with this way of living, a human morality appalled by the violence of it, vestiges of Puritanism that rebelled at such total immersion in satisfying primal needs. Yet even when Stonehaven didn't make me happy, when I was raging at Jeremy or at Clay or at myself, I was in a perverse way still happy, content at least, content and fulfilled.

Everything I'd chased in the human world was here. I wanted stability? I had it in a place and people who would always welcome me, no matter what I did. I wanted family? I had it in my Pack, loyalty and love beyond the simple labels of mother, father, sister, brother. So, realizing that everything I ever wanted was here, was I prepared to cast aside my human aspirations and bury myself in Stonehaven forever? Of course not. I'd always have the need to fit into the larger world. No amount of therapy or self-analysis would change that. I'd still hold down a job in the human world, maybe escape there for vacations when the insulated life of the Pack overwhelmed me. But Stonehaven was my home. I wouldn't run from it anymore.

Nor could I keep running from myself. I don't mean the werewolf part of me. I think I accepted that years ago, maybe even embraced it because it gave me an excuse for so many things in my life. If I was aggressive and snappish, it was the wolf blood. If I lashed out at others, wolf blood again. Ditto for any violent tendencies. Moody? Angry? Hot-tempered? Hell, I had a reason to be that way, didn't I? I was a monster. Not exactly a condition to invoke peace and inner harmony in the best of people. Yet I had to admit the truth. Being a werewolf didn't make me that way. Look at Jeremy, Antonio, Nick, Logan, Peter. Each one might have shared some of my less attractive characteristics, but so would almost any stranger pulled off the street. Being a werewolf made me more capable of acting on my anger, and living with the Pack made such behavior more acceptable, but everything that I was, I'd been before Clay bit me. Of course, knowing that and accepting it were two different things. I'd have to work on the accepting part.

It took almost a month from that day in Toronto for me to realize what Clay had meant when he'd said he knew why I picked Philip and why it couldn't work. The first two weeks after we recovered Clay were hell, some days not knowing if he'd make it to the next. At least, it seemed that way to me. I'd watch him lying unconscious in bed and be sure his chest had stopped rising. I'd call for Jeremy. No, strike that. I'd scream for Jeremy and he'd come running. Of course, Clay was breathing fine, but Jeremy never made me feel I'd overreacted. He'd murmur something about a temporary shortness of breath, maybe minor sleep apnea, and he'd examine Clay thoroughly before settling into the bedside chair to watch for a "relapse." By the third week, Clay was regaining consciousness for longer periods and even I had to admit the danger finally seemed past. That wasn't to say I stopped camping out at his bedside. I didn't. I couldn't. And as long as I insisted on being there, Jeremy insisted taking over bedside watch while I slept or went for a run, even though we both knew such constant vigilance was necessary only for my peace of mind.

Near the end of the third week, I came back from my shower to find Jeremy in my post by Clay's bed, in the exact same vigilant pose I'd left him in twenty minutes before. I stood in the door, watching him, taking in the circles under his eyes, the gaunt prominence of his cheekbones. I knew then that I had to stop, get a grip, and admit to myself that Clay was doing fine and would continue to do fine—if not better—without constant surveillance. If I didn't, I'd run myself into the ground and Jeremy would follow without a word of protest.

"Feeling better?" he asked without turning.

"Much."

He reached back as I approached, took my hand, and squeezed it. "He'll be awake soon. His stomach's growling."

"God forbid he should miss dinner."

"Speaking of which, we're going out tonight. You and I. Someplace requiring a suit and tie and a shave—at least for me. Antonio is driving in with Nick. They'll look after Clay."

"That's not nec—"

"It's very necessary. You need to get out, get your mind off this. Clay will be fine. We'll take your cell phone in case anything happens."

As I nodded and sat in the chair beside Jeremy, the answer to Clay's puzzle hit me with such force I had to gasp. Then I had to beat myself over the head for not having seen it earlier. Why had I chosen Philip? The answer had been staring me in the face since I'd returned to Stonehaven. Who did he remind me of? Jeremy, of course.

In my defense, Jeremy and Philip did not, outwardly at least, have much in common. They looked nothing alike. They didn't share the same gestures. They didn't even act the same way. Philip didn't have Jeremy's emotional control, his authoritarianism, his quiet reserve. But these weren't the qualities I most admired in Jeremy. What I saw in Philip was a shallower reflection of what I valued in Jeremy, his endless patience, his consideration, his innate goodness. Why did I subconsciously seek out someone who reminded me of Jeremy? Because in Jeremy I saw some girlish vision of Prince Charming, someone who would bring me flowers and care for me no matter how badly I screwed up. The problem with this fantasy was that I had absolutely no romantic feelings for Jeremy. I loved him as a friend, a leader, and a father figure. Nothing more. So in finding a human version of my ideal, I'd found a man I was certain to love, but never with the passion I'd feel for a lover.

Did that make me feel better? Of course not. In excusing my inability to fall in love with Philip, I wanted to be able to say that it was because of some problem in him, something he lacked. The truth was that the fault was entirely mine. I'd made a mistake and, as good and as decent as Philip was, he had to suffer for it.

After five weeks of postponing my return to Toronto, I decided to do it. Clay was taking an afternoon nap. I was lying beside him, half dozing, when I realized I had to leave right then, before I changed my mind. I got up and scribbled a note for Clay. Jeremy was out back fixing the stone wall. I didn't tell him where I was going. I was afraid he'd want me to eat dinner first or wait until he could drive me to the airport or some other delay that would give my resolve time to weaken.

I didn't call to tell Philip I was coming. Hearing his voice was one more thing that might make me change my mind. I went straight to the apartment and let myself in. He wasn't there. I settled onto the couch to wait. An hour later, he returned, panting from a run in the early July heat. He swung through the door, saw me, and stopped.

"Hi," I said, managing a weak smile.

I saw the fear in his eyes then and knew it never would have worked between us. No matter how close I got to any human, if they ever learned the truth about me, there would always be fear. You couldn't get past that.

"Hello," he said at last. He hesitated, then closed the apartment door, and mopped off his face. After giving himself time to recover, he laid his towel on the hall table and stepped into the room. "When did you get back?"

"Just now. How are you feeling?"

"Fine. I got your flowers. Thank you."

I inhaled. God, this was awkward. Had it always been this way? I couldn't even remember how we used to talk. Any sense of familiarity had flitted away.

"Your—uh—side must be better," I said. "If you're out jogging."

"Walking. Not jogging. Not yet."

He sat in the recliner opposite me. I inhaled again. This wasn't working. There was no easy way to do this.

"About what you saw that day . . ." I began.

He said nothing.

"About what you—uh—saw me do."

"I didn't see anything." His voice was soft, barely audible.

"I know you did and we need to talk about it."

He met my eyes. "I didn't see anything."

"Philip, I know—"

"No." He spat the word, then pulled back and shook his head. "I don't remember anything about that day, Elena. You went to work. Your cousin came up looking for you. Two other men came up looking for you. Someone stabbed me. Then it's all a blank."

I knew he was lying. For the safety of the Pack, I should pursue it, get him to admit what he'd seen, and find a way to explain it away. Yet something told me that this was better for Philip. Let him explain it his own way. I owed him that much.

"I should go now."

I got to my feet. He said nothing. I saw my bags stacked in the hall, next to a few boxes of his own stuff.

"I've subletted the apartment," he said. "I—" He rubbed the bridge of his nose. "I would have called you, your cell phone. I was . . . working my way up to it."

"I'm sorry."

"I know." He met my eyes for the first time since I'd arrived and managed the barest ghost of a smile. "It was good, still. A mistake, but a good one. If you come back to Toronto someday, maybe you can look me up. Have a drink together or something."

I nodded. As I lifted my bags, my gaze flitted to the hall table.

"It's in the drawer," Philip said softly.

I turned to say something, but he was heading into the bedroom, his back to me. He closed the door.

"I'm sorry," I whispered.

I pushed open the lobby doors and walked out carrying two small pieces of luggage. I'd left a note for Philip to give the rest to charity or throw it in the garbage. There was nothing there I needed. I only took the two bags so he wouldn't think I was abandoning my things in anger. There was only one item in that apartment I'd really wanted back, the item I'd retrieved from the hall table drawer. I still had it in my hand. As I stood in the building vestibule, I put down the luggage, and opened my fist. Clay's wedding band gleamed in the streetlights.

Clay.

What was I going to do about Clay?

Despite all we'd been through, I still couldn't give him what he wanted. I couldn't promise my life to him, swear I'd be by his side every waking and sleeping minute, 'til death do us part. But I loved him. Loved him completely. There would be no other men in my life, no other lovers. I could promise him that. As for the rest, well, I'd have to offer what I could and hope it would be enough.

"You're here."

I looked up sharply. Clay stood in the wavering yellow light of a streetlamp. For a moment, I thought I was imagining things. Then he stepped forward, his left leg dragging, not completely healed after his ordeal.

"Didn't you get my note?" I asked.

"Note?"

I shook my head. "You shouldn't be here. You're supposed to be in bed."

"I couldn't let you leave. Not until I talked to you."

I glanced at the luggage by my feet and realized he must have thought I was waiting to get inside the apartment building, instead of leaving it. Hmmm. Never let it be said I passed up the opportunity to milk something for all it's worth. Yes, I can be cruel, even sadistic on occasion.

"And what did you want to say to me?" I asked.

He stepped forward, putting one hand on my elbow and moving so close I could feel his heart beating through his shirt. It was pounding, but that might have just been from the exertion of the impromptu trip.

"I love you. Yes, you've heard that before, heard it a million times, but I don't know what else to say." He lifted a hand to my face and touched my cheek. "I need you. This last year, when you were gone, it was hell. I made up my mind that when you came back, I'd do whatever it took to get you back. No more tricks. No more tantrums. I know I didn't do a great job. Hell, you probably never even noticed the difference. But I was trying. I'll keep trying. Come back home with me. Please."

I looked up into his eyes. "Why did you go back up to the apartment?"

He blinked. "Huh?"

"The day you were attacked. You saw Daniel and LeBlanc go up to the apartment, didn't you?"

"Right . . ."

"You knew I wasn't up there. You'd just spoken to me on the phone."

"Right . . ."

"So you knew the only person in the apartment was Philip. Yet you went up there and tried to protect him. Why?"

Clay hesitated, then said, "Because I knew it was what you'd want me to do." He stroked his thumb across my cheek. "I know that's not the answer you want to hear. You want me to say I had a sudden flash of conscience and went up there to save Philip. But I can't lie. I can't feel the things you want me to feel. I didn't care whether Philip lived or died. I saved him because I knew you'd want me to, because I knew if anything happened to him, you'd be hurt."

"Thank you," I said, kissing him.

"That was a good answer?" A hint of his old grin slipped into his voice and his eyes.

"The best I can hope for. I know that now."

"So you'll stay?"

I smiled up at him. "I never planned to leave, which you'd know if you'd bothered to read my note before charging all the way here to stop me."

"You—" He stopped, threw back his head, and laughed, then caught me up in a bone-jarring kiss and hug. "I guess I deserved that."

"That and more." I grinned and kissed him, then pulled back and watched him.

"What is it?" he asked.

"When you were gone, I was thinking this story wouldn't have a happily ever after ending. Maybe I was wrong."

"Happily ever after?" He grinned. "As in 'forever after'?"

"Well, maybe not 'forever after.' Maybe 'happily ever after for a little while.'"

"I could live with that."

"Happily ever after for a day or two, at least."

"A day or two?" He made a face. "I was thinking of a bit longer. Not forever, of course. Just eight, maybe nine decades."

"Don't push your luck."

He laughed and lifted me up in another hug. "We'll work on it."

"Yes," I said, smiling down at him. "I'm ready to work on it."

Stolen

PROLOGUE

He hated the forest. Hated its eternal pockets of damp and darkness. Hated its endless tangle of trees and bushes. Hated its smell of decay—dead vegetation, dead animals, everything dying, even the living creatures incessantly pursuing their next meal, one failure away from the slow descent into death. Soon his body would be one more stink fouling the air, maybe buried, maybe left for the carrion feeders, his death postponing theirs for another day. He would die. He knew that, not with the single-minded intent of the suicidal or the hopeless despair of the doomed, but with the simple acceptance of a man who knows he is only hours from passing out of this world into the next. Here in this stinking, dark, damp hell of a place, he would die.

He didn't seek death. If he could, he'd avoid it. But he couldn't. He'd tried, planning his breakout for days, conserving his energy, forcing himself to eat, to sleep. Then he'd escaped, surprising himself really. He'd never truly believed it would work. Of course, it hadn't actually worked, just appeared to, like a mirage shimmering in the desert, only the oasis hadn't turned to sand and sun, but damp and dark. He'd escaped the compound to find himself in the forest. Still hopeful, he'd run. And run. And gone nowhere. They were coming now. Hunting him.

He could hear the hound baying, fast on his trail. There must be ways to trick it, but he had no idea how. Born and raised in the city, he knew how to avoid detection there, how to become invisible in plain sight, how to effect an appearance so mediocre that people could stare right at him and see no one. He knew how to greet neighbors in his apartment building, eyes lowered, a brief nod, no words, so if anyone asked about the occupants of 412, no one really knew who lived there: Was that the elderly couple? The young family? The blind girl? Never rude or friendly enough to attract attention, disappearing in a sea of people too intent on their own lives to notice his. There he was a master of invisibility. But here, in the forest? He hadn't set foot in one since he was ten, when his parents finally despaired of ever making an outdoorsman out of him and let him stay with his grandmother while his siblings went hiking and camping. He was lost here. Completely lost. The hound would find him and the hunters would kill him.

"You won't help me, will you?" he said, speaking the words in his mind.

For a long moment, Qiona didn't reply. He could sense her, the spirit who guided him, in the back corner of his mind, the farthest she ever went from him since she'd first made herself known when he was a child too young to speak.

"Do you want me to?" she asked finally.

"You won't. Even if I want it. This is what you want. For me to join you. You won't stop that."

The hound started to sing, joy infusing its voice with melody as it closed in on its target. Someone shouted.

Qiona sighed, the sound fluttering like a breeze through his mind. "What do you want me to do?"

"Which way is out?" he asked.

More silence. More shouts.

"That way," she said.

He knew which way she meant, though he couldn't see her. An ayami had presence and substance but no form, an idea impossible to explain to anyone who wasn't a shaman and as easy for a shaman to understand as the concept of water or sky.

Turning left, he ran. Branches whipped his face and bare chest and arms, raising welts like the marks of a flagellant. And equally self-inflicted, he thought. Part of him wanted to stop. Give up. Accept. But he couldn't. He wasn't ready to surrender his life yet. Simple human pleasures still held too much allure: English muffins with butter and strawberry jam at the Talbot Café, the second-story balcony, farthest table on the left, the sun on his forearms, tattered mystery novel in one hand, coffee mug in the other, people yelling, laughing on the busy street below. Silly things, Qiona would sniff. She was jealous, of course, as she was of anything she couldn't share, anything that kept him bound to his body. He did want to join her, but not yet. Not just yet. So he ran.

"Stop running," Qiona said.

He ignored her.

"Slow down," she said. "Pace yourself."

He ignored her.

She withdrew, her anger a flash fire in his brain, bright and hot, then smoldering, waiting to flare again. He'd stopped hearing the hound, but only because his blood pounded too loudly. His lungs blazed. Each breath scorched through him, like swallowing fire. He ignored it. That was easy. He ignored most of his body's commands, from hunger to sex to pain. His body was only a vehicle, a medium for transmitting things like strawberry jam, laughter, and sunlight to his soul. Now after a lifetime of ignoring his body, he asked it to save him and it didn't know how. From behind him came the bay of the hound. Was it louder now? Closer?

"Climb a tree," Qiona said.

"It's not the dog I'm afraid of. It's the men."

"Slow down then. Turn. Confuse them. You're making a straight trail. Slow down."

He couldn't. The end of the forest was near. It had to be. His only chance was to get there before the dog did. Ignoring the pain, he summoned every remaining vestige of strength and shot forward.

"Slow down!" Qiona shouted. "Watch—"

His left foot hit a small rise, but he adjusted, throwing his right foot out for balance. Yet his right foot came down on empty air. As he pitched forward, he saw the streambed below, at the bottom of a small gully eroded by decades of water flow. He flipped over the edge of it, convulsed in midair, trying to think of how to land without injury, but again he didn't know how. As he hit the gravel below, he heard the hound. Heard its song of triumph so loud his eardrums threatened to split. Twisting to get up, he saw three canine heads come over the gully edge, one hound, two massive guard dogs. The hound lifted its head and bayed. The other two paused only a second, then leaped.

"Get out!" Qiona screamed. "Get out now!"

No! He wasn't ready to leave. He resisted the urge to throw his soul free of his body, clenching himself into a ball as if that would keep it in. He saw the undersides of the dogs as they flew off the cliff. One landed atop him, knocking out his last bit of breath. Teeth dug into his forearm. He felt a tremendous wrenching. Then he soared upward. Qiona was dragging him from his body, away from the pain of dying.

"Don't look back," she said.

Of course, he did. He had to know. As he looked down, he saw the dogs. The hound was still at the top of the gully, howling and waiting for the men. The two other dogs didn't wait. They tore his body apart in a shower of blood and flesh.

"No," he moaned. "No."

Qiona comforted him with whispers and kisses, pleaded with him to look away. She'd tried to save him from the pain, but she couldn't. He felt it as he looked down at the dogs destroying his body, felt not the pain of their teeth, but the agony of unbelievable loss and grief. It was over. All over.

"If I hadn't tripped," he said. "If I'd run faster . . . "

Qiona turned him then, so he could look out across the forest. The expanse of trees went on and on, ending in a road so far away the cars looked like bugs crawling across the earth. He glanced back at his body, a mangled mess of blood and bone. The men stepped from the forest. He ignored them. They didn't matter anymore. Nothing did. He turned to Qiona and let her take him away.

"Dead," Tucker said to Matasumi as he walked into the cell-block guard station. He scraped the mud of the forest off his boots. "Dogs got him before we did."

"I told you I wanted him alive."

"And I told you we need more hounds. Rottweilers are for guarding, not hunting. A hound will wait for the hunter. A rottie kills. Doesn't know how to do anything else." Tucker removed his boots and laid them on the mat, perfectly aligned with the wall, laces tucked in. Then he took an identical but clean pair and pulled them on. "Can't see how it matters much. Guy was half-dead anyway. Weak. Useless."

"He was a shaman," Matasumi said. "Shamans don't need to be Olympic athletes. All their power is in their mind."

Tucker snorted. "And it did him a whole lotta good against those dogs, let me tell you. They didn't leave a piece of him bigger than my fist."

As Matasumi turned, someone swung open the door and clipped him in the chin.

"Whoops," Winsloe said with a grin. "Sorry, old man. Damn things need windows."

Bauer brushed past him. "Where's the shaman?"

"He didn't . . . survive," Matasumi said.

"Dogs," Tucker added.

Bauer shook her head and kept walking. A guard grabbed the interior door, holding it open as she walked through. Winsloe and the guard trailed after her. Matasumi brought up the rear. Tucker stayed at the guard station, presumably to discipline whoever had let the shaman escape, though the others didn't bother to ask. Such details were beneath them. That's why they'd hired Tucker.

The next door was thick steel with an elongated handle. Bauer paused in front of a small camera. A beam scanned her retina. One of the two lights above the door flashed green. The other stayed red until she grasped the door handle and the sensor checked her handprint. When the second light turned green, she opened the door and strode through. The guard followed. As Winsloe stepped forward, Matasumi reached for his arm, but missed. Alarms shrieked. Lights flashed. The sound of a half-dozen steel-toed boots clomped in synchronized quickstep down a distant corridor. Matasumi snatched the two-way radio from the table.

"Please call them back," Matasumi said. "It was only Mr. Winsloe. Again."

"Yes, sir," Tucker's voice crackled through the radio. "Would you remind Mr. Winsloe that each retinal and hand scan combination will authorize the passage of only one staff member and a second party."

They both knew Winsloe didn't need to be reminded of any such thing, since he'd designed the system. Matasumi stabbed the radio's disconnect button. Winsloe only grinned.

"Sorry, old man," Winsloe said. "Just testing the sensors."

He stepped back to the retina scanner. After the computer recognized him, the first light turned green. He grabbed the door handle, the second light flashed green, and the door opened. Matasumi could have followed without the scans, as the guard had, but he let the door close and followed the proper procedure. The admittance of a second party was intended to allow the passage of captives from one section of the compound to another, at a rate of only one captive per staff member. It was not supposed to allow two staff to pass together. Matasumi would remind Tucker to speak to his guards about this. They were all authorized to pass through these doors and should be doing so correctly, not taking shortcuts.

Past the security door, the interior hall looked like a hotel corridor, each side flanked by rooms furnished with a double bed, a small table, two chairs, and a door leading to a bathroom. Not luxury accommodations by any means, but simple and clean, like the upper end of the spectrum for the budget-conscious traveler, though the occupants of these rooms wouldn't be doing much traveling. These doors only opened from the outside.

The wall between the rooms and the corridor was a specially designed glass more durable than steel bars—and much nicer to look at. From the hallway, an observer could study the occupants like lab rats, which was the idea. The door to each room was also glass so the watcher's view wasn't obstructed. Even the facing wall of each bathroom was clear Plexiglas. The transparent bathroom walls were a recent renovation, not because the observers had decided they wanted to study their subjects' elimination practices, but because they'd found that when all four walls of the bathrooms were opaque, some of the subjects spent entire days in there to escape the constant scrutiny.

The exterior glass wall was actually one-way glass. They'd debated that, one-way versus two-way. Bauer had allowed Matasumi to make the final decision, and he'd sent his research assistants scurrying after every psychology treatise on the effects of continual observation. After weighing the evidence, he'd decided one-way glass would be less intrusive. By hiding the observers from sight, they were less likely to agitate the subjects. He'd been wrong. At least with two-way glass the subjects knew when they were being watched. With one-way, they knew they were being watched—none were naive enough to mistake the full-wall mirror for decoration—but they didn't know when, so they were on perpetual alert, which had a regrettably damning effect on their mental and physical health.

The group passed the four occupied cells. One subject had his chair turned toward the rear wall and sat motionless, ignoring the magazines, the books, the television, the radio, everything that had been provided for his diversion. He sat with his back to the one-way glass and did nothing. That one had been at the compound nearly a month. Another occupant had arrived only this morning. She also sat in her chair, but facing the one-way glass, glaring at it. Defiant . . . for now. It wouldn't last.

Tess, the one research assistant Matasumi had brought to the project, stood by the defiant occupant's cell, making notations on her clipboard. She looked up and nodded as they passed.

"Anything?" Bauer asked.

Tess glanced at Matasumi, shunting her reply to him. "Not yet."

"Because she can't or won't?" Bauer asked.

Another glance at Matasumi. "It appears . . . I would say . . . "

"Well?"

Tess inhaled. "Her attitude suggests that if she could do more, she would."

"Can't, then," Winsloe said. "We need a Coven witch. Why we bothered with this one—"

Bauer interrupted. "We bothered because she's supposed to be extremely powerful."

"According to Katzen," Winsloe said. "If you believe him. I don't. Sorcerer or not, the guy's full of shit. He's supposed to be helping us catch these freaks. Instead, all he does is tell us where to look, then sits back while our guys take all the risks. For what? This?" He jabbed a finger at the captive. "Our second useless witch. If we keep listening to Katzen, we're going to miss out on some real finds."

"Such as vampires and werewolves?" Bauer's lips curved in a small smile. "You're still miffed because Katzen says they don't exist."

"Vampires and werewolves," Matasumi muttered. "We are in the middle of unlocking unimaginable mental power, true magic. We have potential access to sorcerers, necromancers, shamans, witches, every conceivable vessel of magic . . . and he wants creatures that suck blood and howl at the moon. We are conducting serious scientific research here, not chasing bogeymen."

Winsloe stepped in front of Matasumi, towering six inches over him. "No, old man, you're conducting serious scientific research here. Sondra is looking for her holy grail. And me, I'm in it for fun. But I'm also bankrolling this little project, so if I say I want to hunt a werewolf, you'd better find me one to hunt."

"If you want to hunt a werewolf, then I'd suggest you put one in those video games of yours, because we can't provide what doesn't exist."

"Oh, we'll find something for Ty to hunt," Bauer said. "If we can't find one of his monsters, we'll have Katzen summon something suitably demonic."

"A demon?" Winsloe said. "Now that'd be cool."

"I'm sure it would," Bauer murmured and pushed open the door into the shaman's former cell.

CHAPTER I

DEMONIC

"Please tell me you don't believe in that stuff," said a voice beside my shoulder.

I looked at my seat-mate. Mid-forties, business suit, laptop, pale strip around his ring finger where he'd removed his wedding band. Nice touch. Very inconspicuous.

"You shouldn't read crap like that," he said, flashing a mouthful of coffee stains. "It'll rot your brain."

I nodded, smiled politely, and hoped he'd go away, at least as far away as he could on an airplane flying at an altitude of several thousand feet. Then I went back to reading the pages I'd printed from the believe.com website.

"Does that really say werewolves?" my seat-mate said. "Like fangs and fur? Michael Landon? *I Was a Teenage Werewolf*?"

"Michael . . . ?"

"Uh, an old movie. Before my time. Video, you know."

Another polite nod. Another not-so-polite attempt to return to my work.

"Is that for real?" my seat-mate asked. "Someone's selling information on werewolves? Werewolves? What kind of people would buy crap like that?"

"I would."

He stopped, finger poised above my papers, struggling to convince himself that someone could believe in werewolves and not be a complete nutcase, at least not if that someone was young, female, and stuck in the adjoining seat for another hour. I decided to help.

"For sure," I said, affecting my best breathless blond accent. "Werewolves are in. Vampires are so five minutes ago. Gothic, ugh. Me and my friends, we tried it once, but when I dyed my hair black, it went green. "

"That's, uh—"

"Green! Can you believe it? And the clothes they wanted us to wear? Totally gross. So then, like, Chase, he said, what about werewolves? He heard about this group in Miami, so we talked to them and they said vampires were out. Werewolves were the new thing. Chase and I, we went to see them, and they had these costumes, fur and teeth and stuff, and we put them on and popped these pills and presto, we were werewolves."

"Uh, really?" he said, eyes darting about for an escape route. "Well, I'm sure—"

"We could run and jump around and howl, and we went out hunting, and one of the guys caught this rabbit, and, like, I know it sounds gross, but we were so hungry and the smell of the blood—"

"Could you excuse me?" the man interrupted. "I need to use the washroom."

"Sure. You look a little green. Probably airsickness. My friend Tabby has that real bad. I hope you're feeling better, 'cause I was going to ask if you wanted to come with me tonight. There's this werewolf group in Pittsburgh. They're having a Grand Howl tonight. I'm meeting Chase there. He's kinda my boyfriend, but he switch-hits, you know, and he's really cute. I think you'd like him."

The man mumbled something and sprinted into the aisle faster than one would think possible for a guy who looked like he hadn't exceeded strolling speed since high school.

"Wait 'til I tell you about the Grand Howl," I called after him. "They're so cool."

Ten minutes later, he still hadn't returned. Damn shame. That airsickness can be a real son-of-a-bitch.

I returned to my reading. believe.com was a website that sold information on the paranormal, a supernatural eBay. Scary that such things existed. Even scarier was that they could turn a profit. believe.com had an entire category devoted to auctioning off pieces of spaceship wrecks that, at last count, had 320 items for sale. Werewolves didn't even warrant their own classification. They were lumped into "Zombies, Werewolves, and Other Miscellaneous Demonic Phenomena." Miscellaneous demonic phenomena? The demonic part kind of stung. I was not demonic. Well, maybe driving some hapless guy from his airplane seat wasn't exactly nice, but it certainly wasn't demonic. A miscellaneous demonic phenomenon would have shoved him out the escape hatch. I'd barely even been tempted to do that.

Yes, I was a werewolf, had been since I was twenty, nearly twelve years ago. Unlike me, most werewolves are born werewolves, though they can't Change forms until they reach adulthood. The gene is passed from father to son—daughters need not apply. The only way for a woman to become a werewolf is to be bitten by a werewolf and survive. That's rare, not the biting part, but the surviving part. I'd lived mainly because I was taken in by the Pack—which is exactly what it sounds like: a social structure based on the wolf pack, with an Alpha, protected territory, and clearly defined rules, rule one being that we didn't kill humans unless absolutely necessary. If we got the munchies, we pulled into the nearest fast-food drive-through like everybody else. Non-Pack werewolves, whom we called mutts, ate humans because they couldn't bother fighting the urge to hunt and kill, and humans were the most plentiful target. Pack wolves hunted deer and rabbits. Yes, I'd killed and eaten Bambi and Thumper. Sometimes I wondered if people wouldn't consider that even more shocking, in a world where a dog thrown from a car garners more media attention than murdered children. But I digress.

As part of the Pack, I lived with the Alpha—Jeremy Danvers—and Clayton Danvers, his adopted son/bodyguard/ second in command, who was also my partner/lover/bane of my existence . . . But that gets complicated. Back to the point. Like everyone else in the Pack, I had responsibilities. One of my jobs was to monitor the Internet for signs that some mutt was calling attention to himself. One place I looked was believe.com, though I rarely found anything deserving more than a dismissive read-over. Last February I'd followed up something in Georgia, not so much because the listing sounded major alarms, but because New York State had been in the middle of a weeklong snowstorm and any place south of the Carolinas sounded like heaven.

The posting I was reading now was different. It had the alarms clanging so hard that after I'd read it Tuesday, I'd left a message for the seller immediately, and set up a meeting with her in Pittsburgh for Friday, waiting three days only because I didn't want to seem too eager.

The posting read: "Werewolves. Valuable information for sale. True believers only. Two homeless killed in Phoenix 1993–94. Initially believed to be dog kills. Throats ripped. Bodies partially eaten. One oversized canine print found near second body. All other prints wiped away (very tidy dogs?). Zoologist identified print as extremely large wolf. Police investigated local zoos and concluded zoologist mistaken. Third victim was prostitute. Told roommate she had an all-night invitation. Found dead three days later. Pattern matched earlier kills. Roommate led police to hotel used by victim. Found evidence of cleaned-up blood in room. Police reluctant to switch focus to human killer. Decided third victim was copycat (copydog?) killing. Case remains open. All details public record. Check *Arizona Republic* to verify. Vendor has more. Media welcome."

Fascinating story. And completely true. Jeremy was responsible for checking newspaper accounts of maulings and other potential werewolf activity. In the *Arizona Republic* he'd found the article describing the second kill. The first hadn't made it into the papers—one dead homeless person wasn't news. I'd gone to investigate, arriving too late to help the third victim, but in time to ensure there wasn't a fourth. The guilty mutt was buried under six feet of desert sand. The Pack didn't look kindly on man-killers.

We hadn't been worried about the police investigation. In my experience, homicide detectives are a bright bunch, smart enough to know there's no such thing as werewolves. If they found mauling with canine evidence, they saw a dog kill. If they found mauling with human evidence, they saw a psychopath kill. If they found mauling with both human and canine evidence, they saw a psychopath with a dog or a murder site disturbed by a dog. They never, ever, saw a partially eaten body, footprints, and dog fur and said, "My God, we've got a werewolf!" Even wackos who believed in werewolves didn't see such murders as werewolf kills. They were too busy looking for crazed, half-human beasts who bay at the full moon, snatch babies from cradles, and leave prints that mysteriously change from paws to feet. So when I read something like this, I had to worry about what other information the vendor was selling.

The "media welcome" part worried me too. Almost all believe.com listings ended with "media need not inquire." Though vendors pretended the warning was meant to discourage tabloid journalists who'd mangle their stories, they were really worried that a legit reporter would show up and humiliate them. When I went to investigate such claims, I used the guise of being a member of a paranormal society. This time, since the vendor had no problem with media, I was pretending to be a journalist, which wasn't much of a stretch, since that was my profession, though my typical beat was freelancing articles on Canadian politics, which never included any mention of demonic phenomena, though it might explain the rise of the neo-conservatives.

Once in Pittsburgh, I caught a cab, registered at my hotel, dropped off my stuff, and headed to the meeting. I was supposed to meet the vendor—Ms. Winterbourne—outside a place called Tea for Two. It was exactly what it sounded like, a cutesy shop selling afternoon tea and light lunches. The exterior was whitewashed brick with pale pink and powder blue trim. Rows of antique teapots lined the windowsills. Inside were tiny bistro tables with white linen cloths and wrought-iron chairs. Then, after all this work to make the place as nauseatingly sweet as possible, someone had stuck a piece of hand-markered cardboard in the front window informing passersby that the shop also sold coffee, espresso, latte, and "other coffee-based beverages."

Ms. Winterbourne had promised to meet me in front of the shop at three-thirty. I arrived at three-thirty-five, peeked inside, and didn't find anyone waiting, so I went out again. Loitering in front of a tearoom wasn't like hanging around a coffee shop. After a few minutes, people inside began staring. A server came out and asked if she could "help me." I assured her I was waiting for someone, in case she mistook me for a vagrant soliciting leftover scones.

At four o'clock, a young woman approached. When I turned, she smiled. She wasn't very tall, more than a half-foot shorter than my five-ten. Probably in her early twenties. Long curly brown hair, regular features, and green eyes—the type of young woman most often described as "cute," that catchall description meaning she wasn't a beauty but there was nothing to drive her into the realm of ugliness. She wore sunglasses, a brimmed hat, and a sundress that flattered the kind of figure men love and women hate, the full curves so maligned in a world of Jenny Craig and Slim-Fast.

"Elena?" she asked, her voice a deep contralto. "Elena . . . Andrews?"

"Uh—yes," I said. "Ms. Winterbourne?"

She smiled. "One of them. I'm Paige. My aunt will be along shortly. You're early."

"No," I said, returning her smile full-wattage. "You're late."

She blinked, thrown off by my bluntness. "Weren't we supposed to meet at four-thirty?"

"Three-thirty."

"I was sure—"

I pulled the printout of our e-mail correspondence from my pocket.

"Oh," she said, after a quick glance. "Three-thirty. I'm so sorry. I must have jotted it down wrong. I'm glad I stopped by early then. I'd better call my aunt and tell her."

As she took a cell phone from her purse, I stepped away to give her privacy, though with my heightened auditory senses I could have heard the murmured conversation a hundred feet off. Through the phone, I heard an older woman sigh. She promised to join us as soon as possible and asked—warned?—her niece not to start without her.

"Well," Paige said, clicking off the phone. "My apologies again, Ms. Andrews. May I call you Elena?"

"Please. Should we wait inside?"

"Actually, it's a bad place for something like this. Aunt Ruth and I had coffee here this morning. Food's great, but it's much too quiet. You can hear conversations from across the room. I guess we should have realized that, but we're not very experienced at this sort of thing."

"No?"

She laughed, a throaty chuckle. "I suppose you hear a lot of that. People not wanting to admit they're into this kind of stuff. We're into it. I won't deny that. But this is our first . . . what would you call it? Sale? Anyway, since the tearoom turned out to be a bad choice, we had some platters made up and took them to our hotel. We'll hold the meeting there."

"Hotel?" I'd thought she lived in Pittsburgh. Vendors usually arranged meetings in their hometown.

"It's a few blocks over. An easy walk. Guaranteed privacy."

Big warning bells here. Any woman, even one as femininity-challenged as me, knew better than to traipse into the hotel room of a stranger. It was like a horror movie where the heroine goes alone into the abandoned house after all her friends die horrible deaths and the audience sits there yelling, "Don't go, you stupid bitch!" Well, I was the one shouting, "Go on, but grab the Uzi!" Walking headfirst into danger was one thing; walking in unarmed was another. Lucky for me, I was armed with Supergirl strength. And if that didn't do the trick, my Clark Kent act came with fangs and claws. One glance at this woman, barely five-two, nearly a decade my junior, told me I didn't have anything to worry about. Of course, I had to fake concern. It was expected.

"Umm, well . . . " I said, glancing over my shoulder. "I'd prefer a public place. No offense . . . "

"None taken," she said. "But all my stuff is back at the hotel. How about we stop by there, and if you still don't feel comfortable, we can grab my things, meet up with my aunt, and go somewhere else. Good?"

"I guess so," I said, and followed her down the street.

CHAPTER 2

TEA

The hotel was one of those old places with a ballroom-sized front lobby, glass chandeliers, and elevator operators dressed like organ grinders. Paige's room was on the fourth floor, second one left of the elevator. She unlocked the door and held it open for me. I hesitated.

"I could stick something under the door to prop it open," she said.

Her face was all open innocence, but I didn't miss the mocking lilt in her voice, maybe because I was much taller and in better physical condition. Even without werewolf strength, I could take her in a fight. Still, that wasn't to say there wasn't some ape with a semiautomatic lurking behind the door. All the muscles in the world won't stop a bullet to the head.

I glanced around and stepped inside. She took a pad of paper from the table and held it up, gesturing toward the closing door.

"That won't be necessary," I said.

"The phone's right here." She lifted the receiver so I could hear the dial tone. "Would you like me to move it closer? I'm pretty sure Pittsburgh has nine-one-one services."

Okay. Now she was making fun of me. Stupid little twit. Probably one of those airheads who parked in deserted underground lots at night and bragged of their courage. The impulsiveness of youth, I thought, with the maturity of someone almost two years into her thirties.

When I didn't reply, Paige said something about making tea and vanished into the adjoining room of the suite. I was in the living room part, which contained a small table, two chairs, a sofa, a recliner, and a television. A partly open door led into the bedroom. Through it, I could see suitcases lined against the side wall and several dresses hung on a rack. By the front door there were three pairs of shoes, all women's. No sign of a male occupant. So far the Winterbournes seemed to be aboveboard. Not that I really expected some guy with a semiautomatic to leap from behind the door. I was suspicious by nature. Being a werewolf does that to you.

As I sat at the table, I eyed the platters from the tearoom. Sandwiches, cookies, and pastries. I could have devoured all three platefuls as a snack. Another werewolf thing. Like most animals, we spent a large part of our lives engaged in the three Fs of basic survival: feeding, fighting, and . . . reproduction. The food part was necessity. We burned calories like fire burns kindling—without a constant supply, our energy fizzled out. I had to be careful when I ate in front of humans. It wasn't fair. The guys could down three Big Macs and no one batted an eye. I got strange looks if I finished two.

"So this information you're selling," I said as Paige returned. "It's as good as the Phoenix case, right?"

"Better," she said, setting the tea tray on the table. "It's proof that werewolves exist."

"You believe in werewolves?"

"Don't you?"

"I believe in anything that'll sell magazines."

"So you don't believe in werewolves?" Her lips curved in an annoying half-smile.

"No offense, but it's not my thing. I write the stuff. I sell it to magazines. People like you buy it. Ninety percent of the readers don't believe it themselves. It's harmless fantasy."

"Best to keep it that way, isn't it? Harmless fantasy. If you start believing in werewolves, then you have to admit the possibility of other things, witches and sorcerers and shamans. Not to mention vampires and ghosts. Then there's demons, and that's a whole can of worms you don't want to open."

Okay. Now she was definitely making fun of me. Did someone stick a big "mock me" sign on my back? Maybe I was taking this more personally than it was intended. Look at it from her point of view. As a believer, she probably looked on nonbelievers the same way nonbelievers looked at her, as a pathetic ignoramus. Here I was, ready to buy information to perpetrate a myth I didn't even believe in, selling my integrity for next month's rent. A journalistic whore. Didn't I deserve a little mockery?

"Where's the information?" I asked, as politely as I could manage.

She reached over to the side table, where a folder lay. For a moment, she leafed through it, lips pursed. Then she took a sheet and laid it between us. It was a photograph showing the head and shoulders of a middle-aged man, Asian, a pinched nose and dour mouth softened by doe-like eyes.

"Do you recognize him?"

"I don't think so," I said. "But it's a pretty ordinary face."

"How about this one? Not quite so ordinary."

The next photo showed a man in his early thirties. He wore his dark red hair in a long ponytail, a fashion statement that didn't suit anyone over the age of twenty-five. Like most guys who continued the hairstyle past its prime, he seemed to be compensating for a hairline that had already receded farther than the Bay of Fundy at low tide. His face was paunchy, once semi-handsome features vanishing as fast as his hair.

"Now, him I recognize," I said.

"You do?"

"Of course. Come on. I'd have to live in Tibet not to recognize him. Hell, even journalists in Tibet read *Time* and *Newsweek*. He's been covered by them, what, five times in the last year? Ty Winsloe. Billionaire and computer geek extraordinaire."

"So you've never met him personally?"

"Me? I wish. No matter how many interviews he's given, a Ty Winsloe exclusive would still be a career breakthrough for a no-name reporter like me."

She frowned, as if I'd answered the wrong question. Instead of saying anything, though, she fanned both pictures in front of me and waited.

"Okay, I give," I said. "What does this have to do with werewolf proof? Please, please, please don't tell me these guys are werewolves. Is that your game? Put one decent story on the web, lure some dumb journalist down here, then weave a whopper about werewolf billionaires?"

"Ty Winsloe is not a werewolf, Elena. If he was, you'd know it."

"How . . . ?" I shook my head. "Maybe there's some confusion here. Like I said in my e-mail, this is my first werewolf story. If there are experts in the field, that's a scary thought, but I'm not one of them."

"You're not here to write a story, Elena. You're a journalist, but not this kind."

"Ah," I said. "So, tell me, why am I here?"

"To protect your Pack."

I blinked. Words jammed in my throat. As the silence dragged past three seconds, I struggled to fill it. "My—my what?"

"Your Pack. The others. Other werewolves."

"Ah, so I'm a"—I forced a patronizing smile—"a werewolf."

My heart thudded so loudly I could hear it. This had never happened to me before. I'd run into suspicions, but only general questions about my behavior—like "What are you doing in the forest after dark?"—never anything that tied me to being a werewolf. In the normal world, normal people didn't go around accusing other people of being werewolves. One person, someone I was close to, actually saw me Change forms and convinced himself he'd been hallucinating.

"Elena Antonov Michaels," Paige said, "Antonov being your mother's maiden name. Born September 22, 1969. Both parents killed in an auto accident in 1974. Raised in numerous foster homes in southern Ontario. Attended the University of Toronto. Dropped out in her third year. Returned several years later to complete a bachelor's degree in journalism. Reason for the hiatus? A bite. From a lover. Clayton Danvers. No middle name. Born January 15, 1962—"

I didn't hear the rest. Blood pounded in my ears. The floor swayed beneath me. I gripped the table edge to steady myself and struggled to my feet. Paige's lips moved. I didn't hear what she said. I didn't care.

Something snapped me back into my chair. Pressure wound around my legs as if someone were tying them down. I jerked up but couldn't stand. Looking down, I saw nothing restraining me.

Paige stood. I bucked against the chair. My legs wouldn't budge. Panic seeped into my chest. I pushed it back. This was a trick. A simple trick.

"Whatever you're doing," I said. "I'd suggest you stop it. I'm going to count to three."

"Don't threaten—"

"One."

"—me, Elena. I can do—"

"Two."

"—a lot more than bind—"

"Three."

"—you to that chair."

I crashed both fists up into the bottom of the table and sent it jetting into the air. As the pressure on my legs vanished, I vaulted across the now-empty space between us and slammed Paige against the wall. She started saying something. I grabbed her by the neck, stopping the words in her throat.

"Well, it would seem I arrived just in time," a voice said behind us.

I looked over my shoulder to see a woman walking into the room. She was at least seventy, short and plump, with white hair, a flowered dress, and a matching pearl necklace and earring set, the perfect image of a TV grandmother circa 1950.

"I'm Ruth, Paige's great-aunt," she said, as serenely as if I were enjoying tea with her niece instead of throttling her. "Trying to handle matters on your own again, Paige? Now look what you've done. Those bruises will take weeks to fade and we didn't bring any turtlenecks."

I loosened my grip around Paige's neck and struggled for a suitable reply. None came. What could I say? Demand an explanation? Too dangerous, implying I had something to hide. Better to act as if Paige's accusation was crazy and I was getting the hell out of here. Once away from the situation, I could figure out my next move. I shot Paige the wary look people use when dealing with someone of limited sanity and side-stepped toward the door.

"Please don't." Ruth laid a hand on my arm, firm but not restraining. "We must speak with you, Elena. Perhaps I can handle this better."

At that, Paige reddened and looked away. I eased my arm out of Ruth's grip and took another step toward the door.

"Please don't, Elena. I can restrain you, but I'd rather not resort to that."

I lunged at the door and grabbed the handle with both hands. Ruth said something. My hands froze. I jerked them back from the door handle, but they wouldn't come loose. I tried to turn the handle. My fingers wouldn't respond.

"This is the way the spell should work," Ruth said, her voice and face radiating the calm of a seasoned teacher handling a recalcitrant child. "It won't break until I give the command."

She said a few words. My hands flew free, throwing me off-balance. As I stumbled back, Ruth put out a hand to steady me. I recovered and stepped away fast.

"Please stay," she said. "Binding spells have their place, but they're not terribly civilized."

"Binding spells?" I said, flexing my still-numb hands.

"Witchcraft," Ruth said. "But I'm sure you figured that out. Whether you want to believe it may be quite another matter. Let's start over, shall we? I'm Ruth Winterbourne. That impetuous young woman behind you is my niece Paige. We need to speak to you."

CHAPTER 3

HOCUS-POCUS

I wanted to run. Throw open the door, run, and not stop until Ruth and Paige Winterbourne were gone, not just out of my sight, but out of my head as well. I wanted to run until my legs ached and my lungs burned and I could think of nothing but stopping, unable to spare a moment's energy dealing with what had happened. Not the most mature response. I know that. But it was what I was good at. Running. I'd been doing it all my life. Even when I didn't run, when I dug in my heels and confronted my fears, there was always a part of me running as fast as it could.

I knew what I should do. Stay and work this out, refute Paige's claims, and discover how much these women knew. If Paige had simply said she knew I was a werewolf, as disturbing as that would have been, I could have handled it. But when she recited my bio, though it was all accessible through public records, the violation was somehow more personal. Then bringing up my history with Clay as matter-of-factly as she'd recited my birth date, well, every fiber screamed for me to run, get out of there, get some distance, deal with it later. Only Ruth's demonstration of power kept me from running. It also gave me a moment to stop and think.

Did I want to return to Jeremy and say that two strangers had accused me of being a werewolf and I'd bolted? Oh, he wouldn't be angry. He'd understand. That was the worst of it. I didn't want him to understand why I'd screwed up. I wanted him to be proud of me. Yes, I know, I was much too old to be seeking approval from a surrogate father-figure, but that's the way it was. After Clay bit me, Jeremy had taken care of me, putting his life on hold to put mine back together. Each time I undertook one of these investigations, I was showing Jeremy that he hadn't made a mistake, that I'd prove my value to the Pack by repaying his efforts ten-fold. Now, faced for the first time with imminent exposure, was I going to return to New York and say, "Sorry, Jer, but I couldn't deal"? Not in this lifetime. If I ran, I'd keep running. Everything I'd worked so hard for in the last year—letting myself accept my life at Stonehaven, with the Pack, with Clay—would all be thrown away and I'd go back to being as miserable and screwed-up as I'd been eighteen months ago.

So I stayed. Ruth and I came to an agreement. I'd hear her out, admitting nothing. If I wanted, I could treat her story like the ramblings of a senile old woman and pretend I was sticking around just to be polite.

We sat at the table, Paige on the far side, chair pulled back. She hadn't said a word since her aunt arrived.

"Do you believe in witches?" Ruth asked as she poured me a cup of tea.

"Wicca?" I said carefully.

"No. Witches. Hereditary witches. Like hereditary werewolves."

She put up a hand as I started to protest.

"I'm not asking for an admission, remember? You're humoring an old lady. Well, if you don't—or didn't—believe in witches, then I have to assume you don't believe in anything more fantastical. All right, then. Let's start from scratch. Pretend there are witches and . . . other things. Pretend, too, that these beings—races, we call them—know about one another and gather periodically to disseminate information and deal with potential exposure. Now, at one point, werewolves were part of this collaboration—"

I opened my mouth, but Ruth again raised her hand.

"All right," Ruth said. "You don't need a history lesson. We didn't come here for that. As Paige may have said, we came to warn you. Did she get to that part?"

"I showed her the photos," Paige said. "We didn't get to the explanation."

"Allow me then. These men—humans—have been giving us some trouble. Quite a bit of trouble. Confrontations, accusations, kidnappings. It would seem they know more than they should."

"Those two?" I said, pointing at the folder. "Ty Winsloe? Kidnapping witches? You're losing me. This doesn't make sense."

"What does anymore?" Ruth said with a tiny smile. "Once upon a time all we had to worry about was bonfires and Grand Inquisitors. Now we have evil computer magnates. I won't go into detail, partly because I suspect you won't stick around long enough to listen and partly because I'm hoping a little curiosity might bring your Pack to our meeting."

"I really—"

"They know about the werewolves and they're looking for them, just as they're looking for the rest of us."

I leaned back in my chair and looked from Ruth to Paige. Ruth watched me, green eyes bright and sharp. Paige pretended to be watching me, but those same green eyes on her were hooded and distant, looking at me but not seeing me.

"You know how this sounds, don't you?" I said. "Pretend I *am* a werewolf. You two lure me here with some bullshit story and tell me you're witches. Not only are you witches but you're part of some supernatural United Nations. As delegates of this UN, you've decided to contact me with this story about demonic computer geeks—"

"They're not demonic," Ruth said. "As I said, they're human."

"You guys really take this stuff seriously, don't you?"

"It is serious," Paige said, cool stare freezing. "Maybe we made a mistake choosing you—"

"And about that. Why choose me? Or did you put that story on the Internet and assume only a werewolf would reply? Let's say this conspiracy exists and there are guys out there looking for werewolves. What's to stop them from responding to your ad?"

"We did get a lot of inquiries," Ruth said. "But we were waiting for yours."

"Mine?"

"A few years ago, our council had a run-in with a werewolf. Not one of your Pack. An outsider. We've kept tabs on him, in case we ever needed to contact the werewolves. When this trouble began, we found him and . . . persuaded him to share some information with us. He knew about your Pack, who led it, who was in it, where they lived. Moreover, he knew all about you and your background. Being the only female werewolf, it seems you've achieved quite legendary status among your race."

She smiled. I returned a blank stare.

Ruth continued, "He knew you followed up on realistic werewolf sightings, watching for misbehavior. Quite interesting. We do the same, monitoring witches who've left the Coven. So we decided to try getting in touch with you that way before attempting direct contact."

"Why me?"

"You're part of the Pack. As well, being the only female, you seemed a . . . better choice of contact. Perhaps easier to talk to than your male counterparts."

In other words, more gullible? Less likely to counter threat with violence? If they wanted the latter, they should have gone straight to the top. Jeremy was the most levelheaded among us. He was also the most open-minded. He'd have been the best choice for this meeting. Wouldn't it have made more sense to take their concerns directly to the Alpha anyway? Unless, for some reason, they didn't want to do that.

"You still realize how this sounds," I said. "Forget how and why you chose me. You bring me here, issuing B-movie lines like 'We know who you are.' Sorry, but I'm looking for the hidden camera. Let's say I believe all this hocus-pocus. Why, if this UN doesn't include werewolves, would you suddenly want to contact them now? If you are witches, you must have run into bad guys before."

"We risk exposure as often as you do," Ruth said. "But it's always been one race at a time. This is different. This involves all of us, which is why we must band together."

"One for all and all for one," I muttered.

"This isn't a joke," Paige said.

"You still don't believe us, do you?" Ruth asked. "Even about the witch part, despite our little demonstration."

"We could do a bigger one," Paige said. "Say, zip your mouth shut. Permanently."

"Paige," Ruth warned. "Forgive my niece's youthful exuberance. If you'd like, though, I could certainly give you a better demonstration. Nothing as uncivilized as a binding spell, of course."

"No thanks," I said.

"Why?" Paige asked. "Because you don't believe? Or because you don't want to?"

"I did what I said I'd do. I stayed. I listened. Now I'm leaving."

As I stood, Ruth touched my arm. "At least tell your leader what we've said. We're meeting in two days. Delegates from the major races will be there to discuss the problem. We'd like your Pack to join us. Here's my card."

She handed me a business card. I half-expected to see "Ruth Winterbourne, Spells and Potions." Instead, it was a card for "Winterbourne Designs, Custom Apparel for Women." The address listed was in Massachusetts, though disappointingly not Salem.

"Yes," Ruth said with a smile. "It's a real business card for a real business. Not much money in hexes these days."

"I don't—"

"Put it in your pocket and we'll pretend you're going to throw it away once I'm out of sight. If you call, use my cell phone number. We're heading straight from here to the meeting in Vermont. It wouldn't be a long drive from New York if you decide to come out. I hope you do."

I mumbled something noncommittal, pocketed the card, and left.

Afterward, I spent more time thinking about witches than billionaire conspiracy theories. The thought of other "supernatural" beings intrigued me, though I found it hard to believe. Okay, skepticism from someone who routinely morphed into a wolf may sound hypocritical, but I couldn't help it. I'd been a werewolf for nearly six months before *I* believed they existed. I'd Changed forms, I'd seen Jeremy Change forms, yet I still managed to convince myself that it wasn't real. Serious denial. Maybe it was easier to believe werewolves were a onetime aberration of nature, the way some people—myself included—think the universe contains only one populated planet. The thought of zombies and vampires wandering the earth was just too weird. But Ruth hadn't mentioned zombies or vampires. She'd only said witches and . . . other things. I could believe in witches. The idea that some people could harness the earth's powers was much easier to accept than the idea that, say, some people could transform into wolves.

When I walked into my hotel room, the phone was ringing. I stood in the doorway, contemplated a quick about-face, then resigned myself to answering it. Besides, it might not be who I expected.

"What the hell are you doing in Pittsburgh?!" the caller roared before I even got the receiver to my ear. I looked for a volume button on the phone, couldn't find one, and considered "accidentally" hitting the plunger.

"Nice to hear from you, too, Clayton. My flight was fine, thanks. How's Detroit?"

"Hotter than Hades," he muttered, his Southern drawl resurrected as his voice dropped to non-eardrum-shattering decibels. "Smells worse, too. Why didn't you call and tell me you were going to Pittsburgh?"

"Because you would have insisted on meeting me here. I don't need—"

"Too late. I'm already packing."

"I don't need your help, and I don't need your protection."

"And my company, darling? I suppose you don't need that either."

"Give it a rest. You only left yesterday, and I'll be joining you on Monday."

"Then I can save you two flights. I'll drive down tonight, and when you're done there, I can bring you back to Detroit—"

"No."

"I'm just trying to be—"

"Controlling, possessive, overprotective."

"I miss you."

"Nice try. The answer's still no. I can handle this."

"So what exactly are you handling?"

"I'll tell you tomorrow," I said. "After I speak to Jeremy."

"Anything good?"

"Maybe."

"Fun?" he asked.

"Definite mayhem possibilities."

"Come on. Tell me."

"Later."

"Tease," he growled.

"You want to hear teasing?" I asked.

"Sure, if you want me in Pittsburgh in an hour."

"It's a six-hour drive."

"Wanna bet?"

We went on like this for a while, forty-five minutes actually. Before we ended the conversation Clay had agreed—most grudgingly—not to follow me to Pittsburgh. I had to admit that since we'd been back together, he really had been working at being less controlling, possessive, and overprotective. Not that he was giving up and letting me lead a semi-independent life. We kept separate bedrooms, but that was as far as it went. He still expected me to be with him twenty-four hours a day. Even the separate bedroom thing was a joke. Having my own room only meant I had a place to store my stuff. Wherever I slept, Clay slept.

As part of my own relationship-saving efforts, I'd had to admit that this togetherness thing was part of Clay's nature. Bitten as a child, he'd forgotten ever having been human, and nothing in his later experiences convinced him he was missing out on anything. He was more wolf than human. About the togetherness thing, Clay would argue that you'd never see a wolf telling its mate that it had to "get away for a while" or needed "some personal space." They formed lifelong bonds that seemed to work out just fine despite the grievous lack of relationship therapy.

Clay and I had been together nearly twelve years. Well, "together" was a mild exaggeration. We'd started out twelve years ago, then there was the biting thing. After ten years of bouncing back and forth, I'd broken down and admitted to myself that I loved him and couldn't live without him—all that Harlequin romance stuff. Still, our relationship was hardly the sort of thing Harlequin would endorse. Clay and I went together like fire and gasoline—intense heat, incredible fireworks, and, occasionally, devastating destruction. I'd come to realize that was how we were. It wasn't a calm, stable relationship, it never would be, and, frankly, neither of us wanted that. Blissful domesticity was for other people. Give us fireworks and explosions, of both the positive and negative variety, and we were as blissful as could be.

I couldn't sleep that night.

I lay in bed, staring at the ceiling, fighting off an unease that kept me from closing my eyes.

First, there was the question of the witches. Were they witches or not? Either way, I didn't trust their motivation. Too much of what they'd said didn't make sense. I should have called Jeremy as soon as I'd left their hotel. He wasn't going to be happy when he found out I'd waited a full day to tell him. At least two people knew I was a werewolf and I hadn't told either Clay or Jeremy. Where the hell was my head at? Should I call Jeremy now? It was 2:45 A.M. My flight left at 8:00. This could wait. Could it? Should it?

I went for a run to clear my head. Jogging, I mean. While Changing into a wolf and running around Pittsburgh might be fun, it was definitely not the kind of excitement I needed. I pulled on shorts and a T-shirt, left my hotel room, and followed a maze of alleys to a deserted industrial area. Big cities weren't the place for late-night jogs. Anyone seeing a young woman running around Pittsburgh at 3:00 A.M. was going to be looking for the guy chasing her.

I'd jogged about a quarter-mile when I realized someone was following me. No big surprise. Like I said, young women jogging at night attract attention, usually the wrong kind. Sure, if some guy jumped me, I could slam him into the nearest brick wall and there'd be one less potential rapist for the world to worry about. But that meant a body to clean up in a strange city. Not only that, but I couldn't do it. I can talk the talk, but I ain't that tough. Even if some mugger pulled a gun on me and I had to kill him, I'd regret it. I'd wonder if I'd overreacted, if maybe this was the guy's first offense and a good scare would have set him straight, if maybe he had a wife and kids at home and only wanted a few bucks for food. Better to avoid getting into a situation where such action might be necessary. Wild wolves survived by avoiding confrontation with humans. Smart werewolves did the same.

When I heard soft running footfalls nearby, I first made sure it wasn't a coincidence. I turned down the next three streets and circled full around to where I'd been. The footsteps followed. Next I got downwind and checked the scent, in case it was another werewolf. As the only female werewolf in a country with a couple dozen males, I was considered a trophy. The fact that my lover was the most feared and hated werewolf around only added to my value. If mutts didn't want to fuck me, they wanted to fuck Clay over—and the chance to do both at once was more than some could resist. Though I didn't know of any mutts in the Pittsburgh area, they were a nomadic lot and my dossiers were always out of date.

My pursuer wasn't a mutt. Werewolves have a distinct underlying scent and this guy didn't. It was a guy—a man, I mean. Other than that, his smell didn't give me much to go on. No aftershave. A touch of body odor, as if his deodorant had reached its time limit. Otherwise clean. Very clean. I didn't expect that with a rapist or mugger. Yes, I know not every creep is a scruffy, unshaven vagrant. Most aren't. But they aren't usually hygiene fanatics either. Curiosity aroused, I decided to get a look at my stalker.

Still eager to avoid confrontation, I did both at once, getting a closer look while sneaking away. To find him, I stopped in the middle of the empty street, bent over, and retied my shoes. Then I muttered under my breath, yanked them undone, and redid them. By the third tie-up, stalker-guy got antsy, probably cursing me for stopping in the road instead of in some nice shadowy corner. He leaned out of his hiding spot, giving himself away with a blur of motion in the otherwise still street. He was hiding in a building alcove to my left.

Straightening, I launched into a set of hamstring stretches. Midway through my second set, I took off. Running full-out, I raced into the alley alongside the building where my stalker hid. By the time he came after me, I was behind the adjacent building. I stopped in a rear doorway and searched the ground. A few yards to my left, I saw what I wanted. Something dark and missile-like. A half-dozen beer bottles were scattered around the door. Grabbing the nearest one, I pitched it down the back alley. It crashed somewhere behind the next building. Fortunately, my stalker wasn't deaf. When he got to the end of the side alley, he turned toward the crash and headed in that direction, moving away from me.

Keeping in the shadows, I watched the man as he walked away. Six-two, maybe six-three. Average weight. Dressed in dark pants and jacket. Some kind of hat. Baseball cap? He slowed, paused, getting his bearings. Then he hunkered down and crept forward, head moving from side to side, like a sniper creeping through the jungle. Something dangled from his hand. A gun. A big gun. Right, Elena. You're being stalked through Pittsburgh by an armed Vietnam vet. That's what I got for watching

Platoon with Clay last week. The guy was probably carrying a bottle of Wild Turkey.

Sticking close to the wall, I slunk toward my stalker. Light from a naked bulb flashed off what he held in his hand. Definitely a gun. I narrowed my eyes to get a better look at his outfit. He wore black fatigues. Okay, enough with the *Platoon* flashbacks. Fatigues didn't come in black, at least I didn't think they did. The guy wore black baggy pants, an equally baggy jacket, a dark ball-cap, and dark, thick-soled boots.

He stopped. I flattened myself against the wall and waited. Tugging off his ball-cap with one hand, he scratched his head with the other. In the silence of the night, his fingernails rasped through his short hair. Very short hair. Like military buzz-cut short. Keeping his cap off, he took something from his pocket, flicked his wrist, and lifted it to his ear.

"She come out that way?" he murmured into the two-way radio. I assumed it was a radio because I didn't see him punch in a phone number. "Yeah . . . no. She musta made me. Spooked and ran. Caught me off guard . . . yeah . . . no, no. I woulda noticed that. Kinda hard to miss a wolf out here."

Wolf? Did he say wolf?

This really wasn't my day.

CHAPTER 4

Houdini

"No," my stalker said into his radio. "What? . . . Yeah. Probably. You gonna check with Tucker? . . . Nah, I'll walk. Tell Pierce to park it around back . . . Yeah? Well, it's not far . . . See ya in a couple."

He stuffed the radio into his pocket. Then he lifted his gun and did something to make it smaller, folded back the barrel or unscrewed it or something. Hey, I'm Canadian. I don't know street guns. Somehow he made the weapon half the size, lifted his jacket, and stuck it in a holster.

I followed stalker-guy back to the street. There he met up with a second man, also dressed in the whole cat-burglar/gothic-fatigue getup. Both removed their ball-caps and shoved them in a collapsible knapsack. Then they unzipped their jackets, making themselves look as normal as possible without revealing the guns. They headed east. I followed.

By the third turn, I knew where they were going. We were still a half mile away, but I knew. As I expected, they walked three blocks, made a left, made a right, walked three more blocks, and ended up in front of the hotel where I'd met the Winterbournes that afternoon. So my concern about gun-toting men hiding in the Winterbournes' hotel room hadn't been so paranoid after all. Only instead of having their cohorts/minions jump me there, they'd waited to go after me under cover of night.

I expected the men to walk straight in the front lobby. When they didn't I was surprised, then realized two guys dressed in black walking into the lobby of an expensive hotel at 4:00 A.M. would raise a few eyebrows . . . and a few alarms. Invited or not, they were taking the back route. They skirted around to a side door. My stalker leaned against the wall, blocking my view, while his friend fiddled with the lock. Two minutes passed. Then the door opened and they slipped inside. I counted to twenty, then went after them.

The two men took the stairs. They climbed to the fourth floor, opened the exit door, and peered out. After a few moments of discussion, my stalker's companion slipped into the hall, leaving stalker-guy in the stairwell.

348

Now I had a dilemma. From my vantage point below the stalker, I couldn't see anything—not him and certainly not his companion, even though the door was propped open. I did have an option. When I'd come in with Paige, I'd noticed a second set of stairs on the far side of the lobby. I could exit on the third floor, find the alternate stairs, go up to the fifth, and circle back to the staircase. From the steps above, I'd be able to see. Plus, the stalker would be more likely to expect danger from below, someone coming up from ground level. On the other hand, the plan also meant I'd be out of hearing and smelling range for at least a few minutes. Was it better to stay where I could use those two senses? The longer I waited, the more risky it would be to leave. I crept down the stairs to the third floor.

Circling around wasn't a problem. The exits were marked at each end of the hall. I came back to the first stairwell, took off my shoes, slipped through the fifth-floor door, and eased down the stairs until I was a half-dozen steps from the fourth-floor landing where stalker-guy waited. Sliding my shoes back on, I crouched to peer through the railing. Perfect. Now I had sound, smell, and sight. My stalker's partner was at room 406. The Winterbournes. He was crouched before the door, fiddling with lock-pick tools. So they weren't invited guests. Maybe the Winterbournes had been telling the truth about being in danger. At least, telling the truth about *themselves* being in danger. And me? Well, I wouldn't have been in Pittsburgh if it weren't for them, right? Somehow I doubted these militia-wannabes would have been stalking me tonight if I'd stayed home. Whether or not the Winterbournes were complicit in this, I could still blame them for it. Lucky thing, because I definitely wanted to blame them for something.

Stalker-guy rolled from his heels to his toes, muttering under his breath. Down the hall, his companion wiped his sweaty face on his shoulder. He stood, stretched, and crouched again. Several times he tried the door handle, then turned to his partner and shook his head. Finally my stalker waved him back. I quickstepped up three stairs, out of sight. They came into the stairwell and closed the door.

"No go," lock-pick guy said. "I don't get it. I'm sure I popped the lock, but it won't open."

"Dead bolt?"

Lock-pick guy shook his head. "I checked out the place this morning. Old-fashioned key locks."

"Call Tucker. I saw a pay phone out front. Ground line. I'll wait here."

Lock-pick guy trotted down the stairs. As the first-floor door swung shut behind him, I heard another door open, this one on the fourth floor.

Stalker-guy cracked open the exit to look down the hall. Then he made a noise deep in his throat, a stifled chuckle. I sneaked down a few steps, crouched again, and looked through the door crack.

Paige Winterbourne stood in the hall, arms folded across her chest, dressed in a green silk chemise and matching wrap. Frowning, she surveyed the corridor. Then she stopped and stared at the exit where we hid. Though the door was open only a couple of inches, she must have seen light or shadow peeking through. As she watched, stalker-guy hesitated, holding the door handle, ready to close it. If she'd gone back into her room to call security, he would have bolted. But she didn't. She narrowed her eyes and started toward us. Yet another horror movie cliché. When the ditzy ingenue hears a bump in the night, does she retreat to safety and phone for help? Of course not. She has to see what's behind that partly open door. All Paige needed now was to lose the negligee, so she could run naked and screaming down the hall when she flung open the door and found the killer lurking behind it.

Stalker-guy broke from the script. Instead of waiting for Paige to throw open the door, he took out his gun and snapped it back together. Then he eased the door open another half-inch and lifted the gun to the door crack. Last year, I'd seen an innocent woman gunned down because of me. Whether Paige was innocent or not was a matter of some debate, but I doubted she deserved to be murdered in a hotel hallway. I leaped over the railing and landed on the man's back. He fell forward. I grabbed his head and twisted his neck. The simplest, quietest, and cleanest kill.

As he dropped face-first to the floor, I looked up to see Paige holding the door open and staring.

"Stand guard," I said. "Is your room unlocked?"

"My—? Umm, yes."

I hoisted the dead man onto my shoulder and pushed past her into the hall. "I said to stand guard. He wasn't alone."

"Where are you—oh, wait. My room? You can't put him—" She stopped. "Take him to the suite next to ours. The near side. It's empty."

"All the better."

"I can unlock the door with a spell," she said.

She hurried down the hallway alongside me, murmuring words in a foreign language. While she was talking, I covered my hand with my shirt, reached over, and snapped the vacant room's doorknob.

"Run back and get the gun," I said. "Then wake your aunt and get in here."

Paige hesitated, like a knee-jerk reaction against taking orders. She seemed to think better of arguing and paused only a second before jogging to the stairwell. I dragged the dead man into the bathroom, closed the door, and checked his pockets for ID. Nothing. Seeing the two-way radio in his pocket reminded me that there was a second gunman, and Paige and her aunt were taking their sweet time evacuating their room.

I opened the bathroom door as they walked into the vacant room. Paige was still wearing her chemise and wrapper. Ruth's long housecoat covered her nightwear. Both carried a change of clothing and their purses, and Paige had the gun.

"Good idea," I said. "Is all your ID in there?"

"No sense leaving them any clues if they break in," Paige said. "If we have to, we can leave the rest of the stuff behind."

"Paige told me what happened," Ruth said. "We're very grateful. Also very impressed. You have excellent reflexes."

"Self-defense classes," I said.

"Still not admitting to the werewolf thing?" Paige asked.

I walked to the bathroom and held open the door. "Either of you ever see this guy before? Don't touch anything. The cops will dust for prints."

"Cops?" Paige repeated.

"Yes, cops. Who do you think will handle the murder investigation? Hotel security?"

"Murder? You mean he's dead?"

"No. He's resting comfortably," I said. "People always sleep best with their heads at a ninety-degree angle. He looks comfortable, doesn't he?"

"There's no need for sarcasm," Paige said tightly. "Maybe you're used to hauling corpses around, but I'm not."

"Sheltered life. You're supposed to be a witch and you've never had to kill anyone?"

Paige's voice tightened another notch. "We use alternate methods of defense."

"Like what? Cast a spell to make your attackers think happy thoughts? Turn their guns into flowers? Peace and love for all?"

"I'd have used a binding spell," Paige said. "Kept the guy alive so we could question him. Wow. There's a novel idea. If you hadn't killed him, maybe we could have talked to him."

"Oh, that's right. Paige's ultra-efficient binding spell. Tell you what. Next time I see a guy pointing a gun at you, I'll let you do things your way. You start your invocation and see if you can finish before he guns you down. Deal?"

Paige lifted the gun, opened it, removed a tranquilizer dart, and held it up. "No one wanted to kill me."

"Are you sure about that?" a male voice asked.

Paige and I jumped. Even Ruth looked up, startled. In the corner of the bedroom stood a man dressed in the same black fatigues as the dead man on the floor. He was of average height and weight, with average brown hair cut short but not military short. Only one distinguishing feature—a paper-thin scar running from temple to nose—assured me I'd never seen this man before. I glanced toward the hall door. It was still closed and locked. Paige's change of clothing lay undisturbed in front of it. So how'd this guy get in?

"I'm glad to hear you wouldn't have killed poor Mark," the man said, sitting on the edge of the bed, stretching his legs and crossing his ankles. "Very sporting of you. I guess what they say about witches is true. So self-less, so concerned for others, so unbelievably naive."

I stepped toward him.

"Don't!" Paige hissed.

"This is the werewolf?" The man turned dirt-brown eyes on me in a smirking once-over. "Better than I expected. So, are you coming along, wolf-girl? Or do things have to get"—his smirk broadened to a grin—"physical."

I glanced at Paige and Ruth.

"Oh, they're coming too," the man said. "But I'm not worried about them. Only witches, you know. They'll do what they're told."

Paige made a noise in her throat, but Ruth laid a restraining hand on her arm.

"So you're kidnapping us?" I asked.

The man yawned. "Looks that way, doesn't it?"

"What's in it for you?" Paige asked.

"See?" The man looked at me. "That's witches for you. Make me feel guilty. Appeal to my kinder, gentler side. Which might work, if I had one."

"So you're working for Ty Winsloe?" I said.

"Oh, come on, ladies. As much as I'd love to chat about my motivations and the Yankees' chances at the World Series—"

I lunged at him, sailing the five feet between us. My hands went out, ready to catch him in the chest and topple him backward. But they didn't. Instead I hit empty air and tumbled onto the bed, twisting fast to right myself before the counterattack. It didn't come. I whirled around to see the man standing by the bedroom door, the same bored expression on his face.

"Is that the best you can do?" He sighed. "Major disappointment."

I advanced on him, slowly, eyes locked on his. When I was close enough to hear his heartbeat, I stopped. He grinned again and his eyes sparked with boyish anticipation, like a kid impatient for the game to begin. His throat pulsed, words moving up to his mouth. Before he could say anything, I swung my right foot out, hooked his legs, and yanked. He pitched backward. Then he vanished, one second dropping like a brick, the next—not there. Just not there.

"Clever," he said from somewhere behind me.

I spun to see him standing in the bathroom by the dead body.

"You're getting the hang of it," he said, a grin illuminating his eyes. "I'd love to give you another chance, but my compatriots are coming. Can't let them find me playing with the enemy. They wouldn't understand. Humans."

He bent to grab the tranquilizer gun Paige had dropped. Ruth's lips moved. The man stopped in mid-reach, fingers close enough to flex and touch the metal. But his hand didn't move.

"Go!" Ruth said, snatching her purse from the floor. "It won't last."

Paige sprinted across the room, grabbed my arm, and dragged me toward the door. I jerked away and turned back to the man. He was immobilized. It didn't matter if it wouldn't last. I didn't need long. I stepped toward him. Paige grabbed my arm again.

"No time!" she said. "He could break it any second."

"Go on," I said.

"No," Ruth said.

Together they propelled me out the door. I resisted, but it was clear they weren't going anywhere without me, and I wasn't about to risk anyone's life, including my own. So I ran for the stairwell. They followed.

We'd gone down almost two flights of steps when I heard the tramp of footsteps coming up from the bottom. I wheeled around and shoved Paige back up. As we ran for the third-floor exit, someone shouted from below. The clomp of footsteps turned to a fast beat as they hightailed it up the stairs after us.

I pushed past Ruth and Paige and led them down the hall to the opposite stairwell. Our pursuers were just coming onto the third floor as we bolted through the other door. Down the stairs. Out the first-floor emergency exit. Alarms blared.

Paige turned to the north. I grabbed her arm and wrenched her back.

"That's the street," I hissed, pushing her in front of me as we ran south.

"They won't gun us down in front of people," she called back at me.

"Wanna bet? How many people do you think are out there at four-thirty in the morning?"

"Just run," Ruth said. "Please."

The alarms seemed to slow the men down. Maybe someone stopped them. I didn't know and didn't care. All that mattered was that we made it to the south end of the alley, turned west, and were halfway down that one before I heard our pursuers come out of the hotel, barking orders. The west alley ended. Our choices were south to a dead end or north to the street. With Ruth and Paige in their nightgowns, I wasn't sure running to the possible safety of the street was such a good idea. But "dead end" had a really ominous ring to it. So I turned north and kept running. Actually, "running" was an overstatement. Call it a fast jog. While Paige managed to stay beside me, forcing her elderly aunt to run at my normal pace would have been as much a death warrant as leaving her behind.

Partway to the street, we hit a narrow alley that went off to the west and I veered down it. The men were now rounding the north corner, their heavy breathing like the baying of hounds at our heels. I was glad Ruth and Paige couldn't hear it. Ahead, a garbage dumpster blocked the west route. I could see a turn to the south and assumed there was a north fork as well. There wasn't. Worse yet, the south fork ended in an eight-foot wall.

"Over the dumpster," I whispered. "I'll jump on and pull you up."

Ruth shook her head. "Down there," she wheezed, pointing south.

"But there's no—"

"Hide," she said.

I squinted down the dark alley. There was no cover there but shadows. I turned to Ruth to say as much, then saw her face. It was crimson, her chest heaving, such rasping breath making her wince. She couldn't go any farther.

Nodding, I shepherded them down the south alley and motioned for us to stand against the west wall, where the shadows were deepest. I put Ruth, in her pale yellow nightgown, on the far side, sheltered by Paige and me. It wouldn't help. They'd see us. One glance down this alley and we were caught. All I could do now was prepare to confront them.

We were barely settled into the shadows when three men skidded to a halt in front of the dumpster. One was lock-pick guy, the other was Houdini from the hotel room, and the third was yet another military-style clone.

"Don't move," Paige whispered, touching my arm.

I didn't think it would help, but if it made them feel better, I'd stay still until we were discovered. The men looked at the dumpster, then glanced down the south alley, too quick to see us. Lock-pick guy walked from one end of the dumpster to the other.

"Blocked," he said. "No way but over."

"With an old lady?" the new guy said. "No way."

Houdini leaned against the north brick wall, took a cigarette from his pocket, and struck a match. The flame lit his face for a second, then sputtered into darkness. He took a drag while the two military guys argued over the likelihood of our having scaled the dumpster. Hello! We were twenty feet away, in almost plain sight. But no one ever said the military recruited for brains. Besides, the more I saw of these guys, the more I doubted they were acting under the auspices of any wing of the U.S. military. So what were they? Retired military maybe? More likely discharged. Or those militia groups who pop up with alarming frequency on American newscasts. It didn't matter. Bright, they were not.

As I turned back to Houdini, he looked right back at me. He knew exactly where we were. Why didn't he tell his comrades? Because he wanted us to sweat. Extending the game of cat and mouse. He lifted the cigarette and inhaled. The red ember glowed in the night, then fell, end over end, blinking in the darkness before hitting the ground in a shower of sparks. As he stepped toward the south alley, I tensed and held my breath. His eyes scanned the alley, on us then not on us. Cute. Pretend you can't see us. Lull us into a false sense of security. Sadistic bastard. I held my breath and prepared for the attack.

CHAPTER 5

LEGION

Houdini walked less than a foot from me, looked at the opposite wall, then swiveled his gaze my way. Here it comes. He was taking his sweet time, pretending not to see me. Then, he'd suddenly meet my eyes and bingo, lap up the fear he expected to see there. I gritted my teeth as his head turned toward mine. But his gaze kept moving, right over my face, eyes not even flickering to mine. He grunted. A muscle beneath his scar spasmed. He turned to the wall at the end of the alley and looked up. Then he vanished. A crackle of paper erupted from the other side of the wall. A curse. Then he was back, striding toward the military goons.

"Undisturbed trash on the other side of the wall," he said. "They didn't go that way. Either over the dumpster or you guys took a wrong turn. I'll check the other side of the dumpster, but I'm betting on the latter. Humans."

His companions started to grouse, but Houdini had already vanished. A minute later he returned.

"Puddles," he said. "With no wet tracks leading out of them. You fucked up."

Lock-pick guy glared. "If you're such a great tracker, why didn't you take the lead?"

"Not my job," Houdini said, walking east down the alley. "I'm special ops."

"That's right," lock-pick guy called after him. "You have super powers. So you should have been able to beam yourself down to the hotel exit before they escaped. Oh, sorry. I forgot. You're not that powerful, are you?"

Houdini didn't turn, just extended his middle finger in the air and kept walking. Lock-pick guy glanced at the dumpster again, then peered down the south alley. Unless he was night-blind, he should have seen us. But he didn't. He snapped something to the third man and they took off after Houdini.

When they were out of earshot, Ruth leaned toward me and whispered, "Cover spell. I would have mentioned it, but there wasn't time."

I listened to the retreating footsteps, waited until they were gone, then turned to her. "It worked, but I don't suppose you have something a bit more disabling in that bag of tricks, in case they come back."

Ruth chuckled. "Sorry. Our spells are designed for defense, not offense."

"We have some aggressive spells," Paige said. "But they take time to prepare."

Ruth's mouth tightened. "We don't use them. That's not our way."

I remembered what Houdini said about witches. Personally, I'd rather stop my attackers permanently, but witches seemed to have a different philosophy.

Thinking of Houdini, I had to ask, "What was that guy?"

"Half-demon with teleport abilities," Paige said. "Limited range, probably no more than five to ten feet. Offspring of a minor demon, hence the diluted power. My guess is that's the best Winsloe and his bunch have. That's why they want better specimens."

"Specimens?" I said.

"We'll explain at the meeting," Ruth said. "Right now we need to get someplace safe."

"I can get us over the dumpster," I said. "Messy, but safer than heading back to the hotel."

Ruth nodded and we hurried up the alley. Going over the dumpster wasn't the most pleasant route, but it was easy enough. A six-foot jump was nothing for a werewolf. Neither was hauling up two average-sized women. The stench was the worst of it, enough to make me lose my appetite, which was a feat in itself. We made it down the other side without hearing a sound from the other alley. Our pursuers were long gone.

Once over the dumpster, I followed my nose to an all-night doughnut shop. We managed to sneak through the parking lot and scoot into the washroom without attracting attention. I bought coffee and doughnuts and took them into the washroom where Paige and Ruth were cleaning up. While they ate, I snuck through the door labeled "employees only" and raided the staff lockers for clothes. I wasn't sure what would fit, but anything had to be better than nightgowns, so I grabbed what I found and took it into the bathroom. We agreed it was time to split up.

"Take care," Ruth said as I prepared to leave. "Watch your back and go straight to the airport. We'll see you at the meeting."

I hesitated, not wanting to leave the impression that by joining them that evening, I was ready to join their meeting, but Ruth had already turned away and started talking to Paige. So I murmured my good-byes and left.

I returned to my hotel and told the desk clerk I'd gone for an early jog and left my card-key upstairs. He escorted me up to my room, opened it, and waited while I pretended to be looking for the card-key, actually checking for hidden guests. Once he left, I grabbed my stuff, got out, caught a cab to the airport, and called Jeremy.

By the time I called Jeremy, my brain had shifted into overdrive. While I'd been running and worrying about escaping, I hadn't had time to think much about what I was seeing. Now I had too much time, and my mind took full advantage of it. Witches and binding spells. Teleporting demons and armed militia men. Tranquilizer guns and kidnapping plans. Whatever happened to the good old days when all I had to worry about was crazed mutts? Werewolves I could handle. But this? What the hell was this?

I blurted the whole story to Jeremy in a semi-coherent rush of words, thankful I'd found a private phone booth and didn't need to worry about watching what I said. Jeremy waited until I was done, paused to make sure there wasn't more, then said, "That doesn't sound good."

I had to laugh. As I did, I felt the tension ease from my neck and shoulders, and relaxed for the first time that day. Typical Jeremy. Master of understatement. I could have told him a nuclear warhead had escaped from Russia and was heading for New York and he'd have said the same thing in the same calm, unruffled tone.

"And no," I said, "I haven't been drinking or ingesting illegal narcotics."

He chuckled. "I believe you. Where are you now?"

"At the airport."

"Good. Don't fly to Syracuse. Buy a ticket for Buffalo and watch out for curious onlookers. I'll meet you at the airport."

By the time my plane touched down, I'd relaxed enough to feel pretty foolish about calling Jeremy in a near-panic and making him drive nearly three hours to Buffalo. There must be a logical, nonsupernatural explanation for what I'd seen last night. I didn't know what it might be, but I was sure it existed.

As the crowd of disembarking passengers carried me into the waiting area, I looked over their heads for Jeremy and spotted him immediately.

At six-two, Jeremy might not be the tallest guy in the room, but he usually stood a few inches above his neighbors, high enough for me to catch a glimpse of black eyes topped by arching black brows and black bangs always a few weeks overdue for a cut. When he'd last condescended to let me cut his hair, I'd noticed the first strands of white. Not surprising considering Jeremy was fifty-two. We aged slowly—Jeremy looked in his mid-thirties—and he was probably past due for some gray, but I'd still teased him unmercifully. With Jeremy, any flaw was worth picking up on. He didn't have nearly enough of them.

When he finally saw me, his lips curved in the barest of smiles, then he nodded and waited for me to come to him. Typical.

"Okay," I said as I drew up beside him. "Tell me I overreacted."

He took my bag. "Certainly not. Far better than ignoring it and, say, not calling me as soon as you found out about these women."

"Sorry."

He waved off the apology. "We're on top of it now. We're heading straight to Vermont. I've packed our bags. It doesn't seem wise to return to Stonehaven until we know more about this threat."

"So we're going to the meeting?"

"We don't have much choice. These wi—women seem to have all the answers."

"So we're getting information from them, not joining them?"

Jeremy chuckled. "You sound relieved. Don't worry, Elena. The Pack doesn't need any outside help."

"I tried calling Clay from the airport, but he was out. I left a message saying we needed to talk to him. Should I try him now?"

"He got your message and called home. I explained what happened. I think it's best if he doesn't join us for this meeting. Somehow I doubt he'd be on his best behavior."

"I can see it now. Charging into the meeting, demanding answers, and threatening to throw someone out the nearest window if those answers don't come fast enough. And that *would* be his best behavior."

"Exactly. Not quite the entrance I had in mind. So I downplayed the danger and told him you and I could handle it. I'll keep him updated, and if things prove difficult, he can join us."

"What about Nick and Antonio? They're in Europe for another two weeks."

"Three," he said. "I phoned and told Tonio to be on the alert. If we need them, we'll call. Otherwise, even if this threat is real, Europe may be the best place for them. Out of danger."

"So it's just the two of us."

Another chuckle. "I'm sure we'll survive."

We spent the night at a cottage Jeremy had rented in Vermont. Despite the busy season, he'd managed to find a place where the original guests had canceled their reservation at the last minute. Not only was it in a secluded, wooded region, but it surpassed "suitable" and approached perfect, a lakeside chalet far from vacationer traffic. I'd have been lucky to get us reservations at a third-rate highway motel. Trust Jeremy to find Eden with less than a day's notice.

The meeting was being held in Sparta, Vermont. On the drive, Jeremy had called Ruth's cell number and told her we'd arrive Monday, though the meeting started on Sunday. Actually, we planned to show up Sunday, but he figured the lie might help us. If we were walking into a trap, by arriving early, we'd catch them off-guard.

As each passing hour pushed Pittsburgh further into my memory, my skepticism returned. What had I really seen? Nothing a good troupe of magicians or illusionists couldn't pull off. Cover spells and teleporting demons? Right. In the light of day, such things seemed ridiculous. Phantasms of night and nerves. Much more likely we were indeed walking into a trap, a clever but very human trap. At the very least, we were about to meet some seriously deluded people.

The next morning, as we drove down the highway off the mountain, I could see Sparta ahead, nestled in the valley, lone white church on the mountainside, spire wreathed with cloud or late-day fog. Wood-sided houses, all colors of the rainbow, peeked up from the August greenery. Holsteins and red barns dotted the few fields carved out of the wilderness. Pink cottages ringed a lake to the south. It was picture-perfect . . . from a distance. The closer you drove, the more you noticed the signs of decay. The brightly colored houses screamed for paint or vinyl siding. The barn foundations were crumbling into piles of stone that barely supported the woodwork above. Rusty fences and rotted posts let cows escape into neighboring fields. The lakeside cottages didn't look big enough to hold a double bed, let alone a bathroom. On the edge of town we passed a sign welcoming us to Sparta, population 600. The cemetery across the road held more people than the village itself. A dying town, bolstered by one remaining source of tourism, a massive campground outside the village limits, jam-packed with trailers and motor homes and not a tent in sight.

The town center swarmed with tourists, some from the trailer park, others persumably from nearby cottages. Not that downtown Sparta was any kind of shopping mecca. There was an Exxon gas station, the House of Wang Chinese restaurant, Lynn's Cut and Curl, the Yankee Trader general store—with signs boasting of video games and hand-scooped ice cream—and the ever-present coffee shop, called simply Joe's. From what I could see, there were only three streets in Sparta, the highway plus cross streets on either end, Baker to the west and New Moon to the east. The two side streets were lined with houses differentiated only by their colors, everything from baby blue to deep violet to lime green. Despite the abundance of open land beyond the town, lawns were barely big enough to warrant a power mower. Flowers came in two varieties: marigold and begonia. Country-craft wreaths hung from front doors, and signs hung from porches proclaiming "The Millers: John, Beth, Sandy, Lori, and Duke. Welcome All!"

"Odd that they'd pick such a small town for their meeting," I said.

"Maybe," Jeremy said, "but how many of those people walking around do you think actually live here?"

I saw his point. Both sides of the highway were jammed with SUVs and minivans. Families strolled the street, licking ice cream cones and sipping canned diet soda. Strangers probably outnumbered townies ten to one. A few more wouldn't be noticed.

"Ooops, we passed it," I said. "Sign for the Legion Hall back there. Sorry."

Jeremy pulled into a parking lot, waited for a brigade of baby strollers to pass, then turned the Explorer around and headed back. The Legion Hall was at the end of Baker, a good half mile beyond the last house on the street. Jeremy slowed to look at the hall, then continued down another hundred feet and pulled into a dead-end lane. We found a path leading toward the Legion Hall through a patch of woods. We debated taking it, but decided against it. While it might have given us a chance to sneak up and look around, there was also the risk that someone from the meeting would pick that moment to pop outdoors and catch us lurking among the trees. Not exactly a dignified entrance.

Taking the road, we still approached with care. When we got to the hall, I surveyed the parking lot and counted four vehicles: two mid-sized rental cars, a Jeep with California plates, and an Accord with Massachusetts plates.

"I see the witches drove," I said, gesturing at the Accord. "So much for teleport spells and magic broomsticks. And look at this place. It's a Legion Hall. We're going to a meeting of supernatural races in a Legion Hall. On a beautiful summer day, with not even a thunderclap in the background. Couldn't they have found a rotting Victorian mansion somewhere?"

"The mausoleum at the cemetery was booked. If you look up in the far left corner under the eaves, I believe I see a cobweb."

"That's a streamer. A pink streamer. From a wedding reception."

"Well, I'm sure you'll find some cobwebs inside."

"Sure, right next to the Ladies' Auxiliary snack table."

Jeremy bent to read the schedule posted behind a cracked glass case.

"So what are we booked under?" I asked. "The New Age Alternate Lifestyle conference?"

"No, the Corporate Technology Workshop."

"Great. Witches without broomsticks, teleport spells, or imaginations. What's next? If there are vampires in there, they probably drink artificial blood plasma substitute. Sterilized, of course."

"If there are vampires, they'd be in their crypts right now. It's daylight."

"So, in that case, I can logically conclude that vampires don't exist, right? If they did, they'd be at the meeting. And if they were coming to the meeting, it'd be held at night. Ergo a daytime meeting means no vampires. Bonus."

"Not a big vampire fan?"

"It's not that. Think about it. Witches, sorcerers, magicians, whatever . . . they're minor-league bad. If such things existed, they wouldn't be more than gifted humans. Werewolves are major league. No magic sleight of hand can top our big trick. Add superhuman strength, preternatural senses, and a really nasty attitude—"

"Speak for yourself."

"Present company excepted. Point being, witches have nothing on us. But vampires? Vampires could be more powerful. They certainly get better press. I might walk into that meeting and find out I'm not the baddest thing in the room."

"Maybe not, but you'll still be the baddest thing *alive* in the room."

I grinned. "The undead angle. Hadn't thought of that."

"Proper categorization is the key. Now let's get inside."

Jeremy pulled on the door. It didn't budge.

"Locked," he said.

He paused a moment, as if considering whether to knock, but I knew he wouldn't. The Alpha of the werewolves did not wait to be admitted to any so-called meeting of the supernatural. Jeremy yanked on the door, but it didn't break, didn't even quaver.

"Guess the powers are bound to fail once you hit a certain age," I said. "Allow me."

Jeremy stepped aside with a mocking half-bow. I grabbed the door handle and heaved with enough force that the door should have flown from its hinges. It didn't move.

"Oh," I said.

"Oh, indeed. Perhaps you could huff and puff and blow the door down."

An image from Pittsburgh came to me. Lock-pick guy complaining about the Winterbournes' hotel-room door.

"A spell," I said. "They've cast a spell on it. Guess we have to knock."

"Be my guest."

That was embarrassing. Werewolves knocking at the door. What was the world coming to? Still, we had no choice. I knocked and a few moments later, Paige answered.

Her eyes widened as she opened the door. "You're early."

"Is that a problem?" Jeremy asked, his voice pure silk.

Paige glanced up at him, hesitated, then shook her head. "No, of course not. Come in and meet everyone."

CHAPTER 6

Introductions

As Paige led us down the hall, we could see the main room ahead. There were four people on folding chairs around a folding wooden table, the type of furniture found in church basements everywhere. Looking at the four, I was relieved—or perhaps slightly disappointed—to note a complete absence of cloven hooves and unsightly body appendages. The four looked as if they could have really been at a conference, albeit a casual midsummer conference in cottage country.

Ruth sat beside an empty chair. Like Paige, she wore a sundress. Across from them was a woman in her mid-forties, slender with short auburn hair. Beside her sat a young man with broad shoulders, a boyish face, and light brown hair tipped blond. On his left was a man on the far side of middle age, heavyset and graying. He looked aboriginal, probably Inuit, his smooth face a mask of meditative calm. So this was a gathering of the most powerful supernatural beings in North America? Oh, please. Central casting could have found a more likely bunch by plundering the Sunday night television lineup.

Across the room was the Ladies' Auxiliary snack table. Well, not exactly, but close enough. The only thing missing was the blue-haired matron doling out goodies and guarding her cash box. There was a table with a coffee urn, a margarine tub of white powder that was more likely to be creamer than cocaine, a pyramid of Styrofoam cups—one filled with sugar cubes—and a plate of powdered doughnuts. On the rear wall, a handwritten sign reminded snackers that coffee and doughnuts were a quarter each, followed by a line in red clarifying that this meant fifty cents for both a doughnut and coffee, not a quarter for the two combined. I really hoped the Legion folks were responsible for the goodies and the sign. Otherwise . . . well, I didn't want to consider the alternative. Let's just say if anyone passed around a plate for membership dues, I was out of there.

Beside the table was a flip-board and, on the top page of the flip-board, the meeting agenda. I kid you not. They had an agenda, not just a rough list of topics, but a full schedule starting with greetings and refreshments at 10:00, background at 10:30, roundtable at 11:45, followed by lunch from 12:15 to 1:15. I glanced over my shoulder to see Jeremy reading the schedule, lips twitching.

"At least they're organized," he murmured, too low for Paige to hear.

Everyone turned as we walked in. Ruth stood, features rearranging themselves in a welcoming smile as she tried to hide her surprise.

"Hello," she said. "I thought you weren't coming until Monday."

"Our plans for the weekend fell through."

"Oh? Oh, well, yes. Come in then. Everyone, this is Jeremy . . . Jeremy Danvers, the . . . leader . . . I hope that's right, leader? . . . of the—"

"Jeremy is fine," he finished. "This is Elena."

The young man with the blond-tipped hair grinned. "The infamous werewolves? Funny, you don't look like werewolves. No connecting eyebrows, no hairy palms. Damn. Another myth shot to hell. And I thought all werewolves were male. That's definitely not a guy."

"Women's lib," I said. "We're everywhere now."

The young man's grin broadened. "Is nothing sacred?"

"Elena is the only female werewolf," Paige said as she walked to the empty chair. "Werewolves are made two ways, by inheriting the genes or by being bitten. Most werewolves are hereditary, since few people bitten by a werewolf survive. Because the genes pass only through the male line, female werewolves are extremely rare."

The young man rolled his eyes. "Next on the Discovery Channel, an in-depth examination of werewolves and feminism by Paige Winterbourne."

"Go to hell, Adam."

"Don't rush me."

"Ignore them, please," Ruth said. "Adam and Paige have known each other since they were children. Sometimes I suspect they haven't come very far in the intervening years. Now, introductions. This one beside me is Paige and that young man is Adam, in case that wasn't perfectly obvious. Our younger generation. The poor man stuck between the two is Kenneth."

The middle-aged man blinked, as if startled back to earth. He looked at us and gave a confused smile.

"On Adam's other side is Cassandra."

The auburn-haired woman's smile didn't reach her eyes, which studied us with interest but little emotion.

"That's not what you really want to know, is it?" Adam said. "At least, that's not the good part, not *who* we are, but *what* we are, right? Though it's probably better to explain the two separately or it ends up sounding like an AA meeting for the damned. 'Hi, my name is Adam and I'm a half-demon.'"

"A half . . . ?" I said.

"Exactly what it sounds like. Mom's human. Dad's the living embodiment of absolute evil. Luckily, I got my looks from Mom's side. My father's not exactly GQ material. Don't ask me what my mother was thinking. Obviously one too many tequila shots that night."

"Demons take human form to rape or seduce human women," Paige said. "Half-demons are always human in appearance. They inherit other qualities from their fathers. Each has different powers, depending on the type of demon that sired them."

"The X-Men of the underworld," Adam said. "Now that Paige has so neatly summed up my biology, here are the goods on the rest. Paige and Ruth, witches, but you knew that. Cass, vampire. Ken, shaman. You know what a shaman is?"

"Yes," Jeremy said.

"So that's it. The major supernatural races, all in one place, like Satan's Ark."

"Adam, please," Ruth said. She turned to us. "Adam likes to joke, but I can assure you, we are not evil, not Satanists, nothing of the sort."

"Just regular folks," Adam said. "With a few quirks."

I glanced at Adam. So this was a half-demon. Uh-huh. I'd never heard of half-demons before Pittsburgh, but I was sure if such things existed, they shouldn't look like this guy. Any portrayal of demons I'd ever seen was quite clear on several points: They had cloven hooves, scales, horns, and tails. Logically, then, a half-demon should at least have bad skin. He should not be a baby-faced, all-American boy who looked like he should be greeting guests at Disney World. Maybe that was the idea. Maybe half-demons were supposed to look charming and innocuous. It would be far easier to tempt mortals to evil without scales and horns ruining that all-important first impression. Perhaps beneath that wide-eyed exterior lurked a soul of pure evil.

"Chairs," Adam said, scrambling to his feet. "You guys need chairs. Hold on. I'll be back in a flash."

Maybe it was a deeply hidden wellspring of evil. Very deeply hidden.

Then there was Cassandra. A vampire? Who was she kidding? She looked as much like an undead bloodsucker as I looked like a half-wolf monster. Okay, bad analogy. The point was that Cassandra could not be a vampire. It wasn't just her appearance. Granted, she looked less like a crypt-dwelling fiend than a Wall Street exec, the kind of woman whose tailored dresses, perfect manicure, and nearly flawless makeup were a trap waiting to spring on anyone who mistook the outer package as a sign of inner softness. But the problem went deeper than that. Much deeper. First, there were no fangs, not even oversized canines. Second, she sat in a room with sunlight streaming through the windows. Third, there was no way in hell—pardon the pun—you could tell me that any woman could style her hair and apply her makeup that well if she couldn't see her reflection. Even with a three-way mirror, I can't get my hair back in a clip without tendrils escaping every which way.

Jeremy must have been thinking the same thing because he started by saying, "Before we begin, we need to clear up one thing. I don't mean to sound suspicious—"

"Don't apologize," Cassandra said. "You should be suspicious."

Jeremy nodded. "Although Adam so neatly categorized everyone, you can see where we might be in need of more . . . concrete evidence."

I said, "To put it bluntly, how do we know you are what you say you are? You say you're a vampire, but . . . "

"Everyone knows vampires don't exist," Cassandra said.

"It is a bit hard to swallow," I said. "Vampires, witches, shamans, demons."

"Are you listening to yourself?" Paige said. "You don't believe in the supernatural? You're a werewolf!"

"Alleged werewolf."

Paige rolled her eyes. "Here we go again. You still don't believe we're witches, do you? Even after we cast multiple spells to save your life—"

"Save my life?" I sputtered. "You were the one padding down a hotel hallway in your nightgown, so eager to see the bad guy lurking behind door number one."

Adam laughed. Paige shot him a glare.

"Okay," I said, "let's pretend I believe in vampires and witches. How do I know that's what you guys are? Do you know how many wackos out there think they're vampires? Trust me, you don't want to know. It'll keep you up at night."

"I've seen them," Cassandra said. "Black lipstick, black nail polish, absolutely zero fashion sense. Wherever did they get the idea vampires are color-blind?" She lifted her pen and offered it to me. "You could stab me with this. Just not in the heart, please."

"Too messy," I said.

She settled back in her chair, eyes on me as if no one else was in the room. I could feel the curiosity in her gaze now as it moved across my face, studying me. Her lips curved in a smile, still cool, but now tinged with friendly interest.

"I could bite you," she said.

"I'd only bite you back."

The smile touched her hazel eyes. "Interesting thought. What do you think would happen? A vampire/werewolf hybrid? Or would it have no effect? Intriguing idea, but impractical at the moment. We could compare fangs."

"Definitely a guy thing."

She laughed. "Quite right."

"Maybe you can explain something then," I said. "If you *are* a vampire . . . " I looked at the sunlight streaming through the window.

"Why am I not exploding in a cloud of dust? I've often wondered that myself. As Adam would say, 'Damn, another myth shot to hell.' I'm quite glad that one isn't true. An eternity without Caribbean beach vacations would be more than I could handle. It was much more disheartening when I discovered I couldn't fly. But as for a demonstration, perhaps this will do."

Cassandra laid her left hand on the table, lifted the pen, and jammed it down into her outstretched palm, driving it a half-inch into her hand. Ruth shuddered and looked away. Cassandra examined the damage with cool detachment, as if she'd stabbed the tabletop instead.

"A poor job of it," she said. "Unlike werewolves, we don't have super strength. That's the best I can manage, but it should prove my point."

She tugged the pen out, then lifted her palm for me to examine. The puncture was as clean as a nail hole through a waxen dummy. As I watched, the edges of the wound moved together, the flesh reconstituting itself. Within a minute, her skin was smooth and unblemished.

"No pain, no blood, no fuss," she said. "Good enough?"

"Yes," Jeremy said. "Thank you."

"My turn?" Paige said. "What can I do to convince you, Elena? Conjure up a demon?"

"Paige!" Ruth's eyes widened in alarm. She quickly turned to us. "Let me assure you, we do not conjure demons. Besides a few simple self-protection spells, witches practice only benevolent magic."

"And it harm none, do what thou wilt," Cassandra murmured.

Ruth whispered something to Paige, who nodded, shrugged, rolled her eyes, clearly adopting the ever-popular defense of the young: "Geez, I was only kidding." Had she been kidding? Not about conjuring a demon, but about being able to do it? Ruth said they practiced only so-called white magic. Was that all they *could* do? Or all they *would* do? Was a certain apprentice spell-caster not too happy with her predefined role as the direct descendant of the Good Witch of the North? Hmmm.

"That's enough of the demonstrations," Jeremy said. "Right now, I'd like to learn more about these men who stalked Elena."

"I heard about that," Adam said, grinning at me. "The first casualty of war. Way to go. I'm jealous."

"You would be," Paige said.

Ruth glanced at the two with a look 90 percent exasperated affection and 10 percent gentle warning. They shut up as quickly as if they'd received a tongue-lashing. Ruth paused, as if making sure they were going to be quiet, then began her story.

CHAPTER 7

AGENDA

Five weeks ago, a shaman had been kidnapped and had contacted Kenneth via astral projection—whatever that was. By the time he contacted Kenneth, he was in rough shape. A shaman was never physically strong to begin with, so it didn't take much rough treatment to injure one—or so Ruth explained. Because of his weak condition, his report was patchy and at times incoherent. From what Kenneth could make out, the shaman had been kidnapped by two men and taken to a compound a full day's drive from his home in Virginia. There, two other men had questioned him about his powers and abilities. In the early days of his captivity, the shaman had enough strength to astral-project through the compound at night, searching for clues about who had captured him and why. He'd learned the names of the two men who'd questioned him, Lawrence Matasumi and Tyrone Winsloe. Winsloe's name meant nothing to the shaman or Kenneth. Apparently knowledge of current events didn't rank high in shaman priorities.

While this shaman had been astral-projecting, he'd found that he wasn't the only supernatural being in the compound. His captors had a teleporting half-demon—likely Houdini—on their staff. He also heard that a sorcerer was assisting them, though he never saw the man. As for the other captives, when he first astral-projected, he found a witch, two half-demons, and a Vodoun priest. Then the witch disappeared and he learned that another, stronger witch had been targeted to take her place.

That was all the shaman knew. He'd promised to contact Kenneth again the next day but never did. When Kenneth conveyed the information to Ruth, Paige recognized Winsloe's name and used the Internet to track down Lawrence Matasumi, a renowned parapsychology researcher.

"Have you had any luck finding these men?" Jeremy asked when Ruth finished.

"Find them?" Adam said. "Hell, no. We figured we'd hide out and pray they don't find us."

"Actually, we've been debating that very matter," Ruth said, ignoring or missing Adam's sarcasm.

"Have we?" Adam said. "I thought it was decided. Reactive, not proactive. That's our way. Well, it's the way of the witches, and since they lead these meetings—"

"Why, Adam," Paige said, "are you expressing an interest in a greater leadership role? More responsibilities?"

He only grinned. "Perish the thought. I was only saying that, as our esteemed leaders, the witches generally make such strategic decisions, and they've decided we're ducking for cover."

"We need to discuss the matter further," Cassandra said. "This is a new situation for us. We've never had to worry about finding those who threaten us. If someone thinks they have proof of vampires, they aren't interested in exploring the intricacies of our lives. They're calculating how much money they'll get in the book deal. Finding them isn't a problem. They're waving big red flags saying, 'Find me, please'—find me and make me rich."

"But with these guys it's different," I said. "So, different threat, different response, right? They're hiding, so you need to find them."

"And do what?" Paige asked. "Ask them to stop harassing us?"

Jeremy looked at Ruth. "If we find the threat, we eliminate it. That's our way."

"Sign me up," Adam said.

"We are going to take action," Ruth said. "You know that, Adam, although our idea of action may not match yours. This is a serious threat, and I'm not comfortable even gathering here to discuss it. No matter how careful we were in setting up this meeting, we have seven supernatural beings in one place, each of whom these men would love to collect."

"Is that what they're doing?" Jeremy asked. "Collecting?"

"We aren't clear on their motives," Ruth said. "That wasn't something Roger—the kidnapped shaman—was able to determine. From what he observed, we gather that they're studying us, trying to get to the root of our powers."

"So they can find a way to use them for themselves," Paige said.

Ruth frowned. "We aren't sure of that. I don't like jumping to conclusions, but yes, that would seem to be a viable motivation. The presence of Lawrence Matasumi on their team would suggest strong scientific interests."

"And the presence of Ty Winsloe means someone's expecting to cash in big time," Paige said. "Winsloe's no philanthropist. The guy wouldn't cross the road to save an old lady unless she'd leave him her estate for his inconvenience."

A small frown from Ruth. "Perhaps. The point is, though, that they seem to want to harness our powers. For personal gain or in the name of science, it doesn't matter."

"They can't get my powers," Adam said. "Strictly hereditary."

"You sure about that?" Paige said. "Maybe if they take you apart, organ by organ, they can find exactly what in your physiological structure gives you these powers. Of course, whether they found it or not wouldn't matter much to you, since you'd be in a bunch of little autopsy bags."

"Nice visuals, Paige," Adam said.

"The point is," Ruth said, "we don't know what they can get from us. Some things, like minor spells, can be learned. As for becoming a werewolf or vampire, that's a frighteningly simple matter. What if these men began selling the ability to become a werewolf?"

"Hope they wouldn't charge much," I muttered.

"I'm sure plenty of people would see the advantages to superhuman strength," Ruth said.

"Not to mention prolonged youth," Paige added. "You'd have morons lining up ten deep for that one. The latest alternative to plastic surgery: Become a werewolf."

"The point is," Ruth said, again, "that by having the ability to do these things, to freely—or not so freely—distribute these powers, these men could upset the balance of nature. People would die. Humankind would be at risk, threatened by the worst kind of excesses, immortal dictators, spell-casting tyrants, serial killers who could take the form of wolves—"

"Been there, done that," I murmured low enough for only Jeremy to hear. A smile sparked in his eyes, but he kept his face impassive.

"We have to think beyond ourselves," Ruth said.

"Do we?" Cassandra asked. "I know that's how you feel, Ruth, but I'm not terribly concerned with protecting humankind from self-destruction. I care what this threat means to *me*. If you tell me these men want to kidnap me, that's a good enough reason for me to take this seriously. The question is, what are we going to do about it?"

That certainly was the question. And we spent the next seven hours discussing it, sending Adam and Paige out to get lunch at one and barely stopping the debate long enough to eat.

So what was Ruth's plan? Well, step one was for each delegate to notify his or her fellow monsters. Sounds simple and logical, right? Of course, Jeremy would notify the rest of the Pack. He'd never dream of doing otherwise. Now that he realized the extent of the danger, he'd tell Clay to join us right away. That done, he'd only need to make one other phone call. Two deaths in last year's skirmish with the mutts had reduced us to a Pack of five. Besides Clay, Jeremy, and myself there were only Antonio Sorrentino and his son, Nick. There were always a half dozen or so mutts trying to get admitted to the Pack, and with our diminished numbers, Jeremy was considering two or three, but he was in no rush to make a decision, so for now we were five. Two easy phone calls. But that wasn't what the witches wanted. They wanted us to notify the mutts. Say what? As Jeremy explained, mutts were nomadic. Territory was for the Pack. Only one mutt had territory, and that was a special arrangement. Then Ruth wanted us to notify this particular mutt and let him contact the others. Okay. Sure. I could see it now. I'd call Karl Marsten, ask him to pass on the word to his "fellow mutts," and he'd laugh himself into a stomach rupture. He'd still be laughing when he hung up on me.

Ruth didn't understand how things worked. Like us, the witches had a small central group, which they called the Coven. More witches lived outside the Coven than in it, like the Pack and the mutts. Outside witches were considered an inferior class, like the mutts. But, unlike us, witches didn't *admit* the others were inferior. Oh, no. According to Ruth, outside witches were poor misguided souls in need of protection and conversion. She reminded me of an early Christian missionary talking about Native Americans, and I noticed Paige squirming as her aunt spoke. Unlike missionaries, though, Ruth didn't want these outside witches to join their "church"—their Coven. Oh, no. They only wanted them to live good and proper lives on their own. The Coven was special.

If we thought the logistics of notifying werewolves was tough, informing vampires and half-demons was almost impossible. Cassandra knew where to find all of the couple dozen living (should I say existing?) vampires, but she had zero interest in apprising all but a handful and made it clear that she wasn't wasting her time on such a ridiculous task. Let the others look after themselves. As for half-demons, there were apparently over a hundred in North America alone, about 50 percent of whom, if notified, would be lining up to apply for jobs with the enemy.

Now, of course Ruth didn't want us to contact each and every member of our race, but she expected us to at least notify a few and ask them to pass the word along. That was more than anyone, except Kenneth, was willing to do. Jeremy, Cassandra, and Adam all agreed it was a waste of time. After a few hours arguing the point, they abandoned it and moved to step two.

Everyone agreed on step two: Learn more about the enemy. How to go about this was another matter, but everyone agreed on the principle. We had to know more. And step three? Don't even ask about step three. The group was divided between witches and shamans wanting to find a way to discourage or discredit our antagonists, and werewolves and half-demons wanting to eliminate them. Cassandra didn't care much one way or the other, so long as these people went away and left her alone.

At seven we were still talking. Everyone was getting tired and a wee bit cranky. When Ruth suggested we order in dinner, the answer was a resounding "No!" We needed a break. We'd drive to nearby Kingston for dinner, then come back to the meeting. As Ruth said earlier, our gathering was dangerous in itself. We all wanted to decide on a course of action that day and get the hell out of Sparta.

As the meeting disbanded for dinner, everyone except Paige walked to the parking lot en masse. Maybe she had to fix up her notes. Or maybe she was the cleanup crew. When we got outside, Kenneth and Cassandra headed to separate rental cars. Jeremy and I were walking to the Explorer when Ruth called him over. Jeremy motioned me toward the SUV and strode back to Ruth.

"Scary bunch, huh?" said a voice to my left.

I turned to see Adam jog up beside me.

He grinned. "So, what was the scariest part? The flip-board agenda? The powdered doughnuts?"

"Please tell me the witches aren't charging a quarter for coffee and doughnuts."

"No, no, no. Didn't you see the sign. It's *fifty* cents for a coffee and a doughnut. A quarter each. Seriously, though, that's Legion stuff. But the flip-board and the schedule were definitely Ruth's doing. A guy who used to be a delegate told me that, years ago, the witches had a mission statement and a code of conduct for these meetings. I think he was kidding, but I've never been sure."

"So they're always so . . . earnest?"

Adam laughed. "Earnest. That's a good word to describe witches. Well, maybe not Paige, but certainly Ruth and the rest of them. Deadly serious. This is important stuff, damn it." He rolled his eyes. "Everyone's gotta have a hobby, and with the witches, it's organizing these meetings. Hey, is it true you gave Paige those bruises around her neck?"

"It was a misunderstanding."

He grinned. "I'll bet. I'll also bet she deserved it. Paige can be a major pain, but she can also be a lot of fun. You have to be careful which side of her you land on." He glanced back at Jeremy and Ruth. "So, you think your leader can talk these guys into taking action?"

"If he can't, we'll do it ourselves. We aren't accustomed to taking orders from others."

"My kinda people. That's what we need in these meetings. A strong, nonpassive leader."

"A male leader?"

Adam lifted both hands to ward me off. "I didn't say that. It's not a gender thing. It's a race thing. Witches and shamans aren't like us. And vamps? Well, they're not like anyone, which is exactly how they like it. Cass can kick ass if she wants. Not super-strong or anything, like she said, but that regenerative stuff is real handy in a fight. Guy shoots you, you just keep walking and grab the gun. Very cool."

"So they're immortal?"

"Nah. Not exactly anyway. They can regenerate, they live for hundreds of years, and they're damned tough to kill. Close enough to immortal for me."

Before I could ask anything more, Paige joined us.

"I'm going with you," she said to Adam. "Kenneth offered to drive Ruth. I'd go along, but at the speed he drives, I'd faint from hunger before we reached the restaurant." She glanced at me. "Want to come with us?"

I was about to decline when Jeremy waved me over, saving me the trouble of coming up with a polite excuse. I said I'd see them at the restaurant and jogged over to Jeremy.

CHAPTER 8

BURNED

We'd elected to eat at an Italian restaurant. Bad choice. Though it was nearly eight, the place was crowded. This part of Vermont didn't offer much in the way of fine dining, so it seemed as if everyone within a fifty-mile radius who didn't like hamburgers was here. There was no hope of getting a table for seven, so we agreed to split up. When the server found us a table for six and a table for two, Cassandra offered to take the small table. At first, I thought she wanted to eat alone, which wouldn't have surprised me, but instead she invited me to join her. I wasn't the only one shocked by that. Paige stared at me as if trying to figure out what could possibly possess Cassandra to pick me as her dining companion. I think she'd have been less surprised if Cassandra invited me to *be* dinner instead. Even Kenneth blinked, which seemed a sure sign that a dinner invitation from Cassandra was not a common event. I'll admit, I was flattered. Cassandra didn't seem the type who'd need, much less want, company.

Cassandra and I sat apart from the others, out on the patio. I wondered whether she'd eat dinner. She ordered chicken parmigiana and white wine. While she drank the wine, she only had a few bites of the chicken, then shifted the food around on her plate to make it look as if she'd eaten more. Maybe she was eating later. I really didn't want to think about that. Culinary squeamishness may seem absurd coming from someone who chows down on raw rabbit, but there was a difference between what appealed to me as a wolf and what appealed to me as a human. As good as freshly killed deer tasted after a hunt, I didn't like to think about it while eating seafood linguine.

"You're curious," Cassandra said after our meals arrived. "But you don't ask questions. Odd for a journalist."

How much had Ruth and Paige told everyone else about me?

"Depends on the type of journalist," I said. "I do politics and social issues. Strictly public-life stuff. Very little dirt-digging of a personal nature."

"So you avoid personal questions. Probably because you don't want anyone asking them back. If you're curious, you can ask. I don't mind."

"Okay," I said . . . and asked nothing.

After a few minutes of silence, I decided I really should ask something. Not just anything, but the big question. After all, it was staring me in the face, from Cassandra's barely touched dinner.

I gestured at her plate. "So, I guess you're not big on chicken."

"Solids in general. I can eat a few bites, but more gives me a nasty case of indigestion."

She waited, face expressionless, but a smile shimmering in her eyes.

"There's no sense asking, is there?" I said, sipping my wine. "Asking if vampires—you know—would be like asking if werewolves change into wolves. It's the hallmark of the species."

"Actually, in my case, you'd be mistaken. I know, I know, you read so many stories. But they're just not true. I most emphatically do not sleep in a coffin." She paused, then arched her eyebrows. "Oh, isn't that what you meant?"

"I meant, obviously you drink—" I gestured at my wineglass.

"Burgundy? I prefer white. Yes, I can drink wine. Thank heaven for small mercies. It's only solids that give me trouble. Let me help you out, Elena. I believe the word you're looking for is 'blood.'"

"That's it. Slipped my mind."

She laughed, a throaty laugh that startled the server coming out the patio door. We ordered refills on our wine, then waited until he'd left.

"So what is it these days?" I said. "Home deliveries from the blood bank?"

"Afraid not."

"A special deal with the butcher?"

"The FDA would likely disapprove. Sadly, we're stuck getting our meals the old-fashioned way."

"Ah."

"Ah, indeed," she said with another laugh. "Yes, I drink it straight from the source. Some rules, though. No children. No one under thirty. Makes it more sporting."

"Did I mention I'm twenty-eight?"

"That's not what I heard." She grinned. "No need to worry. Common courtesy dictates that we never drain the lifeblood of anyone to whom we've been formally introduced."

She cut a few bits of chicken and moved them around on her plate. "To be honest, I've tried animal blood and blood banks. They don't work.

Living that way is like subsisting on bread and water. We exist, but barely. Some still do it. I'm too selfish. If I'm alive, I want to be completely alive. The only apology I can make is that I try to choose those who welcome death, the old, the sick, the suicidal. I'm deluding myself, of course. I can tell that a man wants to die, but I have no way of knowing if he's about to climb a twenty-story building or is temporarily depressed over a broken affair. Life would be so much simpler if we lost our souls when we were reborn, if we forfeited the ability to feel, to know right from wrong. But I suppose that's why they call it a curse. We still know."

"But you don't have a choice."

"Oh, there's always a choice. Self-annihilation. Some do it. Most consider it, but the will to survive is ultimately too strong. If it means the choice between their death and mine, altruism be damned. The motto of the truly strong. Or the incredibly selfish."

We were quiet a moment, then she said, "I take it werewolves aren't cannibals, then?"

"You mean eating humans, not other werewolves, which strictly speaking, would be cannibalism."

"You don't consider yourselves human?"

"To varying degrees. Myself, I still think half-human, half-wolf. Cla— Others don't. They consider werewolves a separate species. I'm not avoiding the question. Pack wolves are forbidden to eat humans. We wouldn't anyway. It doesn't make sense. Eating humans wouldn't serve any other purpose than to sate a hunger that can as easily be satisifed with a deer."

"It's that easy then?"

"I wish. Unfortunately, there's not just the hunger. There's the hunting instinct, and I'll admit, humans satisfy that far better than any animal."

Cassandra's eyes glittered. "The Most Dangerous Game."

The thought struck me then, how odd it was to be discussing this with another woman. I shook it off and continued, "Trouble is, it's hard to hunt without killing. It's possible, but dangerous, risking the chance you won't be able to stop yourself before the kill. Non-Pack werewolves hunt, kill, and eat people. The temptation is too great, and most aren't interested in controlling their impulses."

The server came out then to get our dessert order. I was about to pass, as I usually did when dining with other women, then realized it didn't matter. Cassandra wouldn't care if I ate three pieces of cake. So I ordered tiramisu and a coffee. Cassandra seconded the coffee. As the server turned to leave, Cassandra reached out and grabbed his wrist.

"Decaf actually," she said.

As she spoke, she kept her hand on his wrist, thumb outstretched across his pulse. The server was young and Latin-handsome, big dark eyes and smooth olive skin. Did he notice she held his arm too long? Not a chance. As she called him back and changed her order, she kept her eyes on his like he was the most fascinating thing in the room. And he stared back like a mouse entranced by a cobra. If she'd asked him to step into the back alley with her, he'd have tripped over his feet to obey. When she finally released his arm, he blinked, then something like disappointment crossed his face. He promised to hurry with the coffees and returned to the dining room.

"Sometimes I almost can't resist," Cassandra said after he'd gone. "Even when I'm not hungry. The intoxication of power. A nasty but unbreakable addiction, don't you think?"

"It's . . . tempting."

Cassandra laughed. "You don't have to pretend with me, Elena. Power is a glorious thing, especially for women. I spent forty-six years as a human woman in seventeenth-century Europe. I'd have killed for a chance at power." Her lips curved in a wicked grin. "But I guess I did, didn't I? The choices one makes." She leaned back and studied me, then smiled again. "I think you and I will get along quite well. A rare treat for me, meeting a huntress who isn't another self-absorbed vampire."

Our coffees and my dessert arrived then. I asked Cassandra what it was like to live as long as she had, and she regaled me with stories for the rest of the meal.

After dinner, Adam repeated Paige's offer to join them on the way back to the Legion Hall. Again, I was about to decline, but this time Jeremy overheard and insisted I go along, probably hoping the two youngest delegates would talk more freely without their elders around. In an aside, he promised to follow us in the Explorer.

Unlike Jeremy, Adam hadn't found parking in the small lot behind the restaurant, so the three of us left the others and headed up a side street. Ahead, on the other side of the road, I saw the old Jeep from the Legion Hall parking lot, the one with the California plates.

"Yours?" I asked Adam.

"Unfortunately."

"That's some drive."

"A long drive. In a Jeep, a very, very long drive. I think I shook loose two fillings this time. Getting above the speed limit is nearly impossible.

And passing? Forget it. It'd be easier driving *over* slow traffic. Next time, I'm saving my pennies so I can fly out."

"You say that every time," Paige said. "Robert would buy you a plane ticket any day, but you always refuse. You love driving that piece of crap."

"The blush is wearing off the romance. One more— Shit!"

I looked up to see a massive Yukon backing into the spot in front of Adam's Jeep. The gap was barely big enough to fit a compact. The behemoth SUV kept reversing until it was mere inches from the Jeep's front bumper. Another car was parked less than a foot from the Jeep's rear end.

"Hey!" Adam called as he jogged toward the Yukon. "Hold on!"

A forty-something woman in the passenger seat turned and fixed Adam with an expressionless stare.

"I'm stuck in behind you," he said, flashing a wide grin. "Could you just pull forward a second? I'll get her out of there and you'll have lots of room."

The passenger window was down, but the woman didn't answer. She looked over at the driver's seat. No words were exchanged. The driver's door opened and a man in a golf shirt got out. His wife did the same.

"Hey!" Adam called. "Did you hear me? You boxed me in. If you can pull forward, I'll be out of there in a flash."

The man clicked his remote. The alarm chirped. His wife fell in step beside him and they headed for the restaurant.

"Assholes," Paige muttered. "Own a fifty-thousand-dollar gas-guzzler and you own the whole damned road."

"I'll talk to them," I said. "Maybe he'll listen to a woman."

"Don't." She grabbed my arm. "We'll catch up with the others and come back for the Jeep later."

"I'm only going to talk to them."

She glanced at Adam, who was starting after the couple. "It's not you I'm worried about."

The man turned now, lip curling as he threw some insult at Adam.

"What did you say?" Adam yelled back.

"Oh, shit," Paige murmured.

The man turned his back on Adam.

"What did you say?" Adam shouted.

As Adam advanced on the man, I made a split-second decision to interfere. We were trying to lie low and couldn't afford to call attention to ourselves with a brawl that might involve the police. Adam should have known this, but I guess even the most easygoing young men can be subject to surges of testosterone.

As I turned to go after Adam, Paige grabbed my arm.

"Hold on," she said. "You don't—"

I shook her off and started running, ignoring her trailing footsteps and warning shouts. As I drew closer to Adam, I smelled fire. Not smoke or burning wood or sulfur, but the subtler odor of fire itself. Ignoring it, I grabbed Adam's wrist and whirled him around.

"Forget it," I said as he turned. "Jeremy can drive us—"

Adam faced me now, and I knew where the smell of fire came from. His eyes glowed crimson. The whites were luminescent red, sparking absolute, bottomless rage.

"Get your hands off me," he rumbled.

There was no trace of Adam's voice in the words, no sign of him in his face. Heat emanated from his body in waves. It was like standing too close to a bonfire. Sweat sprang from my pores. I turned my face from the heat, still holding his wrist. He grabbed me, each hand gripping a forearm. Something sizzled. I heard that first, had a second to wonder what it was, then blinding pain seared through my arms. He let go and I stumbled backward. Red welts leaped up on either forearm.

Paige grabbed me from behind, steadying me. I shoved her away and turned back to Adam. He was striding toward a vacant alley.

"He's okay," Paige said. "He'll get it under control now."

The Explorer rounded the corner. I waved my arms for Jeremy to stop and yanked open the passenger door before the SUV hit a full stop. As I jumped in, Jeremy's gaze went to my burned arms and his mouth tightened, but he said nothing. He waited until I was inside, then hit the accelerator.

CHAPTER 9

Dissection

As Jeremy drove, I explained what happened. Once outside town, Jeremy pulled into a gas station, parked in front of the phone booth, and got out. A few minutes later he returned and took us back onto the highway.

"Ruth?" I asked.

"I told her we're not returning to the meeting tonight. She heard what happened. Very apologetic. She asked if we'd come if they meet again tomorrow. I said I didn't know, so she wants me to call back tonight and see what they decided."

"Will you?"

"Probably. My first priority is protecting the Pack. To do that, we may need to join these people temporarily, while they investigate this threat. They have resources we can't match. At dinner we discussed this astral projection the shamans do, and it sounds like an invaluable tool for learning more about these men you encountered in Pittsburgh. Beyond that, though, I have no intention of sticking around to help them. We fight our own battles."

In the silence that followed, I reflected on our day, on the overwhelming things we'd discovered. Overwhelming for me, at least. Jeremy seemed not only unfazed but unsurprised by it all. I could chalk this up to his usual equanimity, but his response to everything seemed too calm, even for him.

"You knew," I said. "You knew there were other . . . things out there. Besides us."

"I'd heard rumors. When I was a child. Long nights, after a Meet, occasionally talk would turn to the possibility of other creatures, vampires, spell-casters, and the like. Someone remembered an uncle who once encountered a being with strange powers, that sort of thing. Much the way humans might discuss aliens or ghosts. Some believed. Most didn't."

"You did?"

"It seems improbable that we'd be the only legendary creature with its basis in reality." He drove in silence a moment, then continued. "Once, not long before his death, my grandfather told me that his grandfather claimed to have sat on a council of what Ruth would call 'supernatural beings.' My grandfather suspected the story may have simply been the confused imaginings of an old man, but he thought he should pass it on to me. If it was true, if other creatures existed, then someone in the Pack should be aware of the possibility."

"Shouldn't everyone in the Pack have been aware of the possibility?" I said. "No offense, Jer, but I really would have appreciated a warning."

"To be honest, the thought never crossed my mind. I never tried to discover whether my grandfather's story was true or not. The point seemed moot. I have no interest in other beings, and we're safer if they have no interest in us. Yes, I suppose one of you could accidentally come across one, but considering how few of us exist, and how few of them exist, the chances of not only meeting but recognizing each other seemed infinitesimal. Certainly it's never happened before, not in my lifetime or my grandfather's. Now it appears these witches have been aware of us for a very long time. I never considered that possibility."

"Are you admitting you made a mistake?"

His lips twitched in the barest smile. "I'm admitting to an oversight. It would only be a mistake if I considered the possibility and chose to ignore it."

"But if werewolves did sit on this council at one time, why isn't it in the Legacy?" I said, referring to the Pack's history book.

"I don't know. If as Ruth says, werewolves broke from the council, they may have chosen to remove that portion of their history from the Legacy."

"Maybe for good reason," I said, brushing my fingertips over my burned arms.

Jeremy glanced at me and nodded. "Maybe so."

At the cabin, Jeremy washed and dressed my burns, then asked if I was ready for bed or wanted to stay up longer.

"Were you staying up?" I asked.

"If you were."

"If you were, I will, but if you're tired . . . ?"

"Are you tir—" Jeremy stopped. A small half-smile flitted across his lips and I knew what he was thinking. We could go on like this all night, neither of us willing to voice an opinion that might inconvenience the other. With Clay or Nick or Antonio, I made my wants and opinions known without hesitation. Survival of the loudest. With Jeremy, his unerring civility resurrected my upbringing, and a simple choice could evolve into an endless "After you," "No, I insist, after you" farce. If Clay were here, he'd make up our minds for us before the second round of the dance. Without him, we were on our own.

"I'm going to stay up awhile," I said.

"I'll keep you company."

"You don't have to."

"I know. We'll sit on the deck. Go out, and I'll fix us a snack."

I went outside. Minutes later, Jeremy followed with two glasses of milk and a bag of cookies.

"Nothing stronger around to dull the pain," he said, handing me the milk. "You'll have to settle for simple comfort."

Jeremy sat beside me. We gazed out over the water for a few minutes, the crunch of cookies echoing in the silence. Smoke from a campfire floated across the lake.

"We should build a fire," I said.

"No matches."

"Damn. Where's Adam when you need him?"

Jeremy gave a half-smile. "We'll have a bonfire for you back at Stonehaven. Plenty of matches there. Marshmallows too. If only I can remember how to carve a roasting stick."

"You know how?"

He chuckled. "Hard to believe, isn't it? Yes, I did some camping as a child. Dominic used to rent a cottage every summer, get Tonio and his brothers out of the city, back to nature. They'd take me along."

As Jeremy lapsed into silence, I struggled to think of a way to keep him talking. Jeremy didn't discuss his childhood. Not ever. I'd had hints from others that it wasn't the most idyllic youth, but Jeremy kept mum on the subject. Now that he'd cracked opened that window, I wasn't about to let it close again so easily.

"Where did you go?" I asked.

"Not far. Vermont, New Hampshire."

"Was it fun?"

Another half-smile. "Very. I didn't care about the back to nature part. Stonehaven has all that. But it let Tonio and me play at being real kids, to play *with* other kids. Of course, we met other children at school. But we always went to private school. As Alpha, Dominic enforced that for Pack sons. If their fathers couldn't afford to send them, he paid for it. Strict

environmental control. Home for weekends and holidays, minimal interaction with humans. On vacation, though, we could cut loose, so long as
we used false names and all that."

"You had to use fake names? How old were you?"

"Young. Tonio was older, of course. But I was the one who made up
our stories. It was fun, actually, inventing a new identity every summer.
One year we were minor nobility visiting from England. Our accents were
atrocious. Another year we were Mafia brats. Tonio loved that one. Gave
him a chance to practice his Italian and make the local bullies quake."

"I can imagine."

"Great fun, until the kids started offering us their ice cream money.
Tonio drew the line there. Integrity above all, even if it meant turning
down extra food. We were debating whether to admit the whole mob
thing was a hoax when Malcolm showed up to take me back to Stonehaven.
Early as always."

Malcolm had been Jeremy's father, though I never heard Jeremy call
him by anything but his first name.

"He missed you?" I asked.

Jeremy laughed. Not his usual chuckle or half-smile, but a whoop of
laughter that startled me so much I nearly dropped my cookie.

"No," he said, composing himself. "Malcolm most assuredly did not
miss me. He did that every summer, stop by to see how I was doing. If
I was having fun, which I always was, he decided it was time for me to
come home."

I didn't know what to say to that, so I said nothing.

Jeremy continued, "After a few years, I started outmaneuvering him.
As soon as Malcolm arrived, I'd have a massive attack of homesickness.
Desperately miserable. Dying to leave. Then, of course, he'd make me stay
the rest of the summer. The Sorrentinos played along. They knew what it
was like for me at home." He gave a wry half-smile. "You, Clayton, and
me. Three housemates, all with rotten childhoods. What are the chances?"

"Clay had a good childhood."

"Barring the small matter of being turned into a werewolf at the age
of five and spending the next few years hiding in the bayou, eating rats
and drunks."

"I meant after that. After you rescued him. He's always said he had
a good childhood at Stonehaven."

"When he wasn't being expelled from school for dissecting the class
guinea pig?"

"It was already dead."

Jeremy chuckled. "I can still hear him saying that. Over thirty years later and I can hear it perfectly. Clay's first Pack meeting. I'm trying to pretend everything's fine, not let anyone know about the expulsion. Then Daniel roars in and announces it to the whole Pack. 'Clayton got kicked out of school for cutting up a guinea pig.' Clay tears into the room, marches over to Daniel, glares up at him—they were the same age, but Clay was at least a head shorter—and shouts, 'It was already dead!'"

"Which explained everything."

"Absolutely." Jeremy smiled and shook his head. "Between the dissected class pet and the toy animal fiasco, I had to question whether I was cut out for surrogate parenthood."

"Toy animals?"

"Clay hasn't told you that one?" Jeremy drained his glass, picked up mine, and stood.

I grabbed his pant leg. "Tell me."

"When I come back."

I groaned and waited. And waited. Took him much too long to pour that milk. Playing the whole thing for full effect.

"Toy animals," I said when he finally returned.

"Right. Clay had problems with the other children at school. I assume you know that."

I nodded. "He didn't fit in and didn't try. Small for his age. Antisocial. The accent only made it worse. I wondered about that when I met him. He said he'd lived in New York State for twenty years, but he sounded like he'd just stepped off the train from Louisiana. He said when he was a kid, other children mocked his accent. So he kept it. Clay's perverse logic."

"Anything to set him apart. So, after the guinea pig disaster, I homeschooled him until the following September, then sent him to a different school and asked the principal to notify me of any behavioral problems. I swear I spent three afternoons a week in parent-teacher conferences. Mostly it was little things, but one day the teacher said Clay was having trouble at recess. The other kids were complaining that he was following them around, watching them, that sort of thing."

"Stalking them," I said. "Scouting for weaknesses."

"Exactly. Now, I wasn't worried he'd do anything. I was very strict on that point. No devouring classmates." Jeremy rolled his eyes. "Other parents warn their kids not to talk to strangers. I had to warn mine not to eat them. Anyway, this teacher says Clay isn't showing an interest in normal recess pursuits, like playing with toys. Toys. I knew I was missing something. Clay was the most un-childlike child I'd ever met, so I tended to forget he should be doing childish things. After the conference, I drove straight to the toy store and bought bags of toys. He ignored them all . . . all except this set of plastic animals—cows, horses, sheep, deer, camels, and so on. He'd take them into his room and stay there for hours. I congratulated myself on my great insight, assuming he liked the animals because he felt some kinship to them. Then I found the book."

Jeremy paused.

"What book?" I asked, because I knew I was supposed to.

"*Gibson's Guide to Animal Anatomy.* He'd stolen it from the school library and dog-eared a bunch of pages. So I took a closer look at the plastic toys. They were all marked with strategically placed red Xs."

"Identifying the vital organs," I said. "For hunting."

"Exactly."

"So what'd you do?"

"Gave him a long lecture about stealing and made him return the book immediately."

I threw my head back and laughed. Jeremy rested his hand around my waist, a rare gesture of closeness that I enjoyed for as long as possible.

"How about a run?" he asked after a few minutes. "We could both use one to work off some stress after today."

I was getting tired, but I never would have said so. Werewolves preferred to run with others—the Pack instinct. As with so many other things, Jeremy was different. He preferred solitude when he Changed. He'd sometimes join us in a Pack hunt but rarely went for a regular run with a partner. So, when he offered, I could have been ready to drop from exhaustion and I wouldn't have refused.

We walked into the woods, taking the path until we were deep enough to find places for our Change. We'd gone about twenty feet when Jeremy turned to stare over my shoulder.

"What?" I asked.

"Headlights slowing at the top of the drive," he murmured.

The driveway sloped steeply from the road to the cottage, putting the car on a hilltop, so all we could see was the glow of twin lights. As we waited, the lights vanished and the rumble of the engine died. A car door opened and shut. Footsteps walked to the edge of the hill. A stone pinged from beneath a shoe, clattering down the incline. A pause. Someone listening for a response to the noise. Then the whisper of long grass against pant legs. A glimmer of darkness above us, movement without form. Then moving south, downwind. Intentionally downwind. A tree creaked to our right. I jumped. Only the wind.

Jeremy was watching, listening, smelling, only a tightness in his jawline betraying his tension. I looked at him, but he didn't look back. Too busy watching. And waiting. The scuffle of dead twigs underfoot. Silence again. A loon cried across the lake. Again I jumped. Then a rock tumbled down the hillside to my right. As I turned, I caught a blur of motion to my left. Misdirection. Shit. Too late. The blur was on me, knocking my legs out from under me. Hands grabbed me as I went down, flipping me onto my back and pinning my arms at my sides. I hit the ground with my attacker atop me.

CHAPTER 10

GUESTS

"Miss me?" Clay asked, grinning down at me.

I kicked up, somersaulting him over my head and into a stack of firewood. The wood toppled over him, knocking his breath out.

"Guess not," he wheezed, somehow still grinning.

"Can I kill him?" I asked Jeremy. "Please."

"Maim, but don't kill. We may still need him." Jeremy offered Clay a hand and yanked him to his feet with a bit more force than necessary. "I'm glad to see you got my message, but I didn't think you'd be here this fast. Did you have any trouble getting out of your course?"

No, Clay wasn't a student at the University of Michigan. He was a professor. Well, not actually a professor. I mean, not permanently. He was a research-based anthropologist who occasionally did short lecture series, not because he liked to—Clay didn't *like* doing anything that involved contact with humans—but because the odd foray into the world of interpersonal academics was an evil necessary for keeping up his network of contacts and thus maintaining his career. Most people who'd met Clay, on hearing his occupation, said something along the lines of "I thought you needed a Ph.D. to do that." Clearly the vision of Clay and a doctorate degree did not go together. Yes, he had one—I can vouch for that, having seen the diploma at the bottom of his sock drawer. Anyone who met Clay, though, could be forgiven for the mistake. He didn't talk like someone with an advanced degree. And he sure didn't look like a Ph.D. Clay was one of those detestable people blessed with both genius-level intelligence and drop-dead-gorgeous looks. Blue eyes, dark blond curls, and a rugged face straight out of a magazine. Match that with a powerful body and you have a package that wouldn't go unnoticed in the middle of a Chippendales convention. He hated it. Clay would have been overjoyed to wake up one morning and find himself transformed into the kind of guy who got lingering gazes only when his fly was down. I, on the other hand, shallow creature that I am, would not be so pleased.

Clay told Jeremy that his lecture series had been part of an interim course, so he'd had no problem talking to the regular prof and rescheduling his portion for the end of the session. As he explained this, I practiced my grade-three math skills.

"You left Clay a message on my cell phone, which he took with him to Detroit, right?" I asked.

Jeremy nodded.

"And when did you leave that message?"

"Before dinner. After you left to sit with Cassandra I used the pay phone in the lobby."

"Uh-huh. About four hours ago, then. So assuming Clay took the shortest route from Detroit, through Ontario, into Quebec and down, that's well over six hundred miles. A Porsche traveling at, say, ninety miles an hour, with no stops or slowdowns, would take at least seven hours to make the trip. Anyone see a problem with this math?"

"I wasn't actually in Detroit when Jer called," Clay said.

"Uh-huh."

"I was a bit . . . closer."

"How close?"

"Ummm, say . . . Vermont."

"You sneaky son of a bitch! You've been here the whole time, haven't you? What did you do, follow us around?"

"I was protecting you."

I resisted the urge to stomp my foot on the ground. Not the most mature way to launch an argument, but sometimes frustration blew maturity out of the water. Clay did that to me. I settled for one ground-shaking stomp.

"I don't need protection," I said. "How many scrapes have I been in? Too many to count, and no one's killed me yet, have they?"

"Oh, there's good logic. Shall I wait until someone does, darling? Then I'm allowed to protect you? Guard your grave maybe?"

"I ordered you to stay in Detroit, Clayton," Jeremy said.

"You said I didn't *need* to come along," Clay said. "You didn't say *couldn't*."

"You knew what I meant," Jeremy said. "We'll discuss this later. Come back to the cottage now and we'll fill you in on anything you don't already know."

We headed back toward the cabin. When we were nearly out of the woods, Jeremy stopped and raised a hand, silencing us.

"Did you rent a pickup?" he whispered to Clay.

"Nah, some little shit-box. Figured the Boxster might be a bit conspicuous in these parts. Why?" He followed Jeremy's gaze. "That's not mine."

I looked up the hill to see a pickup truck parked at the end of the drive.

"What time is it?" Clay asked.

"Too late for making out," I said. "Too early for hunting or fishing."

"I'd say we have company," Jeremy said. "I'll stand watch. You two circle the cottage and greet our guests."

Clay and I crept from the forest. The south side of the cabin was dark and quiet. As I listened, I caught the crunch of dead leaves from the north side. I waved for Clay to take the lake side while I slipped across the drive.

On the north side of the cottage I found my quarry, a single man standing lookout. I crept through the trees until I was beside the man. He was probably fifty, but with the physique and bearing of a man half that age. His stance was ramrod straight, eyes trained on the driveway, unblinking. A professional. Retired military, possibly, given the half-inch buzz cut and clothes so stiff I suspected he starched his underwear. He held his gun at his right side, lowered but tense, ready to flip up and fire like a pump-action toy. Where did Winsloe do his recruiting? *Soldier of Fortune?* With the way these guys were popping up, it looked like he'd bought himself a whole damned army.

Clay stepped from the forest, coming out behind the gunman. He caught my eye through the trees. I nodded and crouched. As he eased forward, some drunken lout across the lake yelled. The lookout spun around, but Clay was already in mid-flight. I leaped and knocked the gun from the man's hand as Clay grabbed him around the neck. A dull snap. Then silence.

Clay lowered the dead man to the ground. I opened the gun chamber. The bullets inside shone too brightly for lead. I flashed them to Clay as he dragged the body into the woods.

"Silver bullets," I whispered. "Not standard equipment for a B&E."

Clay nodded.

"Front or back?" I asked.

"You pick."

I headed for the front door. It was cracked open. As I slunk along the wall, there was a muted pop from behind the cabin as Clay broke the rear lock. When I was close enough to see through the front-door crack, I paused. No light, sound, or movement came from within. With my toe, I prodded the door open farther. Still nothing. I crouched and crept through, staying low enough that I wouldn't catch anyone's attention—or catch a bullet fired blindly at chest level.

The front and back doors were opposite each other, linked by a common hall, so as soon as I sneaked inside, I saw Clay. He lifted his brows. Hear anything? I shook my head. As we stepped into the main room, he pointed overhead and mouthed "light." I looked toward the staircase. Upstairs a light flickered, like a moving flashlight. Clay gestured from me to him, then pointed up again. We were both going. He led.

Three-quarters of the way up the stairs, one creaked. That was inevitable, wasn't it? I think carpenters do that on purpose, make at least one creaky step so no one can ever steal up or down undetected. We froze and listened. Silence. Clay stepped on the next tread, stooped, and leaned forward, peeking into the upper hall. He shook his head. Nothing. After a moment's pause, he climbed the last three steps. He went left into the back bedroom, where the light was coming from. I stood at the top of the stairs, back to the far wall, guarding the front bedroom, the steps, and Clay all at once.

"Shit," he whispered.

I turned. Jeremy had been using the back bedroom. He or one of the intruders had left on the nightstand light. In front of it, a pedestal fan rotated at the slowest speed, blades intermittently blocking the bulb, giving the impression of flickering light. As I shook my head, footsteps sounded on the main level. The hatch to the basement slapped shut.

"That's it," a man's voice said. "They're not here."

"Then we'll wait," another said. "Get Brant and we'll leave."

Footfalls on the front porch. "Brant's gone."

"Probably taking a piss. Fucking wonderful lookout. Go start the truck, then. He'll figure it out."

Clay whispered, "I'll head them off at the back. You take the front. Get them into the woods. Away from their truck—and Jeremy."

I hurried toward the stairs, expecting Clay to follow me. I should have known better. Why take the stairs when there was a more dramatic departure at hand? Still, it wasn't pure theatrics. Clay's exit did distract the two men from hearing me run out of the house. I was leaping off the front porch when the second-story bathroom window smashed. A shower of glass rained down on the men. As they looked up, Clay dropped to the ground in front of them.

"Going somewhere?" he said.

Before either man could react, Clay kicked the pistol from the hand of the man on the left. The man on the right spun, saw me, lifted his gun, and fired. I dodged sideways, but something pricked my calf. A tranquilizer dart. Clay had realized which man had the more dangerous weapon and disarmed him, leaving the tranquilizer gun for round two.

The first man ducked Clay's next kick and thundered into the forest. Clay followed. The other man stood watching me, tranquilizer gun poised. I plucked the dart from my leg and charged. His eyes widened as if he'd expected me to keel over on the spot. Obviously anyone who thought he needed silver bullets to kill a werewolf also didn't know he'd need an elephant-sized wallop of sedative to drop one. As he aimed again, I dove for his legs, caught them and jerked backward, pulling him down with me. The gun sailed to the side. His hand flew up, not toward me, but left, reaching out across the ground. Shit. The other gun. The real gun.

I rolled sideways and knocked the gun out of his reach. He got to his knees, raised his fist, then paused. Guys did this. It was like some ingrained school-yard rule. Boys don't hit girls. Not ever. They usually only hesitated a moment before realizing there were exceptions to every rule. Still, it gave me time to duck, which I did. I brought my fist up into his gut. He doubled over, still kneeling. I grabbed his hair and slammed his face into the ground. He recovered fast, though. Too fast for me to snap his neck. His gaze went straight for the gun. As he lunged forward, I snatched it out of his reach, swung my arm back, and plowed the barrel into his heart. His eyes went wide, and he looked down at the gun protruding from his chest, touched the trickle of blood oozing from the wound, frowned in confusion, swayed once on his feet, then toppled backward.

Clay stepped from the forest, looked down at the man, and tilted his head.

"Hey, darling," he said. "That's cheating. Werewolves don't use guns."

"I know. I'm so ashamed."

He laughed. "How you feeling after that dart?"

"Not even a yawn."

"Good, 'cause we have one left. Guy headed into the bog. Figured I'd come back and see if you needed help before we give chase. He won't get far."

"Change, then," Jeremy said, walking up behind us. "It's safer. Are your arms all right, Elena?"

I peeled off the bandages, wincing as they came free. We healed fast, but the process still took longer than a few hours.

"I'll be okay," I said.

"Good. Go on, then. I'll look after these two."

Clay and I left to find places to Change.

After twelve years, I had Changing down to a science, a simple set of steps that I followed to keep myself from focusing on the upcoming pain. Step one: Find a clearing in the woods, preferably well away from everyone else, since no woman, vain or not, wanted to be seen in the middle of a Change. Step two: Remove clothing and fold neatly—this was the plan, though somehow my stuff always ended up hanging inside out from tree branches. Step three: Get into position, on all fours, head between my shoulders, joints loose, muscles relaxed. Step four: Concentrate. Step five: Try not to scream.

When I'd finished my Change, I rested, then stood and stretched. I loved stretching as a wolf, exploring the differences in my structure, the new way my muscles interacted. I started from the paws, pressing my nails into the soil and pushing against the ground with all four legs. Then I arched my back, hearing a vertebra or two pop, luxuriating in the total absence of any back or neck stiffness, the little aches and pains of bipedalism that humans learn to accept. I moved the end of my spine, curling my tail over my back, then let it drop and swung it from side to side, tail hairs swishing against my hind legs. Finally, the head. I rotated my ears and searched for at least one new sound, maybe a woodpecker a mile away or a beetle burrowing in the earth beside me. I played the same game with my nose, sniffing and finding something new, cow manure from a field five miles off or roses blooming in a cottage garden. I couldn't do the same with my eyes. If anything, my sight was worse as a wolf, but I blinked and looked around, orienting my night vision. I didn't see in black and white, like most animals, but in a muted palette of colors. Finally, I pulled back my lips in a mock snarl and shook my head. There. Stretches complete. Time for the workout.

CHAPTER 11

AMUSEMENTS

S ince Clay left him, the man had covered a lot of ground. He'd run at least two miles—all in the same quarter-mile radius, circling and zig-zagging endlessly. Some people have no sense of direction. Tragic, really.

Clay had driven him into a boggy area where no cottagers had reason to venture and thus no cottagers had carved paths. As we drew close, we could hear the man out there, the squelching of his boots constructing an aural map of his movements. East a dozen feet, veering a few inches south with each step, then turning abruptly southwest, moving twenty feet angling north, another turn, a few more steps—and he was pretty much back where he'd started. Clay's sigh tremored through his flanks. No challenge. No fun.

At this point, we should have finished the guy off—gone down into the bog, one in front, one in rear, jumped him, torn out his throat, and called it a day. That would have been the responsible thing to do, dispatch the threat without risk or fuss. After all, this was a job, damn it, it wasn't sup-posed to be fun. Still, there was one problem. Mud. Mud oozed between my toes, and the cold water inched up my forelegs. I lifted one front paw. It came up a thick, black club, mud coating every hair. As I put my paw down, it shot forward on the slick ground. I couldn't work like this. It wasn't safe. There was only one option. We had to get the guy out of the bog. Which meant we had to chase him. And, damn, I felt bad about that.

We split up, circling in opposite directions around the man fumbling in the mud. I took the south and found the ground was still marshy. When we met up at the far side, Clay swung his head north, telling me the ground there was dry. I paused then and audibly located the man again. Southwest, maybe fifty feet away. Clay rubbed against my side and growled softly. He circled me, brushing along my flank, tail tickling across my muzzle, then walked around the other side. I shifted closer, ducked my muzzle under his throat and pressed it there. Anticipation quavered through his body, a palpable vibration against my cheek. He nuzzled my ear and nibbled the edge of it. I nudged him, then stepped back. "Ready?" I asked with a glance. His mouth fell open in a grin, and he was gone.

I slogged through the mud after Clay. We went south-southwest. About twenty feet south of our target, we stopped. Then we headed north. Ahead, the man was still squelching through the bog, punctuating every few steps with a muttered oath. Having decided he'd lost Clay miles back, he was intent on getting out of what must have seemed the largest bog in North America. As we drew closer, we slowed, trying to quiet the sound of our approach. Not that it really mattered. This guy was so engrossed in escaping the endless bog that we probably could have bounded up wearing castanets and he wouldn't have heard us. We came within a dozen feet of him and stopped. Although the breeze was at our back, we were now close enough to smell him even upwind. Clay brushed against my side to get my attention. When I looked over, he lifted his muzzle to the sky, miming a howl. I snorted and shook my head. Warning our prey had its attractions, but I wanted to try something different.

I inched through the scrubby brush. When the man's scent hit gagging intensity, I paused and checked his direction. Moving due north, his back to me. Perfect. I ducked my head, eased my belly to the mud and crept along until I could see the man pushing through a sumac. He could just as easily have gone around the scraggly tree, but he was fumbling in near darkness, having either dropped his flashlight or left it with his dead partner. Other than the sumac, the area surrounding him was clear. I backed up—much tougher to coordinate as a wolf than a human. Clay slid forward to meet me. When he was alongside, I dropped my forequarters to the ground and waggled my rear in the air. He grunted and tilted his head to one side, a clear "What the hell are you doing?" I snorted, stood, and repeated the performance, this time bouncing back and forth. It took a second, but he finally got it. He brushed against me one last time, burrowing his muzzle into my neck. Then he turned and loped northwest.

I went north again, creeping only a few feet farther before seeing the man. He was plowing through ankle-deep water, curses coming at two for every step. I swiveled my ears right and caught the sound of Clay's paws clumping through the mud. When he was parallel to me, he stopped, blue eyes glinting in the darkness. I didn't need to communicate my location to him. My pale fur glowed under all but the darkest skies. Turning toward the man, I double-checked his location. He'd gone maybe two steps in the intervening moment. I added those extra two feet to my position. Then I crouched, forequarters down, rear in the air, wiggling as I shifted position and tested my back legs. Up, down, side, side, down again, tense, hold . . .

perfect. I moved my concentration to my front legs, coiling the muscles. One last check on the target. No change in position. Good. Now launch.

I sailed through the air. The undergrowth crackled on takeoff. The man heard it, turned, and lifted his hands to ward me off, not noticing that my trajectory wouldn't bring me within a yard of him. I landed to his right. I dropped my head between my shoulders and growled. His eyes flashed from surprise to comprehension. That was what I wanted, why I hadn't let Clay warn him. I wanted to see his expression when he realized exactly what he was facing, for once not being mistaken for a wolf or wild dog. I wanted to see the understanding, the horror, and, finally, the bladder-releasing panic. He gaped for one long moment, jaws open, no part of him moving, not even breathing. Then the panic hit. He whirled around and almost tripped over Clay. He shrieked then, a rabbity squeal of terror. Clay drew back his lips, fangs flashing in the moonlight. He growled, and the man bolted for the clearest opening, north toward the dry ground.

It wasn't much of a chase in the bog, more like two mud wrestlers pursuing a third, all three sliding more than they were running. Once we hit dry ground, the man broke into a headlong run. We sprinted after him. It was an unfair race. Running full-out, a wolf is faster than most professional athletes. This guy was in excellent shape, but no professional, and he had the additional disadvantages of near exhaustion, mounting panic, and lousy night vision. We could have taken him with one burst of speed. Instead we slowed to a lope. We had to give the guy a chance, right? Of course, fairness was our only motivation. We weren't really trying to prolong the chase.

We loped after him for a good mile across an open field. The stink of his panic rushed back at us, filling my nose and saturating my brain. The ground flew under my feet, my muscles contracting and expanding in a syncopation so absolute that the feeling was nearly as heady as the scent of his fear. His labored breaths rasped like sandpaper against the silence of the night. I blocked that out, listening instead to the steady huff of Clay's panting as he ran beside me. Once or twice Clay veered close enough to brush against me. The intoxication of the chase was complete. Then, with one new scent on the breeze, reality took over. Diesel fumes. There was a road ahead. Alarm zinged through me, then was washed away in a wave of common sense. It was approximately 3:00 A.M. on a Monday morning in the middle of cottage country. The chances of hitting traffic congestion ahead were zero. The chances of encountering even one car were nearly as low. All we had to do was get this guy across the road and keep going.

Though I could still smell diesel, it wasn't intermingled with the scent of asphalt. A dirt road. Better still. We crested a small rise and saw the road ahead, an empty ribbon of brown weaving through the hills. The man clambered up the ditch on the near side. As we leaped off the hillock, a flash of light illuminated the road for one second, then vanished. I paused. For a moment, all was dark. Then the light flashed again. Two round lights in the distance, bobbing over the hills. The man saw it too. He found a last burst of speed and ran toward the oncoming vehicle, arms waving. Clay shot out from behind me. As the car dipped into the last valley, Clay vaulted across the road, sprang at the man, and knocked him flying into the ditch. A pickup came over the last hill, motorboat rumbling behind it. It cruised up alongside us and kept going.

I raced across the road. Clay and the man were at the bottom of the ditch, tumbling together, Clay snapping, trying to get a good hold as the man squirmed to escape. Both were covered in mud, making Clay's job tougher and the man's easier. The man contorted sideways and reached for the bottom of his pant leg. In a flash, I realized what he was after. I yelped a warning to Clay. The man's hand clamped on something under his cuff. As he yanked it out, Clay dove for his hand. A flash of light. A crack of thunder. A shower of blood. Clay's blood.

I flew down the ditch, knocked the gun from the man's hand, and turned on him. His eyes widened. I leaped at him, grabbed his throat, and tore. Blood jetted. The man convulsed. I flung him from side to side until his throat tore away and his body sailed into the bushes. Something prodded my flank and I spun to see Clay there. Blood streamed from the back of his fore-haunch. I pushed him down on his side, licked the wound clean, and examined it. The bullet had passed through the skin and muscle connecting his front leg to his chest. It stank of gunpowder and burned flesh, and as soon as I cleaned the wound, it filled with blood again. I cleaned it again, than gauged the flow of blood. No longer streaming, it had slowed to a steady drip. Ugly, but not life-threatening. As I pulled back for another look, Clay licked the side of my muzzle and burrowed his nose against my cheek. A low rumble, like a growling purr, vibrated through him. I bent to check his wound again, but he blocked my view and nudged me backward into the woods. Mission accomplished. No mortal injuries. Time to Change back.

After I Changed, I returned to where the corpse lay on the ground. Clay leaped out behind me, swatting my rear, and grabbing me around the waist before I could retaliate. As he bent to kiss me, I dodged his lips to check his wound. The gunshot was now through the back of his upper arm, several inches from his torso—one spot on us as wolves didn't always correspond to the same spot as humans. Blood oozed from the hole. I bent for a closer look, but he snatched my chin, lifted it, and kissed me.

"You need to get that checked," I mumbled through the kiss.

He hooked my left foot and I fell backward against his good arm.

"You really need to—"

He lowered me to the ground. I dug in my heels and locked my knees.

"Jeremy should look—"

He stifled the rest by kissing harder. I wrenched free of his arm and danced backward. He grinned and started to advance.

"Arm's fine, then?" I said.

"Don't care if it isn't."

"Good. Then you won't mind working for it."

I spun and bolted. I didn't get far. This side of the road was forest, and thick woods weren't kind to humans, particularly naked running humans. I circled a clump of trees. Clay followed me around once, then changed direction and tried to grab me from the other side. I laughed and raced back and across the clearing. As I darted around again, he dove at my feet and snagged one. I stumbled, but regained my balance as he hit the ground, hand still around my ankle. Squirming out from his grasp, I broke free and scrambled away. A hoarse laugh resounded through the trees, followed by scuffling as he got to his feet. I shot behind a stand of trees and waited to see which direction he'd pick. I heard him run toward me. Then silence. I waited. More silence.

Crouching below eye level, I inched clockwise around the trees. Nothing. I spun around, expected him at my rear. He wasn't there. I paused, then crept counterclockwise until I was back on the clearing side of the trees. No sign of him. I listened, sniffed, looked . . . nothing. As I stepped backward into the clearing, I caught a blur of motion to my left, from behind a massive oak. I wheeled away, but too slowly. Clay grabbed me around the waist and sent us both to the ground with a hard thump.

His mouth went back to mine, tongue slipping between my teeth. I tossed him on his back. As I struggled to get up, he flipped me over again, hands pinning mine to the ground. I struggled, more for the feel of it, his body moving on mine, the weight of him, the rough scratch of his chest and leg hairs against my skin, the contractions of his muscles as they worked to keep me down. The blood from his wound smeared across us, mixing with the man's dried blood on me. There was blood on his lips and in his mouth. Closing my eyes, I tasted the sharp tang and explored deeper with my tongue.

The ground below us was slick with damp leaves coated in layers of fresh mud and blood. We slipped and slid across it, grappling and laughing and kissing and groping, then Clay grabbed my hips and plunged into me. I gasped, and he threw his head back, laughing. We wrestled some more, rolling and thrusting together, not bothering to find a rhythm. The ground chafed and twigs poked in the damnedest places, but we kept going, kissing until we were out of breath, then laughing and tussling some more. I closed my eyes and drank in everything, the tripping of my heart, the smell of damp leaves and blood, the sound of Clay's glorious laugh.

When I opened my eyes, he was grinning down at me. He never closed his eyes when we made love, never looked away, always watching my face and letting me see everything in his eyes. I saw the first shudder of climax, the widening of his eyes, the slow moving of his lips saying my name. Gasping, I felt my body tense in waves of perfect sensation as I joined him.

"Miss me?" he said a few minutes later, still lying on me, slowly slipping from inside me.

I tilted my head back to look up at him and grinned. "In ways."

"Ouch. Cruel. Very cruel."

"At least I appreciate you for one thing."

"Only one thing?"

His hand moved to my breast, teasing the nipple between his fingers, then bringing his lips down for backup. I closed my eyes and groaned.

"Or maybe several things," I murmured. "That's one of them. Want to compile a list?"

He chuckled, the vibration tingling through my breast.

"No list, please," said a deep voice somewhere to our right. "I'll be waiting here all night. I already had to wait through round one."

I turned my head to see Jeremy walk through the trees.

"Sorry," I said.

"Don't be. But I'd like to get this cleaned up before dawn."

Clay groaned and lifted himself onto his elbows, still lying on me.

"Yes," Jeremy continued. "Terribly inconsiderate of me, expecting you to dispose of the corpses you created before you finished your reunion romp. I apologize most sincerely. Now get off your ass, Clayton, and get to work."

Clay sighed, gave me one last kiss, and got to his feet. I stood and walked over to the body of the dead man. Yes, I was still naked, and, yes, Jeremy was standing right there, and, no, I didn't try to cover myself or anything so ridiculously prudish. Jeremy had seen me naked, had sketched me naked, had tripped over me lazing around naked. We were werewolves, remember? That meant that after we Changed, we were always naked and, most often, nowhere near our clothing. We got used to being naked and, after a while, clothed/unclothed, it was all pretty much the same.

"I don't suppose you brought our clothes?" I said. "Shouldn't matter, so long as we don't meet any early morning anglers on the way back."

"Actually, I did bring them, but considering the amount of mud and blood on both of you, I think we'd better stick to nudity for a while longer. You'll be clean soon enough."

I didn't ask what he meant by that. I dropped to my knees beside the dead man and searched for a wallet or ID. Jeremy walked back to the ditch and returned with a spade, which he tossed to Clay.

"Bury him here?" Clay asked.

"No. Dig a hole by his neck, turn him over, and drain the blood. We'll take him back to the cottage for disposal. It's about a half mile back. I was hoping for a closer kill."

"No choice in the matter," I said. "We found him in a bog, chased him here to dry ground, then he pulled a gun. Shot Clay in the arm."

Jeremy frowned, walked over to Clay, and examined the wound.

"Clean shot," he said. "Does it hurt?"

Clay lifted his arm above shoulder level. "Only if I do this."

"Then don't do that."

"Couldn't resist, could you?" I said.

Clay grinned. Jeremy's lips curved in the barest smile, then he clapped Clay on the back.

"Get to it, then. Drain the body so we can move him."

"There's no ID," I said.

Jeremy nodded. As Clay lifted the shovel to dig, Jeremy and I jumped in at the same time, both realizing it wasn't something he should do with a bad arm. After a brief argument—I argued, Jeremy held the shovel and refused to release it—I let Jeremy dig the hole, then I tipped the body over it. Once the blood had drained, we filled in the hole with the surrounding blood-soaked leaves, then covered it with soil and took the corpse back to the cottage.

⚜

It was still deep night when we returned to the cabin. Jeremy and I carried two corpses to a treed strip of bank along the lake. Clay stayed back with the third, saying he had to "do something" with it. Neither Jeremy nor I asked for details. With Clay, it was better not to know.

I stood on the embankment, still naked. We'd tied thick rope around the neck and legs of each corpse and weighted them with concrete blocks from a cottage demolition up the road.

"Wow," I said to Jeremy as I lowered myself to the ground and dipped my legs into the icy water. "I get to make someone 'swim with the fishes.' This is cool. My first Mafia-style disposal. You realize what this means. If I get caught, I'm going to have to turn state's witness against all you guys. Then I'll sell my story for a million bucks. But I'll never get to enjoy it, 'cause I'll live out the rest of my miserable existence in a shanty in the Appalachians, eating muskrat stew, jumping every time I hear a noise, waiting for the day when one of you hunts me down like the traitorous bitch I am." I paused. "Hold on. Maybe this isn't so cool after all. Can't we just bury him?"

"Get in the water, Elena."

I sighed. "Being a gangster ain't what it used to be. Al Capone, where have you gone?"

Jeremy pushed me off the bank. I hit the water with a splash.

"And try to be quiet," he said.

"I didn't—"

He threw the man down to me, dunking me underwater with the weight. When I resurfaced, Jeremy was gone. I swam into the middle of the lake, dragging the weighted corpse behind me. Then I dove to check the depth. It was at least fifty feet. This guy wouldn't surface any time soon. To be sure, I snagged him in a tangle of some underwater plants. Then I returned for the second body.

Clay still wasn't back when I got to the shore. Jeremy passed me corpse number two, and I swam back out to repeat the procedure, dropping this one a hundred feet farther west, in hopes that if one surfaced, the other wouldn't also be found. Sometimes it scared me that I even thought of such considerations. I had too much experience with these things. Way too much.

As I resurfaced after dumping the body, arms grabbed me around the waist and jettisoned me out of the lake. Coming down I hit the water with a tidal-wave splash. I grabbed Clay by the neck and dragged him under, holding him there for a second—maybe longer—before releasing him.

"Did Jeremy tell you the part about being quiet?" I hissed as he came up for air.

He grinned. "I am being quiet. You're the one splashing around."

I lunged for him. He grabbed me, pulled me against him and kissed me. His lips were ice-cold, his breath steaming hot. I kissed him deeper, wrapping my arms and legs around him, then ducking him under the water again.

"I *did* miss you," I said as he surfaced.

He tilted his head and knocked his open palm against one ear. "Sorry, darling. Water in the ears, I think. I coulda sworn you admitted that you missed me."

I pulled a face, then turned and started to swim, heading for shore. Clay caught my leg and hauled me back.

"I missed you, too," he said, pulling me upright against him. He traced his fingers up my inner thigh. "We should be getting in. Think we can trick Jeremy if we come to shore farther down?"

"For a few minutes."

"Long enough?"

"Long enough for now."

He grinned. "Good. Wanna race?"

"What's the prize?"

"Winner's choice."

I lunged forward. He grabbed my ankle again, yanked me back, then took off ahead.

By the time we got to the cabin, Jeremy already had the Explorer packed. We wouldn't stay at the cottage any longer, for obvious reasons. Before leaving, Jeremy disinfected Clay's wound and my burned arms, then dressed both. Then we left to find a place for the night. While we'd been disposing of the bodies, Jeremy had called Ruth and, without mentioning our guests, discovered the group was convening again in the morning. Someone had told these men where to find us. Only five other people knew we were in Vermont. All five of them would be at the meeting in a few hours. So would we.

CHAPTER 12

Confrontation

The meeting was due to start at eight. We got up at seven but were still late. An hour wasn't enough time for three people in our tiny motel room to shower, shave (no, being a werewolf doesn't give me extraneous hair; the guys shaved, not me), dress, leave, grab takeout, eat, and drive to Sparta. To save time, Clay and I even shared a shower, which for some reason didn't manage to save any time at all. Go figure.

Before we'd dumped the bodies, Jeremy had emptied their pockets. Even if we weren't curious about their identity, it was standard operating procedure to destroy the ID before dumping a body. Like I said, we had way too much experience with this stuff. As with the guy I'd checked, one of the other two didn't have any wallet, ID, or cash on him. The third guy had two twenties and a driver's license in his rear pocket. Emergency cash and a license in case he was pulled over. Bare minimum. These guys had known what they were doing. Jeremy had checked the driver's license and proclaimed it a fake. An impressive fake, but a fake. Jeremy would know. He manufactured all our phony IDs, something else we had far too much experience with.

We arrived at the Legion Hall at nine-thirty. All four cars were in the lot. Again the witches used a spell to lock the door, but this time we didn't knock. Clay tore the door off the hinges and we walked inside. As I entered the room, Ruth stopped talking. Everyone looked up.

"Where have you been?" Ruth asked.

I grinned, baring my teeth. "Hunting."

"Wanna see what we caught?" Clay asked from behind me.

He strode to the table and tossed a garbage bag on it. Cassandra was the only one who looked at him, wondering who he was. Everybody else stared at the bag. No one moved to take it. Then Cassandra reached forward, lifted one side of the bag, and looked in. After a second, she let the plastic fall from her hand and sat back in her chair. Her eyes moved from Clay to me and back to Clay, face blank, no shock, no disgust, nothing. Paige peeled back the plastic and recoiled fast.

The third man's head lay on its side, eyes wide and dull. Paige jumped to her feet and tried to yank the plastic back over it. The head rolled with the sudden movement. She bit off a scream.

"Interesting form of introduction," Cassandra said, looking at Clay. "May I ask who you might be?"

"Clayton Danvers," Paige muttered between her teeth. "The werewolf Pack's guard dog."

"The question isn't who's Clay," I said, "but who's that guy in the bag? Anyone up for volunteering information?"

"We found this man at our cottage last night," Jeremy said. "He was with two others who, I can assure you, are equally dead. They came armed with silver bullets."

"Silver—" Adam began. "Shit, isn't that supposed to—" He stopped and looked around at the others. "You think we sent these guys?"

"Look at him," Paige said, turning to me. "Clean-shaven, military brush cut. Just like the guys in Pittsburgh. Obviously—"

"Obviously nothing," Clay said. "Either the whole Pittsburgh thing was a setup or you dressed these guys to look like Elena's stalker so, if it backfired, we'd draw the *obvious* conclusion. If these men were part of this kidnapping scheme, why would they come after Jeremy and Elena when you guys were all holed up here in a late-night meeting? You'd be the *obvious* choice."

"Maybe they wanted a werewolf," Paige said. "Besides, we always cast protective spells around our meetings. They wouldn't have been able to get to us."

"So you expected trouble?" I said. "Thanks for warning us. But that doesn't explain how they got here. First they show up in Pittsburgh, then here. How?"

"They must have followed"—Paige stopped, then murmured—"someone."

"They followed you," Cassandra said, turning on Ruth. "You led them right to us."

"Perhaps you weren't behind last night's attack," Jeremy said, "but you can hardly be absolved of blame. Ensuring you weren't followed from Pittsburgh is an elementary safety precaution. If that's how this group operates, then I have no interest in aligning my Pack with you, even temporarily. As you can see"—he gestured at the bag—"we can take care of ourselves. We will continue to do so without your help. Anyone who comes after us or interferes with us again will be treated the same as those three men last night. Anyone. For any reason."

We left. No one came after us.

I drove the Explorer back to the motel. It was packed and ready to go. All we had to do was pick up Clay's rental car.

"Where to next?" I asked as we stood in the motel parking lot.

"Montreal," Clay said. "We need to return the car."

I turned to the econo-box rental, noticing the Quebec license plates. "Why the hell did you leave your car in Montreal?"

"You think I was gonna cruise Vermont looking for a rental agency when I was driving right past a big city?"

"How about I drive straight home and you guys meet me there?"

"You're coming to Montreal, Elena," Jeremy said.

Jeremy headed to the econo-box and folded himself into the tiny passenger seat. Yes, he would have been more comfortable in his Explorer, but that would mean listening to Clay curse the loathed SUV for a few hundred miles. Given the choice between leg cramps and a migraine, Jeremy would choose the former. Riding in the SUV with me and leaving Clay alone in the rental wasn't an option. Until the danger had passed, Clay would stick close to Jeremy, protecting his Alpha as instinct dictated.

Once Jeremy was in the car, Clay walked over, wrapped his hands around my waist, and pulled me against him.

"I'll make it up to you," he murmured against my ear. "Tonight. We'll go for a run."

"In the city?"

He grinned. "You arguing?"

"Jeremy will."

"We'll take him along. I'll talk him into it on the drive. Speaking of which, you wanna liven the ride up a bit?"

"Race?"

"You read my mind, darling."

"A four-banger verses a V6?"

"It's the driver, not the car."

"You're on. First one to Montreal gets to pick where we run tonight."

"One catch," Clay said. "We have to play safe and stay in sight. If I can't see you in my rearview mirror, I'm slowing down."

"Rearview mirror? Baby, you ain't seeing me through nothing but the windshield."

He grinned. "We'll see about that."

Racing through the back roads of Vermont was great fun. Once we got to Highway 87, things would get decidedly dull, but on the two-lane back roads we had to contend with mountains, valleys, towns, blind curves, lane-hogging campers, and poky sightseers. Plenty of close calls. Plenty of excitement. The bad guys didn't need to kill us. If they waited long enough, we'd do it ourselves.

After about a half hour, I was stuck behind Clay. My fault. We'd been leapfrogging for miles. I'd been in the lead, then I'd come up behind a fifth-wheeler with a camper on the back and made the mistake of leaving a safe cushion between it and me, which Clay, of course, had zipped into. Now we were stuck on a winding road behind this dullard who insisted on doing the speed limit. Finally, I noticed a straightaway long enough to pass. But Clay didn't pull out. After a moment's thought, I realized why. He couldn't see past the fifth-wheeler. I could. The advantage of driving an SUV—improved vision. Hah! So on the next suitable straightaway, as Clay fishtailed trying unsuccessfully to see around the fifth-wheeler, I pulled out and passed. Once around the truck, I zipped past a car and a tractor trailer. Then I floored it. Clay's subcompact vanished amid an unending stream of tourist traffic. He'd be pissed that I'd broken his "stay in sight" rule, but it served him right, thinking he could outrace me no matter what he drove. Clay's self-confidence could always use a shake-up. He'd catch me soon enough.

I burned up ten miles with no sign of Clay in the rearview mirror, then slowed. No sense pushing my luck or I'd have Jeremy on my back, too. Jeremy let us play our games, but if I went too far, he'd tear a strip off of me. Besides, I was getting near the highway, and I wanted to be sure Clay was behind me by then. So I eased down to the speed limit, turned the corner onto the gravel road leading to the highway, cranked up the radio, and relaxed.

A mile or two later, as I was cruising along enjoying the scenery, something appeared in front of me. Something big. Right in front of me. So close I didn't have time to see if it was a moose or a deer or a person. Nor did I have time to think. I reacted. I jerked the steering wheel and hit the brakes. Too hard on both counts. I saw the flash of a face on the roadway. Then the Explorer spun left, and for a second, I thought it might flip over. It didn't. Instead it slammed into the far ditch. The airbag exploded, knocking me in the face like a punching bag. Before I could recover, the driver's door clicked open.

"Are you okay?" a woman's voice asked. She pulled the airbag from my face and frowned. "Are you okay? That man ran right in front of you. I couldn't believe it."

I gave my head a shake, groggy, punch-drunk. "A man? Did I hit him?"

"No. Would have served him right if you had." The woman shook her head. "I guess I shouldn't say that. Let's get you out of there."

As she helped my out, I got a better look at her. Mid- to late forties. Dark blond hair cut in a chin-length pageboy. Linen dress. Simple gold-chain necklace. Face drawn in concern.

"Come sit in the back of my car," she said. "I've called an ambulance."

I hesitated, swaying on my feet. "My friends are coming."

"Good." She guided me to her car, a sleek black Mercedes, opened the back door, and helped me inside. "We'll wait here for them. How do you feel?"

"Like someone KO'd me in round one."

She laughed. "Can't say I know what that feels like, but I can imagine. You're pale, but your color's coming back. Pulse feels fine."

I felt her fingers against my wrist. Then I felt something else there. A prick. A rush of icy cold. As I yanked my hand back, the driver's door opened. A man got in. He turned to grin back at me.

"Just couldn't wait for another sparring match, huh?"

His face flashed in my memory, but my brain was fogging fast and I couldn't place him. Then, as my muscles went slack, I remembered.

The half-demon from Pittsburgh. Houdini.

My head hit the seat. Everything went black.

CHAPTER 13

PRISON

For hours, I fought to regain consciousness, rousing enough to know something was wrong but unable to pull myself awake, like a swimmer who sees the water's surface above but can't reach it. Each time I jetted toward awareness, the tranquilizer's undercurrent dragged me back. Once I felt the rumbling of a van. Then I heard voices. The third time all was still and silent.

On the fourth round, I managed to open my eyes and kept them open, certain if I closed them I'd be lost. For at least an hour, I lay there, winning against the urge to sleep, but without the strength to do more than stare at a beige wall. Was it beige? Or taupe? Maybe sand. Definitely latex. Eggshell latex. Scary that I knew so much about paint. Scarier still that I was lying there, paralyzed from the eyelids down and trying to figure out what shade my captors had painted my prison. My encyclopedic knowledge of paint was Jeremy's fault. He redecorated obsessively. I mean obsessively. He had his reasons, which were no one's business but his own. If wallpapering the dining room every two years quelled whatever ghosts haunted him, I bit my tongue and pasted. As for why I was thinking about paint at such a ridiculously inopportune moment, well, there wasn't much else I could think about, was there? I could fret and worry and drive myself into a panic wondering where I was and what my captors planned to do with me, but that wouldn't change anything. I couldn't lift my head. I couldn't open my mouth. I couldn't do anything but gaze at this stupid wall, and if brooding over the paint color kept my nerves calm, so be it.

Taupe. Yes, I was pretty sure it was taupe. My upper lip tingled, like dental anesthesia wearing off. I wrinkled my nose. Slight movement. A smell. Fresh paint. Wonderful. Back to the decorating again. I inhaled deeper. Only paint, the scent so strong it drowned out anything else. No, wait. Something else mingled with the paint. Something familiar. Something . . . Blood. Mine? I sniffed again. Not mine, which wasn't terribly reassuring. As I rolled my eyes up, I could see dark splotches under a hastily applied layer of paint. Blood-sprayed walls. Never a good sign.

I screwed up my face. All muscles functional. Great. Now if someone attacked me, I could bite him, provided he was helpful enough to put some vital body part in my mouth. The tingling moved down my neck. I looked up. White ceiling. Distant noise. Voices. No, one voice. Someone talking? I listened closer and heard the hyper-babble of a DJ. After a Guinness-breaking feat of long-windedness, he stopped. A guitar twanged from the far-off radio. Country music. Damn. They'd resorted to torture already.

Hand and arm movement. Hallelujah. Digging my elbows into the bed, I propped up my torso and looked around. Four walls. Three taupe. The fourth mirrored. One-way glass. Lovely. By my feet, a bathroom. I could tell it was a bathroom and not a closet because I could see the toilet, not through the door, but through the front wall, which was clear glass. Grade-school bathroom peeping had left someone with a very disturbing fetish.

More smells. A woman. The room was permeated with her smell. The bed on which I lay had been fitted with fresh, lemon-scented sheets, but the other woman's smell had soaked through to the mattress below. A note of familiarity. Someone I knew? The woman who'd drugged me? No, someone else. Teasingly familiar . . . The association clicked. I recognized her scent because it bore overtones from the smell of the blood on the walls. Not a good way to make an acquaintance, and judging by the quantity of dark splotches under the paint, a face-to-face meeting wouldn't be forthcoming. Not in this life at least.

Hold on. I had hips. Well not really—my baggy-seated jeans always proved otherwise. I mean my anatomical, curve-free hips had movement and feeling. Then legs. Yes! I swung my legs over the edge of the bed and pitched forward onto the floor. Okay, the legs weren't quite back yet. Nice carpet though. Industrial-weave loom. A pleasing blend of gray and brown, great for hiding those pesky blood splatters.

After a few minutes, I was able to struggle to my feet. I looked around. Now what? Assuming these were the same people who'd captured that shaman, there should be other prisoners in adjoining cells. Maybe I could communicate with them.

"Hello?" I said. Then louder. "Hello?"

No response. Doubtless the walls were too thick for jailhouse whispering. Even the air coming through the foot-square ceiling vent smelled filtered and processed. Still, if I could hear a radio playing . . . I looked around for a speaker. There was an intercom by the door, but the music didn't sound tinny, so I doubted they were piping it in. As I listened, I caught the sound of someone shouting, voice raw, screaming barely intelligible curses. I gauged the distance of the noise. Very muted, probably more than fifty feet away. So it was good soundproofing, but it wasn't werewolf-proof.

As the shouter took a much-needed vocal break, I heard scratching. Rats? Mice? No, I'd smell them. Besides, my cell was nothing if not clean, as sterilized as a McDonald's kitchen on health inspection day. I rotated my head to pick up the sound. It came from the corridor. Scratch, scratch, pause, scratch, scratch, scratch, swoosh. The swoosh of paper. Someone lifting a page, shuffling it, then scratch, scratch—pen on paper. Someone writing outside my cell. I stood, turned away from the hallway, walked three steps, then whirled to face the door. The noise stopped. I bared my teeth, snarled, then inclined my open mouth closer to the mirrored wall and picked at a piece of imaginary food caught between my teeth. Frenzied scribbling ensued. Okay, now I knew *what* the note-taker was watching. And I didn't recall signing any consent forms.

I strode to the door and pounded on the glass. Though it didn't budge under the onslaught, my fists boomed with each strike. I didn't shout. If they couldn't hear my pounding, they certainly wouldn't hear my yelling. A long minute passed. Then the intercom above my head buzzed.

"Yes?" a woman's voice. Young. Studiously neutral.

"I want to speak to someone in charge," I said.

"I'm afraid that won't be possible," she said, pen scribbling.

I pounded harder.

"Please don't do that." Calm, approaching boredom. Pen still scratching.

I drew my fist back and slammed it into the glass. The blow shuddered through the glass and my arm. The pen stopped.

"I understand you're upset, but that won't help. Violence never solves anything."

Says who?

I turned away, as if backing down, then whammed a roundhouse kick against the side wall. One chunk of plaster flew free, revealing a strip of solid metal. I hooked my fingertips behind the metal and gave an experimental tug. No give. But I wasn't really trying. Now if I ripped away enough of this plaster, I could get my fingers behind the metal and give a real good pull . . .

Heavy footsteps clomped outside my cell. Ah, progress.

The intercom clicked.

"Please step away from the wall," a male voice intoned.

He sounded like one of those car alarms from the '90s, where if you made the ghastly error of walking within six inches of some yuppie's Beemer, a mechanical voice warned you to move away, like you might brush against it and leave fingerprints. The last time we'd encountered one of those, Clay had leaped onto the hood of the car, leaving much more than fingerprints. The car owner had been within hearing distance. You've never seen a pudgy forty-something move so fast. Then he'd seen Clay and decided the damage really wasn't so bad after all. Following Clay's example, I did not step away from the wall. I smashed my fist into the plaster between the metal brackets, leaving a nice hole into the adjoining cell.

The door flew open. A man's face flashed into the room, then withdrew. The door slammed shut. A radio squawked.

"Base one, this is alpha. Request immediate backup to cell-block one, unit eight."

"You messing with my girl?" a lazy Midwest drawl asked, voice hissing with static. Houdini. "You sound a wee mite panicked there, soldier-boy. Want me to come down and hold your hand?"

"Reese? What the hell are you doing in the— Never mind."

Click. End of static.

"Cocky bastard."

"No kidding," I said.

Silence. Then "Shit," and a snap as the intercom died.

"Get me someone in charge," I said. "Now."

A muttered exchange, indecipherable through the glass. Then boots stalking away. I decided not to worry the hole in the wall further. Not yet at least. Instead I hunkered down and peered through it. I might have been gazing into a mirror, a reverse image of my own cell. Only this one was empty. Or so it appeared. I thought of calling through the opening, but hadn't heard the note-taker leave, and there was no sense talking to a potential cell-mate while I had an audience. So I waited.

Twenty minutes passed. Then the intercom clicked on.

"My name is Doctor Lawrence Matasumi," a man said in perfectly unaccented American, the region-free tones usually heard only from national news show anchors. "I would like to speak to you now, Ms. Michaels." As if it was his idea. "Please step into the bathroom, lower the seat, straddle the toilet facing the tank, place your hands outstretched behind you, and do not turn your head until instructed."

Somehow he made such ludicrous instructions sound perfectly rational.

I thought of a comeback, but squelched it. This didn't sound like a man who'd appreciate bathroom humor.

While I was sitting on the john, the exterior door whooshed open, like breaking a vacuum seal. Footsteps entered. One set of loafers, one set of low heels, and two—no, three—pairs of boots.

"Please do not turn your head," Matasumi said, though I hadn't moved. "Keep your hands outstretched. A guard will enter the bathroom and secure your hands behind your back. Please do not resist."

He was so polite about it, how could I disobey? Especially considering the twin snaps of gun safety catches that accompanied his instructions. Someone walked into the bathroom and grasped my hands, his touch firm and impersonal—just business, ma'am. He pulled my arms together and clapped cold metal bands around my wrists.

"The guard will now lead you into the main room. You may take a seat on the chair provided. When you are seated comfortably, the guard will secure your feet."

Okay, this was getting tedious.

"You sure you don't want him to secure my feet first?" I asked. "Throw me over his shoulder and carry me to the chair?"

"Please rise from the toilet and proceed into the main room."

"Can I look now?" I asked. "Maybe you should blindfold me."

"Please proceed to the main room."

Geez, this guy was scary. As I walked from the bathroom, I saw the man from Paige's picture, short, round-faced, doe-like eyes watching me impassively. To his left was a young woman with spiked burgundy hair and a snub nose adorned with a diamond chip stud. She kept her gaze on my chin as if not wanting to look higher. Both were seated in chairs that hadn't been in the room five minutes ago. Flanking them stood two guards, more military types. Like the guy accompanying me, they wore fatigues, had buzz cuts, carried guns, and looked buff enough to give WWF champs a good whupping. They stared at me with expressions so blank you'd think they were guarding the chairs instead of live people. I caught one's eye and gave a shy half-smile. He didn't even blink. So much for seducing the guards. Damn. And they looked so cute . . . in a GI Joe, molded-plastic, automaton kind of way.

Once I was seated, my escort secured me to the chair with arm restraints and leg irons.

Matasumi studied me for at least three full minutes, then said, "Please do not use this opportunity to attempt escape."

"Really?" I looked at the metal bands strapping my wrists and ankles to the chair, then at the trio of armed guards behind me. "There goes that plan."

"Good. Now, Ms. Michaels, we will skip the denial phase and begin our discussion based on the premise that you are a werewolf."

"And if I refuse that premise?" I asked.

Matasumi opened a teak box filled with bottles and syringes and tools, the uses of which I preferred not to ponder.

"You got me," I said. "I'm a werewolf."

Matasumi hesitated. The young woman lifted her pen from the pad, glancing at me for the first time. Maybe they'd expected me to resist. Or maybe they were just hoping for a chance to use their toys. Matasumi ran through some baseline lie-detection questions, the sort of things anyone who'd done the most basic research would know: my name, age, place of birth, current occupation. I wasn't dumb enough to lie. Save that for the big stuff.

"Let me begin by telling you that we already have a werewolf in custody. Your answers will be compared against information he has already provided. So I would suggest you tell the truth."

Damn. Well, that changed things, didn't it? So much for wholesale prevarication. On the other hand, it was possible that Matasumi was lying about having a mutt. Even if he did, I could pepper my lies with enough truth to keep them guessing which of us wasn't being completely honest.

"How many werewolves are in this . . . Pack?" Matasumi asked.

I shrugged. "It depends. It's not static or anything. They come and go. It's not a close-knit group. Kind of arbitrary, actually, who the Alpha lets in and kicks out, depending on his mood. He's a very temperamental guy."

"Alpha," his assistant interjected. "Like the alpha in a wolf pack. You use the same terminology."

"I guess so."

"Interesting," Matasumi said, nodding like an anthropologist who's just discovered a long-lost tribe. "My knowledge of zoology isn't what it should be."

Behind me, the door clicked and air whooshed out. I turned to see the woman who'd lured me into the car.

"Tucker told me you'd started early," she said. She turned a pleasant smile on me, as if we were new acquaintances meeting for cocktails. "I'm glad to see you're up and about so quickly. No lasting effects from the tranquilizers, I hope."

"Feeling peachy," I said, trying hard to smile without baring my teeth.

She turned back to Matasumi. "I'd like Doctor Carmichael to check her out."

Matasumi nodded. "Tess, please call Doctor Carmichael from the hall phone. Tell her to bring her equipment down for a checkup at seven o'clock. That should give us sufficient time with the subject."

"The subject?" the older woman laughed and glanced at me. "Please excuse us. Our terminology isn't the most civil, I'm afraid. I'm Sondra Bauer."

"So pleased to meet you," I said.

Bauer laughed again. "I'm sure you are. Hold on, Tess," she said as the assistant headed for the door. "No need to buzz Doctor Carmichael. She's expecting us in the infirmary."

"Infirmary?" Matasumi frowned. "I don't believe this subject—"

"Her name is Elena," Bauer said.

"I prefer Ms. Michaels," I said.

"I'd like Elena checked by Doctor Carmichael immediately," Bauer continued. "I'm sure she'd appreciate the chance to stretch her legs and have a look around. We can continue our discussion with her in the upstairs room. She'll get tired of these four walls soon enough."

"May I speak to you privately?" Matasumi asked.

"Yes, yes. You're concerned about security. I can see that," she said, lips twitching as she looked from my restraints to the guards. She slanted an eye-roll at me, as if sharing a joke. "Don't worry, Lawrence. We'll make sure Elena is properly restrained, but I don't see the need for excess. Handcuffs and armed guards should be quite sufficient."

"I'm not sure—"

"I am."

Bauer headed for the door. My picture of the power structure here was developing fast. Research assistant, guards, half-demon, all roughly equal—the hired help. Scientist above them, mystery woman above scientist. And Ty Winsloe? Where did he fit in? Was he even involved?

My guard unstrapped me from the chair and removed the restraints from my arms and legs, then herded me into the corridor. My cell was the last one on the end, across from a recessed metal door with two red lights above it. At the other end was a matching door with matching red lights. Twin rows of one-way glass flanked the hall. I counted doorknobs. Three more on my side, four opposite.

"This way, Elena," Bauer said, walking right.

Matasumi gestured to the closer door. "This route would be quicker."

"I know." Bauer gestured me forward, smiling encouragingly, like I was a toddler taking her first steps. "This way please, Elena. I'd like to show you around."

Really? A guided tour of my prison? Well, I couldn't argue with that, could I? I followed Bauer.

Chapter 14

Exhibition

As I walked toward Bauer, I passed a chair facing my cell, presumably where Tess had been taking notes. When I glanced at the chair, it started to shake. I'd like to think it was scared of me, but I rarely evoked that response in living things, let alone inanimate objects.

"Earthquake zone?" I asked.

"Shhh!" Matasumi said, holding up his hand.

Matasumi crouched beside the chair and studied it. The chair rocked from one diagonal to the other, back and forth, faster, then slowing, then regaining speed, tilting almost to the point of tipping, then reversing.

Matasumi motioned me forward. When I didn't move fast enough, he waved impatiently. I stepped toward the chair. It kept rocking. Matasumi thrust his palm at me, telling me to move away. I did. No change. He crooked his finger to motion me back, eyes never leaving the chair. I walked beside it. The chair kept rocking, speed unaffected. Then it stopped. Bauer flashed me a wide, almost proud smile.

"What did you think of that?" she asked.

"I'm really hoping it doesn't mean this place is built on a fault line."

"Oh, no. We chose the environment very carefully. You didn't feel a tremor, did you?"

I shook my head.

"You'll see that sort of thing quite often down here," she said. "Don't be alarmed if you wake up in the morning to find your magazines in the shower stall or your dining table upside down."

"What's causing it?"

She smiled. "You are."

"Ms. Bauer means all of you," Matasumi said. "Our subjects. I doubt you personally would have much impact. Werewolves are known for physical, not mental powers. These events began several weeks ago, as our collection of subjects grew. My hypothesis is that they result from the high concentration of diverse psychic energy. Random spurts of energy causing equally random events."

"So it just happens? No one's doing it?"

"There's no discernible pattern or meaning to the events. They're also quite harmless. No one has been injured. We're monitoring it closely, as there is always the possibility the energy could build to dangerous levels, but at this point, we can safely say you have no reason for concern."

"If objects start flying, duck," Bauer said. "Now, let's resume the tour before we have any further interruptions." She motioned to the ceiling. "We're underground. The outer walls are several feet of reinforced concrete. Perhaps not impossible to break through—if you had a wrecking ball, plus a bulldozer to dig your way out. The second floor is also subterranean, so this level is more than fifty feet down. The ceiling is solid steel, as is the floor. The one-way glass is a special experimental design. It will resist—how many tons of pressure, Lawrence?"

"I don't know the precise specifications."

"Let's just say 'a lot,' then," Bauer said. "The doors at either end are reinforced steel, at least as strong as the glass. The security system requires both hand and retinal scans. As you've already discovered, the walls between the cells are not quite so impenetrable. Still, there's not much to be gained by knocking peepholes into the next cell since, as you can see, it's currently unoccupied."

She gestured at the adjoining cell. It was empty, as was the one across from mine.

"Our next guest might be familiar," Bauer said, leading me farther and motioning left.

The man was watching television. Average height, trim and fit, dirty-blond hair made several shades dirtier by a lengthy interval between showers, whisker shadow growing into a full-scale beard. Familiar? Only vaguely. By Bauer's introduction, I guessed he was a mutt, but I couldn't be sure without smelling him. Of the few dozen mutts in North America, I'd recognize about half by sight alone. For the others, I needed a scent to jog my memory.

"Werewolf?" I asked.

"You don't know him?"

"Should I?"

"I thought you might. He knows you quite well. By reputation, I suppose. Do you have any contact with the werewolves outside your Pack?"

"As little as possible."

It was true. We didn't go out of our way to associate with mutts. Unfortunately, that didn't mean we lacked contact with them. I'd probably had a run-in with this one before, but I'd had so many run-ins with so many mutts that I could scarcely separate one from the next.

Bauer moved on. Matasumi was right behind us now. Tess had resumed her note-taking, jotting down my every word. I'd have to start being more eloquent. If they were recording me for posterity, I wanted to sound at least moderately intelligent. "Clever" would be good, but a stretch.

"Next on the right we have a Voodoo priest."

"'Voodoo' is the common name," Matasumi said. "The correct terminology is 'Vodoun.'"

Bauer waved off the distinction, then tilted her hand like a spokesmodel toward the cell on the right. I knew I'd have nightmares about this, dreaming that I was sitting in my cage scratching my butt while Vanna White here conducted tours of the ward—"And on the left we have a rare example of the female *Canis lupis homo sapiens*, common name 'werewolf.'"

The man in the cage had dark skin, short dreadlocks, and a close-cropped beard. He glared at the one-way glass as if he could see through it, but his eyes were focused a few feet left of our group. His lips parted and he muttered something. I couldn't make out the language, but I recognized the raspy voice as that of the man who'd been shouting earlier.

"He's cursing us," Bauer said.

Matasumi made an odd chortling sound. Tess stifled a giggle. Bauer did one of her eye-rolls, and they all laughed.

"Voodoo priests have only the most negligible powers," Bauer said. "They're a minor race. Are you familiar with that term?"

I shook my head.

Matasumi took over. "We have the good fortune to have someone on staff who was able to supply us with the details of classification. Major and minor refer to the degree of power a race possesses. Major races include witches, half-demons, shamans, sorcerers, necromancers, vampires, and werewolves. These groups are relatively small. Minor races are much larger. In fact, it would be a misnomer to even call them 'races' because they often have no blood ties. Typically, they are normal people who display a certain aptitude and may have been trained to hone these talents. These minor races include Vodoun priests, druids, psychics, and many others. To a layperson these people may appear to have great power, but in comparison to a witch or a werewolf—"

"There is no comparison," Bauer cut in. "Not for our purposes. This 'priest' has no skills that the weakest witch or shaman couldn't top. Our first and last foray into the world of the minor races."

"So for now you're keeping him here . . . ?" I prompted.

"Until we need the cell," Bauer said.

Guess it would be too much to hope that they'd release subjects who proved unworthy.

"Trial and error," Bauer continued. "More often than not, we've made excellent choices. For example, take a look at the guest in the room next door."

The next prisoner was another man, this one in his late thirties, small, with a compact build, light brown skin, and finely drawn features. He lifted his gaze from a magazine, stretched his legs, then resumed reading. As he'd looked up, I amended my age estimate to mid-forties, maybe closing in on fifty.

"Can you guess what he is?" Bauer asked.

"No idea."

"Damn. I hoped you could tell us."

Matasumi forced a pained smile. Tess gave an obligatory laugh. Obviously an old joke.

"You don't know what he is?" I asked.

"No idea," Bauer said. "When we picked him up, we thought he was a half-demon, but his physiology is all wrong. Like most of the major races, half-demons have common physical traits, as we've learned in examining the three specimens we've acquired so far. Armen doesn't share any of them. His anatomical quirks are all his own. His powers aren't half-demon, either."

"What can he do?"

"He's a human chameleon." She waved off Matasumi's protests. "Yes, yes, Doctor Matasumi will tell you that's not an accurate description, but I like it. Much more catchy than 'unknown species with minor facial contortion abilities.'" She winked at me, again as if sharing a private joke. "Marketing is everything."

"Minor facial contortion abilities?" I repeated.

"Mr. Haig can willfully alter his facial structure," Matasumi said. "Minor changes only. He cannot, for example, turn himself into you or me, but he could change his face enough so he would no longer resemble his passport photo."

"Uh-huh."

"It doesn't sound very useful for everyday life, but it is incredibly significant in the larger scheme of things. This particular power is completely undocumented in the annals of parapsychology. I'm postulating a new evolutionary shift."

He smiled then, the first smile I'd seen from him. It shaved decades from his face, lighting his eyes with childlike excitement. He watched me and waited, lips twitching as if he could barely contain the urge to continue.

"Evolutionary shift?" I echoed.

"My hypothesis is that all supernatural races—the true races, the major races—are the result of evolutionary anomalies. For example, with the werewolves, somewhere in the very distant past one man somehow developed the ability to Change into a wolf. A complete quirk of nature. Yet a quirk that improved his ability to survive and therefore was reflected in his DNA, which he passed to his sons. The minor powers of a werewolf—longevity, strength, sensory enhancement—may have been part of this initial change or may have evolved later, to make werewolves better suited for the lives they lead. Similar anomalies would explain the beginnings of all the major races."

"Except half-demons," Bauer said.

"That goes without saying. Half-demons are a reproductive hybrid. They rarely transmit their powers to their offspring. Now, back to Mr. Haig. If my theory is correct, these random evolutionary changes must happen with some frequency—not commonly, but more often than would explain the few existing major races. Perhaps some of these deviations are so recent that there aren't yet enough members to classify as a race. If that is true, then Mr. Haig may be the forefather of a new species. Over generations, his power could develop exponentially. Where Mr. Haig may only be able to fool a traffic officer, his great-great-grandson may be able to alter his physical structure enough to *become* the officer."

"Uh-huh."

Matasumi turned around and gestured to the last pair of cells across the hall. "Here are two more interesting specimens. Look to your left first, please."

In the cell beside the mutt, a woman lay on the bed, eyes open, staring at the ceiling. She was roughly my age, maybe five-six, 120 pounds. Dark red hair, green eyes, and enviably clear skin that looked like it had never sprouted a blemish. She radiated vibes of sturdy good health, the sort of woman I could imagine cheerfully manning some National Park outpost.

"Witch?" I asked.

"Half-demon," Bauer said.

So half-demons could be female? No one had said otherwise, but I'd assumed they were all male, maybe because the only two I'd ever met were men or maybe because when I thought "demon" I thought "male."

"What's her power?" I asked.

"Telekinesis," Bauer said. "She can move things with her mind. Leah is the daughter of an Agito demon. Are you familiar with demonology?"

"Uh—no. The shortcomings of a modern education."

Bauer smiled. "Not much call for it these days, but it's a fascinating subject. There are two types of demons: eudemons and cacodemons. Eudemons good, cacodemons bad."

"Good demons?"

"Surprising, isn't it? Quite a common religious belief, actually. Only in Christian mythology do you find demons so thoroughly . . . demonized. In truth, both kinds exist, though only the cacodemons procreate. Within each of the two types there's a hierarchy based on the demon's relative degree of power. An Agito is quite high on the scale."

"So I guess telekinesis is more than a parlor trick, then."

"Much more," Matasumi said. "The implications and applications of such a power are infinite."

"What can she do?"

"She can move things with her mind," Matasumi said, parroting Bauer's earlier description.

In other words, they had no idea what the "implications and applications" were either. Sure, telekinesis sounded fine, but what could you really do with it? Besides grab the salt from the counter without leaving the dinner table.

"Are there many female half-demons?" I asked.

"Males are more common, but females aren't unknown," Matasumi said. "We actually selected Leah for her gender. We've had some difficulties with our male subjects, so I thought females might be easier to manage. More passive."

"Watch it," Bauer said. "You're surrounded by women here, Lawrence. Yes, women seem to make better subjects, but it has nothing to do with passivity. Women are better able to assess the situation and see the futility of resisting. Men seem to feel an obligation to fight back, no matter what the odds. Take our Voodoo priest. Rants and curses all day, every day. Does it help? No. But he keeps doing it. How does Leah react to the same situation? She stays calm and she cooperates." She turned to me. "Have you ever seen telekinesis?"

"Uh, no," I said. "I don't think so."

She smiled. "Time for a performance, then."

CHAPTER 15

SAVANNAH

Bauer reached for the intercom button on the half-demon's cage. Something in my gut tightened, and I opened my mouth to stop her, then bit back the protest. Why did I care if Bauer talked to this woman? Maybe I just didn't like the idea of my fellow captives knowing they were being watched and discussed like zoo animals.

"Leah?" Bauer said, leaning into the speaker.

"Hey, Sondra," Leah said, rising from the bed. "Did my appointment get bumped up again?"

"No, I'm just passing by. Showing a new guest around. She's very interested in your powers. How about a demonstration?"

"Sure." Leah turned to the small table. After a second, a coffee mug rose from the surface and spun around. "How's that?"

"Perfect. Thank you, Leah."

The woman smiled and nodded. If she had any objection to being treated like a trained monkey, she gave no sign of it, just stood there awaiting further commands.

"I'll see you later, Leah," Bauer said.

"I'm not going anywhere. Say hi to Xavier for me. Tell him to stop by some time. Bring a deck of cards."

"I'll do that."

Bauer clicked off the intercom.

"Xavier is our other half-demon," she said to me. "You've met him."

"Houdini."

Bauer smiled. "Yes, I suppose so. No bonds will hold that one, as we soon discovered. Lucky for us he was happy to cooperate with our questions and experiments for the right financial incentive. Quite the mercenary, our Xavier. A valuable asset to the team, though."

"Like the sorcerer," I said.

Bauer shot me a studiously blank look.

"I heard you hired a sorcerer, too," I said.

Bauer hesitated, as if pondering whether to lie, then said, "Yes, we have a sorcerer. He helps us find our supernaturals. You're not likely to encounter Mr. Katzen though, if that puts your mind at ease."

"Should it?"

"Sorcerers have an . . . unsavory reputation among some supernatural races. Not entirely unwarranted."

Matasumi coughed discreetly, but Bauer ignored him and rapped her nails against the Vodoun priest's cell wall. He glanced up, maybe sensing someone there, and cast a baleful glare at the mirrored glass.

"Untrustworthy egomaniacs, most of them," Bauer went on. "Our Mr. Katzen, I'm afraid, is no exception. As I said, though, you don't need to worry about him. He doesn't associate with what he considers the 'lower' races. Now Xavier is much more sociable."

"He keeps Leah entertained, I see."

"Actually no. He's not likely to take her up on her offer. Sad, really. When Leah found out we had another half-demon here she was thrilled. I don't think she's ever met another of her kind. But Xavier won't have anything to do with her. He met her once and has since refused to go near her. We've even tried bribes. Keeping our guests happy is very important to us. Leah is a very gregarious young woman. She needs social stimulation. Fortunately we've found other ways to accommodate her. She's taken quite an interest in two of our other guests."

"Curtis and Savannah," Tess said.

Bauer nodded. "Who are also our two guests most in need of companionship, someone to cheer them up. I think Leah has a knack for that. An innate sense of altruism. Curtis and Savannah both enjoy her company immensely. Which only makes Xavier's animosity all the more unfathomable. He won't even talk to her. It's causing some concern for us. We'd like to bring Leah on the team, but we can't afford the tension it would cause."

"Have a lot of cap—guests joined 'the team'?"

Bauer's eyes sparked as if I'd asked the million-dollar question. "Not many, but it's certainly possible. Particularly for our more honored guests, like yourself. Once we're assured of a guest's cooperation, we're quite happy to make an offer. It's something to strive for."

In other words, if I was a very, very good girl, I too could kidnap and torture my fellow supernatural beings. Oh, joy.

"Any idea why Xavier doesn't like Leah?" I asked.

"Jealousy," Matasumi said. "Within the half-demon hierarchy Leah has higher standing."

"Are they aware of this hierarchy?" I asked. "I thought half-demons didn't have much contact with one another. They don't have any central or ruling group, right? So how do they know who has what status?"

Silence.

After a moment Matasumi said, "At some level, I'm sure they're aware of their status."

"An Agito demon ranks over an Evanidus, Xavier's sire," Bauer said. "And an Exustio ranks over both. That's Adam Vasic's sire, right? An Exustio?"

"Never came up in conversation, surprisingly."

Disappointment flashed across her face, then vanished in another false-hearty smile. "We'll have Doctor Carmichael check those burns. I'm assuming Adam gave them to you."

She paused. I said nothing.

"An Exustio half-demon is very powerful," she continued. "Right at the top. He'd be a first-rate catch. Maybe you could help with that. I'm sure those burns don't tickle."

"They're healing," I said.

"Still, we'd be very grateful—"

Matasumi interrupted. "We don't even know if Adam Vasic's sire is an Exustio, Sondra. We only have one person's secondhand account on that."

"But it's a very good account." Bauer turned to me. "One of our early captives was a shaman who served on Ruth Winterbourne's council back when Adam's stepfather started bringing him to the meetings. He's a Tempestras half-demon. The stepfather, that is. He's also supposedly an expert on demonology, and he was convinced Adam's sire was an Exustio."

"Though he's never given any indication of having such an advanced degree of power," Matasumi said. "Skin burns are more likely the sign of an Igneus. An Exustio would have incinerated Ms. Michaels."

"Still, even an Igneus half-demon would be quite a coup. And I'd love to get his stepfather. There's very little data on Tempestras demons."

"I'd like to meet the mother," Tess said. "What's the chance that a woman is going to be chosen to bear a demon's offspring and end up marrying a half-demon? There must be something in her that attracts them. It could be very useful research. And interesting."

This was creeping me out. How much did these people know about us? It was bad enough that they knew what we were, but to have delved into our personal lives like this was downright disturbing. Did they do this a lot, stand around discussing us like we were characters in some modern *Dark Shadows* soap opera?

"Why didn't you grab Adam instead of me?" I asked.

"Don't underestimate your own importance to us, Elena," Bauer said. "We're thrilled to have you with us."

"And we couldn't find Adam," Tess added.

Gee, thanks.

Bauer continued, "And, beside Leah, our last, but certainly not least guest."

I turned. In the cell behind me was a girl. No, I don't mean a young woman. I mean a child, no more than twelve or thirteen. I assumed her youthful appearance was the manifestation of some unknown supernatural race.

"What is she?" I asked.

"A witch," Bauer said.

"Does a spell do that? Make her look young? Handy trick, but if it were me, I sure wouldn't want to return to that age. Either long before or long after puberty for me, thank you very much."

Bauer laughed. "No, it's not a spell. Savannah's twelve."

I stopped. If I'd been shivering before, I was frozen now, a block of ice lodged in my gut.

"Twelve?" I repeated, hoping I'd heard wrong. "You captured a twelve-year-old witch?"

"The absolute best age," Matasumi said. "Witches come into their full powers with the onset of their first menses. Being on the brink of puberty, Savannah presents us with the perfect opportunity to study mental and physiological changes that might explain a witch's ability to cast spells. We had a remarkable stroke of luck finding her. An accident really. Savannah is the daughter of a former Coven witch we targeted several weeks ago. When our men picked up the mother, the daughter was unexpectedly home from school, so they were forced to bring her as well."

I scanned the cell. "You don't keep her with her mother?"

"We had some trouble with her mother," Bauer said. "Her powers were stronger than our sorcerer led us to believe. Dark magic, you might call it, which would likely explain her split with the Coven. Eve was . . . well, we had to—"

"We removed her from the program," Matasumi cut in. "The best thing, really. She proved much too difficult to be a useful subject, and her presence distracted the child."

The ice expanded to fill my stomach. These people were holding a child in an underground cell, congratulating themselves on having found her, and extolling the advantages of killing her mother? I watched the girl. She was tall for her age, whip-thin, with a face that was all planes and sharp angles. Waist-length jet-black hair fell so straight it seemed weighted down. Huge dark blue eyes overpowered her thin face. An odd-looking child with the promise of great beauty. She stared intently at a crossword puzzle book, pencil poised above the page. After a moment she nodded and scribbled something. She held the book at arm's length, studied the completed puzzle, then tossed it aside, got up from the table, paced a few times, and finally settled for surveying the contents of a bookshelf behind the television set.

"She must get bored," I said.

"Oh, no," Bauer said. "This isn't easy for Savannah. We know that. But we do our best to accommodate her. Anything she wants. Chocolate bars, magazines . . . we even picked up some video games last week. She's quite . . . " Bauer paused, seeming to roll a word on her tongue, then discarded it and said quietly, "She's comfortable."

So she knew how bad it sounded. "Sorry we executed your mom, kid, but here's some *Tiger Beat*s and a Game Boy to make up for it." Bauer tapped her manicured nails against the wall, then forced a smile.

"Well, that's it," she said. "You're probably wondering what all this is for."

"Perhaps later," Matasumi murmured. "Doctor Carmichael is waiting and this isn't really the place . . . "

"We've shown Elena around. Now I think it's only fair we offer some explanation."

Matasumi's lips tightened. So this wasn't usually part of the tour? Why now? A sudden need to justify herself after showing me Savannah? Why did Bauer care what I thought? Or was she defending it to herself?

Before Bauer continued, she led me out of the cell block. I studied the security procedures. Once through, we passed two armed guards stationed in a cubbyhole beyond the secured door. Their eyes passed over me as if I was the cleaning lady. One of the advantages to hiring guards with some form of military background: Curiosity had been drilled out of them. Follow orders and don't ask questions.

"Some sort of military connection?" I asked. As long as Bauer was in a mood to answer questions, I should ask them.

"Military?" She followed my gaze to the guards. "Using supernatural beings to build the perfect weapon? Intriguing idea."

"Not really," I said. "They did it on *Buffy the Vampire Slayer*. A subpar season. I slept through half the episodes."

Bauer laughed, though I could tell she had no idea what I was talking about. I couldn't picture her lounging in front of a TV set, and even if she did, I was sure the only thing she watched was CNN.

"Don't worry," she said. "This is a completely private enterprise. Our choice of guards was merely practical. No governmental overtones intended."

We walked through another set of doors into a long corridor.

"In our post-industrial society, science is constantly pushing the boundaries of technology," Bauer said, still walking. I glanced overhead for speakers, half-certain I was hearing Bauer's voice on some prerecorded tour tape. "The human race has taken great strides in the field of technology. Massive strides. Our lives get easier with each passing day. Yet are we happy?"

She paused, but didn't look back at me, as if not expecting an answer. Rhetorical question, dramatic pause. Bauer knew her public-speaking tricks.

"We aren't," she said. "Everyone I know has a therapist and a shelf of self-help books. They go on spiritual retreats. They hire yogis and practice meditation. Does it do any good? No. They're miserable. And why?"

Another pause. I bit my lip to keep from answering. It wouldn't have been the sort of reply she wanted.

Bauer continued, "Because they feel powerless. Science does all the work. People are reduced to technological slaves, dutifully pumping data into computers and waiting for the great god of technology to honor them with results. When the computer age first arrived, people were thrilled. They dreamed of shorter work weeks, more time for self-improvement. It didn't happen. People today work as hard, if not harder, than they did thirty years ago. The only difference is the quality of the work they perform. They no longer accomplish anything of value. They only service the machines."

Pause number three.

"What we propose to do here is return a sense of power to humanity. A new wave of improvement. Not technological improvement. Improvement from within. Improvement of the mind and the body. Through studying the supernatural, we can affect those changes. Shamans, necromancers, witches, sorcerers—they can help us increase our mental capabilities. Other races can teach us how to make immense improvements in our physical lives. Strength and sensory acuteness from werewolves. Regeneration and longevity from vampires. Countless other advances from half-demons. A brave new world for humanity."

I waited for the music to swell. When it didn't, I managed to say with a straight face, "It sounds very . . . noble."

"It is," Matasumi said.

Bauer pressed a button and elevator doors opened. We stepped on.

Chapter 16

Trick

The infirmary was exactly what one would expect from such a high-tech operation: antiseptic, white, and cold. Filled with gleaming stainless-steel instruments and digital machines. Not so much as a faded "symptoms of a heart attack" poster on the wall. All business, like its doctor, a heavyset middle-aged woman. Carmichael covered all opening pleasantries with a brusque hello. From there it was "open this, close that, lift this, turn that." Zero small talk. I appreciated that. Easier to swallow than Bauer's unwarranted chumminess.

The examination was less intrusive than the average physical. No needles or urine samples. Carmichael took my temperature, weight, height, and blood pressure. She checked my eyes, ears, and throat. Asked about nausea or other tranquilizer aftereffects. When she listened to my heart, I waited for the inevitable questions. My heart rate was well above normal. A typical werewolf "physiological anomaly," as Matasumi would say. Jeremy said it was because of our increased metabolism or adrenaline flow or something. I didn't remember the exact reason. Jeremy was the medical expert. I barely passed high school biology. Carmichael didn't comment on my heart rate, though. Just nodded and marked it on my chart. I guess they already expected that from examining the mutt.

After Carmichael finished with me, I rejoined my party in the waiting room. Only one of the three guards had accompanied me into the infirmary. He hadn't even sneaked a peek when I'd changed in and out of my medical gown. Serious ego blow. Not that I blamed him. There wasn't much to see.

Matasumi, Bauer, Tess, and the three guards led me down the hall away from the infirmary waiting room. Before we got to our destination, a guard's radio beeped. There was some kind of "minor incident" in the cell block, and someone named Tucker wanted to know if Matasumi still needed the guards. It was dinner hour and most of the off-duty guards had gone into town. Could Matasumi spare the three accompanying us?

Matasumi told Tucker he'd send them down in five minutes. Then we all trooped into an area Bauer referred to as the "sitting room."

The sitting room was an interrogation chamber. Anyone who'd seen a single cop show wouldn't be fooled by the comfortable chairs and Art Deco prints on the walls. Four chairs were arranged around a wooden table. A pool-table-sized slab of one-way glass dominated the far wall. Video cameras and microphones hung from two ceiling corners. Bauer could call it a goddamned formal parlor if she wanted. It was an interrogation room.

My escort led me to the near side of the room, facing the one-way glass. Once I was seated, he opened flaps in either side of the chair and pulled out thick reinforced straps, which he fastened around my waist. Though my wrists were still cuffed, he used another set of straps to bind my elbows to the chair arms. Then from the floor he pulled a heavy buckle attached to chains that retracted under the carpet. This he affixed to my feet. All four chair legs were welded to the floor. Damn, we needed one of these for our sitting room at Stonehaven. Nothing like a steel-bonded restraint chair to make a guest feel at home.

Once I was secured, Matasumi released the guards. Wow, he was taking a big chance there. No armed guards? Who knew what havoc I could wreak. I could . . . Well, I could spit in his face and call him really nasty names.

As for the questioning, it was pretty boring. More of the same sort of questions Matasumi had fired at me in the cell. I continued to mix my truths and lies, and no one called me on it. About twenty minutes into the session, someone knocked at the door. A guard came in and told Matasumi and Bauer that this Tucker guy requested their presence in the cell block to advise on an "issue." Bauer balked, insisting Matasumi could handle it, but it involved some special project of hers, and after a moment's argument, she agreed to go. Tess followed Matasumi out, though no one had invited her. Guess she was afraid of being spit on. Bauer promised they'd be back as soon as possible, and they were gone. Leaving me alone. Hmmm.

My optimism faded fast. There was no way I was getting out of this chair. No adrenaline rush would give me the strength to break these bonds. With the way I was tied up, someone could perform open-heart surgery on me and I couldn't do more than scream. I couldn't even Change into a wolf and hope to slip out. The straps and chains were tethered with a device that gobbled up slack like a seat belt. If I were to Change, I would only risk hurting myself.

As I examined my bonds, the door behind me opened. A man stumbled into the room, tripping over leg irons. Before I could see his face, a smell hit me and the hairs on my arms rose. A mutt. I twisted my neck to see the mutt from the cage downstairs. Patrick Lake. The name leapt to consciousness at the first whiff of his scent. I'd only met him once, and not a memorable meeting at that, but a werewolf's brain categorizes smells with the efficiency of a top-notch filing clerk. With a few molecules of scent, the accompanying information is at our mental fingertips.

Patrick Lake was a drifter and a man-eater. He wasn't a prolific killer—a body here, a body there, like most mutts, savvy enough to know each kill brought him closer to exposure, but unable or unwilling to quit. The Pack didn't bother much with mutts like Lake. Maybe that sounds bad, like we should be out there stopping every mutt who kills humans, but if we did that, we'd need to exterminate three-quarters of our race, and really, it wasn't our job. If humans were being killed, let other humans deal with it. Harsh but practical. We became concerned only when a mutt called attention to himself, thereby endangering the rest of us. Lake did that about four years ago by killing the daughter of a city official in Galveston, Texas. Clay and I had flown down to do our respective jobs. I'd investigated the status of the murder case. If Lake became a suspect, he had to die. Since it never got that far, Clay settled for beating the crap out of Lake as a warning, then making sure he caught the next plane out of Texas. Patrick Lake hadn't given us any trouble since.

When Lake staggered into the room, I jerked up in my seat, snapping the bonds tight. Houdini—Xavier—walked in behind him. Seeing me, he stopped and blinked, then looked around the room.

"All alone?" he asked.

I didn't reply. Unless there were half-demon guards with the power of invisibility, it was quite apparent I was alone. Still, Xavier leaned out the door to check the hall. Then, shoving Lake ahead of him, he crossed to the one-way glass, peered through, frowned, zapped into the next room, and returned.

"Alone," he said, shaking his head. "You gotta love this place. Military efficiency, high-tech security, the latest communication gadgetry. And for all that, as disorganized as my mother's kitchen cupboards. I can't believe they left you alone. It is eight o'clock, isn't it?"

"Let me check my watch," I said.

He chuckled. "Sorry. They sure have you tied down, don't they? Somebody's not taking any chances. But I'm sure it's eight, and I was supposed to bring Lake up here at eight. Now they can't even keep their scheduling straight. Someone's gotta hire a secretary."

Lake stared at me. He'd never met me before, not officially anyway. In Galveston, I'd come close enough to smell him, but I'd stayed upwind and out of sight. That was a complication Clay hadn't needed. Mutts got a little . . . excited the first time they met me. A hormone thing. I'd been told that I smelled like a bitch in heat—not the most flattering description, but it explained a lot. After a mutt got to know me, his human brain usually kicked in and overrode the signals, but the first few meetings were always dicey. Sometimes I could use the reaction to my advantage. Usually it was just a major pain in the ass.

"Like her?" Xavier asked.

Lake muttered something and tried to wrench his gaze away, but he didn't succeed in breaking visual contact. He walked behind my chair, leg chains sparking static against the carpet. I stared straight ahead. Get it over with, asshole. Lake circled the table twice. When Xavier snickered, Lake paused only a second before instinct impelled him forward again, circling, eyes shunting back to me.

"I'll admit, she's a good-looking girl," Xavier said. "But don't you think you're overdoing it, buddy?"

"Shut up," Lake growled and kept circling.

"Don't worry," Xavier said, turning to me. "If he tries to sniff your crotch, I'll snap a muzzle on him."

Lake turned on Xavier, tensed as if to lunge at him, then thought better of it and settled for growling a string of epithets. The spell was broken, though, and when he wheeled back to face me, his eyes were still blazing, but with fury, not lust.

"You were there, weren't you?" he said. "In Galveston. With *him*. When he did this to me." He lifted his cuffed hands and thrust them out. His left palm was permanently fixed in handshake position, the rest of the forearm gnarled and wasted, the result of too many breaks and insufficient setting.

"Who's 'he'?" Xavier asked.

"Clayton," Lake spat, gaze still skewering mine.

"Oh, the boyfriend." Xavier gave a mock sigh. "Did you have to mention the boyfriend? I saw him in Vermont, and I'm still feeling pretty inferior about the whole thing. Please tell me that guy's got some nasty habits. Body odor. Picks his nose. Give me something."

"He's a fucking psycho," Lake snarled.

"Perfect! That's exactly what I wanted. Thank you, Pat. I feel much better now. Whatever my questionable mental status, no one has ever accused *me* of being a psychopath."

Lake stepped closer and eyed my bonds.

"Don't be getting any uncivilized ideas," Xavier said. "You touch her and I'll have to let her touch you back. You don't want that. She's a strong girl."

Lake snorted.

"You don't believe me?" Xavier said. "She's been here a few hours and she already put a hole in her cell wall. You've been here two weeks and haven't even dented yours. Could be she's stronger than you."

"Not likely."

"No, maybe not. You're bigger. More muscle mass. Male advantage. But she's definitely smarter. Figured out how to knock me down on her second try. You and I went ten times as many rounds and you never laid a finger on me. The female of the species is more deadly than the male. Who sang that?"

"It's from Kipling," I said.

"See? She is smarter than us."

"Better educated," Lake said. "Not smarter."

"How about a bet then? A match. If she takes you, I get your diamond ring."

"Go to hell," Lake muttered.

"Sociable guy, isn't he? Brilliant conversationalist. No wonder you won't let him in your Pack."

"Go to hell," Lake enunciated more slowly now, turning his glare on Xavier.

"Touched a sore spot, did I? Oh, come on. Play my game. Show me what a big bad wolf you are. You want some comeuppance for that arm, don't you? How about it, Elena? Feel like a few rounds with Mr. Personality?"

"I don't fight on command," I said.

Xavier sighed and rolled his eyes. Then he strolled over to me and undid all the straps holding me to the seat, leaving only the handcuffs.

"Hey!" Lake said, striding toward us.

Xavier stopped him with an outstretched hand, knelt to undo Lake's leg irons, then unlocked his handcuffs. Lake shook the cuffs off and drew his arm back for a swing at Xavier. But his fist connected with empty space. Xavier was gone.

I'd stayed in my seat. No point in facing off with this mutt. Better to sit here, refuse to play the game, and hope Matasumi and Bauer returned soon.

Lake stepped back and surveyed me. A grin tickled the corners of his mouth.

"Don't bother," I said. "It's been tried before under far more advantageous circumstances. You know what'll happen if you even try. Clay will ensure you can't ever try again."

"Really?" Lake's eyes widened and he looked around. "I don't see him here. Maybe I'm willing to take the chance."

"Fine," I said. "Knock yourself out."

I didn't move. Werewolf fights were 70 percent bravado. These days, Clay won most of his battles simply by showing up. His reputation was enough. At least it worked for male werewolves. I wasn't so lucky. No matter how many bouts I won, mutts still figured I was helpless without Clay to protect me.

Lake circled the chair. I didn't move. He grabbed my hair, wrapping the long stands around his fist. I set my teeth and still didn't move. He yanked my head back. I only glared up at him. With a growl, he released my hair, grabbed my shoulders, and shoved me forward out of the chair. I twisted, trying to brace myself against the table, but, unlike my chair, it wasn't bolted to the floor. When I hit the table edge, it skidded out of reach and I collapsed to my knees, my manacled hands shooting forward to break my fall. Lake slammed a foot into my ass and sent me crashing onto my face. I stayed still, face against the carpet.

"Whoa," Lake said. "That was hard."

"My hands are cuffed," I muttered against the carpet pile.

"Yeah? Well, my left hand doesn't work so good, thanks to lover boy. Maybe I should do the same to you. Nah. Not the arm. The face. Maybe then he won't find you quite so appealing."

"Face or arm, it doesn't matter. Touch me and you're a dead man."

"I'm already a dead man, honey. With you here, these bastards don't want me anymore. Might as well get my kicks while I can."

While we traded volleys, I kept my arms tucked under me and concentrated. Sweat broke out across my forehead. Lake knelt in front of me and grinned.

"Looking a little pale there, honey. Not as tough as you pretend."

I shifted, pulling my weight off my arms. Lake leaped to his feet and stomped one foot into the center of my back. Something cracked. Pain arced through me. Stifling a cry, I closed my eyes and focused on my hands. I eased my belly off the carpet and twisted my palm up. I felt the weight of Lake's foot on my back, resting there. Without warning, he pushed down, grinding me into the carpet. Five needles drove through my shirt and into my stomach. I gasped and smelled blood.

"Does that hurt?" Lake said. "Geez, I feel sooo bad. Do you know how much this arm hurt? Do you have any idea? Unable to go to the hospital, to a doctor? Tracking down some quack who'd had his license revoked—"

I flipped over fast, catching Lake off guard. He stumbled backward. In a second, he'd regained his balance and drew his foot back, aiming at my chest as I twisted upright. I swung my right hand up and caught his leg. My nails tore through his jeans and sank into flesh. When I had a good grip, I yanked, ripping his leg open. Lake screamed and stumbled away.

"Fuck! What the fuck—?"

He looked at my hand. Only it wasn't a hand. It was a claw, the grip and fingers of a human hand, the fur of a wolf, nails long, razor-sharp, and rock-hard. The cuffs hung from my other hand. The partial Change had narrowed my hand enough to pull it through the bracelet.

"What the fuck?!" Lake repeated backing against the wall.

"Pack trick," I said. "Takes concentration. Too much for a mutt."

I advanced on him. He hesitated, then launched himself at me. We went down. I clawed his back. He yelped and tried to wrestle free. I grabbed the back of his shirt with my left hand and flung him off me. As I scrambled to my feet, the door flew open. Bauer hurried into the room with Matasumi, Tess, and two guards at her heels. All five stopped inside the doorway and stared. Then Bauer strode across the room, barreling down on Lake.

"What the hell is going on here?" Bauer said.

"She started it," he said.

"Oh, please," I said, getting to my feet.

My hand was normal now. I'd even slipped it back through the cuff. Xavier strolled through the doorway.

"*He* started it," Lake said.

"Just following orders." Xavier leaned against the doorjamb, hands in pockets. "The ring's mine, Pat. She whupped your ass."

"Is it on tape?" Matasumi asked.

Xavier yawned. "Of course."

Bauer spun on both of them. "Orders? Tape? What happened in here?"

I knew what had happened. I'd been set up, and I was furious for not seeing it earlier. Shouldn't I have wondered why security-paranoid Matasumi released my guards? Why he then left me in the room alone? Why Xavier was strolling around alone with another werewolf after Matasumi had argued over letting me leave my cell even under armed guard? Matasumi must have arranged everything while I was in the infirmary. As long as I was out of my cell, why not try a little experiment? Find out what happens when you put a Pack werewolf in the same room as a mutt.

Bauer started reaming out Matasumi, then stopped herself. She dismissed Xavier and Tess for the night, then asked the two guards to escort me back to my cell. Once we were out of normal earshot, she lit into Matasumi again.

CHAPTER 17

Contact

I'd been back in my cell for about twenty minutes when Bauer brought my dinner. Ham, scalloped potatoes, baby carrots, cauliflower, salad, milk, coffee, and chocolate cake. Decent enough food to fend off any notion of a hunger strike—not that I would have done that anyway. No protest was great enough to warrant starvation.

Before I ate, Bauer showed me around the cell, pointing out the toiletries, demonstrating how the shower worked, and explaining the meal schedule. A nightgown and a single day's worth of clothing were kept in a drawer under the bed. Why only one change of clothes? Bauer didn't say. Maybe they were afraid if we had too much fabric, we'd rig up a way to hang ourselves from the nonexistent rafters. Or did they think there was no sense providing more when we might not live long enough to need it? Cheery thought.

Bauer didn't leave after conducting my cell tour. Maybe she expected a tip.

"I apologize," she said after I sat down to eat. "What happened upstairs . . . I didn't know they planned that. I don't believe in tricking our guests. This whole arrangement is difficult enough for you without having to worry about stunts like that."

"It's okay," I said through a mouthful of ham.

"No, it isn't. Please tell me if anything like that happens when I'm not around. Would you like Doctor Carmichael to look at your stomach wounds?"

"I'm fine."

"There's clean clothing if you want to change out of that shirt."

"I'm fine," I said, then added a conciliatory "Maybe later."

She was trying to be nice. I knew I should reciprocate. Knowing and doing were two different things. What was I supposed to say? Thanks for caring? If she cared, she wouldn't have kidnapped me in the first place, right? But as she watched me eat, her look of concern seemed genuine.

Maybe she didn't see the contradiction here, abducting me, then worrying about how I was treated. She stood there as if waiting for me to say something. Say what? I had little enough experience with other women. Making chitchat with someone who'd drugged and kidnapped me was well beyond my set of social skills.

Before I could think of suitable small talk, Bauer left. Relief mingled with my guilt. As much as I knew I should try to be friendly, I really wasn't in the mood for conversation. My back hurt. My stomach hurt. I was hungry. And I wanted to go to bed, which didn't mean I was tired, but that I wanted to talk to Jeremy. Jeremy could communicate with us mentally. The catch was he could only do it while we slept. After the incident with Lake, anxiety had begun oozing from behind my carefully erected barricades. I wanted to talk to Jeremy before my stress got out of control. He'd already be working on a rescue plan. I needed to hear it, to know that they were taking action. Even more than that, I needed his reassurance. I was scared, and I needed some comforting, someone to tell me everything would be okay, even if I knew that was an empty promise. I'd be friendly and polite to Bauer tomorrow. Tonight I wanted Jeremy.

Once I'd finished my meal, I took a shower. Definite privacy issues with the shower setup. The bathroom walls were see-through. The glass door on the shower stall was only slightly opaque, marring features but leaving very little to an observer's imagination. I fashioned a half-curtain by stretching the bath towel from the toilet to the shaving mirror over the sink. Waltzing around Stonehaven naked was one thing. I wasn't doing it in front of strangers. When I used the toilet, I draped the towel over my lap. Some things demand privacy.

After my shower, I put my clothing back on. They may have provided a nightgown, but I wasn't wearing it. Nor would I wear their fresh clothing tomorrow. I'd take another shower in the morning and hope nothing started to smell. My clothes were the only personal thing I had left. No one was taking them away from me. At least, not while the odor was bearable.

Jeremy didn't contact me that night. I don't know what went wrong. The only time I'd known Jeremy to be unable to contact us was when we were unconscious or sedated. I was sure the sedatives were out of my system, but I clung to that excuse. It was also possible that Jeremy was unable to contact me here, below ground, but I preferred not to consider that since it meant not only wouldn't I have Jeremy's help planning my escape, but he might assume I was dead and not try effecting any rescue. Deep down,

I knew that last part was bullshit. Clay would come for me. He wouldn't give up until he saw a corpse. Still, there was always that insecurity, that nagging voice forever trying to destroy my faith, telling me I was wrong, he wouldn't risk his life to save me, no one could or would care for me that much. So, despite everything I knew to the contrary, I awoke in a cold sweat, certain I'd been abandoned. No amount of reassuring self-talk would help me. I was alone and I feared I would remain alone, forced to rely on my own wits to escape. I didn't trust my wits that much.

In the late hours of the night, nearing dawn, someone did contact me. But it wasn't Jeremy. At least, I didn't think it was. I was dreaming that I was in a Mongolian yurt with Clay, arguing over who got the last red M&M. Just when I'd begun to consider giving in, Clay gathered his furs and stormed out into the howling wind, swearing never to return. The dream startled me up from sleep, heart thudding. As I tried to settle back to sleep, someone called my name: A woman's voice. I was sure it was a woman, but I was in that confused state between sleeping and waking, unable to tell if it was someone in my cell or a voice calling from a dream. I struggled to lift my head from my pillow, but plunged into a fresh nightmare before I could rouse myself.

The next morning, I stayed in bed as long as I could, stretching out sleep in the unlikely event that Jeremy was still trying to contact me and only needed a few more minutes. At eight-thirty, I admitted defeat. I wasn't sleeping, only keeping my eyes closed and faking it.

I shifted my legs out of bed, doubled over, and almost collapsed to the floor. My stomach felt like someone had sliced open all the muscles while I slept. Who'd think five little puncture wounds could hurt so much? The fact that they were self-inflicted didn't help. One day into my captivity and I was already doing more damage to myself than to my enemies. Maybe Patrick Lake was in more pain than I was. Not likely. My back had seized up overnight from Lake's stomping, and as I struggled to stand straight, my body revolted from both sides, stomach and spine. I hobbled to the shower. Steaming water helped my back but set my stomach afire. Cold water soothed my stomach but tightened my back again. Day two was off to a wonderful start.

My mood sank when Bauer brought my breakfast. No complaints about the meal, of course, and not really any complaint about Bauer bringing it, but one look at her sent my spirits plummeting. Bauer sauntered in wearing snug-fitting beige suede pants, a billowing white linen shirt, and knee-high boots, her hair artlessly swept up in a clip, cheeks flushed with pink that didn't come from a bottle, smelling faintly of horse, as if she'd just breezed in from a morning ride. I was dressed in a ripped and blood-stained shirt, my too-fine hair knotted from the harsh shampoo, and my eyes bloated from a rough night. When she called out a cheery good morning, I stumped over to the table, unable to stand fully erect or manage more than the most monosyllabic grunt in greeting. Even bent over, I was four or five inches taller than Bauer. I felt like a Neanderthal woman—big, ugly, and none too bright.

When Bauer tried to entice me into conversation, I was tempted to thwart her efforts again, but a peaceful breakfast wasn't a luxury I could afford. If I had to plot my own escape, I needed to get out of this cell. The best way to get out of this cell would be to "join" my captors. And the best way to join them would be to secure Bauer's favor. So I had to play nice. This was tougher than it sounded. Oddly enough, I had a problem sitting around chatting about the weather with the woman who'd thrown me into captivity.

"So you live near Syracuse," she said as I tore into my bagel.

I nodded, mouth full.

"My family's from Chicago," she said. "Bauer Paper Products. Have you heard of it?"

"It sounds familiar," I lied.

"Old money. Very old."

Should I be impressed? I feigned it with a wide-eyed nod.

"It's odd, you know," she said, settling into her chair. "Growing up with that kind of name, that kind of money. Well, not odd for me. It's all I know. But you see yourself reflected through other people's eyes and you know you're considered very lucky. Born with the proverbial silver spoon. You're supposed to be happy, and God help you if you aren't."

"Money can't buy happiness," I said, the cliché bitter on my tongue. Was that what this was about? Poor little rich girl? I'm rich and unhappy so I kidnap innocent strangers—well, maybe not so innocent, but unwitting nonetheless.

"But *you* are happy," Bauer said. A statement, not a question.

I managed a half-genuine smile. "Well, at this very moment, being held captive in a cell, I wouldn't exactly say—"

"But otherwise. Before this. You're happy with your life."

"No complaints. It's not perfect. There's still that nasty werewolf curse—"

"You don't see it that way, though. As a curse. You say it, but you don't mean it."

She stared at me now. No, not at me. Into me. Eyes blazing, leaning forward. Hungry. I pulled back.

"Some days I mean it. Trust me." I polished off my bagel. "These are great. Real New York bagels. I don't suppose there's any chance of seconds."

She leaned back, flames in her eyes extinguished, polite smile back in place. "I'm sure we can arrange something." She checked her watch. "I should be getting you up to Doctor Carmichael for your physical."

"Is that a daily routine?"

"Oh, no. Yesterday was just a checkup. Today is the full physical."

Bauer lifted her hand. The door opened and two guards walked in. So that's where they'd been hiding. I'd wondered, hoping maybe Bauer felt comfortable enough to forgo the armed entourage. Guess not. The appearance of trust, but a lack of substance. Or perhaps just a lack of stupidity. Damn.

I had a neighbor. When I stepped from my cell, I saw someone in the room across from mine. A woman seated at the table, her back to me. It looked like . . . No, it couldn't be. Someone would have told me. I would have known. The woman turned half-profile. Ruth Winterbourne.

"When . . . ?" I asked.

Bauer followed my gaze and smiled as if I'd uncovered a hidden present. "She came in with you. We were in Vermont near the meeting hall that morning. When we saw you leave with the Danverses, Xavier and I decided to follow. The rest of the team stayed near the others. We knew someone would be alone eventually. Fortunately, it was Ruth. A very good catch. Of course, any one of them would have been good. Well, except her niece. Not much use in an apprentice witch of that age. Savannah is another matter, given her youth and what we know of her mother's powers."

"How come I didn't see Ruth yesterday?"

"The trip was unusually . . . difficult for her. Her age. The very thing that makes her valuable is something of a liability. We overestimated the sedative dosage. But she's quite fine now, as you can see."

She didn't look fine. Maybe someone who'd never met Ruth would mistake the dull eyes, yellow-hued skin, and lethargic movements for normal signs of aging, but I knew better. Physically, she seemed well enough. No signs of illness or broken bones. The damage was deeper than that.

"She looks pretty down," I said. "Depressed."

"It happens." Statement of fact. No emotion.

"Maybe I could speak to her," I said. "Cheer her up."

Bauer tapped her long nails against her side, considering. If she saw an ulterior motive in my altruism, she gave no sign of it.

"Perhaps we could arrange something," she said. "You've been very cooperative, Elena. The others were worried, but other than the wall-punching, you've been surprisingly well behaved. I believe in rewarding good behavior."

Without another word, she turned and left me to follow. Inwardly I balked, but outwardly I trailed along at her heel like a well-trained puppy. Trained puppy indeed. Forgive me, but "well-behaved" is not a term one ought to apply to a grown woman, yet Bauer said it without malice or insinuation. Be a good puppy, Elena, and I'll give you a treat. The temptation to show Bauer exactly what I thought of her reward system was almost overwhelming. Almost. But I did want to talk to Ruth. She was my only contact in this place, and I wasn't above asking for help. A spell had gotten us out of that doomed situation in the Pittsburgh alley. With her spells and my strength, we should be able to devise a way out of here.

So I was a good puppy. I suffered through the physical without protest. This time my visit to the infirmary wasn't nearly so unintrusive. They took X-rays, blood samples, urine samples, saliva samples, and samples of bodily fluids I didn't know I had. Then they attached wires to me and took readings of my heart and brain. Carmichael poked and prodded and asked questions I'd blush answering for my gynecologist. But I reminded myself that this was the price of talking to Ruth, so I ignored the intrusions and answered the questions.

The physical lasted several hours. At noon, someone knocked, then opened the door without waiting for a reply. Two guards walked in. They might even have been the ones who'd brought me up here, but I couldn't be sure. By this point, the crew cuts had blended into a nameless, faceless blob. Seen one, you've seen 'em all. One of the guards—maybe one of these two, maybe not—had stayed in the infirmary with me earlier, but after an hour or so, he'd muttered something about a shift change and told Dr. Carmichael to call for backup. She hadn't. When these two arrived, I thought they were coming to take the place of that missing guard. Instead they escorted in the "human chameleon," Armen Haig.

"I'm running behind," Carmichael said, not turning from a series of X-rays clipped to a lighted wall.

"Should we wait outside?" one guard asked.

"Not necessary. Please take the second table, Doctor Haig. I'll be right with you."

Haig nodded and walked to the table. His guards promised to return in an hour, then left. Unlike me, Haig wasn't even manacled. I suppose his powers weren't any great security risk. Even if he made himself look different, the guards were bound to notice an apparent stranger prowling the compound. Escape wasn't likely.

For the next twenty minutes, Carmichael bustled around the infirmary, checking X-rays, peering through microscopes, jotting notes on a clipboard. Finally she stopped, surveyed the room, then snatched a tray of fluid-filled vials from a metal cart.

"I need to run a test in the lab before we finish up here, Ms. Michaels."

Déjà vu or what? Bring another captive into a room with me, find an excuse for leaving that room, and see what fun and exciting chaos ensues. Couldn't these guys think up more than one ruse?

Carmichael headed for the exit, then stopped and looked from me to Haig. After a pause, she laid the tray on the counter and picked up the intercom phone. Though she turned her back and lowered her voice, her words were impossible to miss in the silent room. She asked someone in security whether there were any "issues" with leaving Haig and me together for a few minutes, if I was manacled. There weren't.

"Don't forget to turn on the camera," Haig murmured as she hung up. His voice was rich and honey-smooth, with traces of an accent.

Carmichael snorted. "I can't program my damned VCR. You think I can operate that thing?" She waved at the video camera mounted overhead. "A word of warning, though. Don't think of leaving. I'll be locking the door behind me. There's a perfectly functioning camera in the waiting room and guards in the hall. They won't look kindly on an escape attempt."

She took her tray of vials and left the room.

CHAPTER 18

PARTY

After Carmichael left, I studied the video camera for signs of activity, but it stayed silent and still.

"So," Haig said. "What are you in for?"

"Raping and pillaging."

The corners of his mouth turned up. "That would have been my first guess. Are you finding the accommodations to your liking?"

"My kennel, you mean?"

Another quarter-smile. "Ah, so you *are* the werewolf. I didn't know whether it was polite to ask. Emily Post doesn't cover circumstances such as this. Werewolf. Hmmm. I had a patient with lycanthropy once. Felt compelled to turn around three times before settling onto the couch. Quite trying. But he always brought in the paper from the front stoop."

I remembered how Carmichael had addressed him. "Doctor Haig," I said. "So you're a shr—psychiatrist?"

"A shrink, yes. My special abilities aren't very profitable in everyday life. I suppose they might help if I were to become an international assassin, but I'm a terrible shot. And please call me Armen. Formality seems rather out of place here."

"I'm Elena. Psychiatry, eh? So did you know Matasumi? Before you came here?"

"I'd heard of him." Dark lips curved in a moue of distaste. "Parapsychology. With a reputation for skirting the code of research ethics."

"Really? Go figure. You must have no shortage of people to analyze here, between the captives and captors."

"Frighteningly enough, the ones in the cages would be more likely to earn my recommendations for early release."

"Matasumi's got some definite issues," I said. "And Bauer?"

"One of the sanest, actually. Just sad. Very sad."

That wasn't the impression I got, but before I could press for details, Armen continued. "The one I'd most like to get on the couch is Tyrone

Winsloe. Though once I had him there, I'd be sorely tempted to tie him to it and run like the devil."

"What's wrong with him?"

"Where do I start? Tyrone Winsloe is"—Armen cocked his head toward the door; footsteps entered the waiting room, then stopped—"out of town on business at the moment." He lowered his voice. "If you need any help . . . adjusting, please ask. This isn't a very pleasant place. The sooner we can be out of it, the sooner we'll all feel much better."

As he fixed me with a knowing look, I knew he wasn't offering help with my psychological adjustment.

"As I said, my special ability isn't very useful," he murmured. "But I'm very observant . . . as a psychiatrist. And like everyone, I can always use companionship. For moral support. Additional resources and strength. That, I believe, is your specialty. Strength."

The doorknob turned. Carmichael bumped it open with a clipboard and walked in, flipping through pages.

"Off you go, then, Ms. Michaels," she said. "Your escort is in the waiting room."

"A pleasure to meet you, Elena," Armen said as I left. "Do enjoy your stay."

Bauer and the guards took me back to the sitting/interrogation room. One guard fastened me to the leg and torso restraints, and removed my arm restraints, which pleased me until I realized they'd only left my hands free so I could eat lunch. Once I finished, on went the handcuffs. Then Matasumi and Tess joined us, and I endured round two of interrogation.

A couple of hours later, as Bauer walked me to my cell, I checked across the hall. The opposite cell was empty.

"Where's Ruth?" I asked.

"A slight setback. She's in the infirmary."

"Is she okay?"

"There's no immediate danger. We're probably overreacting, but our guests' health is very important."

"Can I see her when she comes back?"

"I'm afraid that won't be possible," she said, reaching for the door to my cell. "But I have arranged for company of a different sort."

"I'd like to speak to Ruth."

Pushing open my door, Bauer walked through as if I hadn't said anything. The guards prodded me forward. I stepped into my cell, then stopped. My hackles rose, and some ancient instinct warned me that my den had been invaded.

"You remember Leah, don't you?" Bauer said.

The red-haired half-demon sat at my table, pouring a glass of wine. She glanced up and smiled.

"Hey," she said. "Elena, right?"

I nodded.

"Welcome to the party," she said, raising her glass in a toast. "Can you believe this? Wine, cheese, fancy crackers. I don't eat this well at home. Are you joining us, Sondra?"

"If you don't mind."

"The more the merrier." Leah beamed a smile 100 percent sarcasm-free. "May I pour you ladies a glass?"

"Please," Bauer said.

I didn't answer, but Leah filled two more glasses. As Bauer stepped forward to take hers, I could only gape. A wine and cheese party? Please tell me they were kidding.

"Do you like white?" Bauer asked, extending a glass to me. "It's a very good vintage."

"Uh—thanks." I took the wine and managed to fold myself into a chair, a task that seemed far more onerous than it should.

"Elena's a journalist," Bauer said.

"Really? TV or radio?" Leah asked.

"Print," I murmured, though it came out as a guttural mutter, dangerously close to a grunt.

"She does freelance work," Bauer said. "Covering Canadian politics. She's Canadian."

"Oh? Interesting. You guys have a prime minister, right? Not a president."

I nodded.

Leah gave a self-deprecating laugh. "Well, there's the extent of my knowledge of international politics. Sorry."

We sipped our wine.

"Leah's a deputy sheriff in Wisconsin," Bauer said.

I nodded, struggling to think of some germane comment to make and coming up blank. Oh, please, Elena. You can do better than this. Say something. Say anything. Don't sit there like a grunting, nodding idiot. After we'd touched on my career, I should have asked Leah about hers. That was how small talk worked. My experience socializing with other women was embarrassingly slight, but certain rules held true no matter who you were talking to.

"So you're a police officer," I said, then winced inwardly. Duh. If I couldn't come up with something more intelligent than that, I should keep my mouth shut.

"Not as exciting as it sounds," Leah said. "Especially not in Wisconsin. Cheese, anyone?"

She cut wedges from a round of Gouda and proffered the cheese board. We each took one, along with a lacy cracker that crumbled most unbecomingly as I bit into it. As we munched, Bauer refilled our half-empty wineglasses. I downed mine, praying it might help, then noticed both women watching me.

"Thirstier than I thought," I said. "Maybe I should stick to water."

Bauer smiled. "Drink all you want. There's more where that came from."

"So, do you live in Canada?" Leah asked.

I hesitated, but realized if I didn't answer, Bauer would. My life wasn't exactly a secret around here. "New York State."

"Her husband's American," Bauer said. "Clayton is your husband, isn't he? We couldn't find a marriage record, but when we were following you, I noticed he wears a wedding ring." She glanced at my left hand. "Oh, but you don't. That's an engagement ring you have, though, isn't it?"

"Long story," I said.

Leah leaned forward. "Those are always the best."

I inched back in my chair. "So, how about you two? Married? Boyfriends?"

"I've run through the marriageable material in my little town," Leah said. "I've put my name in for a transfer before the seventy-year-old widowers start looking good."

"I've been married," Bauer said. "Youthful rebellion. Married him because my father forbade it and soon realized that sometimes father does know best."

"What does your husband do?" Leah asked me.

"Clayton's an anthropologist," Bauer answered before I could deflect the question.

"Oh? That sounds . . . fascinating."

Sipping her wine, Bauer gave a giggling laugh. "Admit it, Leah. It sounds perfectly awful."

"I didn't say it," Leah said.

Bauer drained her glass and refilled everyone's. "No, but you were thinking it. Trust me, this guy is no tweedy academic. You should see him. Blond curls, blue eyes, and a body . . . Greek god material."

"Got a photo?" Leah asked me.

"Uh, no. So, how do you like—"

"We have some surveillance pictures upstairs," Bauer said. "I'll show them to you later. Elena is a very lucky girl."

"Looks aren't everything," Leah said, flashing a wicked smile. "It's performance that counts."

I studied the bubbles in my wineglass. Oh, please, please, please, don't ask.

Leah downed her wine. "I have a question. If it's not too personal."

"And even if it is," Bauer said with a giggle.

Oh, please, please, please—

"You guys Change into wolves, right?" Leah said. "So, when you and your husband are wolves, do you still . . . you know. Are you still lovers?"

Bauer snorted so hard wine sprayed from her nose. Okay, that was the one question even worse than asking how Clay was in bed. This was a nightmare. My worst nightmare. Not only thrown into a wine and cheese party with two women I barely knew, but with two women who knew everything about me and were getting a wee bit tipsy. Let the floor open up and swallow me now. Please.

"This is really good cheese," I said.

Bauer laughed so hard she started to hiccup.

The door whooshed opened. A guard stuck his head inside.

"Ms. Bauer?"

In an eye-blink, Bauer was sober. She coughed once into her hand, then straightened up, face as regal as ever.

"Yes?" she said.

"We have a situation," he said. "With prisoner three."

"They're not prisoners," she snapped, getting to her feet. "What's the problem with Mr. Zaid?"

"His clothes are gone."

Leah snorted a laugh and covered her mouth with her linen napkin.

"What's he done with them?" Bauer asked.

"He—uh—hasn't done anything, ma'am. He finished his shower and they were—uh—gone. Started raising a hel—ruckus. Cursing, ranting. All that voodoo stuff. Demanded we get you. Immediately."

Annoyance flitted across Bauer's face. "Tell Mr. Zaid . . . " She stopped. Hesitated. "Fine. I'll speak to him. Step inside. I'll be right back."

CHAPTER 19

GHOSTS

B auer wasn't gone long enough for Leah and I to exchange more than a few sentences. When she returned, she brushed past the guard she'd left in the cell with us. She didn't looked pleased.

"How's Curtis?" Leah asked.

Bauer blinked, as if distracted by her own thoughts. "Fine," she said after a moment's pause. "He's fine. Just . . . unnerved by all this."

"Where were his clothes?" Leah asked.

Another blink. Another pause. "Oh, on his bookshelf." She settled into her chair and refilled her wineglass. "Neatly folded on the top shelf."

"The spirits are at work," Leah intoned, grinning mischievously.

"Don't start that," Bauer said.

"Did you move—" I began. "I mean, can you do things like that?"

Leah waved a cheese-topped cracker, scattering crumbs. "Nah. It would be fun, though. Telekinesis is limited to a half-demon's range of vision. If I can't see it, I can't move it. My powers aren't very precise either. If I tried lifting a pile of clothes—" She turned and looked at my bed. The folded blanket at the end levitated, floated over the side, and fell in a heap on the carpet. "Gravity takes over. I could throw it against the wall or toss it in the air, but when I let go, it would never fall nicely folded."

"So it's that random psychic energy thing, then?" I asked Bauer.

"They're back," Leah said in a high-pitched child's voice.

Bauer laughed, covering her cracker-filled mouth with one hand and wagging her free index finger at Leah. "Stop that." She turned to me. "That's what I meant. Leah's pet theory. She thinks we have a poltergeist."

"Poltergeist?" I repeated. "Don't tell me you built this place over an Indian burial ground. After three movies, you'd really think people would learn."

Leah laughed. "There, see? Thank you, Elena. Sondra hasn't even seen the first *Poltergeist*. All my pop culture references are lost on her."

"So you're kidding," I said. "About the poltergeist."

"Uh-uh."

"Don't get her started," Bauer said.

"You don't really believe in ghosts," I said.

"Sure," Leah said, grinning. "But I draw the line at werewolves. Seriously, though, how much do you know about poltergeists?"

"I walked out during the second movie and skipped the third. That's it."

"Well, I'm something of a self-taught expert. When I was in high school, I read everything I could find on poltergeists. Because of the similarities with my 'condition.' I wanted to know more about myself and my kind and figured maybe so-called poltergeists were really manifestations of tele-kinetic half-demons."

"Sounds plausible," I said.

"It does, until you learn more about it. Poltergeists typically appear around children approaching puberty. Half-demons don't come into their full powers until closer to adulthood. Poltergeists are also associated with noises and voices, which aren't part of my repertoire. Neither is stuff like rearranging furniture or neatly moving objects from one place to another, other marks of a poltergeist."

"We haven't heard any strange noises," Bauer said.

"But not all poltergeist manifestations involve sound. Everything else about these occurrences points to a poltergeist."

"A poltergeist who just happened to appear here?" I said. "Of all places?"

"It's *not* Savannah," Bauer said, slanting a warning look at Leah.

"The young witch?" I said.

"Just another theory," Leah said. "Savannah is at the perfect age, and with her powers, she'd be an ideal conduit, especially under these strained circumstances."

"You think she conjured up—"

"Oh, no, no," Leah said. "Savannah is a sweetheart. A total innocent, I'm sure. Now, her mother was a real piece of work, and I wouldn't have put anything past her, but I'm certain Savannah didn't inherit any of her darker powers."

"If," Bauer said. "And I repeat, *if* Savannah has caused some kind of poltergeist to materialize, which I doubt, I'm sure she isn't aware of it."

"Certainly," Leah said. "She probably can't even control it. There's been no evidence to the contrary . . . well, except for . . . "

Bauer sighed. "A few of the more alarming disturbances have revolved around Savannah. When she becomes upset, the activity increases."

"If that poor guard hadn't ducked . . . ," Leah said. "But no, I still say it's beyond Savannah's control. More likely, her anger spurs the poltergeist to react. An unwitting emotional connection, though potentially, it could be quite dangerous if someone were to cross—"

"It's random psychic energy," Bauer said firmly. "Until Doctor Matasumi or I see anything to the contrary, that's the assumption."

The door opened.

"Yes," Bauer snapped, then turned to see Matasumi's assistant hovering in the doorway. "I'm sorry, Tess. What is it?"

"It's nearly four-thirty. Doctor Matasumi thought I should remind you—"

"Oh, yes. The conference call. I'm sorry. I'll be right with you. Could you please send the guards in to escort Leah back to her room?"

"Party's over," Leah said and chugged the rest of her wine.

After dinner, the voice I'd heard the night before called again. This time I was sure I was awake. Well, reasonably sure, at least. I still held out hopes that the whole wine and cheese party had been a nightmare.

"Who's there?" I said aloud.

"It's me, dear. Ruth."

I hurried to the hole I'd punched between my cell and the next, crouched, and peered through. No one was there.

"Where are you?" I asked.

"Across the hall. It's a ranged communication spell. You can speak to me normally and I'll hear you as if I were there in the room. Thank goodness I finally got in touch with you. I've been having the devil of a time. First the sedatives. Then the blocking field. Just when I figured out a way around that, they whisked me out of here because my white blood cell count was low. What do they expect at my age?"

"Blocking field?" I repeated.

"I'll explain. Sit down and make yourself comfortable, dear."

To ensure our privacy, Ruth cast a sensing spell that could detect anyone in the corridor. Useful things, spells. Not my cup of tea, but far more practical than I would have imagined.

Our captors had taken Ruth around the same time Bauer and Xavier had trapped me, so she hadn't known I'd been kidnapped, which meant she didn't know whether Jeremy and Clay had returned to the others or even if they knew what had happened to me. When I told her I hadn't been able to contact Jeremy, she was surprised to the point of shock, not that we couldn't make contact, but that any werewolf had telepathic abilities.

We all have our stereotypes, I guess. Witches equaled mental power, were-wolves equaled physical power, and never the twain shall meet.

"What happened when you tried to contact him?" she asked.

"I can't do that," I said. "He's the one with the powers. I have to wait for him to make contact."

"Did you try?" she asked.

"I wouldn't know how."

"You should try. It's very simple. Relax and pretend— Never mind. It won't work anyway."

"Why won't it work?"

"They've put up a blocking field. Have you met their spell-caster?"

I shook my head, realized she couldn't see the motion and said, "No. I've heard of him, though. Katzen, I think they called him."

"Isaac Katzen?"

"You know him?"

"I know of him. He was with one of the Cabals, I believe. Oh dear, I hope they aren't involved. That would be the devil of a problem. Sorcerer Cabals are—" She stopped. "Sorry, dear. Spell-casting business. You don't need to know anything about that."

"What about this Katzen guy? Do I need to know anything about him? Bauer says I'm not likely to run into him. How'd she put it? He doesn't associate with 'lower races'?"

A short chuckle. "That is most definitely a sorcerer. No, dear, I shouldn't think you'd have to worry about Isaac Katzen. Sorcerers have little use for non-spell-casters. Little use for witches, too. Sorcerers aren't male witches. Completely different race. Nasty bunch, I'm sad to say. No sense of themselves as part of something greater. An absolute absence of altruism. They'd never dream of using their powers to help—" A sigh and a chuckle. "Stop digressing, Ruth. Age, you know. It's not that the mind starts to wander; it's that it's so stuffed full of information that it's forever jumping off track and zipping down tangents."

"I don't mind."

"Time, my dear. Time."

I turned toward the door. "Is someone coming?"

"Not yet. If they have Isaac Katzen 'on staff,' as you'd say, then he has almost certainly cast a spell to block telepathy, among other things."

"What other things?"

"Well, he could monitor communications, provide added security—"

"Monitor communications? You mean he could be listening to us right now?"

"No, dear. He'd need to be close by to do that, and I've already ascertained there's no one down here but our fellow captives. Do be careful, though. If he does visit the cells, he could listen without using the intercom system. For most spells, he'd need to be nearby, but he can block telepathy remotely."

"But you've figured out a way around that. Can you contact someone outside the compound?"

"I believe I can, though I haven't had a chance. I will later. I'll get in touch with Paige and tell her you're here, so she can communicate with you. She's had the proper training. Never had the need to use it, but it should go well. She'll be a very powerful spell-caster someday. She has the potential and more than enough ambition. Some difficulty accepting her boundaries right now, so it may not go as smoothly as she'd like. Be patient with her, Elena. Don't let her become frustrated."

"Why do I need to communicate with Paige at all? You can do that, right? You talk to her, I'll talk to you . . . "

"I have something else I need to do. I don't mean to be rude, my dear. I'm not abandoning you. With Paige's help, you'll get along fine without me. There's someone else who needs me more. They have another witch here. A child."

"Savannah."

"You've met her?"

"Seen her."

"Horrible, isn't it?" Ruth's voice clogged with emotion. "Just horrible. A child. How anyone could be so callous—but I can't dwell on that. I need to help her."

"You can get her out of here?"

Silence. As it dragged past ten seconds, I wondered if someone had entered the hall. Then Ruth continued, "No. Sadly, that's beyond my capabilities or I'd get you both out, along with every other poor soul in here. The best I can do is give the child the tools she'll need to survive. At her age, she has only the most rudimentary knowledge and can cast only very benign spells. I need to give her more. Accelerate her development. Not the path I'd choose under any other circumstances. It could be . . . well, it may not be the best thing, but given the choice between that and perishing . . . I'm sorry, my dear. I don't need to bother you with the details. Suffice it to say, I'll be busy with the child, though I'll contact you when I can. Now, here's what you'll need to do to help Paige communicate with you."

Ruth told me how to prepare for Paige's telepathic spells. "Be receptive" was the condensed version. Nothing terribly complicated. I might feel something like the grains of a tension headache. Instead of ignoring it, I had to relax and concentrate on clearing my mind. Paige would do the rest. Ruth would contact her tonight, let her know we were both safe, and give her some tips on how to work the spell so it would overcome the blocking field. Once I communicated with Paige, I could tell her how to contact Jeremy.

"Now," Ruth said when she'd finished. "One caution. You mustn't let Paige know about Eve's child. Savannah, I mean."

"Did she know her?" I asked.

"Savannah? No. Eve left when she was pregnant. Paige probably doesn't even remember her. She was only a child herself then. No one was close to Eve. It doesn't matter. If Paige knows there's a young witch here, she'll insist on rescuing her immediately. If she couldn't get to her and something happened . . . " Ruth inhaled sharply. "Paige would never forgive herself."

"It won't matter. When we break out, we'll take Savannah."

Ruth paused. When she spoke, there was a pain in her voice so deep I could feel it. "No, you can't concern yourself with the child. Not now. I'll give Savannah what powers I can. You must concentrate on getting yourself out."

"What about you?"

"It's of no consequence."

"No consequence? I'm not leaving—"

"You'll do what you must, Elena. You're the important one now. You've met these people. You've seen this place. That knowledge will be invaluable in helping the others fight this threat. As well, your escape will secure the aid of your Pack. If you don't get out— But you will. You'll get out, and your Pack will help the others to stop these people before they capture more of us. Then, when you return, you can worry about the child. If—when—you get her free, take her straight to Paige. That's important. After what I'm going to do for Savannah, only Paige will be able to control the damage. At least, I hope . . . " Her voice trailed off. "I can't worry about it. Not now. The important—"

She stopped and fell silent. Then, "Someone's coming, dear. I'll speak to you when I can. Be ready for Paige."

"Expect the second ghost when the clock strikes two."

Ruth chuckled. "Poor Elena. This must be quite unsettling for you. You're doing fine, dear. Just fine. Now get some sleep. Good night."

CHAPTER 20

REJECTION

B auer brought my breakfast the next morning, along with a coffee for herself. We settled at the table and, after getting the "How's breakfast? How did you sleep?" formalities out of the way, I said, "I'd really like to see Ruth. If it's possible." I kept my eyes downcast, voice as near to groveling as I could manage. It stung like hell, but I had more important things than wounded dignity to consider.

Bauer was silent a moment, then laid her hand atop mine. I fought the urge to pull away and kept my gaze down so she wouldn't see my reaction.

"It isn't possible, Elena. I'm sorry. Doctor Matasumi and Colonel Tucker think it's a security risk. I can only push things so far before they start shoving back."

"How is Ruth?" I asked. "Still depressed?"

Bauer paused, then nodded. "A bit. More adjustment problems than usual."

"Maybe if she saw me. A familiar face."

"No, Elena. Really, I can't. Please don't ask again."

I picked up a slice of apple and nibbled at it, then said, "Well, maybe she could have another visitor, then. What about Savannah? That might perk her up."

Bauer tapped her nails against her mug. "You know, that might not be such a bad idea. But, again, there's the security issue."

"Is there? I thought Savannah hadn't come into her powers yet. Now with me, there's the danger that Ruth and I could plot something together. I understand that. But what kind of spells could Savannah cast that Ruth couldn't already do herself?"

"That's a good point. I'll mention it to Lawrence. Doctor Carmichael and I are worried about Ruth. A visit from Savannah might be just what she needs. Very thoughtful of you, Elena, to think of it."

Hey, I'm a thoughtful kind of gal. No ulterior motives here. "It might be good for Savannah, too," I said. "An older witch to talk to, now that her mother's dead."

Bauer flinched at that. Good shot, Elena. Nice and low. I decided to pluck out the barb before it had time to fester. Continue my thoughtful ways . . . and keep worming into Bauer's good graces.

"I enjoyed meeting Leah yesterday," I said. "Thanks for arranging it."

"I'll do what I can, Elena. I know this isn't . . . the best of circumstances."

"Not as bad as it could be. Though I am going to miss a publication deadline if I'm not out by next week. I don't suppose there's any chance . . . "

Bauer gave a tiny smile. "Sorry, Elena. No promises."

"Worth a shot." I finished my orange juice. "So, when we were discussing careers yesterday, we forgot to ask you about yours. Do you work for the family business? Pulp and paper, right?"

"That's right. My father retired a few years back, so I head the business now."

"Wow."

A wan smile. "There's very little 'wow' about it. I'm only there because my father had the misfortune to sire only two children. My younger brother took over the company after my father retired. Actually, 'took over' is a minor exaggeration. My father handed him the company. It proved to be too much for my brother. He killed himself in ninety-eight."

"I'm sorry."

"After that, I was the heir by default, much to my father's chagrin. If he hadn't had a stroke after my brother's death, he'd probably have taken the reins back rather than hand them to a woman. Like I said, old company, old family. A daughter's place is to marry well and bring fresh blood to the board of directors. Technically, I run the company, but in reality I'm only a figurehead, a woman still reasonably young and attractive enough to trot out at major functions, show the world how progressive the Bauer family is. CEOs, VPs, they do all the work. They think I can't handle it. It doesn't matter if I'm twice as smart as my brother was. Twice as ambitious. Twice as driven. But you must know what that's like."

"Me? I don't really—"

"The only female werewolf? A bright, strong-willed young woman invading the last bastion of male exclusivity? Come on. This Pack of yours. They treat you like some kind of pet, don't they?"

"Jer— They aren't like that."

She was quiet. I glanced up from my breakfast to see her watching me with a smile of satisfaction, as if I'd said exactly what she wanted to hear.

"You get respect?" she asked.

I shrugged, hoping it would wipe the satisfaction from her smile. It didn't. Instead she inched forward in her chair. Her eyes burned with the same intensity I'd seen yesterday when she'd asked me about my life.

"You enjoy special status, don't you? The only female."

"I wouldn't say that."

She laughed. Triumph. "I've talked to that other werewolf, Elena. Patrick Lake. He knew everything about you. You speak for the Pack leader. You intercede with outside werewolves on his behalf. You can even make decisions in his stead."

"I'm just a glorified mediator," I said. "When it comes to mutts, I do more housecleaning than policy-making."

"But you are entrusted with the power to speak for the Alpha. Immense power in your world. The trusted aide of the most important werewolf and the lover of the second most important. All because you're the only female."

She smiled as if unaware she'd just insulted me. I wanted to tell her that Clay and I fell in love before I became "the only female werewolf" and that I'd *earned* any status I had with the Pack. But I wouldn't rise to the bait. I didn't need to. She only paused for breath before continuing.

"Do you know what's the worst thing about my life, Elena?"

I thought of rhyming off a list, but doubted she'd appreciate the effort.

"Boredom," she said. "I'm tied to a job no one will let me do, stuck in a life no one will let me lead. I've tried to take advantage of it, the spare time, the money. Mountain-climbing, alpine skiing, deep-sea diving. You name it. I've done it. The riskier and more expensive, the better. But do you know what? I'm not happy. I'm not fulfilled."

"Huh." A headache knotted behind my eyes.

Bauer leaned forward. "I want more."

"It must be difficult—"

"I deserve more," she said.

Before I could try another response, she stood and sailed from the cell like a prima donna after her greatest performance.

"What the hell was that about?" I muttered after she'd left.

The headache tightened. Damn it, I was a mess. Trampled spine, punctured stomach, and now a headache. I thought about Bauer. Enough of your problems, lady, let's talk about mine. I chuckled to myself, then gasped as the laugh sent splinters of pain coursing through my skull. I rubbed the back of my neck. The pain only worsened. When I lay on the bed, the light overhead scorched my eyes. Damn it. I didn't have time for a headache.

I had so much to do. Finish breakfast, shower, scrub the bloodstains off my shirt, plot how to escape this hellhole, and foil the villians' evil plans. A very busy timetable for someone confined to an underground cage.

I forced myself up from bed. The sudden movement felt like needles stabbing through my eyes. Tension headache? All things considered, I was entitled to one. Rubbing the back of my neck again, I headed for the shower.

"Elena?"

I turned and looked around. No one was there.

"Ruth?" I said, though the voice didn't sound like hers. It wasn't the way Ruth had communicated with me either. Ruth's voice had been audible. This one was more something I sensed or felt rather than heard.

"Elena? Come on!"

This time, I smiled. Though the voice was still a whisper, too faint to recognize, the exasperation was remarkably identifiable. Paige.

I closed my eyes, prepared to reply, and realized I had no idea what I was doing. It wasn't like talking to Jeremy. With Jeremy, communication took place in a dream state, where I imagined I could both see and hear him. It sounded and felt like natural conversation. This didn't. Paige's summons was the proverbial "hearing voices in your head," and auditory delusions weren't part of my normal psychopathology. How did I answer back? I tried mentally forming a response and waited.

"Come . . . ena. Answer . . . !"

Okay, she couldn't hear me and I was losing her. I concentrated harder, picturing myself saying the words. Silence returned.

"Paige?" I said, testing the words aloud. "Are you there?"

No response. I called her again, mentally this time. Still nothing. The knot in my head loosened and I began to panic. Had I lost her? What if I couldn't do this? Damn it, concentrate. What had Ruth told me? Relax. Clear your head. My head was clear . . . well, excepting the frustration zipping through my brain. Concentrate, concentrate. No good. The harder I tried, the more I feared I couldn't do it. Now I was stressed. And Paige was gone. I took a deep breath. Forget this. Go have a shower. Dress. Relax. She'd try again . . . I hoped.

Paige's second attempt came about two hours later. This time I was lying in bed, reading a boring magazine article and half asleep. It must have been the perfect telepathy environment. When I heard her call, I responded without thinking, answering in my head.

"Good," she said. " . . . there."

"I can barely hear you," I said.

"That's . . . you don't . . . experience."

Although I couldn't hear the full sentence, I could guess at the missing content. I couldn't hear her because I was new at this. The problem had nothing to do with *her* inexperience. Naturally.

" . . . Ruth?"

"She's okay."

"Good." Louder, clearer, as if the reassurance added to the signal. "How about you? Are you okay?"

"Surviving."

"Good. Hold on then."

"Hold—?"

Too late. The signal disconnected. I was alone. Again. Damn her.

Twenty minutes later. "Okay, I'm back."

Paige. Another easy contact, probably because, once again, I wasn't expecting it.

"You ready?" she asked.

"For what?"

The floor slid out from under me. I twisted to break my fall, but there was nothing there. No floor. No "me." The order to move came from my brain and went . . . nowhere. I was pitched into complete blackness, but I didn't lose consciousness. My brain went wild, issuing commands, move this, do that, look, sniff, listen, scream. Nothing. There was nothing to respond. I couldn't see, hear, speak, move, or smell. Every synapse in my brain exploded with panic. Absolute animal panic.

"Elena?"

I heard something! My mind scrambled back to sanity, clinging to that one word like a life raft. Who said that? Paige? No, not Paige. A man's voice. My heart leaped with recognition before my brain even figured it out.

"Jeremy?"

I said the word, didn't think it, but said it and heard it. Yet my lips didn't move and the voice I heard wasn't my own. It was Paige's.

I saw light. A blurred figure in front of me. Then a mental pop and everything became clear. I was sitting in a room. Jeremy stood in front of me.

"Jer?"

My words. Paige's voice. I tried standing. Nothing happened. I looked down and saw my hands resting on the arms of a chair, but they weren't my hands. The fingers were shorter, soft, bedecked with silver rings. I followed the line of my arm. Brown curls spilled over my shoulder, lying atop a dark green lily-of-the-valley–print sundress. A sundress? This was definitely not my body.

"Elena?" Jeremy crouched in front of me—or not me. He frowned. "Did this work? Are you there, sweetheart?"

"Jer?" I said again.

At the bottom of my field of vision, I saw my—the—lips move, but I felt nothing. Even my field of vision itself was skewed, the angle all wrong, like I was watching the scene through an oddly placed camera. I tried to shift upward, add some height to my position, but nothing happened. The sensation was unsettling to the point of panic. Was this what it was like to be paralyzed? My heart fluttered in my chest. I didn't feel it pounding, only perceived it in my mind, some gut-level awareness of my body's normal responses to fear, knowing that my heart should be fluttering, even if it wasn't.

"What—" I began. The voice was so alien in my ears that I had to stop. Swallowed. Mentally swallowed, I mean. If my throat moved, I wasn't aware of it. "Where am I? *Who* am I? I can't move."

Jeremy's face clouded. "Didn't she—?" He muttered something under his breath, then started again, calm. "Paige didn't explain?"

"Explain what? What the hell is going on?"

"She's transported you to her body. You can see, hear, speak, but you won't have any sort of mobility. She didn't explain—?"

"No, she dumped me into limbo and I woke up here. Showing off."

"I heard that," a distant voice in my head said. Paige.

"She's still here," I said. "There. Somewhere. Eavesdropping."

"I'm not eavesdropping," Paige said. "You have my body. Where am I supposed to go? I wasn't showing off. I knew you'd want to speak to Jeremy, so I wanted to surprise you. It should have been a smooth transition, but I guess your lack of experience—"

"*My* lack of experience?" I said.

"Ignore her," Jeremy said.

"I heard that," Paige said, quieter.

"How are you?" Jeremy asked. He laid his hand on mine. I saw it, but couldn't feel it and felt a pang of loss.

"Lonely," I said, surprising myself. I lightened my tone. "Not for lack of company, though. Seems I'm quite the popular 'guest' around this place. But it's—I'm—" I inhaled. Pull yourself together, Elena. That was the last thing Jeremy needed, to hear me on the verge of an emotional breakdown. Where had this come from?

"I'm tired," I said. "Not sleeping well, not eating well, no exercise. So I'm touchy. Cabin fever, I guess. Physically, I'm fine. They aren't torturing me, beating me, starving me. Nothing like that. I'll be okay."

"I know you will," he said softly. He pulled up a chair. "Do you feel up to talking about it?"

I told him about Bauer, Matasumi, rattled off some details on the guards and the other staff like Xavier, Tess, and Carmichael, giving him a rough picture of the situation. I explained as much as I could about the setup of the compound, then about the other captives, remembering Paige's silent presence and stopping myself before talking about Savannah.

"I'm only interested in getting you out," Jeremy said when I'd finished. "We can't worry about the others."

"I know."

"How are you holding up?"

"Fi—"

"Don't say 'fine,' Elena."

I paused. "Is Clay . . . around? Maybe I could talk to him . . . Just for a few minutes. I know we have to keep this short. No time for socializing. But I'd like—if I could . . . "

Jeremy was quiet. Inside my head, Paige muttered something. Alarm zinged through me.

"He's okay, isn't he?" I asked. "Nothing's happened—"

"Clay's fine," Jeremy said. "I know you'd like to speak to him, but it might not be . . . a good time. He's . . . sleeping."

"Sleep—?" I began.

"I am not sleeping," a voice growled from across the room. "Not voluntarily, at least."

I looked up to see Clay in the doorway, hair tousled, eyes dimmed by sedatives. He lumbered into the room like a bear awaking from hibernation.

"Clay," I said, heart tripping so fast I could barely get his name out.

He stopped and fixed me with a scowl. My next words jammed in my throat. I swallowed them and tried again.

"Causing trouble again?" I asked, forcing a smile into my voice. "What did you do to make Jeremy drug you up?"

His scowl hardened with something I'd seen in his face a million times, but never when he looked at me. Contempt. His lips twisted, and he opened his mouth to say something, then decided I wasn't worth the effort and turned his attention to Jeremy.

"Cl—" I began. My gut was solid rock. I couldn't breathe, could barely speak. "Clay?"

"Sit down, Clayton," Jeremy said. "I'm talking to—"

"I can see who you're talking to." Another twist of the lips. The briefest glare in my direction. "And I don't know why you're wasting your time."

"He thinks you're me," Paige whispered.

I knew that. Deep down, I knew that, but it didn't help. I saw the way he looked at me, and it didn't matter who Clay *thought* was there, he was looking at me. Me.

"It's not Paige," Jeremy said. "It's Elena. She's communicating through Paige."

Clay's expression didn't change. Didn't soften. Not even for a second. He turned his stare to me and I saw the disdain there, stronger now, hard and sharp.

"Is that what she told you?" he said. "I know you want attention, Paige, but this is low. Even for you."

"It's me, Clay," I said. "It's not Paige."

He sneered, and I saw everything there that I'd never wanted to see in Clay's face when he looked at me, every drop of contempt he had for humans. I'd had nightmares of this, seeing him turn that look on me. I'd woken sweating, blood pounding, absolutely terrified, the way no child-hood nightmare had ever frightened me. Now I looked at him and something snapped. The world went black.

CHAPTER 21

REBIRTH

I awoke on the floor of my cell. I didn't get up. Had I been dreaming? I wanted to believe it, then chided myself for such a silly wish. Of course, I didn't want it to have been a dream. I wanted to believe I'd talked to Jeremy, conveyed all my observations to him, set the wheels of rescue in motion. Who cared about Clay? Okay, I cared. Cared more than I wanted to most times, but I had to put this thing in perspective. Clay hadn't looked at *me* that way. At least, he hadn't intended the look for me. Obviously he wasn't getting along with Paige, and frankly, that didn't surprise me. Where humans were concerned, Clay wasn't Mr. Congeniality at the best of times, and certainly not when said human was an overconfident, outspoken witch young enough to be one of his students. I lay on the floor and told myself all this, and it didn't help a bit. I felt . . . My mind clamped shut before the last word escaped, but I pried it back open. Admit it. I had to admit it, if only to myself. I felt rejected.

So what, right? I felt rejected. Big deal. But it was a big deal. Too big a deal. The second I owned up to the emotion, it engulfed me. I was a child again, taking the hand of a new foster parent, clasping it tight and praying I'd never have to let go. I was six, seven, eight years old, faces flipping before me like pages in a photo album, names I'd forgotten but faces I'd recognize if I saw them for a split second on a passing train. I heard voices, the drone of a television, my small body held tight against the wall, barely daring to breathe for fear of being overheard, listening to them talk, waiting for "The Conversation." The Conversation. Admitting to each other that it wasn't working out, that I was "more than they bargained for." Convincing themselves they'd been tricked by the agency, fooled into taking a blond-haired, blue-eyed doll, a broken doll. They hadn't been tricked. They hadn't listened. The agencies always tried to warn them about me, about my past. When I was five, I'd seen my parents killed in a car accident. I'd sat on the country road all night, trying desperately to wake them up, crying for help in the dark. No one found me until morning, and after that, well, I wasn't quite right after that. I withdrew into my mind, emerging only to throw fits of rage. I knew that I was spoiling things for myself. Every time a new foster family took me in, I swore to myself I'd make them fall in love with me; I'd be the perfect little angel they expected. But I couldn't do it. All I could do was sit in my head, watch myself scream and rant, wait for the final rejection, and know it was my fault.

I never tell that story. I hate it. Hate, hate, hate it. I refuse to let my past explain my present. I grew up, I grew stronger, I overcame it. End of story. From the time I was old enough to realize that my problems weren't my fault, I'd decided not to shift the blame to all those foster families, but to get rid of it. Throw it out. Move on. I could imagine no fate worse than becoming someone who tells the story of her dysfunctional childhood to every stranger on the bus. If I did well in life, I wanted people to say I did well, not that I did well "all things considered." My past was a private obstacle, not a public excuse.

Clay was the only person I'd ever told about my childhood. Jeremy knew bits and pieces, the parts Clay felt necessary to impart in those early days when Jeremy had to deal with me as a newly turned werewolf. I'd met Clay at the University of Toronto, where I was an undergrad with an interest in anthropology and he was giving a short lecture series. I fell for him. Fell hard and fast, not impressed by his looks or his bad-boy attitude, but by something I can't explain, something in him I hungered for, something I needed to touch. When he favored me with his attention, I knew that was something special, that he didn't open up to people any more than I did. As we grew closer, he told me about his own screwed-up childhood, glossing over details he couldn't impart without revealing his secret. He told me about his past, so I told him about mine. As simple as that. I was in love and I trusted him. And he betrayed that trust in a way I'd never completely recovered from, as I would never recover from that endless night on the country road. I hadn't forgiven Clay. We'd moved past talk of forgiveness. It wasn't possible. And he'd never asked for it. I don't think he expected it. Over time, I'd learned to stop expecting myself to be able to give it.

Clay's motive for biting me was inexplicable. Oh, he'd tried to explain it. Many times. He'd brought me to Stonehaven to meet Jeremy, and Jeremy had been planning to split us up, and Clay had panicked and bit me. Maybe it was true. Jeremy admitted he'd intended to end Clay's relationship with me. But I don't believe that Clay's bite had been unplanned. Maybe the timing was, but I think in some deep part of his psyche, he'd always been ready to do it if the need ever arose, if I ever threatened to leave him. So what happened after he bit me? Did we make up and move on? Not on your life. I made him pay and pay and pay. Clay had made my life hell, and I returned the favor tenfold. I'd stay at Stonehaven for months, even years, then leave without a moment's notice, refusing all contact, cutting him from my life completely. I'd sought out other men for sex and, once, for something more permanent. How did Clay react to this? He waited for me. He never looked for revenge, never tried to hurt me, never threatened to find someone else. I could be gone for a year, walk back into Stonehaven, and he'd be waiting as if I'd never left. Even when I'd tried to start a new life in Toronto, I'd always known that, if I needed him, Clay would be there for me. No matter how badly I fucked up or how badly fucked up I was, he'd never leave me. Never turn his back on me. Never reject me. And now, after more than a decade of learning that lesson, all it took was one look from him, one single look, and I was curled up on the floor, doubled over in pain. All the logic and reasoning in the world didn't change how I felt. As much as I wanted to believe I'd overcome my childhood, I hadn't. I probably never would.

Lunch came and went. Bauer didn't bring it, for which I was grateful. I didn't see her again until nearly six. When she opened my cell door, I double-checked the time, figuring either dinner was early or my watch had stopped. But she didn't bring food. And when she stepped through the door, I knew no early meal was forthcoming. Something was wrong.

Bauer walked in with none of her usual assertive grace. She half-tripped over an imaginary wrinkle in the carpet. Her face was flushed, cheeks bright spots of crimson, eyes glittering unnaturally bright, as if she had a fever. Two guards followed her in. She waved them toward me, and they bound me to the chair where I'd been reading a magazine. The whole time they were tying me up, Bauer refused to meet my eyes. Not good. Really not good.

"Go," she said when they were done.

"Should we wait outside—" one began.

"I said go. Leave. Back to your posts."

Once they were gone, she began to pace. Small, quick steps. Back and forth, back and forth. Fingers tapping her side, the mannerism changed now, not tapping with thoughtful slowness but fast. Manic. A mania to her pacing. To her eyes. To everything.

"Do you know what this is?"

She whipped something from her pocket and held it up. A syringe. Quarter-filled with a clear liquid. Oh, shit. What was she going to do to me?

"Look," I said. "If I did anything to upset—"

She waved the syringe. "I asked if you knew what this was."

The syringe slipped from her hands. She scrambled to retrieve it, as if the plastic would shatter upon striking the carpet. As she fumbled, I caught a whiff of a familiar smell. Fear. She was afraid. What looked like mania was a struggle for control, as she desperately tried to disown an emotion she wasn't accustomed to feeling.

"Do you know what this is, Elena?" Her voice rose an octave. Squeaked. Was she afraid of me? Why now? What had I done?

"What is it?" I said.

"It's a saline solution mixed with your saliva."

"My what?"

"Saliva, spit, gob." Voice racing up the scale. Nervous giggle, like a little girl caught saying a bad word. "Do you know what this can do?"

"I don't—"

"What will it do if I inject it into myself?"

"Inject—?"

"Think, Elena! Come on. You're not stupid. Your saliva. You bite someone. Your teeth pierce his skin, like this needle piercing mine. Your saliva goes into his bloodstream. My bloodstream. What happens?"

"You'd turn—You could turn—"

"Into a werewolf." She stopped pacing and went still. Completely still. A small smile tugged up her lips. "That's exactly what I'm going to do."

It took a moment for this to register. When it did, I blinked and opened my mouth, but nothing came out. I swallowed, fought for calm. Don't panic. Don't make it worse. Treat it as a joke. Diffuse the situation.

"Oh, come on," I said. "Is that the answer to your problems? You don't get respect at work so you'll become a werewolf? Get a good job with the Pack, knock some heads together, find yourself a handsome lover? 'Cause if that's what you're thinking, trust me, it doesn't work that way."

"I'm not an idiot, Elena."

She spat the words at me, spittle flinging from her lips. Ooops, wrong tactic.

"What I want is change," she continued. "To reinvent myself."

"Becoming a werewolf isn't the answer," I said softly. "I know you're not happy—"

"You know nothing about me."

"Then tell—"

"I came to this project for one reason. For the chance to experience something new, something more dangerous, more exhilarating, more life-altering than scaling Mount Everest. Experiences all my money and influence can't buy. Spells, immortality, extrasensory perception, I didn't know what I wanted. Maybe a little of everything. But now I know exactly what I want, what I was looking for. Power. No more kowtowing to men, pretending I'm dumber than they are, weaker, less important. I want to be everything I have the potential to be. I want this."

My brain still skidded, unable to find traction long enough to understand what Bauer was saying. The suddenness of it all overwhelmed me, almost convinced me I must be dreaming or hallucinating. Yet how sudden was it? Unbelievably so, from my perspective, but what about from hers? How long had she been watching the parade of inmates, waiting for the one who could give her the power she craved? Now, having found what she thought she wanted, perhaps she was afraid to hesitate, afraid she'd change her mind. I had to change it for her. But how?

Bauer held up the syringe. As she stared at it, she blinked, almost blanched. Fear so thick it clogged my nostrils, unwittingly started my adrenaline pumping. When she looked back at me, the anger was gone. What I saw in those eyes stopped me cold. Pleading. Fear and pleading.

"I want you to understand, Elena. Help me. Don't make me use this thing."

"You don't have to use it," I said quietly. "No one's going to make you."

"Do it for me then. Please."

"Do—?"

"Bite my arm."

"I can't—"

"I have a knife. I'll cut the skin. You can just—"

Panic settled in my chest. "No, I can't."

"Help me do it right, Elena. I don't know how well the saline solution will work. I could only guess at the amount, the proportion. I need you—"

"No."

"I'm *asking* you—"

I strained against my bonds, locking eyes with her. "Listen to me, Sondra. Give me a minute and let me explain what'll happen to you if you use that. It isn't the way you think it is. You don't want to do this."

Her eyes glittered then. All mania gone. Ice-cold. "I don't?"

She lifted the syringe.

"No!" I shouted, bucking in my chair.

She buried the needle into her arm, shoved the plunger down. And it was done. One second. One split second. As much time as it had taken Clay to bite me.

"Goddamn you!" I yelled. "You stupid bitch— Call the infirmary. Now!"

Her face was preternaturally calm, lips curving in something like bliss. Blissful relief at having done it. "Why, Elena? Why should I call the infirmary? So they can reverse it? Suck the gift from my veins like snake venom? Oh, no. We'll have none of that."

"Call the infirmary! Guards! Where the hell are the guards?"

"You heard me send them away."

"You don't know what you've done," I snarled. "You think this is some great gift. One prick of the needle and you're a werewolf? You did your research, didn't you? You know what happens now, right?"

Bauer turned her dreamy smile on me. "I can feel it coursing through my blood. The Change. It's warm. Tingling. The beginnings of metamorphosis."

"Oh, that's not all you're going to feel."

She closed her eyes, shuddered, reopened them, and smiled. "Seems I've gained something tonight and you've lost something. You're no longer the only female werewolf, Elena."

Her eyes widened then. Bulged. Veins in her neck and forehead popped up. She gasped, choked. Hands going to her throat. Body jerking upright. Spine snapping rigid. Eyes rolling. Rising to her toes, pitching forward and back, like a convict on the end of a hangman's noose. Then she collapsed, pooling to the floor. I screamed for help.

Chapter 22

WINSLOE

"What did you do to Ms. Bauer?" Matasumi asked.

Guards had collected Bauer soon after I started shouting. Twenty minutes later, they'd returned with Matasumi. He now stood there accusing me without a trace of accusation in his voice.

"I told the guards." I sat on the edge of my bed, trying to relax, as if this sort of thing happened every day. "She injected herself with my saliva."

"And why would she do that?" Matasumi asked.

"The bite of a werewolf is one way of becoming a werewolf."

"I realize that. But why—" He stopped. "Oh, I see."

Did he? Did he *really* see? I doubted it. None of them could understand what was coming. I could, and I was trying very, very hard not to think about it.

Matasumi cleared his throat. "You claim Ms. Bauer injected herself—"

"The syringe is on the floor."

His eyes flickered to the needle, but he made no move to pick it up. "You claim she used this syringe—"

"I don't *claim* anything. I'm telling you what happened. She injected herself in the arm. Look for the needle mark. Test the contents of the syringe."

The door opened. Carmichael hurried inside, lab coat billowing behind her.

"We don't have time for this," she said. "I need to know what to do for her."

Matasumi waved Carmichael aside. "First, we must establish the exact nature of Ms. Bauer's ailment. It's all very well for Ms. Michaels to claim—"

"She's telling the truth," Carmichael said. "I saw the needle mark."

It would have been hard to miss. Even as the guards had carried Bauer from the cell, I'd seen the injection point, swollen to the size of a Ping-Pong ball. A memory of my own bite leaped to mind, but I shoved it back.

Cold, clinical observation. That was the only way I could deal with this. Take notes from Matasumi.

Carmichael turned to me. "I need to know how to deal with this. Sondra's unconscious. Her pressure's dropping. Her temperature's sky-rocketing. Her pupils won't react to stimuli. Her pulse is racing and becoming erratic."

"There's nothing I can do."

"You've been through this, Elena. You lived through it."

I said nothing. Carmichael advanced on me. I eased back on the bed, but she only came closer, pushing her face into mine until I could smell her frustration. I turned my head. She grabbed my chin and wrenched my face back to hers. "She's dying, Elena. Dying horribly."

"It'll only get worse."

Her fingers tightened, digging into my jaw muscles. "You are going to help her. If it were you up there, I wouldn't stand by and watch you die. Tell me how to help her."

"You want to help her? Put a bullet through her head. Skip the silver variety. Regular lead will do."

Carmichael flung my chin aside and stepped back to stare at me. "My God, you are cold."

I said nothing.

"This isn't helping," Matasumi said. "Treat the symptoms as you see them, Doctor Carmichael. That's the best we can do. If Ms. Bauer inflicted this misfortune on herself, then all we can do is treat the symptoms and leave the rest to fate."

"That's not the best we can do," Carmichael said, her eyes boring into mine.

I didn't want to defend myself. I really didn't. But the weight of that glare was too much.

"What exactly do you think I can do?" I asked. "I don't run around biting humans and nursing them back to health. Do you know how many newly bitten werewolves I've met? None. Zero. It doesn't happen. I've never even been around a hereditary werewolf who's come of age. I don't know what to do."

"You've been through it."

"You think I took notes? Do you know what I remember? I remember Hell. Complete with fire and brimstone, demons and imps, red-hot pinch-ers and bottomless pits of lava. I remember what I saw up here." I smacked my palm against my forehead. "I remember what I imagined, what I dreamed. Nightmares, delirium, that's all there was. I don't know shit about temperatures and blood pressure and pupil response. Someone else dealt with that. And when it was all over, I didn't want to know what he did. All I wanted was to forget."

"These visions of Hell," Matasumi said. "Perhaps you could describe them for me later. The connection between the supernatural and Satanic ritual—"

"For God's sake, leave it alone," Carmichael said. "For once. Leave it alone."

She strode from the room. Matasumi bent for the syringe, then stopped, motioned for a guard to pick it up, and followed Carmichael.

Would I have helped Bauer if I could? I don't know. Why should I? She kidnapped me and threw me in a cage. Did I owe her anything? Hell, no. If the woman was stupid enough to turn herself into a werewolf, that wasn't my problem. Did I do or say anything to make her embrace such unbelievable folly? Did I regale her with stories of the wonderful, fun-filled life of a werewolf? Anything but. Did I seek revenge by encouraging her to plunge that needle into her arm? Absolutely not. Yes, she was my enemy, but she'd brought this on herself. So why did I feel responsible? I wasn't. Yet part of me wished I could help, at least alleviate her suffering. Why? Because I understood that suffering. This was another woman who'd become a werewolf, and as different as our circumstances were, I didn't want her to suffer. The outcome would almost certainly be death. I hoped it came quickly.

At midnight, Winsloe walked into my cell. Through the shadows of an impending nightmare, I heard the door open, subconsciously realized the sound came from the real world, and forced myself awake, grateful for the diversion. I rolled out of bed to see Tyrone Winsloe standing in my cell doorway, framed by the hallway light, presenting himself, waiting for my acknowledgement. A disconcerting surge of awe ran through me. It was like having Bill Gates show up on my doorstep—no matter how much I wanted to be *not* impressed, I couldn't help myself.

"So this is the female werewolf." He stepped inside, flanked by two guards. "A pleasure to make your acquaintance," he said with a mock bow. "I'm Ty Winsloe."

He introduced himself, not with modesty, as if I might not recognize him, but with a smarmy self-importance, an introduction as phony as the bow. When I didn't respond fast enough, a tremor of annoyance unsettled his features.

"Promethean Fire," he said, prompting me with the name of his world-famous company.

"Yes, I know."

His face rearranged itself back into a gratified smirk. Motioning the guards to stay put, he stepped farther into the cell. His gaze inched over me, walking around, giving my backside a slow once-over, scrutinizing me without embarrassment, as if I were a potential slave in a Roman market-place. When he circled back to my front, his gaze paused at my chest, lips curving downward in a disappointed frown.

"Not bad," he said. "Nothing a couple of implants couldn't fix."

I narrowed my eyes. He didn't seem to notice.

"Ever thought of that?" he asked, gaze settling on my chest.

"I don't plan to have kids, but if I ever do, I'm sure they'll find this set quite adequate."

He threw back his head and laughed as if this were the funniest thing he'd ever heard. Then he leaned around me and swept his gaze over my rear again.

"Great ass, though."

I sat down. He only smiled and continued studying my lower half. Then he tossed a bundle of clothes on the table.

"You can leave the jeans on," he said. "I brought a skirt, but I like the jeans. That ass was made for jeans. I don't like big, flabby asses."

He liked women with little butts and big tits? Someone had played with one too many Barbie dolls as a kid. I glanced at the pile of clothes but made no move to take it.

"The shirt has to go," he said. "There's a halter top there. Skip the bra."

I stared at him, unable to believe what I was hearing. This was a joke, right? Billionaires were supposed to be eccentric, so this must be Winsloe's warped idea of a practical joke. Yet as I stared, his lips compressed, not in a smile but in pique.

"Take the clothes, Elena," he said, all joviality draining from his voice.

Behind him, the two guards stepped forward, fingering their guns as if to remind me of their presence. Okay, maybe it wasn't a joke. What was with the people in this place? Within several hours I'd seen an intelligent woman turn herself into a werewolf and met a billionaire with the matu-rity and mind-set of an adolescent boy. Compared to this bunch, I was downright normal.

Still, I reminded myself, Tyrone Winsloe was in charge here, and he was a man accustomed to getting what he wanted when he wanted it. But if he thought I was changing into a halter top so he could leer at my substandard breasts—well, a girl's gotta set limits, right? I'd been treated this way by mutts, though I knew how to handle them. If they talked like that, I told them off. If they touched me, I broke their fingers. They wouldn't want it any other way. As Logan always said, mutts liked their women with balls. Ty Winsloe wasn't a mutt, but he was a guy with his hormones in overdrive. Close enough.

"My arms are still burned," I said, turning away from the clothing. "They look like shit."

"I don't mind."

"I do."

One long moment of silence.

"I asked you to put on the top, Elena," he said. He looked down at me, lips twisted in a humorless, teeth-baring grin that any wolf would have recognized.

I glanced from him to the guards, snatched the halter top from the pile, killed the urge to return Winsloe's warning snarl, and settled for stalking into the bathroom.

Going into the bathroom to change was a waste of time, considering the see-through wall, but I could still turn my back to him as I switched shirts. The halter top would have fit a prepubescent girl—a short prepubescent girl. It rode up to my rib cage and cut furrows in my shoulders. Looking down, I saw that it left absolutely nothing to the imagination. First, it was skintight. Second, it was white. Twin dark circles pressed against the fabric. If I caught even the slightest breeze, that wasn't all that would be pressing against it. A wave of humiliated fury flooded me. After everything that had happened in the last twelve hours, this was the pinnacle. The proverbial straw. I would not take this. I would—I stopped. I would do *what*? I remembered the look in Winsloe's eyes when I'd challenged his command to change. I remembered Armen Haig's comments on Winsloe's mental state. What would Winsloe do if I refused? Was I willing to take that risk over something as ultimately trivial as not wanting to wear a revealing shirt? I rubbed my hands over my face, resisted the urge to cross protective arms over my chest, and marched back into the cell.

Winsloe studied my chest for two whole minutes. I know because I counted the seconds, struggling not to spend the time fantasizing about retaliation. This was nothing, I told myself. Nothing. But it was. Somehow, being forced to parade my tits in front of this man was worse than any torture Matasumi could have devised with his box of toys. I realized then that this juvenile farce had nothing to do with getting me into a tank top. It was about power. Winsloe could make me put on this tank top and there wasn't a damn thing I could do about it. He wanted to make sure I knew it.

"At least they're firm," Winsloe said. "Not bad, really, if you like them small. I think implants are still our best bet, though."

I bit my lip. Bit it hard enough to taste blood and wish it was his.

"Amazing tone," he said, circling me. "Lean and tight, but no bulk. I was worried about bulk. Muscles on a girl are downright creepy."

"Oh, I have muscles," I said. "Wanna see them?"

He only laughed. "That hole in the wall tells me all I need to know. Plus I saw the video of you and Lake, though I guess that wasn't so much strength as cunning. Quick wits. Very quick."

"How's Ba— Ms. Bauer?" I asked, hoping to change the subject.

"You know about that?" He wriggled his butt onto my dining table and perched there. "I guess you would. Bizarre, huh? No one saw it coming. Sondra's always been so together. Uptight, even. Guess it's the rigid ones that snap the hardest, huh? About that video—"

"How is she?" I repeated. "What's the prognosis?"

"Shitty, last I heard. Probably won't make it through the night. Now, speaking of that video, I have some news you'll like." He smiled, his partner's impending death already forgotten. "Wanna guess what it is?"

"I couldn't begin to imagine."

"Tonight I'm sending your fellow combatant to his final reward. The great doggie bone in the sky—or the other direction. We're gonna have ourselves a hunt."

"A . . . hunt?"

He jumped off the table. "A hunt. A big ol' wolfie hunt. Tonight. Larry's done with your 'mutt' and we're gonna give him a proper send-off." Winsloe snapped his fingers at the two guards, whose presence at this debacle I'd been trying hard to ignore. "Chop-chop, boys. Get on the horn and tell your buddies to prepare the guest of honor. We'll meet them at the lookout."

I'd spent most of the last half hour gaping at Winsloe. Now my disbelief was mingled with something else. Dawning horror. Did he mean what I thought he meant? He was going to hunt Patrick Lake? Release him and hunt him down like the prize quarry at some big-game reserve? No, I must be mistaken. I had to be mistaken.

"Well?" he said, turning to me. "Grab that jacket from the table. It's getting cold out there. Wouldn't want you to catch pneumonia."

"I'm going outside?" I said slowly.

Winsloe laughed. "We sure as hell can't hunt him in here."

He threw back his head, barking a laugh, slapped me on the rear, and waltzed from the cell.

CHAPTER 23

GAME

The night was cold for late summer. It was still August, wasn't it? I calculated back. Yes, still August. It only seemed like I'd been gone longer.

If I'd hoped to pick up any clues to our location by going outside, I was disappointed. We took an elevator two flights up to ground level, exited through a secured door, and emerged a dozen feet from a forest that could have existed anywhere from Cape Breton to northern California. Maybe if I'd known my regional fauna better, I could have narrowed the possibilities, but examining trees was the furthest thing from my mind.

My wrists were manacled. Winsloe walked in front of me. The two guards, guns now drawn, followed behind. A path wove through thick forest to a clearing where a lookout stand towered a hundred feet in the air. Patrick Lake stood at the base of a wooden pillar, stamping his feet against the cold, both hands cupped around a lit cigarette.

"Hey," he said as we neared. "What's going on? It's fucking cold out here."

"Finish your smoke," Winsloe said. "You'll be plenty warm soon enough."

"I asked—"

One of Lake's guards jabbed him with a rifle butt.

Lake snarled, lifted a hand to swat the guard, then stopped himself. "I was only asking—"

"It's a surprise," Winsloe said, grabbing the ladder railing. "Finish your smoke."

"What's she doing here?" Lake waved his cigarette at me.

Winsloe was five steps up. He leaned over the railing.

"It's a surprise," he repeated. "We'll start as soon as you're ready."

Lake pitched his cigarette to the ground and stomped it. "I'm ready now."

"Then we begin."

"Release point two?" a guard asked.

"As planned," Winsloe said. "Everything as planned."

Winsloe continued his ascent. I followed, with our two guards close behind. By the time we reached the top, Winsloe was puffing. I surveyed the forest below. Lake and his guard duo had disappeared into the darkness.

"Over there," Winsloe panted, waving to the east. "Release point two. Release point one just below. Release point three by the river."

Not only was there a predesignated release point, but there was more than one. Why? I opened my mouth to ask, then realized I might not want to know.

"The choice of release point depends on the quarry," Winsloe continued. "So far I've done a witch and a half-demon."

"You—hunted them?"

He made a face. "Not much of a hunt. Especially the witch. You'd think she'd have been more of a challenge, casting spells and all that. In RPGs the magical races can be your strongest players once they gain enough experience. But in real life? She fell apart. Couldn't take it. Cast a few penny-ante spells and quit. Found her curled up under a bush. No survival instinct. Like that old lady they picked up with you. First sign of trouble and she sinks into depression. Can't take the pressure."

I eyed the ground below. Wondered if it was hard enough to kill Winsloe if he took a tumble.

"The half-demon was a minor improvement. At least he tried. Then there was the shaman. I didn't hunt him, though. That was an escape. We fixed the problem soon enough, so don't let that give you any ideas. He didn't get far anyway. Dogs took care of him. From what I hear, he was even worse than the witch. Ran full-out until he collapsed."

"So now—" I cleared my throat, forced calm. "So now you're going to hunt Lake."

"A werewolf." Winsloe lowered his binoculars to grin at me. "Cool, huh? The hunter becomes the hunted. That's the trick, the challenge. All that 'Most Dangerous Game' bullshit is just fantasy crap. Put your average modern guy in the woods and he freaks. Take away his tools and his weapons and you might as well go deer-hunting. At least deer have some experience eluding hunters. Humans have nada. But wolves? They *are* the hunters. They have their own tools, their own weapons. They know the forest. Combine that with human intelligence and bingo: You've got yourself the ultimate big game." He held out the binoculars. "Want to have a look?"

I shook my head.

"Go on. They're night vision. Not that you'd need them, I guess. I hear you guys can see in the dark. That's why I'm doing this at night. Added challenge. Of course, I have all the latest toys, like these. Wouldn't want it to be *too* much of a challenge."

I lifted the binoculars to my eyes. Looking out, all I saw was forest. Endless forest. Then a flash of orange light.

"The flare," Winsloe said, voice rising with excitement. "They've stunned Lake. Now they'll take off. In ten, maybe fifteen minutes he'll wake up all alone in the woods. If he has half a brain, he'll realize it's a trick, but he'll run anyway. My guess is he'll smell the river and run west. Better be careful, though. If he takes the easy route, he'll find himself in a bear pit." Winsloe laughed, the sound taking on a grating edge. "Traps everywhere. Here, here, over here."

I turned to see him pointing at places on a laminated map. When I stepped closer, he whisked it out of sight and waggled a finger at me.

"Uh-uh. Can't have you learn all my secrets. You like those binoculars?"

"They . . . work well."

"Of course they do. I wouldn't buy them otherwise. Wait until you see the rest of my gadgets. And the weapons." He rolled his eyes in near lust. "The weapons. Unbelievable what they come up with these days. I have lockers of them scattered all over the playing field, so I'll have variety. Only thing missing is a nail gun. That's the pisser. The nail gun's always my favorite."

"You hunt with a nail gun?"

"Not out here. In games, of course. The nail gun is the absolute best. The shredding factor can top grenades."

"Games," I repeated. "You mean video games."

"What other kind is there?"

I looked out at the forest beyond. The playing field, he'd called it. A giant, custom-designed playing field stocked with high-tech gadgets, booby traps, and an arsenal of weapons.

"That's what this is," I said slowly. "A video game. A real-life video game."

"One step up from virtual reality. Actual reality. What a concept." He grinned and slapped me on the rear again. "Let's move. The game is afoot."

We met Lake's two guards before we reached the main path. They confirmed that the release had gone smoothly, then they took up positions in front of Winsloe, guns drawn, flanking him for protection. I walked behind Winsloe. The other two guards followed, side by side, at my rear. Everyone except me wore night-vision goggles. Even I could have used a pair. The darkness was nearly complete, a weak crescent moon darting between clouds and treetops, no stars in sight. My vision faded in and out with the moon. Not that there was much to see. Nothing but trees, trees, and more trees.

Despite the ball of dread nestled in my gut, my heart began tripping with anticipation as we moved deeper into the woods. Even while my brain knew what I was doing here, my body refused to believe it. It took in the stimuli—the crisp night air, the scent of rotting leaves and damp earth, the sounds of voles and mice scampering from our path—and formed its own interpretation, based on years of experience. I was walking through the woods at night, ergo I must be going for a run. Ignoring all commands to the contrary, my body reacted like an excited puppy straining at its leash. My skin prickled. My blood drummed. My breathing quickened. On the plus side, my senses sharpened, letting me hear and smell twice as well. On the minus side, there was that niggling worry about contorting body parts and unsightly hair growth.

Before quashing my body's reaction, I used my heightened awareness to get a better sense of my surroundings. Sight-wise, it didn't help much. No matter how well I could see, I didn't have X-ray vision, so I couldn't see through the damned trees. My other senses were more helpful. A few minutes of listening convinced me there was nothing to hear. Well, there was plenty to hear—creaking branches, whispering breezes, predators and prey hooting, squealing, bolting, and diving—but that wasn't what I wanted. I hoped for some distant sounds of civilization, and the only ones I detected were the chugs and wheezes of the machinery that kept the compound running. I switched to smell, my best sense. Again, I searched for human life and found only the stink of the main building and the gravel road that led to it. The odor of the road was faint, indicating it ran south of the compound. Unfortunately, the forest was to the north, which was the direction I'd run if I escaped the compound. While there might be an easy way out to the south, it was safer to stick with what I knew, and right now all I'd seen was this forest.

Beyond the compound, the wilderness gave off only its own scents. Nature reigned here. Even the path bore mere traces of human scent, as if nature fiercely wiped it clean the moment human trespassers were gone. Again, my brain and body vied for interpretation. My body thought it was in heaven, a natural paradise as pristine as that at Stonehaven and— even better—a fresh paradise ripe for exploration. My brain decided it was in hell, an endless forest with no civilization in sight. If I escaped, I had to go somewhere. Somewhere meant a house, a town, a public place where my pursuers might fear to follow.

Escaping now was out of the question. Even if I made it past the armed guards, I'd only become an added attraction on Ty Winsloe's hunt. I'd have to wait, but I still hoped to break out of the compound at some point, preferably before my captors got bored with me as they had with Patrick Lake. If I—no, *when* I—escaped, where would I go? There was nothing out here but forest. Endless forest. I could run and run for hours and— Wait a second. What the hell was I saying? I was a wolf. Half-wolf, at least. Gee, what's a wolf going to do in the wilderness? Duh. Survive, of course. Here I could escape my pursuers better than I could in any concrete jungle. This was my element. Even now, in human form, I was at home here, able to see in the near-dark, able to smell water and food, able to hear the quietest owl swoop overhead. I didn't need the safety net of civilization. Well, eventually, I would need to find a way back to the others, but I could outlast any human that tried to recapture me—night-vision goggles, high-powered telescopes, and all. I'd need to be careful, but the only danger I'd face would come from my pursuers. I certainly didn't need to worry about dying of starvation, dehydration, or exposure.

"Where's his clothing?" Winsloe snapped.

I skidded to a halt before I ran into Winsloe's broad back. Surfacing from my reverie, I blinked and looked around. We stood beside a tree bedecked with strips of fluorescent orange plastic.

"This is release point two," Winsloe said.

"Yes, sir," said one of the front guards, pulling a map from his pocket and holding it out.

Winsloe smacked the map to the ground. "I wasn't *asking*. I was *telling*. I know this is release point two. I want to know if you morons know it. Is this where you released Lake?"

The guard's jaw tightened, but his voice remained deferential. "Of course, sir."

Winsloe spun on me. "He has to undress to Change into a wolf, doesn't he? Either that or he'd rip his clothes, right?"

I nodded.

"So either way, there should be clothes here. Where are they?"

I made a show of looking around, though I could tell with a single sniff that Lake hadn't left anything behind. "If they're not here, then he hasn't Changed forms."

Winsloe wheeled to one of the rear guards. "Pendecki. Checkpoints."

The guard to my left rear wore a black bandolier covered in gadgets, with looping wires connecting them to a battery pack. He calmly pulled one from its holster and flicked a switch. The device blipped, red LED lights blinking, like one of those early handheld video games.

"The target has passed checkpoints five and twelve, sir."

"We have visual at five," Winsloe said.

"Yes, sir. Checkpoint five has a motion-sensor camera and—"

"I'm not *asking*! I'm telling!" Winsloe said. "Show me the fucking tape!"

Still unruffled, Pendecki unclipped another gadget, unfastened its connecting wire, and held it out to Winsloe, who snatched it with a curse. Pendecki's expression didn't change. Either he was accustomed to dealing with Winsloe or he'd worked with men like him before. The other three guards weren't nearly so cool under pressure. One of the fore-guards had begun to sweat. The other kicked his toes against the earth as if trying to stay warm. Pendecki's partner stood motionless, tensed for trouble.

Winsloe held a small back-and-white screen. Out of the corner of my eye, I watched as he pounded tiny buttons. A tape rewound and played, showing a few seconds of infrared video. An arm and leg appeared on screen, then vanished. Winsloe hit buttons and watched it again.

"He's not a wolf," he said, lifting his head. "Can someone tell me why he isn't a wolf?"

Of course, no one could. Except me. I waited until all eyes turned my way, then said, "A lot of non-Pack werewolves can't Change on demand." Even as the words left my mouth, I regretted them. They led to a painfully obvious next question.

"Non-Pack," Winsloe said. "So Lake can't shape-shift when he wants. But you can."

"It depends on—"

"Of course you can," Winsloe said. "I saw the tape."

I realized then why I was here. I'd assumed Winsloe had invited me along to impress me with his game, one hunter showing off to another. Maybe that was part of it. But there was a deeper reason why he'd told me about his gadgets and traps and weapons but hadn't let me near his map. He was warning me. If I screwed up, if I displeased him, this would be my fate. Matasumi might not be done with me, but Winsloe wouldn't care. He was young and rich and powerful. Delayed gratification wasn't in his vocabulary. Right now, he wanted a hunt. If Lake couldn't provide it, I could.

I felt my lips move, heard words come out. I tried to persuade myself that what I said next was born of my will to survive. But it didn't feel that way. It felt like cowardice. No, worse than cowardice. It felt like treason.

"He'll Change if he's frightened."

Winsloe smiled, all teeth. "Then let's frighten him."

Chapter 24

Failure

"Checkpoint eight four minutes ago," Pendecki said. Winsloe glanced over his shoulder at me, boyish excitement back in his eyes. "Just so you know, I don't use checkpoint tracking when I hunt. Not terribly sporting, old chap. The camera setup wasn't even my idea. Tucker insisted on it. You know Tucker? Head guard?"

I nodded, teeth chattering. I told myself it wasn't that cold, but I couldn't stop shivering.

"Old-style military. So rigid you couldn't shove a dog tag up his ass. After the shaman got loose, he figured we needed these trip-wire cameras. Later, when we got Lake, I decided the cameras might come in handy for my hunts. Like I said, not to use them for tracking, but to make sure he stays within the perimeter of the playing field. We have miles to go until we reach the edge of the property, but I figure werewolves are the one monster that might be able to run that far."

"What if he does get that far? Will you let him go?"

"Oh, sure. A hundred yards beyond the perimeter is home free. That's my rule. Of course with these cameras, we pretty much ensure he'll never make it that far."

"Checkpoint twelve, sir. Sorry to interrupt, but we're close enough that there's no delay on the signal."

"He just passed it?"

"Affirmative."

Winsloe grinned. "Pick up the pace, then."

As a group, we jogged along the path.

"Checkpoint twelve again, sir."

"Circling," Winsloe crowed. "Perfect. Good doggie. Wait right there."

"We're coming up to twelve—"

Winsloe raised his hand for us to stop. His head bobbed in the darkness. Then he pointed to the northeast, where I could smell Lake about seventy feet away. Undergrowth crackled. Winsloe's grin broadened. He reached into his jacket. With his other hand, he waved a complex series of motions. The guards nodded. The front two lifted their rifles. The rear two silently laid theirs on the ground and pulled pistols from beneath their coats. Winsloe withdrew a grenade from his jacket. He turned to me with a grin and a wink, as if he hadn't been contemplating my death only minutes before.

Winsloe pulled the pin from the grenade and pitched it through the air. The moment he released it, the rear guards took off, each circling in opposite directions around the grenade's path. The front guards pointed their rifles farther afield. As the grenade detonated, the guards fired. The forest exploded with firepower.

"Run, fucker, run," Winsloe chortled. He grinned back at me. "Think that'll scare him?"

"If it didn't kill him."

Winsloe waved aside my pessimism, then paused and grinned. "Hear that? He's on the move. Fall out, boys. We have a runner."

Chaos ensued. At least to me it was chaos. Six humans running half-blind through thick forest after a panicking werewolf was not my idea of graceful pursuit. The more we ran, the more racket we raised, the more we spooked Lake, the more he ran. A vicious circle that ended only when Winsloe stopped, panting and leaning against a tree for support.

"Gotta give him a chance to Change forms," Winsloe wheezed.

"Good idea, sir," Pendecki said, darkness hiding the sarcastic glint in his eyes from all but me.

Winsloe bent double at the waist, gasping for breath. "Is the air thinner up here?"

"Could be, sir."

Had we run up a hill? Hmmm, can't say I noticed it.

"So, he'll Change forms now?" Winsloe asked me.

"He should," I said.

If he's not worn out, I thought. With any luck, after the initial run and this chase, Lake would be too exhausted to Change. Why did I hope this? Because I didn't want Winsloe to get his hunt. I wanted this game to be as disappointing as the others. If Lake didn't give Winsloe the adrenaline rush he wanted, Winsloe would abandon werewolves as his theoretical "ultimate" prey and look elsewhere, as he had after hunting a witch and a half-demon. If Lake fulfilled Winsloe's expectations, he'd soon be scouring the cells for another victim and, seeing as how I was the only remaining werewolf, it wasn't hard to guess where his attention would fall. He might like to tart me up and concoct a few jerk-off fantasies, but I suspect Ty Winsloe got off on his hunting conquests more than he did with the sexual variety.

A moan shivered through the trees. Winsloe stopped panting and lifted his head. Another moan, deep, drawn out. The hairs on my arms pricked.

"Wind?" Winsloe mouthed.

Pendecki shook his head.

Winsloe grinned and motioned us toward the noise. We crept through the forest until one fore-guard lifted his hand and pointed. Through the brush, something pale flickered. I inhaled, then choked on a sudden gasp. The stink of fear and panic flooded the clearing, the scent so strong I wondered if Lake had lost control of his bowels.

Winsloe hunkered down and inched forward.

"No," I hissed, grabbing the back of Winsloe's jacket. "He's Changing."

Winsloe only grinned. "I know."

"You don't want to see that."

The grin broadened. "Oh yes, I do."

One of the nameless guards butted his rifle against my arm, knocking my hand from Winsloe's jacket. I turned to glare at him, but he was already past me, overtaking Winsloe. I crouched and waited for him to stop Winsloe. Instead, the guard circled past him and tugged a sheaf of greenery from Lake's hiding spot.

"Jesus Christ!" the guard yelled, leaping to his feet. "What the fuck—!"

As he'd jumped up, he'd torn the fern from its roots, exposing the clearing. A blur of pale flesh flashed from within, then a shriek that set my teeth on edge. Lake rolled to the ground, legs up, protecting his underbelly. For a moment, he moved too fast for anyone to see more than skin. Then he lay still and everyone saw more. Much more.

A hairless, lipless muzzle protruded from the middle of Lake's face, his still-human nose grotesquely stuck on top, nostrils flared wide. His eyes were on the sides of his head where his human ears should have been. His ears had grown, bat-like now, stopped midway on their ascent to the top of his skull. Sparse fur webbed his fingers and toes. A naked stump of tail batted the ground between his legs. The slice I'd cut in his leg pulsated bright pink where his stretching skin had ripped the scabs free. His back was hunched and twisted, swallowing his neck and pulling his head into his chest.

"What the fuck happened to him?" the guard shouted, still falling back, hand going to his gun.

Fury filled me. This was not something anyone should see, the absolute most private part of a werewolf's life. This was a werewolf at his most vulnerable, naked and hideous, a true monster, but one stripped of even the most basic means of self-protection. Mutt or not, at that moment, Lake was closer to me than these gaping, stinking humans.

"He's Changing," I snarled. "What the hell did you think it looked like?"

"Not like that," Winsloe said, staring like a kid at a carnival freak show. "Holy shit. Can you believe that? That is the most disgusting—"

Lake's lipless muzzle contorted in a bellow of pain. The guard poked his rifle into the clearing and prodded Lake.

"Stop that!" I shouted, turning on the guard. "Back off and let him finish."

Lake writhed on his back, clubbed hands crossed to protect his vital organs. The guard pushed his gun forward again. Pendecki lunged and grabbed the barrel.

"She's right," Pendecki said. "If you want your hunt, sir, I'd suggest we do as she says. Back off and let him finish . . . whatever he's doing."

Winsloe sighed. "I suppose so. But some time I've gotta see this."

"Wait a few days," I said. "You can watch Sondra Bauer go through it."

"If she lives." He sighed, not at the prospect of his colleague's death, but at the thought that her imminent death might ruin his chance to see a werewolf Change. "Okay. Stop teasing the brute, Bryce. About-face, boys. Fall back."

Pendecki and the two other guards backed out of the clearing. Bryce ignored the command, but Winsloe didn't notice, his attention engrossed in the spectacle before us. As Lake lay still curled in the fetal position, his flesh began to writhe, as if snakes were trapped under his skin. Hair sprouted like reverse dominos, leaping up in a straight line from his wrist to his shoulder.

"Jesus!" Winsloe said.

The hair retracted and Lake convulsed, moaning.

"Get back," I hissed. "He can't—"

Winsloe waved me into silence and inched forward. Lake's head spun wildly, trying to watch Winsloe from both skewed eyes at once. His back arched and twin rows of muscles sprang from his neck, thickening it to twice its width. The tendons pulsated, grew, shrank, grew, shrank. The Change stopped there, only the neck muscles moving from human to wolf and back again.

"What's wrong?" Winsloe asked, not taking his eyes from Lake.

Lake was stuck between forms. I didn't say that to Winsloe. I didn't dare open my mouth for fear that, if I moved at all, it would be to grab

Winsloe by the shoulders and fling him into the bushes beyond, which would earn me a certain bullet from the guards. As I watched Lake, I prayed the seizure would end. Let him become a wolf or a human. Something. Anything. He was doomed, but to die like this? My guts went cold at the thought. Every werewolf's subconscious nightmare was to become stuck between forms, caught in this monstrous, misshapen body, unable to change either way. The ultimate horror.

Lake rolled from side to side, panting and sweating and making ghastly mewling sounds. Muscles jerked and spasmed at random. Only his neck changed forms, tendons growing and shrinking. He gave one huge, gagging convulsion and flipped onto his other side. Looking straight at me. I turned away.

"Shoot him," I said quietly.

"What the fuck?" Winsloe scrambled up to glare at me. "Who's giving the orders around here? You don't tell me what to do. Not ever."

"He's caught," I said. "He can't finish and he can't Change back."

"We'll wait."

"It won't—"

"I said, we'll wait."

"Then move back." I forced myself to add, "Please. Give him some privacy."

Winsloe grunted and shot me another lethal glare, but waved the others back, though the other three guards were already ten feet from the thicket. Bryce couldn't resist one last prod. As he pushed his rifle forward, Lake's hands flew to his sides.

"Watch—!" I began.

With an inhuman shriek, Lake pushed off on his arms and flung himself at Bryce. The guard fired. Lake squealed and tumbled backward, hit the ground, and skittered into the undergrowth, trailing blood in a slug's path behind him.

"What the hell are you doing?" Winsloe bellowed. "You shot him!"

"He attacked—"

"Get back!" Winsloe shouted, spittle flying. "All of you. Get back. Now!"

The undergrowth rustled. Everyone jumped. Bryce and another guard lifted their weapons.

"Guns down!" Winsloe said. "Put the fucking guns down!"

We all froze and listened to the silence. Lake's smell was everywhere. I swiveled my head, homing in on it.

"Okay," Winsloe said, inhaling deeply. "Well, that was a royal fuckup.

Now, here's what we're going to do, and if I hear one more goddamn gunshot, it better be from me. Is that—"

The bushes exploded. Bryce raised his rifle.

"Don't you fucking dare!" Winsloe screamed.

Lake's misshapen body sailed through the air. Two shots rang out. I dropped. The ground shuddered once, then twice. A moan. A very human moan. I lifted my head to see Bryce beside me on the grass, his head to the side, eyes locked with mine. His mouth opened. Bloody foam bubbled out. He coughed once. Then he went still. I tore my gaze from his dead eyes and looked around. Lake lay on my other side, a bloody hole in his forehead.

I struggled to my feet, trying to figure out how Lake could have killed Bryce so quickly. As I stood, I saw the bullet hole in Bryce's chest. Behind him, Winsloe flung his pistol to the ground.

"Can you believe it?" he shouted. "Can you fucking believe it? I ordered him not to fire. A direct order. He killed my werewolf. He fucking shot my werewolf."

Only Pendecki moved, but his limbs wouldn't coordinate. He dropped awkwardly, knelt beside Bryce's corpse, fingers trembling as he felt for a pulse.

"Dumb fuck!" Winsloe shouted to the sky. He clenched his fists at his sides, face purple with rage. Stepping forward, he kicked Bryce's body. "I ordered him not to fire. Did anyone hear me order him not to fire?"

"Y—yes, sir," Pendecki said.

Winsloe spun on me. My heart stopped.

"Get her out of here," he said. "Take her back to her fucking cage. Go. All of you. Get out of my fucking sight before I—" He strode to where his pistol lay in the grass.

We were out of his sight before he turned around.

CHAPTER 25

ПURSE

I was next.

When the guards returned me to my cell, I sat on the edge of my bed and didn't move for three hours. Winsloe's hunt had been a bigger disaster than I could have dreamed. That was what I'd wanted, right? In the forest it had seemed so clear to me. If the hunt failed, I'd be safe. But I wasn't safe. I was next.

I'd reasoned that if Winsloe didn't get what he wanted from Lake, he'd move on. I'd been wrong. Tonight hadn't been a minor disappointment for Winsloe. It had been failure. Abject failure. How would he react to that? Get pissed off, stomp his feet, murder a guard, and move on to a new source of amusement? Sure. That was just the kind of reaction to failure that would have helped Winsloe build one of the biggest corporations in the computer industry. No, this "setback" wouldn't stop Winsloe. To people like Tyrone Winsloe failure wasn't an obstacle simply to be overcome, but to be blown into the stratosphere, destroyed so thoroughly that it wouldn't leave even as much as a scorch mark on his pride. Having failed—and failed before an audience of inferiors—he'd step back, analyze the situation, home in on the source of his defeat, fix it, and start over. When he'd determined what had gone wrong and ensured it wouldn't happen again, he would come for me. I couldn't wait around to be rescued. I had to act.

Now, this made perfect sense, this talk of action. But I'd hardly spent the last three days lounging around my cell ignoring perfectly good avenues of escape. If I knew how to get out, I'd damned well have done it. My one and only plan had been to ingratiate myself with Bauer. Great plan, really, barring the small matter of her turning herself into a were-wolf and dying. Okay, she wasn't dead yet, but even if she recovered, she'd be in no shape to help me. Or would she? I hadn't lied to Carmichael when I'd said I couldn't help Bauer. But Jeremy could. If I could communicate with him, maybe I could save Bauer's life, and if I saved her life, maybe she'd feel indebted enough to help me. Way too many ifs and maybes in that plan, but it was all I had.

I formulated my course of action with a logical detachment that half-impressed and half-scared me. Sitting on the bed, watching the digital clock flip past minutes, then hours, I felt nothing. Absolutely nothing. I remembered Clay's rejection and felt nothing. I remembered Bauer plunging the syringe into her arm and felt nothing. I remembered Lake caught in his Change, the guard lying dead beside me, Winsloe's frustrated rage. Still I felt nothing. Two-thirty, three, three-thirty. The passage of time engrossed every particle of my attention. At four o'clock I came up with my plan. At four-thirty I looked at the clock and realized a half hour had passed. Where had it gone? What had I done? It didn't matter. Nothing mattered, really. Jeremy and Paige would be sleeping. I shouldn't bother them. Five o'clock. Maybe I should try contacting Paige. Be ready with Jeremy's advice when the guards brought my breakfast. Still, it took effort. So much effort. Much easier to watch the clock and wait. All the time in the world. Five-thirty. Perhaps Jeremy would be up by now. I wouldn't want to wake him. It wasn't really that important. I could try, though. It might take a while to get hold of Paige. No sense delaying. Six o'clock. Six—? Where—? Never mind. Give it a try.

I tried. Nothing happened. Of course nothing happened. What made me think it would? I wasn't the one with the telepathic abilities. Yet this thought never occurred to me. I mentally called for Paige, and when she didn't answer, I thought, "Huh, that's strange," and kept trying. Okay, so my brain wasn't working on all cylinders. In the last eighteen hours I'd been rejected by my lover, watched my only hope for freedom turn herself into a werewolf, and discovered that the leading investor in this project was a psycho with a fetish for athletic women and monster-hunting. I was entitled to blow a few mental circuits.

Eventually I accepted that I couldn't contact Paige. So I waited for her to contact me. And I waited. And waited. Breakfast came. I ignored it. Breakfast went.

At nine-thirty, Paige tried to contact me. Or I think she did. It started with a headache, like the day before. On the first twinge of tension, I'd leaped into bed, stretched out, closed my eyes, and waited. Nothing happened. The headache decreased, vanished, then returned a half hour later. I was still in bed, afraid even to change position for fear I'd screw up Paige's transmission. Again, nothing happened. I relaxed. I imagined opening myself up, imagined talking to Paige, imagined every possible bit of conducive imagery I could. Not so much as the barest whisper rewarded my efforts.

What if Paige couldn't contact me? What if she wasn't strong enough, if the last time had been a fluke? What if *I'd* screwed things up when I'd inadvertently severed the connection? What if, even now, some deep part of my psyche resisted contact, terrified of further rejection? What if the damage was permanent? What if I was on my own . . . for good?

No, that wasn't possible. Paige would be back. She'd find a way, and I'd talk to Jeremy and everything would be fine. This was temporary. Maybe she hadn't even been trying to contact me. Maybe I just had a headache, completely understandable given the circumstances.

Paige would be back, but I wouldn't sit around waiting. Action was the only true cure for panic. I had a plan. Yes, it would be easier if I had Jeremy's advice, but I could start on my own. All I needed to do was remember my own transformation by reaching into the deepest, most carefully suppressed crevices of my psyche and dredging up memories of Hell. No problem.

Two hours later, drenched in sweat, I tore free of my memories. For the next twenty minutes, I sat on the edge of my bed, collecting myself. Then I went and had a shower. I was ready.

At lunch I told the guards I wanted to see Carmichael. They didn't respond. They never spoke to me more than necessary. A half hour later, as I'd begun to suspect they'd ignored my request, they returned with Matasumi. That complicated my plan. While Matasumi seemed to want to help Bauer, he was not inclined to do so at the cost of letting me out of my cage. If he had his way, I don't think captives would set foot outside their cells from the moment they were captured until someone came to dispose of the carcass.

Eventually I persuaded Matasumi to take me upstairs, provided I was manacled, in leg irons, and accompanied by a cadre of guards to prevent me from getting within ten feet of Matasumi. At the infirmary, Matasumi left to find Carmichael. Three guards escorted me inside while the others blocked the exit through the waiting room.

Bauer lay on the first bed. Beside her, Tess read a paperback mystery and worried a cuticle. When Tess saw me, she jerked up in alarm, then noticed the guards and settled for scooting her chair back six inches before she resumed reading.

Lying on the hospital bed, Bauer looked even more regal and composed than she had in life. Her dark blond hair fanned out across a pristine white pillow. The fine lines around her eyes and mouth had vanished, smoothed into the face of someone half her age. Her eyes were closed, lashes lying against flawless white skin. Her full lips curved in the faintest of smiles. Absolutely still, composed, and ethereally beautiful. In short, she looked dead.

Only the graceful rise and fall of her chest told me I wasn't too late, that they hadn't laid Bauer out for a viewing. Still, the urge to compliment the mortuary cosmetician was almost overwhelming. Almost. I kept my comments to myself. Somehow I doubted my audience would appreciate them.

"Peaceful, isn't she," Carmichael's voice said from behind me.

"She's not restrained," I said as Carmichael walked around the bed and waved Tess out.

"The sides of the bed are high enough to prevent accidents."

"Not the type I'm thinking of. She needs arm and leg restraints. The best you can find."

"She's sleeping soundly. I'm not—"

"Restrain her or I leave."

Carmichael stopped checking Bauer's pulse and looked up sharply. "Don't threaten me, Elena. You've admitted to Doctor Matasumi that you can help Sondra, and you will, with no conditions. At the first sign of a violent reaction, I'll restrain her."

"You won't be able to."

"Then the guards will do it. I want her to be comfortable. If that's all I can do, that's good enough."

"Noble sentiments. Ever wonder how comfortable we are in the cell block? Or don't we count? Not being human and all, I suppose we aren't covered under the Hippocratic oath."

"Don't start that." Carmichael resumed her survey of Bauer's vital signs.

"You have your reasons for doing this, right? Good, moral reasons. Like everyone else here. Can I guess yours? Let's see . . . discover unimaginable medical breakthroughs that will benefit all of humankind. Am I close?"

Carmichael's mouth tightened, but she kept her eyes on Bauer.

"Wow," I said. "Good guess. So you justify imprisoning, torturing, and killing innocent beings in the hopes of creating a human super-race? Where'd you get your license, Doctor? Auschwitz?"

Her hand clenched around her stethoscope, and I thought she was going to hurl it at me. Instead, she gripped it until her knuckles whitened, then she inhaled and looked past me to the guards.

"Please return Ms. Michaels to her—" She stopped and swiveled her gaze to mine. "No, that's what you want, isn't it? To be sent back to your cell, relieved of your obligations. Well, I won't do it. You're going to tell me how to treat her."

Bauer's body went stiff. One tremor shuddered through her. Then her arms flew out, ramrod straight. Her back arched against the bed, and she started to convulse.

"Grab her legs," Carmichael shouted.

"Restrain her."

Both Bauer's legs flew up, one knee knocking Carmichael in the chest as she leaned over to hold her down. Carmichael flew back, air whooshing from her lungs, but she rebounded in a second and threw herself over Bauer's torso. The guards jogged across the room and fanned out around the bed. One grabbed Bauer's ankles. Her legs convulsed, and he lost his grip, sailing backward and toppling a cart to the floor. The other two guards looked at each other. One reached for his gun.

"No!" Carmichael said. "It's only a seizure. Elena, grab her legs!"

I stepped away from the table. "Restrain her."

Bauer's upper body shot up, hurling Carmichael to the floor. Bauer sat straight up, then her arms flew up, windmilling in a perfect circle. When they passed her head, they didn't veer from their course to allow for the normal range of motion. Instead they went straight back. There was a dull double snap as her shoulders dislocated.

Carmichael grabbed the slender straps that hung from the bedsides. I was about to say that Bauer needed to be restrained with something ten times stronger, but I knew I'd already gone too far, turning this into a battle of wills that the doctor wouldn't forfeit. The guard who had grabbed Bauer's legs earlier took a tentative step forward.

"Get back!" I snarled.

I walked toward the end of the bed, ignoring Carmichael's frantic efforts to attach the bed restraints, paying attention only to the movements of Bauer's legs. As I passed the spilled cart, I picked up two rolls of bandages. I counted the seconds between convulsions, waited for the next one to subside, then grasped both of Bauer's ankles in one hand.

"Take this," I said, throwing one bandage roll at the nearest guard. "Tie one end to her ankle, the other to the bed. Don't make it tight. She'll break her own legs. Move fast. You have twenty seconds left."

As I talked, I tied Bauer's left leg to the bedpost, leaving enough room for her to move without hurting herself. Carmichael picked up another bandage roll from the floor and reached for Bauer's arms, ducking as one flailed awkwardly.

"Count off—" I began.

"I know," Carmichael snapped.

We managed to get Bauer's arms, legs, and torso loosely tied to the bed, so she could convulse without hurting herself. Sweat poured from her in musky, stinking rivulets. Piss and diarrhea added their own stench to the bouquet. Bauer gagged, spewing greenish, foul-smelling bile down her nightgown. Then she started to seize again, torso arching up in an impossibly perfect half-circle off the bed. She howled, closed eyes bulging against the lids. Carmichael ran across the room to a tray of syringes.

"Tranquilizers?" I asked. "You can't do that."

Carmichael filled a syringe. "She's in pain."

"Her body has to work through this. Tranquilizers will only make it harder the next time."

"So what do you expect me to do?"

"Nothing," I said, collapsing into a chair. "Sit back, relax, observe. Maybe take notes. I'm sure Doctor Matasumi wouldn't want you to ignore such a unique educational opportunity."

Bauer's seizures ended an hour later. By then her body was so exhausted she didn't even flinch when Carmichael fixed her dislocated shoulders. Around dinnertime we had another mini-crisis when Bauer's temperature soared. Again, I warned Carmichael against any but the most benign first-aid procedures. Cool compresses, water squeezed between parched lips, and plenty of patience. As much as possible, Bauer's body had to be left alone to work through the transformation. Once her temperature dropped, Bauer slept, which was the best and most humane medicine of all.

When nothing else happened by ten o'clock, Carmichael let the guards return me to my cell. I showered, put my clothes back on, and left the bathroom to find I wasn't alone.

"Get off my bed," I said.

"Long day?" Xavier asked.

I hurled my towel at him, but he only teleported to the head of the bed.

"Touchy, touchy. I was hoping for a more hospitable greeting. Aren't you bored with talking to humans yet?"

"The last time we spoke, you tossed me—handcuffed—into a room with a very pissed-off mutt."

"I didn't toss you in. You were already there."

I growled and grabbed a book from the shelf. Xavier vanished. I waited for the shimmer that presaged his reappearance, then launched the book.

"Shit," he grunted as the book hit his chest. "You learn fast. And you carry a grudge. I don't know why. It wasn't like you couldn't handle Lake. I was right there. If something had gone wrong, I could have stopped him."

"I'm sure you would have, too."

"Of course I would. I was under strict orders not to let anything happen to you."

I grabbed another book.

Xavier held up his arms to ward it off. "Hey, come on. Play nice. I came down here to talk to you."

"About what?"

"Whatever. I'm bored."

I resisted the urge to pitch the book and shoved it back on the shelf. "Well, you can always turn yourself into a werewolf. That seems to be the common cure for ennui around here."

He settled farther back on the bed. "No kidding. Can you believe that? Sondra, of all people. Not that I can't imagine a human wanting to be something else, but she must have a few screws loose to do it like that. It's bound to happen, though. All the exposure. Inferiority complexes are inevitable."

"Inferiority complexes?"

"Sure." He caught my expression and rolled his eyes. "Oh, please. Don't tell me you're one of those who thinks humans and supernaturals are equal. We have all the advantages of being human plus more. That makes us superior. So now you get these humans who, after a lifetime of thinking they're at the top of the evolutionary ladder, realize they aren't. Worse yet, they discover they *could* be something better. They can't become half-demons, of course. But when humans see what the other races can do, they'll want it. That's the rotten core of this whole plan. No matter how high-minded their motives, they'll all eventually want a piece. The other day—"

He stopped, glanced at the one-way glass as if checking for eavesdroppers, then vanished for a second and reappeared. "The other day, I walked into Larry's office, and you know what he was doing? Practicing a spell. Now, he says he was conducting scientific research, but you know that's a pile of horseshit. Sondra is only the beginning."

"So what are you going to do about it?"

"Do?" His eyes widened. "If the human race is intent on destroying itself, that's its problem. So long as they pay me big bucks to help, I'm a happy guy."

"Nice attitude."

"Honest attitude. So tell me—"

The door clicked and he stopped. When it whooshed open, two guards walked in, led by an older uniformed man with a grizzled crew cut and piercing blue eyes.

"Reese," he growled at Xavier. "What are you doing here?"

"Just keeping our inmates happy. The female ones at least. Elena, this is Tucker. He prefers Colonel Tucker, but his military discharge was a bit iffy. Borderline court-martial and all that."

"Reese—" Tucker started, then stopped, pulled himself upright, and turned to me. "You're wanted upstairs, miss. Doctor Carmichael asked for you."

"Is Ms. Bauer okay?" I asked.

"Doctor Carmichael asked us to bring you up."

"Never expect a direct answer from ex-military," Xavier said. He hopped from the bed. "I'll take you upstairs."

"We don't need your help, Reese," Tucker said, but Xavier had already hustled me out the door.

As I passed Ruth's cell, I noticed it was empty.

"Is Ruth okay?" I asked.

"No one told you?" Xavier said. "I heard you made a suggestion to Sondra before she flipped out."

"Suggestion? Oh, right. For Ruth to visit with Savannah. They let her?"

"Better yet. Come take a look."

Xavier headed down the row of cells.

CHAPTER 26

CRISES

"Doctor Carmichael wants her upstairs now," Tucker said.

Xavier kept walking, so I followed. I glanced in each cell as we passed. Armen Haig sat at his table reading a *National Geographic*. Leah napped in bed. The Vodoun priest's cell was empty. Had Matasumi "removed" him from the program? I shivered at the thought, yet another reminder of what happened when captives outlived their usefulness.

When we came to Savannah's cell, Xavier reached for the door handle.

"Don't you dare," Tucker hissed, striding toward us.

"Relax, old man. You'll give yourself a heart attack."

"I'm in better shape than you'll ever be, boy. You're not taking this . . . young lady into that cell."

"Why? Afraid of what'll happen? Four supernatural beings in one place. Imagine the incredible concentration of psychic energy," Xavier said in a passable imitation of Matasumi.

Xavier pushed open the door. Savannah and Ruth sat at the table, heads bent together as Ruth drew imaginary lines on the tabletop. As the door opened, they jerked apart.

"Oh, it's just you," Savannah said as Xavier stepped inside. "What's the matter? Can't zap through walls anymore? That'd be a shame, losing your one and only power."

"Isn't she a sweetheart?" Xavier said, looking back at me as Ruth shushed Savannah.

Ignoring the older woman, Savannah stood and craned her neck to see behind Xavier.

"Who's with you?" she asked.

"A guest," Xavier said. "But if you're not going to be nice—"

Savannah dodged past him and looked up at me. She smiled. "You're the new one, the werewolf."

"Her name's Elena, dear," Ruth said. "It's not polite—"

"A werewolf. Now that's a *real* power," Savannah said, shooting a look at Xavier.

"Come in, Elena," Ruth said. When I did, she embraced me. "How are you, dear?"

"Surviving."

"I heard the most awful thing about that poor Miss Bauer—"

"So what happens when you Change into a wolf?" Savannah asked. "Does it hurt? Is it gross? I saw this movie once, about werewolves, and the muzzle came right through this guy's mouth and ripped his head—"

"Savannah!" Ruth said.

"It's okay," I said, smiling. "But we don't have much time. They're taking me upstairs." I glanced at Ruth. "Is everything going well?"

Ruth looked at Savannah. A beam of pride penetrated her exasperation.

"Very well," Ruth said.

"Tucker's getting restless," Xavier said. "We should go."

"Bring her back some time," Savannah said, returning to her seat. "I'm out of Mars bars, too."

"And remind me what should compel me to do you these favors?" Xavier said. "Your boundless charm?"

Savannah gave a mock sigh, eyes twinkling with a cunning that was half-child, half-woman. "Fine. Get me some candy bars and I'll play Monopoly with you. Since you get so bo-o-o-red."

"I don't think that's such a good idea, dear," Ruth whispered.

"It's okay," Savannah said. "He's a really shi—crappy player. We can both beat him."

There was still something I needed to say to Ruth, but I had no idea how to do it without Xavier overhearing. I didn't dare ask to speak to Ruth in private. Even if I could, where would we find privacy in a glass cube?

"You're having trouble contacting Paige," Ruth said.

I jumped and glanced over at Xavier. He was still bantering with Savannah.

"He can't hear me," Ruth said. "Don't answer aloud, though. The spell only works for me. Just nod."

I nodded.

Ruth sighed. "I was afraid of that. I spoke to her yesterday, but when I tried this morning, I couldn't contact either you or her. Perhaps it's because I'm concentrating too much of my energy on the child. I had no idea how powerful Savannah would be. Her mother had great potential, but she never lived up to it. Too undisciplined. Too inclined toward . . .

darker things. With the proper training, this one could be—" She stopped. "But that's witch business. I won't bore you with it. Just please make sure you get her to Paige. After what I'm doing, Savannah must not be left on her own. As for renewing contact, try to relax, dear. It will come. If my energy returns, I'll communicate with Paige myself and get a message to you."

"—poker?" Savannah was asking me.

"Hmmm?" I said.

"Do you play poker?" she said. "Xavier says he won't play because we need a fourth person, but I think he's just scared he'll get beat by a girl."

"Good night, Savannah," Xavier said, ushering me out of the cell.

"Not the dark Mars bars," Savannah called after him. "They give me zits."

Xavier chuckled and pulled the door shut. Tucker still stood in the hall, arms crossed.

"So?" Xavier asked him. "See any unidentified flying objects? Did the walls come crumbling down?"

Tucker only glared. Xavier grinned and led me toward the exit.

"You don't believe that psychic energy explanation?" I asked as we walked. "What do you think it is? A poltergeist?"

"Pol—?" he started, then his lip curled. "Leah."

"She seems to think—"

"I know what she thinks." Xavier opened the security door. "Her poltergeist theory."

"There you are!" a voice called.

I looked to see Carmichael bearing down on us.

"You," she said to Xavier. "I should have guessed. I asked for Elena over twenty minutes ago."

"If it was an emergency, you'd have come yourself," Xavier said.

"It's an emergency now." She waved him off. "Go make yourself useful for once. Maybe you can help—"

Xavier vanished. Carmichael sighed and shook her head, then grabbed my elbow and propelled me to the elevator. As we headed down the corridor to the infirmary, I caught a few snatches of conversation from behind a closed door. Soundproofing muffled the voices nearly to the point of obscurity, even for me. One sounded like Matasumi. The other was unfamiliar, male with undertones of a lilting accent.

"Vampires?" the unfamiliar voice said. "Who gave him permission to capture a vampire?"

"No one needs to give him permission," Matasumi said, his voice a near-whisper, though nobody except a werewolf could possibly hear through the soundproofed walls. "With Sondra incapacitated, he's start-ing to throw his weight around. He wants you to tell us where we can find a vampire."

"He" had to be Winsloe. And the second man? Bauer said the sorcerer was helping them find potential captives. Was this the elusive Isaac Katzen? I slowed to listen as we passed the door.

"You're wasting your time with this, Lawrence," the man said. "You know you are. You have to put your foot down. Tell him no. I gave him two werewolves. That's enough. We have to stick with the higher races. Werewolves and vampires are common brutes, driven entirely by physical needs. They have no higher purpose. No higher use."

"That's not entirely true," Matasumi said. "Though I agree that we should concentrate on the spell-casters, the werewolves are providing invaluable insights into the nature of physical and sensory power. A vam-pire might be useful for—"

"Goddamn it! I don't believe this! You're as bad as Sondra! Seduced by . . . "

His voice trailed off as Carmichael propelled me down the hall. I pre-tended to stumble, giving myself time to hear more, but the voices hushed until I couldn't stall any longer and followed Carmichael into the infirmary.

There was no emergency. The spot where Bauer had injected herself was gushing a thick, stinking, blood-streaked pus and had swollen to the size of a golf ball, which threatened to cut off circulation to her lower arm. Okay, maybe that would normally seem like a cause for alarm, but in the metamorphosis from human to werewolf it was only one of several dozen potentially life-threatening hurdles. Again, I advised Carmichael against fancy medical cures. The transformation had to run its course. Simple, almost primitive medicine was the only solution. In this case, that meant draining the wound, applying compresses to reduce the swelling, and watch-ing for temperature spikes. During it all, Bauer stayed asleep. She hadn't once regained full consciousness since collapsing in my cell. Nature had taken over, shutting the brain down to divert all resources to the body during this crucial period.

Once the crisis passed, Carmichael decided I should move permanently into the infirmary. Hey, I wasn't arguing. Anything to be out of my cell and one level closer to freedom. Naturally, Matasumi wasn't fond of the idea. He argued with Carmichael and, as usual, lost. I was given a cot in the infirmary and round-the-clock guards, one in the room and two outside the door. Then I made a demand of my own. I wanted my manacles removed. If Bauer regained consciousness, I needed to be able to defend myself. The three of us argued over this, but Matasumi and Carmichael finally relented, agreeing to remove my handcuffs in return for posting a second guard inside the room.

Still convinced I'd hear from Paige, I mentally compiled a list of questions to ask Jeremy. There were so many things I couldn't recall from my own transformation. I remembered him explaining that he couldn't give me anything for the pain, constantly reiterating the "nature must run its course" line, but on one occasion he'd administered sedatives. Why? I couldn't remember, but it meant there must be exceptions to the "no drugs" rule. So what were they? How bad did things have to get before *not* drugging Bauer would be more dangerous than drugging her? What about the restraints? How tight was too tight? How loose was too loose? Madness added strength, but did that make Bauer stronger than an experienced, physically fit werewolf like myself? And what about the saliva transfer? A bite injected a limited amount of saliva. Bauer had overdosed. Was that a problem? Would the fact that she'd injected the saliva instead of receiving it through a bite cause problems? I was sure Jeremy would know. All I needed to do was talk to him.

It didn't happen. I lay awake as long as I could, but after thirty-six stress-filled, sleepless hours, I couldn't fend off slumber for long. Paige never contacted me.

The next day began with back-to-back medical crises. First, more seizures. Then, before Bauer recovered from that, she stopped breathing. Her throat swelled and the muscles thickened as she started to Change from human to wolf. Her underlying anatomy wasn't ready yet for the transformation, so while her neck altered, the inside of her throat—windpipe, esophagus, whatever—remained human. Don't ask me for specifics. I'm no doctor. Even Carmichael seemed baffled. The point was that Bauer stopped breathing. If we spent time wondering why, she would have suffocated. I tilted her head back, straightening her windpipe, and massaged her neck, pressuring it back into human form. That worked, but too slowly. Carmichael began worrying about oxygen deprivation, and I had to agree. So she performed an emergency tracheotomy. Lots of fun. Once Bauer was breathing, we could relax. For a while.

Being in the infirmary had more advantages than I'd imagined. Not only was I closer to freedom, but after the first day people treated me much the same way they did Tess. I became not an inmate, but Carmichael's assistant, unimportant enough in the overall hierarchy that my presence was ignored. In other words, people talked around me as though I were part of the furnishings. Matasumi talked to Carmichael, the guards talked to one another, Tess talked to the cute janitor. Everyone talked. And I listened. Amazing what I could pick up, not only tips about the compound and its organizational structure, but petty things like which guards had a reputation for slacking off. Fascinating stuff.

Later that day, I even got to see Armen Haig again and the Vodoun priest, Curtis Zaid, who was still very much alive. I didn't have much luck with Zaid. If, as Bauer had implied, Leah had befriended the Vodoun priest, she had even better social skills than I thought. When I tried talking to Zaid, he blocked even such pleasantries as "good morning" with baleful glares and silence. Definitely not a potential ally. Armen, on the other hand, was a very promising prospect. He not only wanted to escape—and wanted help—but he'd been doing his homework. He knew the security system, the guards' rotations, and the compound layout. Better yet, he managed to convey this information to me right in front of Carmichael, working it into such banal conversation that she never even noticed. Observant, canny, and extremely bright. My kind of guy . . . for an escape partner, that is.

CHAPTER 27

Exit

The next crisis was another bout of seizures. After we'd subdued Bauer, I couldn't sit still. I prowled the infirmary, touching this, playing with that, until my knee banged a steel cart and Carmichael finally looked up from her paperwork.

"Would you sit down?" she snapped. "Before you break something."

I walked to the chair, looked at it, then paced to Bauer's IV.

"Don't—" Carmichael began.

"What's in there?"

"It's a general solution, mostly water with—" Carmichael stopped, seeing that I'd already moved on, my attention now caught by the beeping heart-rate monitor. "Is it close to your time to Change?"

I considered it. I'd last Changed early Monday morning, five days ago. Like most werewolves, my cycle ran weekly. That meant, although I could Change as often as I liked, I needed to Change at least once a week, or risk having my body force a Change. Already I could feel the restlessness coursing through me. Soon my muscles would start to twinge and ache. For now, though, I could control it. I had a few days left. If I had to Change in this place, they'd probably put me in a secure cell with a full audience and a videographer. I'd endure a whole lotta aches and pains before I let that happen.

"No, not yet," I said. "I'm just restless. I'm not used to being in such a confined space."

Carmichael capped her pen. "I could probably arrange for you to take a walk through the compound. Under sufficient guard. I should have recommended some exercise in your program."

"Exercise?" said a voice from the door. "Don't be talking like that in my compound."

"Hello, Tyrone," Carmichael said without turning to face him. "Did you need something?"

Winsloe sauntered into the room and grinned at me. "Just what

502

you've got there. Thought I'd keep Elena company for a while, let you do your work."

"That's very . . . considerate of you, Tyrone, but I'm afraid you'll have to wait if you need to speak to Ms. Michaels. I was about to call for some additional guards to take her for a walk. She's restless."

"Restless? Is she ready to Change?"

"No, she is not." Carmichael thumped her clipboard onto the counter and headed for the intercom.

"It should be soon. Maybe she needs—"

"She doesn't."

Carmichael hit the intercom button. Winsloe walked behind her and clicked it off.

"You said she needs exercise?" Winsloe said. "What about the weight room? Get some extra guards and I'll escort her myself."

Carmichael paused, looked from Winsloe to me, then said, "I don't think that's such a wise idea. A walk—"

"Won't be enough," Winsloe said, grinning his little-boy grin. "Will it, Elena?"

I considered it. While I'd rather walk and explore the compound, I also had to ingratiate myself with Winsloe, to give him a reason to keep me alive. "A weight room would be better."

Carmichael's eyes met mine, conveying the message that I didn't have to go with Winsloe if I didn't want to. When I glanced away, she said, "Fine," and punched the intercom button.

We left my two in-room guards at the infirmary, gathered the two at the door, and added three more, meaning I was guarded by more than double the firepower and muscle they'd left with Bauer. Skewed priorities, but nobody asked my opinion, and I'd only waste my breath offering it. I was surprised Carmichael didn't send all the guards with me and cover Bauer by herself.

The weight room wasn't any larger or better equipped than the one at Stonehaven. It was little more than fifteen feet square with a multi-use weight machine, free weights, a punching bag, a treadmill, a ski machine, and a StairMaster. We didn't have any cardio equipment at Stonehaven. No matter how bad the weather, we'd rather be jogging outside than running on an indoor hamster wheel. As for the StairMaster—well, buns of steel weren't high on any werewolf's priority list, and from the looks of the dust on this machine, the guards didn't think much of it either.

Three guards were working out when we arrived. Winsloe ordered them to leave. One did. Two stuck around for the show. A girl lifting weights. Wow. What a novelty. Obviously they hadn't been to a public gym in a very long time.

I didn't pump iron for long. Every time I sat down, Winsloe was there, checking my weight load, asking how much I could manage, generally annoying the hell out of me. Since dropping a fifty-pound barbell on his foot didn't seem a wise idea, I abandoned the weights. I tried the treadmill but couldn't figure out the programming. Winsloe offered to help and only succeeded in jamming the computer. Obviously his technical know-how didn't extend beyond PCs. It didn't matter. I didn't want to jog anyway. What I really wanted to do was hit something—hard. The perfect outlet for that was in the far corner. The punching bag.

As I strapped on hand guards, the onlookers edged closer. Maybe they hoped I was going to pummel Winsloe. I strode to the punching bag and gave it an experimental whack. A collective inhalation went up from the crowd. Oooh, she's going to fight. Wow. If only it was another girl standing there instead of a punching bag. But you can't have everything, can you?

I knocked the bag a few times, getting the feel of it, reminding myself of the stance, the motions. A few slow jabs. Then faster. Slowing. A right hook. Winsloe sidestepped close enough so I could see him in my field of vision, and if I scrunched up my eyes just right, I could shift his image in front of the punching bag. Bam-bam-bam. Three lightning-fast punches. Out of the corner of my eye, I saw him staring, lips parted, eyes glowing. Guess it was as good for him as it was for me. All the better. I danced back. Pause. Inhale. Ready. I slammed my fist into the bag, once, twice, three times, until I lost count.

Thirty minutes later, sweat plastered my hair to my head. It dripped from my chin, it stung my eyes, the smell of it wafted up stronger than anything the best deodorant could disguise. If Winsloe noticed the stink, he gave no sign of it. His eyes hadn't left me since I'd started. Every few minutes my gaze dropped to the bulge in his jeans and I hit the bag harder. Finally, I couldn't take it any longer. I wheeled around and slammed a roundhouse kick into the bag, crashing it into the wall. Then I turned to Winsloe, letting the sweat drip from my face.

"Shower," I said.

He pointed to a door behind the StairMaster. "In there."

I strode toward it. He followed, along with two guards he waved forward. I stopped, turned on my heel, and glared at them. Winsloe only watched me, lips twitching with the anticipation of a ninth-grader sneaking into the girls' locker room. I met his gaze and something in me snapped. Grabbing my shirt, I ripped it off, then hurled it into the corner. My bra followed. Then my jeans, my socks, and finally my underwear. Pulling myself straight, I glared at him. This what you want to see? Fine. Get your fill. When he did—and all the guards did—I stormed into the shower room.

Now, at this point, you'd think even the most callow voyeur would rethink his actions, maybe experience a twinge of embarrassment. If Winsloe felt any such twinges, he probably mistook them for indigestion. Still grinning, he followed me into the communal shower room, gesturing for the two guards to follow, and proceeded to watch me bathe. When he offered to wash my back, I slapped his hand away. Winsloe lost his grin. He stomped to the faucets and turned off my hot water. I made no move to defy him by turning the hot back on and finished my ice-cold shower. That placated him enough to hand me a towel when I was done. A lesson here. Winsloe liked me tough, so long as that toughness wasn't directed at him. Like those women pictured on a certain type of fantasy paperback— long-limbed, lean-muscled, and wild-haired . . . with jewel-studded slave collars. His personal Amazonian love-slave.

When we emerged from the shower room, a guard told Winsloe that Carmichael had been calling. She needed me. Winsloe walked me to the infirmary. After he left, I discovered there was no real crisis, just a mild spell of seizures. If Carmichael had used the excuse to rescue me from Winsloe, she gave no sign of it, her demeanor as curt as ever, commands interspersed with bouts of annoyance at my medical ineptitude. After two days together, though, we'd established a routine of tolerance and borderline courtesy. I respected her. I can't say she felt the same about me—I suspected she saw my refusal to defy Winsloe as a sign of weakness—but at least she treated me as if I was an actual person, not a scientific specimen.

That evening there was a disturbance in the cells. A guard came to the infirmary with head wounds, and since I was there with Bauer, I was privy to all the excitement and discussion that ensued.

The guard had been retrieving the dinner dishes from Savannah and Ruth. When he'd opened the door, a plate had flown at his head. He'd ducked, but it struck the door frame with such force that pieces of exploding china had embedded themselves in his scalp and one side of his face, narrowly missing his eye. Carmichael spent a half hour picking shards from his face. As Carmichael stitched up the longest slice, she and Matasumi discussed the situation. Or, more accurately, Matasumi explained his theories and Carmichael grunted at appropriate intervals, seeming to wish he'd take his hypotheses elsewhere and let her work. I guess with Bauer gone, Matasumi didn't have anyone else to talk to. Well, he could have talked to Winsloe, but I'd gotten the impression no one really discussed anything important with Winsloe—he seemed to exist on another level, the dilettante investor who was indulged and obeyed, but not included in matters of compound operation.

Apparently the level of paranormal activity in the cells had increased recently. Leah, whose cell was next to Savannah's, complained of spilled shampoo bottles, ripped magazines, and rearranged furniture. The guards were another favored target. Several had tripped passing Savannah's cell, all reporting that something had knocked their legs from under them. Annoying, but relatively benign events. Then, that morning, the guard who'd brought Savannah's and Ruth's daily change of clothing had rebuked Savannah for spilling ketchup on the shirt she'd worn the previous day. As he'd left the cell, the door had slammed against his shoulder, leaving a nasty bruise. Matasumi suspected this rash of activity was caused by having Ruth and Savannah together. Yet even after the potentially serious accident with the flying plate, he didn't consider separating the two. And lose such a valuable opportunity to study witch interaction? What were a few scarred or crippled guards compared to that? As he expounded on the situation's "potential for remarkable scientific discoveries," I thought Carmichael muttered a few epithets under her breath, but I may have been mistaken.

That night, curled on my cot, I tried to contact Ruth. Okay, maybe I was in denial about my lack of psychic abilities. I guess I figured if I tried hard enough, I could do anything. Supremacy of the will. The incident with the guard worried me. If the "psychic events" in the cell were increasing, I suspected it was related to Ruth's training of Savannah. I wanted to warn her: Tone it down or risk separation. After an hour of trying, I gave up. This failure only reminded me of my inability to contact Paige, which reminded me that I was out of contact with Jeremy, which reminded me that I was on my own. No, I admonished, I was not on my own. I was temporarily out of contact. Even if I was cut off from Jeremy, I was quite capable of plotting my own strategies. Last year I'd single-handedly planned and executed Clay's rescue. Of course, there'd been a few bugs . . . well, more than a few, actually, and I'd almost gotten myself killed . . . but, hey,

I'd saved him, hadn't I? I'd do better this time. Live and learn, right? Or, in this case, learn and live.

"Not that—no, the *left*-hand drawer. Your *other* left hand!"

I tossed in my sleep, dreaming of Carmichael barking orders.

"The crash cart. Goddamn it! I said the *crash* cart, not that one."

In my dream, a dozen identical carts surrounded me as I stumbled from one to the next.

"Give— No, just move. Move!"

Another voice answered, male, mumbling an apology. My eyelids flickered. Fluorescent light stabbed my eyes. I clenched them shut, grimaced, and tried again, squinting this time. Carmichael was indeed in the infirmary, but for once I wasn't the object of her frustration. Two guards scrambled around the room, grabbing this and that as she snatched an instrument tray from the counter. My two in-room guards watched, stupefied, as if they'd been half-asleep.

"Can I do anything?" one said.

"Yes," Carmichael said. "Move!"

She thrust him out of the way with the crash cart and pushed it out the door. I tumbled from bed and followed, my drowsiness making me either brave or stupid. Either way, it was the right move. Carmichael didn't notice me tagging along. When she was this preoccupied, I'd have to stab her with a scalpel to get her attention. The guards didn't say anything either, maybe assuming that I was now Carmichael's assistant in all matters and, if she didn't want me, she'd have stopped me herself.

By the time the guards and I arrived at the elevator, the doors were closing behind Carmichael. We waited and got on when it returned. I hoped we'd head up to the surface. No such luck. We went down. To the cells.

"What's happened?" I asked.

Three guards ignored me. The fourth paid me the courtesy of a shrug and a muttered "Dunno." When the elevator opened on the lower level, the guards remembered their job and flanked me as we headed down the hall. Once through the secured door, I heard Savannah's voice.

"Do something! Hurry!"

The door to Ruth and Savannah's cell was open, letting voices stream into the hall.

"Calm yourself, Savannah," Matasumi said. "I need the guards to explain what happened."

I winced. Another guard accident? So soon? Now Ruth and Savannah would definitely be separated. I tried to hurry, but the guards blocked my path and kept me at their pace.

"I didn't do anything!" Savannah shouted.

"Of course you didn't," Carmichael snapped. "Now get out of the way. All of you."

"There's no need for all this equipment," Matasumi said. "There weren't any vital signs when I arrived. It's too late."

"I'll say when it's too late," Carmichael said.

No vital signs? That sounded bad. When I wheeled into the room, Savannah launched herself at me. Reflexively, my hands flew up to ward off an attack, but she wrapped her arms around my waist.

"I didn't do anything!" she said.

"I know," I murmured. "I know."

I touched her head awkwardly and stroked it, hoping I wasn't petting her like a dog. Consoling distraught children wasn't one of my strengths. Actually, I could say with some certainty that it was something I had never been called on to do before in my life. I scanned the room for Ruth. The cell was filled to capacity. Carmichael and three guards huddled over the bed as the doctor worked on a prone figure. The four guards that had accompanied me all crowded in for a better look, shoving Savannah and me into the corner. I craned my neck to see over their heads.

"Where's Ruth?" I asked.

Savannah stiffened, then pulled back. My gut tightened. I looked at the bed. Carmichael and the three guards still blocked my view, but I could see a hand dangling over the side of the bed. A small, plump, liver-spotted hand.

"Oh no," I whispered.

Savannah jerked away. "I—I didn't do it."

"Of course not," I said, pulling her back to me and praying she hadn't seen my initial reaction.

Matasumi turned on the four guards who'd come down with me. "I want to know what happened."

"We just got here," one said. He motioned to the guards surrounding the bed. "They were on the scene first."

Matasumi hesitated, then stepped toward the bed and tapped one guard's arm. As the guard turned, a commotion erupted in the hallway. Two more guards burst in, guns in hand.

"Please!" Matasumi said. "We didn't call for reinforcements. Return to your posts."

Before they could move, another guard entered, accompanied by Leah.

"What—" Matasumi sputtered. He stopped and regained his composure with a quick intake of breath. "Why is Ms. O'Donnell here?"

"When I passed her cell, I noticed she was quite agitated," the young guard said, traces of color blossoming on his cheeks. "I—uh—used the intercom to inquire and she—uh—asked if she could see what was going on."

"You do not release a subject from a cell. Ever. Return her immediately."

Leah pushed past Matasumi, edging through the group until she was right at the bedside. When she saw Ruth, she gasped and wheeled to face Savannah and me.

"Oh," she said, hands flying to her mouth, eyes fixed on Savannah. "I am so sorry. How— What happened?"

"As I've been asking for the past ten minutes," Matasumi said.

The guard he'd tapped stepped away from the bed. "I was walking past on my rounds and I saw the old—Miss Winterbourne on her bed. The kid was leaning over her. I thought something was wrong, like maybe she'd had a heart attack, so my partner and I opened the door. We found the clock beside them on the floor. Blood splattered on it. Miss Winterbourne's skull bashed in."

Savannah tensed in my arms, heart pounding.

"Oh, you poor thing," Leah said, hurrying toward us. "What a horrible accident."

"It—it wasn't me," Savannah said.

"Whatever happened, it's not your fault, hon."

Leah reached for Savannah. The girl hesitated, still clinging to me. After a moment, she reached for Leah's hand and held it tight, her free arm still around me. A flash of disappointment crossed Leah's face. Then she nodded, as if realizing this wasn't a popularity contest. Leah squeezed Savannah's hand and stroked the back of her head.

After a moment, Leah turned to the group surrounding the bed. She cleared her throat and said loudly, "Can I take Savannah to my cell? She shouldn't be here."

Carmichael glanced up from her work, sweat streaming down her broad face.

"What's she doing here?" she said, waving at Leah. "Put her back in her cell."

The guards jumped to obey, as they hadn't for Matasumi. Two hustled Leah out. Savannah watched her go with such sadness that I wanted to implore Carmichael to let Leah stay, but I was afraid if I did, I'd be kicked out too. Savannah needed someone. While Leah would have been preferable, Savannah would have to make do with a not-so-empathic female werewolf. When Leah was gone, Savannah deflated and leaned against me. She was quiet for several minutes, then she glanced around at the others. Everyone was busy with Ruth.

"I think—" she whispered.

She stepped closer. I laid a tentative hand on her shoulder and she melted against me. I patted her back and murmured wordless noises that I hoped sounded comforting. It seemed to calm her, probably not so much because of any consolation I offered, but because she saw me as her only remaining ally in a roomful of enemies. After a minute, she looked up at me.

"I think," she whispered again, "I think I might have done it."

"You couldn't—" I began.

"I wasn't sleeping. I was thinking about things—things Ruth told me. My lessons. Then I saw it. The clock. It flew—like the plate with the guard. I think I did it. I'm not sure how, but I think I did."

The impulse to deny her culpability sprang to my lips, but I bit it back. The look on her face wasn't that of a child begging to be consoled with well-meaning lies. She knew the truth and trusted me with it.

"If you did, it wasn't your fault," I said. "I know that."

Savannah nodded, brushed back streaks of tears, and leaned her head against my chest. We stood like that, not speaking, for at least five minutes. Then Carmichael stepped away from the bed. Everyone stopped what they were doing. The only sound in the room was the tripping of Savannah's heart.

"Time of death—" Carmichael began.

She lifted her arm, but she must not have put on her watch when summoned from bed. For a long moment, she stared at her wrist, as if expecting some magical timepiece to appear. Then she dropped her hand, closed her eyes, exhaled, and walked from the cell.

It was over.

Chapter 28

Changes

Once everything quieted down, Matasumi realized I was there. Of course, he'd seen me there earlier, but he hadn't realized what it meant, namely that I was someplace I definitely should not have been. He hustled me back to the infirmary with four of the remaining guards.

I spent the next few hours lying on my cot, staring at the lights blipping on Bauer's machines. Ruth was dead. Could I have done something to prevent that? Should I have? She'd known the risks. That didn't make me feel any better. Now she was dead and Savannah blamed herself. I should have been more comfort to Savannah. I should have known the right gestures, the right words. Ruth's death would be a turning point in her life, and all I'd been able to manage were the most awkward solaces. Shouldn't I have been able to dredge up some deeply rooted maternal instincts and known what to do?

Of course, Savannah hadn't intended to kill Ruth. But had she done it? I feared so. More than that, I was afraid it hadn't been an accident. No, I didn't think Savannah had sent that clock flying on purpose. Absolutely not. Her pain at Ruth's death had been too raw, too real. Yet I was afraid that some unconscious part of Savannah had killed Ruth, that something in her nature, in her genes, something she couldn't help, had made her unwittingly attack those guards and kill Ruth. Maybe I'd seen too many "demon child" horror movies. I hoped that was it. I prayed that it was. I liked Savannah. She had spirit and intelligence, an engaging mix of childish innocence and preteen sass. She was a normal kid, part angel, part devil. Surely there was no more to it than that. But the psychic events revolved around Savannah. As Ruth had trained Savannah, the events had rapidly escalated from harmless to lethal. What had Ruth said about Savannah? Great power, incredible potential . . . and a mother inclined toward the "darker side" of magic. Was there such a thing as a genetic predisposition to evil? Had Ruth overlooked it? Had she refused to see anything bad in someone so young? In giving Savannah more power, had she signed her own death warrant? Please, let me be wrong. For Savannah's sake, let me be wrong.

With morning came breakfast. I didn't touch it. Carmichael arrived at her usual time, shortly before eight, a brusque "How are you?" the only indication that anything had happened the night before. When I said I was fine, she studied me for an extra second, grunted, and began her paperwork.

I spent the early morning dwelling on Ruth's death, how it changed things, how I could have prevented it. I spent a lot of time on the last one. Maybe I shouldn't have. Life and death were beyond our control here. At any moment, Matasumi could have decided Ruth was no longer a viable subject or Winsloe could have strolled into her cell and taken her on one of his hunts. Still, I shouldered part of the blame, maybe because it gave me some sense of control in an uncontrollable situation.

Around mid-morning a soft moan roused me from my thoughts. I glanced up. Bauer moaned again. She dug her head back into the pillow, face contorting in pain.

"Doctor?" I said, standing. "She's coming to."

As Carmichael strode across the floor, I leaned over Bauer. Her eyes flew open.

"Hello, Sondra," I said. "We—"

She bolted upright, thin restraints snapping, and slammed against my shoulder. As I fell back, I caught Bauer's gaze, saw something hard and blank there. Before I could react, she grabbed my shoulders and flung me into the air. For a moment, everything slowed, and there was that split second of suspension before gravity took over and I hurtled across the room and crashed into the wall.

Carmichael helped me stand and shouted for the guards. Bauer sat upright, struggling to get out of bed, sheets twisted around her legs. Her face was contorted with rage, her eyes were blank, lips moving soundlessly. When the sheets didn't give way, she roared in frustration and jerked her legs sideways, tearing through the cloth. I ran to the bed and threw myself across Bauer.

"Keep your fucking hands off me!" Bauer roared. "All of you! Get back! Don't touch me!"

"Delirium," Carmichael panted as she raced to the bed with stronger restraints. "You said it was one of the steps."

"Right," I said, though at the moment, lying atop Bauer as she flailed beneath me, a medical diagnosis wasn't exactly a priority. "Where the hell are the guards?"

The guards were right there, doing what they did best—holding their guns and waiting for the signal to fire. Carmichael threw the restraints at them.

"Tie her!" she said. "Now!"

Before they could move, Bauer bucked and sent me flying again. This time I stayed on the floor an extra moment to regain my breath. Let the damned guards handle it. Let Carmichael handle it. She was the one who'd refused to properly restrain Bauer.

Bauer stopped struggling and sat still as a statue. The four guards surrounded the bed, tensed, restraints in hand, looking like animal-control officers waiting to throw a net on a rabid dog, none wanting to make the first move. Sweat streamed down Bauer's face and her mouth hung open, panting. She moved her head from side to side, eyes scanning the room. Wild and blank, they passed the guards, me, Carmichael. They stopped at an empty spot to her left, and she lunged forward, held back only by the ripped sheets.

"Get the fuck out of here!" she yelled.

No one was there.

I crawled to my feet, keeping my movements careful as if trying to avoid the notice of a wild animal.

"We have to restrain her," I whispered.

No one moved.

"Give me those," Carmichael said, reaching to snatch the restraints from the nearest guard.

"No," I said. "Let them do it. I'll get closer and run interference if she attacks. You get a sedative ready and stand back."

Oh, sure, give myself the life-threatening job. And for what? No one would notice. No one would care. Still, the job had to be done. If I didn't do it, one of these yahoos would fire his pistol at the first sign of trouble. Then where would my plans be? Dead and buried with Bauer.

Carmichael turned to the guards. "Wait until Elena is beside the bed. Then move quickly, but carefully. Sondra doesn't know what she's doing. We don't want to hurt her."

Which of course, was easier said than done. While I crept across the room, Bauer kept still, staring and cursing at unseen intruders. Yet the moment the guards touched her, she exploded, summoning up the unexpected strength of delirium. All of us working together could barely wrestle her onto the bed.

Once Bauer was down, I helped the nearest guard fasten his restraint. As my fingers worked at the clasps, Bauer's arm seemed to shimmer and contract. I shook my head sharply, feeling the pain inside it bounce around like a red-hot coal. My vision blurred.

"Elena?" Carmichael grunted as she fought to tie Bauer's other arm down.

"I'm okay."

As I worked on the knot, Bauer's arm convulsed, the wrist narrowing, the hand twisting and contorting into a knot. It hadn't been a trick of my eyes. She was Changing.

"Elena!"

At Carmichael's shout, I jumped. Bauer's hand flew from its bindings and tore at the empty space where my throat had been. Webbed fingers and misshapen claws swung through the air. I threw myself over Bauer's chest as she bolted upright again.

A snarl of rage erupted and she shoved me off her. Both hands now free, Bauer grabbed a guard and threw him across the room. He collapsed, unconscious, against the wall. Bauer's back shook and contorted, great lumps moving under the skin. She howled and fell onto her side.

"Sedate her!" I shouted.

"But you said—" Carmichael begun.

"It's too soon! She's not ready! Sedate her! Now!"

Hair sprouted from Bauer's back and shoulders. Bones lengthened and shortened, and she cried out, half-howling, half-whimpering. Her whole body convulsed, clearing the bed, me still clinging to her. Her face was unrecognizable, a hellish mask of writhing muscles that was neither wolf nor human. Fangs jutted over her lips. Her nose had stopped midway on the transformation to muzzle. Hair sprouted in tufts. Then there were the eyes. Bauer's eyes. They hadn't changed, but they were bulging and rolling, agony pouring out in waves. She met my gaze, and for a second I saw recognition. Some part of her had passed the delirium and was conscious, trapped in that hell.

Carmichael jabbed the syringe into Bauer's arm. Bauer flew upright and hung there, with me draped over her lap. Her body jerked several times, then she gave a low snuffle, and her eyes widened as if in surprise. She blinked once. Then she slid down onto the bed.

I tensed, waiting for the next round; then the Change reversed. This time there was no violence or pain to the transformation. She melted peacefully back into human form, like a computer-generated morphing. When she was fully human again, she curled into semi-fetal position and fell asleep.

Armen made another visit to the infirmary. Yesterday had been his regular checkup. Today he feigned a migraine headache with such finesse that even Carmichael never doubted his symptoms, though I suppose that wasn't surprising, considering he was a psychiatrist and therefore had a medical degree himself. We picked up our conversation where we'd left off. He had a plan for escaping that involved another medical ruse, thereby bringing him up to the second floor with me, which was much easier to escape from than the well-secured cell block. Again, he worked this into such ordinary small talk that I had to keep my own brain revving to keep up with the subtext interpretation.

The more I talked to Armen, the more I viewed my ploy with Bauer as a backup plan. Armen was an ally far more to my liking. First, he was conscious, which was a definite advantage over the comatose Bauer. Second, he reminded me of Jeremy, which increased my comfort level tenfold. He was quiet, courteous, and even-tempered, an unassuming exterior disguising a strong will and razor-sharp mind, someone who took charge instinctively, yet tempered that authoritarianism with enough grace and wit that I didn't mind letting him take the lead. I trusted Armen and I liked him. An ideal combination.

The rest of the day passed quietly, but the night made up for it, plaguing me with strange and disturbing dreams. I started the night at Stonehaven, playing in the snow with Clay and Nick. We were in the middle of a snowball fight when a new dream overlapped that one, cutting in like a more powerful radio station. In the other dream, I was lying in bed while Paige attempted to contact me. The two dreams spliced together: One minute I'd feel icy snow dripping down my neck, the next I'd hear Paige calling me. Some part of me chose the snowball dream and tried to block the other, but it didn't work. I lobbed two last snowballs at Nick, then a wave of snow engulfed me, swallowing that dream and spitting me into the other.

"Elena? Damn it, answer me!"

I struggled to return to my winter games, but to no avail. I was stuck in the dream of Paige. Wonderful.

"Elena. Come on. Wake up."

Even in my dream, I didn't want to answer, as if I knew that imagining myself speaking to Paige would only depress me more, reminding me that

I'd been out of contact with her for three days, a situation that now seemed permanent.

"Elena?"

I mumbled something unintelligible even to myself.

"Ah-ha! You *are* there. Good. Hold on. I'm going to bring you into my body. Fair warning this time. Jeremy's here. Now, on the count of three. One, two, three, ta-da!"

Five seconds of silence. Then,

"Oh, shit."

Paige's curse faded behind me as I tumbled through bits and pieces of dreams, like someone was flipping channels, refusing to pause long enough for me to see what was on. When it stopped, I was a wolf. I didn't need to see myself; I could feel it in the way my muscles moved, the perfect rhythm of each stride. Someone ran ahead of me, a shape flickering through the trees. Another wolf. I knew that, though I couldn't get close enough to see anything but shadow and blurred motion. Although I was the pursuer, not the hunted, fear strummed through me. Who was I chasing? Clay. It had to be Clay. That degree of panic, of blind fear, fear of loss and abandonment—I could only associate it with Clay. He was there, somewhere, ahead of me, and I couldn't catch up. Each time my paws struck the ground, a name echoed through my skull, a mental shout. But it wasn't Clay's name. It was my own, repeated over and over, beats matching the rhythm of my legs. Glancing down, I caught sight of my paws. They weren't my paws. Too large, too dark—a blond nearly gold. Clay's paws. Ahead a bushy tail flashed in the moonlight. A white-blond tail. I was chasing myself.

I started awake and bolted upright in bed. Leaning forward, chest heaving, I ran my hands through my hair, but it wasn't my hair, not a long, tangled mess, but close-cropped curls. I dropped my hands to my lap and stared at them. Thick, squared hands, nails clipped back to the quick. Workman's hands, yet ones that rarely handled a tool larger than a pen. Uncallused, but not soft. Bones broken more times than I could count, each time meticulously reset, emerging unmarred except for a road map of minute scars. I knew each one of those scars. I could remember nights lying awake, asking, "Where'd you get this one? And this one? And—whoops, I gave you that one."

A door opened.

"It didn't work, did it?" Clay's angry drawl, not from the doorway, but here, from the bed.

Jeremy shut the door behind him. "No, Paige wasn't able to make contact. She thought she did, but something went wrong."

"And aren't we all shocked to hell. You're entrusting Elena's life to a twenty-two-year-old apprentice witch. You know that, don't you?"

"I know that I'm willing to use any tool possible to find Elena. Right now, that apprentice witch is our best hope."

"No, she's not. There's another way. Me. I can find Elena. But you won't believe it."

"If Paige is unable to reestablish contact—"

"Goddamn it!" Clay grabbed a book from the nightstand and whipped it across the room, denting the far wall.

Jeremy paused a moment, then continued, voice as unruffled as ever. "I'm going to get you something to drink, Clayton."

"You mean you're going to sedate me again. Sedate me, shut me up, keep me quiet and calm while Elena is out there—alone. I didn't believe it was her talking through Paige and now she's gone. Don't tell me that wasn't my fault."

Jeremy said nothing.

"Thank you very much," Clay said.

"Yes, you're to blame for us losing contact that time, though it probably doesn't explain why we can't recontact her. We'll keep trying. In the meantime, perhaps we can discuss this other idea of yours in the morning. Come see me if you change your mind about that drink. It'll help you sleep."

As Jeremy left, the dream evaporated. I tossed and turned, thrown back into the channel-surfing world again. Snap, snap, snap, bits of dreams and memories, too scattered to make any sense. Then darkness. A knock at the door. I was seated at a desk, poring over a map. The door was behind me. I tried to turn or call out a welcome. Instead, I felt my pencil move to scratch a few words on a pad. I looked at the writing and, with no surprise, recognized Clay's scrawl.

The room swirled, threatening to go dark. Something tugged at me with the gentle insistence of the tide, reaching out to pull me back. I fought it. I liked where I was, thank you very much. This was a good place, a comforting place. Just sensing Clay's presence made me happy, and damn it, I deserved a bit of happiness, illusory or not. The tide grew stronger, swelling to an undertow. The room went black. I wrenched myself free and slammed back into Clay's body. He'd stopped writing now and was studying a map. A map of what? Someone knocked again at the door. He didn't respond. Behind him, the door opened, then shut.

"Clayton." Cassandra's voice, butter-smooth.

He didn't answer.

"A grunt of greeting would suffice," she murmured.

"That would imply a welcome. Don't you need to be invited into a room?"

"Sorry. Another myth shot to hell."

"Feel free to follow it."

Cassandra chuckled. "I see Jeremy inherited all the manners in the Danvers family. Not that I mind. I've always preferred honesty and wit over polish." Her voice drew closer as she crossed the room. "I noticed your light on and thought you might care to join me in a drink."

"Love to, but I'm afraid we don't share the same taste in fluids."

"Could you at least look at me when you turn me down?"

No answer.

"Or are you afraid to look at me?"

Clay turned and met her eyes. "There. Piss off, Cassandra. How's that?"

"She's not coming back, you know."

Clay's hand clenched around the pencil, but he said nothing.

I felt the tugging at my feet again and braced myself against it. Somewhere in my head Paige called my name. The undertow surged, but I held firm. This was one scene I definitely wasn't leaving.

"They won't find her," Cassandra said.

"According to you, we should stop trying."

"I only mean that it's a waste of our time. Better we concentrate our efforts on stopping these people. Save all our lives, not just Elena's. If, in stopping them, we rescue her, that's wonderful. If we don't . . . it's hardly the end of the world."

The pencil snapped between Clay's fingers. Cassandra stepped closer. When the undertow threatened again, I kicked and fought with all my might.

Cassandra took yet another step toward Clay. I felt him tense and start to step back, then stop and hold his ground.

"Yes, you love her," Cassandra said. "I can see that and I admire that. Really, I do. But do you know how many men I've loved in all these years? Loved passionately? And of those men, do you know how few names I remember? How few faces?"

"Get out."

"I'm asking you to join me for a drink. One drink. Nothing more."

"I said, get out."

Cassandra only smiled and shook her head. Her eyes gleamed now with the same look I'd seen her give the server at the restaurant, only stronger. Hungrier. Her fingers grazed Clay's forearm. I wanted to scream for him to look away, but I was powerless to do anything but watch and wait.

"Don't pull that shit, Cassandra," Clay said. "It doesn't work on me."

"No?"

"No."

Clay looked Cassandra squarely in the eyes. She went completely immobile, only her eyes working, glowing brighter as she stared at him. Several minutes passed. Then Clay stepped toward Cassandra. Her lips curved in a triumphant smile. My heart stopped.

"Get out, Cassandra," Clay said, his face only inches from hers. "Ten seconds or I throw you out."

"Don't threaten me, Clayton."

"Or you'll do what? Bite me? Think you can sink your teeth into me before I rip your head off? I hear that's a good cure for immortality. Five seconds, Cassandra. Five . . . four . . . "

The scene went black. No swirling, not tugging. Just a sudden stop. I blinked. Harsh light blinded me. I squeezed my eyes shut. Through my lids, I saw the light swing away. Fingers gripped my shoulder and shook me.

"Rise and shine, sleepyhead."

A voice. Unfortunately, not Clay's voice. Not Cassandra's voice. Not even Paige's. This was worse. Ten times worse. Ty Winsloe. From pleasant dreams to unsettling visions to outright nightmares. I clenched my eyes shut.

"Whaddaya think, boys?" Winsloe said. "Does our sleeping beauty need a kiss to wake her up? Of course, in the original fairy tale, she needed more than a kiss . . . "

My eyes snapped open and I bolted upright. Winsloe chortled and beamed a flashlight in my face, then skimmed it over my body.

"You always sleep with your clothes on?" he asked.

"This isn't exactly a private suite," I said, snarling a yawn. "What time is it?"

"Just past three. We need your help. There's been a breakout."

I sat on the edge of my cot, blinking, brain struggling to get past visions of Clay and Cassandra. Three o'clock? In the morning? Breakout? Did he mean someone had escaped? Who? Why did they need my help? Had there been an accident? Did Carmichael want me?

"Huh?" I said. So much for intelligent and articulate questions. What do you expect at three A.M.?

Winsloe prodded me from bed. "I'll explain on the way."

Chapter 29

BLOODHOUND

Armen had escaped. When Winsloe told me, my breath caught, and for a long moment I couldn't breathe. Armen had escaped . . . without me. On the heels of my panic came a flash of hurt, then the realization that Armen must have been presented with an opportunity that he couldn't ignore. Could I blame him? Of course not, though that didn't make things any better. My escape partner was gone, taking our plan with him. Worse still, Winsloe wanted me to stop him.

"You want me to track him down?" I said.

"That's what I said. Use your nose. Sniff him out."

"Like a bloodhound."

Winsloe glanced over sharply at my tone. "Yes, like a bloodhound. Is that a problem?"

Of course that was a problem. I was a person, not an animal, not a sideshow attraction. I didn't perform for anyone's amusement. I wanted to say so, but the edge in Winsloe's voice dared me to defy him. I didn't have the guts. Or, more accurately, my instinct for self-preservation was too strong. I remembered Winsloe's reaction when I'd slapped his hand away in the shower and knew I couldn't afford another show of defiance. That didn't mean I'd betray Armen. I might have to track him, but I didn't have to find him.

Flanked by guards, I followed Winsloe downstairs to the cell block. Two more guards waited outside Armen's cell. Inside, Tucker knelt beside a guard, who sat on the floor, cradling his head. The guard looked familiar, but I couldn't put a name to him. The only time I ever bothered to note a guard's name was when he'd done something to distinguish himself from the others. Most hadn't.

"Did you find out what happened?" Winsloe asked, in a voice that implied he didn't give a damn what had happened, he only wanted to get on with the hunt.

"Seems like Haig made himself a weapon," Tucker said. "Something sharp, like a knife. Caused a commotion when my men were doing their rounds, then pulled this weapon on them when they opened the door. Knocked Ryman here out cold. Must have taken Jolliffe along to get past security. Ryman's okay, but we'd better move if we want Jolliffe alive. We'll need to track him. I've sent Pendecki to get the tracking—"

"No need," Winsloe interrupted. "I've got a world-class tracker right here."

Tucker looked at me and frowned. "That's one of my men out there, sir. With all due respect, I don't think we should fool around—"

"Fool around?"

Tucker's jaw clicked as if biting something back. "I didn't mean it that way . . . sir. I'm concerned about—"

"Of course you are. So am I. That's why I brought Elena. Ryman, feeling up to joining us?"

Ryman struggled to his feet. "Yes, sir."

"I think—" Tucker began.

"Don't think," Winsloe cut in. "That's not what I pay you for. Come on, Ryman; we'll see if we can't get this bastard. Maybe get you a little payback for that goose egg on your head."

Outside the compound, Winsloe dismissed the two guards accompanying me, leaving only the injured Ryman. I wondered at this, knew it wasn't a good sign, but was still too sleep-drugged to make sense of it. Other thoughts clogged my tired brain. Armen had made a weapon? He'd attacked a guard? Knocked him unconscious? Was this the same Armen who'd been looking to me to provide the brute force for an escape?

As we headed into the woods, someone shouted "Hey!" behind us. Ryman whirled, gun poised, reflexes unhampered by any lingering effects from his head injury. No one was there. Dead grass crackled farther up the path, and we all spun back around to see Xavier twenty feet away.

"Easy, soldier," Xavier said, hands in the air. "Don't be shooting the friendlies."

"I should," Ryman muttered. "Teach you a lesson."

"What's up?" Xavier asked, sauntering toward us. "I hear Haig made a break for it. We doin' the search-and-rescue thing? Or the search-and-destroy thing?" He saw me and stopped. "Whoa, what's wolf-girl doing out of her cage?"

I glowered at him. He sidestepped fast, as if ducking my glare, then bobbed back grinning.

"That's one lethal look you have there. Deadlier than Ryman's bullets." He turned to Winsloe. "So what's the deal? Fun and games time? Can I play?"

"Maybe next time," Winsloe said.

"Oh, come on. Don't be a spoilsport. I wanna play."

"Yeah?" Ryman said. "How about you be the practice target?"

Winsloe waved Ryman to silence. "That's enough. Back inside, Reese. I said, next time."

"Fine." Xavier rolled his eyes, then vanished. Obviously someone else who knew enough not to push Winsloe.

"Are we still on track, Elena?" Winsloe asked.

"Hmmm? Oh, right." I sniffed the air. "Yes, Ar—Haig was here. With someone else."

"Jolliffe," Winsloe said. "Good. Tucker will be pleased. Lead on, then. Ryman, stay behind her."

We headed into the woods.

"Are you sure this is the way?" Winsloe asked ten minutes later.

It wasn't. I'd branched away from Armen's true path ten yards back. Winsloe shone his flashlight on my face. I swallowed a quick assertion and made a show of sniffing the air. Out of the corner of my eye, I watched him, gauging his credulity, and decided to test the water before making a potentially fatal leap.

"I thought it was," I said slowly. "The trail seemed to turn this way."

"Undergrowth looks pretty dense," Winsloe said.

Did it? It appeared passable to me, but maybe I was looking as a wolf, not a panicked human running for his life, captive in tow. I hunkered down and inhaled close to the ground. Behind me, Ryman snickered.

"You're right," I said. "They didn't come this way. I must have been picking up their scent on the breeze. Better retrace our steps."

"Maybe you should stay on all fours," Ryman said. "Keep your nose to the trail." He smirked.

"That's okay, Elena," Winsloe said. "Take it slow. Don't feel pressured."

Me? Feel pressured? Why on earth would I feel pressured? Just because I was being asked to hunt down a fellow captive, with a loaded pistol at my back and a psychotic megalomaniac calling the shots?

"Maybe I am a little nervous," I said. "Sorry."

Winsloe beamed a magnanimous smile. "That's okay. Just take it easy."

Sure, boss. No problem. I inhaled, backtracked to the real trail, and started again. About fifty yards farther along, Armen's trail veered east. I decided to keep heading south. I didn't get three steps.

"You sure that's the right way?" Winsloe called from behind me.

I froze.

"Seems to me they went east," he said. "There's some bent branches here."

I turned to look at the bushes surrounding the wide gap Armen had gone through. Not a single twig was broken. There was no way Winsloe could tell Armen had turned here. Unless he already knew. The warning tingle I'd felt since we'd begun this expedition surged to an Arctic chill. Winsloe knew exactly where Armen had fled to, probably had him tracked and captured before he even came to the infirmary. He was testing me— my abilities and my honesty. Had I already failed?

Quelling the urge to stammer excuses, I looked from the bushes to the path I'd chosen, pinched the bridge of my nose and tried to look exhausted, which wasn't much of a stretch. I crouched and sniffed the ground, crept over and smelled the bushes, then stood and sampled the air. With a sigh, I rubbed the back of my neck.

"Well?" Winsloe said.

"I'm smelling a trail both ways. Give me a sec."

I rolled my shoulders and took a deep breath of chilly night air. Then I got down on all fours, ignoring Ryman's snickers, and followed both potential paths for several yards.

"That one," I said, pointing at the real trail as I got to my feet. "He took a few steps the other way, then backed up and turned down that gap between the bushes."

Plausible, and impossible to refute unless you had a werewolf's nose. Winsloe nodded. It worked for him. Good.

As I followed the trail, I wondered how Winsloe planned to end this charade. They'd obviously recaptured Armen already. Would we bump into the troop of guards holding him? Or would the trail loop back to the compound? What was the point? To amuse himself by making me per-form like a circus dog? Humiliate me while testing my trustworthiness? Was he hoping I'd screw up or make a run for it, giving him an excuse to hunt me? I wouldn't give him the satisfaction. If he wanted a loyal two-legged hound, that was exactly what he'd get.

I didn't try to trick him again. What was the use, if he already had Armen? We trekked another half mile into the forest. The scent grew stronger, until I could pick it up in the wind.

"They're close," I said.

"Good," Winsloe said. "Slow down then and—"

Ahead, a clump of bushes exploded with crackles and curses. Two figures flew out of the shrubbery, Armen atop a guard, hands grappling against the man's throat. Winsloe raced forward, yanking a gun from under his jacket. Ryman fired a warning shot. Armen froze. Winsloe launched himself at Armen and knocked him off Jolliffe.

Anger flared in my gut, white hot. I clenched my fists to keep from acting on it. I wanted to scream at Winsloe, denounce his "tracking exercise" for what it was. A game. Another juvenile game choreographed right down to leaping on Armen *after* the poor man was paralyzed by the sound of gunfire. You trying to impress me, Tyrone? Oh, I'm impressed. I'd never seen such a pathetic performance.

"There," I said, barely able to unhinge my jaw enough to force words out. "You have him. Good job. Can we go now?"

Everyone ignored me. Winsloe had Armen spread-eagled on the ground and was patting him down looking for weapons. Jolliffe sat in the shadows, as if too stunned to move. Ryman walked over and extended a hand, helping his partner to his feet.

"What happened here?" Winsloe said.

"He had a weapon, sir," Jolliffe said. "He forced me from the cell, took my gun, and made me open the doors, then dragged me into the woods. He tried to kill me. I escaped a ways back, followed, and caught up to him here."

At which time you held him until we arrived, I thought. After having probably been in radio contact with Winsloe since you escaped from Armen.

"He was hiding in those bushes," the guard said, continuing his story. "He shot at me. I disarmed him and we fought, then you showed up."

"Wh—what?" Armen said, struggling to lift his head from the ground. "I didn't—you came to my cell. You brought me out here. You—"

Winsloe slammed Armen's face back into the dirt. Again, it took every ounce of restraint not to fly at him. Then the impulse vanished and I couldn't move if I'd wanted to. My legs turned to cold lead as I saw the look on Armen's face, the confusion and disbelief beneath a layer of blood and bruises. Jolliffe said something. My gaze swiveled to him. I saw his face, really saw it, and recognized it, as I'd earlier recognized Ryman. Watching them together, I knew where I'd seen them. At the hunt. The two nameless men with Pendecki and Bryce the night we'd hunted Patrick Lake. That wasn't the last time I'd seen them, either. They'd been the two who'd accompanied me into the shower with Winsloe. His pet guards. Handpicked for another special mission.

Armen hadn't escaped. It made no sense. Armen was a thinking man, not the sort who'd take such a risk on a sudden impulse. He wouldn't know how to fashion a makeshift prison weapon. And he certainly wouldn't attack two armed guards, each twice his size. No, he hadn't escaped. He'd been brought here. Beaten and dragged into the forest. For what? To play a role in Winsloe's latest game? Winsloe wanted me to track someone, so he'd gone to the cell block, chosen a target, and enlisted his pet guards to help build the scenario. Was it worth it, you sick bastard? Did you get your rocks off this time?

"Can we go now?" I asked again, raising my voice to be heard over their conversation. "We have him. We should head back."

Winsloe shifted so he was sitting sideways atop Armen, leaning back like he was in a comfortable chair. "Can't do that, Elena. Wish we could, but we can't. We aren't done yet."

He glanced at Ryman and Jolliffe. The two guards grinned back, and my gut turned to ice.

"We can't have prisoners escaping, can we, boys? Escaping their cells, then escaping punishment. No siree. We have to set a standard. No one escapes my compound and lives."

I struggled for breath. "But—but I thought Haig was an important subject. Doctor Matasumi said—"

"Larry will understand. A prisoner escapes, we hunt him down, we try to bring him back alive, but . . . well, things happen. Capturing a prisoner is a delicate matter. So much could go wrong, and of course, we can't risk letting anyone get away and put the project at risk."

I could not let this happen. I'd felt sick enough over hunting Patrick Lake, and he'd been a vicious killer. Armen Haig was no monster. He was a decent man, an innocent in a world where most of us, myself included, had forfeited our innocence when we became something other than human. The monsters here were the three with no excuses for their behavior.

What did Winsloe see when he looked at Armen, at me, at Patrick Lake, at the guard he'd killed, or anyone else who inhabited his world? Did he see people, conscious beings? Or did he see cardboard cutouts, actors, characters in some grand game designed for his amusement?

"You can't kill him," I said, keeping my voice as neutral as possible.

Winsloe stretched his legs, settling his weight onto Armen. "You're right. I can't. Well, I *could*, but I won't."

"Good. Now can we—"

"I'm not killing him. You are."

Chapter 30

Sacrifice

I stopped short, words jamming in my throat. "I—I—"

"That's right. You're killing him. You're going to Change into a wolf and hunt him." Winsloe stood and put a foot on Armen's back. "Is that a problem, Elena?"

For one brief second, I was certain Winsloe knew about my collaboration with Armen, that this was his way of foiling our plans, killing my ally, and letting me know that he knew, but I quickly realized that Winsloe couldn't know. Armen had been too shrewd, had kept our discussions well disguised. We hadn't progressed far enough in our plans for even the most quick-witted listener to realize what we were plotting. If someone had been listening, he would have only heard two people carrying on a conversation. With an icy jolt, I wondered if that had been enough. Had Winsloe overheard me with Armen and detected a blossoming friendship? Did that explain why he'd chosen Armen from all the other captives, risking Matasumi's displeasure? Why not take Leah or, better yet, Curtis Zaid, the useless Vodoun priest? Because it wouldn't hurt me enough. It wouldn't be sadistic enough.

Winsloe stepped closer. "I said, is that a problem, Elena?"

"Yes, it's a goddamned problem," I snarled. "I will not kill a man for your amuse—"

I reeled back. Felt the imprint of his hand burning my cheek. Stumbled. Recovered. Spun around, fist barreling toward his jaw. A bullet seared my side. Threw me off-balance, half impact, half surprise. Grabbed a tree. Broke my fall. Stood there, facing the trunk, chest heaving, a serpent of rage whipping through my body. I gripped the tree hard enough to puncture bark holes in my palms. Closed my eyes. Inhaled. Fought for control. Found it. Took deep breaths and stepped back. I dropped my fingers to my side and felt the wound. Straight through, nicking a rib and nothing more.

"One more time, Elena," Winsloe said, walking up behind me. "Is that a problem?"

I turned slowly, keeping my eyes off his. Winsloe gave a grunt of satisfaction, interpreting my lack of eye contact as a sign that I was cowed, not that I didn't dare look at him for fear I'd rip his face off if I did.

"Answer the question, Elena."

"I can't." Inhaled. Forced apology into my tone. "I can't do—"

I saw his hand go up, this time with the gun in it. Saw the pistol careering toward my face. I backpedaled but too late. The gun glanced off the side of my skull. Lights flashed. Then went dark. When I recovered, I was lying on the ground with Winsloe standing over me.

"This is how it's going to work, Elena," he said, leaning down into my face. "You're going to Change into a wolf. Right here. Right now. Then you're going to hunt Mr. Haig. When you capture him, you will hold him until I arrive. Then you will kill him. Any deviation from this plan and you will both die. Understood?"

I tried to sit. Winsloe's foot landed on my stomach, forcing me down and knocking the breath from my lungs.

"It's—it's not that easy," I gasped between gulps of air. "I might not be able to Change. Even if I do, I won't be able to control myself once I catch him. It doesn't work that way."

"It will work any way I say it will work." Winsloe's voice held all the emotion of a golf pro explaining the rules of the course. "If you fail, you will answer to me. And when you're done answering to me, my boys will take their turn, and when they've tired of you, you die. Is that incentive enough, Elena?"

I started to shake. No anger now. Just fear. Uncontrollable terror. Killing Armen would be an act of cowardice I would never forgive myself for, even if I could do it. But if I didn't? Rape and death. To me, the idea of being raped was more terrifying than that of dying. Ghosts of my childhood filled my brain, voices that said I'd promised such a thing would never happen again, that I was too strong, that I could never again be forced to submit to anyone.

"I can't," I whispered. "I just can't."

I saw Winsloe's foot fly back. Squeezed my eyes shut. Felt his boot connect with my side, landing square atop the bullet wound. Heard a woman's scream. My scream. Hated myself. Hated, hated, hated. I would not die this way. Not raped. Not forced to kill an innocent man. If I had to die, I'd do it my way.

I flung myself up, throwing Winsloe clear. He landed on his back. I scrambled to my feet and turned on him.

"No!" A shout. Armen.

I whirled, saw Ryman raise his gun. Armen lunged at me. The gun spat a stream of bullets. Armen's body stopped in midair, chest exploding, body jolting with the impact. As he hit the ground, I dropped beside him.

"More merciful. For both of us." His voice was paper thin, too low for anyone's ears but mine. Bloody froth bubbled from his lips.

"I'm sorry," I whispered.

"Don't—" His eyelids fluttered once. Twice. Then closed.

I hung my head, felt tears clog my throat. In the silence that followed, I braced myself for what was to come. Winsloe would kill me for this. For attacking him. For ending his game. When I finally turned to face him, though, I saw only satisfaction in his eyes. He hadn't lost at all. The outcome was still the same. Armen was dead. It was my fault. I knew it and I'd suffer for it.

"Take her back to her cell," Winsloe said, brushing off his jeans. "Then get someone out here to clean up this mess."

As he glanced down at Armen, his mouth tightened and he skewered me with a glare. The outcome may have been the same, but his game had been ruined. I'd pay for it. Not tonight. But I would pay.

Ryman and Jolliffe led me into the forest. We were about halfway to the compound when Ryman suddenly shoved me hard. I tripped. As I steadied myself and turned to glare at him, I found myself glaring into the barrel of his gun. I clenched my jaw, wheeled around, and continued walking. I'd gone about five feet when a kick from Jolliffe cut my legs from under me. I stumbled against a tree and took a moment to compose myself before turning. Both men trained their guns on me.

"What do you want?" I said. "An excuse to shoot me?"

"We don't need one," Ryman said. "We just tell Tyrone that you made a break for it and we had to take you down."

"Like a rabid dog," Jolliffe said.

Both men laughed. Rage shot through me. What had happened back in that grove made me sick with guilt and self-loathing. I wanted nothing more than to find another target for that anger, someone else I could blame for Armen's death. These two morons were screaming for the job. I sized them up. Could I bring them down without getting shot? I estimated my odds at five to one. When those odds struck me as reasonably good, I knew I was in trouble. My rage was fast consuming my common sense. I tore my gaze away from the two guards and continued walking.

Ryman strode up beside me and grabbed my arm. As he slammed me against a tree, I started to lash out, then felt the cold metal of a gun barrel at my temple.

"Don't ever turn your back on me, bitch," he breathed in my face. "Cliff and I were looking forward to some fun tonight. You ruined it. Maybe Ty's willing to overlook that, but we aren't. Who the hell do you think you are anyway? Defying Tyrone Winsloe? Attacking him? Spoiling our game?"

"Take your hands off me."

"Or what?" He jammed his knee into my crotch. "What are you going to do if I don't?"

Someone chuckled to our left. "How about . . . rip out your fool throat, tear off your testicles, and carve you up like a Thanksgiving turkey. Not necessarily in that order."

We turned to see Xavier leaning against a tree, puffing on a cigarette. He threw down the stub, strolled over, and tugged me out of Ryman's grasp.

"You don't wanna be messing with this gal," Xavier said. "Did you see what she did to that other werewolf? Ripped his leg open . . . while wearing handcuffs. Now you boys might have guns, but I wouldn't want to see how much damage she could do before she went down."

Before either guard could open his mouth, Xavier hooked his arm around my waist and led me back to the open path, heading for the compound.

"She seems to tolerate you just fine," Jolliffe muttered as he walked up behind us. "Something we should be telling Ty about, Reese?"

"I'm not crazy enough to trespass on the big man's territory," Xavier said. "Can I help it if the poor girl's got a thing for me?"

He grabbed my ass. I whirled to slug him, but he vanished, reappearing on my other side.

"It's one of those love-hate things," he called back to the guards. Under his breath he murmured, "Play nice, Elena. You don't want me to take my marbles and go home."

He was right. As much as I hated being indebted to Xavier, he was the only thing standing between me, the two guards, and a potentially nasty situation.

Xavier rested his arm around my waist again and glanced over his shoulder. "Think Tyrone will let me have her when he's done? We could run away together, build a hut on some deserted island, live off coconuts, sunshine, and sex. What do you say, Elena? We'd make beautiful babies. Think about it. We could single-handedly turn wolves into a vanishing species."

"Ha-ha," I said.

Xavier paused, cocked his head. "No laughter from the peanut gallery. Guess they don't get the joke. Want me to explain it to you, guys?"

"We want you to fuck off, Reese," Ryman said. "Like right now."

"In front of you guys? I'm a demon, not an exhibitionist." Xavier walked a bit faster, propelling me alongside him. "Anyway, we're almost at the compound. Larry was wondering what happened. Getting pretty worried about his star subject. I volunteered for the search party. Think I'll win a prize?"

"Not when Matasumi finds out what happened to that star subject," I murmured.

Something flashed across Xavier's face, but before I could decipher the expression, it did its own disappearing act, hiding behind his usual cocky nonchalance. He kept up a running monologue until we arrived at the compound. Then Xavier took me through the security door, letting it bang shut on the two guards. We almost made it into the elevator without them, but Jolliffe grabbed the doors at the last moment. They got on and pushed the button for the cell block. When the car stopped on the middle floor, Xavier tried to lead me off. Ryman snatched my arm.

"Ty said return her to her cell."

Xavier sighed. "He meant the infirmary. That's where she sleeps now. He must have forgotten."

"He said the cell."

"He made a mistake."

The two men locked gazes. Then Xavier straightened up and leaned out the elevator door. Carmichael's voice and footsteps echoed down the hall.

"Doc?" Xavier called. "I have Elena here. These guys tell me Tyrone wants her taken back to her cell."

"He must have made a mistake," Carmichael said as she approached.

"That's what I told them."

Carmichael stopped in front of the open elevator doors. "Cliff, Paul, take Ms. Michaels to the infirmary. I'll be right there."

Xavier accompanied me to the infirmary and didn't leave until Carmichael showed up. He tried to stay longer, but she shooed him out, grumbling that my sleep had been interrupted enough and she needed my help in the morning. As he left, Xavier mouthed, "You owe me." I did. And I was sure he wouldn't let the IOU go unpaid.

As I settled onto my cot, Carmichael bustled around the room, prepping equipment and checking Bauer. Once she asked me if there was anything I'd like to talk about. There was, but I couldn't do it. I didn't want to see my guilt reflected in another person's face. A good man had died that night. He'd been shot by a vicious guard, after being sentenced to death by a sadistic tyrant, but ultimately the weight of his demise lay on my shoulders. I couldn't share that with Carmichael. The one person in the world I could have unburdened myself on was hundreds of miles away, fighting his own battles in a motel room. Thinking about that only reminded me how alone I was. Before Carmichael left, she fixed me a cup of tea. From the medicinal smell, I knew it contained a sedative, but drank it anyway. That was the only way I was going to fall asleep that night and I desperately wanted to sleep, to sleep, to forget . . . if only for a few hours.

CHAPTER 31

EXILE

After breakfast the next day, Bauer awoke.

I was sitting beside her bed, absorbed in my thoughts, as I had been all morning. When she first opened her eyes, I thought it was a reflexive action. Her eyes opened, but she didn't move, just stared at the ceiling, expressionless. Then she blinked.

"Doctor?" I said.

Carmichael made a noise and glanced up from her paperwork. A split second later, she was at the bedside. It took a while for Bauer to rouse herself. I guess if you've been out cold for days, you don't exactly jump up screaming—at least, we should be thankful she *didn't* jump up screaming, all things considered.

It took about twenty minutes for Bauer to awaken enough to move. She tried shifting onto her side, but the restraints held her back. She glanced down sharply, frowning, saw the bonds, and shot a glare at Carmichael. Her mouth opened, but only a whisper came out, so faint even I couldn't distinguish words. Carmichael got the message, though, and quickly loosened the arm restraints.

"Uh, that's not such a good idea," I said.

"She's too weak to talk, much less move," Carmichael said.

Bauer's eyes went from me to Carmichael, following our exchange. She searched my face with no flicker of recognition. Then I saw the flash. She remembered me. Her eyes narrowed.

"Wh—" She stopped and swallowed. "Wh—why's she here?"

"Elena's been helping me, Sondra. Since your . . . mishap."

"Mi—?" Bauer swallowed again, tongue flicking over her dry lips. "What mishap?"

"Grab Sondra a glass of water, Elena."

Again Bauer's gaze settled on me. "Wh—why's she here?"

"Get the water and then have the guards take you for a walk. I need to speak to Sondra."

I retrieved the water and tried to ignore the second half of the request, but Carmichael shooed me away. I knew I shouldn't leave Carmichael alone with Bauer. I also knew there was no sense arguing with the doctor. So I settled for leaving with the in-room guards and advising the door guards to take up posts inside. To my surprise, they obeyed. It would have been a heartening sign of my growing power and position if I hadn't suspected they were hightailing it into the infirmary so they could regale their colleagues with tales of being the first to see the new werewolf awake.

After my walk, Tucker met us outside the infirmary.

"Drop her off with Peters and Lewis inside," Tucker said. "Then get down to the cells and escort Miss O'Donnell into Zaid's cell."

"I thought Doctor Matasumi canceled all visits," one of my guards said.

"Katz—Doctor Matasumi changed his mind."

"But I thought he said—"

"He changed his mind. Miss O'Donnell will visit Zaid for one hour, followed by a one-hour visit with Miss Levine."

"How is Savannah?" I asked.

Three pairs of eyes turned on me, as if the walls had spoken. For a moment it seemed no one was going to answer me, then Tucker said brusquely, "She's fine."

"You know, I wouldn't mind seeing her myself," I said. "Maybe cheer her up a little."

"Miss O'Donnell can do that," Tucker said, then turned and headed down the hall.

The two guards led me into the room. Bauer still lay on the bed. Carmichael sat beside her, holding her hand. I assumed Bauer had fallen back asleep, then noticed her eyes were open. Carmichael motioned me to silence.

"I know it's a shock," Carmichael murmured. "But you're in good health and—"

"Good health?" Bauer spat, turning to skewer Carmichael with blazing eyes. "Do you know what I feel like right now? This—this—" Her left hand tried to punch the air, but only succeeded in a weak flutter before collapsing back at her side. "This *isn't* my body. It's not me. It's—it's wrong. Horribly, disgustingly wrong. And the dreams." She gave a choking gasp. "Oh, God. The dreams."

Carmichael touched Bauer's brow. Bauer closed her eyes and seemed to relax. Then she opened her eyes and saw me.

"Get her out of here," Bauer said.

"I realize Elena might not be the person you most want to see right—"

"Get her out of here."

Carmichael squeezed Bauer's hand. "I know she's a reminder of what's happened, but you need her, Sondra. She understands what you're going through, and she can help us. Without her—"

"Without her?" Bauer looked at me and pulled back her lips in a snarl. "Without her, I wouldn't be here."

"I understand your anger, Sondra. If it hadn't been for Elena coming here, this would never have happened. But you can't blame her—"

"Can't blame her? Can't blame her?" Bauer's voice rose. "Who the hell do you think did this to me?"

An hour later, I was back in my cell.

After everything I'd done, every risk I'd taken, one accusation from a newly turned, half-mad werewolf and I was in my goddamned cell. I'd nursed Bauer back to health. I'd prevented Carmichael from administering potentially life-threatening medicines. I'd thrown myself between Bauer and the gun-happy guards. How did she repay me? She blamed me, and not just in a figurative sense—because she'd used my saliva—but literally accusing me of turning her into a werewolf. Madness, right? What about the syringe? The needle mark? The evidence exonerated me. What did they think, that I'd stolen a syringe from the infirmary during my physical, filled it with my spit, and jabbed it into Bauer's arm? That was exactly what they thought. Or what Matasumi thought. Carmichael seemed to have the sense to realize this was preposterous. She hadn't said so outright, but she'd argued to keep me in the infirmary, and when I'd been forced to leave, she'd walked me to the door and promised to "get things straightened out."

How much good would Carmichael be as an ally? She was an employee with no real authority. When only Matasumi and Winsloe had been in charge, Carmichael's strong will had metamorphosed into true power. In battles of personality, Matasumi was defenseless. Winsloe had the requisite willpower to challenge anyone, but he kept out of the day-to-day running of the compound. So, in Bauer's absence, Carmichael had little trouble getting me into the infirmary against Matasumi's wishes. But now Bauer was back. Where did that leave Carmichael? I weighed the personalities of both women, assessing their chances.

There was one more factor to consider. How hard would Carmichael fight for me? She made little secret of her contempt for Winsloe and Matasumi but seemed fond of Bauer. Would she subject her weakened patient to a battle of wills? It depended on one thing: Bauer's convalescence. If Carmichael felt she needed me to help Bauer, she'd fight. But if Bauer recovered without relapse, I was shit outta luck. My best hope was for something horrible to happen, for Bauer to lose control, and for Carmichael and Matasumi to realize they needed my help. Knowing what a newly turned werewolf was capable of, it was an awful thing to wish for.

I had truly been cast out of favor. If there'd been any doubt, it soon vanished. The guards brought my breakfast two hours late, dropped it off, and left. Then they brought my lunch. Nothing happened in the interim. Absolutely nothing. Carmichael didn't summon me for a checkup. Matasumi didn't come down to question me. Xavier didn't pop by for a visit. Even Tess didn't take up observation duty outside my cell. I was left with my thoughts, consumed by memories of the night before. Alone with my fears, my self-recriminations, and my grief, reflecting on Armen's death, then Ruth's, then my own situation, which was growing bleaker with each passing hour.

Around mid-afternoon my door opened, and I leaped from my seat so fast you'd have thought Ed McMahon stood there with a Publishers Clearing House check. Okay, so it was only a guard, but at this point, any face was welcome. Maybe he was coming to take me upstairs. Maybe he was coming to deliver a message. Hell, maybe he was just coming to *talk* to me. Six hours of exile and I already felt as if I'd spent a week in solitary confinement.

The guard walked in, set a vase of flowers on the table, and left.

Flowers? Who'd be sending me flowers? Carmichael trying to cheer me up? Right. Matasumi apologizing for sending me back to the cell? Oh, yeah. Bauer thanking me for all my selfless work on her behalf? That's gotta be it. With a bitter laugh, I turned the flowers around and read the card.

Elena,
Sorry to hear what happened.
I'll see what I can do.
    Ty

I slammed the vase off the table and clenched my fists, seething with fury. How dare he! After last night, how did he dare send me flowers, feign concern over my exile. I scowled at the flowers strewn across the carpet. Was this his idea of a joke? Or was he trying to fool me into thinking he still cared? Was he taunting me? Or did he, in his twisted way, really still care? Goddamn it! I snarled and kicked the vase across the room. When it didn't shatter, I strode over, scooped it up in one hand, and whirled to pitch it into the wall. Then I froze in mid-throw, fingers still wrapped around the vase. I couldn't do this. I couldn't afford to incur Winsloe's anger. The impotent fury that swept through me was almost enough to make me hurl the vase into the wall, damn the consequences. But I didn't. Giving in to the rage would only give him an excuse to hurt me again. He wanted to play mind games? Fine. I dropped to my knees and began gathering the flowers, obliterating all signs of my anger. Next time Tyrone Winsloe stepped into my cell, he'd see his flowers nicely displayed on the table. And I'd thank him for his thoughtfulness. Smile and thank him. Two could play this game.

At seven o'clock that evening, the door opened. A guard walked in.

"They need you upstairs," he said.

Elation rushed through me. Yes! And not a minute too soon. Then I saw his face, the tightness of his jaw failing to conceal the anxiety in his eyes.

"What's happened?" I said, getting to my feet.

He didn't answer, only turned and held the door. Two more guards waited in the hall. All had their guns drawn. My stomach plunged. Was this it, then? Had Bauer ordered my death? Had Winsloe tired of toying with me and decided to hunt me? But that wouldn't make the guards anxious. Some, like Ryman and Jolliffe, would be fairly licking their chops at the prospect.

As I stepped through the door, the first guard poked me in the back with his gun, not a hard jab, more of an impatient prod. I picked up speed and we quick-marched through the security exit.

The infirmary waiting room was jam-packed. I counted seven guards, plus Tucker and Matasumi. As I stepped through the door, time slowed, giving me a montage of visual impressions bereft of smell and sound, like a silent movie cranking through one frame at a time.

Matasumi seated, face white, eyes staring at nothing. Tucker at the intercom barking silent orders. Five guards clustered around him. One guard sat beside Matasumi, head in his hands, palms over his eyes, chin damp, a wet smear staining one shirt sleeve. The last guard faced the far wall, bracing himself with arms outstretched, head bowed, chest heaving. As I shifted my weight forward, my shoe slid. Something slick on the floor. I glanced down. A thin puddle of opaque yellowish brown. Vomit. I looked up. The infirmary door was closed. I stepped forward, still in slow motion. Faces turned. The crowd parted, not giving me room but stepping away. Nine pairs of eyes on me, expressions ranging from apprehension to disgust.

"What's going on here?" Winsloe's voice behind me shattered the illusion.

I could smell now: vomit, sweat, anxiety, and fear. Someone muttered something unintelligible. Winsloe shoved past me to look through the infirmary door window. Everyone paused, collectively holding their breath.

"Holy shit!" Winsloe said, his voice filled not with horror but with wonder. "Did Elena do—oh, shit, I see. Jesus fucking Christ, would you get a look at that!"

Almost against my will, my feet moved toward the infirmary door. Winsloe sidestepped to give me room and put his arm around my waist, pulling me in.

"Can you believe that?" he said, then laughed. "I guess you can, right?"

At first, I saw nothing. Or nothing unusual. Beyond the window was the counter, shining antiseptic white, stainless-steel sink gleaming like something in a kitchen showroom. A row of bottles stood at attention along the back of the counter. Carmichael's binder lay at a perfect ninety-degree angle beside the sink. Everything ordered and spotless, as always. Then something along the base of the counter caught my eye. An obscenity amid the pristine cleanliness. A star-shaped splatter of blood.

My gaze traversed the floor. A smear of blood six inches from the counter. Fat drops zigzagging to the crash cart. The cart upended, contents scattered and broken. A puddle of blood. A shoe print in the puddle, edges razor perfect. Then another smear, bigger, the bloodied shoe sliding across the floor. The filing cabinet. The hundred-pound steel cabinet toppled over, blockading the far corner as if someone had tipped it and hidden behind its imperfect barricade. Papers scattered across the floor. Blood spattered over them. Beneath the bed, a shoe with a bloodied bottom. Above the shoe, a leg. I whirled to face the others, to tell them someone was in there. As I turned, my gaze traveled up the leg to the knee, to a pool of bright crimson, to nothingness. A severed leg. My stomach leaped to my throat. I spun away, fast, but not fast enough. I saw a hand lying a few feet from the bed. Closer to the door, half-obscured under a spilled tray, a bloody hunk of meat that had been human.

Something hit the door, reverberating so hard I stumbled back with the impact. A roar of fury. A flash of yellowish brown fur. An ear. A blood-soaked muzzle. Bauer.

"Tranquilizers," I wheezed as I regained my balance. "We need to sedate her. Now."

"That's the problem," Tucker said. "It's all in there."

"All of it?" I inhaled, blinking, struggling to get my brain working again. I rubbed a hand across my face, straightened up, and looked around. "There must be a backup supply. Where's Doctor Carmichael? She'll know."

No one answered. As silence ticked by, my guts heaved again. I closed my eyes and forced myself to look through the window. Back at the foot under the bed. The shoe. A sensible, sturdy black shoe. Carmichael's shoe.

Oh, God. That wasn't fair. It was so, so, so not fair. The refrain raced through my head, chasing out all other thoughts. Of everyone in this god-damned place. Of all those who I'd gladly see die. Of those few I'd even be happy to see die a death as horrible as this. Not Carmichael.

Rage surged through me. I clenched my fists, gave in to the anger for a moment, then shoved it back as I turned to face the others.

"She's fully Changed," I said. "You have a fully Changed, half-mad werewolf in there, and if you don't act fast, she'll come right through this door. Why's everyone standing around? What are you going to do?"

"The question is," Tucker said. "What are *you* going to do?"

I stepped away from the door. "This is your problem, not mine. I warned you. I warned and warned and warned. You used me to help her recover, then you threw me back in my cell. Now things have gone wrong and you want me to fix it? Well, I didn't screw it up in the first place."

Tucker waved at the guards. One moved to the door, checked through the window, and turned the handle.

"You'll find sedatives in the cupboards along the far wall," Tucker said.

"No way," I said. "No fucking way."

Four of the remaining guards lifted their guns. Trained those guns on me.

"I will not—"

The door opened. Someone shoved me. As I stumbled in, the door slammed shut, catching my heel and knocking me to the floor. Scrambling to my feet, I heard nothing but silence. Then a sound vibrated through the room, more felt than heard. A growl.

CHAPTER 32

RAMPAGE

S till on all fours, I looked up slowly. A 120-odd-pound wolf stared back, yellow-brown fur on end, making Bauer seem as big as a mastiff. She stared me in the eyes, ears forward, teeth bared, lips curled in a silent snarl.

I looked away and stayed down, holding myself a few inches lower than Bauer. The submission rankled, but my life was worth more than my pride. And yes, at that moment, I was very worried about my life expectancy. Even Clay would avoid tackling a werewolf who was in wolf form when he was not. As a wolf, Bauer had the advantage of teeth and claws. Moreover, the human shape itself is awkward for fighting an animal—too slow, too tall, too easily thrown off-balance. The only superior weapon humans have is their brain, and that doesn't help much against something with an animal body and a human brain. Against a newly turned werewolf, the human brain is actually a disadvantage. Our minds are fundamentally logical. We assess a situation, devise possible strategies, and pick the one that represents the best compromise between likelihood of success and likelihood of survival. If I'm late for work, I can floor the gas pedal all the way to the office, but considering the risk of personal injury, I'll choose instead to drive ten or fifteen miles over the speed limit and arrive at work slightly late but alive. A new werewolf in wolf form loses that ability to reason, to assess the consequences. It is like a rabid beast, fueled by instinct and fury, ready to destroy everything in sight, even if it kills itself in the process.

I could fight Bauer only if I Changed into a wolf. But even under ideal conditions, that took five to ten minutes. Like Lake, I'd be completely vulnerable during that interim, too deformed even to stand and run away. Bauer would tear me apart before I sprouted fur. Yet no one was letting me out of here until I stopped Bauer. The only way to do that would be to sedate her.

To knock Bauer out, all I had to do was run across the room, grab a sedative-filled syringe from the cupboard, and jab it into her. It sounded so easy. If only there wasn't a blood-crazed wolf between the cupboard and me. Even if Bauer didn't pounce on me before I ran past, she'd attack the second my back was to her. I inhaled. First step: I had to find the proper mix of submission and self-confidence. Too submissive and she'd see me as easy prey. Too assertive and she'd see me as a threat. The key was to not show fear. Again, it sounded so easy . . . if you weren't in a room littered with bloody body parts, reminding you that with one false move your limbs and vital organs would join them.

I inched forward, keeping my gaze focused below Bauer's eyes. As I moved, I scrutinized her body for signs: bunched muscles, tense tendons, all the signals that presaged an attack. In five steps, I was parallel to her, about six feet to her left. Sweat stung my eyes. Did it stink of fear? Bauer's nose twitched, but the rest of her remained motionless. As I sidestepped past, I swiveled, keeping my face to her. Her eyes followed me. I kept moving sideways. A dozen steps to go. Bauer's hindquarters shifted up, the first sign of an impending leap. With that early sign, I thought I'd have time to react. I didn't. By the time my brain registered that she was about to lunge, she was airborne. There was no time to turn and run. I dove past her, hit the ground, and rolled. Behind me, Bauer hit the floor, all four legs skidding. As I watched her slide, I realized I did have an advantage here. Like a new driver plunked behind the wheel of a Maserati, Bauer was unprepared for the power and precision handling of her new body. If I could take advantage of her mistakes and inexperience, I could survive.

As I lurched to my feet, Bauer was veering around. I sprinted past her and vaulted onto the counter. Throwing one cupboard open, I grabbed the wooden partition between the doors to balance myself and spun around. Bauer flew at me. I kicked her under the jaw and she somersaulted backward, skidding across the floor. As I flipped to face the cupboards, I saw faces crowding the infirmary window. Were they enjoying the show? Damn, I hoped so.

While Bauer recovered, I threw open the second cupboard door and searched both sides for syringes filled with sedative. Instead, I saw a box of plastic-encased syringes and rows of labeled bottles. A do-it-yourself job. Shit! Were these the right syringes? Which bottle did I need? How much should I fill it? I pushed my questions aside, grabbed a syringe, and started scooting down the counter toward the bottles. Then I stopped, plucked a second packaged syringe from the box, and shoved it into my pocket. Klutz insurance. When I reached the bottles, I scanned them for a familiar name. Behind me, Bauer struggled to her feet. Move, Elena! Just grab one! I saw pentobarbital, recognized it from Jeremy's medical bag, and reached for it.

Bauer leaped at the counter but miscalculated and crashed into it. The whole structure shook as my fingers grazed the pentobarbital. My hand knocked the bottle. I fumbled for it, but it toppled from the cupboard, bounced off the countertop, and rolled across the linoleum. As Bauer circled for another attack, I reached for a new bottle of sedative. There wasn't another one. Frantically, I scanned the shelf, but saw nothing I recognized. Bauer leaped. I swung around to kick her again, but missed by a hairsbreadth. This time I hadn't braced myself, and the motion propelled me off-balance. I pitched forward and jumped from the counter before I fell. Bauer grabbed my left leg at the knee. Her fangs sank in. Pain clouded my vision. Blindly I swung my fist at the source of the pain, connected with her skull, and sent her reeling, probably more from surprise than pain. When she jerked away, her fangs ripped through my knee. My leg buckled as soon as I put weight on it. Gritting my teeth, I stumbled to the bottle of pentobarbital on the floor, found it—unbroken—snatched it up and sailed awkwardly over the first bed. As Bauer leaped after me, I thrust the bed at her and knocked her off her feet.

I tore the seal off the bottle and filled the syringe. Did I use too much? Did I care? If it stopped Bauer—temporarily or forever—that was good enough. Bauer flew over the bed. I started to scramble over the second bed, but Bauer caught my foot. Her fangs scraped my ankle as my shoe came free in her mouth. The shoe snagged on her teeth and she tumbled back to the floor, shaking her head wildly to free herself from this new enemy. Still atop the second bed, I lifted the syringe over Bauer and plunged it down, feeling a momentary elation as the needle penetrated the deep fur behind Bauer's head. Now all I had to do was hit the plunger. But I'd put so much force into the downswing that I wasn't prepared for the next step. I released the syringe to get a better grip and Bauer twisted away, leaving the needle stuck harmlessly in her shoulder.

As Bauer lunged at my legs, I jumped to the floor. At this rate, I was fast running out of obstacles. I raced around the end of the bed as Bauer hurtled over it. I shoved the bed, trying to hit her again, but she'd leaped high enough this time and cleared it easily. While she circled around, I sprinted across the room. Could I get close enough to depress the syringe plunger? Not without getting close enough for Bauer to rip out my throat. Could I fill the second syringe and try again? I searched for the bottle, but I didn't see it and couldn't remember if I'd recapped it. Unlikely.

I grabbed a metal cart and flung it at Bauer as she came at me. It knocked her back. I turned to find some new weapon. At my feet lay a bloodstained piece of white cloth. With a gnawed torso inside it, and a head atop it, neck bitten through almost to decapitation, eyes wide, disbelieving. Carmichael.

Her eyes paralyzed me. I could have saved her. If they'd brought me up here earlier . . . How long did they wait? How long was Carmichael in here with Bauer? Running for her life? Feeling teeth rip through her flesh? Knowing it was over but still hoping, praying for rescue? Had she been dead before Bauer began ripping her apart? Before Bauer started to eat her? Oh, God. I doubled over, faintly registering a blur of motion to my left, knowing Bauer was coming but unable to move, unable to wrench my gaze or my thoughts from Carmichael. Out of the corner of my eye, I saw Bauer leap. That broke the spell.

I dove out of Bauer's path, but she caught my pant leg in her teeth and I tripped, crashing to the floor. As I flipped over, she leaped onto my chest, jaws wide, slashing down at my throat. I brought my fists up into the underside of her jaw, skewing her aim. Wrapping both hands in her neck fur, I fought to keep her head away from mine. Her jaws snapped so close a rush of hot air hit my throat. The stink of her breath enveloped me, the stench of blood and rage and raw meat. I arched my head up to meet her eyes, trying to assert my superiority with a glare. It didn't work. It would never work. She was too far gone to recognize a dominant wolf. Grappling with her, I managed to get both my legs up and thrust them into her stomach. She fell back. As I scrambled from under her, something moved to my left. Xavier. He waved his arms.

"Here doggy, doggy," he called. "Time for a new chew-toy."

Bauer kept coming at me. Xavier lunged and grabbed a handful of tail fur. When she whipped around, he vanished and reappeared a few feet away. She charged. He popped to the other side of the room.

"Over here, doggy," he called. "Come on, Elena. You have to hit the plunger for the stuff to work."

"I know that," I snarled.

Bauer wheeled and charged Xavier again. This time, I tore after her. Xavier waited until the last second, then disappeared. Bauer tried to stop but had built up too much speed and plowed into the wall. I jumped on her back and slammed the syringe plunger down. Relief flooded me. Then I realized Bauer was twisting around, jaws open. What had I expected? That she'd drop the second the sedative went in? I whacked my open hand against the sensitive top of Bauer's muzzle. Then I ran like hell. Behind me, I heard a thud, but I didn't turn around until I'd leaped onto the countertop. Bauer lay crumpled on the floor. For a moment, I stood there, rigid, heart pounding. Then I slumped onto the counter.

⚜

An hour later I was back in my cell. I sensed a pattern here—save the day, get thrown into solitary confinement. Great motivation.

Though Bauer had only scraped my foot, she'd done a bang-up job on my knee. Without Carmichael, there was no one to tend to my wounds. Matasumi had examined my leg and pronounced that the muscles and tendons may or may not have been torn. Gee, thanks. Tucker had stitched up the two longest tears. He hadn't used anesthetic, but I'd been too exhausted to care.

Once inside my cell, I went into the bathroom, undressed, and sponge-bathed with a facecloth. A shower would have been heaven, but I couldn't get my bandages wet. As I scrubbed blood from the tear in my jeans, I remembered the blood splatters in the infirmary and, remembering the blood, remembered the mangled pieces of Carmichael scattered across the floor. I stopped and inhaled. Damn her. Why hadn't she listened to me? If she'd heeded my warnings, if she'd properly restrained Bauer, if she'd kept Bauer under guard, if she'd fought harder to keep me in the infirmary . . . So many ifs.

I closed my eyes and inhaled again. I didn't even know Carmichael's first name. As that thought skittered guiltily through my brain, I realized it didn't matter. I'd known enough about her to know that, however misguided the aspirations and dreams that brought her to this place, she hadn't deserved to die like that. She'd been the only person who'd given a damn about Bauer, and Bauer's first act as a werewolf had been to slaughter her. How do you like your new life now, Sondra? Is it everything you imagined?

The door of my cell opened. I glanced up to see Xavier, for once using the conventional method of entering a room. He closed the door behind him and waved a bottle of Jack Daniel's.

"Thought you could use this," he said. "Probably not up to your standards, but Winsloe keeps moving his stash of the good stuff."

I wrung out my jeans over the sink and tugged them on. Xavier could see my state of undress through the glass wall but didn't comment on it. Maybe the tragedy upstairs had shaken him. Or maybe he was just too tired for one-liners.

When Xavier had come to my rescue in the infirmary, I'd assumed Matasumi or Tucker had sent him in, but later, when the two of them discussed the situation while examining my knee, I'd learned Xavier had acted on his own. Of course, with his powers, he'd never been in any real danger from Bauer, but at least he'd put himself out enough to help. So, for once, I didn't tell him to get the hell out of my cell. Besides, I really did need a drink.

While I finished dressing, Xavier filled the two tumblers he'd brought. He handed me one as I walked from the bathroom.

"How did that happen?" I asked. "Where were the guards?"

"They'd decided guards weren't necessary. Sondra was still partially restrained last time I saw her. Either she broke free or the good doctor released her. A guard stopped by at six-thirty and found Sondra chowing down on her first wolf meal."

"No one heard anything?"

"Hey, they bought the best soundproofing on the market, remember? I'd bet Carmichael hit the intercom buzzer but didn't have time to stand around and chat. Of course, no one in central security admits he heard the buzzer."

I downed my whiskey and shook my head.

"I've saved your ass twice now," Xavier said. "With Ryman and Jolliffe yesterday and now with Sondra."

"Sorry, but they confiscated my checkbook when I arrived. You'll have to bill me."

He grinned, unoffended. "Money isn't everything. Or so they keep telling me. This seems a good time to test the theory and try an even more time-honored method of commerce. The barter system. A tax-free exchange of services."

"Uh-huh."

"Oh, don't give me that look," he said, tipping another few ounces into my glass. "I'm not talking about sex. You'd eat me alive." He paused and made a face. "Bad choice of words. My apologies to the good doctor. What I meant is that you owe me big-time, and someday I will collect."

"I'm sure you will."

"And so long as you're running a tab, here's a bit of advice you can add to it. You've overstayed your welcome, Elena. We both have. The big man is plenty pissed with both of us right now."

"Winsloe." I closed my eyes and winced. "Now what did I do?"

"Enough. I know you must be making escape plans, so I'd suggest you bump them up before he erupts." He lowered his voice to a near-whisper. "Now, two things you have to be careful of when you break out. First is Katzen—"

"The mysterious sorcerer. I haven't even met the guy."

"Neither have I. He's a paranoid son of a bitch. Won't deal with anyone except—"

My cell door opened. Winsloe walked in with Ryman and Jolliffe.

"Too late," Xavier murmured around the rim of his glass. He took a slug, then waved the empty glass at Winsloe. "See what I have to resort to? Jack Daniel's. Barely drinkable. You get me hooked on the good stuff, then keep hiding it on me. Sadistic bastard."

Xavier grinned, and I detected more than a hint of satisfaction in that grin, the pleasure of being able to call Winsloe that to his face and get away with it.

"You owe me a bottle of cognac anyway," Xavier continued. "I like the Remy Martin XO, not the VSOP. You can have someone drop it off at my room later."

Winsloe arched his brows. "And how do you figure that?"

"I saved your girl. Twice now, actually." He grinned at Ryman and Jolliffe. "But we won't get into that first time, will we, guys? I'm no tattletale. Besides, that wasn't a big deal. But upstairs there? Whew. Another minute and she'd have been a goner."

"You think?" Winsloe said.

"Oh, yeah." Xavier slapped my back. "No offense, Elena, but you were in way over your head."

"Thanks," I said, and managed to almost sound like I meant it.

"So you owe me, Ty. Drop off that bottle anytime."

Winsloe laughed. "You've got balls, Reese. Fair enough then. I owe you. You'll get your cognac. Stop by my room in about an hour and pick it up. Maybe I can rustle up a few glasses of the Louis XIII for us, make that XO taste like bad moonshine."

"Sounds like a plan."

Under Xavier's quick grins and Winsloe's easygoing camaraderie thrummed a current of tension so strong you could almost see it. Xavier had been right. He was in deep shit. Yet both men chatted away as if nothing were wrong, as if they were just two old buddies planning to get together later for a few drinks. Masters of bullshit, both of them.

"So I'll see you in my room?" Winsloe said. "In an hour?"

"You bet," Xavier said. And I knew he had no intention of keeping that appointment, just as I knew that when he bade me good night he was really saying good-bye and that if he ever collected on that IOU, it wouldn't be within these compound walls. Like all successful gamblers, Xavier knew when to take the money and run.

After Xavier zapped from the room, Winsloe's gaze slithered over me and he pursed his lips.

"That's the same clothing you arrived in," he said. "They've given you other stuff to wear, haven't they? What about that shirt I brought you?"

Actually, I'd tried using it as a spare washcloth, but there wasn't enough fabric to get decent sudsing action. Be nice, I reminded myself. If Xavier was right, I was already on Winsloe's bad side. Again. I couldn't afford to make things worse. No matter how badly I'd been torn up that night, physically and emotionally, I had to play nice. Had to. Whatever he said. Whatever he did. I could not fight back. It would be a greater game of wits and fortitude than my match with Bauer, but I could handle this. I really could.

"It's a werewolf thing," I said, injecting apology into my tone. "Laundry soaps, fabric softeners—the smell's too strong."

"You should have said so. I'll tell the staff to get unscented detergent. Don't bother with the clothes Sondra supplied. I'll order new things for you."

Oh, joy.

Winsloe plopped onto my bed. I stayed standing, back to the bookshelf, trying hard not to feel cornered.

"Can you believe what Sondra did to the doc?" Winsloe asked, eyes glinting like a little boy who's seen his first NHL blood-on-ice brawl.

"It . . . happens."

"You ever do stuff like that?"

"I'm a Pack werewolf."

He hesitated, as if this was a non sequitur. Then he leaned forward. "But you could do it. Obviously. You're stronger and *much* younger."

When I didn't answer, he hopped to his feet and rocked on his heels. "You did a helluva job evading Sondra. Better than the doc, that's for sure." He laughed. The sound grated down my spine. "Too bad Xavier interfered. I'd hoped you'd fight Sondra."

"Sorry."

I should have explained why I hadn't fought, but I couldn't. My exhaustion was too great. An apology would have to suffice. Maybe if I was polite but not encouraging, he'd take the hint and leave.

"You should have fought her," Winsloe said.

I shook my head, eyes downcast, and slumped into a chair.

"I would have liked it if you'd fought her," he continued.

How 'bout you fight her next time, Ty? Now *I'd* like that. I kept my eyes down so he wouldn't see the flare of contempt.

"I would have liked that, Elena," he repeated, ducking his head to look at me.

"Why didn't you say so?" Damn! Too sharp. Retreat, retreat. "I guess I got the impression you guys wanted Bauer alive. I should have asked."

Silence. Had that still sounded sarcastic? Damn it! Change tack, double-time. I yawned and rubbed my hands over my face.

"I'm sorry, Ty. I'm so tired."

"You didn't look tired when I walked in. Standing around, chatting it up with Xavier. You two seem pretty tight."

"I was just thanking him. He did me a big favor, jumping in—"

He snapped his fingers, pique vanishing in an eye blink. "Favor. That reminds me, there's something I need to ask you about. Hold on and I'll be right back."

I wanted to ask if it could wait until morning. I really did. But after last night, I desperately needed to get back into his good graces. I couldn't deny him a favor. Besides, he seemed to be in a chipper mood. That was a good sign. So I summoned my last bits of strength, managed a clumsy half-smile, and nodded. Not that my consent mattered. Winsloe and his guards were already gone.

CHAPTER 33

TORTURE

When Winsloe returned I was dozing in my chair. He burst into the cell waving a manila envelope.

"Devil of a time finding these buggers," he said. "Larry had already filed them in his to-do box. Way too efficient."

I roused myself. Tried to look interested. Accidentally yawned.

"Am I boring you, Elena?" Winsloe asked. The edge in his voice twisted his grin into a teeth-baring grimace.

"No, no." Bite back another yawn. "Of course not. What do you have there?"

"Surveillance photos of a werewolf I'd like you to identify."

"Sure"—Damn it, Elena. Stop yawning!—"if I can, but my memory for faces is pretty bad."

"That's okay. This one doesn't have a face." Winsloe chortled. "Not a human face, I mean. He's a wolf. If you ask me, all wolves look the same, which is why Larry didn't bother asking you for an ID. But then I thought, maybe that kind of thinking is too race-centered. You know, like those witnesses who get on the stand and finger the wrong black guy because all black men look the same to them?"

"Uh-huh." Get to the point. Please. Before I drift off.

"So, I thought, maybe all wolf faces don't look the same to a wolf. Or to a part-time wolf." Another chortle that set my nerves on edge.

"I'll do my best," I said. "But if I've seen this mutt before, I've probably only seen him as a human. A scent would be better."

"Scent." Winsloe snapped his fingers. "Now why didn't I think of that. See? Race-centered again. I think I'm sharp if I can identify the smell of pepperoni pizza."

I reached for the envelope. He thumped onto the bed and tossed it beside him, as if he hadn't noticed me reaching for it.

"Could I see—?" I began.

"A team spotted this guy late last night. No, I guess that'd be early this morning. The wee hours anyway."

I nodded. Please, please, please get to the point.

"Very bizarre circumstances," Winsloe mused. "Ever since we snatched you and the old witch, we've had a team trying to find the rest of your group. We could always use another werewolf, and Larry's pretty keen on getting that fire-demon guy. We lost track of them after we grabbed you two. That's not exactly a secret, though I'd rather you didn't tell Larry I told you. He's not too pleased about the whole thing, but I'm sure it makes you feel better, knowing your friends got away."

Winsloe paused. And waited.

"Thanks," I said, "for telling me."

"You're welcome. So, we've had this team scouting the area, picking up tips, most of them useless. Yesterday Tucker recalled that group, and sent a fresh one to replace them. Keeping up morale and all that. The first team was heading back and spent the night in some backwater motel. Next morning, they get up for a pre-dawn start, go outside, and what do you think they see there, on the edge of the woods?"

"A—uh—" Come on, brain, wake up. "A—umm, a wolf?"

"Glad to see you're paying attention, Elena. Yes, it was a wolf. A big fucker of a wolf. Standing right there, watching them. Now either this is the biggest coincidence in the universe or this werewolf had been following them. Searching for the search party."

Brain kicking in now. "Where was this?"

"Does it matter?"

"All werewolves are territorial. Technically mutts can't hold territory, but most stick to a familiar piece of ground, like a state, just moving from city to city. If I knew where this took place, it would help me figure out who it might have been."

Winsloe smiled. "And help you figure out where *you* are. None of that, Elena. Now let me tell my story. So, the guards see this wolf and they figure out that it's a werewolf. One grabs a camera and snaps some photos. The other two go for the tranquilizer guns. Before they can unpack them, though, the wolf vanishes. So they gear up and head into the woods. And do you know what? He's right there, like he's waiting. They get close, he runs, then stops and waits. Luring them in. Can you believe that?"

"Werewolves retain human intelligence. It's not that strange." But it was. Why? Because luring prey was an animal tactic and mutts didn't use animal tactics. No, I corrected quickly. They *rarely* used animal tactics. Of course they *could*. Some did.

"Wait," Winsloe said, grinning. "It gets weirder. You know what this wolf does next? He separates them. Takes a commando team, including a former Navy Seal, and figures out how to separate them. Then he starts picking them off. Killing them! Can you believe that?" Winsloe laughed and shook his head. "Man, I wish I'd been there. One werewolf turning those military goons into blithering idiots, wandering around the woods, getting picked off like blonds in a horror flick. The wolf kills two and goes after the third. And what do you think he does?"

My heart was pounding now. "Kills him?"

"No! That's the topper. He doesn't kill him. He runs him ragged. Like he's trying to exhaust him, like he wants to keep him alive but too weak to fight. Okay, maybe I'm reading too much into this, attributing human motivations to an animal. Anthro—what do they call that?"

"Anthropomorphism," I whispered, feeling as if all the air had been knocked from my lungs, knowing this was no accidental segue.

"Right. Anthropomorphism. Hey, that's what your boyfriend studies, right? Anthropomorphic religions. Boring as hell if you ask me, but people say that about computers, too. Each to his own. Now where was I?"

"The wolf," I whispered. "Running down the last survivor."

"You don't look so good. Maybe you should come over here and lie down. Plenty of room. No? Suit yourself. So the wolf is running circles around this last guy. Only something goes wrong."

I wanted to stop up my ears. I knew what was coming. There was only one way Winsloe could have the photos in that envelope, only one way he'd know this story. If the last team member had survived. If the wolf—

"Somehow that canny fucker screwed up. Miscalculated a turn or a distance maybe. He got too close. The guard fired. Pow! Dead wolf."

"Let—let me see the photos."

Winsloe tossed the envelope at me. As it tumbled to the floor, I scrambled after it, ripping it open and yanking out the contents. Three photos of a wolf. A golden-haired, blue-eyed wolf. I felt a whimper snake up my throat.

"You know him?" Winsloe asked.

I crouched there, clutching the photos.

"No? Well, you're tired. Keep them. Get some rest and give it some thought. Xavier's probably waiting for me upstairs. I'll come back in the morning."

Winsloe left. I didn't see him go. Didn't hear him. All I could see were the photographs of Clay. All I could hear was the pounding of my blood. Another whimper crept up from my chest, but it died before reaching my mouth. I couldn't breathe. Couldn't make a sound.

Suddenly my body convulsed. A wave of agony blinded me. I toppled, photos fluttering the carpet. My leg muscles all knotted at once, like being seized by a thousand charley horses. I screamed. The waves hit in rapid succession and I screamed until I couldn't breathe. My limbs flailed and jerked as if being wrenched from their sockets. Some dim part of my brain realized I was Changing and told me to get control before it tore me apart. I didn't. I gave into it, let the agony rip through me, welcomed each new torment even as I screamed for release. Finally it was over. I lay there, panting, empty. Then I heard something. The faintest scratch from the hallway. Winsloe was there. Watching. I wanted to leap up, charge the wall, and batter myself against it until it broke or I did. I wanted to tear him apart, mouthful by mouthful, keeping him alive until I'd wrenched every last shriek from his lungs. But grief crushed me to the floor, and I couldn't even find the energy to stand. I managed to pull my belly off the ground and hauled myself into the narrow crevice between the foot of the bed and the wall, the one place where Winsloe couldn't see me. I wedged into the tiny space, tucked my tail under me, and surrendered to the pain.

I spent the night replaying Winsloe's words, fighting against my grief to recall each one. Where had the guards seen the wolf? Behind the motel or beside it? Exactly when did it happen? What did Winsloe mean by "predawn"? Had it been light out yet? As I asked these questions, part of me wondered if I was just allowing my mind to stutter through inanities rather than confront the soul-numbing possibility of Clay's death. No. These questions held clues, minute clues that would reveal the lie in Winsloe's words. I had to find that lie. Otherwise, I feared my breath would jam up in my throat and I'd suffocate on my grief.

So I tortured myself with Winsloe's story, his hated voice invading and filling my brain. Find the lie. Find the inconsistency, the misspoken word, the detail so obviously wrong. But no matter how many times I replayed his story, I couldn't find a mistake. If Clay found the search party, he'd have done exactly what Winsloe claimed he did: lure them into the forest, separate them, and kill them, leaving one alive to torture for information. There was no way Winsloe could make up something so true to Clay's character. Nor was there any way Winsloe could have guessed what Clay would do in that situation. So he'd told the truth.

My heart rammed into my throat. I gasped for breath. No, it had to be a lie. I'd know if Clay was dead. I'd have felt it the moment the bullet hit him. Oh, God, I wanted to believe that I'd know if he was dead. Clay and

I shared a psycho-physical connection, maybe because he was the one who had bitten me. If I was hurt and he wasn't around to see it, he'd feel it, knowing something was wrong. I'd experience the same twinges, the same floating anxiety and unease if he was hurt. I hadn't felt anything that morning. Or had I? I'd been asleep at dawn, drugged by Carmichael's sedative. Would I have felt *anything*?

I stopped myself. There was no sense dwelling on vagaries like premonitions and psychic twinges. Stick to the facts. Find the lie there. Winsloe said the last guard killed Clay, then returned with the photos and the story. If I could talk to that guard, maybe he wouldn't be as accomplished a liar as Winsloe. Maybe—I inhaled sharply. The guard had brought back the photos and the story. What about the body?

If that guard had killed Clay, he'd have brought back his body. At the very least, he'd have taken photos of it. If there'd been a corpse or photos of one, Winsloe wouldn't have settled for showing me pictures of Clay alive. He'd known exactly who the wolf was and he'd told me the story to torture me, to punish me. This was my comeuppance for disobeying him the night before. One small misstep and he'd lashed out with the worst punishment I could imagine. What would he do if I really pissed him off?

Eventually, after I'd persuaded myself that Clay was alive, the exhaustion took over and I fell asleep. Though I'd fallen asleep as a wolf, I awoke as a human. It happened sometimes, particularly if a Change was brought on by fear or emotion. Once we relaxed into sleep, the body morphed painlessly back to human form. So I awoke, naked, with my head and torso sandwiched between the bed and the wall and my legs sticking out.

I didn't get up immediately. Instead, I thought of ways to catch Winsloe in a lie, so I'd be certain about Clay. I had to be certain. Winsloe had left the photos. Maybe if I studied them I'd see something—

"Open this fucking door now!" a voice shouted.

I bolted upright, knocking my head against the bed. Dazed, I hesitated, then wriggled from my hiding place.

"Let me out of here!"

A woman's voice. Distorted, but familiar. I winced as I recognized it. No. Please no. Hadn't I suffered enough?

"I know you hear me! I know you're out there!"

With great reluctance, I moved to the hole in the wall between my cell and the next. I knew what I'd see. My new neighbor. I bent to peer through. Bauer stood at the one-way glass wall, banging her fists soundlessly against it. Her hair was snarled and matted, face still streaked with blood. Someone had dressed her in an ill-fitting gray sweat suit that must have belonged to one of the smaller guards. No more meticulously groomed heiress. Anyone seeing Sondra Bauer now would take her for a middle-aged mental patient coughed up from the bowels of some gothic asylum.

After last night's rampage, they'd put Bauer in the next cell. The last wisp of hope in my dream of escape evaporated. Bauer was now as much a prisoner as I. She couldn't help me one whit. More than that, I now had a crazed, man-killing werewolf in the next cell, with a hole through the wall that separated us. Was this Winsloe's doing? Wasn't last night's torture enough? I realized it would never be enough. As long as I was in this compound, Winsloe would find new ways to persecute me. Why? Because he could.

I wanted to crawl back into my hidey-hole and go to sleep. I wouldn't sleep, of course, but I could close my eyes and blot out this whole nightmare, dredge up some happy fantasy world in my mind, and live there until someone rescued me or killed me, whichever came first.

Instead, with great effort, I plunked onto my bed and surveyed the room. My Change had shredded my clothing. So much for my wardrobe rebellion. I exhaled. No time for brooding. I'd have to wear whatever they'd given me. First step: Get presentable. Then I'd find out why Bauer was in the next cell.

When I emerged from the bathroom, clean and dressed, I returned to the hole and peeped through, in case Bauer's presence there had been a sadistic twist of my imagination. It wasn't. She lay huddled at the foot of the door, whimpering and scratching the glass like a kitten caught in the rain. I might have felt sorry for her, but I was fresh out of pity.

I sensed someone in the halls. Maybe it wasn't so much "sensing" as assuming Tess or Matasumi would be observing the new werewolf. I raked my fingers through my hair, straightened my shirt, and walked to my own one-way glass wall.

"Could I please speak to someone?" I asked, calmly and clearly, hoping to set myself apart from the lunatic next door.

Moments later, two guards entered my cell.

"Could someone please tell me why Ms. Bauer is next door?" I asked.

They looked at each other, as if debating whether to answer. Then one said, "Doctor Matasumi felt it was necessary to confine her. For security reasons."

No shit. "I certainly understand that. But could you tell me why she's in *that* particular room? There's a hole in the wall joining our cells."

"I believe they are aware of that."

"They?" I asked, all wide-eyed innocence.

"Doctor Matasumi and Mr. Winsloe."

"Ah." I inhaled softly. My teeth ached from all this saccharin. "So they are aware they've given Ms. Bauer a cell with access to mine?"

"Mr. Winsloe felt it fulfilled all necessary security requirements."

With as sweet a smile as I could muster, I thanked them for their time and they left. So I'd been right. This was Winsloe's idea. Put Bauer in the cell next to mine, leave the gaping hole unrepaired, and see what happens.

Once they were gone, I checked the hole. I'd torn it open nearly to the steel bracing, and it was less than a foot square. So there was no real risk of Bauer breaking through. The most we could do was communicate.

Without warning, Bauer leaped to her feet and slammed her fists against the glass. "Open this door, you fucking bastards! Open it or I'll rip out your goddamned hearts! I'm the big bad wolf now. I can huff and I can puff and I'll blow you to smithereens." Her voice trailed off in a high-pitched hiccuping laugh.

Well, *theoretically* we could communicate.

I examined the photos of Clay for clues as to when and where they were taken. The date stamp on the back said August 27. I mentally counted days. August 27 had been yesterday. So Winsloe's story had been true—at least the part about someone taking these pictures of Clay the morning before. I still refused to believe he was dead. Judging by the realism of Winsloe's tale, I assumed Clay really had killed several members of a search party. That made sense. If Jeremy discovered these guards were following the group, he'd have sent Clay after them with instructions to bring one back alive for questioning. But the last time I'd seen Clay, he'd been in no shape for high-risk missions.

"Do you recognize him?"

I whirled to see Winsloe and his two guards in my cell.

Winsloe smiled. "Werewolf hearing not up to par this morning, Elena?"

Come to see what damage your sadistic ploy has wrought, Ty? Well, last night's breakdown was all the reward you're going to get. I was back and ready to play the game.

"Sorry," I said. "I was busy studying these pictures. He looks vaguely familiar, but I'm not coming up with a name." Eyes still riveted on the photos, I asked, "So, how did Xavier like the cognac?"

A split second of hesitation. I peeked out of the corner of my eye and saw Winsloe's mouth tighten. Score one for me. I bit my cheek to keep from grinning. Winsloe rolled his shoulders and crossed the room. When he looked my way again, he'd replaced his smile.

"Bastard never showed up," Winsloe said. "Probably passed out somewhere sleeping off that Jack Daniel's."

Oh, yeah. Sleeping it off in a five-star hotel somewhere with a wallet full of Winsloe's cash.

"Probably," I said. "Now, about this wolf you want me to ID, like I said last night, a scent would be better. Get me a scent and, if I've met the guy, I'll know it."

"You're that good?"

I smiled. "The best. If you had an article of clothing or—" I jerked my head up. "I know. The body. You have the body, right? Doctor Matasumi wouldn't leave the body in the woods for anyone to find. Take me to it and I'll give you that ID."

Winsloe pulled out my dining chair and lowered himself onto it, buying a few extra seconds. Come on, asshole. Think fast.

"Well, that's a problem," Winsloe said. "The guard was really shaken up after he shot the brute. Hightailed it back here. Larry and Tucker lit into him like you wouldn't believe. Leaving a werewolf corpse in the woods? We didn't hire these guys for their brains, that's for sure. Tucker rounded up a new team yesterday afternoon and sent them out to retrieve the body. Only they couldn't. Guess why."

"It was gone."

Winsloe laughed and tilted his chair back. "A fellow horror-flick buff. You got it. They found the spot and they found the blood, but no body. Now Larry's furious, thinking the project's in jeopardy because someone found the body. But there's another possibility, isn't there? That the werewolf is still alive." Winsloe hummed the theme to *Halloween*. "So I ordered another team to start looking for our mystery immortal. But don't worry."

"About what?"

Winsloe grinned. "I know what you're thinking, Elena. Don't put on the tough-chick face for me. You're worried that we'll find him. Am I right?"

"I really don't care—"

"Sure you do. You're worried that we'll bring this 'mutt' back here and he'll try to hurt you, like Lake did. Or, worse yet, that he'll usurp your position here, that we'll find him a more interesting specimen and dispose of you. But that won't happen. I won't let that happen, Elena. You're too important to me. No other werewolf will take your place. I've made sure of that. Before that last team left, I took them aside and promised a hundred-thousand-dollar bounty for the guy who brings me the head. Just the head. I made that clear. I don't want the live werewolf."

He stood to leave. I clenched my fists, nails digging into my palms until I smelled blood. Winsloe took five steps. Ryman smirked at me, then pulled open the door for Winsloe. Before stepping through, Winsloe snapped his fingers, pulled a smaller envelope from his pocket, and tossed it at my feet.

"Almost forgot. New surveillance photos. Fresh from last night. Seems Tucker was using his brains, sending a new team to find your friends. They found them. For a few hours at least. They've lost track since, but I'll keep you posted. I know you're concerned."

I gritted my teeth. Daggers of fury threatened to split my skull.

"Seems they're looking for someone," Winsloe continued.

"Me," I managed to say.

"Oh, I assume that, but now someone else has gone missing. Our team managed to capture some bits of conversation. Someone's jumped ship. Someone important. Problem is, we're having trouble figuring out who it is. Larry's working on it, comparing these new pictures with our old ones. Maybe you can see who's missing. You don't have to tell me, though. I wouldn't ask you to rat out your friends."

Winsloe left. I closed my eyes, felt the pain stab through my skull and palms. It took several more minutes before I was ready to look at the photos. When I did, I found pictures of the group conferring and milling about. I didn't need to figure out who was missing. One look at Jeremy's expression told me. Clay was gone. He hadn't been acting under Jeremy's command the morning before, when he'd tracked down the former search team. He was on his own. Alone.

Clay was coming after me.

I spent the rest of the morning racking my brain for a new escape plan. I had to get out. Not eventually, not soon, but now, immediately, before Winsloe tired of this latest game and upped the ante yet again. The harder I struggled to come up with an idea, the more I panicked, and the more I panicked, the harder it was to come up with an idea. I had to calm down or I'd never think of anything.

⚜

Bauer settled down later than morning. When I was sure she was lucid—which I determined by the fact that she'd stopped screaming and started eating her cold breakfast—I went to the hole and tried to talk to her. She ignored me. When she finished her meal, she rummaged for a pencil and paper in a drawer and wrote a two-page letter, then walked to the door and politely asked someone to deliver it. I could guess the contents: a plea for release, a more reasonable version of what she'd been ranting about for the last few hours.

So Bauer wanted out. Well, so did the rest of us. Did she feel like a "guest" now? As I thought this, a plan formed in the back of my brain. Bauer wanted out. I wanted out. When I'd first gone to nurse her, I'd hoped that in her gratitude she'd help me escape. Gratitude was out of the question now. But what about escape? What if I offered to take her with me? Bauer knew the compound's weaknesses and its security system—that is, if she was sane enough to remember. Combine my strength and experience with her knowledge and we could be a formidable team. Not exactly a complete and foolproof plan, but it was a start.

One remaining problem—well, okay, there were lots of remaining problems—but a big one was how to escape the cells. I pondered the possibility of staging something that would get me out of my room. Sure, I could probably do it, but could I get Bauer out at the same time? Unlikely. When the guards brought my lunch, I studied the door as it opened, seeing how it operated, looking for a weakness. Then I noticed something so blatant I kicked myself for not seeing it before. The guards didn't completely shut the door. They never did. Why? Because the door opened only from the outside and they never brought an extra guard to stand in the hall and let them out, as Bauer and Matasumi had always done. When they entered, they left the door a half-inch ajar, giving them finger room to pry it open. How could I use this to my advantage? Well, I could knock out one guard while the other pulled his gun and shot me—okay, bad idea. I could say, "Hey, what's that crawling down the wall?" and make a break for it when they turned away. Umm, no. Better give this one some thought.

CHAPTER 34

ALLIANCE

The guards dropped off my lunch at one. When they opened the door to leave, I sneaked a peek into the hallway. Tess wasn't there. Lunchtime for everyone. Good. While Bauer was lucid and no one was listening in, I could broach the subject of escape with her. Was it safe? She could try to garner favor with Matasumi by selling me out, but I doubted she was desperate enough to grovel. Not yet. Besides, given her circumstances and animosity toward me, no one would believe her if she did tattle.

Listening for telltale noises from the hall, I moved my chair close to the hole, sat, and peered through. Bauer was pacing.

"Feeling any better?" I asked.

She kept pacing.

"I don't want to make things worse," I said. "But you know they won't let you out of that cell. To them, you've switched sides."

Pace to the door, to the TV, back to the door.

"If you want out, you'll have to get yourself out."

Still no response. Not so much as an eye flicker in my direction.

"You have to escape," I said.

Bauer wheeled on me. "Escape?" A harsh laugh. "To what? Life as a monster?"

I could have reminded her who chose that monstrous life, but I didn't. "I know it's bad now, but it'll get easier—"

"I don't want it to get easier!" she snarled, striding toward the hole. "I want it gone! That's what I want them to do for me. Get rid of it. Suck this curse from my veins and make me normal again."

"They can't do that," I said softly. "Nobody can do that."

"Bullshit!" Spittle flew from her lips. "You want me to suffer, don't you? You're enjoying this. 'Sondra got what she deserved.' Ha-ha-ha. Well, I didn't deserve this. You never said it would be like this. You tricked me!"

"Tricked you? I warned you not to do it."

"You didn't tell me everything."

"Oh, well, excuse me. When you barged in here like a madwoman waving a syringe and ranting about starting an exciting new life, I should have whipped out my handy 'So You Wanna Be a Werewolf' disclaimer form and made you sign on the dotted line."

Bauer grabbed a chair, hurled it at the hole, then stomped into the bathroom.

I had to work on my approach.

A few hours later, Bauer's sanity made another guest appearance. I was ready. Plan two: Be more empathetic. While I found it hard to work up much sympathy for someone who'd done this to herself, somewhere deep in me there was a faint, fluttering urge to empathize. Bauer was another female werewolf, likely the only one I'd ever meet. Remembering the horror of my own transformation, I understood what she was going through. Winsloe had asked if I'd ever done anything like Bauer did to Carmichael. My reply hadn't been entirely honest. Back when I'd escaped from Stonehaven, my already demon-plagued brain had plummeted into uncontrolled madness and rage. I'd killed two people before Jeremy rescued me. Unlike what Bauer had done with Carmichael, I hadn't known my victims and I hadn't tormented them or torn them to pieces. Yet I had done one thing I would never forget. I'd eaten my victims. Was I that different from Bauer? I hadn't shot myself up with werewolf spittle, but I'd fallen in love with a man I suspected was dangerous. I hadn't killed a friend, but I had killed innocent people. As much as I resisted, I understood Bauer. And I wanted to empathize.

The question was: *Could* I empathize? As my awkward episode consoling Savannah had proven, I was not a naturally empathic person. Pushing past my doubts, I stationed myself by the hole and looked into Bauer's cell.

"How're you doing?" I asked.

Bauer spun to face me. "How the fuck do you think I'm doing?" She inhaled sharply, eyes closing as if in pain. "This isn't me. This body, this personality. It's not me. I don't use this language. I don't throw tantrums. I don't plead for my life. But do you know what's worse? *I'm* still here, trapped inside, looking out."

"Your brain is still accepting the transformation. It'll get—"

"Don't tell me it'll get easier."

I knew what I had to say, what I had to share, but the words caught in my chest. Biting back my pride, I forced them out.

"When I was first bitten, I—"

"Don't."

"I just wanted to say—"

"Don't compare yourself to me, Elena. We have nothing in common. If I gave you that impression before, it was only because I wanted something from you."

"Maybe so, but we have something in common now. I'm—"

Her voice went cold. "You're nothing, Elena. A nobody who became a somebody by accident. Becoming a werewolf was the defining accomplishment in your life, and you didn't even take a hand in it. Your money, your youth, your strength, your position, your lover, they're all yours only because you were the only female werewolf."

"I—"

"Without that, what are you? A no-name part-time journalist whose annual salary wouldn't cover my wardrobe."

With that, she wheeled around, stomped into the bathroom, and started the shower.

You know, empathy really is a two-way street.

At seven the guards brought my dinner. As usual, one carried the tray while the other stood watch, gun at the ready. I ignored them, having given up hope of bringing a guard over to my side or gaining any valuable information from them. Best to treat them as deaf-mute waiters. I had other things to worry about.

When they came in, I was on my bed, thinking up escape plans. After a moment, I noticed the tray-bearing guard lingering at my table, looking at the photos of Clay. He nodded at his partner and nudged his attention to the pictures. "It's him," he mouthed.

"You know him?" I asked.

The guard started, as if the bed had spoken.

"You know him?" I repeated. "The wolf in the photos?"

Both men looked at me as if I'd joined Bauer in her private asylum, probably thinking I should be the one who'd recognize a werewolf, not them.

"Tyrone dropped those off," I said, still on my back, feigning all the nonchalance I could muster. "He figured I might be able to ID the guy, but I couldn't. Seems he caused some hoopla at a motel."

Now they were definitely looking at me like I was ready for a straitjacket.

"You don't recognize him?" the one by the door asked.

I stifled a half-yawn. "Should I?"

"Isn't this your mate?"

"Clay? No. He'd never leave the Alpha—our leader."

"Then why—" The guard stopped, turned to his partner, and lowered his voice. "Does Matasumi know this?"

"Why?" the other guard said, not bothering to whisper. "It doesn't matter who the werewolf is. If anyone sees him around here again, we kill him. That's the order."

My hands clenched, but I forced myself not to make a noise, not to say a word, not to ask a question. The second guard shrugged, and they left without so much as a glance in my direction.

Clay was nearby. I'd been right. He was coming for me. I couldn't let him do that. There was too much he didn't know, too much he was unprepared for. Clay had bested Tucker's search party easily enough, but here there were at least five times as many guards, plus a fortified underground building with a top-notch security system, all surrounded by a forest laced with Ty Winsloe's traps. I had to stop Clay before he tried to rescue me. To do that, I needed to escape—fast. I glanced at Bauer's cage. Time to throw off the kid gloves.

It was nearly midnight before Bauer was lucid again. For the past two days, I'd been honing my ability to judge when someone was in the hall. Part of it was hearing, part of it was sensing. Though it was difficult to know if someone was watching us, there was a definitive way to tell if they were listening in. The intercom. When turned on, it gave an audible click, then hissed softly until someone turned it off. After Bauer regained her senses, I waited until the guards passed on their hourly tour, listened carefully for the intercom buzz, then reclined onto my bed.

"You still think they're going to let you out, don't you?" I called.

Bauer didn't answer, though I knew she could hear me.

"You know," I continued, "there was someone who would have let you out. Who probably wouldn't have let you get thrown in that cell in the first place. Unfortunately, you tore her to pieces."

Bauer inhaled but didn't reply.

"I know you remember," I said. "It's like you said, part of you is still there, a sane part, watching. Do you remember what it was like? Chasing her? Seeing her confusion? Her disbelief? Listening to her plead for her life? You can still picture it, can't you—the look on her face when you tore out her throat." I paused. "Do you remember what she tasted like?"

A clatter from the other cell. Then retching. I waited. Bauer stayed in the bathroom.

"Who's going to let you out, Sondra?" I called. "Who's going to risk becoming your next meal? Who out there gives a damn? Only one person did and now she's in a garbage bag . . . or several garbage bags."

"Stop it." Bauer's voice was quiet, almost quavering.

"Maybe you plan to escape by yourself. Then what? Where will you go? Back home, snack on mom and dad?"

"Stop it." Stronger, but still shaky.

"That's what'll happen. You won't be able to end the hunger and the Changes. Eventually you might gain enough control to survive, but at what cost? How many will die first? You'll start killing because you have to, then keep doing it because you can, because after a while you develop a taste for it, the power and the meat. That's what happens to mutts."

I paused before continuing. "Speaking of mutts, the first one you meet will kill you. Of course, he'll probably rape you first, as it will be his only chance to screw a female of his own species."

"Shut up."

"I'm foretelling your future here, Sondra. Free of charge. Only one person can help you avoid all that. The Pack Alpha. The question is, how do you get his help? Well, if you escape by yourself, you could show up at his doorstep, plead for mercy. He'll be very nice about it. Invite you in, take your coat, show you to the parlor, offer you coffee. Then he'll introduce you to Clayton. And that handsome face you admire will be the last thing you see. That is, if I'm still alive. If I die here, I really wouldn't recommend you go anywhere near New York State. The hell you're going through now is nothing compared to what Clay will do to you if I die."

The bathroom door slammed. "You're trying to scare me."

I laughed. "You know better, Sondra. You met Patrick Lake. You know what mutts are like. You know Clay's reputation. I'm offering you a way out. Help me escape and I'll make sure Jeremy helps you."

"Why should I believe you'd keep your word?"

"Because I'm a Pack wolf, and I wouldn't degrade myself by lying to a mutt. To me, that's what you are. A useful mutt, but a mutt nonetheless."

Bauer didn't reply. For an hour we stayed silent in our respective cells. Then quietly, her voice barely above a whisper, Bauer agreed. And we went to sleep.

BREAK

We spent the next day planning, working around the observation schedule, the guards' cell-block tours, mealtimes, and Bauer's recurring bouts of madness. The last was the most troubling. What if Bauer flipped out in the midst of our escape? Her lucid periods were growing longer, but would they be long enough?

According to Bauer, Winsloe's security system was hardwired with the identities of all compound staff. This hardwiring ensured it was almost impossible for a captive to tamper with the computer, adding his own retinal and fingerprint scans. Of course, that meant it was equally difficult to remove an ID. What did this mean for us? Bauer's ID would still work. Since she had top clearance, she could enter and exit all levels of the compound with one unauthorized guest.

Would Bauer be leaving with only one companion? I still hadn't decided. As bad as I felt for Leah and Curtis Zaid, I couldn't take them with me. Ruth had been right. The more people I added to my escape plan, the greater the likelihood of failure. Better to assuage my conscience with a personal commitment to free them when I returned with the others. But what about Savannah? Ruth had told me to leave her. Should I? Could I? Two very different questions. Given Savannah's certain link to Ruth's death and the other incidents, was it safe to set her free? I feared that Ruth's teachings had only intensified Savannah's powers, made her more dangerous. Was it wise to take Savannah out of here and dump her into the care of an apprentice witch like Paige? Or should I leave her here, where her powers could be safely contained, until we could make arrangements with the other Coven witches? Perhaps Ruth had anticipated the danger and that was why she'd told me not to take Savannah when I escaped. So I should leave Savannah.

But *could* I? Could I abandon a child here, knowing something could happen to her before I returned? Granted, that child might be capable of evil, but through no fault or will of her own. She was innocent. I was certain of that. So how could I leave her behind? I couldn't. Bauer could get us both through the exits simply by taking one person at a time. It would slow us down, but that didn't justify abandoning Savannah. If possible, I'd take Savannah. I just wouldn't tell Bauer about it. Not yet.

We planned to escape that night, when the guards brought my bedtime snack at ten-thirty. Were we ready? Probably not, but I didn't dare wait any longer. I had to stop Clay. We needed tomorrow as a backup day, in case I couldn't get out of my cell that night.

I spent the early part of the evening resting in bed. Of course, I didn't really rest—not mentally, at least. I lay awake worrying about everything that could go wrong. Before the guards arrived, I would pick off the scabs on my torn knee, inducing it to bleed again, then use this distraction to kill them and get free. What if the bleeding-knee trick failed to incite the guard's concern? What if I wasn't fast enough, if the second guard pulled his gun while I killed the first? I had to kill them. I couldn't risk them recovering consciousness before we escaped—

Whoosh.

I froze, recognizing the sound before my brain registered it. My cell door had opened. Instead of jumping up to see who was there, I lay still, tensed and waiting. What time was it? Nine-twenty. Too late for Matasumi. Too early for my snack. Xavier was gone. That left Winsloe. Please, no. Not tonight. I stayed still, listening and smelling the air, hoping I'd misheard the noise.

A full minute passed with no word of greeting, no scent of an intruder, no whoosh of the door closing. I lifted my head from the pillow and turned toward the door behind me. No one was there. I shifted onto my elbows for a better look. The door was closed. No, wait. Not closed. Open a half-inch, maybe less. Again, I braced myself. Was Winsloe in the hall, giving last-minute instructions to Ryman and Jolliffe? Yet I heard and smelled nothing. I counted off sixty seconds, then eased my legs over the side of the bed, and crept to the door. Leaning toward the open crack, I inhaled. Only old scents answered. How was that possible? Someone had opened the door only minutes before. Why couldn't I smell him?

Shifting into a semi-crouch, I edged the door open an inch, then another, then a full foot. I stretched my hamstrings, rolled onto the balls of my feet, and peered out the door. Someone was in the hall. I jerked back, then realized who I'd seen and leaned out again. Bauer stood outside her cell, looking one way, then the other. When she saw me, she straightened.

"Did you—?" she whispered.

I shook my head and stepped into the hall. Before I could say anything, a door opened at the opposite end of the hall and Savannah came out, half-stumbling with sleep, hair a dark tangle, one thin shoulder peeping from a red plaid nightgown. Seeing us, she rubbed a hand over her face and yawned.

"What happened?" she asked.

I motioned for silence and beckoned her closer. Since I couldn't smell anyone else in the hall, the doors must have opened automatically, some kind of mechanical malfunction. Too coincidental? Maybe, but I wasn't going to ignore the opportunity. Yes, it could be a trap, but to what purpose? To see whether we'd try to escape? That would be more of an intelligence test—anyone who'd stay in prison when the doors were open clearly lacked a few brain cells. It could be one of Matasumi's research experiments, like when he'd put me in that room with Patrick Lake. Worse yet, it could be another of Winsloe's sick games. So should I sit in my cell and do nothing? Maybe I *should,* but I couldn't. If this was real, I had the chance to save the three people whose safety concerned me most: Savannah, Bauer, and, of course, myself.

"We're leaving," I whispered, leaning down to Savannah's ear. "Bau— Sondra can get us out. Sneak back to your cell and get your shoes."

"We're going now?" Bauer whispered.

"We're out, aren't we?"

As Savannah scampered back to her cell, Bauer hesitated, confusion clouding her eyes. I told myself she was only sleepy, but feared worse. Bauer's addled mind wouldn't respond well to changes in routine. She'd thought we were leaving in a few hours, and even this small deviation from the plan might throw her brain off track. I smiled as encouragingly as I could and steered her toward her cell.

"Just grab your shoes," I said.

Bauer nodded and reached for the door handle. She turned it, frowned, glanced over her shoulder at me, then jiggled the handle, and pushed against the door. It wouldn't open. Prodding her aside, I wrenched the handle and slammed my shoulder against the door. It didn't budge.

"It should open," Bauer said, panic creeping into her voice. "It *has* to open. There's no external lock."

"I can't get back in my cell," Savannah said as she ran back to us. "The door's stuck."

"So is this one," I said. "I guess if a mechanical malfunction can open them, it can jam them shut, too. We'll have to leave as we are."

"What about Leah and Mr. Zaid?" Savannah asked. "Shouldn't we get them out?"

"If we can."

We couldn't. I started with Curtis Zaid. The Vodoun priest lay huddled atop his bedcovers, fast asleep. His door was shut tight.

"Jammed," I said.

Savannah raced across the hall and tried Leah's door. "Same here."

"They'll have to stay behind for now," I said. "Sondra, the exit by Savannah's cell is the one with the guard station, right? The one by mine only has a camera linked to the station."

Bauer nodded.

"Good."

I headed for the exit on Savannah's side. Bauer grabbed my arm.

"That's the guarded one," she said.

"I know."

"But you can't—we can't—they'll shoot us!"

I disengaged her hands from my arm and met her wild eyes. "We discussed this, remember, Sondra? Both doors link to a common hall with the elevator at the midpoint." I chafed at the extended explanation, but I knew this was what Jeremy would do, how he'd calm Bauer's mounting hysteria. "If we go out the camera-monitored door, the alert will notify the guards. They'll see us through the camera and meet us before we can get on the elevator. With the other door, the guards will be right on the other side. They'll only seconds to react before I burst through. They won't have time to call for help. I'll ki—disable them and we can sneak upstairs."

I nudged Bauer forward and motioned for Savannah to follow me. As Bauer walked to the door, something fell from the ceiling. I lunged forward, knocking her out of the way. The object hit the floor with a sharp pop and tinkling of glass.

"Just a lightbulb," Savannah said. "You sure moved fast."

As Bauer recovered, I glanced up. Overhead was a row of six bulbs, the first now only an empty socket. A tiny squeak caught my attention, and I noticed the second bulb in the line move. As I watched, the bulb twisted slowly, unthreading from the socket.

"Wow," Savannah said. "It almost looks like—"

Crack, crack, crack! The whole row of lightbulbs smashed to the floor, plunging us into darkness. Bauer yelped.

"It's okay, Sondra," I said. "Your eyes will adjust. You have night vision now. The light from the security door will be enough. Move toward it and—"

Savannah shrieked. I whirled and reached into the darkness to calm her. Something tickled my left arm. I slapped my right hand over the spot and felt blood welling beneath my palm. Bauer screamed. A white blur flew at my face and slashed my cheek. As I snatched it, razor-sharp glass bit into my palm. Another piece struck my scalp. My eyes adjusted then, and I saw a whirlwind of broken glass flying around us.

"The door!" I yelled. "Sondra! Grab the door!"

Dimly I saw her outline huddled against the far cell, arms pulled in, head tucked down against the onslaught. Shards of glass pricked and sliced my bare arms and face as I pitched toward her. I grabbed her arm and yanked her to the exit, positioning her in front of the retina camera. As I reached for the button, I noticed her eyes were squeezed shut.

"Open your eyes!" I shouted.

She clenched them tighter, pulling her chin into her chest.

"Open your goddamned eyes for the scanner!"

I was reaching up to pry them open when she blinked. I hit the button. The first red light flickered, then died and the whole panel went black. I smacked the button again. Nothing happened. I jabbed it over and over, eyes skimming the panel for any sign of life. Nothing. No lights. No sound. It was dead. I spun around. At the other end of the hall, a dim red glow reflected around the corner.

"The other door still has power," I said. "Let's go."

"I can't," Bauer whispered, cradling her head against the flying glass. "I can't."

I ignored her. "Savannah, run to my cell. I didn't shut my door. Get inside while we unlock the other exit."

I grabbed Bauer with both hands, and half-carried, half-dragged her down the corridor. The maelstrom of glass followed, whirling around us, biting like a thousand wasps.

In the darkness and my haste, I passed Savannah, and arrived at my cell ahead of her. With a spasm of relief I saw my door was still open. I remembered I needed my shoes and darted inside to grab them. As I turned, the foot of my bed moved. It bounced a half-foot off the ground, then shot straight up in the air and hurtled toward me. I barely had time to backpedal out of the cell before the mattress struck the back of the door, slamming it shut.

"What—what—" Bauer stammered.

I shoved her toward the other exit. A staccato series of pops rang out. Expecting gunfire, I dropped to my knees. The hall filled with deafening static, as if someone had cranked every intercom up full blast. Savannah brushed against me. I squeezed her shoulder and tried to tell her everything would be okay, but the static drowned me out. Giving Savannah one last reassuring pat, I grabbed Bauer and propelled her in front of the security door. This time, perhaps realizing it was her only escape from the flying glass, Bauer positioned herself in front of the retinal scanner and hit the button. The red light flickered out, and for a moment everything went dead. Then a green light flashed. Bauer grasped the handle and the second light changed from red to green. She yanked open the door and flew into the hall. I knew that Bauer's security pass only allowed one other person, so as soon as Savannah and I both went through, an alarm would sound somewhere. I couldn't worry about it. The guards would see us through the camera anyway.

I slammed the door behind us. A few stray shards of glass fell harmlessly to the floor.

"What happened in there?" Savannah whispered.

"I don't know," I said. "Are you both all right?"

Savannah and Bauer nodded. Yes, every inch of our bare skin seemed to be bleeding, but no one had taken a piece to an eye or a major artery, so we seemed to realize that made us "all right."

Voices echoed from the other end of the hall. Savannah's head jerked up.

"We aren't going to make it," she whispered.

"Yes, we are," Bauer said. She straightened, brushing a trickle of blood from over her eye. "I am not going back in there. I'm out now and I'm staying out. Elena will take care of the guards. We'll stay here where it's safe."

From whimpering jellyfish to group leader in sixty seconds flat? Nice to see Bauer regain her poise, but this wasn't the sort of change I'd have wished for. Never mind. At least she wasn't cowering in a corner. Besides, I *was* the one who should go after the guards. Bauer would only get in my way.

As I started forward, Savannah grabbed my shirt.

"I'll help," she whispered. "I'll cast a spell."

I hesitated, wanting to tell her not to bother, but realized that giving Savannah a chance to feel useful might calm her fears. Besides, she was only a twelve-year-old neophyte witch. She'd only know the simplest sort of spells.

"Okay," I said. "As long as you can cast it from here. Keep down and quiet."

As I crept forward, a crash shook the hallway. Then another. Then smashing glass, louder than the falling lightbulbs. Then pitch dark. Yes! This time I welcomed the blackness. It would give me an advantage . . . so long as the broken glass didn't start flying again.

"Goddamn it!" a voice—presumably a guard's—hissed. "First, exit one dies, then the camera at exit two, now this. A fucking power failure."

"I'll grab the flashlight," a second voice said.

"We both will. I'm not standing around in the dark."

So there were only two guards? Better and better. I quickened my pace to a lope, rounded the corner, and hit the elevator button. Then I headed for the guard station. Partway there, I stumbled over something and looked down to see a fluorescent light cover. I sidestepped and brought my stockinged foot down squarely on a shard of glass. Biting my cheek against a yelp, I brushed my foot left and right, clearing the path as I eased forward. Light darted from around the corner. The guards had found their flashlight. Damn.

Behind me, the elevator doors creaked open. A voice called out, not in front of me, but from the rear. I froze in mid-step. The guards rounded the corner, flashlight beam bouncing off the walls. Someone behind me shouted. I whirled, saw a gun, and dropped to the floor. Shots rang out from front and back. A bullet grazed my leg. I gasped and crawled to the side of the hall. A scream. A shout of rage. A curse. I glanced up. The guards were shooting at each other, the two from the station firing at three by the elevator. Two more lay on the floor, one screaming and writhing. Bullets whizzed past me. I got up on my hands and knees, pitched forward, and ran doubled-over to the others. I raced right past the second group of guards. They didn't even notice.

"Go back!" I yelled to Savannah and Bauer. "Get inside!"

Chapter 36

Corñered

Bauer pushed past Savannah and flew through the security sequence. The exit opened and all three of us clambered through. I slammed the door behind us. Savannah shouted that the door was now open to the empty cell across from mine. We dove inside.

"I was peeking around the corner," Savannah said as I gulped air. "When the guards came with the flashlight, I saw the other ones get off the elevator. I cast a confusion spell so you could get past them. It worked pretty good, huh?"

"Very good," I said, not mentioning that I'd been nearly caught in the crossfire. What the hell had Ruth taught this kid? A twelve-year-old witch should be casting spells to calm frightened kittens, not making armed men blast one another to bits.

"Hey," a voice said from the doorway. "Did I miss my party invitation?"

We all jumped. Leah stepped inside, yawning and raking her fingers through her sleep-mussed hair.

"Don't close that!" Bauer said, grabbing the cell door.

Did it matter now? Though I said nothing, I certainly didn't foresee another breakout attempt in our near future. While the opened cells may not have been a trap, they hadn't been a lucky break either. The opposite, in fact. My great escape plan had vanished in that hailstorm of bullets outside. Even if we got through this mess, Winsloe would only need to check the computer logs to realize I'd used Bauer to get past security. He'd make sure it never happened again. I tried not to think of the multitude of ways he could ensure that.

Leah walked to a chair and slumped into it. "Cut my damned foot walking down here. There's glass all over the floor. And how come the doors are open? Not that I'm complaining but— Whoa, what happened to you guys?"

"Flying glass," I said.

"Geez. Not sorry I missed it. Is anyone hurt? I know first aid."

"We're fine," Bauer said, moving to the bed.

While we talked, Savannah leaned out the doorway. "I don't see anyone. Are they all dead?"

"Dead?" Leah repeated as I yanked Savannah away from the open door. "Who's dead?"

I explained what had happened. As I spoke, Leah kept shooting discreet glances at Savannah, who'd collapsed onto the carpet and didn't seem to notice.

" . . . we should stay in here," I said. "Remain calm and hope they do the same. No sudden moves. Nothing to set them off."

Savannah pushed herself up from the floor. "I know this calming spell—"

"I'm sure you do, hon," Leah said. "But maybe that's not such a good idea."

Savannah's face fell. Leah put her arm around the girl's shoulders and gave her a squeeze.

"Elena and I can handle the guards," Leah said. "We'll find a safe place for you, hon, in case there's trouble when the guards arrive."

Slanting a look sideways, Leah directed my gaze from Savannah to the stray lightbulb pieces on the floor. My heart sank. Savannah. Who else could have been responsible for the whirlwind of flying glass? There'd been only three of us in that hallway and only one who'd been known to propel dangerous objects through the air. It was a big step up from hurling plates, but I'd already seen a demonstration of Savannah's increased powers with that lethal confusion spell. Of course, she hadn't done it deliberately—she'd been hurt as badly as any of us—but that wasn't the point. Whether she intended it or not, Savannah was dangerous. Put her under emotional stress and she reacted with violence.

"Good idea," I said. "We should get Savannah someplace safe." Safe for her and safe for us.

"Sondra, how about you go with Savannah?" Leah said. "My cell's open. Hide in there."

Bauer sat on the bed, knees pulled up, staring at the wall. Back to whimpering jellyfish.

"I'm fine," she whispered.

"You've had a rough go of it," Leah said. "Elena and I can handle this. How about you take Savannah and—"

"I'm fine!" Bauer snarled, head jerking up, lips curling. Then she froze, as if realizing what she'd done. She closed her eyes and shuddered. "I'm fine," she said firmly. "I want to help."

"Maybe we can talk to the guards," I said. "Explain what happened. Is there an intercom, Sondra? Some way we can communicate with them?"

Bauer shook her head.

Outside the cell, something thudded against the exit door. We all stopped to listen. Two more thuds in quick succession, then silence.

"They can't get in," Bauer whispered. "The exit door must have lost power or jammed."

"So much for hoping they were all dead," Leah said. "How many guards are there in total?"

"Three doz—no, thirty," Bauer said. "We—they started with thirty-six, but there's been casualties."

"Lousy odds. Well, let's get Savannah out of here before things get bad."

Leah reached for Savannah, but she ducked and ran to me.

"I want to help," she said, looking up at me.

As if I didn't feel guilty enough just suspecting Savannah of causing the flying glass. But if Leah and I were going to fight this, we had to get Savannah someplace safe where she could calm down.

"We aren't trying to shut you out, Savannah. I know you could help. That confusion spell"—I managed a wry smile—"well, I was impressed, I'll tell you that."

"But . . . " Savannah sighed, with the weary resignation of a child who could hear "but" coming a mile away.

"But if you stay, Leah and I will be too worried about you to concentrate on the danger."

"We'd be *very* concerned if you stayed," Leah said, sneaking me a look. "We'd all feel *much* better if you were someplace else . . . safe. I'll take you to my cell."

"Fine," Savannah said, in a voice that said our decision was anything but fine.

Leah reached for Savannah's hand, but the girl brushed her off and stalked out the door. Leah jogged after her.

Several minutes later, Leah hurried back. The guards were still beating at the exit door.

"She's in my cell," Leah said. "Hidden under the bed. I closed the door."

I started to nod, then stopped. "You closed the door? What if it jams? How will we get her out?"

"Right now I'm more worried about Savannah getting herself out. If I didn't lock her in, she'd be down here in two minutes flat, trying to help us. We don't need that kind of help." She glanced at the broken glass. "She's helped quite enough already."

"If Savannah made the glass fly, it wasn't intentional."

Leah shrugged. "You're probably right. Anyway, it's not her fault. What can you expect, with a mother like Eve."

"You think that's it? Just because her mother was into black magic doesn't necessarily mean—"

"Eve wasn't just a witch, Elena. Her father was a demon, meaning she was a half-demon/witch hybrid. A brutal combination. Now, I'm pretty laid-back. I don't scare easily. But Eve scared the crap out of me. Sondra, remember when she first got here—"

Bauer whirled to face us. "Who the fuck cares, Leah?! We have God knows how many armed guards pounding at the exit door and you're discussing Savannah's genealogy!"

"Chill out, Sondra. Elena and I have everything under control. We're used to this kind of stuff. All I'm saying, Elena, is to be careful around Savannah. Remember, she's a preteen girl, hormones kicking in and all that shit. It only makes things worse. Who knows—"

"Goddamn it!" Bauer shouted. "They're breaking down the fucking door!"

"You think they'll get in?" Leah asked me calmly, as if Bauer were some lunatic screaming inside a padded room.

"Eventually," I said.

She sighed. "Okay, then. Time to prepare the welcoming party."

When we'd finished planning, we turned off the light. With our night vision, Bauer and I would be fine, and Leah had decided that the overall advantages of darkness outweighed the personal disadvantage of limited vision.

We slipped into the hall, staying behind the corner in case the guards broke through, guns blazing.

"Hello!" Leah shouted. "We're trapped in here! Some of us are hurt! What's going on out there? Can you hear us?"

No one replied. As Bauer had warned, the door was soundproof. Leah tried a few more times, then I motioned her to silence and listened. I could hear only snatches of muffled voices.

"—when's that—getting here?"

"—other door—power out—"

"—radio—again—"

"—off-duty guys?—Matasumi, Winsloe?"

Leah leaned against my shoulder. "Can you tell how many there are?"

I shook my head. "Three, maybe four voices, plus those who aren't talking. Wait, I hear something else."

A loud hissing sounded from the other side of the exit. As I tried to identify the noise, it suddenly rose to a grating whir, loud enough even for a non-werewolf to hear.

"Blowtorch," Leah said. "That'll work. We'd better get ready."

We never got a chance to put our plan into motion. As I swung into the empty cell, the exit door suddenly opened. The guards' shouts of surprise broke into a barrage of commands. Leah darted into the first cell with me. As I wheeled to close the door, I realized Bauer wasn't with us.

"She bolted," Leah said.

"Shit!"

I threw open the door. Bauer was running down the hall.

"Sondra!" I shouted.

She stopped. Instead of turning around, though, she started pounding on the cell door to her right.

"Open up!" she yelled. "Goddamn you! Let me in!"

At first, I thought she'd lost it. Then I realized she was at the one remaining occupied cell, that of the Vodoun priest. Of course, Zaid couldn't hear her. The wall was soundproof. Despite everything happening out here, the poor guy was probably sound asleep. I leaned out the doorway to tell her to hide, but she was already gone, vanishing into Armen Haig's former cell.

As I closed the door, I realized we had a problem. Leah and I were hiding behind a one-way pane of glass. Any guards in the hall could see us, but we couldn't see them. Not good. I scanned the cell for a hiding spot, knowing I wouldn't find one. We were exposed. Any second now the guards would come around that corner—I stopped. Why hadn't they come around the corner already? When I cracked open the door, I heard frantic shouts, then a scream, an inhuman shriek that made my hackles rise.

I motioned Leah back. "I'm taking a look."

"Crouch," she said. "Stay below eye level."

We both hunkered down. I eased the door open. A flash of light ricocheted off my eyes and I jerked back, only to see the beam skitter from wall to floor to ceiling, like someone wildly brandishing a flashlight. Over the screaming, I heard a male voice; then a high-pitched alarm swallowed all sound. I sniffed and smelled something so unexpected I doubted my own senses. The acrid stench of burned meat filled the air. As I inhaled again, second-guessing myself, a guard rocketed by so fast I didn't have time to retreat into the cell. It didn't matter. He flew past, mouth open in a scream swallowed by the siren. Something flapped at his side. I squinted in the near dark, then shuddered. It was his arm, almost severed above the elbow, swinging back and forth as he ran.

The flashlight beam continued to bounce around the walls. Shapes flickered, casting contorted shadows on the wall. The siren wavered and gave one last coughing blip. As it died, sound filled the air: the hissing of the blowtorch, shouts from the guards still hidden around the corner, the endless screams of the guard with the severed arm. Another guard stumbled around the corner, the blowtorch flickering beside him. As he passed our cell, he slid on something, his legs flying out. The blowtorch sailed into the air. Then it stopped. Stopped eight feet above the ground and hovered there, spitting blue flame. The fallen guard sprang to his feet. The blowtorch flew down and sliced him across the back. His arms shot up and he pitched forward, screaming as his shirt ignited. The stink of charred flesh and fabric filled the air.

"Open the fucking door!" a guard yelled from around the corner. "Get us out of here!"

"They're trapped," I whispered to Leah. "I can't see what's going on. The blowtorch—"

Bang! A gunshot. Then three more in quick succession. Four loud metallic clangs.

"They're shooting the door," Leah said. "We should stay put."

"Trust me. I'm not going anywhere."

A sudden roar overlapped the screams and shouts.

"What's that?" Leah asked.

I knew. Even as I squinted down the hall, I knew what I'd see. Bauer had Changed into a wolf. She charged the guards. I threw open the door. Leah grabbed my arm.

"The guards are still around the corner," I said. "I can stop Sondra before they see her."

"Then what?"

Bauer reared as she collided with the fiery guard. Yelping, she back-pedaled and skittered away from the flames. Then human instinct overtook animal. Wheeling around, she skirted the burning body and continued charging down the hall.

"Just let me—" I began.

"No. Think, Elena. You can't help her."

Bauer barreled past us and rounded the corner. A guard screamed. He raced into the main stretch of hall, blood spattering from his torn shoulder.

Bauer ran after him. Before they even reached our cell door, she pounced, landing on his back. As they fell, she sank her teeth into the back of his neck, tearing out a mouthful. Blood and gore sprayed.

"I'll use the distraction to run down to the other exit," Leah said. "Maybe it's open now."

"What—?" I began, then realized she couldn't see what was happening, wasn't affected by it.

Leah brushed past me.

"Watch out!" I yelled, but she was gone and Bauer was too engrossed in her current victim to chase down another.

Bauer ripped chunks from the guard's shoulders and back, throwing them into the air. The guard's body convulsed. His face was stark white, eyes impossibly wide and blank. A guard around the corner shouted, as if just realizing his comrade was missing.

I couldn't watch any longer. I threw open the door and leaped out, no plan in mind other than somehow saving Bauer. Did she deserve saving? Was her life worth risking mine? It didn't matter. She was a werewolf, a female werewolf born from my genes. I had to protect her.

As I tore from the cell, another guard came around the corner, gun raised. He fired. The shot blazed through the darkness and hit Bauer in the left haunch. She lunged at him. He lifted the gun, but she was on him, teeth ripping at his throat. As I ran toward them, two shapes sprang from the darkness. Gunfire resounded down the hall. I dove, twisting around just in time to see the bullets hit Bauer, blasting her in the chest and head.

In that second, even as blood and brain exploded from Bauer's shattered skull, even before her body collapsed to the floor atop the dead guard, I saw the exit door swing open. I saw it and I saw my chance. My only chance. I felt my feet move, my body turn. Savannah flashed through my mind. I couldn't leave without her. Yet even as I thought this I felt my body diving for the open door. I didn't have time to go back for Savannah. Even if I could, should I? Who knew what she was capable of if things got really bad? With Savannah in tow, I might never escape, might die trying. Better to leave her here, underground, where her powers could be controlled, where she was too important to be killed. I'd come back for her later with the others.

I was already in the hall, my body having made the decision even as my brain floundered. What about Leah? Was I abandoning her, too? Coward! But my feet kept propelling me toward the elevator. Once there, I pounded my fist against the button, slamming it over and over, feeling the pain course down my arm and only hitting it harder, punishing my cowardice.

The elevator doors opened. I stepped in.

GONE

"Elena!"

Leah's voice. I grabbed the elevator door before it closed. Leaning out, I saw Leah jogging from the opposite exit.

"I couldn't get to Savannah," I called.

"Me neither. Shit! All hell's broken loose in there. We'll never get back inside."

"Hurry then."

As she ran, the elevator door jerked, as if trying to close. I shoved it back, but it kept moving, pushing harder and harder until I had to lean against it, straining to hold it open.

"Come on!" I yelled. "Something's wrong with the doors."

When Leah was less than five feet away, the door jolted violently, slamming into my shoulder. I stumbled. Leah reached to grab me, but I fell backward into the elevator car. The doors clanged shut. I jumped up and pounded on the button to reopen the elevator.

"It won't open!" I yelled. "Hit the call button!"

"I am!"

The elevator lurched suddenly. It heaved upward, rocking and jerking so hard I nearly lost my balance. As I grabbed the side rail, a shrill grinding noise split the air. I white-knuckled the rail, brain scrambling to remember what to do in an elevator crash. Bend my knees? Get on the floor? Pray? The elevator slowed, then ground to a halt. I barely dared to breathe, waiting for the floor to give way beneath me. Then the doors opened.

I found myself staring at a waist-high wall. No, not a wall. A floor. The elevator had stopped between levels. As I stepped forward to look out, the elevator jerked again. Machinery groaned in the shaft overhead and the car began sinking. The floor inched from my waist to mid-chest. My window of escape was vanishing—literally. Grabbing the edge of the floor, I vaulted up, lost my grip, and fell back into the car. I clambered to my feet and tried again. This time I managed to keep my hold and wriggle through just as the elevator vanished down the shaft.

As I looked around, I recognized the top floor. So the elevator had brought me all the way up. Praise be. If I'd been let off on the middle level, I wouldn't have had a clue where to find a staircase.

I took a moment to compose myself and remember where the exit was. To my left, at the end of the hall. As I turned, voices echoed through the corridor, coming toward me from the rear. I looked around for a hiding place. There was a door about twenty feet down the hall. I sprinted for it, threw the door open, and was jumping inside when I realized the voices had stopped. The guards were back at the elevator. As I listened, they argued over what to do about the broken elevator, then unanimously decided to hand the decision to someone else—namely Tucker. A minute later, they were gone.

I waited until the sound of their boots receded into silence, then I eased from my hiding spot, looked both ways and ran. The corridor ended in a small room. Inside was the door to freedom. All I had to do was open it. And to open it, all I needed was the retina and handprint of an authorized person. Goddamn it! Why hadn't I thought of this? Getting *to* this level was only half the problem.

The voices near the elevator returned. Back already? I raced for the closet again. Once inside, I listened. Only two voices this time. They were waiting for their companions to return with Tucker. I didn't have time to think up a foolproof plan, or much of any plan at all. I didn't stand a chance against more than two guards. If I hesitated, I'd be trapped in this closet until someone found me.

Pushing open the door, I checked the hall and made sure I couldn't see the guards—meaning they couldn't see me. As quietly as possible, I hustled toward the elevator. I stopped at the corner, crouched, and peered around it. The guards faced the opposite wall, one peering into the elevator shaft, the other bitching about the delay. I took one breath, then launched myself at the first guard, knocking him into the elevator shaft. His arms windmilled once, and he plunged out of sight. I nearly stumbled in after him and managed to avoid it only by using the momentum to twist and spring at the second guard. His hand went for his gun. As he yanked out the pistol, I snatched it from his hand and flung it down the elevator shaft. Then I slapped my palm over the guard's mouth and shoved him forward. When he resisted, I heaved him off the ground and carried him. His feet kicked frantically. One struck my torn kneecap, sending such a jolt of pain through my leg that I pitched forward. A hairsbreadth from dropping him, I regained my grip and started to run, half-stumbling, half-loping toward the exit.

I dragged the guard to the door. The security panel was the same as those on the cell-block exits. I hit the button Bauer had used and jammed the guard's chin upward. As the camera whirred, the guard realized what I was doing and shut his eyes. But it was too late. The first light flashed green. I grabbed the guard's hand and wrenched open his fist. Bones snapped. I forced his broken fingers around the door handle. The second light turned green. Placing my hand over his, I yanked open the door. Then I snapped his neck. I didn't hesitate, didn't wonder whether I had to kill him, if there wasn't some other way. I didn't have time for a conscience. I killed him, dumped his body on the floor, grabbed his boots, and bolted.

I raced into the forest, eschewing the network of paths and heading for the thick brush. No one came after me. They would. The question was how far I'd get before they did. How many miles to the nearest town? Which direction? I pushed back the first tendrils of panic. Finding civilization couldn't be my first priority. Getting someplace safe was more important. While the residual human in me equated public places with safety, I knew that any hiding place far enough from the compound would suffice. Run far, take cover, and recuperate. Then I could concentrate on finding a telephone.

It was another night like the one when Winsloe had hunted Lake: cold, damp, and overcast, the moon dimmed by cloud cover. A beautiful night for a prison break. The darkness would cover me, and the cold would keep me from overheating. As I soon discovered, though, body temperature wasn't a problem. I couldn't move fast enough to work up a sweat. Off the paths, the woods were rain-forest thick. Every ground-level inch was clogged with vines and dead vegetation. Every aboveground inch was covered with bushes and spindly trees, all vying for pockets of sunlight unclaimed by the towering old-growth forest. Here and there I stumbled onto paths trodden by deer, but I kept losing them as they petered out into thin trails already reclaimed by wilderness. A place for animals, not humans. Now, unlike most prison escapees, I had the option of turning into an animal, but I couldn't spare ten minutes to Change. Not while I was still so close to the compound. Any pursuing guards would be on foot so, for now, I could afford to share their disadvantage.

As I barreled through the forest, I realized I had one—or several— physical disadvantages not shared by the guards. First, I was wearing a pair of men's size twelve boots on women's size ten feet. More important,

I was injured. Cuts covered my arms and face, stinging each time a branch whipped back against me. I ached from the zillion other still-healing wounds accumulated in the past week. I could live with that, though. Grit my teeth and be a big girl. My knee was another matter. Since Bauer had ripped it open in the infirmary, the fire had died to a dull, constant burning. The guard's kicks had reignited the flames, and running through the forest was only adding oxygen to blaze. After twenty minutes, I was limping. Limping badly. Hot blood streamed down my shin, and raw flesh rubbed against my pants, telling me Tucker's sewing job had come apart. I had to Change. Simple arithmetic: One bum leg out of four was twice as good as one out of two.

I slowed, moving more carefully now so I wouldn't leave an obvious trodden path. After I zigzagged for five minutes, I found a thicket, crawled inside, and listened. Still no sound of pursuers. I pulled off my clothes and Changed.

I was still straining with the final stages of my Change when something knocked me to the ground. Leaping up, I twisted to face my attacker. A rottweiler stood three feet away, growling, a stalactite of drool quivering from his curled upper lip. To his left was a large bloodhound. A tracking dog and a killer. These two hadn't strayed from a neighboring farm. They'd come from the compound. Damn it! I hadn't even realized they had any dogs. The kennel must have been outside. If I'd paused before bolting into the woods, I would have smelled the dogs and have prepared. But I hadn't taken the time.

My Change finished, I pulled myself up to my full height. The hound wheeled and ran, not so much intimidated as confused, seeing a canine and smelling a human. The rottweiler stood his ground and waited for me to take the next step in the dance of ritualized intimidation. Instead, I leaped at him. Screw ritual. Now was no time to stand on ceremony. Tracking dogs meant pursuing guards, and pursuing guards meant guns. I preferred to take my chances with the rottweiler.

My sudden attack caught the dog off guard, and I sank my teeth into his haunch before he tore away. He twisted to grab me, but I darted out of reach. When I lunged again, he was ready, rearing to meet me in mid-jump. We crashed together, both struggling for the crucial neck hold. His teeth grazed my lower jaw. Too close for comfort. I broke away and sprang to my feet. The rottweiler scrambled up and leaped at me. I waited until the last second, then feinted left. He hit the ground, all four legs flying out to stop his slide. I dashed behind him and vaulted onto his back. As he fell, he twisted, jaws snapping onto my foreleg. Pain shot through me, but I resisted the urge to jerk away. I slashed at his unprotected throat, teeth ripping through fur and flesh. The rottweiler convulsed, bucking to throw me free. My head shot down again, this time grabbing his mangled throat and pinning him to the ground. I waited until he stopped struggling, then let go and ran.

Already the baying of a hound reverberated through the night air. The ground vibrated with running paws. Three dogs, maybe four. The hound had rediscovered his courage in a backup team. Could I fight four dogs? No, but experience had taught me that one or two would run from a werewolf, as the hound had. Could I handle those that remained? As I wondered this, someone shouted, making the decision for me. In the time it would take me to challenge and fight the dogs, the guards would be on us. My options narrowed to two: Throw the hound off my trail or lead the dogs away from their handlers. Either way, I had to run.

The best way to lose the hound would be to run through water. Winsloe had mentioned a river. Where was it? The night air was so damp, everything smelled like water. I'd run about a half mile when the humidity content in the westerly wind tripled. As I veered west, I found a path and took it. Speed was now a bigger concern than laying a difficult trail. On the open path, I ran full tilt, head low, eyes narrowed against the wind. I dashed across a spongy patch of ground, covering it in three strides. As my front paws hit firmer earth, the ground beneath my back legs suddenly gave way. Grappling for a hold, I dug my front claws into the soil as my back legs pedaled air. Behind me, my hindquarters disappeared into the darkness of a deep hole. I recalled what Winsloe had said about Lake running for the river: " . . . if he takes the easy route, he'll find himself in a bear pit." Why couldn't I have remembered that five minutes ago?

The hound's baying crescendoed, then split into two voices. Two hounds. Both getting very, very close. My right rear paw struck something on the side of the pit, a stone or a root. I pushed off it, getting enough leverage to launch my hindquarters almost out of the pit. Cursing my lack of fingers, I gripped the earth with my front nails, sank my rear claws into the side of the pit, and managed to wriggle my backside out. A dog yipped behind me. I didn't turn to see how close it was. Better off not knowing.

I ran for the river. An earsplitting yowl sounded to my left, so close I felt the vibration. I veered right and kept going. The thunder of running paws shook the ground. I hunkered down and picked up speed. I was faster than any dog. All I had to do was keep out of their reach long enough to outpace them. So long as I didn't hit any more traps, I could do it. The sound of running water grew until it drowned out the panting of the dogs. Where was that river? I could smell it, hear it . . . but I couldn't see it. All I could see was the path extending another fifty yards. And beyond those fifty yards? Nothing. Meaning the ground dropped off to the river. How much of a drop? A small riverbank or a hundred-foot cliff? Was I willing to take the risk, keep running until I fell off the edge? The water sounded close, so it couldn't be too steep a drop. I had to take the gamble. Not slowing, I raced toward the trail's end. Then, less than thirty feet away, a shape flew from the forest's edge and landed in my path.

CHAPTER 38

GETAWAY

All four of my legs shot out, like brakes on a car careering out of control. I caught a glimpse of fur, a flash of canines, and braced for the attack. A tawny underbelly sailed over me. Stupid dog. They never did have any sense of aim. I wheeled around to meet my assailant on the backlash and saw only a flicker of tail fur as he raced away. Huh. Well, that was easy. As I began to run for the riverbank, a roar of fury split the night air, and I again skidded to a stop. I knew that roar. Inhaling, I caught my attacker's scent and realized why he hadn't attacked me.

Wheeling, I saw Clay fly at a pack of five dogs. I tore after him. Before I could cover the fifty feet between us, both hounds and one rottweiler turned tail and ran. That meant we only had to fight two dogs, a rottweiler and German shepherd. Perfect! Hey, wait a minute—Clay was running after the cowards, leaving me with both remaining dogs. Goddamn it! Couldn't he just let them go? Of all the egotistical— The rottweiler turned on me, cutting short my mental tirade. As I spun to face him, the shepherd lunged at my haunch. The rottweiler sank its teeth into my shoulder. I topped backward, trying to knock him off. The shepherd leaped at my throat, but I saw the flash of teeth and snapped my head down to protect my neck. As the shepherd pulled back, I grabbed his ear between my teeth and wrenched, shredding it. He yelped and stumbled away. The rottweiler grabbed my shoulder again and shook me. My legs struggled for a foothold. Pain ripped through my shoulder. My traitorous knee joint flared, doubling the agony. As my good rear leg scuffed the ground, I dug in, got some leverage, and rolled, jerking the rottweiler off his feet. We tumbled down, somersaulting together, snapping at anything within biting distance. Then, in mid-roll, the rottweiler flew off me. Literally flew. One second his teeth were plunging into the thick fur around my neck, then next he was hurtling skyward. Blood sprayed my eyes. Blinded, I lurched to my feet, tossing my head to clear my vision. The first thing I saw was the rottweiler hanging from Clay's jaws. Then I noticed a movement to my right. The shepherd. It dove at Clay. I spun, catching it in mid-flight, and tore out its throat before we even hit the ground. Its body was still twitching when I heard the shouts of the guards.

I ran for the riverbank. Clay cut me off and shoved me toward the woods. As I snapped at him, I saw the bodies of both hounds lying farther up the path and I understood. Clay had gone after the fleeing hounds to ensure they couldn't double back and pick up our trail. With the hounds dead, we didn't need to head for the water.

We dove into the underbrush and circled north, coming within thirty feet of the guards as they jogged toward the river. They didn't stop, nor did the rottweiler loping beside them. They were making enough noise to cover ours, and the southeasterly wind kept our scent from the dog.

I followed Clay through two miles of forest, heading northeast. When he stopped, I sniffed for the stink of a road but smelled only forest. As I searched the breeze, he brushed along my side, rubbing close enough for me to feel the heat of his body through his fur. He circled me, then paused at my injured shoulder, licked it twice, and circled again. This time he stopped at my left back leg and nudged it out from under me, forcing me to my haunches. He snuffled my torn kneecap, then started to lick it. I jerked up, straining forward, motioning that we had to keep running, but he knocked my rear legs out again, less gently this time, and went back to work on my knee before moving his attention to my shoulder. Every few minutes, he'd move his muzzle to my cheek, breath whooshing hot against my face, nuzzle me, then return to cleaning my injuries. As he worked, my ears pivoted constantly, listening for the guards, but they didn't come. Finally, Clay prodded me to my feet, brushed along my side one last time, then headed northeast at a slow lope. I followed. A half hour later, I picked up the distant scent of a road. Time to Change.

Even after I'd Changed back, I stayed in my hiding place. While Clay paced beyond the thicket, I crouched there, listening to the crunch of dead leaves under his feet and wondering what the hell I was doing. For nine days, I hadn't known whether I'd ever see Clay again. For one endless night, I'd even thought he might be dead. The moment my Change ended, I should have run to him. Instead I knelt close to the ground, heart thudding, not with anticipation, but something closer to fear. I didn't know how to face Clay. It was like a stranger was waiting for me and I wasn't sure how to react, wanting nothing more than to huddle here until he went away. Not that I wanted Clay to go away. I just . . . I wished Jeremy were there. Wasn't that awful? Wanting a buffer to protect me against a reunion with the man I loved? Clay was the only person with whom I ever felt completely comfortable. And now I felt as if I were confronting a stranger? What kind of bullshit was that? Yet even as I railed at my lunacy, I couldn't bring myself to go to him. I was afraid. Afraid I'd see something missing from his eyes, see traces of the look he'd given me when he'd thought I was Paige.

Clay stopped pacing. "Elena?" he said softly.

"Ummm—I don't have any clothing."

Of all the idiotic things I could say, that topped the list. I expected Clay to fall over laughing. He didn't. He didn't make a sound, just reached into the thicket and held out his hand. I closed my eyes, took it, and let him pull me out.

"Lousy time for joking, eh?" I said.

But he wasn't smiling. Instead he stood there, eyes searching my face, hesitant, almost uncertain. Then he pulled me against him. My knees gave way, and I stumbled into his arms, burying my face against his shoulder, inhaling his smell as a sound frighteningly close to a sob burst from my lips. I breathed in his scent, filling my brain with it, crowding out everything else. My body shuddered, then started to shake. Clay hugged me tight, one hand entwined in my hair, the other rubbing my back.

When I stopped shaking, I bent my knees, lowering us to the ground. His hands slid behind my back, cushioning it against the cold earth. I touched my lips to his, tentatively, as if there was still a chance he'd pull away, reject me. His lips moved against mine, soft, then harder, increasing in pressure and intensity until I couldn't breathe and didn't care. I guided my hips up to his and pulled him into me.

Afterward, as we lay on the dew-damp ground, I listened for human sounds and heard only the tripping of Clay's heartbeat, slowing with each breath. It would be just my luck to have the guards find us now, lying in the grass twenty feet from freedom, having postponed our getaway to make love. Was that the ultimate in balls, recklessness, or plain stupidity? Probably a combination of all three. Never let it be said that Clay and I ever did anything as conventional as actually completing an escape from near-death before indulging in a quick round of reunion sex.

"We should go," I said.

Clay chuckled. "You think?"

"Probably. Unless you brought food. Then maybe we could squeeze in a picnic before we leave, watch the sun come up."

"Sorry, darling. No food. There's a town about ten miles from here. We'll grab breakfast there."

"No sense rushing things. Sex. A relaxing meal. Hell, maybe we can find time for some sight-seeing before we go."

Clay laughed. "I'm afraid the only local sight we'll be seeing is the nearest restaurant drive-thru. I was in kind of a hurry to get away and I didn't grab a change of clothes. We'll have to share what I've got. Of course, that'll make it easier if we decide to stop for more sex after breakfast."

"Just take me home," I said.

"I wish I could, darling."

"I meant, take me wherever Jeremy and the others are."

He nodded and retrieved his clothes from behind a nearby tree. Then he handed me his shirt, boxers, and socks, leaving him with his jeans and shoes. Once we'd dressed—or half-dressed—he carried me to the waiting car. No, it wasn't some great romantic gesture. The ground was wet and I'd have drenched my socks if I walked. Plus my knee still throbbed when I put any weight on it. So maybe it was romantic after all. Practical romance. The kind we did best.

We were in Maine. Not seaside, vacation-land Maine, but the middle of the remote northern section. Before Clay had left Jeremy to look for me, the others had narrowed my location to upper Maine. In Clay's absence, Jeremy had moved everyone to New Brunswick, deeming it the safest location from which to search for both of us. Clay learned this by calling Jeremy from a roadside pay phone. Jeremy still had my cell phone and was able to give him directions.

On the way to New Brunswick we stuck to the back roads for as long as we could, but in that part of Maine, the non-highway roads were often so insignificant we couldn't find them on the map. We soon turned onto I-95. Forty minutes later we arrived at the Houlton–Woodstock border crossing. As usual, crossing the border into Canada was a snap. Pull up to the booth and answer a few simple questions. Citizenship? Destination? Length of stay? Bringing any firearms/liquor/fresh produce? Enjoy your stay. I hoped we would.

Jeremy had taken the others to a motel a few miles off the Trans-Canada Highway, near Nackawic. Why had Jeremy chosen western New Brunswick for their base camp? Two reasons. First, it was outside the United States. Tucker and his guards were American and knew all of us—except me—were American, so they'd assume we'd stay in the States, even if Canada was a few scant hours away. Second, western New Brunswick was primarily French-speaking. That might seem like an obstacle—and Jeremy hoped it would—but in reality the language barrier was as easily crossed as the international border. Jeremy and I both spoke French, and even if we hadn't, most locals would be bilingual. It was difficult to live in Canada and not speak at least some English, despite our official national bilingualism. If Tucker even thought to send a search party across the border, he'd gravitate toward the English-speaking regions in eastern New Brunswick. So, although we were less than two hundred miles north of the compound, we were safer here than if we'd run all the way down the coast to Florida.

Throughout the trip, Clay and I barely spoke. Anyone else would have peppered me with queries about my captors, the compound, my escape. Eventually I'd have to answer these questions, but right then, I wanted nothing more than to lean back in my seat, watch the scenery pass, and forget what I'd left behind. Clay let me do that.

We reached the motel at nine-thirty. It was an old but well-kept motor lodge with a huge roadside sign proclaiming "Bienvenue/Welcome." Only a half-dozen cars dotted the parking lot. Come evening, it would fill with vacationers making the trek from Ontario and Quebec to the Maritimes, but for now everyone was gone, up early and on the road by breakfast.

"Is this the right place?" I said. "Do you recognize any of the rental cars?"

"No, but they'd have traded them for new ones. I do recognize that guy by the fence, though."

Jeremy stood before a caged pen of grouse and pheasant, his back to us. I threw open the door and leaped out before the car stopped rolling.

"Hungry?" I called as I jogged toward Jeremy. "They look fat enough."

Jeremy turned, giving me a half-smile, as unsurprised if I'd been standing behind him the entire time. He'd probably seen us drive in and stood here, watching the birds. At one time, not even so long ago, I'd have taken this as a snub, spent hours agonizing over why he hadn't come to greet me. But I knew Jeremy hadn't been ignoring me. He'd been waiting. Jeremy would no more come running out to welcome me back than he'd scoop me up in a bear hug and tell me he'd missed me. Anyone else in the Pack would, but that wasn't Jeremy's way, never would be. Yet when I threw my arms around him and kissed his cheek, he hugged me back and murmured that he was glad to see me. That was enough.

"Have you eaten?" he asked. Again, typical Jeremy. I'd spent nine days locked in a cell and his first concern would be that they hadn't fed me properly.

"We grabbed breakfast," Clay said as he approached. "But she's probably still hungry."

"Starved," I said.

"There's a restaurant a mile down," Jeremy said. "We'll get a proper meal there. First, though, I suggest you put on more clothing. Both of you." He steered me toward the motel. "We'll take my room. My kit's in there. Judging by the looks of that knee we'll need it."

A room door opened and Paige emerged, but Jeremy continued leading me toward the opposite end of the motel. I managed a quick smile and wave before Jeremy ushered me into his room.

"They're eager to see you, but it can wait," he said.

"Preferably until after I shower," I said.

"First, medical attention. Then a shower, food, and rest. There's no rush to talk to anyone."

"Thanks."

"Her knee's the worst," Clay said as I sat down. "The shoulder looks bad, but it's all surface tearing. The knee damage goes deeper. Partially healed and torn open again. The arm and facial cuts are superficial, but they need to be cleaned up. Same with the slice on her hand and the powder burns on her shoulder and side. There's also some healed puncture wounds in her stomach you should check."

"Should I?" Jeremy said.

"Sorry."

I knew Clay was apologizing not so much for giving Jeremy medical instructions but for the last few days, for taking off on his own. No one spoke as Jeremy examined my wounds. While he bent over my knee, my stomach growled.

Jeremy glanced over his shoulder at Clay. "The restaurant is on the east side of the highway. Head south around the bend. They should have pancakes."

"*Et le jambon, s'il vous plaît,*" I said.

"They speak English," Jeremy said, lips twitching as Clay hesitated by the door. He gingerly pulled a half-dozen broken threads from my kneecap before adding, "She said she wants ham as well. *Naturellement.*"

"Right," Clay said. And left.

RECUPERATION

After examining and cleaning my myriad wounds, Jeremy restitched my leg. Now, one might wonder how he *happened* to have a surgical needle and thread on hand, but Jeremy was more likely to go on a trip without his toothbrush than his medical kit—and he was very conscientious about oral hygiene. From past experience, Jeremy had learned to take his kit pretty much every time he stepped out with Clay or me. We had a habit of turning even the most innocuous events into medical emergencies, like the time we went to the opera and I ended up with a fractured collarbone—my own stupidity really, but Clay had started it.

I persuaded Jeremy to forgo binding my wounds. A hot shower was more important. Once he'd tied off my stitches and warned me against getting them "too wet," I bolted for the bathroom. I waited for the water temperature to hit scalding before I stepped into the shower. For several minutes I stood motionless, letting the hot water cascade over me, sloughing away all remnants of the last week. When the shower door opened, I didn't turn. Sure, I'd seen *Psycho*, but no knife-wielding intruder would get past Jeremy, and I knew it wasn't Jeremy opening the door—a knife-wielding intruder would be more likely to interrupt my shower. Cool skin brushed against my bare legs. As the shower door slid closed, fingers tickled down my hip. I closed my eyes and leaned back against Clay, feeling his body slide into the contours of my back. I felt him lean forward, reaching for the shampoo. As I tilted my face up to the pelting water, his hands went to my hair, fingers tugging through the tangles, the sharp smell of soap perfuming the steam. I stretched my head back into his hands, nearly purring with contentment.

When he'd finished my hair, he shifted away for a moment, then returned. Soapy hands caressed my arms, then slid down to the outside of my legs, tracing circles there before gradually moving to the inside of my thighs. I parted my legs and Clay chuckled, the sound reverberating against my back. He ran his fingertips in slow zigzags up and down the inside of my thighs, teasing, then slipped inside me. I moaned and arched against him. His free hand went around my waist, pulling me closer, his erection pushing against the small of my back. I shifted onto my tiptoes and wriggled, trying to guide him into me. Instead he turned me around to face him and lifted me onto him. I bent my head back into the water, pulling Clay along as he kissed me. The water had cooled to chill pellets that beat down on my face. Reaching up, I entangled my fingers in Clay's drenched curls, feeling rivulets of water tickle along the insides of my wrists. He made a noise deep in his throat, half-groan, half-growl, and pushed into me, nearly toppling us into the tub. Then he shuddered and pulled out.

"Please don't tell me you're done," I said, still hanging backward over his arms.

Clay laughed. "Would I do that to you? I'm fine, but your breakfast is getting cold."

"Trust me, I'm not worried."

I reached to pull him back into me, but he eased away, got a better grip on my waist, opened the shower door, and carried me out. Once in the bedroom, he tossed me onto the bed and was inside me before the mattress stopped bouncing.

"Better?" he asked.

"Ummm, much."

I closed my eyes and arched into him. As I moved, the smell of breakfast on the nightstand wafted between us. I hesitated a split second. My stomach growled.

"Upstaged by ham and pancakes," Clay said. "Again."

"I can wait."

Clay thrust into me with a mock growl. "You're too kind, darling."

I moved my hips against his. My stomach chortled and wheezed. Clay shifted up and forward. I reached out to pull him back, but he didn't withdraw, instead reaching for something over my head. As I closed my eyes again, grease dripped onto my cheek, and a slice of ham pressed against my lips. I opened my mouth and chomped it down in a few bites, then sighed, and lifted my hips to meet Clay.

"Mmmm."

"Is that for me or the ham?" he whispered against my hair.

Before I could assuage his ego, he pushed another slice of ham into my mouth, then bent his head to lick the dripped grease, his tongue tracing circles across my cheek. We moved together for a few minutes and I forgot the food. Honest. Then Clay reached up again, this time returning with a folded pancake. I sank my teeth into the bottom half and pushed the rest up to his mouth. He laughed and took a bite. When I finished, I lifted my head and licked the crumbs from his lips. He took another pancake and dangled it above me. I jerked my head up to snatch it. My teeth sank into something he hadn't been offering.

"Yow!" he said, shaking his injured finger.

"Don't be dangling the food, then," I mumbled through a mouthful of pancake.

Clay growled and lowered his face to the side of my neck, nibbling a sensitive spot. I yelped and tried to wriggle away, but he pinned me down and thrust into me. I shuddered and gasped. Then I really did forget the food.

Twenty minutes later, I was curled up beside Clay, one arm draped over his back, tracing designs in the sweat between his shoulder blades as he nibbled the hollow between my neck and shoulder. I yawned, stretched my legs, then wrapped them around his.

"Sleep?" he asked.

"Later."

"Talk?"

"Not yet." I buried my face in his chest, inhaled, and sighed. "You smell so good."

He chuckled. "Like ham?"

"No, like you. I missed you so much."

His breath caught. One hand went to my hair, stroking it back from my ear. I didn't usually talk like that. If I said I missed him, there was usually a punch line. If I said I loved him, it was almost always in the middle of making love, when I couldn't be held accountable for anything I said. Why? Because I was afraid, afraid that by admitting how much he meant to me, I'd give him the power to hurt me even worse than he had by biting me. Which was stupid, of course. Clay knew exactly how much I loved him. The only person I was fooling was myself.

"I was scared," I said. Another thing I hated to admit, but as long as I was on a roll . . .

"So was I," he said, kissing the top of my head. "When I realized you were gone—"

Someone knocked on the door. Clay swore under his breath.

"Go away," he murmured, too low for the visitor to hear.

"It could be Jeremy," I said.

"Jeremy wouldn't bother us. Not now."

"Elena? It's me," Paige called.

Clay lifted himself onto his forearms. "Go away!"

"I just wanted to see how Elena—"

"No!"

Paige's sigh fluttered through the door. "Stop shouting, Clayton. I'm not going to harass her. I know she's been through a lot. I only wanted to—"

"You'll see her when everyone else does. Until then, wait."

"Maybe I should talk to her," I whispered.

"If you open that door, she won't go away until she's pestered every iota of information from you."

"I heard that, Clayton," Paige said.

He snarled at the door and muttered under his breath. Something told me Clay and Paige hadn't become fast friends in my absence. Fancy that.

"Ummm, Paige?" I called. "I'm kind of tired, but if you'll give me a minute to dress—"

"She won't go away," Clay said. "You need time to relax. You don't need to be answering questions for a bunch of strangers."

"I'm *not* a stranger," Paige said. "Could you be a little less rude, Clayton?"

Clay was right. If I let Paige in, she'd want to know everything. I wasn't ready for that. Nor did I want to lie here while Clay and Paige argued through a closed door.

I crawled from the bed and tossed Clay his jeans. When he opened his mouth to protest, I jabbed a finger at the window, then lifted it to my lips. He nodded. As I slid into Clay's T-shirt and boxers, he eased the window open and unhooked the screen. Then, while Paige patiently waited for us to open the door, we escaped into the surrounding forest.

"That probably wasn't very nice," I said as we tramped deeper into the woods.

Clay snorted. "Won't catch me losing any sleep over it."

"I know Paige can be difficult, but—"

"She's a pain in the ass, darling. And that's being generous. The kid is barely out of school and she thinks she's a leader, pushing her way into everything, arguing, second-guessing Jeremy. Until she met you in Pittsburgh, she'd never been within screaming distance of real danger and suddenly she's an expert." He shook his hand. "Don't get me started."

"Seems I already did."

"Nah, that's nothing, darling. Give me a few hours and I'll tell you what I really think of Paige Winterbourne. *Nobody* talks to Jeremy that way, especially not some little girl with an overinflated sense of her own importance. If I had my way, Paige would have been sent packing last week. But you know Jeremy. He doesn't put up with her crap, but he won't let it get to him, either." He pushed through a tangle of tree branches. "Where're we going?"

"How about a run? Even Paige wouldn't pester a wolf."

"Don't count on it."

After our run, we made love. Again. Afterward we lay in the grass, soaking up the late summer sun that pierced the canopy of trees overhead.

"You smell that?" Clay asked.

"Hmmm?"

"I smell food."

"Dead or alive?"

Clay laughed. "Dead, darling. Dead and cooked."

He heaved himself up, looked around, then motioned for me to wait and vanished into the woods. A half-minute later he returned with a picnic basket. Well, a cardboard box actually, but the smells drifting from it were definitely of the picnic variety. Laying it on the grass, he unpacked cheese, bread, fruit, a covered plate of chicken, a bottle of wine, and assorted paper and plastic eating tools.

"Picnic fairies?" I asked, then caught a whiff of scent that answered my question. "Jeremy." I grabbed a drumstick and tore a chunk from it. "I'm spoiled."

"You deserve it."

I grinned. "I do, don't I?"

We polished off the meal and the wine in under ten minutes. Then I reclined on the grass and sighed, content and sated for the first time in nearly two weeks. I closed my eyes and the first seductive tug of sleep washed over me. Sleep. Uninterrupted sleep. The perfect cap to a perfect day. I rolled against Clay, smiling drowsily, and let the waves of slumber pull me under. Then I bolted awake.

"We can't sleep out here," I said. "It's not safe."

Clay's lips brushed my forehead. "I'll stay awake, darling."

As I opened my mouth to argue, Jeremy's voice drifted from the distance. "You can both sleep. I'm here."

I hesitated, but Clay pulled me back down, entwining his legs around mine and cushioning my head with his arm. I wrapped myself in his warmth and fell asleep.

It was late afternoon when Jeremy nudged us awake. Clay grunted between snores but didn't move. I yawned, rolled over, and kept rolling until I was lying on my other side, whereupon I promptly fell back asleep. Jeremy shook us harder.

"Yes, I know you're still tired," he said as Clay grumbled something unintelligible. "But Elena needs to speak to the others today. I can't postpone it until morning."

Clay muttered under his breath.

"Yes, I know I *could*," Jeremy said. "But it would be rude. They've been waiting all day."

"We need—" I began.

"I brought your clothing."

"I need to brush—"

"There's a comb and mouthwash with the clothes. No, you're not going back to your room or I suspect I won't see either of you until morning. We're meeting in fifteen minutes. I'll keep it short."

The meeting was to be held in Kenneth and Adam's room. As we crossed the parking lot, I saw Paige pacing the crumbling sidewalk. Her arms were crossed, probably against the cool night air, but it looked as if she was holding in a barrage of questions she'd been waiting half a day to fire at me. Just what I need— No, that wasn't fair. Of course, Paige was anxious to speak to me. I'd been in the enemy camp. I'd seen what we were up against. It was understandable that she'd be bursting with questions about the compound, my captors, the other prisoners— Oh, God. Ruth. Paige didn't know about Ruth. The past week was such a jumble that I'd completely forgotten Paige had contacted me *before* Ruth died. The last she'd heard, her aunt was alive. Damn it! How could I have been so insensitive? Paige had been waiting for news of her aunt. She'd held off while Jeremy treated my wounds, given me time to shower, then came to ask about Ruth. And what had I done? I'd snuck out the bedroom window.

"I have to talk to Paige," I said.

"Stay in sight," Clay called as I jogged away.

As I approached, Paige turned and nodded, acknowledging my presence, but saying nothing. Her face was expressionless, any annoyance hidden under a veneer of good manners.

"How are you feeling?" she asked. "Jeremy says your wounds aren't too bad."

"About earlier," I said. "I'm—I wasn't thinking—it's been a hell of a day." I shook my head. "Sorry, that's a lousy excuse. You wanted to know about your aunt. I never thought—I shouldn't have—"

"She's gone, isn't she?"

"I'm so sorry. It happened after we lost contact, and I forgot you didn't know."

Paige's eyes moved from mine, turning to stare over the parking lot. I struggled for something to say, but before I could think of anything, she spoke, her gaze still fixed on some far-off point.

"I knew," she said, her voice as distant as her gaze. "I sensed she was gone, though I'd hoped I was wrong." She paused, swallowed, then shook her head sharply and turned back to me. "How did it happen?"

I hesitated. Now wasn't the time for the truth. Not until I'd spoken to Jeremy first.

"Heart attack," I said.

Paige frowned. "But her heart—"

"Welcome back!" Adam shouted from across the parking lot.

I turned to see him running toward me, grinning.

"You look good," Adam said. "Well, except for those cuts. We'll get them back for that. How are your arms? The burns, I mean. I never got a chance to explain. I didn't mean it, which I guess you figured, since Clay didn't kill me for it. Anyway, I'm sorry. Really sorry."

"To be honest, I'd forgotten all about it."

"Good. Then forget I mentioned it." He turned as Clay reached us. "How come you didn't take me along? I could have helped with the rescue."

"There was no rescue," Clay said, looping his arm around my waist. "While I was trying to find a way inside, Elena escaped. All I did was provide the getaway car."

"See?" Cassandra said as she joined us. "I told you Elena was a resourceful girl."

Paige rolled her eyes at the use of "girl," but Cassandra ignored her.

"Congratulations, Elena," she said, laying a cool hand on my arm. "I'm glad to see you out and looking well."

She sounded as if she meant it. I stopped myself. Why wouldn't she mean it? Because I'd dreamed that she'd counseled the others to abandon me and made a play for Clay? A dream, I reminded myself. A manifestation of my own insecurities. Cassandra's welcoming smile was genuine

enough. If Clay's arm seemed to tighten around me, well, that was probably coincidence. Or my imagination.

"We should get this meeting started," Paige said. "We'll keep it brief.
I'm sure you're exhausted, Elena. We won't pester you for details tonight.
I promise."

LOYALTIES

At the meeting, Jeremy summarized what my escape added to our knowledge. By combining my info with Clay's, we had a good picture of the internal and external geography of the compound. Perhaps most important, we knew where to find our enemies. Given the size and complexity of the operation, it was unlikely they'd move camp anytime soon. So, Jeremy reasoned, we could take the time to plan an infiltration strategy, end the threat permanently, and release Ruth and the others.

As Jeremy said this, I realized everyone assumed Ruth was still alive. Why wouldn't they? I hadn't said otherwise.

"Ruth—uh—didn't make it," I said.

"What?" Adam's gaze darted to Paige. "You mean she—"

"She's gone," Paige said, her voice hollow and small.

"Shit." Adam walked over to Paige and put his arm around her shoulders, then looked at me. "What happened?"

Now I was trapped. Would I lie in front of the entire group, knowing they'd learn the truth after I explained everything to Jeremy? Or would I be honest and have Paige wondering why I'd lied only minutes before? How did I get into these scrapes? Better make a clean breast of it before I dug myself in any deeper.

"It's—uh—complicated," I began.

"They murdered her, didn't they?" Paige said. "I know the kidnapping must have been stressful, but she was in excellent health."

In other words, Paige hadn't bought my heart-attack story. I mentally thanked her for giving me a graceful way out and not calling me on my lie.

"Actually, no," I said. "They didn't kill her. Not the people who kidnapped us, anyway. It was one of the other captives. But it wasn't her fault."

Paige frowned. "An accident?"

"Umm, kind of, but not exactly." I inhaled. "Ruth didn't tell you everything when she contacted you. There was another witch there. A young girl."

I told the whole story: Ruth's training of Savannah, the unexplained events in the compound, the attacks on the guards, Ruth's death, and the mayhem Savannah caused during our escape attempt.

"So you're saying this kid's evil," Adam said.

"No. She's not," I said. "She just does—"

"—evil things," Cassandra finished. "I'm sorry, Elena, but that sounds like evil to me. Whether it's intentional or not is hardly the point. We have to consider the wisdom of freeing a child with this capacity for destruction. From what I've heard, I seriously doubt any of us is capable of controlling her. Especially the Coven."

Cassandra slanted a look at Paige. The young woman's cheeks burned, and she opened her mouth as if to argue, then closed it.

"It's settled, then," Cassandra said. "We can't worry about the girl—"

"Savannah didn't do these things," Paige said quietly.

Cassandra sighed. "I understand why you'd like to think that, Paige. No one wants to believe a child capable of evil, much less condemn her to death, but the fact remains—"

"She didn't do it," Paige said, stronger now. "A witch can't do things like that. We just can't. A spell for moving an inanimate object? Yes. For moving the object with enough force to crush someone's skull? Absolutely not. The best a witch could do would be to knock a plate off the table, not hurl it across a room."

"But Eve was also a half-demon," Adam said. "We were only kids when she left, but I remember that."

"Her father was an Aspicio," Paige said. "That means Eve's power was limited to vision. She had enhanced sight and could cause temporary blindness. That's it. Besides, powers from a half-demon aren't transmitted to offspring. You know that."

A long minute of silence passed.

"Look," Paige said. "Cassandra's right. I don't want to believe there's something wrong with this girl. But would I lie to save her if it meant endangering others? Of course not. Give me credit for a little common sense. If Savannah could kill Ruth, she could kill me too."

"There was another theory," I said. "Some people thought it was a—uh—poltergeist."

"A what?" Clay said.

I scowled at him. "I'm just repeating what I heard, okay?"

"It wasn't a poltergeist," Paige said. "And yes, Clayton, such things do exist, but this isn't how they manifest themselves. Someone inside that compound was responsible. What other supernaturals were there?"

"On the opposite side?" I said. "The teleporting half-demon we met in Pittsburgh, but he left a few days ago. Plus they supposedly had a sorcerer named Isaac Katzen on staff, though I never met the guy."

"A sorcerer could do it," Adam said.

"Some of it," Paige said. "Opening the cell doors, playing with the intercom system, jamming the exits. All possible sorcerer spells. But hurling objects and unscrewing lightbulbs? No way. That requires a very specific talent."

"Telekinesis," I murmured.

"Exactly," Paige said. "Several races have varying degrees of telekinetic power, such as—"

"Such as a telekinetic half-demon," I said. A lump of ice settled in my stomach. "But she said— Damn it!" I inhaled sharply. "There was one at the compound. A captive. She said she wasn't capable of stuff like that. And I believed her. I know that sounds incredibly stupid, but *everyone* believed her. Besides, she wasn't even around when most things happened."

"That doesn't matter," Paige said. "A Volo, the highest level of telekinetic half-demon, wouldn't need to be present to exercise her powers. I remember hearing about one case where a Volo could find an arrow in an adjoining room and fire it into a bull's-eye with enough force to shatter the shaft into matchsticks."

I closed my eyes. "How could I have been so stupid?"

"It's not your fault," Paige said. "Like you said, everyone believed her. When people think of telekinesis, they picture a person bending a spoon, but in reality Volos might well be the most dangerous type of half-demon. They could throw a person out a tenth-floor window without lifting a finger."

I cursed myself for having bought into Leah's whole girl-next-door routine, the displays of concern, the offers of help, the overtures of friendship. I'd believed Leah. I'd listened as she wove a web of lies and deceit around an innocent child, spreading the tendrils of doubt until Savannah herself believed she was guilty. Had Leah known about Ruth's training? Had she killed her to stop it? Whatever Leah's agenda, it involved Savannah. And I'd left them together.

Suddenly, I couldn't breathe. I staggered to my feet and ran from the room.

I heard Clay behind me. Not slowing, I loped around the motel and headed for the forest. He didn't call for me to stop or wait, just jogged up beside me as I walked into the forest.

"Paige is right," he said after a few minutes. "It wasn't your fault."

"Yes, it is. I wanted to get Savannah out. But I didn't. The moment came and I choked. I told myself that I was doing the best thing, leaving her in there, but deep down I knew better. I saw my chance to escape and I took it. To hell with everyone else."

"I don't believe that. If you left her behind, it's because you had to. We'll get her out when we go back."

"But it doesn't sound like we're going back anytime soon."

Jeremy stepped up behind us. "We'll return as soon as we're ready, Elena. You're safe, so I won't rush."

"But Savannah—"

"Our main objective is to stop these people, not to rescue anyone."

"But you were planning to go in for me."

"That's different. Clay and I were willing to take the risk. Everyone else was free to make their own decision. I won't risk your life or Clayton's by rushing in to rescue a stranger. Even a child."

"What if I decide to take that risk myself?"

"You're not free to make that decision, Elena. So long as you're part of the Pack, I can make it for you, and I am forbidding you to return."

"That's not—"

"Not fair," Jeremy finished. "Yes, we've been through this before. But it's Pack law. And don't threaten to leave the Pack because I will make certain you don't go back to that compound alone, no matter what rights to self-determination you claim. I take the responsibility for this decision. We'll make every effort to save this child when we return. If anything happens to her before we get there, blame me, not yourself."

I started to argue, but Jeremy was already walking away.

I didn't chase Jeremy down to pursue the matter. After ten years of living under his roof and his rules, I knew what worked and what didn't. Hounding him didn't. Once Jeremy made up his mind, the only way to change it was to erode the obstacles with logic and persuasion. Bring out the battering rams and he only doubled the fortifications. I'll admit, patience isn't one of my virtues, but I resolved to give the matter some time. A few hours at least. Maybe overnight.

⚜

"So the security system requires both a fingerprint check and a retinal scan?" Jeremy asked.

He was seated at the tiny dining table in our room. Clay and I were sprawled across the bed, Clay dozing, me trying hard not to join him.

"Uh, right," I said.

He jotted something onto his papers. "Index finger?"

"Huh? Oh, no. Sorry. It's a handprint, not a fingerprint. You grab the handle and it reads your handprint."

"We don't have to do this tonight. We'll have plenty of time later."

Not if I had anything to say about it. "I want to do it now, while it's fresh in my mind."

"Have we had dinner?" Clay's muffled voice floated up from the pillows.

"What?"

He rolled onto his back. "I'm counting meals. We had breakfast in Maine, then another breakfast here. Or was that brunch? If so, was the picnic lunch or dinner?"

"I'm counting it as lunch," I said.

"Good. Then let's go get dinner."

Jeremy insisted on being polite and inviting the others to join us. As Clay knocked at Kenneth and Adam's room, the neighboring door opened and Adam stepped out, turning to say a few words to someone inside. When Kenneth opened his door, Clay went in. I waited outside for Adam.

"We're going to dinner," I said. "Have you eaten?"

"Nope. I was just about to ask you guys the same thing. Let me grab my car keys."

"Was that Paige?" I said, nodding to the next room.

"Yeah. She's pretty upset."

"Should I ask her to join us?"

He shrugged. "You can ask, but I don't think she's feeling up to it. If not, tell her I'll bring something back."

I'd rather Adam asked Paige himself, but he vanished into his room, leaving me to it. I was probably the last person Paige wanted to see. Her aunt was dead and I hadn't even had the decency to tell her straight off. I inhaled, walked to her door, and rapped lightly, half hoping she might not hear me. After a second's pause, I turned to leave. Then I heard the clank of the chain lock and the door opened.

"Hey, there," Paige said, managing a wan half-smile. "You still up? How are you feeling? I've got some sleeping teas if you're having trouble."

How was I feeling? Oh, about two inches tall. Paige's eyes and nose were splotched red, as if she'd spent the last couple of hours crying, and she was worried that I might not be able to sleep?

"I'm really sorry," I said. "About your aunt. I don't mean to intrude, but we're heading out for dinner and I was wondering if you felt like joining us."

"No," she said. "Thanks, but no thanks."

"Adam said he'd bring something back for you."

She gave a distracted nod, paused, then said quickly, "Could you—I don't mean to be a pain. Really. I know you're tired and sore, and I hate to pester you, but could you stop by when you come back? I have—"

She stopped and looked over my shoulder. I heard Clay's footsteps behind me. Paige paused, then straightened up, as if bracing herself, and went on. "Clayton, I was just asking Elena if you could spare her for a while tonight. Thirty minutes tops. I promise."

"You're not coming to dinner?" he asked.

"I'd rather not."

"No one stays alone," he said. "That's Jeremy's rule." I shot him a glare, warning him to be more sensitive, but he didn't catch it and continued. "Cassandra will stay with you."

"Oh, she'll love that," Paige said.

"If she doesn't like the rules, she can leave."

"We should all be so lucky," Paige murmured under her breath. "Seriously, though. You don't need to leave someone behind with me. I have plenty of protection spells."

"Those are the rules," Clay said. "No one stays alone. It's not like Cassandra eats anyway." He started to leave, then added, "If Elena's feeling up to it, she can stop by with your dinner. Twenty minutes. Then she needs her rest."

"Gee, does that mean I have your permission?" I called after him.

"I'm not answering that," he said without turning.

"Smart man." I looked at Paige. "I'll pop by afterward."

"Thanks. I appreciate it."

CORONATION

A t ten I returned to Paige's room, her still-warm dinner in hand. I found
her alone.

"Where's Cassandra?" I asked.

"Out. Trolling for dinner or companionship. I refuse to be the former
and I don't qualify to be the latter. Wrong gender."

"No one is supposed to be alone. Does Jeremy know she's taking off
on you?"

"No, and I'm not tattling, so let's keep it between us. Personally, I feel
safer when she's gone. A vampire isn't exactly my ideal choice for a
roommate. One attack of the midnight munchies and I'm a goner. I was
bunking up with Adam, but sharing a room with Cassandra was putting
a definite strain on Kenneth's nerves, so we switched."

"So you and Adam are . . . together?"

She frowned, then caught my meaning and laughed. "Oh, God, no.
We've been friends since we were kids. Trust me, we know each other too
well for anything else." She walked to the mini-fridge. "Can I get you something to drink? I have bottled water, diet soda. Nothing stronger, I'm afraid."

"That's okay."

"Just get on with it, right?"

"I didn't mean—"

She waved a hand. "Don't worry. I know you're tired and, again,
I apologize for bugging you. It's just, well, I'm working on specs, blue-
prints and such for the compound. I know we don't need them right away
but, well, I want to keep busy. It's easier—" She nibbled at her lower lip,
looked away. "Easier if I have something to do, keep my mind occupied."

I knew what she meant. Last year when two of my Pack brothers died,
only action had assuaged my grief. I'd thrown myself into plotting against
the mutts who'd killed them, partly for revenge and partly to keep from
dwelling on their deaths. In preparing for our onslaught against those
who'd killed Ruth, Paige was doing the same. I understood that.

"I've got most of it done already," she said, passing me a notebook from the table. "All I need is for you to fill in a few blanks."

I flipped through her notes. "Actually, Jeremy has most of this. You could—"

"Get it from him. Right. Sure." She turned, but not before I saw disappointment flicker across her face. "Guess I should have known he'd be two steps ahead of me. Okay, then, well, that's all I wanted. Sorry about that. I wasn't thinking."

"Oh, wait. There's a couple of things here Jeremy hadn't asked," I lied. "Tell you what. I'm not tired yet. How about I fill in everything you're missing. Even if I've already told Jeremy, it never hurts to have two copies."

"Oh?" For the first time since I'd arrived, her smile touched her eyes. "That's great. Thanks."

Like I said, I knew how she felt. Well, I didn't know exactly how she felt, having no idea how close she'd been to her aunt, but I understood that she needed something to do, something to make her feel that she was taking action. Providing that was the least I could do.

When we finished, I offered to spend the night in Paige's room, arguing that Cassandra seemed in no rush to return and that Jeremy was sharing our room, so no one would be alone even if I stayed. Paige refused. She assured me her lock spells would keep out most intruders and her protection spells would warn her if anyone bypassed the locks. I suspected she wanted to be alone with her grief, so I didn't push the matter.

That night I dreamed of escaping the compound. Over and over. Each time the circumstances differed, but one element remained the same. I left Savannah behind. Sometimes I forgot about her until I was outside and it was too late. At other times my guilt was more obvious. I ran past her cell and I didn't stop. I heard her calling my name and I didn't stop. I saw Leah reach out to grab her . . . and I didn't stop. Finally as the dream replayed its umpteenth version, I was running for the open exit door. Then Savannah appeared on the other side, urging me on. I stopped. I turned around. And I ran the other way.

I bolted upright, gasping for breath. Clay was awake, holding me, brushing the sweat-sodden hair from my face.

"Do you want to talk about it?" he asked.

As I shook my head, his arms tightened, but I didn't look at his face. Didn't want to. This wasn't something I could discuss with him. He'd only try to convince me that I'd done the right thing getting myself out safely. If the situation were reversed, would I want Clay risking his life to save a stranger? Of course not. But the point would be moot because Clay would never take any risk to save a stranger. He'd throw himself in front of a bullet to protect his Pack, but he wouldn't stop to help an accident victim. If I was there, he'd do it to please me, but if he was alone, the thought would never cross his mind.

I didn't expect Clay to care about Savannah. Well, maybe I still held out hope that he'd develop a social conscience, but I'd learned that such a change ranked alongside world peace on the scale of well-meaning but naive wishes. Clay cared about his Pack and only his Pack. How could I expect him to understand my guilt over Savannah?

As I eased back into Clay's arms, I noticed Jeremy across the room, propped on his elbow, watching me from the cot. He lifted his brows in an unspoken question. Did I want to talk to him instead? I gave a small shake of my head and lowered myself onto the bed. I could sense them both watching me, but closed my eyes and feigned sleep. Eventually the room went still. When it did, I slipped onto my back and lay there in the dark, thinking.

Had I jumped to conclusions earlier, when I decided it had been Leah causing the trouble and framing Savannah? What if I persuaded Jeremy to strike early, then discovered I'd been mistaken? What if people died because of that mistake? And what if I did nothing and Savannah died because of *that* mistake? I had to find a middle ground. If we had enough information, acting swiftly would be to our advantage. Did we know enough? Or, more accurately, what were our chances of learning more? Pretty slim. We had the data I'd gathered from inside the compound, plus what Clay had learned from scouting the site, plus what the others had uncovered in their research. Whatever we didn't know by now, we'd likely never find out. We had to concentrate on formulating a plan—

Outside, a neighboring door clicked. I tensed and listened. Our group occupied all the rooms at this end. Was someone going out? No, wait. It was probably Cassandra returning. I checked the clock. Two thirty-five. Oh, that's great. We ask her to keep an eye on Paige and she takes off for half the night. Paige might not want to tattle, but I would. Jeremy needed to know we couldn't rely on Cassandra to back up Paige.

As I reclined onto the pillow, I heard shoes scuff against pavement outside. I glanced at Clay and Jeremy. Sound asleep. I eased out of bed and tiptoed to the window. Lifting a drapery corner, I peered out to see Paige stealing across the parking lot, suitcase in one hand, notebook in the other. Shit!

Being careful not to wake the guys, I tugged on my jeans and shirt and crept out the door. Paige rounded the bird pen and vanished into the darkness beyond. Barefooted, I scampered after her, one eye on my target, the other on the pavement, watching for broken glass. When I reached the bird pen, a pheasant roused itself, opened one sleepy eye, then squawked and jetted into the air. Damn it! Sometimes there were serious disadvantages to being a werewolf. Even as I lunged away from the cage, several other birds awoke and added their voices to the din. So much for a stealthy approach. I raced through the grove of trees where I'd last seen Paige and found her in an auxiliary parking lot. She stood beside a car, frowning in the direction of the panicking birds. When she saw me, she fumbled with the keys, barely getting the door open before I arrived.

"Uh, hi," she said, faking a bright smile. "You're out late."

"Going somewhere?" I asked.

"Ummm, just out for something to eat." She backed into the driver's seat. "The stuff you brought me got cold so I thought I'd go see if I can find a 7-11 or something."

"You won't mind if I join you then," I said as I snapped the passenger door lock and slid inside. I gestured to her suitcase. "Hell of a purse you've got there."

She laid her hands on the steering wheel spokes, paused, then glanced at me. "I'm leaving, Elena. I know this is a bad way to do it, but I was afraid someone would try to stop me. It's too much for me. I'm backing out."

"I'm sorry about your aunt."

"She—" Paige looked out the windshield. "She wasn't my aunt."

"Oh, well, your Coven sister or whatever you—"

"She was my mother."

"Your—?"

"That's how it works in the Coven," Paige said, keeping her eyes on the windshield. "Or how it used to work. The old way, from my mother's time. Witches didn't marry, so they avoided the stigma of single-motherhood by raising their daughters as nieces. No one outside the Coven knew the truth. In my case Adam knows, but that's about it. When my mother was young, she was too busy preparing to be Coven leader to think about an heir. Once she became leader, she realized the Coven was faltering and decided she needed a daughter, someone she could train and prepare in her own way. So when she was fifty-two, she used magic to have a daughter. Me."

"So that means you're . . . ?"

"The official new Coven leader." Her lips twisted in a sardonic smile.

"It'd be funny if it wasn't so ridiculous. A twenty-two-year-old leader." She inhaled sharply and shook her head. "Doesn't matter. The point is that I've been trained for this. For the responsibility. I can't expect Jeremy or Kenneth or Cassandra to accept me as a fellow leader yet, but I know I can do it. Right now, though, I have to go home. There are things to be done, arrangements to be made."

"I understand." I leaned over her lap and lifted the notebook she'd let slip between her seat and the door. "But if you're going home, you won't be needing this."

She grabbed the book from me. "Oh, actually, I do. For the Coven records."

"You aren't going home, Paige. You're going to the compound."

She forced a laugh. "By myself? That'd be crazy."

"My sentiments exactly. I understand you must want revenge for your mother, and I promise you'll get it when we go back, but there's no—"

As confusion flitted across her face, I realized revenge wasn't her motive. Then I recalled Ruth's warning, telling me not to let Paige know about Savannah or she'd insist on rescuing the girl.

"You're going after Savannah," I said.

"I have to," she said quietly.

"Because your Coven expects it?"

"No, because *I* expect it. How can I be Coven leader if I let this girl die? How could I live with myself? Look, I'm not stupid and I'm not suicidal. I'm not going in there, spells blazing, tearing the place apart. I couldn't do that anyway. All I want is Savannah. I'll be careful. I'll take my time, scout the place out, and find a way to get her. You guys don't need to worry about this. It's witch business. I—"

Paige's door flew open, nearly toppling her to the ground. Clay shoved his head into the car. Paige jumped and edged toward me.

"What's going on?" he asked.

"Paige wants to go after Savannah."

"Oh, fuck!" He slammed the door and strode around to my side. "Let me guess. She's going after the kid and she needs your help."

"I don't—" Paige began.

"She's not asking for my help," I said, getting out of the car. "She wants to do it alone."

"So she decided to tell you about it first? Call you out here, tell you what she's up to, and expect you'll let her go alone? Bullshit. She's playing on your sympathy. You'll insist on going with her and—"

"She didn't call me out," I said. "I followed her."

Paige slid from the car, straightened, and met Clay's eyes. "I'm doing this alone, Clayton. I'm not asking for or accepting any help."

"Are you crazy?" He walked over and tried to pluck the keys from her fist, but she backpedaled. He stopped and held his hand out. "Give me those, Paige. You're not going anywhere."

She looked from Clay to me, as if assessing her chances of escape.

"Not a prayer," I said. "There's two of us. We can outrun you. We can outfight you. Unless you've got a doomsday spell up your sleeve, you ain't leaving."

She glanced over her shoulder and seemed ready to make a break for it when Jeremy stepped from the bushes behind her. She hesitated. Then her shoulders sagged and the keys slid from her hand.

"Come inside," Jeremy said. "We'll talk."

"I have to get Savannah out," Paige said as we walked into our motel room. "You guys don't get it. I don't expect you to. Like I told Elena, it's witch business."

"We understand that you're concerned for her," Jeremy began.

Paige spun to face him. "Concerned? I'm terrified for her." She flipped through her notebook and jabbed a finger at a page. "Look, I wrote down everything that happened that night Elena escaped. I divided the events into potential sorcerer versus telekinetic half-demon activity. There's some overlap, but between the two they cover everything. Now, what are the chances that this sorcerer and half-demon independently decided to raise hell on the same night? Sure, it's possible that one started things and the other joined in, but I doubt it. This half-demon is working with a sorcerer."

"Okay," I said.

Paige's gaze traveled across our faces. "See? You *don't* get it. You can't."

"Explain it to us," Jeremy said.

She inhaled. "Sorcerers hate witches. And vice versa. The biggest feud in the history of supernatural races. Our version of the Hatfields and the McCoys. Only the sorcerers do all the shooting. We're an ugly reminder—" She inhaled again. "You guys don't need a history lesson. Just trust me on this one. If Leah is working with Katzen, and she's blaming Savannah for murder, then that's trouble. Big trouble. I can't begin to fathom their motivation, but I know Savannah is in danger. In one night, Winsloe and his cohorts have lost both their werewolves and suffered untold damage to their facility. Who will shoulder the blame for all that? The child witch. Isn't that what this Leah told you before you escaped? That Savannah did it?"

"They won't kill Savannah," I said. "She's too important."

Even as I spoke the words, I heard my own doubt. With Bauer and Carmichael dead, Winsloe and Matasumi were the only principals left. Matasumi might want Savannah alive, but he was just a scientist. Winsloe had the cash, so he was in charge. I remembered the conversation I'd overheard between Matasumi and the man I assumed to be Katzen. At that time, Winsloe had already begun throwing his weight around, picking and choosing the sort of captives he wanted. Winsloe had no interest in witches. I knew that. Savannah was alone now, without even Xavier to protect her.

"This is all speculation," Clay said.

"Which I fully admit," Paige said. "Which is why I'm not endangering any lives but my own."

"You can't do that," Jeremy said. "If you're the new Coven leader, you have to consider the best interests of your Coven. What happens if they lose both Ruth and her successor? You have a responsibility to stay alive, if only until you've selected and trained the next leader."

"But—"

"Let's see what we can do," he said. "Give me your notes and we'll review what we have."

Chapter 42

Return ·

Two days later, we checked out of the motel. We were going back.

We'd spent the last two days planning. Finally Jeremy agreed that we had all the information we were likely to get and there was no sense delaying our return. Paige had chafed at the delay, but she hadn't tried to bolt, probably because either Jeremy or I had been with her nearly twenty-four hours a day, making sure she didn't. I'd even moved into her room, letting Cassandra have her own, which not only helped ensure Paige wouldn't disappear in the night but made me feel a lot better about her personal safety. As for Cassandra, well, she could look after herself.

For the trip to the compound, we split the group into two carloads, based on the two groups we'd form once we arrived. The plan was for Jeremy, Cassandra, and Kenneth to wait in the background while Clay, Adam, Paige, and I broke in and cleared all initial resistance. We'd debated which group Paige should be in. As Coven leader—and someone unaccustomed to fighting—she should have stayed back with Jeremy. However, she argued that her spells could prove invaluable in protecting the front-line group. She could unlock doors, cover us, confuse attackers, communicate with Kenneth—the list went on. Besides, she really wanted to do this, unlike Cassandra, who'd shown no interest in taking a more active role. In the end, Paige's persistence had paid off, and we'd agreed she should join my group.

I drove the second car, because Paige refused to set foot in any vehicle with Clay behind the wheel and Clay refused to take the backseat to any apprentice witch—Coven leader or not—so if we were ever going to leave the parking lot, the task of driving fell to me. Before we piled into the car, I noticed Clay shooting glances at Jeremy as he climbed into the other vehicle.

"You can go with him if you want," I said.

"No," Clay said. "He's right. We need to discuss our strategies on the trip, so this makes sense. Besides, it's not like I haven't left him alone before."

"I'm sorry."

"About what?"

"Taking off that day. Not being careful. Getting myself kidnapped. Losing contact with you guys. Making you—"

He pressed his lips to mine, cutting me short. "You didn't make me do anything. I chose to come after you."

"It's just that I hate . . . " I trailed off and shrugged. "You know, putting you in a position where . . . " I cut a look at Jeremy and exhaled. "Making you choose."

Clay laughed. "Making me choose? Darling, we live with the guy. We share a house, bank accounts, even vacations. We're never alone and I've never heard you utter one word of complaint. You have *never* asked me to choose, and you have no idea how grateful I am for that, because if I ever had to pick, it would be you, no matter what that meant for the Pack."

"I'd never do that to you."

"Which is why I know how much you love me. Yes, I feel shitty about having abandoned Jeremy, but he understands, and I don't regret it, even if you did get yourself free without my help." He pulled back to look at me. "Now, are you okay with this? Going back in? 'Cause if not . . . "

"I'm fine. I want to get it over with. I want to finish this, say good-bye to all these nice people, and go home, to our own home, our own beds, and be alone."

"Reasonably alone," Clay said with another glance toward Jeremy.

"Close enough."

"Let's do it, then."

When Clay and I had escaped the compound grounds, we'd used the main service road that bisected the west end of the property. Definitely not the safest route, but Clay hadn't been able to find another one. This time we were using an overgrown rutted road that dated back several property owners. Paige had discovered it by hacking into property records and old surveys. Yes, I said hacking, as in computer hacking. When she told me how she got the information, I'd asked her to repeat herself—several times. Perhaps my prejudices were showing, but when I pictured a hacker, I thought of some guy like Tyrone Winsloe, only with no money and worse hygiene. Paige quickly corrected me: She was not a hacker; she was a professional computer programmer who knew how to hack. Sounded like hairsplitting to me, but I kept my mouth shut. However she got the information, I was grateful. We all were . . . even Clay. The old surveys had shown all previous roads crisscrossing the compound property. We sampled several and chose one that fell midway between secluded and accessible. I drove a few hundred feet along it, then pulled over for our final pre-assault rendezvous with Jeremy.

Twenty minutes later, I sat on an old tree stump talking to Paige while Clay and Adam pored over the maps. Jeremy had given us our instructions and was now discussing last-minute details with Kenneth. Paige and Kenneth would act as telepathic liaisons between the two groups, allowing us to communicate without two-way radios or cell phones. Telepathic liaisons. The phrase slid so easily from my mental tongue. Scary, really. Binding spells, sorcery, astral projection, telepathy, telekinesis, teleportation—did I ever expect to hear those words outside of an *X-Files* episode? Now I was standing in a forest grove with a witch, a half-demon, a vampire, and a shaman, planning to put an end to a nefarious plot to usurp our powers and alter the path of humankind. Talk about your conspiracy theories.

After a few minutes of speaking to Kenneth, Jeremy waved Paige over. I stayed where I was.

"Does it bother you?" Cassandra asked, walking over to me. "Being back here?"

I shrugged. We hadn't spoken much in the last few days. My choice. No matter what Cassandra may or may not have done in my absence, her abandonment of Paige at such a sensitive time was unforgivable. Despite what Clay thought of Paige, I liked her. She had spirit and a depth of altruism I truly admired. Even Clay had started cutting her some slack over the last couple of days, which only made Cassandra's callousness all the more incomprehensible. Even after I'd told Cassandra, point-blank, that I was bunking up with Paige because she was shirking her responsibilities, she hadn't shown a twinge of remorse. And I accused Clay of being self-absorbed.

"Be careful in there," Cassandra continued. "Remember what Jeremy said. You don't know what kind of extra security measures they may have taken since your escape. I meant what I said before you were taken. I'd like to get to know you better, Elena. Let's make sure we have that opportunity." She laid her hand on my forearm and smiled, eyes sparkling with a feral gleam. "I must admit I'm looking forward to this. Not many opportunities for mayhem in my life these days."

Paige joined us. "Well, Cass, if you really want some fun and excitement, you could always change your mind and join us on the front line.

Oh, but that's not what you meant, right? You want controlled, risk-free mayhem."

"My skills are better suited to the second wave of attack," Cassandra said, smiling at Paige as if humoring a rude child.

Clay walked up. "And I don't want anyone with us who doesn't want to be there." He took my arm, not-so-subtly disengaging it from Cassandra's grasp. "Jeremy has some last-minute instructions for you, darling."

"Let me guess," I said. "Be careful. Don't show off. Don't take unnecessary risks."

Clay grinned. "Nah. Jeremy trusts you. It's more like: 'Make sure Clay's careful,' 'Make sure he doesn't show off,' 'Make sure he doesn't take unnecessary risks.' Babysitting instructions."

I rolled my eyes and headed for Jeremy. He was alone, leaning over a map spread on the hood of one car. As I approached, he folded the map without looking up.

"You'll be in charge out there, Elena," he said as he turned.

"I know the routine. I look after Clay. I set the tone. I make sure he keeps it under control."

"You call the shots. He knows that."

"What about Adam and Paige? Do they know that?"

"It doesn't matter. Adam will follow Clay's lead. Paige will know better than to engage in leadership squabbles on the battlefield. Take control and they'll follow."

"I'll try."

"One more thing. Stay with Clay. If you separate, you'll be too worried about each other to concentrate on your tasks. No matter how bad things get, stick together. Don't take any chances."

"I know."

"I mean it." He reached out and brushed an escaped strand of hair from my shoulder. "I know you're sick of hearing it, but don't take any chances. Please."

"I'll look after him."

"That's not what I mean. You know that."

I nodded and kissed his cheek. "I'll be careful. For both of us."

Step one: Inspect the grounds.

Clay, Paige, Adam, and I followed the overgrown service road for two miles, at which point the road looped north, away from the compound, meaning we had to finish the journey with a half-mile trek through thick brush. Once we were close enough to see the compound, we stopped and circled the perimeter, staying as far in the forest as we could while still being able to see the open strip of ground surrounding the building. We looked, listened, and sniffed for anyone outside the compound walls. According to Clay, from his earlier observations, people came outside for three reasons only: to smoke, to feed the dogs, and to leave the grounds. Leaving the grounds meant driving one of four SUVs stored in a nearby garage. No one left on foot and no one went for walks in the forest. Nature lovers these guys were not. Our walk around the perimeter confirmed that no one was outside.

Step two: Kill the dogs.

During Clay's earlier reconnaissance, he'd found the kennel. It was a cinder-block building tucked thirty yards into the woods, as if purposely placed away from the compound to eliminate noise. These dogs were for tracking and killing, not for guarding. As we drew near the kennel, I could tell why. Every few minutes one of the dogs would start a hellish racket, barking at something in the forest, barking at a cell-mate, or just barking from sheer boredom. Although the dogs wouldn't alert anyone to our presence, we still had to get rid of them. I'd seen what they were capable of doing to me as a wolf. I didn't want to think of how much damage they could do to me when I was in human form. Once the guards realized we were in the compound, someone would get the dogs, and they'd do what they'd been trained to do, namely rip us to shreds.

We circled the kennel from the south, moving with the wind. The building was roughly twenty by ten with a fenced yard half that size. As Clay had discovered on his earlier visit, no guards were posted at the kennel. Nor were there any security measures in place to protect the animals. Only a garden-variety padlock secured the gate.

Once we were downwind of the kennel, I counted the dogs by separating their scents. Three. As Clay, Adam, and I crept forward, Paige cast a cover spell. This was the same spell Ruth had cast in the Pittsburgh alley, meaning we were invisible only if we stayed still. When we moved, our images were distorted, but visible. It worked fine with the dogs, confusing them long enough for Clay to snap the padlock and the three of us to get inside. Clay and I killed our targets easily enough. Adam fumbled the choke hold we'd shown him. Not his fault. Most people aren't neck-snapping experts. The dog managed to graze four bloody furrows in Adam's arm before Clay finished the job. Paige tried to inspect the injury, but Adam sloughed it off and helped Clay drag the dog carcasses into the kennel building.

Step three: Disable the vehicles.

This was one thing Clay and I could not do. Why? Because we were both so mechanically challenged we rarely pumped our own gas for fear we'd somehow screw up and the car would burst into flames before our eyes. Here was Adam's chance to make up for the botched choke hold. After we snapped the door locks, Adam flipped up the hoods, pulled a few wires and metal things, and declared the vehicles unusable. All Clay and I could do was watch. Worse yet, Paige advised Adam on a few ways to make the damage less detectable, so even the mechanically inclined guards couldn't quickly deduce and fix the problem. Not that I was envious. Who cared whether you could change motor oil when you could snap a rottweiler's neck in 2.8 seconds? Now there was a practical skill.

Step four: Get inside the compound.

Okay, now things got tough. In the movies, heroes always get into seemingly impenetrable buildings through a heating duct or ventilation shaft or service entrance. In real life, if someone goes through all the hassle of creating an elaborate security system, they don't have a 3'×3' ventilation shaft secured only by a metal grate and four screws. Unless they're really, really stupid. These guys were not. Hell, they didn't even have one of those massive air vents with the slowly rotating, very sharp fan that would chew us to bits if we didn't dash through the blades at exactly the right moment. Nope. None of that fun stuff. Not even old-fashioned windows. Just one way in and out. The front door.

When Clay had scouted the compound during my captivity, he'd discovered that guards engaged in that sacred ritual of workers everywhere—the hack pack: die-hard smokers condemned to huddle together against the elements. Obviously even nefarious secret projects were smoke-free these days. Having determined there was only one way into the compound, we needed to get past the security system. That meant we needed a valid hand and retina. Since we didn't need a good pair of lungs, one of the smokers would work fine.

We positioned ourselves in the woods beside the exit door and waited. Twenty-five minutes later, two guards came out and lit up. Clay and I each targeted one and killed him. Neither guard even saw us, perhaps being too enraptured by that first flood of nicotine. They'd barely finished a quarter of their cigarettes before we cured them of the habit.

We dragged the corpses a hundred feet into the woods. Then Clay dropped his and pulled a folded garbage bag from his back pocket.

"He's not going to fit in that," Paige said.

Clay shook open the bag. "Parts of him will."

"You're not—" Paige paled and I could almost see flashbacks of the "decapitated head in the bag" incident running through her mind. "Why can't you just hold him up to the security camera?"

"Because, according to Elena, we'll need to get past more security inside, and if you'd like to drag along a two-hundred-pound corpse, be my guest."

"I don't see why—"

Adam started to hum. As Paige turned to glare at him, I recognized the tune.

"'Little Miss Can't Be Wrong,'" I murmured . . . and tried very hard to stifle a laugh.

Adam grinned. "Clay called her that once when you were away. If she starts getting bossy, sing it. Shuts her up every time."

"Try singing it again and see what happens," Paige said.

Adam's grin broadened. "What are you going to do, turn me into a toad?"

Paige pretended not to hear him. "Elena, did you know that one of the major accusations against witches during the Inquisition was that they caused impotence?"

"Ummm, no," I said.

"Not just psychological impotence either," Paige said. "Men accused witches of literally removing their penises. They thought we collected them in little boxes where they wriggled around and ate oats and corn. There's even this story in the *Malleus Maleficarum* about a guy who went to a witch to ask for his penis back. She told him to climb a tree, where he'd find some in a bird's nest. He did and, of course, tried to take the biggest, but the witch said he couldn't have that one because it belonged to the parish priest."

I laughed.

"Men," Paige said. "They'll accuse women of anything." She paused and slanted a look at Adam. "Of course, it's such an outlandish charge, one can't help but wonder if there isn't a grain of truth in it."

Adam feigned a gulp. "Personally, I'd rather be a toad."

"Then give up the singing career or you'll be doing it as a soprano."

I laughed and glanced at Clay. He was holding his right arm out straight and bracing it with his left hand. Sweat dappled his forehead as the muscles beneath his forearm began to pulse.

"What are you—?" Paige began.

I motioned her to silence. Now was really not a good time to pester Clay. Since we couldn't exactly lug around a box of tools, he had to improvise a way to remove the dead man's head and hand.

Adam stared at Clay's hand as it began transforming into a claw. "That has got to be the coolest thing I've ever seen. Or the grossest."

"Come on over here," I said to Paige. "This isn't something you want to see."

We moved farther into the woods. Paige kept her gaze trained on a tree in the distance, cheek twitching, as if trying unsuccessfully not to think about what was happening behind us. There was a wet tearing sound, then a dull thud as the guard's decapitated head hit the ground.

"Nope," Adam said. "*That* was the grossest. Hands down."

"Heads down," Clay deadpanned. "The hand is next."

Adam hurried over to Paige and me.

"You know," Paige said, looking at Adam. "I always thought 'turning green' was only an expression. Guess not."

"Go ahead and laugh," Adam said. "That's one advantage to my powers, though. Burning flesh might smell awful, but at least it's bloodless."

"Okay," Clay said, stepping from the woods. "I'm ready. We're going in."

Chapter 43

Infiltration

We headed for the exit, checking first to ensure no one else had come outside for a nicotine fix. Once there, Clay removed the head and hand from the bag. I took the hand. As he lifted the head to the camera, I poised the still-warm hand beside the door handle, ready to grab it as soon as the first light turned green. Instead, the indicator stayed red and something beeped. I turned to see a numeric keypad attached to the wall. "ID#?" flashed on the tiny screen.

"Shit!" I said. "A key code. How did I miss that?"

"Because you were breaking out, darling, not breaking in," Clay said. "I didn't notice it either. Must be added security for getting inside."

"No problem," Paige said. "Let's break this down logically. First, find the number of digits." She started pressing the "9" button.

"Don't!" Adam said, snatching her hand. "If we punch in the wrong code, we might set off an alarm."

"I know that. All I'm doing is seeing how many digits it'll accept. Looks like five. Okay. So let's go back to this guy's body and see if we can find a five-digit number."

"Maybe tattooed on his chest," Adam said.

"No need for sarcasm," she said. "He might have a card or something with the number on it. Even if it's a secret, like a PIN, lots of people write it down and hide it in their wallet. We just look for anything with five digits."

"This is stupid," Adam muttered.

"No," I said. "It's logical, like Paige said. I'll run back—"

"We don't have time!"

"We'll make time," Clay said. "You two step into the woods and stay hidden."

Clay and I returned to the headless corpse and searched the pockets, finding neither a wallet nor anything bearing a number of any sort. When we returned, Adam was pacing just beyond the forest's edge.

"Nothing, right?" he said.

I nodded, then turned to Paige. "Okay, so we know it's a five-digit number. Can you hack into the system? Break the code?"

"Not without a laptop and a lot of time." She glanced at Adam, who'd strode out of earshot, then she lowered her voice. "He's wired. I don't think he slept much last night."

"He'll be fine," I said. "Let's check out that keypad again."

We returned to the door.

"Well?" Adam said. "Do we have a plan yet?"

"We're working on it," I said.

"What about you two?" Paige asked. "Can you turn into wolves and get us in?"

"How?" Clay said. "Whine and scratch at the door until someone opens it?"

"Is that all we've got?" Adam snapped. "What about the backup plan?"

"Cool it," Clay said. "We're working on one."

"Working on one? You mean we don't have one?"

Paige laid her hand on Adam's arm. He shook it off.

"What the hell are we standing around for?" he said. His voice tightened, taking on a shrill note of panic. "We have to hurry. Using that scanner probably set off an alarm. Even if it didn't, someone's bound to come looking for those two guards. Goddamn it!"

The whites of Adam's eyes suffused with red, as rage replaced panic. The smell of fire flared. Clay grabbed Adam by the back of the shirt just as Adam's fist connected with the door. There was a loud pop. The door shimmered. Clay hauled Adam back and threw him to the ground, then pushed Paige and me out of the way and stood over Adam.

"Control it, Adam," Clay said. "Concentrate."

Adam lay facedown on the ground. He balled his outstretched hands into fists, grabbing handfuls of grass and earth. The grass sizzled and smoked. When Adam started to stand, Clay put his foot on his back.

"Got it under control?" Clay asked. "I'm not letting you up until you do."

Adam nodded and Clay backed off, but stayed tense. Adam sat up, buried his face in his hands, and groaned like a college freshman with a killer hangover. Then he gave his head a sharp shake and looked at us.

"Sorry, guys," he said. "I didn't mean—" His head jerked up. "Did I do that?"

I followed his gaze and saw that the exit door was open. I blinked, looked again, and realized it wasn't open. It was gone. Only a pile of ash remained.

"Holy shit," Paige whispered. "You incinerated it."

"I did?" Adam stood, walked to the door, and touched the edge of it, then yelped and jerked his hand away. Red welts emblazoned his fingertips. He grinned. "Look, Ma, no door!" He punched the air and whooped. "Guess I'm not your average fire demon after all. See this door, Paige? Remember it next time you decide to bad-mouth me."

. "Congratulations," Clay said. "Now get the hell inside."

Adam nodded and tried to plaster on a serious face, but his grin slipped through. Clay motioned for him to lead the way. As he stepped over the pile of ash, he stooped and raked his fingers through it, then turned to Paige and grinned, eyes shining. She smiled back, then prodded him through the doorway. We were in.

Our next task was to disable the alarm and radio system. From my trips to and from the infirmary, I knew the communication center was located on the second floor, around the corner from the elevator. Several guards were on duty there at all times, manning the equipment. Tucker's office adjoined the guard station. With any luck, he'd be there. Killing Tucker was another high-priority job. Of all the remaining staff, Tucker was the most dangerous, not for any personal qualities—I didn't know the man well enough to assess that—but because he commanded the troops. When someone discovered that we'd infiltrated the compound, Tucker would rally them to action. Without Tucker and without the radio system, any sense of order among the guards would break down—or so we hoped. The only other person who could possibly control the men would be Winsloe. The guards might not like or respect Winsloe, but he paid their wages, which they wouldn't receive if they cut and ran at the first sign of trouble. So Winsloe would be next on our target list.

Once Winsloe and Tucker were dead, we'd be more concerned with fighting individual guards than tracking down the remaining staff members. Oh, sure, Tess might pull a nail file on us, but I could probably take her. That left Matasumi, a guy who couldn't fight his way out of a locked bathroom. Oh, right, I was forgetting someone. The sorcerer. Paige assured me she'd know Katzen if she saw him. Witches intuitively recognized sorcerers . . . or so she'd heard, though she'd never met one herself. Very comforting.

We'd planned to take our time moving from the exit to the guard station, avoiding confrontations, taking side routes if necessary. The incinerated exit door kiboshed that plan. We had to get to the guard room and disable the radios before anyone saw the damage.

Fortunately, we arrived at the communication center without incident. Our luck continued when we found only two guards manning the station. One was chomping on a granola bar. The other was doing the crossword in a week-old newspaper. We could only see slivers of their profiles, but it was enough to send a cold thrill through me. I smiled. These were two guards I recognized, two I'd never forget: Ryman and Jolliffe, the men who'd helped Winsloe hunt Lake, who'd played key roles in Armen's death, who'd taken such pride and vicious pleasure in their jobs. And now this dedicated duo was so engrossed in their work that Clay and I managed to sneak up behind them without either noticing. The temptation to shout "Boo!" and watch them hit the rafters was almost too great. But we were in a hurry. So Clay grabbed Ryman in a headlock and I snapped Jolliffe's neck as he pondered a nine-letter synonym for stupidity. We needed to keep one guard alive and had chosen Ryman, hoping his mouth would be too full of granola for him to scream. It was. Unfortunately, it was so full that when Clay grabbed him by the throat, he almost choked to death, thereby necessitating a flurry of discussion over the proper way to perform the Heimlich maneuver. It was a sad state of affairs when you had to save someone's life before you killed him.

Ryman finally coughed up a soggy chunk of oats, then let loose a stream of vulgarity.

"Now that doesn't sound like 'thank you,'" Clay said, clamping his hand over Ryman's mouth.

"There's gratitude for you," I said. I leaned into Ryman's face. "Remember me?"

His face went white. I grinned, baring my teeth.

"These are the two I told you about," I said to Clay.

His eyes sparked, and he returned my grin. "Good."

Ryman made a noise that sounded suspiciously like a whimper. I flashed him one last smile, then stepped away, leaving him to Clay. As Adam disconnected the communication equipment, I snapped the lock on Tucker's office, leaned inside, looked, and sniffed.

"Seems our luck stops here," I said. "No sign of the colonel."

"That's why we have this one." Clay slammed Ryman's head and upper torso onto the desktop, knocking over a bottle of mineral water. "Let's keep this brief. Where do we find Tucker?"

Blood trickled from Ryman's nose. He blinked, orienting himself, then cleared his throat and lifted his head.

"Paul Michael Ryman," he said, voice clipped, robotic. "Former corporal with the United States Army. Currently serving under Special Operations Colonel R. J. Tucker."

"What the hell is that?" Clay said.

Paige muffled a laugh. "I—uh—think it's his version of name, rank, and serial number. Sorry, Paul, but that's really not going to help us."

Clay leaned over, stretched Ryman's hand flat against the desktop, then smashed it with his fist. There was a sickening crunch, like the snapping of bird bones. Ryman shrieked, cut off in mid-note by Clay's hand over his mouth.

"Doctors will have a hell of a time fixing that," Clay said. "I'd call it a write-off. That was the left hand. Next I do the right. Where is Tucker?"

"Paul Michael Ryman," Ryman gasped when Clay uncovered his mouth. "Former corporal with the United States Army. Currently serving under Special Operations Colonel R. J. Tucker."

"Oh, for pity's sake," Paige said. "Come on, Paul. We all appreciate your loyalty, but trust me, no one else is going to give a damn. Just tell the man what he wants to know and get it over with."

"Paul Michael Ryman. Former corporal with the United States Army. Currently serving under Special Operations Colonel R. J. Tucker."

"Men," Paige muttered, shaking her head.

Clay spread Ryman's right hand on the desktop. A spurt of static from one set of speakers made me jump. Clay only glanced at Adam.

"Sorry," Adam said. "I'm almost done."

He jacked down the volume on the static-spewing speaker, then bent to look at the wiring on the other one.

"Okay," Clay said. "One last chance. Wh—"

The still-functional speaker broke into an earsplitting whine. As Adam reached to flick it off, a voice sounded.

"Jackson to base. Base, do you read? Repeat, security has been breached. Over."

"Hold on," Clay whispered before Adam turned it off. He motioned for me to hold Ryman still and quiet, then snatched the mike from Adam. "How do you work this thing?"

"Push the button to talk. Release to listen. They can't hear anything unless the button's down."

Clay cranked up the volume on the disconnected speaker. Static filled the room. He pushed the talk button.

"Base to Jackson," Clay said, swallowing his accent. "Ryman here. We're having equipment problems. Repeat. Over."

"Shit, Paul," the voice came back. "I can barely hear you. I said we have a breach. The fucking door's been blown off. I'm guessing explosives, but shit, you should see this. Nothing left but ash. One helluva bomb."

"No," Adam said, grinning. "One helluva half-demon."

Clay motioned him to silence, then pressed the mike button. "Where's Tu—Colonel Tucker?"

"Last time I saw him, he was on level two, taking inventory in the gun locker. He isn't answering his radio?"

"I'll try again. Maintain your position. I'm sending backup."

Clay handed the mike to Adam, then gestured from me to Ryman.

"You want him?" he asked.

I met Ryman's eyes with a cold stare. "Not really. Go ahead and kill him."

Ryman's eyes bulged. His mouth opened but before anything came out, Clay snapped his neck. Once Adam finished disconnecting the radio and security systems, we headed for the gun locker.

Now, we didn't know exactly where to find the gun locker. The guard had said level two, which narrowed it down somewhat. From my infirmary excursions, I'd learned that the second floor was laid out much like the lower level, one large block with a single corridor looping around and joining at the elevator. That made it easier. All we had to do was start at one end and check every room until we found Tucker. Getting Ryman to divulge the exact location of the gun locker would have taken too much time.

On our search, we found and killed two kitchen workers. No, they didn't threaten us. No, we didn't perceive them as a threat. The unpleasant truth was that we had to kill everyone. No matter how harmless they might seem, even the lowliest staff member possessed the most dangerous weapon of all: knowledge. They knew we existed, and for that, they couldn't be allowed to leave the compound.

While searching for Tucker, we found Matasumi in a locked room—or I should say, I smelled him through a locked door. We listened for a moment, then Paige cast a minor spell to open it. She admitted the spell worked only on simple locks, but since it was silent, we decided to try that before employing more physical techniques. It worked and we eased the door open. I peered inside and saw Matasumi seated at a computer. He was alone. I eased the door shut, bumping Paige in the chin as she craned her neck for a look inside.

"All clear," I whispered. "He's working at a computer. Doesn't seem to even realize there's a problem."

"He knows," Paige said. "Did you see the Zip disks? The knapsack? He's backing up data and clearing the hard drive before he runs."

"And he's about to encounter a fatal error," Adam said, grinning. "Mind if I handle this one?"

"I saw a gun on the desk," Paige said. "A big one. He probably grabbed the largest one he could find."

Clay glanced at me.

"I doubt he has any idea how to use it." I nodded to Adam. "Sure, go ahead. We'll cover you. Just be—"

"Careful," Adam said. "I know."

I eased open the door. Matasumi faced the side wall. His fingers flew across the keyboard. As Adam stepped into the room, Matasumi bent to put another disk into the drive. He saw Adam and froze, then sneaked a glance at the gun on the corner of the desk. His hand darted out, but Adam snatched the rifle before Matasumi got close.

Adam brandished the gun and whistled. "This is one wicked piece of firepower. You got a license for it, Doc?"

Matasumi froze again, hand still outstretched.

"Didn't think so," Adam said. "Neither do I, so how about we get rid of this before someone gets hurt."

Adam started to toss the gun to Clay, then thought better of it, laid it on the floor, and scooted it to us with his foot.

"Adam Vasic," Matasumi murmured.

"You know my name? I'm flattered."

Adam grabbed Matasumi's hand and shook it. Matasumi yelped and yanked his hand back. He stared at the bright red splotches on his palm, then gaped at Adam, as if unable to believe he'd burned him.

"Whoops," Adam said. "Sorry about that, Doc. Haven't quite got the fiery stuff under control yet." Adam turned to the computer. "Whatcha working on? That's some piece of hardware. Paige, you see this? What is it?"

Adam bent and squinted at the tower box. He reached out and touched it. Sparks flew. Circuits popped. Matasumi jerked back.

"Damn!" Adam said. "That looks bad. Think you can fix it, Paige?"

"Sorry, I'm not a technician."

Adam shook his head. "Guess we're shit outta luck, then, Doc. Sorry about that. What were you doing anyway? Downloading files?" Adam popped the disk from the drive. It sizzled, then melted like wax between his fingers. "Oops. Hope you have backups."

Matasumi's eyes flickered to a locked shelf overhead. Clay stepped forward and snapped it open. Adam scooped up a handful of disk cases. This time they disintegrated at his touch, leaving only charred bits of plastic and metal.

"See?" he said, showing Clay his fistful of ash. "That's what happens when you help me strengthen my powers. Even worse than King Midas's curse. At least gold's valuable." He turned to Matasumi and shrugged. "Sorry, Doc, but it's really for the best. We can't let that information get outside these walls, can we? Oh, wait. There's one more memory bank I need to shut down. My apologies in advance."

Adam tore a wire from the computer and wrapped it around Matasumi's neck. For a second, Matasumi didn't seem to realize what was happening. Then his hands flew to his throat. Too late. As Adam wrenched the wire tight, it ignited, flared, then died as Matasumi slumped sideways, garroted.

"You enjoyed that far too much," Paige said.

Adam only grinned. "What do you expect? I'm a demon."

"*Half*-demon."

"And a full demon would have tortured the poor guy first. At least I was merciful."

"Finish destroying the files and the computer," Clay said. "Then we move."

"Should I contact Kenneth now?" Paige asked as we left the room.

Clay shook his head and kept walking.

"But Jeremy said to notify them once we were inside and had the systems down."

"No, he said to notify him when Elena told you to."

Paige glanced at me.

I shook my head. "Not yet."

"But we could use their help."

"Whose help?" Clay said, stopping suddenly and wheeling on her. "Kenneth's? He can't fight. Cassandra's? She might fight, *if* she feels like it. We'll call them in when it's clear."

"But—"

"But nothing." Clay glowered at Paige. "You're asking me to put my Alpha in a potentially dangerous position where he's not only the lone fighter, but where he's responsible for two other people. I won't do that."

"I'm sorry," Paige murmured as Clay turned away.

Clay spun on her. "What?"

"I said, I'm sorry."

Clay hesitated, gave a brusque nod, then motioned us to silence and started forward again.

We found the gun locker. To my surprise, it was actually a whole room. Hey, I've never been in the military. I hear the term "gun locker" and I picture a high-school locker stuffed with AK–47s and grenades instead of smelly socks and week-old ham sandwiches.

I sneaked up to an open doorway, peeked around the corner, and saw Tucker scribbling on a clipboard. Not only was he alone, but he had his back to us. Maybe Bauer had a point when she made that little speech about overreliance on technology in the post-industrial age. These guys were so convinced of the impenetrability of their high-tech security system that, so long as no alarms blared, they felt safe. Tucker wasn't even armed. Really, where was the challenge?

I backed away from the door and motioned to Clay. He crept to my side, glanced around the door, and shook his head. We broke into a flurry of sign language. Then I nodded, stepped back, and waved Adam and Paige forward. Clay glided around the door, shoes silent on the linoleum. When Adam tried to follow, I put out my hands to stop him. Clay could handle this alone. Better if we stayed hidden.

I closed my eyes to sharpen my hearing and tracked the whisper of Clay's breathing, mapping it against Tucker's. The gap between them closed. Then, as I waited for the scuffle of the attack, two loud clicks shattered the silence. Guns.

I lunged into the open doorway. Paige grabbed the back of my shirt, stopping me just as two guards stepped from their hiding places, guns trained on Clay's head.

Annihilation

Clay froze in mid-step. His eyes flickered from one guard to the other, but he didn't move, didn't even complete his stride. Tucker turned to face him, smiling.

"So it *is* you," Tucker said. "The brute who took out my men near Augusta. If we hadn't found the camera, I wouldn't have believed it. Three of my best men. Killed by one rabid dog."

Clay said nothing. Adam, Paige, and I stood in the open doorway. Tucker ignored us.

"Not a bad idea, disabling the radios and alarms," Tucker said. "Not bad, but not brilliant either. You underestimated how well I've trained my men. As soon as Jackson realized we had a breach, he sent one of his team to warn me personally."

Paige held my arm. As Tucker spoke, she squeezed it. Thinking she was frightened, I didn't brush her off. Then she pinched me so hard I had to bite back a yelp. When I glared down at her, she nodded almost imperceptibly toward the nearer guard. I returned an equally discreet head shake. No way was I endangering Clay's life by attacking a guard. Paige squeezed my arm harder and shot me an impatient look. I turned away.

Tucker continued, "Yes, I know it's four to three right now. Not outstanding odds for our side, but I expect them to improve at any moment. One of my men is gathering backup as we speak." He tilted his head. "Do I hear footsteps? I think I do. But you're the one with bionic hearing. Tell me, how many men are approaching? Four? Six? Ten?"

Paige murmured under her breath. It didn't sound like English . . . Shit! She was casting a spell. Before I could stop her, the guard who was farther from us tensed. He looked from side to side, only his eyes moving, slowly flooding with panic. I knew then what Paige had cast: a binding spell. Paige released her grip on my arm and I flew at the nearer guard. As I slammed into him, a shot fired at the ceiling. I wrenched the gun from his hands as we fell to the floor. The second guard was turning now, the spell broken.

Adam hurdled over me and threw the other guard into the wall. Clay grabbed Tucker by the neck. As I drove my fists into my target's gut, his knee caught me in the chest, winding me. The stink of burning flesh filled the room. The other guard screamed. At the sound, my guard hesitated just long enough for me to catch my breath. I heaved him over my head and into a set of heavy steel shelves. The back of his head slammed into the top shelf corner. He hung there a minute, suspended in midair. His eyes blinked once, then he toppled face first to the floor, blood gushing from a crevice in the back of his skull. Clay checked the guard's pulse as I stood.

"Dead," he said.

One glance at Tucker and the other guard told me they suffered from the same condition.

"Can you hear anyone coming, darling?" Clay asked.

"Tucker was bluffing earlier," I said. "But they're coming now. At least four. As many as seven. We should run."

"Run?" Adam said. "Their seven to our four? That's decent odds."

"I want excellent, not decent. Seven to four almost guarantees a loss on our side. Are you volunteering for the position?"

Adam glanced at Clay.

"Elena's right," Clay said. "We run now and hope they split up. If they don't, we pick the battlefield. Here, we're cornered."

We left the gun locker.

Though I could hear the guards coming, they weren't in sight yet. We made it around the corner. Then we ducked into an open doorway.

"They're at the gun locker," I whispered as I listened. "They're talking . . . they see Tucker. One—no, two are staying to check for vital signs. The rest are going to keep looking. They've slowed to a walk, but they're coming this way."

"They've separated," Clay murmured. "But not for long."

I turned to Paige. "Can you cast that cover spell?"

"Sure," she said.

"Does it work . . . reliably?"

Her face darkened. "Of course—" She stopped herself and nodded. "It'll work. It's a level-three spell. I'm a level-four apprentice. Binding is fourth level, which is why it gives me some trouble."

"Good. You three wait here in the doorway. Paige will cast her cover spell. Stay still and they won't see you. Don't cover me, Paige. I'll be the decoy and lead them past you three. Clay and Adam can attack from behind. Once the guards' attention—and their guns—are off me, I'll join the fight."

Paige shook her head. "*I'll* be the decoy."

"We don't have time to argue," Clay said.

"You, Adam, and Elena are fighters. I'm not. Better to have you three attack. Besides, Elena may not look too threatening, but when these guys see me, the words 'kick-ass bitch' won't even enter their minds. They won't expect a fight."

"She's right," Clay said.

I hesitated.

"We'll be right here," Clay whispered to me, too low for the others to hear. "She'll be okay."

"Places everyone," Paige said. "Here they come."

In the ensuing battle, Adam took a bullet to the shoulder. Painful, but not incapacitating. The guards died. All of them—the four who'd come around the corner, plus the two who'd stayed behind to check Tucker, plus three more who showed up before Paige finished casting a healing spell to stop Adam's bleeding. Nine guards. All dead. When it was over, Paige stood amid the dead guards, looked down at the bodies, and excused herself. She spent the next few minutes in an empty room. We didn't bother her. She wasn't the only one who'd seen enough death that day. As I thought of all the killing still to come, the guards and other staff we hadn't yet encountered, my own resolve began to falter. It was all too much. Yes, I'd killed before, but those had been mutts, stone-cold killers themselves, and their deaths had been spaced out over all my years as a werewolf. To kill so many people, in so short a time . . . I knew I'd have nightmares about this day, that I'd see their faces, wonder if they had wives, girlfriends, children. I told myself I couldn't think about that. They had to die to protect our secrets. They'd understood the danger when they signed on to this project. Knowing that didn't make it any easier. The bodies piled up, and I desperately wanted to find some way to avoid the killing. But there was no other way. Everyone had to die.

Adam, Clay, and I didn't exchange a single word while Paige was gone. When she returned, her face was pale but grim.

"Let's get this over with," she said.

Adam blinked and looked around in confusion, like a sleepwalker waking up in the backyard. His face was as pale as Paige's. Shell shock.

Clay looked from Paige to Adam to me. He rested his fingertips on my arm and half-turned from the other two, facing me.

"I'll finish," he said. "You guys have had enough. Show me where to look and cover my back. I'll do the rest."

I met his eyes. He looked as tired as I felt. Not physically exhausted, but mentally wiped out. He'd had enough, too. When I touched his hand, he squeezed my fingers.

"Let's find a safe place for them," I murmured, too low for Paige and Adam to hear. "Then you and I will finish."

Clay hesitated.

"Jeremy told us to stay together," I said. "I'm not letting you fight alone."

Clay searched my face, then exhaled slowly. "Okay, darling. Let's get this over with so we can go home."

We left Paige and Adam behind. Paige agreed without comment. Adam protested, but I took him aside and explained that we were worried about Paige and didn't dare leave her without someone to stand guard. I think Adam knew better, but after seeing a way to exit the action with his dignity intact, he accepted the change in plans and escorted Paige into an empty room.

Clay and I covered the whole second level twice. When we found no sign of Winsloe, we went upstairs, exited the compound, and checked for potential escapees. All four vehicles were still in the garage. We killed two guards frantically tinkering with a busted Bronco. Then we circled the perimeter of the compound, listening and sniffing for anyone who might have bolted into the woods. Nothing. No trace of Winsloe either.

When we returned to Paige and Adam, I asked Paige to go ahead and contact Kenneth. Time for Jeremy to join us. It would take at least thirty minutes for the three of them to get through the woods. By then, we'd be ready for their help cleaning up and destroying the evidence. First, though, we had one last task: Clear the cells.

EMANCIPATION

Paige and Adam insisted on accompanying us downstairs. By my count, most of the guards were already dead, so we let them come along. As I expected, there were only the usual two men manning the cell-block guard station. Clay and I dispatched them, then we headed into the cells. Adam's work disconnecting the system meant all the security doors were now open, so we were able to discard the bag o' body parts Clay had retrieved from outside.

Before entering the cell block, Clay and I split up. Yes, Jeremy had warned us not to, but I understood that he didn't mean we weren't to leave each other's sight at all. He trusted me to use my discretion, and that discretion said it would be better for the two of us to enter the cell block from opposite doors. We were out of contact for only a few seconds as we passed from the corridor to the cell block. Entering through separate doors meant no one could escape out the other side as we went in. An unnecessary precaution. Winsloe wasn't hiding in the cell hallway. No one was. Paige and I entered from the guard-station side, and as we walked through the door, Adam and Clay were already heading toward us from the other end.

"We should let everyone out," I called as they approached.

Clay nodded. "Gives us a chance to check the cells for Winsloe."

"That's her?" Paige whispered.

I turned to see that she'd stopped at Savannah's cell. Inside, Savannah played on a Game Boy, nose scrunched in concentration.

"She's okay," I said. "Good."

"Can we let her out?" Paige said, still whispering, as if Savannah could overhear us.

I shook my head. "Let's check on Leah first. Make sure she's secured in her cell."

Leah's cell was still next to Savannah's, and unfortunately she was also alive and well, sitting in her chair, feet propped on a table, reading *Cosmo*.

Adam peered into the cell. "That's her? The evil Leah? Doesn't look very dangerous to me. I could take her."

Paige rolled her eyes. "Unbelievable. One disintegrated door and fire-boy thinks he's king of the demons."

"Boy?" Adam sputtered. "I'm a year older than you."

"Move along," Clay said. "So long as she's secured, we'll leave her there until Jeremy decides what he wants done."

Adam cast one last, longing glance at Leah, then turned to me. "Now what?"

"You and Clay can check how many other cells are occupied while Paige and I talk to Savannah."

As Clay and Adam headed down the hall, Paige and I approached Savannah's cell. Inside, she was still playing her video game. We paused outside the door.

"Did my mother tell Savannah about me?" Paige asked.

I nodded. "She knows what to expect, that you're going to look after her. Or, that was the plan, though I suppose as long as you take her back to your Coven, that would be good enough. I doubt Ruth really expected you to adopt a twelve-year-old."

"She did," Paige said. "Though I'm not sure what Savannah will think of the idea."

"Oh, she'll be fine." I reached for the door handle. "Ready?"

Something akin to panic flitted across Paige's face. Then she exhaled, straightened her shirt, and ran a hand through her curls, as if prepping for a job interview.

"Okay," she said. She stretched past me, opened the door, and walked inside. "Hello, Savannah."

Savannah leaped up, Game Boy crashing to the floor. Her eyes flickered past Paige and saw me. Grinning, she raced over and threw her arms around me.

"I knew you'd come back," she said.

Ouch. That hurt. Really hurt. But I had come back, hadn't I? I only wished I'd had enough faith not to abandon her in the first place.

"This is Paige Winterbourne," I said. "Ruth's . . . "

"Daughter," Paige finished.

Savannah turned to Paige. They were the same height.

"This is the witch who's supposed to take me?" Savannah looked from me to Paige, then back to me. "How old is she?"

"I'm twenty-two," Paige said, smiling.

Savannah's eyes widened in horror. "Twenty-two? She's barely older than me!"

"We'll discuss that later," I said. "Right now—"

"Who's that?" She pointed at Clay, standing in the doorway, then realized she was pointing and turned the gesture into a wave.

"Clayton," I said. "My—"

"Ruth told me about him. Your husband, right?"

"Uh—right."

Savannah gave Clay the adolescent girl's version of a once-over, which didn't extend lower than his neck. She nodded approvingly, then leaned forward, nearly tripping over me.

"Who's that?"

"Adam Vasic," Adam said, stepping into the room with a mock bow.

Savannah stifled a giggle. "Ruth mentioned you. The fire-demon. That doesn't sound *too* bad, but what can you do? Besides start fires?"

"We really should—" Paige began.

"It's Savannah Levine, right?" Adam asked.

Savannah nodded. Adam extended his hand with a flourish, paused, then put his finger to the wall. The drywall smoked. Using his finger, he scorched S. L., then drew a heart around it.

Savannah's face lit up, but she struggled to hide it under a veil of indifference. "Not bad. But anyone can do that with a magnifying glass. Don't you have any *real* powers?"

"Later," Clay said. "We have two more cells to empty."

Adam stepped aside to let Savannah pass, holding the door open for her. She pretended to ignore him, but couldn't hide a tiny smile and one last glance at his artwork on the wall. Poor Xavier. So easily ousted from Savannah's affections by a younger, more powerful half-demon. How fickle the heart of a twelve-year-old girl.

As Savannah walked past Adam, she collided with Clay blocking the exit.

"She stays here," he said. "Paige can look after her."

Savannah yelped.

"We should have released her last," Clay said. "There could still be some guards left. I don't want her wandering about."

"I won't wander—"

Clay cut her off with a look. They locked eyes, then Savannah dropped her gaze.

"Fine," she said. She turned on her heel, stalked to her bed, and threw herself atop it, arms crossed, facing the wall.

"Adam, stay with them," Clay said. "Stand guard."

"I don't need anyone to protect me," Savannah said, flipping over and sitting up, pique vanishing as Adam approached. "But you can look after *her.*" She jerked her chin toward Paige. "She looks like she might need help."

"This is going to be fun," Paige murmured under her breath. "Couldn't you have found me a sweet little eight-year-old witch?"

"It could be worse," I said. "She could be sixteen."

"Someday, she will be."

Two prisoners left. Curtis Zaid, the Vodoun priest, and a new captive in the cell across from my old one.

"What do you think he is?" I asked Clay, tilting my head to study the newcomer. "I heard they were trying to capture a vampire, but this guy doesn't look too anemic, does he?"

That was an understatement. The man in the cell was at least six foot three, with broad shoulders and plenty of muscles, shown off by a sleeveless sweatshirt and well-worn jeans. Definitely not anemic.

"You can stop drooling, darling," Clay said.

I made a face at him and looked back at the stranger. "You think he's a vampire?"

"Want me to stick my neck in and find out?"

"Maybe later. For now, I think we should leave him where he is. Just to be safe."

We walked to Curtis Zaid's cell. I watched him through the one-way glass, trying to assess his mental stability.

"He looks okay," I said. "No ranting and cursing. I think the poor guy's lost it, but he isn't dangerous. He doesn't have any true power. More likely to be a nuisance than a threat."

"Let's get him out, then," Clay said, opening the door.

As we stepped into the cell, Zaid turned and pulled something from his head. Earphones, connected to a CD player on the table. He closed his book and laid it on top of a VCR. CDs? Videos? Hell, all I ever got was old books and a television with two fuzzy stations. Maybe I should have taken up cursing.

"We're here to let you out, Curtis," I said.

Zaid didn't appear the least bit surprised. Maybe he was too far gone. Ignoring us, he stood and headed for the door. We moved back to let him out. He stepped into the hall, stopped, and looked around, as if expecting a trap. Then he started for the exit.

"Uh, you don't want to leave just yet," I called. "It's a long hike to the nearest town."

Zaid kept walking.

"Let him go," Clay said. "He won't get far. We'll find him before we leave."

Savannah ran from her cell. Adam whirled from his guard-post position and tried to snatch her arm but missed.

"Are you done yet?" she called. "Can we go now? Hey, is that Mr. Zaid?" She stopped a few feet from Zaid, stared up at him, and took a tiny step back. "That's not a Voodoo—"

"Savannah!" Paige said, running from the cell. "I told you to stay—"

She pulled up short. I followed her gaze to Zaid, who'd stopped and was slowly turning to face the two witches. Paige went white. Stark white. Zaid lifted his hand as if in greeting. Savannah's feet flew from under her. She sailed through the air.

"Savannah!" Paige screamed and threw herself at the girl.

Savannah's body hovered in midair for a second, then hurtled toward us like a rock from a slingshot. No, not toward *us*. Toward the wall behind us. Clay and I wheeled around, arms out to grab her. Her body stuck my shoulder hard enough to slam me into the wall. Clay lunged, catching us both before we hit the floor.

I looked over Clay's shoulder and saw Paige standing five feet from Zaid. They faced each other, both silent. Zaid's lips curved in a tiny smile.

"It's been a long time since I had the pleasure of confronting a witch," he said. "And here I have two at once. Pity they're only apprentices. We could have had some fun."

He fluttered one hand and Paige's knees buckled. She stumbled, but caught herself.

"Better an apprentice witch than a back-stabbing sorcerer," she said.

"Katzen," I whispered.

While I crouched on the floor holding Savannah, Adam and Clay stepped toward Katzen from opposite sides. He glanced at them and waved a circle with one hand. Clay stopped short, blinking. He reached forward. His hand seemed to hit something hard but invisible. He swung his fist, but his hand stopped in mid-swing. Katzen slanted a bored glance at us.

"Don't bother," he said. "This is between me and the witch. Enjoy the show, but don't make yourselves too comfortable. It won't last long." He turned to Paige. "I'm feeling magnanimous today, witch. Concede and I'll let you go."

"No deal," Paige said. "But if you concede, I'll let *you* go."

Katzen flipped his wrist. This time Paige mumbled a few words and stayed his hand. He flexed his fingers, easily snapping the binding spell, but when he tried the gesture again, Paige cast another spell, stopping his hand before he completed the motion.

"Good try," he said. "But you're wasting your time. No witch, particularly an apprentice, can hope to out-fight a sorcerer. I'm sure you know your history. You witches are so *good* at remembering the past. All you have left, really. Rather sad."

"I know my history lessons," Paige said. "Any true powers sorcerers have came from witches. We taught you everything, but when the Inquisition began, did you protect us? No. The moment you were targeted, you handed them our heads on a silver platter. We gave you power and you betrayed us."

"Perhaps I was wrong," Katzen said. "History isn't all you have left. There's bitterness, too. Bitterness and envy."

Katzen lifted both hands. Paige's lips moved, but before any spell came out, she vaulted into the air. She hit the ground rolling from the impact, then vanished. Disappeared. Katzen scanned the floor.

"A cover spell. How original." He turned, stomped down one foot, turned again, stomped again, as if trying to squash a fleeing ant.

Katzen's barrier surrounded him and Paige, trapping Adam on the far side of the hall. Adam's eyes glowed red as he pounded at the barrier, but even his power couldn't break through. Clay paced along our side, running his hands over the barrier, trying to find a breach. I cradled Savannah as I checked for broken bones. She seemed okay, just bruised and dazed.

Katzen continued to stomp the floor, moving a few inches with each blow. "Tell me when I'm getting close, witch. You know I'll find you. All you have to do is move and you're caught. That's the trouble with witch spells, isn't it? You can only defend yourself. You can't fight back."

A shape shimmered a few feet from Katzen. Paige, lips moving.

"Paige!" I shouted, warning her that she was revealing herself.

Before Katzen could turn, a fiery ball swooped from the ceiling, struck him in the chest, and exploded. He reeled back, coughing, clothing singed. He whipped his head around, searching for Paige. One of his short dreadlocks ignited and smacked his cheek, leaving a bright red patch. He snarled and slapped the fire out, then looked around again. Paige was gone.

"Well done, witch," he said. "Been reading sorcerer grimoires?"

He started to say more, then stopped, turning as if something had caught his eye. His lips curved in a slow grin. I followed his gaze to Leah's cell. Katzen's grin broadened, and he flipped his hand, murmured a few words. There was a click, too soft for human ears to detect. Then Leah's door creaked open an inch. Inside, she sat up, her magazine sliding to the floor. She walked to the door, opened it, and stepped out.

Chapter 46

Demonstration

"You're missing all the fun, my dear," Katzen said as Leah stepped from her cell. "Why don't you take the girl someplace safe while I deal with this one."

Leah blinked, momentarily disoriented as she scanned the hall, gaze crossing the unfamiliar figures of Clay, Adam, and Paige. I eased Savannah off my lap and stood. Leah saw the motion and turned.

"I should have guessed," she said. "Welcome back, Elena."

Clay was easing toward us, trying not to attract her attention until he was close enough to lunge. On the other side of the invisible barrier, Adam paced, eyes smoldering. I sidestepped in front of Savannah.

"Don't even think about it," I said.

"Leah?" Savannah said, still sounding dazed. She struggled to her feet behind me. "Can—can you help us?"

Leah smiled. "Of course I can."

I threw myself at Leah. Something struck me in the back of the head. As I pitched forward, everything went dark. I jolted back to consciousness as I hit the cement floor. Clay's arms were around me, pulling me up.

"Savannah," I said, clambering to my feet.

I staggered, still woozy from the blow. The room swirled. Blood dripped hot against the back of my neck. Clay tried to steady me, but I pushed him away.

"Help Savannah," I said.

Clay grabbed for Savannah, who now stood in front of us. But his hand didn't make contact. It stopped short as it had when he'd hit the invisible barrier around Katzen and Paige.

"No interference from you, wolf-man," Katzen said. "We don't need your kind or the fire-demon. Take your friend and your mate, and leave before this witch whets my appetite for a stronger challenge."

I tottered forward and bumped into the barrier surrounding Savannah and Leah. My head still spun. When I pounded my fists against the invisible wall, the recoil from my own blows sent me stumbling back. As Clay caught me, I saw something on the floor. A book, presumably from Katzen's cell. The corner was flecked with blood. My blood. I stared at it. A book. Leah had hit me with an ordinary book, thrown hard enough to knock me out and draw blood. I looked at Savannah and fear filled me.

"Let her go," I said. "She's only a kid."

Leah rolled her eyes. "Don't go pulling that 'innocent child' crap on me, Elena. Savannah is twelve years old. Hardly a little girl. And hardly innocent." She smiled at Savannah. "But I don't mind that. I'll look after you."

Savannah looked from me to Leah, still confused. In that moment I realized what Leah had been up to, staging all those flying-object events and blaming Savannah. She'd tried to make herself the girl's only ally, the only one who would accept her no matter what she did. In addition, Leah had somehow allied herself with Katzen, as Paige suspected. Together they'd staged the whole horror show the night I escaped. But to what purpose? It didn't matter. Right now all that mattered was that Paige was trapped with Katzen, and Savannah was in danger of leaving with Leah. I couldn't do much about the first part, but the second . . .

"She *is* innocent," I said. "Innocent of everything that happened in here. Why don't you tell her who really attacked all those guards, who really killed Ruth Winterbourne. Flying objects . . . telekinetic half-demon. Hmmm, could there be a connection?"

"But—" Savannah blinked, looking from me to Leah. "You—wouldn't do that."

"Of course I wouldn't," Leah said. "I'd never hurt you, Savannah."

"No?" I said. "What about that flying glass? Do you think that tickled? But you weren't there, were you? You conveniently appeared after that was over."

Savannah's gaze swiveled from Leah to me and back.

"Okay," she said quietly. "If you're my friend, Leah, then let them go. Tell him to let Paige go. She didn't do anything wrong. Let them go and come with us."

"I can't do that, Savannah," Leah said. "They don't understand you. They'll take you away and, when things go bad, they won't understand. I'm the only one—"

"No!" Savannah shouted.

Her body jerked upright. For a moment, I thought Katzen had her again. I threw myself at the barrier, then saw the look on Savannah's face. Her eyes blazed and her features were contorted in rage. Her lips moved.

Leah reached for the girl, then froze in mid-motion. Confusion flickered in her eyes, then dawning comprehension, then the faintest stain of fear. She didn't move. Didn't even twitch a muscle. I looked at Savannah. Her eyes were fixed on Leah.

"My God," Paige whispered. "She's bound her."

Katzen didn't seem to notice Paige had reappeared, breaking her cover spell. Instead he stared at Savannah, then started to laugh.

"Now there's power," he said. He looked down at Paige sitting on the floor. "*That's* a binding spell, witch. Maybe you should have asked her for lessons before you decided to take me on. Too bad. I would have enjoyed a real workout."

He snapped his hand and Paige sailed backward into the wall. She hit the floor rolling and vanished. Katzen renewed his stomping quest. Behind them, Savannah stood with her back to the action, binding Leah. Adam, Clay, and I watched, helpless, our attention torn between the two battles.

Paige shimmered as she cast a spell. Katzen whirled in time to see her just two feet behind him, and his foot flew out, catching her in the stomach before she finished the words. Wheezing, Paige rolled out of his way and struggled to her feet. She repeated the spell. Another fiery sphere erupted from nowhere, this one striking Katzen between the shoulder blades and knocking him to his knees. As he fell, he lifted his hands and Paige catapulted into the air, rushing at the ceiling. She said something and the sorcerer's spell broke abruptly, dropping her to the floor with a bone-jarring thud. She rolled and disappeared behind another cover spell.

"An impressive but sadly limited repertoire," Katzen said, getting to his feet. "Those fire balls won't kill me, witch. You know that."

"Oh, I know," Paige said, appearing a dozen feet behind him.

Katzen spun to face Paige. She sat cross-legged on the floor, making no move to stand.

"But I'll bet I can kill you," she said. "In fact, I can do it without touching you, without even standing up."

Katzen laughed. "Ah, here it comes. The bluff. Do your best, witch. Then I'll do mine."

Paige closed her eyes and said a few words. Katzen braced himself. I held my breath. But nothing happened. Katzen hesitated, then started to laugh. Paige turned her head and looked at Clay. He caught her eye and nodded, then sidestepped toward the invisible wall . . . and walked right through it. The barrier was gone. Katzen didn't notice.

"Damn," Paige muttered. "Can I—uh—try that again?"

Katzen roared with laughter. I sprang to my feet and leaped at him. Clay and Adam lunged at the same time, and all three of us hit Katzen together. His hands flew up to cast a spell. I snatched his wrists, clasping them so tight the bones snapped. Katzen gasped. Clay grabbed his head and twisted. The sorcerer's body convulsed, striking Adam in his wounded side and knocking him backward. Then Katzen went limp. Clay checked his pulse, waited for his heart to stop, then dropped him.

"He's dead."

The pronouncement came not from Clay, but from across the hall. From Savannah. We all turned to see her still holding Leah in the spell, her back to us. She hadn't turned. Hadn't seen the fight, unable to tear her eyes from Leah without breaking the spell.

"He's dead," she said again, and I realized she was talking to Leah. "It's over."

Leah's face went white. Outrage and grief flooded her eyes. A rumbling filled the room. A loud crack. Then another. A chunk of plaster flew from the wall behind me. The lightbulbs exploded. I wheeled toward Savannah as a chair shot from Katzen's cell. It struck Savannah in the back and she crumpled. I rushed at her, but not fast enough. She toppled backward onto the floor. Paige and I grabbed her at the same time. Glass swirled around us, mingling with a whirlwind of dust from falling plaster. Clay shouted. Then Adam. Paige and I bent over Savannah, protecting her from the hailstorm of debris. Then, as suddenly as it had begun, it stopped. And Leah was gone.

Clay and I followed Leah's trail outside, but we didn't get far before a familiar voice hailed us. Jeremy stepped from the woods, Cassandra and Kenneth in tow.

"What happened?" Jeremy asked, taking in our dust-covered clothes and glass-nicked skin.

Reaching out, he wiped a dribble of blood from my cheek. I leaned back against him, closing my eyes to indulge in a brief moment of peace.

"You're okay?" he murmured.

"Alive," I said. "Everyone is."

I gave Jeremy a full report, concluding with Leah's escape. Although I wanted to go after her immediately, Jeremy nixed that plan. He was more concerned with stopping Tyrone Winsloe and finding any remaining staff members. If Leah was on the run, she posed no immediate danger. It was a long walk to the nearest phone. We could stop her later. Right now we needed to make sure no humans left the compound and took our secrets with them.

"Clay and I will go look for Winsloe," I said.

"I'll come with you," Cassandra said. "We found only one guard, and Jeremy took care of him. Tyrone Winsloe may be my last chance for some actual combat."

"Elena and I can handle this," Clay said. "If you want something to do, Cassandra, go skulk around the second floor, see if you can find any warm food."

Cassandra only smiled. "No, thank you, Clayton. I'll wait for Winsloe. He should be quite warm when you finish with him."

"Oh, that reminds me," I said. "There's still one captive left. He might be a vampire, but we're not sure. Would you mind taking a look, Cassandra? If he is a vampire, you can tell me whether it's safe to release him. You'd know, right?"

She nodded. "There aren't many vampires in North America. If he's one of us, I should recognize him."

After we all returned to the cell block, I led Cassandra down the hall toward the remaining captive. As we walked, I tried to think up a way to keep Cassandra from accompanying Clay and me on our search for Winsloe. I didn't want her there. Winsloe was mine. I owed him for everything he'd done, everything he'd threatened to do. His death would be a private matter, something I would share only with Clay.

We arrived at the cell before I came up with a plan. Cassandra took one look at the man inside and blinked. Hard.

"You know him?" I asked.

She paused, seeming to debate whether to lie. "He's a vampire."

I interpreted that to mean she did know him. "Is he dangerous?"

"Not really. Not very useful either. I wouldn't be in any rush to release him. He'll only get in the way. We can come back later."

She turned to go. I grabbed her arm. Her skin was cool to the touch, like someone who'd spent the day in an air-conditioned office.

"What if something happens and we can't release him later?" I said. "Or is that a chance you're willing to take, like when I was being held captive?"

The words were out of my mouth before I realized it. Cassandra turned and studied my face.

"So Clayton told you," she said. "I'd have thought he'd want to spare your feelings. It wasn't like that, Elena. You're a werewolf. A warrior. A bright, resourceful warrior. You didn't need my help to escape. There was nothing I could have done."

"And the others? You counseled them not to help me. To let me rot here."

Cassandra sighed. "It wasn't like that, Elena."

"And the thing with Clay? Making a pass at him before my side of the bed was cold?"

"I wouldn't call it a 'pass.' Clayton is a very intriguing man. Perhaps I was a little too intrigued, but you can hardly blame me for that. Now you're back. He's your man. I respect that. You needn't worry about me."

I smiled, baring my teeth. "Trust me, Cassandra, I wasn't worried." I glanced at the man in the cell. "But I am concerned for this poor guy. I'm letting him out."

Cassandra blanched, then quickly recovered her composure. "Suit yourself."

She turned and headed down the hall, walking faster than I'd ever seen her move. Fleeing the scene? Hmmm.

I opened the cell door. The man turned and gave me a wary once-over.

"Yes?" he said, polite but cool.

"Hi, I'm Elena." I extended my hand. "Your rescuer for today."

"Oh?" Still cool. Brows arching. No effort to shake my hand.

"You want out?" I asked.

He smiled, a touch of warmth defrosting the chill. "Actually, I was getting quite comfortable here, but if you insist, I suppose I could tear myself away."

"We have an old friend of yours with us. She's eager to see you."

"Friend?"

"Cassandra . . . I'm not sure of the last name. Auburn hair. Green eyes. Vampire."

"Cassandra?" His eyes narrowed. "Where?"

"Right down that hall."

I leaned out the door. The man brushed past me and marched into the hall.

"Cassandra!" he yelled.

Halfway down the hall, Cassandra turned. Slowly.

"Aaron!" she called. Her lips stretched in a wide smile as she headed back to us. "My God, is that really you? How long has it been? All these years and you know, you haven't changed a bit."

"Very funny," Aaron said. "Now, Cass—"

She gathered his hands in hers and pecked his cheek. "I can't believe this. When did I last see you? Nineteen seventeen, wasn't it? Philadelphia?"

"Nineteen thirty-one, Romania," Aaron growled, disengaging himself from Cassandra's embrace. "Fifth stop on our Grand Tour. We could have gone to Prague, Warsaw, Kiev, but no, you had to stop in some Romanian backwater so you could amuse yourself playing Dracula for the peasants. And I'm sure it would have been very amusing if *you'd* been the one locked in a church cellar for three days and almost drowned in a vat of holy water."

"It was a mistake," Cassandra murmured.

"Mistake? You left me there!"

"She abandoned you?" I said. "Fancy that."

"Oh, no," Aaron said, his glare boring through Cassandra. "She didn't just abandon me. She *gave* me to them. Her little prank got out of hand, and when the mob came, she saved herself by handing me over."

"It wasn't like that," Cassandra said.

"I'm sure it wasn't," I said. "Well, I guess you two have a lot of catching up to do. Go ahead, Cassandra. Clay and I can handle Winsloe on our own."

As I walked away, Cassandra tried to follow, but Aaron grabbed her arm. They were still getting reacquainted as Clay and I left the cell block to find Winsloe.

CHAPTER 47

RETALIATION

The dog was in the kennel.

We smelled Winsloe as soon as we got within twenty feet of the out-building. We scouted the perimeter as I whispered my plan to Clay. Before I finished, he reached for my arm, stopping me.

"You sure about this, darling?" he asked.

"Oh, I'm sure. Aren't you?"

Clay pulled me closer and tipped my face up to his. "I'm sure I want to do it, and I'm damned sure the bastard deserves it. It's certainly poetic justice. But is it *really* what you want?"

"It's what I want."

"All right, then. If there's any trouble, though, I'm taking him down."

"No, I will."

Clay hesitated. "Okay, darling. If we have a choice, he's yours. But I won't hold back if you're in danger."

"Agreed."

We headed for the kennel.

Winsloe sat in the rear of the middle dog run. His back was to the wall, knees up, pistol trained on the door. Once we'd determined his position by peering through the dusty windows, we chose a course of action. Obviously, barreling through the door was out of the question. We weren't bulletproof. Since the entrance was to Winsloe's left, I selected the window closest to his right. Clay hoisted me, and I carefully unhooked the latches, pulled the pane free, and handed it down to Clay. The opening was roughly two feet square, too small for Clay, so I had to go it alone. He boosted me higher, and I wriggled through feet first, straining to hear Winsloe below, ready to yank myself out if he so much as moved. He didn't. Once my lower torso cleared the window, I grabbed the upper sill with both hands, swung sideways, and pounced, landing on Winsloe's head and shoulders. He screamed. I grabbed his gun and flung it over the wire fence into the adjoining cage.

"Nice scream, Tyrone," I said as I brushed straw from my jeans. "Very macho."

Clay strolled through the doorway. "Sounded more like a shriek to me, darling."

Winsloe jerked around to stare at Clay.

"Yes, that's Clayton," I said. "Looking pretty good for a dead guy, eh?"

As Winsloe struggled to stand, Clay strode over, grabbed him by the neck, slammed him against the wall, and patted him down.

"Unarmed," he said, dropping Winsloe.

"What?" I said. "No grenade? No nail gun? And you call yourself a hunter."

"How much do you want?" Winsloe said. His voice was steady, edged more with anger than fear. "What's a life worth these days? One million? Two?"

"Money?" I laughed. "We don't need money, Tyrone. Jeremy has plenty and he's more than willing to share."

"A combined net worth of maybe two million bucks?" Winsloe snorted. "That's nothing. Here's the deal. You caught me fair and square. I'm willing to pay a forfeit. Ten million."

Clay frowned. "What's this? You never said nothin' about a deal, darling. You promised me a hunt."

"I'm sorry, Ty," I said. "Clay's right. I promised him a hunt, and if I don't deliver, he'll sulk for days."

"Hunt?" Trepidation flashed through Winsloe's eyes, but he quickly doused it. "You want a hunt? Okay. That's fair. Like I said, you caught me. Here's the deal, then. Let me get my equipment and we'll have a real hunt. If I kill both of you, I win. You corner me and you'll get fifteen million."

"The man has balls, darling," Clay said. "Gotta give him that." He hauled Winsloe up by the shirtfront. "You wanna deal? Here's the deal. We let you go. You run for your fucking life. You make it off the game field and we let you go. We catch you first, we kill you. Okay?"

"That's not fair," Winsloe sputtered.

Clay threw back his head and laughed. "Hear that, darling? It's not fair. Weren't those *your* rules? The rules you planned to use if you hunted Elena. She'd be released and hunted by a team of trained professionals. If she escaped the game field, she'd live. Otherwise, she'd die. Am I missing something?"

"It's not the same," Winsloe said, glaring. "I'm not a werewolf. A human can't fight without weapons."

"What about those equipment lockers you have out there?" I said.

"They're locked."

"Fine," I sighed. "Let's make it 'fair,' then. We wouldn't want it too easy. No challenge, no fun."

I walked into the adjoining cage and picked up the gun. Upon examining it, I figured out how to open the chamber and dumped the bullets onto the floor. Then I returned to Winsloe and handed him the empty gun.

"What the hell am I supposed to do with this?" he said.

Clay shook his head. "I thought this guy was supposed to be bright. Let's think about this. We need to Change forms to hunt you. That means we'll be occupied for a while. We're not going to leave you with a loaded gun so you can shoot us while we're Changing."

"You could find us and beat us over the head with the empty pistol," I said. "But I wouldn't recommend it. We'll take turns Changing. If you come near us, we'll kill you. While we're busy, you'll have time to do something. How much time? Well, I'm not going to tell you that. What I will tell you is that you have time to do *something*. You can run for your life. Or you can go back into the compound and find ammo for that gun. Or you can race to the nearest equipment locker and try to spring the lock. Or you can head for the garage and see if you can get one of the disabled vehicles running."

"There," Clay said. "We spelled it out for you. Fair enough?"

Winsloe stood eye to eye with Clay. "Twenty million."

"Twenty seconds," Clay said.

"Twenty-five mil—"

"Nineteen seconds."

Winsloe set his jaw, looked from Clay to me, then stalked from the kennel.

"He's taking this remarkably well," I said when Winsloe was gone.

"Disappointed?" Clay asked.

"I must admit, I had hoped he'd piss his pants. But this isn't so bad. At least he'll try. More challenge."

Clay grinned. "More fun."

We weren't stupid enough to Change in the kennel. We went outside and found a clearing about fifty feet into the forest. Clay Changed first while I stood guard. Then we switched. When I finished, we returned to the kennel, where I picked up Winsloe's scent and followed it.

Winsloe hadn't returned to the compound. Nor had he tried the garage. He'd gone straight into the woods, either running for his life or entertaining the pitiable hope that he could jimmy the lock on an equipment shed before we caught up with him. Worse yet—at least, worse for Winsloe—he'd taken the main path. Had he cut his own trail through the undergrowth, he'd have slowed us down. On the wide path, we could run full-out, side by side. Which we did. There was little need for caution. With only an empty pistol, the worst Winsloe could do was hide in the bushes and pitch it at us as we raced past. Not exactly cause for grave concern.

We passed the lookout tower. Halfway to release point two I caught a whiff of metal. My memory looped through that initial hunt with Lake, and I remembered the next landmark: an equipment locker. So that was Winsloe's plan? Unless he had lock picks handy, he was in for a big surprise. And we were in for a very short hunt.

I rounded the corner and saw the locker ahead. No sign of Winsloe. Had he given up and run? As I drew closer to the shed, I noticed something on the ground. Night-vision goggles. Beside them, a carton of ammunition. And binoculars. I skidded to a halt. The locker doors were open. Sunlight glinted off a metal key in the lock. Winsloe had had a key all along, or he'd known where to find one. Now he was armed with god knows what kind of artillery.

As I stared at the mess, Clay slammed against my shoulder, knocking me into the bushes. A round of gunfire shattered the silence. Clay prodded me farther into the undergrowth. When I didn't move fast enough, he bit my haunch. I scrambled into the bushes, belly scraping the ground. Clay followed. Another round of automatic gunfire showered bullets in a wide arc far above our heads. Wherever he was hiding, Winsloe couldn't see us and was aiming by sound alone. I slowed to a crawl, slinking noiselessly through the brush. When we were out of range, I found a thicket and stopped. Clay crept in behind me. He snuffled along my flank, up to my neck, sniffing for blood. When he finished, I checked him over. We'd both escaped unscathed . . . so far. How many guns did Winsloe have now? How much ammo? Any grenades or other surprises? When I'd said I wanted a challenge, this wasn't what I'd had in mind.

We huddled in the thicket, not so much hiding as staying still and safe while we pinpointed Winsloe's location. After a few minutes, Clay nudged my shoulder and pointed his muzzle northeast. I lifted my nose, but the wind blew from the south. Clay flicked his ears. Listen, don't sniff. I closed my eyes, concentrated, and heard a faint shuffling, the sound of fabric rubbing against fabric. Winsloe was northeast, at least a hundred feet away, back by the equipment locker. Judging from the sound, he was arranging his equipment or shifting to a better vantage position, but staying close to one spot. Good. I indicated to Clay that we should split up and circle around. He snorted softly and eased from the thicket. By the time I got out, he was gone.

From Clay's scent, I could tell he'd gone left, so I went right. Giving Winsloe a wide berth, I crept through the bush until I calculated I was directly north of him. Then I slowed, slunk down, and crept south. Now the wind was in my favor, blowing Winsloe's scent into my nostrils with each breath. I should have sent Clay this way. His sense of smell was poorer than mine and the wind would have helped. It didn't matter. Clay would manage fine without the extra aid. He always did.

Another twenty feet brought me close enough to see flashes of Winsloe's gray jacket as he moved. Hunkering down, I sniffed for Clay and found his scent. Homing in on it, I squinted through the trees and picked up the faint sparkle of gold fur against the drab undergrowth. Clay was closer to Winsloe than I was, so I slid forward until I'd made up the difference. Now I could poke my muzzle through the brush and see Winsloe clearly. He was crouched in a clearing, hands wrapped around a large automatic weapon, eyes darting from left to right. As I watched, he shifted position, turning south, surveying the forest, then rotating north and checking from that viewpoint, never leaving his back to any direction for long. Smart. Very smart. As he moved, I scanned his clearing for weapons but could see only the gun. I was sure he had more, likely hidden in or under his jacket.

As I watched, I heard a soft growl to my left. It was Clay, warning me he was there, rather than suddenly appearing at my side and scaring the crap out of me. As I turned, he stepped through the last stand of trees between us. This was not part of the plan. I huffed and glowered at him. He shook his head. With one look, I knew what he meant. The game was over. Winsloe was heavily armed, tipping the odds too far in his favor. Time for a quick kill. Clay made a circling motion with his muzzle, then jerked it toward Winsloe. Again, I understood. We use the usual routine, boring but reliable. Clay would circle south again. I'd scare Winsloe and drive him into Clay's waiting jaws. I exhaled a canine sigh and lay down to wait until Clay got into position. But he didn't leave. Instead he prodded me to my feet and motioned from Winsloe to me. Ah, a change in routine. Clay would roust Winsloe from the south and drive him into *my* waiting jaws. At first, I thought Clay was being considerate, granting me the kill I'd asked for. Then I realized he wanted us to switch roles because scaring Winsloe would be more dangerous than killing him. Okay, I guess he was still being considerate, not wanting me to get blown to bits or anything. I would have argued the point, but I wanted the kill too badly.

Clay disappeared into the forest. I tracked the whisper of his footfalls. When he was partway around Winsloe's hiding place, Winsloe suddenly stood. I froze. Had he heard Clay? Tensing for the attack, I listened. All I heard were the normal chirps and rustles of the forest. Still, if Winsloe so much as pointed that gun in Clay's direction, I'd be through the bushes in a second, caution be damned. Winsloe straightened, rolled his shoulders in a stretch, then looked up into the trees, craning his neck and surveying the sky. Was Clay in position yet? If so, this would be the perfect time to attack. But I didn't smell Clay on the breeze, so he must still be working his way south. Damn! Winsloe rubbed the back of his neck, then checked his gun, gave a last look around, and stepped from the clearing, heading west.

I edged closer to the now-vacant clearing. When I reached the perimeter, I saw Clay on the southeast side, partially hidden in the bushes. Noticing me, he pulled back and vanished. Seconds later, he reappeared at my side. I looked at him. Now what? Our quarry was on the move. Scaring him and steering him in the proper direction would be ten times more difficult. An ambush would be our best bet, but that meant circling in front of Winsloe, conjecturing his path, and finding a well-hidden place to lie in wait. Difficult enough when we knew the terrain, near-suicidal when we didn't. From the look in Clay's eyes, he couldn't think up a decent plan either. Finally he snorted, brushed against me, then headed in Winsloe's direction. We'd wing it.

We emerged from the clearing into a thick stand of forest. Ahead, Winsloe's jacket bobbed among the trees. Moving carefully to avoid noisy piles of dead leaves, we crept after him. He didn't turn. He was moving fast. As we picked up speed, the forest thinned. Late afternoon sunlight pierced the thick canopy overhead, speckling the ground with ever-widening pools of light. The forest was ending. We broke into a slow lope. Winsloe disappeared in a flood of sunlight. A clearing. A big clearing. I sniffed the air. Water. We were coming to the river. I glanced at Clay. He grunted, telling me he smelled the water and wasn't concerned. Did Winsloe think he could lose us in the river? Swim away or douse his trail? It wouldn't work. We could swim just fine, doubtless much better than Winsloe. As for losing his trail, it was true that we couldn't track him through water, but we were so close that it didn't matter. Even if we lost sight of him, I could pick up his scent in the air.

Winsloe walked to the water's edge, stopped, and wheeled fast, flourishing his gun. Seeing nothing behind him, he turned to the river, looked up and down it, then began pacing the bank. Clay snorted impatiently. So long as Winsloe was thirty feet from the forest's edge, we didn't dare move closer or he'd have time to shoot before we brought him down. If he waded in and started walking, we could move alongside him, staying in the trees until the forest weaved nearer to the riverbank, bringing us close enough to attack.

Winsloe finally stopped pacing. He stood at the foot of a huge oak, tilted his head back, and shaded his eyes to look up at it. Then he grasped the lowest branch and gave an experimental tug. As he slung the gun over his shoulder, Clay shot from the forest. Winsloe didn't notice. With his back to us, he grabbed the branch again and hauled himself up. It was then that I realized what Winsloe was doing. Climbing the tree. Okay, so I'm a bit slow on the uptake. By the time I leaped from our hiding place, Winsloe was ten feet off the ground. Still running, Clay crouched and sprang. Only then did Winsloe see him. He glanced over his shoulder a split second before Clay's teeth sunk into his knee. Winsloe howled. He kicked with his free leg, knocking Clay in the side of the skull. Clay hung on. Blood sprayed his muzzle as Winsloe flailed, shouting and fighting to keep his hold on the tree. I was still several yards away, running full-out. I could see deep furrows in Winsloe's calf where Clay's teeth had ripped through his leg clear to the bone. As the flesh tore, Clay began losing his grip. He danced on his hindlegs, not daring to release Winsloe long enough to get a fresh hold. I covered the last few feet and leaped at Winsloe's free leg. He kicked at exactly the right moment, catching me in the eye. I yelped and fell back. As I got to my feet, Clay's grasp slipped to Winsloe's shoe. Before I could jump at Winsloe again, his shoe slid off and Clay tumbled backward. Winsloe swung his legs out of reach, scrambled to the next branch, and grabbed his gun. We bolted. A round of gunfire rang out, but we were well clear, hidden in the forest again.

We stopped behind a thick stand of trees. Clay motioned for me to stay put, then turned and headed back for a better look at the situation. I didn't follow, not because Clay had told me not to—I'd never been good at taking orders—but because it was safer for only one of us to venture out. As much as I hated to admit it, Clay was the better stalker. If I tried to help, I'd only triple the likelihood of making noise and getting us shot.

Winsloe climbing a tree posed a problem. A big problem. Next time, I'd be a lot more careful about asking for a challenge. I knew Winsloe was smart, but I hadn't expected him to keep so cool under pressure. Given what I'd seen of Winsloe—that cocky self-importance masking an easily bruised ego—I'd thought he'd panic when he realized his life was in danger. Maybe he didn't think it was. Maybe this was all still a game to him. Unfortunately for us, it was a game he was winning. Talk about ego-bruising. First, he'd tricked us and armed himself. Now he'd gone up a tree, the one place we couldn't follow. The tree not only provided him with safety, but it was the perfect vantage point for shooting. How could we even get close—

The forest exploded in a flurry of gunfire. I bolted from my hiding place, then stopped in mid-run. I shouldn't go out there. I was safer here. *Clay* was safer with me here. But what had happened? Was Winsloe shooting blindly? Or had he seen Clay?

Another rapid-fire round of shots. Then silence. I stood there, legs trembling as I listened. When Winsloe fired again, I nearly jumped out of my hide. That did it. I barreled down the incline toward the river clearing. More shots. I stopped on the edge of the clearing, hunkered down, and crept forward until I could see what was happening. Ahead was the old oak with Winsloe perched twenty feet up, squinting south, gun poised. Other than that, the clearing was empty. Empty and quiet. Suddenly a crackling of leaves broke the silence. I swung my head north. A flash of gold darted through the trees. Winsloe turned and fired, shooting at the noise. Clay was long gone. A waste of bullets. I realized that was the idea. Get Winsloe to empty his gun firing at phantasms. A good plan, and one I would have thought of . . . eventually.

I considered retreating to my hiding place, but couldn't do it. I knew it would be safer to let Clay do this alone, but I'd go crazy with worry if I couldn't see what was happening. Before long, Clay smelled me there. He came over and tried to prod me deeper into the woods, but I wouldn't budge. I lay down, put my head on my front paws, and stared into the clearing. He got the idea. I needed to watch, to be sure he was safe. He settled for a quick nuzzle, then grabbed the back of my neck in his jaws, not biting but pinning my head, telling me to stay here and stay down. I grunted my assent. He brushed his muzzle against mine, then disappeared into the forest.

Winsloe emptied his automatic quickly, going through several reloads of ammunition. Then he pulled a pistol from under his jacket. He was more careful now, less willing to waste bullets on mere noises in the woods. So Clay had to be more daring. At first, he'd only come near the edge of the clearing, allowing Winsloe to see a flash of fur. Eventually, though, even that didn't work and he had to dart into the open. By that point, my eyes were firmly closed. My heart pounded so loudly I almost expected

Winsloe to hear it. Eventually, though, it was over. The last shot was fired. After several minutes, Clay slipped from the forest. He stood there, in plain view, muscles tensed, and waited. Winsloe threw the empty pistol at him and cursed. Clay walked closer, slowly, presenting the perfect target if Winsloe should have another weapon stashed under his jacket. Nothing. Winsloe was done.

Now I had a plan. Good thing, too, or my ego would have been more than just bruised. This was my hunt, and I'd done almost nothing, made no plans, taken no risks. It was my turn. While Clay ensured Winsloe was out of firepower, I crept farther into the forest, found a likely spot, and started my Change.

Less than ten minutes later, I walked to the edge of the clearing and whistled. Winsloe's head shot up and he scanned the forest.

"Hear that?" he called to Clay. "Someone's coming. Guess you didn't kill every guard after all."

He leaned over the tree branch and peered down, but Clay was gone. Seconds later, Clay burst through the forest perimeter and looked up at me. His eyes flashed a question. Did I want him to Change too? I shook my head, knelt, and whispered my plan. As I talked, he moved closer, fur rubbing against my bare skin. Without thinking, I ran my fingers through his thick fur. As I finished, I realized what I was doing and stopped. My face heated. On rare occasions when the situation was reversed, and I was a wolf while Clay was human, I freaked out if he touched me. It was . . . well, it was too weird. This time, when I pulled back, Clay nudged my hand and licked between my fingers, telling me it was okay. And it was. Clay was Clay no matter what form he took. Yet another baby step toward accepting my own duality.

"Sound good?" I whispered when I'd finished outlining my plan.

He tilted his head, considering it, then snorted his agreement.

I grinned. "Can't argue anyway, can you?"

He gave a mock growl and nipped my hand, then prodded me to my feet. I stood and we headed for the oak tree.

By the time I emerged from the forest, Winsloe had climbed partway down, staying a dozen feet from the ground, obviously thinking Clay had run away but not willing to descend completely until help arrived. When he heard me coming, he called, "Over here!"—then saw who it was. Disappointment flitted across his face. Not fear, just disappointment. Seeing Clay at my side, he climbed to the next branch.

"How long you planning to stay up there?" I called.

"As long as it takes." His eyes flickered over my naked body, and he managed a humorless smile. "Hoping to entice me down?"

"If I could stomach the thought of seducing you, I'd have done it while I was trapped in that cell."

His mouth tightened. Amazing. Even treed by two werewolves, Winsloe was more concerned about his pride than his life. I walked to the base of the tree and grabbed the bottom branch. He only watched me. It was still a game to him.

I swung onto the first branch. He climbed higher. I went to the next branch. So did he. Beneath us, Clay circled the tree. Ten more feet up and Winsloe's stockinged foot slipped. The branch he held gave way and he grabbed the tree trunk for support. After steadying himself, he squinted at the remaining branches above.

"They won't hold your weight," I said. "But don't take my word for it."

He didn't. He grabbed a branch and tugged. It snapped in his hand. He hesitated, then lowered himself onto the branch under his feet until he was sitting on it. When I got close enough, he kicked at me. As if I wouldn't see that one coming. I ducked easily and seized his injured leg. He gasped and jerked back, nearly tumbling off the branch.

"You want to fight me, go ahead," I said as I climbed onto his branch. "But you'd better have a spare gun under that jacket if you hope to win."

He said nothing. I teetered on the branch, getting my balance. Winsloe sat still, as if resigned to this. Then his hand shot out and smacked my ankle. I grabbed the limb overhead and steadied myself. The branch beneath us swayed.

"Don't be doing that," I said. "If this branch breaks, I can jump to the ground. Even if you survive the fall, you won't survive what's waiting at the bottom."

Winsloe muttered something and made a move to settle, then slammed both hands into my calf. I grabbed his collar, hauled him to his feet, and smashed him backward into the tree trunk.

"You want to fight?" I said. "Okay, let's fight."

He didn't move. His gaze flicked down. I whacked his head against the tree.

"Thinking of knocking my legs out from under me? Don't bother. You do and we both fall. Now, in case you hadn't noticed, I'm not trying to kill you. In fact, I haven't laid an unprovoked hand on you, have I?"

A glimmer of cunning lit his eyes. "You want to negotiate."

"Maybe."

"Fifteen million."

"I thought we were up to twenty-five?"

"Twenty then."

"Oh, so that's how it works? Once I show some interest, the offer goes down. A true businessman."

His mouth tightened. "Fine. Twenty-five."

I pretended to consider it. "You know, Clay was right. We don't need money. We have enough. Wanting more would be greedy."

"Thirty million."

I grabbed him by the shirt collar and swung him over the side. His feet scrambled for purchase, finding only air. I shifted sideways and rested my back against the tree. When he clawed at me, I thrust him out to arm's length.

"Offer me more," I said.

His mouth tightened. I let him slip to my fingertips. He flailed, all four limbs jerking, convulsing, lashing out. I started to release my grip.

"Fifty million," he said.

"Not enough." I let him slip another half-inch. "Offer me everything."

"What?!"

I released one hand from his shirtfront.

"Okay, okay! Fine!"

I grabbed and steadied him. He gulped air, then cast a surreptitious glance at the ground and shuddered.

"Let's clarify that," I said. "What exactly are you offering?"

"My estate. All of it."

"Your personal estate? Not good enough. I want your business holdings, too. Every dollar, every share, every last thing you own. Offer me that."

"Wh—what would I live on?"

"Start over. You're a smart guy. You could make a living. At least you'll be alive. That's more than we can say for Lake and Bryce, isn't it?"

"I'll give you my holdings in everything but Promethean Fire."

I let go. He shrieked, arms windmilling. Before he fell, I grabbed him by the shirtfront, hauled him up, and bent over him.

"Wanna try again?" I said.

His shirt tore, just an inch, but the sound ripped through the silence like a chainsaw.

"All of it," he said. "Goddamn you. Take it all."

"'Cause nothing's worse than dying, right? Tell me, Ty, what would you have done if Armen Haig had made you the same offer? Promised you everything he had? Would you have let him live?"

Winsloe's shirt tore another inch. He stared at me, wild-eyed, lips moving soundlessly.

"Let me answer that for you, Ty. It's 'no.' He could have offered you millions and you still would have killed him. Why? Because his death was worth more than all the money he could give. The few seconds of amusement his death offered was worth more."

"Please," he said. "Please, I'm going to—"

"Fall? Hah. Too easy. You fall. Clay rips your throat out. Game over."

"It's not a fucking game!"

I cupped my hand behind my ear. "What's that, Ty? I think I misheard you."

"I said this isn't a fucking game. It's my life!"

"No, it's your death. Hey, there's an idea. Not a game, but a game show. *This Is Your Death.* Now, I've got to admit, I'm a bit young to have seen *This Is Your Life.* I only know the title, so I'll have to improvise. Cross it with something I do remember watching as a kid. *Let's Make a Deal.*"

I pulled him back onto the branch and helped him get his balance, keeping my hands wrapped in his shirtfront.

"You—you want to negotiate." He wiped sweat from his face and swallowed loudly. "Okay. Good. Let's negotiate."

"Negotiate? Hell, no. I'm making a deal regarding the *method* of your execution, Ty. You're going to die. That's a given. The only question is *how*?"

"N—no. No. Wait. Let's talk—"

"About what? You've already offered me everything you own. You have nothing else to offer, do you?"

He stared, mouth working soundlessly.

"You've offered everything. I rejected that offer. So you're going to die. Why? Because I finally see your point of view. You've convinced me. Watching someone die can be worth more than all the money in the world."

His face drained of blood, mouth opening and closing like a fish on land.

"Behind door number one we have the most obvious choice. You fall from this tree. Only I'll make sure Clay doesn't kill you. And I won't drop you, I'll throw you. Hard enough to break every limb, but not hard enough to kill you. Then we'll gag you and leave you to die, slowly and painfully.

"Behind door number two—"

"No," he said, his voice nearly inaudible. "No. Don't—"

"Hey, I'm just getting warmed up. You know what I admire most about you, Ty? Your creativity. Your ingenuity. Like giving me the choice between killing Armen or being gang-raped. You've inspired me to new heights of creativity, so shut up and listen.

"Option two. Remember that video you saw of me fighting Lake? The one where I change my hand into a claw? Cool trick, huh? Well, here's my idea. I change my hand and slice open your guts. Not a lot, maybe pull out a bit of intestine, start a steady blood drip. You know what they say about gunshot wounds? That the gut shot is the absolute worst. Takes forever to die and hurts like the fires of Hell. Which, if you ask me, would be a good precursor to what you can expect from your eternity. I kind of like that one. Very appropriate. To hell with the game, I'm going for this one."

I pressed my hand against his stomach. He convulsed and a strong, acrid scent wafted up. I looked down to see a wet stain spreading down his pant leg.

"Shit, Ty. I was only kidding." I waved my hand in front of him.

"Stop it," he whispered. "Just stop—"

"Can't. You remember *Let's Make a Deal*, don't you? You're about my age, so you must have seen it as a kid. There's a door number three left. And behind this one we have . . . hmmm." I looked around, then caught a glimpse of something overhead. "There. See that bird flying to the east? Know what that is? A turkey vulture. Also known as a buzzard. A scavenger. That will be the last choice. Death by scavenger. I take you down from this tree and stake you out on the ground. Then I slice you up. Lots of little, nonlethal slices, just enough to draw blood. Before long, you'll get a firsthand view of every scavenger in these woods. Oh, and I'll need to cut out your tongue so you can't scream. A definite sadistic improvement over gagging, don't you think? You should be proud of me, Ty. I'm your star pupil. Oh, speaking of pupils, I won't blindfold you. That way you can see the vultures and stray dogs as they feed on you. Well, until the vultures take your eyes—"

"Stop!" His voice rose, nearly shrill. "I know what you're doing. You want me to beg for my life. To offer you more."

"What more? You've offered everything, Ty. And I said no."

His eyes rolled, rabid with fear and denial. "No. You won't kill me. I'm worth too much."

"You're worth nothing. Only your death is worth something to me."

"No! You won't do it, Elena. I know you won't. You want to scare me, but you'd never—"

"Never?"

"You don't have it in you."

"Option one, two, or three. Pick now."

"You're torturing me. That's all. You only want to see me squirm. You don't have it—"

I grabbed him by the throat and hauled him off his feet. Then I pressed my face against his.

"Don't tell me what I don't have in me."

I growled. Saw the terror in his eyes and drank it in. Then I let him go. Clay ripped out his throat before his body hit the ground.

CLEANUP

After killing Winsloe, Clay Changed, and we returned to our clothing. No time for lingering. There was still work to be done at the compound. Every bit of evidence had to be found and destroyed. Then we had to remove all traces of our presence. Eventually someone would find the compound and the bodies within. To decrease the likelihood of a large-scale police investigation, Paige had hacked into the computer system early this morning and transferred the property deed to a Colombian drug cartel. Don't ask me how she even knew the name of a South American dope lord. Some questions are better left unanswered. As for Winsloe, we'd disposed of his body in a way that ensured he'd never be found. How? Well, that's another one of those questions. The point was that no one would ever find Winsloe or link him to the compound, which would avoid the media blitz that would surround his death.

"Did Savannah look okay to you?" I asked as we finished dressing. "She hit that wall pretty hard."

"She seemed fine. Jeremy will look after her."

"Do you think Paige will be able to handle her?"

"If Paige could handle that sorcerer, she can handle a twelve-year-old kid. She'll be fine, darling. They both will."

"I hope so."

Clay pushed aside a branch for me. "Watching you with Savannah, I was thinking—"

"Don't."

"I didn't say anything."

"Good. Don't."

"I was just thinking—"

"No kids."

He laughed and put his arm around me. "That sounds definite."

"It is. Me as a mother?" I shuddered. "I can only imagine one thing worse. You as a father."

"Thanks a hell of a lot. I'd make a . . . fairly good father. And if not, there's Jeremy. He's a great parent. He'd compensate for my shortcomings."

"Great idea. We have the kids and dump the responsibility on him. He'd love that."

"He wouldn't mind."

I groaned. "No kids."

Clay walked a few more feet, then grinned. "Hey, you know what else? If we had children, you couldn't leave. You'd be stuck with me. Now there's a thought."

"You—that's—oh!"

I threw up my hands and stomped off. Clay's laugh echoed through the forest. He jogged up, swung me off the ground, and tickled me.

"I'm hiding my birth control pills," I said, gasping for breath.

"We'll discuss it later."

"Nev—"

He cut me off with a kiss. A few minutes later, there came a rustling in the bushes.

"They're kissing." A young voice. Savannah.

I twisted to see Jeremy yank Savannah back. Then he peered through the bushes.

"Oh, you're dressed," he said, and released Savannah.

I wriggled out of Clay's grasp. "Of course we're dressed. Since when have we ever stopped in the middle of a dangerous situation to have"— I glanced at Savannah—"a rest."

Jeremy rolled his eyes.

"Did you kill Winsloe?" Savannah asked.

"Kill—" I choked. "Um, no, we—uh—"

"He's been taken care of," Jeremy said. "Now I think we should get you back to Paige before—"

"There you are!" Paige said, bursting through the bushes, face glistening with sweat. "I told you to stay close."

"I did stay close," Savannah said. "You didn't say who I had to stay close to."

"I was out here trying to pick up Leah's trail," Jeremy explained to us. "There's no trace of her. Perhaps you two can do a better job."

"I'll go with Elena," Savannah said. "If we find Leah, I can use my binding spell again."

Paige and I both opened our mouths to protest, but Jeremy beat us to it.

"Why don't we go find Adam?" he said. "Perhaps we can help him."

Savannah's eyes sparked at the mention of Adam, but she only shrugged and allowed that she *supposed* that would be an acceptable alternative. When Jeremy headed toward the compound, Savannah trailed behind him.

Paige sighed. "I may have finally met a challenge I'm not ready for. Thank God I have my Coven sisters. They'll probably die of shock when I actually admit I need help."

"Do you want to come with us and look for Leah?" I asked. "Take a break?"

"No, you two go on. Be careful."

I grinned. "Now, what would be the fun in that?"

Paige laughed and jogged after Jeremy and Savannah.

When we left the compound at dawn there was no evidence to suggest anything out of the ordinary had happened there. Okay, a building filled with dead bodies isn't exactly commonplace, but there was no evidence of anything supernatural. Before leaving, Adam started a series of small fires, not enough to be seen by passing planes, but enough to fill the building with thick smoke, further damaging anything that remained.

Oh, and Leah? We never did find her. I spent two hours scouring the grounds outside the compound. If she'd left, I should have found a trail. Since I didn't, we had to assume she'd holed up somewhere in the compound, where she would have eventually been overcome by smoke. And if she did manage to escape? Well, let's just say none of us planned to visit her home state of Wisconsin anytime soon.

Beginnings

Chapter I

Elena

"Your hours will be four to eight Tuesdays, nine to five Saturdays, and the occasional Sunday afternoon." Ms. Milken looked up at me, watery blue eyes swimming behind her thick glasses. "I trust that won't be a problem."

"Twelve hours a week?" I said. "When you interviewed me, you said a minimum of twenty."

"Business needs change, Elena," she said, enunciating slowly as if I might be too dim to understand this concept. "I believe I said a *possibility* of twenty hours a week."

I clamped the tip of my tongue between my teeth. I knew she'd said a *minimum* of twenty, and damn it, I needed every one of them.

I pushed my chair back, hitting one of the two-foot drifts of paper that blanketed the floor. It didn't look like business was slow. And how the hell could her "business needs" have changed so much since she interviewed me two weeks ago?

As I composed myself, I glanced around the office. Blown-up copies of news articles covered the walls, struggling to convince the visitor that this was a real newspaper, instead of a weekly classified ad rag that scattered a few amateurish features among the advertisements.

When I saw those articles, so proudly displayed, I knew what had happened. I'd walked in for that interview—a third-year journalism student applying for a minimum-wage job—and Ms. Milken had seen her chance to hire a trained reporter at a bargain-basement rate. I needed twenty to thirty hours a week? Well, what a coincidence; that's just what they had in mind. She'd flat-out lied, and I desperately wanted to call her on it, but I didn't dare. I needed this job . . . any job.

So I forced a shrug and said, "Maybe I misheard. But if you ever need someone to work extra hours, I can always use the money. I'll leave a copy of my schedule. I'm free anytime that I don't have classes. Even at the last minute. Just give me a call."

Ms. Milken pursed her lips, then reached over to a stack of paper, plucked a single sheet from the middle, and handed it to me.

"Tips for winterizing gardens," she said. "Turn it into an article. Ten inches. For this week's edition."

I took the sheet. An article on gardening tips? I smiled my keenest cub reporter smile. "I'll drop it off first thing in the morning."

"This week's edition goes to bed in two hours."

"Two—?" My smile collapsed. "I have a class at three."

"Is this going to be a problem, Elena? I've hired students before, and I was reluctant to do so again. I need to know that your priorities are here. Not with boys or parties or bar-hopping or sororities."

"I have my priorities straight," I said, slowly and—I hoped—calmly. "My job is second only to my classes."

"That won't do."

My fingernails bit into my palms, but I kept my voice even. "Maybe, after today, I can skip the occasional class, if it's for something critical." *Like a gardening-tip article.* "But this is the first week of classes, and it's my first time in this particular class, so I really can't miss it." I met her gaze, and knew she was already mentally thumbing through her list of applicants. "But . . . well, maybe I could give it a shot. I still have an hour."

"There's a desk out front."

At 2:37, I handed the article to Ms. Milken. I'd worked on it for fifty-five minutes, but she'd informed me that the company paid in fifteen-minute increments, so I'd be reimbursed for forty-five.

Any other time, I'd have suddenly remembered that I'd forgotten to add something, and tinkered until I reached a full hour. But nothing makes a worse impression than being late for your first class . . . especially one you aren't officially registered in. So I accepted my loss and hurried out the door.

The office was on Grosvenor Street, within easy walking distance of the University of Toronto, which had been a major factor in my accepting the job. I'd been offered a proofreading position at a small press in Pickering, and it had paid better, but the round-trip on the GO Train three times a week would have seriously cut into my earnings. And a job writing articles, however crappy, would look better on my résumé than proofreading.

Now, though, proofreading—as much as I hated it—didn't sound so bad. Nor did the coffee shop job or the clothing store job or any others that had phoned me back after I'd showered the city with my résumé.

Maybe I could call them, see whether any jobs were still open. Or I could do what I'd done last year—work two jobs. Oh yeah, and that had gone *so* well for me—stressing over scheduling, giving up all pretense of a social life, dropping off the running team, studying over breakfast, lunch, dinner . . . even reading while walking to class.

I'd nearly worked my way into a breakdown . . . and almost lost my A average, which would have ended my partial scholarship and made it impossible to finish my degree.

That officious, conniving bitch. From "Of course you can expect twenty hours a week" to "Is this going to be a problem, Elena?" I should have complained. Hell, I should have told her where to stuff her gardening tips and her twelve-hour-a-week job and her ugly mauve suit and her condescending—

I took a deep breath and rubbed my hands over my face. Think of something else, like this next class.

I was looking forward to it, the only optional course on my schedule. Like last year, I'd chosen anthropology. It wouldn't help my future career one whit, but that was why I chose it, as a mental break in a life where everything was—and had to be—focused on the goal of a degree and a job.

In last year's anthro course, I'd had to do a paper on ancient religion. After some research, I'd decided to focus on animal symbolism in religious ritual, which sounded marginally more interesting than anything else. There I'd stumbled across a doctoral thesis by a guy whose specialty was gods that were part human and part animal.

He had some really fascinating ideas, and I'd based my paper on them. A few weeks later, I'd been writing a student paper article on staff changes when a name had jumped out at me. Clayton Danvers, the guy whose thesis I'd used. Seemed he'd participated in a lecture series the year before, and the school had invited him back to cover a partial term for a prof on sabbatical. I'd noted that in my planner so I could sign up for one of his courses. Then just before registration, my life had careened off course.

A former foster brother had tracked me down. After a lifetime of dealing with guys like Jason, I'd learned that most were cowards. Taking a firm stance usually scared them away. Jason was different.

Short of holding a gun to his head, there was nothing I could do to make him back off. After two weeks of darting between friends' apartments and cheap motel rooms, I'd finally persuaded the cops to enforce the damned restraining order.

Then I'd gone back to school, and registration had been the last thing on my mind. When I'd finally remembered, I'd discovered that Danvers's general-level anthropology course was full.

I was third on the waiting list, though, and in my two years at university, I'd learned a bit about waiting lists. Being third usually meant you were in, but sometimes it took a couple of weeks before a spot cleared, and by then you'd have missed those critical first classes. What you had to do was go to class anyway, on the assumption you'd eventually get a place. Most profs didn't mind. Hell, most profs didn't even notice. So that's what I planned to do: show up, sneak in, and start learning.

Chapter 2

Clayton

"An eight o'clock class," I said, gripping the phone as I dropped into my office chair. "I only asked for one thing: no classes before ten. Probably think they're doing me such a big favor, letting me teach at their damned school, that I shouldn't dare ask for anything special."

"Uh-huh," Nick said. "Well, at least—"

"What the hell am I doing here anyway? Oh, sure, I'd *love* to teach in Canada. It's only a few hundred miles from every goddamned person I know."

"Jeremy was right. You *are* in a pissy mood."

I swung my feet onto the desktop. "Bullshit. He'd never say that."

"No, he said you were in a foul mood. Not like I needed anyone to tell me that. I can even predict them now. Every fall, you're this way for at least a month. Like an annual round of PMS."

"What?"

"Never mind. Point is, I know what you need, and if you'd stop being so damned stubborn, we could fix this little problem. Why don't I come up this weekend, we'll hit the town—" He paused. "Do they have bars in Toronto?"

"How the fuck should I know? But if you mean what I think you mean—"

"Hey, you're going to need something—or someone—to keep you warm up there. How bad is it, anyway? Blizzards and stuff?"

"It's the second week of September."

"Yeah, so?"

"Was it snowing when you went with your dad to Minneapolis last week?"

"Course not."

"Well, Toronto is a few latitudes south of that."

He snorted. "Right. I might have failed geography, but I know where Canada is. North. Now, stop trying to change the subject."

A tentative rap at the door.

"You gonna answer that?" Nick said.

"No."

The door creaked open and a student popped her head in. "Professor Danvers?"

Nick's laugh echoed down the line. "Oooh, sounds cute. You—"

I dropped the phone, got to my feet, and turned on the intruder—a dark-haired girl in a skirt too short for any student who hoped to be taken seriously.

"Professor Danvers, sir? I was just wondering—"

"Was that door shut?"

"Uh, yes, but—"

"When you knock on a closed door, you're supposed to wait for it to be opened. Isn't that the point of knocking?"

The girl took a slow step back into the hall. "Y—yes, sir, but I wasn't sure you heard me. I just wanted to ask about your class this afternoon. I heard it's full—"

"It is."

"I was hoping maybe—"

"You want a spot? That's what waiting lists are for. If a place opens up, someone will call you."

"Is it okay if I just sit in—?"

"No."

I slammed the door. When I picked up the phone, Nick was laughing.

"Oh, Professor," he said. "Nasty boy. No wonder the little coeds line up for your classes, all hot for teacher."

"Yeah, you think it's funny? You wouldn't think it was funny if you were teaching classes full of those idiots, taking spots away from serious students—who might actually listen to my lecture instead of giggling with their girlfriends about me."

"Oh, you've got a rough life, buddy. If *I* was teaching your classes, and having your 'problem' . . . let's just say I'd be a very tired, but very happy, guy."

"Yeah? Well, thanks for taking my problems so seriously, *buddy*. Next time you get the urge to call and cheer me up? Don't bother."

I slammed the phone into the receiver. Ten seconds later, it rang again. I ignored it. I'd call him back tonight. I knew Nick didn't mean anything by it, but we'd had the same damned discussion a million times, and you'd really think that by now he'd know how I felt—or didn't feel— about women.

In Nick's world, it wasn't possible for a guy not to want all the women he could get. Well, there *was* one logical explanation, and five years ago he'd tricked me into a gay bar, just to check. But when that didn't seem to be the answer, he'd returned to his quest, certain that if he just kept pushing, I'd "stop being so damned stubborn" and give in.

I slumped into my chair and stared out the window. Since the day Jeremy brought me home to Stonehaven, I'd never spent more than a week away from it or him, and balked at even being gone that long. Now here I was, voluntarily embarking on a two-month sojourn where I'd be lucky to get home every other weekend.

When the offer first came, I'd made the mistake of mentioning it to Jeremy, and the moment I'd seen his reaction, I'd known I was going to Toronto. He'd thought I was considering it, and he'd been so damned proud of me that there'd been no way I could back down without disappointing him.

This was what he'd once wanted for me—a life and a career that extended beyond the Pack. I'd kiboshed that plan before I'd even graduated from high school. Stonehaven was my home, Jeremy was my Alpha, and I wasn't going anywhere. He'd accepted that, but he still liked to see me make the occasional foray into the human world. As much as I loathed every minute away, I did it to please him. So I was here in Toronto until November. And I sure as hell hoped it would tide him over for at least the next decade.

I knew I was overreacting. I'd survive this, much like I'd survived having Jeremy pull out the odd batch of porcupine quills when I'd been a child—grit my teeth and suffer through it. But right now, I was, as Nick said, in one of my fall moods.

They'd started after my eighteenth birthday, but back then, they were mild enough that I'd passed them off as just another bout of moodiness. By my midtwenties, though, that annual dip had become a month-long crater. Edgy all the time, snapping at everyone, haunted by the constant gnawing feeling that I was missing something, that I was supposed to be doing something, *looking* for something.

As I looked out the window, my gaze lifted to a distant line of treetops. That's where I wanted to be—in the woods, someplace deep and dark and silent, where I could lose myself for a few hours. A run wasn't the answer to whatever was bothering me, but if I ran far enough and fast enough, if I hunted and killed and fed, the blackness would lift for a day or so.

I'd do that tonight. Then, when I was feeling more myself, I'd call Nick back and make amends.

A good plan. If only I didn't need to get through the rest of my day to reach it. I scowled at the stack of notes for my next class. It was the general-level course, the one the girl had been trying to squeeze into. According to the clock, I had about five minutes before class began. Might as well get it over with.

I grabbed the notes, stuffed them into my satchel, and left.

CHAPTER 3

ELEПA

I cut through Queen's Park. Once through the university gates, I veered toward Sidney Smith Hall, then stopped dead. I didn't have the classroom number. My timetable was in my knapsack, which I'd left in my dorm room, wanting to look professional for Ms. Milken. I'd assumed I'd have plenty of time to grab it. But my dorm was on the other side of the campus, and I only had a few minutes to get to class.

I hurried into University College, found a phone, dialed my room, and crossed my fingers. Penny, my roommate, picked up on the fourth ring. I directed her to my knapsack and my timetable.

You'd really think that someone who was in her third year would know how to read a timetable. But Penny's inability to decipher the paper probably explained why she was still in her dorm room half asleep. That and the fact that she'd told me on our first meeting that she was a night person, and would I mind not turning on any lights or opening the blinds before noon? Her parents wanted her at university, so she'd go, but damned if she was going to let it affect her social life.

If someone had been paying *my* tuition, I'd have been so happy—

I cut the thought short. With any luck, by the end of the term I'd have enough saved to move into the off-campus apartment two of my friends shared. Or so I'd thought, until Ms. Purple Polyester cut my hours.

Penny finally deciphered the schedule enough to give me the room number. I had three minutes to get there.

"Oh, and the bookstore called," she said. "About some job you applied for."

"Oh? That's great. Do they want—?"

"I told them you already had one. Oh, and tonight? Don't lock the door when you go to sleep, okay? I had a bitch of a time getting it open when I came in."

She hung up.

I let out a string of curses. Not out loud, of course. Too many people around for that.

I'd really wanted that campus bookstore job. It would have been perfect. And now I was stuck with—

Hold on. What if I called the bookstore back and said my roommate was mistaken, that I didn't already have a job? But that wasn't fair. I'd accepted this other position in good faith.

Yes, and she screwed you around! Cut your hours before you even started!

I rubbed my temples. Did everyone else have these mental battles? The two sides of my brain were at war, one telling me to stand up for myself, not to be afraid to get angry, the other side telling me to be nice and to be polite and everything else I'd been taught. The good-girl side usually won, much to my relief. It was easier that way.

This time, though, the fight wasn't so easily won. I didn't want to take the moral high road—I wanted a decent job that would give me enough money to free me from a full year of hell trapped with an inconsiderate party-girl roommate.

By the time I reached the classroom, I was seething, and more than prepared to let a little of that ire seep onto the next person who pushed the wrong button. I didn't need to wait long. I arrived at the lecture hall less than a minute late, and the TA was already closing the door.

The prof wasn't even there yet, just his teaching assistant, a blond grad student who had the audacity to glare at me as if I'd waltzed in midclass and did a cheerleading routine in front of the lectern. That did it. I might have to put up with a condescending new boss and a brain-dead new roomie, but I didn't need this shit from a damned assistant.

So when he glowered at me, mouth opening to make some sarcastic comment like "Glad you could join us," I cut him off with a glower of my own. Our eyes met. He blinked. And closed his mouth. I swept past him and stalked up the steps into the lecture hall.

"Elena!" someone hissed.

I turned to see a girl from my anthropology class last year. Tina . . . no, Trina. I vaguely recalled her saying she'd signed up for this class, too. She tugged her knapsack off the seat beside her and waved me into it.

"Thanks," I whispered as I sat down.

"Seemed like it was filling up fast, and I knew you were coming. Did you get off the waiting list?"

I shook my head. "Not yet."

"Did you check out the TA? Oh my God. I heard the prof was cute, but that TA is gorgeous. I'm already planning to have some trouble with this course." She grinned. "I'll need serious assistance."

I smiled and shook my head as dread settled in my gut. A TA might not wield as much power as a professor, but he had some clout. I'd just pissed off one of the people who would be grading me in this course. How could I be so stupid? I took a deep breath and told myself it wasn't that bad. After all, it *was* only a TA.

When I looked up from my fretting, the guy had closed the door and returned to the lectern. Where was the prof? Please don't tell me he was skipping the first class, after I busted my ass to get here on time.

The TA began. "If you're here for Anthropology 258, Ritual and Religion in the Americas, you're in the right place. If not, you have fifteen seconds to get out the door without disturbing those who know how to read a room number."

"Oh my God," Trina whispered as two kids snuck, shamefaced, out the door.

"Unbelievable, huh?" I said. "Nothing like a TA with an attitude."

"No, I mean his accent. That is the sexiest drawl I've ever heard. Where do you think he's from? Tennessee? Texas?"

I shrugged. The southern drawl definitely pegged him as American, if the rudeness didn't. Okay, that wasn't fair. I knew plenty of Americans, and most of them were great, but occasionally, you met an asshole like this who explained the stereotype. I took out my notepad as he continued talking.

"So, now that the rest of you know where you are . . . or think you do, let's get started. My name, in case you didn't read the syllabus, is Clayton Danvers. I'm your professor for this class."

My head whipped up so fast I nearly dropped my notebook. I looked down at the podium, and I swear he was looking straight at me.

Oh, shit.

Chapter 4

Clayton

When I ended the lecture five minutes late, half the class had already packed away their notes, not even waiting to write down the reading assignment. As the last words left my mouth, students vaulted from their chairs and flew for the door. And for what? There were few, if any, five o'clock classes. They just wanted to leave. I've never understood that mentality, that school was a chore to get through. If you're not there to learn, what the hell are your parents paying thousands of dollars a year for? Babysitting?

As the students thundered from the lecture hall, a gaggle of girls enveloped me, questions flying.

"Is this the right textbook?"

"What are your office hours?"

"Is the final exam going to be multiple choice?"

Life-and-death questions, and every one right on the goddamned sheet that I'd handed out at the beginning of class. I slammed an extra sheaf of those sheets onto the lectern, pointed at it, and strode toward the door.

I wasn't leaving. But someone else was . . . the blond girl who'd glared at me coming in—and then hadn't responded to any of the names on my class list.

She'd ducked out the door without so much as a glance my way. I swung into the hall to see her disappear into a mob of students, her white-blond ponytail swinging. In a sea of brunettes and bottle-blondes, that ponytail was as easy to follow as deer prints through a maze of mouse tracks.

"You!" I called as I strode after her.

A few students turned. One girl pointed at herself, mouthing a hopeful "Me?" But my quarry kept moving, neither slowing nor speeding up.

I jogged right up behind her and called again, but she just continued weaving past the other students, giving them wide berth, careful not to jostle or even brush against anyone else. I found myself watching that, the subtle but clear buffer she kept around herself. Paid so much attention to it that I let her get a dozen steps ahead of me before I realized it.

She zipped around a corner and was gone. Damn it. I had to find out who she was, and why the hell she'd been in my class.

When I rounded the corner, I saw her ponytail bobbing through a small crowd. I called again, but it was clear that unless I used a name, she wouldn't respond. So I grabbed her arm. A last resort—as physical contact with strangers always was—and I would have let her go as soon as I had her attention, but she whirled, wrenching her arm away.

A flash of something crossed her face—pique mingled with wariness. I recognized that look as well as if I'd been standing in front of a mirror, the same reaction I'd have to a stranger grabbing me from behind.

The look vanished as she recognized me. Her shoulders slumped.

"Professor Danvers," she said, sliding backward out of the main thoroughfare.

"You know who I am? Good. Now maybe you'll extend me the same courtesy."

She tilted her head, nose scrunching. A smattering of freckles dotted that nose, invisible to anyone more than a few feet away. I don't know why I noticed that, just as I don't know why I noticed that she was tall, only a couple of inches shorter than me, with a lean, athletic build; that she wore little or no makeup and smelled only of soap, a clean tang that I found myself committing to memory.

"Your name," I said finally. "You didn't answer roll call."

"Oh. Right. Elena. Elena Michaels."

In human society, an introduction is typically a jumping-off point for further conversation, at least followed by a handshake and an inane question or two. But she said it as a closing, her gaze sliding past me, hefting her bag to her shoulder, clearly hoping that answering my question would secure her release.

When I made no move to step back, she gave the softest sigh, inaudible to anyone with normal hearing, then backed against the wall, hugging her bag to her chest.

"I'm not in your class. I'm on the waiting list. Third."

"Classes are for registered students only."

One thin shoulder lifted in a shrug. "Sure, but I tried to register—"

"Not hard enough. The class didn't fill until near the end of the registration period, meaning you obviously couldn't be bothered—"

"Couldn't be bothered?" Her eyes flashed and she opened her mouth to say more, then snapped it shut, and looked away. "Fine."

"Fine? Fine what?"

Another blaze, doused just as quickly as the first, but lingering in a brittle clip to her words. "Fine, meaning I'll stay out of your class until I get a spot. *If* I get a spot."

This wasn't the answer I'd been aiming for, though I realized it only as the words left her mouth. I suppose I'd been digging for a reaction. Well, I got one. Just not the one I wanted.

"Excuse me," she murmured, jaw tight as she slipped around me.

She got two feet away before I swung into her path.

"Why?" I said.

"Why what?"

She snapped the reply, then tensed and winced, just barely, and I knew she was telling herself she shouldn't snap at me, shouldn't let me goad her. I've never been good at empathy, so to see someone—a human no less—react, and to understand, was a shock that knocked aside the last traces of my foul mood.

"The class," I said, softening my tone. "Why did you want to take the class? Is this your area in anthropology?"

She hesitated, eyes studying mine, wary. After a moment, she relaxed and leaned against the wall again. "No, I'm not in anthro. Sorry. Journalism."

"Journalism?"

The softest laugh. "Yes, people do choose to become reporters. Shocking, isn't it?" She shifted her bag to her shoulder. "I take anthropology as my annual extra. Last year I did my term paper on religion. I came across your thesis, read it, thought it was interesting, and used it. Then I saw you were teaching the first half of this course. I wanted to take it, but—" Another half-shrug, gaze disconnecting from mine. "Things came up. I registered late."

"You read my thesis?"

Her gaze met mine, and her smile dissolved. "You think I'm lying? It's published. There's a copy right here at—"

"Do you still have your paper?"

"You *do* think I'm lying."

"If you still have last term's paper, I want to see it. Then you can sit in while you wait for an opening."

Her eyes blazed again, and this time she had to struggle to put the fire out. I knew she wanted to tell me where to stuff my course, but she didn't want to cave either and walk away having me think she'd lied.

The battle raged in her eyes for longer than I'd expected. Had I made a misstep? I didn't doubt for a second that she'd read my thesis or that this was the reason she was in my class. No more than I doubted that I'd let her into that class. I'd just wanted to—I don't know. Maybe see whether I could rile her up. Maybe find an excuse to continue this conversation.

"Fine," she said. "I'll drop it by your office tomorrow—"

"What's wrong with now?"

Her jaw tightened, and I knew then that I had gone too far. When she told me, through clenched teeth, that she had a seven o'clock class and hoped to eat dinner, I agreed to let her drop it off tomorrow at ten, after my morning class.

CHAPTER 5

ELENA

I strode down the quiet hall, last year's anthro paper in hand. Danvers's office was at the far end, probably a spare used for storage, then cleared out when the department had to find space for visiting lecturers.

For almost an hour last night, I'd sat in the computer lab, my paper on the screen, my fingers ready to strike the print sequence, but holding back. Finally I'd grabbed my floppy disk from the drive and left, getting all the way to the coffee kiosk in the next building.

Did I still want to take this course? My gut reaction was "no," that it was too much bother, that the prof was an arrogant jerk and I didn't need this.

And yet . . . well, the truth was that the more hurdles he made me jump to get into this class, the more I wanted in.

As for "proving" that I'd read his thesis, that just got my blood boiling all the more. Who did this guy think he was? There might be some girls who'd sneak into his class for the eye candy, but did that give him the right to assume that all female students were interested in *him* rather than his lectures?

I'd continued struggling until the lab was about to close, and I printed out the paper just in case. I'd only made up my mind that morning, after the campus bookstore called me back, and set up an interview for ten-thirty. Since I was passing Sidney Smith Hall anyway, I might as well make that ten o'clock drop-off for Professor Danvers. Whether I still wanted to take the class didn't matter. At this point, it would be enough to prove I hadn't lied.

I brushed past two students trying to decipher a professor's handwritten office-hours chart. The next door was Danvers's. I didn't even get a chance to knock before he yanked it open. He must have been leaving. Five minutes later and I'd have had an excuse for leaving my paper with the department secretary instead. Damn.

"Just dropping this off," I said, stepping out of his way.

"Come in."

"That's okay. You were heading out, so I'll—"

He frowned. "I wasn't heading out. I was opening the door for you."

"How did you—?" I shook my head and held out my paper. "Here it is."

"Come in."

He turned and walked back in without waiting for an answer. The door shut behind him. Seemed like a good chance to escape. If only I wasn't still holding the damned term paper.

I opened the door. Danvers was taking his seat behind the desk. That desk, and two chairs, were the only furnishings in the cubbyhole office. On the bookcase sat two opened boxes of books. The desk was littered with papers, books, and professional journals.

"If you're busy unpacking . . ." I said.

"Unpacking?" He frowned.

"Never mind. Here's that paper." I started to lay it on the desk, then thought better of it and put it on an empty bookshelf instead. "My phone number is inside the cover. If I don't hear from you by Friday, I'll assume it's okay to show up in class."

"Sit."

"What?"

He waved at the chair across the desk. "Sit."

I resisted the urge to bark, and answered by not answering . . . and not sitting.

"Suit yourself," he said. "Pass me that paper."

I did. He opened it. I waited, expecting him to flip through. Instead he leaned back in his chair, put his feet on the desk, paper crumpling beneath his loafers, and began to read. I checked my watch.

"I have an appointment in twenty minutes."

He glanced at the clock. "I'll keep you for fifteen, then."

"It's way over in the Koffler Center. At the bookstore."

"You can buy your texts later."

"It's for a job interview."

He lowered the paper. "What the hell do you need a job for?"

"Excuse me?" As soon as I said it I regretted my tone. Well, kind of.

"College is for learning. If you work during school, sure, maybe you'll be able to afford a few extra drinks at the pub, but your grades will suffer."

I pried my jaws open enough to speak. "While I appreciate your concern, *sir*, I'm afraid I don't have much choice. If I don't work, I don't go to school."

"Your parents won't pay for it?"

"My parents are dead."

The moment the words left my mouth, I wished I could suck them back in. I braced for the inevitable "I'm sorry" or "That's too bad."

He just nodded. "Well, I guess you would need to work, then."

"So, may I leave?"

"Come back when you're done."

The interview did not go well. I couldn't even blame it on Professor Danvers. By the time I'd walked across campus, my initial outrage had worn off and I realized he probably didn't mean to be rude. Some people just say whatever comes to mind, bypassing the propriety filter.

The problem with the interview had nothing to do with my mood, but rather with my lack of experience. I knew my way around books, and I could be as courteous and helpful as any nervous first-year student could want, but when it came to sales and cash handling, my résumé boasted only a single summer job at a ballpark concession stand. I could tell that this wasn't enough.

So it was back to Ms. Purple Polyester and her gardening tips. Not for long, though. After calling back the bookstore yesterday, I'd felt rather silly for having struggled with the decision and resolved to work for that classified ad rag only until something better came along.

This time when I arrived at Danvers's office, I had a chance to knock. As my knuckles grazed the wood, the door creaked open. I called a hello, then peeked inside. The office was empty. Not very safe, leaving the door ajar, though I suppose there was nothing in the office worth stealing—not unless there was a black market in dog-eared, coffee-stained copies of *Anthropological Quarterly.*

From the door, I could see my paper on a stack of papers. There was a note on it. I slipped inside and picked it up.

Two words. *Elena* and *wait.*

"Woof," I said.

I looked at the note again. At the bottom was a letter. C. It took me a moment before I remembered his given name. Clayton.

Wasn't that an odd way to sign a note for a student? I reminded myself that, given his age, this was likely his first teaching gig. He probably wasn't used to calling himself "Professor Danvers" or "Dr. Danvers." And for a guy who considered a single-word command an appropriate mode of correspondence, signing with a letter was probably more a matter of economics than of familiarity.

The real question was: Would I do as he'd asked—or demanded? My first reaction was to get my back up. Yet when I thought it through, I simmered down. This wasn't a personal slight. Rude, yes. Condescending, maybe. Yet from what I'd seen in the classroom, no more rude or condescending than he'd be to anyone else.

My next class wasn't until after lunch. No reason why I couldn't pull out a textbook and study here for ten, fifteen minutes. If he didn't show up by then, I'd leave a note and go.

I'd only read two pages when the door banged open, hitting the wall so loudly I jumped.

"Good," he grunted, seeing me there. He tossed an armful of books onto the desk, sending an avalanche of paper to the floor. "You get the job?"

"It was just an interview."

He gave me a look, as if this didn't answer his question. Not much experience with the job market, I guess.

"I don't know yet," I said. "They'll call."

His eyes studied mine. "But you don't think you got it?"

I shrugged. "Probably not. Now, about—"

"Forget the bookstore," he said, thumping down into his desk chair. "I have a job for you."

I hesitated, not sure I'd heard right. "Uh, thank you, but—"

"I need a TA."

I stopped, mouth still open. A teaching assistant position had always been my dream job—good pay, work on campus, flexible hours . . .

My brain slammed up a big stop sign. A teaching assistant? In anthropology? I was a journalism major. And an undergrad at that.

Maybe I'm too suspicious, but after years of dealing with abusive foster daddies and brothers, I've earned the right to be. When a guy offers me something that doesn't sound kosher, my brain automatically jumps to one conclusion: He wants sex.

In this case, I dismissed it, even felt a little silly for thinking it. Clayton Danvers didn't need to offer teaching positions to get sex. From the way he'd brushed off those girls yesterday, bedding coeds was *not* on his agenda. He probably had a girlfriend or fiancée at home—some gorgeous neurosurgeon or physicist who modeled for Victoria's Secret in her spare time. Might even have a picture of her for his desk . . . once he found it under that blanket of papers.

"I'm not an anthropology student," I said slowly, in case he'd forgotten.

"So?"

"I need to be in this discipline to be a teaching assistant. Isn't that a requirement?"

He brushed my words aside with a wave. "The school wouldn't be hiring you. I would. I'm a temp, so that's how it works. They hire me, and I hire an assistant if I need one."

I'd never heard that, but it sounded logical.

"What about grading papers?" I said. "I'm not qualified for that. And I sure can't teach your classes if you're off sick."

Another wave. "I never get sick. And you won't need to grade essays. I'll just give you the multiple-choice parts of tests. That and . . . uh, administrative work."

"What kind of administrative work?"

"You know . . . departmental . . . stuff. Whatever I need done."

I cast a pointed look at his desk. "Like filing?"

"Sure. Filing. More important, though, I need research—"

A tentative knock at the door cut him short. His nostrils flared, then his mouth set in a hard line. He made no move to stand. Another rap. I arched my brows. He shook his head. We stayed quiet until footsteps tapped away down the hall.

"That's another thing you can do," he said. "Handle my office hours. Talk to students."

"They probably want to speak to *you*. Especially if they're having problems with the course."

"Oh. Right."

He looked so disappointed that I felt a glimmer of empathy.

"I suppose I could screen student visits," I said. "If it's taking papers or answering easy questions, I can handle it. Otherwise, I could have them make appointments, maybe discourage the ones that don't seem too serious."

He smiled then, his eyes lighting up like a kid's. "That'd be great."

My cheeks heated. "Uh, and research. You were saying something—"

"Right. That's really what I need. I'm working on a paper, and I need someone to do the legwork for me, track down articles, print them up, maybe do some extra digging. You cover all that in journalism, right? Research?"

"Right up my alley."

"Good. We're all set, then. You can start—"

"Wait," I said. "Can I think about it? I should hear what the bookstore says first."

He rapped his pen against the edge of the desk, then leveled it at me.

"What's the pay?" he said.

"Huh?"

"The bookstore. What are they offering to pay you?"

"Uh, minimum . . . well, slightly above."

From his expression, that didn't answer his question.

"Five dollars an hour," I said.

"How the hell do you live on that? I'll pay you eight."

"That's very generous. But wages aren't the only thing I need to consider. Hours are another factor, and you might only need me for five, six hours a week—"

"Hours are negotiable. I need help with this paper, and I want to work on another one after that. How many hours would you need?"

I calculated quickly. "Fifteen, if you're paying eight dollars. That would leave me plenty of time to study."

"Fifteen it is, then. When you're busy with school, take less. When things are slow, take more. I'm not running a nine-to-five business. As long as the work gets done, I'm in no hurry."

That sounded damn close to the most perfect school job I could imagine, which had me wondering what the catch was. Well, I suppose the catch was that I had to work with *him*, but I could handle an abrasive boss.

Next question: Why me? He could hire a hundred students who were better qualified. Maybe part of that was just dumb luck. I'd mentioned that I needed work, and that had reminded him that he needed a TA, so he offered me the job.

As a future employee, I wasn't *that* bad of a choice. I clearly wanted to work—a quality that could be hard to come by in students. Plus, I wouldn't sit and moon over him, and I suspected that was a major qualification. I also knew his work better than most students.

Anyone could grade multiple-choice tests, file his papers, and shield him from students. And if he needed a researcher, a journalism student was a good fit. Why me? Why *not* me?

"Does this mean I get to sit in your class until I get a spot?"

"Huh?" He frowned. "Oh, right. The class. Hell, yeah. You're in."

I smiled. "Good. About the job, then . . . when can I start?"

Chapter 6

Clayton

Elena was due to arrive for work in five minutes, and I still had no idea what *work* I was going to ask her to do. I didn't need a TA. Now, here I was, having volunteered not only to spend at least fifteen hours each week cooped up in this tiny office with a human, but paying her for the privilege.

I blamed temporary insanity, a new symptom of my fall moods. I could tell myself that I'd offered her a job because I'd been flattered that she'd picked my thesis for her term paper. Or that I'd been struck by a sudden wave of generosity, compelled to help a stranger in need. And if either of those explanations was right, then my fall moods weren't just making me moody, they were fucking up my entire personality.

I knew only that the moment she'd said her interview hadn't gone well, the idea had jumped into my brain and out my mouth before I could stop it. Every hurdle she'd raised had only made me more determined. When I'd succeeded, it felt like pulling down a buck single-handedly—a thrill of victory that had lasted right up until ten minutes ago, when I'd fully comprehended what I'd done.

Maybe I could tell her I'd made a mistake, that I'd reevaluated my workload and decided I didn't need a TA after all. Even as I considered that, a lick of shame ran through me. I pride myself on being fair in my dealings with humans. Sure, my idea of fairness and theirs may not always coincide, but I was never intentionally cruel to anyone who hadn't earned it. Elena had done nothing to earn it.

I'd hired her, so I'd have to find work for her to do . . . preferably someplace else. She could do research in the library or—

Footsteps sounded in the hall. The soft slap of sneakers. I inhaled and caught the faintest touch of her scent coming through the half-open door. My pulse revved up, as if I'd scented an intruder . . . and yet not like that at all.

She paused outside the door. Hesitating? Why was she hesitating? Had she changed—

A knock. A *tentative* knock, as if hoping it wouldn't be answered. She *had* changed her mind about the job.

Wait, that's what I wanted, wasn't it?

I yanked open the door to see her turning away.

"Elena!"

She spun. I mentally kicked myself for yelling at her. Was I *trying* to scare her off?

"Come in," I said. "We have a lot to do."

She stepped inside, shucked off her knapsack, and looked around for a place to put it.

"Just toss it wherever," I said.

Another nod, and she tucked it into the corner, under the empty coatrack. My heart was galloping like a spooked stag. Something was wrong. She was *too* quiet. Not that she was usually noisy, but she was giving off palpable waves of distraction, as if she really didn't want to be here.

She was going to quit. The bookstore had called to give her the job, and she didn't quite trust my offer—

"Is this okay?" she said, tugging at her short-sleeved blouse to straighten it. "I wasn't sure if there was, you know, a dress code or something—"

"There isn't. Wear what you like."

She looked around. When her gaze skated past mine, I noticed purplish half-moons under her eyes. She'd slept poorly. Nightmares? Anxiety?

My gaze slid to a faint reddish blotch, the size of a fingerprint, on the side of her throat. A bruise? A lover's kiss?

Did she have a lover? My gut clenched. I shook it off. She was young, pretty. Why wouldn't she have a boyfriend?

"Do you, uh, want me to start filing?" she asked.

She turned toward the desk, and the light illuminated the mark on her throat. Not a bruise or a kiss, but a birthmark or an old, long-healed burn.

"Filing?" she said again. "Should I start—"

"No. Not today. Today we have to talk."

Her blue eyes clouded. "Is something wrong?"

"No, no. We just need to talk about—" *About you. Tell me about yourself. Do you have a boyfriend? What kept you up last night? Is something bothering you? Is it me?* "—your paper. We didn't get time to discuss that yesterday, so I wanted to spend a few minutes on it today."

"Sure." She moved the spare chair over to the desk, sat down, then looked up at me with a faint smile. "So, how badly did I mangle your theory?"

⚜

Elena had only been scheduled to work for two hours that day, and we spent the whole time talking, first about her paper, then shifting into the more general area of my work, my interests, theories, past and current projects. As happy as I'd have been to segue our next discussion into her own life, I knew I wouldn't get away with it.

Any other student would have been content to sit and chat with a prof. Well, she would if she was being paid eight bucks an hour to do it. But Elena expected to work. That was obvious when her shift ended and she thanked me, not for the stimulating conversation, but for the "background." That's how she saw it. That's what she was comfortable with. Still, it was a start . . . even if it did mean I'd have to find actual work for her to do.

When Elena came the next day, I let her file. Can't say I really understood why this seemed so important to her, but no one has ever accused me of being intolerant of other people's eccentricities. So I let her put my papers into neatly labeled folders. Since my handwriting was somewhat indecipherable, I had to stick close by and explain each page to her so she could file it properly.

When she finished, I had a file drawer every bit as beautifully organized as the file cabinet at Stonehaven. Not that I'd seen the inside of the one at Stonehaven lately—it'd been locked ever since Jeremy made the mistake of asking me to retrieve the property tax records, and spent nearly a week refiling the mess.

I'd be more careful with this one. First, though, I'd have to figure out where she'd put everything. Still, the desktop looked very neat and clean, with the pencils and pens in a mug, the stapler and desk calendar arranged just so. Jeremy would have been impressed. Well, actually, he'd probably have a heart attack, but he made it a rule never to visit me during one of my human-world sojourns, so I didn't need to worry about him seeing it.

After that, we had thirty minutes of Elena's shift left, so I spent it making a semipermanent schedule for her. I took into consideration her course load, extracurricular activities, and study habits, giving her a flexible schedule with short shifts, sometimes two per day to reach her goal of fifteen hours a week.

"Wow, that's great," she said, reading it over. "This will work out perfectly." She smiled up at me. "Thanks."

I'd have enjoyed that smile more if I hadn't known that I'd split her shifts to guarantee I'd see her at least once every weekday. And because it'd given me the excuse to ask her a ton of personal questions—what courses she was taking, what sports and activities she enjoyed, etcetera. Good enough, though. For now.

I soon discovered that my ingenious "teaching assistant job" plan was not as foolproof as I'd thought.

I was heading for the cafeteria to grab a second dinner, when a hand thudded onto my shoulder. I wheeled, jerking away.

"Professor Danvers." My assailant flashed a greasy smile. "Just the man I wanted to see."

When he sidled closer, I stepped back and crossed my arms. He moved closer still, checking over his shoulder for students, as if thinking I was getting out of their path. As body-language illiterate as most humans.

The man was middle-aged, dressed in corduroy pants and a tweed jacket that wouldn't have buttoned over his gut no matter how hard he sucked it in. A professor. Had I met him yet? Maybe, but obviously not someone I'd deemed important, or interesting, enough to remember.

"I hear you have a new teaching assistant," he said.

"What?" I hadn't told anyone on staff.

He laughed. "Rumors travel fast. One of my students went by your office yesterday to see whether you needed a TA and you told her you already had one." His fleshy features twisted into a mock frown. "Which seems odd, considering the department has no record of such a position being offered."

"It wasn't. I hired her myself. I'll be paying her myself."

"That's . . . generous of you, Dr.—may I call you Clayton?"

I settled for a shrug he could interpret as he liked.

He continued, "While we appreciate you funding your own TA, surely you can see where that might raise certain questions."

"Of what?"

He gave me a look, as if to say the answer should be obvious. I stood my ground and met his gaze with a level stare. He broke first, beads of sweat popping out across his broad forehead. I took a slow step forward, closing the narrow gap between us.

"Of what?" I said.

His gaze flicked to mine, then skittered away. Confusion fluttered behind his eyes, instinct warning him to back down, human reason wondering why.

"I hired her myself because she'll be working for me," I said. "As a research assistant for studies unconnected to the school. That seemed the only fair way to handle it."

"Yes, well . . ." The man blinked, struggling to recoup his composure. "That's all very sensible, I suppose, but there's another problem. She's taking one of your classes. If she graded papers for her own class—"

"She won't."

"Perhaps if she dropped out of your class—"

"That isn't necessary. She won't mark or grade papers or do any other teaching assistant duties for that class." Did that mean she couldn't cover my office hours? Shit.

A slow, reluctant nod. "I suppose that would be acceptable." His gaze rose to mine. "But, remember, we must always take care when dealing with students, particularly attractive young women."

"That won't be a problem."

He clapped me on the back. "Of course it won't. I just thought I should mention it. Eyes will be watching. Eyes are always watching. And minds are always thinking—usually the worst. Don't forget that."

The next day I told Elena about her job changes. When I finished, she busied herself hanging up her knapsack.

"Okay," she said. "That makes sense. I guess I should have known that—"

"*I* should have known," I said, boosting myself onto the edge of my desk.

A brief smile, one that almost met her eyes. "Not your fault. You're as new at this as I am. So, uh, I guess we'll need to rework that schedule. How many fewer hours—?"

"That won't change. I'll just give you more research work."

The smile grew a quarter-inch, still hesitant. "Really? I mean, you don't need to—"

"More time for research means more research I can do. Publish or perish, that's the law of academics. We'll stick to the original schedule, and if you need more hours, just ask."

Her smile flashed full strength, so brilliant my breath caught.

"Thank you," she said, started to turn away, then stopped. "Oh, and what about your student drop-ins? That's more reception work than teaching assistance, right?"

"It is." *Whew.*

"We're all set then. So—"

Someone rapped at the door. I inhaled and scowled. Student. One who'd been here before, on business no more pressing than a sudden need to have me confirm, in person, the test schedule I'd handed out on the first day.

Elena pointed at herself, then the door. Did I want her to answer it? My nod was so emphatic she choked back a laugh. Then she arched her brows and pointed to a spot behind the door, mouthing "Wanna hide?" with lips twitching in a teasing grin. When I hopped off the desk and ducked behind the door, a small laugh finally escaped her. She tossed me one last breathtaking smile, then answered the door.

Over the next week, our working relationship hit a comfortable stride. When it came to any type of personal relationship, though, the ramparts stayed firmly in place. The moment I worked a conversation away from business, her body language cues were strong enough for a blind man to read, and they screamed "Back off." So I did.

But that left me with a quandary. I didn't just *want* to get to know her better, I needed to—a need that gnawed at my gut worse than hunger, that woke me up in the middle of the night.

As for why I wanted to know so much about her, I tried not to think about that. It made me nervous. A weak word, but there's no better way to describe it. Trying to understand my interest only brought on a strange feeling of apprehension. So I settled for accepting the situation at face value—I found her intriguing, and I was alone in Toronto, lonely, missing my Pack, and in need of companionship.

Yet it soon became obvious that she wasn't letting our relationship deepen until I'd earned her trust. And that, I suspected, would take a while—at least as long as it would take me to learn to trust a human stranger. But the need to know more was so overwhelming that within a week it took me to a place I'd rather not have gone. I started following her.

I'm not proud of that. Studying her when she was in my office or classroom was one thing, but I crossed a line when I started to follow her. I told myself it wasn't stalking. I didn't want to hurt her or scare her. I just wanted to learn more about her.

Despite my best justifications, I hated the way that following her made me feel, and after only a few evenings of it, I vowed to quit. Whether I would have been able to stick with that vow is debatable, but on that final night, fortune favored me with an alternative.

That evening, I spent an hour in the Laidlaw Library, sitting in a carrel, pretending to study a book I'd grabbed off the shelf. My real object of study sat at a table twenty feet away. Elena was working on an essay, driven from her dorm room yet again by her selfish roommate.

Her writing was going badly, a sentence stroked out for every two written, the strokes becoming harsher, angrier, each time. Any second now she'd give up and . . . And then what? I knew how I'd work off my frustration, but how would she?

I peeked over my book. She leaned back, pen in hand, staring at the paper. Then she shoved the pages into her knapsack, threw it over her shoulder, and strode out of the study area. I counted to ten and followed.

When Elena returned to her dorm, I felt a trickle of disappointment. Was that how she resolved her frustration? Give up and go home? Maybe she'd gone upstairs to blast her roommate, tell the brat that this was her room, too, and she wasn't being run off. That's what I would have done, but I suspected Elena wasn't ready for that.

I'd just started back toward my apartment when I caught Elena's scent on the breeze. I turned to see her hurrying across the dorm lawn, knapsack over her shoulder, but carried higher, as if she'd emptied out the load of books. She crossed to the sidewalk, jaw set, gaze forward, ponytail bouncing with each firm stride, moving fast into the gathering darkness. I waited until she vanished around a building, then followed.

Elena cut through the campus up to Bloor Street, then headed west. Although many of the small stores had closed, the nightlife was heating up as people spilled from restaurants and wandered the streets looking for entertainment.

Elena had already eaten. Was she heading to a bar? A date maybe? The question brought a now familiar tightening in my gut. Of all the questions I had about Elena, this topic obsessed me more than most.

I was pretty sure there was no steady boyfriend at school. I'd managed a few casual questions about Friday- and Saturday-night plans, and usually found that they entailed hanging out with friends.

I'd never smelled a man on her. Did that mean there wasn't one? Maybe he was going to school elsewhere or was working back at home . . . wherever Elena's home was.

The answer to *that* question had proved the most elusive. She had to have someone who'd raised her, someplace she called home. Whenever I broached the topic, though, she changed the subject.

Elena passed through the bar and restaurant district without slowing. As the crowds waned, I had to pull further and further back, until I was following her by scent, catching glimpses of her distant form only when she passed under a streetlight. Dusk had deepened to dark, yet she kept walking. At least two miles passed before she turned off. When I saw where she turned off, my heart did a double flip.

As I followed her trail into the park, I had to check my pace. I kept speeding up, anxious to see where she was going, hoping that I knew. I told myself I had to be wrong. Surely there was another good reason why she'd be here.

Like what? Nighttime lawn bowling league? Moonlight skinny-dipping? I knew where she was going.

When she ducked behind a building, I thought I was wrong. But then she stepped out again, the jeans and long-sleeved jersey gone, replaced by shorts and a T-shirt. She looked around the dark, empty park, then headed for the hiking path.

Near the head of the trail, she stopped. Another scan of her surroundings, more careful this time, head tilting to listen. She took something from her knapsack, and tucked the bag beneath some undergrowth. When she straightened, she gave another long, careful look around. Then she held out the small cylinder she'd removed from the bag and pressed a button. A blade shot out. A nod of satisfaction, and she snapped it shut again, cupped it in her palm, walked to the head of the trail, and began her warm-up exercises.

When she finally stopped her stretches, she looked around one last time, then faced the trail, took a deep breath, and vaulted forward, off and running.

For a moment, I stood there, hidden in the trees, watching her. Only when she disappeared around a corner did I snap from my reverie and find a changing place of my own.

CHAPTER 7

CLAYTON

I Changed in a small clearing, as deep in the strip of woods as I could get. When I finished, I stretched, front paws sliding out as far as I could reach. My skin itched, like clothes kept in the closet too long, dusty and stale. More than any other, I hated this part of being away from home—Changing in the shadows, furtive, always on alert. A dangerous undertaking, meaning it couldn't be undertaken any more than necessary. Not like at Stonehaven, where I could Change anytime the urge struck.

I sprang to my feet and ran back to the path. I'd been gone long enough for Elena to get a good head start. Luckily, she was running upwind, meaning I could catch her scent on the breeze. I breathed it in, inhaling so deeply the cold air scorched my lungs.

When I was in human form, Elena's scent teased and intrigued me with unformed thoughts and vague urges. Now there was no vagueness or uncertainty. The smell of her cut through the night air like a drug, and I raced after it, as blind to my surroundings as if I'd been on a treadmill.

Finally, she was there, just ahead of me, ponytail bobbing in the darkness. I threw my front paws out, nails digging into the path, forcing the rest of my body to a skidding halt.

I should have slipped into the woods, then approached hidden along the side, but the tree cover was so far from the path's edge . . . so far from her. Just a little closer, then I'd cut to the shadows.

When I was close enough to hear the chuff of her breathing, I knew I should stop. But it was so dark, with only a sliver-moon illuminating the path. She'd never see me. I could get closer.

She was sweating now, dripping scent. I drank in the smell, eyes narrowing to slits as I inhaled. I slipped off the path to run along the grassy edge, where I'd make less noise. Just a little closer, and then I'd—

Elena stopped, so fast she stumbled. I raced for the tree cover, stopped just inside, and hunkered down, holding myself still.

After a moment, I peered out. She was still there, where she'd stopped, squinting to see in the near-darkness. She held her switchblade out, finger over the trigger, the blade still sheathed. Her gaze traveled over both sides of the path, searching the shadows. She cocked her head, listening. Then, with a soft sigh and a slow shake of her head, she tucked the knife back into her palm, checked her watch, then sighed again. After one longing look down the path, she turned around and started running back the way she'd come.

I stayed in the woods. As much as I wanted to be closer, I wouldn't risk spooking her again. So I ran alongside her, far enough away to keep silent, but close enough that I could hear the pound of her feet, and if I glanced over, see her pale form against the night.

Partway back, she slowed. I could tell from her breathing that she was far from exhausted. Had she heard me? I'd been running silently, skirting dead leaves and undergrowth.

Elena looked around, a casual sweep of the forest. She checked her watch. Her nose scrunched up, head tilted, as if considering something. A pause. Then she strode off the path, heading to my side. I stayed absolutely still. A few feet from the tree line, she lowered herself onto the ground beside a boulder.

I waited, then slunk closer and peered out. She sat on the grass, leaning back against the rock. After another minute, her eyelids began to flag. They closed halfway, then she sat there, relaxing in the quiet night.

I hunkered down to my belly and crept forward until my muzzle poked out into the clearing. Sweat trickled down her cheek. I watched it fall, wondered what it would taste like, imagined it, tangy and salty, imagined the feel of her cheek under my tongue. A shudder ran through me and I closed my eyes.

Something tickled my tail. My eyes flew open. A chipmunk scampered along my side. I stared, marveling at its stupidity. It must have figured I was a dog and stayed focused on its quarry, the human a few feet away. Around here, humans meant food, not danger. It'd probably smelled her and woken up, hoping to be given a late-night snack.

As the chipmunk raced toward Elena, I let out the softest growl. It just kept scampering along, determined to intrude on her solitude.

I slapped down my paw, pinning it. The chipmunk let out a tiny shriek and twisted in panic. I stretched forward, bringing my jaws a hairbreadth from its head, and drew back my lips in a silent snarl. When I was sure it got the message, I lifted my paw. The chipmunk tore back into the woods.

I looked over at Elena. She was still resting, undisturbed. I stretched out, lowered my muzzle to my forelegs, and watched her.

⚛

The way to get to know Elena better was now obvious. She liked to run; I liked to run. Maybe not in the same way, but I could be flexible. The important thing was that this was a common interest that could get us out of that damned office and into an environment where I could be myself. Well, not really myself, but closer to it.

The problem was how to work the topic into conversation. Not only that, but how to formulate it into a request. I didn't have much experience with that—making requests. I told people what I wanted—whether they chose to give it to me was their concern.

I'd had friendships with humans before. Okay, maybe *friendships* is stretching it, but I'd had acquaintances. I never initiated the relationship, though. Even with something as inconsequential as partnering up for a school project, I'd always sat back and waited for someone to come to me, and eventually someone would, a classmate who'd learned to over-look my rudeness, or one who wanted my brains badly enough that he didn't care how unfriendly I was.

Even with Nick, I never said, "Hey, do you want to catch a movie tonight?" I told him I wanted to see a show, and he knew me well enough to understand that the matter was open for negotiation . . . at least in theory.

Yet I knew there was no way in hell I could go up to Elena and tell her to take me along on her next run. Even if I did manage to come up with a rational story to explain how I knew she ran, I suspected the demand-and-wait-for-results approach would leave me waiting for a very long time . . . probably on the opposite side of a slammed door.

This would take finesse. Finesse and patience. Had I possessed either, I'm sure things would have gone much smoother.

When Elena came to work the next day, it was obvious that her run had done its job, clearing her head and her mood. But if I'd hoped that somehow our shared experience had gone both ways, I was soon cured of that fantasy.

Elena came in and did her work, as pleasant as could be. But the moment I tried turning the conversation away from the paper she was researching for me, she steered it right back on track. Even a desperate "So, what did you do last night?" only earned me a murmured "Not much."

The next time she asked me a research question, I'd work conversation in the right direction . . . though I had no idea how I'd segue from prehistoric bear cults to jogging. So she continued skimming through the stack of books, making notes, while I graded quizzes. It went really well for the first ten minutes. Then I got tired of waiting and slapped the stack of quizzes down onto the desk.

"Do you run?" I said.

From the look she gave me, you'd think I'd asked whether she wore men's underwear.

"Do I what?" she asked after several long seconds of silence.

"Run. You know, jog, run, whatever."

She continued to stare at me. I probably should have worked it into the conversation better. Or started a conversation first, so I'd have one to work it into. So now I had to think up one on the fly, which would have been easier if she wasn't sitting there, nose scrunched, waiting for me to say something profound.

"Running is good," I said. "A good hobby—sport. A good sport. Good for you."

Her lips twitched. "Uh-huh."

"Well, it is, right? Gets you outside, in the fresh air, exercising. All good."

The phone rang—a sound I have never been so grateful to hear. As I lifted the receiver, she shook her head, smiling, and I knew my fumble hadn't been fatal—more of a pratfall, the kind of thing she was getting used to.

"Hello?" a woman's voice said on the other end of the line.

I started to hang up, but she spoke again, louder. Elena motioned at the phone, as if maybe I'd thought there was no one there. Damn.

I lifted the phone to my ear. "What?"

Elena sighed and rolled her eyes.

"Is Elena Michaels there?" the woman asked.

"No."

"Her roommate said she was there. She gave me this number and . . ."

The woman droned on, but I didn't hear. As tempting as it was to hang up, this could be urgent. I couldn't argue that talking to me about running was more important than a sick relative . . . not a close relative anyway.

So I passed the phone to Elena. She hesitated, brows knitting, then took it with a cautious "Hello?" No sooner did I hear the woman respond than Elena's eyes went wide with dismay, and I knew I'd made a mistake.

"This isn't—" Elena began. "No, I'm at work. I can't talk about this now. I—"

The woman's voice cut in. I caught a few words, none that made any sense out of context. But the next one required no context at all. And when

I heard it, I reached over to slam down the plunger. Before I could, Elena caught my eye, and her cheeks went scarlet as she realized I was listening. She grabbed the phone from under my hand and twisted around, moving as far from the desk as the cord would allow.

"I can't—" she whispered. "Look, whatever he said, I didn't—"

The woman continued to rant. This time, though, when she called Elena a bitch, Elena's back went rigid.

"This is not my problem," Elena said, voice icing over. "No, *you* listen to *me*. I have never done anything—" The woman yelled something and Elena's back went so tight it looked ready to snap. "He's the one with the problem, not me, and I'm not going to—"

The line went dead. Elena stood there, fingers white around the receiver. After a moment she lowered her arm stiffly, and replaced the receiver in the cradle.

"I am so sorry," she said as she turned to me.

"Sorry? Don't be sorry. What the hell does that woman think—?"

"I'm sorry and it won't happen again."

Elena enunciated each word with care, and as her gaze met mine, my own words died in my throat. From her look, I knew if I continued, I'd cross a line that wasn't ready to be crossed.

"I don't know how she got this number," Elena said.

"Your roommate gave it to her."

Anger sparked in her eyes. "Then I'll have a talk with her."

She turned, still stiff, and looked around the room, as if trying to remember what she'd been doing before the phone rang. Her gaze lit on the stack of books. She reached for the open one.

"Running," I said.

She stopped, lips pursing in a frown, then cracking into a tiny smile. "Ah, right. Running. It's good."

I hoisted myself onto the desktop. "It is, and the reason I was asking is that I run, but I can't seem to find a decent track around here. So I thought, even if you don't run, you might be able to recommend a spot for me."

Elena took her seat. "Well, I do. Run, that is. There are a few good places around here. It depends on whether you like the street or the beach or—"

"Where do you run?"

"Uh, well, that depends. Usually in a park—"

"Good. I'll go with you, then."

She stared at me, as if replaying my words, making sure she'd heard right. Then she pulled back in her chair.

"I'm not sure that's such a . . ."

She let the sentence trail off and her gaze searched mine, wary, almost reluctant, as if looking for something she didn't really expect to find, but had to be sure.

"You like to run alone?" I said. "That's fine. Me, I like company. Back at home, no problem, but here . . . ?" I shrugged. "Not a lot of running buddies to pick from."

She smiled. "I'm sure I could find one for you. I'll make an announcement at the next class and—"

"I want someone to run with, not from."

She laughed.

I continued, "Now, this park you mentioned. Maybe you can show it to me sometime, or draw me a map."

She hesitated, then shrugged. "I don't mind company, I guess. Sure, I'll take you there, show you the trails. I usually run at night, but—"

"Night's fine."

"The park's actually closed after dark. That's one reason I go there. It's very quiet, and I usually have the whole place to myself. Technically, of course, I am trespassing."

"So if we hear sirens, we run faster."

She smiled. "Exactly."

"I'll go with you next time, then. So when's that? Tonight? This weekend?"

A laugh. "Eager to get back to it? Well, you should have plenty of running buddies this weekend."

"Huh?"

"You *are* going home this weekend, aren't you? That's what you said on Monday. Going home for Thanksgiving. Well, not *your* Thanksgiving— that's in November. For you, this is just a long weekend."

"Uh, right. That's right. I'm going home."

Any other time, it would have been a welcome reminder. Right then, though, I wondered whether there was some way I could get out of it.

"So we'll do it next week," she said. "And this weekend, you can run with your regular partners. Assuming you'll see them."

"I will. It's a Meet . . . ing. Meeting. Bunch of buddies coming over."

"Sounds like fun." She settled back into her seat. "You have trails near your place?"

"*At* our place."

Her brows went up.

"Big backyard," I said. "A few hundred acres."

"Oh, wow. Woods?"

I nodded. "Mostly forest, some field. Got a pond, a couple of streams. Lots of trails."

"Now that's the kind of place I'd like to have. Not that I've ever lived in the country. I'm probably one of those people who'd get out there and start missing the city life." She paused. "You're in New York, right? The state, not the city."

"We're up by Syracuse. Nearest neighbor is at least a half mile . . ."

We spent the rest of Elena's shift talking. Okay, I did most of the talking, but she listened, and she was interested, and every now and then she'd let a little of herself slide into the conversation.

Early the next morning, I headed home. There wouldn't have been much use in staying behind. As Elena said, it was the Canadian Thanksgiving, so she'd be going home herself. I'd asked about her plans but, as usual, she'd ducked the question. I'd try again when I came back.

And, if I could, I'd broach the topic of that phone call again. That bugged me, someone tracking Elena down just to tell her off. I was sure Elena had done nothing to warrant that kind of treatment.

More on that later. In the meantime, I had a Meet to attend. And unlike the past few fall Meets, this time I was in the mood to enjoy it.

CHAPTER 8

CLAYTON

B y the time the plane touched down in Syracuse, any urge to skip the Meet had passed, and I couldn't believe I'd ever considered it.

No one met me at the terminal, and I hadn't expected it. I'd come in on the red-eye flight, which I preferred, since it usually meant I didn't need to sit next to anyone. It made sense, then, for someone to drop off my car the day before, rather than get up at four A.M. to come and get me. Of course, it would have made even more sense for me to take a cab, but no one dared suggest that. Airplanes were bad enough.

At just past seven, I reached Stonehaven. As I drove down the long tree-lined drive, the road vanished behind me and the stone walls of the house appeared. The upper windows were black rectangles. Everyone was still in bed, probably sleeping off a late night. On the main floor, strips of light glowed around the drawn dining-room blinds, borrowed illumination from another room, probably the study.

As I passed the cars flanking the drive, a light came on in the furthest upstairs room. Jeremy's bedroom. I hit the garage-door opener, then pulled in beside his truck, left my bag on the seat, and bounded for the house.

Once inside, I saw that my earlier guess had been right. Someone was in the study. The door was ajar, light seeping out into the dark hall.

Logan sat in Jeremy's armchair. Being still fairly new to the Pack, Logan didn't fully understand the protocol, so he always chose the chair he liked best. His favorite just happened to be Jeremy's. He meant no disrespect, but still, whenever I saw him there, my hackles rose. No matter how many times I booted him out of it—with a snarl or a good-natured chair-tipping, depending on my mood—he kept doing it.

Logan was studying, hunched forward over his textbook, highlighter in hand, braids hanging in a short curtain around his face. No . . . not braids. What did they call them? Dreadlocks. A fitting name—they did look pretty damned dreadful.

Apparently, Logan wasn't over his new "search for cultural identity" phase. Made no sense to me. Who cared who your parents were, what their racial or cultural background was? I didn't give a shit about mine. As Jeremy explained, though—and explained often—my own attitude toward this, and most other things, was not the best ruler by which to measure others.

I should be supportive of Logan's identity quest, and if I couldn't be supportive, at least I could keep silent. And if I couldn't *voluntarily* keep silent, then I would do so under direct order. So I was forbidden to comment on the dreadlocks. Which was fine; Logan and I found enough to argue about as it was.

Logan had been with the Pack for three years. Although he was a hereditary werewolf, he'd grown up as a human—the product of an affair that ended after his conception. A few months before his first Change, when he'd been grappling with the initial physical and sensory changes, he'd received a letter from his father. It directed him to 13876 Wilton Grove Lane, near Bear Valley, New York, where he'd find answers to his questions. So he arrived on our doorstep.

To me, this was the height of parental neglect. First you leave your kid with his human mother, who has no clue about her son's true nature, and therefore risk exposure with every childhood trip to the doctor. Then, you let him go crazy wondering what's wrong with him when his werewolf secondary powers kick in. And finally, when you *do* decide to intervene, you foist him off on strangers.

The identity of Logan's father was still a mystery. Logan assumed the guy was black. His mother refused to confirm it, but considering she came from a line of blond-haired, blue-eyed Norwegians, and Logan had deep brown eyes, brown skin, and brown hair, he figured it was a pretty good guess.

With that to go on, Jeremy had been helping to narrow down the paternal possibilities. His most recent theory was that Logan's father was Caribbean. Hence the dreadlocks. As for why Logan would even want to know his father—a mutt who'd abandoned him—that was beyond me. But, apparently, no one cared to hear my thoughts on the matter.

I snuck up behind Logan and loomed over the chair, casting a shadow on his book. He jumped, streaking highlighter across the page.

"Jesus fucking—!" He twisted and saw me. "Goddamn it, Clayton. Do you have to do that?"

"Honing your senses. A duty and a pleasure." I grabbed the text, swung over to the sofa, and dropped onto my back. "*Business Law: Ethical and Economic Considerations.* No wonder you were drifting off."

He stood. "There, I'm leaving the sacred chair. Now can I have my book back?"

"Sit down. Jeremy's shower's still running."

I flipped the page, keeping my finger in at his spot. When he didn't say anything, I lowered the book. He stood next to the chair, hovering like a dragonfly looking for a place to land.

"Well, sit down," I said, reaching out and kicking the chair.

"It's a test, right?"

"Huh?"

"If I sit down, you're going to pounce."

"That wasn't the plan, but if it's what you expect, I'd hate to disappoint you. Better yet, I could yank the chair out from under you." I looked up at him. "Let's test those reflexes. See if you can sit before I can pounce."

Logan snorted. "Yeah, like I'm stupid enough to—"

He dropped toward the chair, but not before I kicked it away from him. He hit the floor.

"Damn," he muttered, then peered up at me. "That was cheating. You said *yank*, not kick."

"Misdirection," I said. "A good try at it yourself, but you tipped your hand by glancing over to see how far back the chair was."

I helped him off the floor.

"Sit." I waved at Jeremy's chair.

He cautiously lowered himself into it.

"So how's school going?" I said. "You get all your courses okay?"

"Most of them. I missed out on an elective I wanted, but squeezed it in next term. How about you?" He slid a sly smile my way. "Maybe Jeremy should send you away every fall. That seems to cure your moods. Torture you with teaching for a month, and you'll be so glad to come home you'll be bouncing off the walls."

I shrugged. "It's not that bad."

He arched his brows. "Come again?"

"The teaching." I tossed his book onto his lap. "I'm happy to come home and torment you and Nick for a couple of days, but it's going okay."

"Uh-huh." He studied me. "Did you have anything to drink on the plane?"

"Water."

"Did you leave it unattended? Close your eyes for a few minutes? 'Cause I'm pretty sure someone slipped something into it."

"Funny. I'm—"

At a noise from the hall, I shot off the couch and bounded to the door as Jeremy walked through. Behind me, Logan slid over to the sofa.

"Hey," I said. "I'm home."

Jeremy's lips curved in a half-smile. "So I heard. As did everyone else, I think. You seem to be in a good mood. I'm glad to see it."

I glanced over at Logan. "At least someone is."

"I'm glad to see it, too," Logan said. "Just exercising a healthy dose of caution. We've all been bracing for the storm, and I'm not quite ready to unlash myself from the mast."

Jeremy shook his head. "I told them you seemed better on the phone, and Nick agreed. A change of scenery was what you needed. I suspected that might be it. Seasonal restlessness."

"I was voting hormones," Logan said. "One of those weird wolf things you're so attuned to. Of course, that could still be it." He grinned at me. "Things getting a little steamy up in the frozen north? Taking Nick's advice when he's not around to gloat over it?"

"No, and if you want me to stay in a good mood, you'll leave Nick's advice where it belongs—with Nick."

"Speaking of whom, I believe I heard him stirring," Jeremy said. "And, if not, I'm sure you can fix that. I'll start breakfast—"

"Why don't we let Nick sleep in? I'll make breakfast." I turned to Logan. "Come and give me a hand."

He groaned.

"Fine, I'll go bug Nick then, and Jeremy can make breakfast—"

Logan leapt up. "I'll start the bacon."

"Good. I'll take the eggs and toast."

"And I'll try not to take it personally," Jeremy said.

"Nah, it's not about you," I said, grinning as I squeezed past him. "It's about me. I'm hungry and I want food I can eat."

I ducked his lethal glare and herded Logan toward the kitchen.

As the weekend slipped past, I found myself, for once, able to relax and enjoy it, not anxiously watching the clock, wishing I could stretch my time at home into infinity.

Nick, Logan, and I began Sunday afternoon with a workout. Within an hour, though, it was down to me pumping iron in the basement alone. Nick worked out to build muscles for girls, not fights. By the thirty-minute mark, he'd done all the body-polishing he wanted. He stuck around a little longer, lounging on the benches and talking to me before wandering off in search of more interesting diversions.

Logan was more dedicated to improving his fighting strength. As the newest and youngest Pack member, he was the one most likely to be targeted by mutts looking to challenge a Pack wolf. He went to Northwestern, in Illinois, which was outside Pack territory, so mutts considered him fair game. I'd tried to help with that, but he'd have none of it, and insisted on defending himself.

It was that streak of independence that usually had him fleeing the exercise room first. When Logan had joined the Pack, Jeremy put me in charge of his physical training. Logan had gone along with it, as he went along with everything Jeremy asked, but the moment he'd considered himself trained, he'd dumped his trainer.

Now, when we worked out together, I tried to give him tips and pointers, but he always acted as if I was criticizing him. It never took long before he was stomping back upstairs. That afternoon, though, he did a full workout, accepting what few tidbits of advice I offered with only the barest roll of his eyes.

I kept on for another half hour after Logan left. At school, my workouts were barely adequate—I had to pick times when no one was around to see how much I was bench-pressing. I was wiping my eyes, getting ready to quit, when I lowered the towel to see Antonio in the doorway.

"You gonna work out?" I asked. "Let me wipe down the machines."

He shook his head and took a seat on the leg-press bench.

"What's up?" I said.

A half-shrug, but his eyes bored into mine as if they could see clear through to the other side.

"So . . . how are you doing?" he asked.

"Fine." I grinned. "Better than fine. Damned near perfect."

"I see that."

I whipped the towel at him. "Not you, too. Come on. Am I not allowed to be in a good mood without everyone wondering what's wrong? Logan's been joking about spiked drinks all weekend. Nick keeps giving me funny looks. Peter took me aside yesterday for a little heart-to-heart on how lonely it can be living away from the Pack, and how tempting it can be to start taking something to make things easier. The only person who seems happy to see me happy is Jeremy."

"I don't think there's anything *wrong*, Clay."

"Good."

He started to say something, then grabbed a dumbbell and began doing arm curls.

He smiled at me. "Still at ninety pounds?"

"Yeah, yeah. And I'm not going any higher for that one. I'm not built the same as you."

His smile grew. "Good excuse. So . . . I hear the teaching is going very well."

"*Very* well would be stretching it, but it's going fine."

He nodded, attention fixed on the weight. "Meeting new people, I suppose."

"Uh-huh."

He did a few more reps, then cleared his throat. "If there's ever anything you want to talk about, Clay, anything you don't feel you can discuss with Jeremy, anything you don't think he'd understand . . ." He met my gaze. "I'm always here. You know that. Just because Jeremy's my best friend doesn't mean I tell him everything. I know better than anyone that there are some things Jeremy doesn't understand. If you haven't experienced a thing, you don't know much about it. Like I wouldn't know how to paint a picture and he wouldn't know how to run a business."

After a moment's hesitation, I glanced at the door, then looked overhead.

"Jeremy's outside," Antonio said, laying down the weight. "He can't hear us."

"Well, there is something," I said.

"Yes?"

"It's not that I don't want to discuss it with Jeremy. I just—Like you said, he just doesn't *get* some things. I know he wants what's best for me, and I know he worries about me, but . . ."

Antonio shifted to the edge of his seat. "Go on."

"I need your advice. You have some experience in this area."

Something flashed behind his eyes. "Yes, I probably do."

"It's about motorcycles."

"Motor—" He blinked. "Motorcycles?"

"You had one, remember? Until you wiped out, and Dominic didn't want you getting another one, went on and on about your responsibilities as a father—"

"I can still hear him every time I take my car up over a hundred."

I laughed and grabbed a fresh towel. "I've been thinking of getting a motorcycle for Toronto. I know Jeremy doesn't want me taking my car up there. He thinks using public transit is good for me, that the more I do it, the more comfortable I'll get with it." I looked at Antonio. "It's not working."

His lips twitched. "And exactly how many times have you taken public transit since you've been there?"

"Once or twice, but that's not the point. I need my freedom. My own transportation. I could afford a motorcycle. Buy it there, ride it until I'm done, then bring it home. Jeremy said no cars, but he never said no bikes."

The smile broke through. "If you think that's really what he meant, then why not just tell him—"

"Too complicated. Point is, a motorcycle would be perfect. Nick and I rode dirt bikes in Arizona last summer. Easy enough."

"You need a license and—"

I waved him off. "If I get pulled over, I'll play ignorant foreigner. But I'd need some help picking the right size bike, the right type, and all that. If I decide that's what I want to do, can I call you?"

He nodded. "A motorcycle might be just what you need. A car, well—" He looked over at me. "It's not as if you need room for more than one, right?"

I shrugged. "I can always buy an extra helmet, just in case, but—"

Nick barreled through the doorway. "You still down here?" He looked at his father. "Giving Clay workout tips? Hey, Logan! Come quick. Clay's getting told how to lift weights."

"Yeah, but is he listening?" Logan said as he walked in. He paused and looked from me to Antonio. "I think we're interrupting something, Nick. How about we—"

"We're not interrupting," Nick said, dropping down beside me. "We're rescuing. Time to get Clay out of here before my father tells him all the things he's been doing wrong and shatters his delusions of perfection."

I snapped the towel at him and got to my feet. "We're done. So what's up? You guys ready for more?"

Nick snorted. "Not more of this. We have"—he made a show of checking his watch—"exactly six hours before we need to drive Logan to the airport. The question is, how to make the most of those hours. I say—"

"I say we let Clay pick something," Logan said.

"Like he's not going to do that anyway," Nick said.

"Yes, but letting him pick, and letting him bully us into letting him pick, are two different things." Logan looked at me. "We were thinking of heading into Syracuse. What'll it be? Dinner? A movie?"

"Dinner and a movie. Then dinner again."

Logan laughed. "Sure, why not? My last chance to pig out before school. Nick? Pick a movie."

"Are we actually going to see what I choose?" Nick said. "Or just pretend to consider it?"

"You pick the movie," I said. "I'll pick the first restaurant. Logan can pick the later one."

"Whoa," Logan said. "That sounds almost democratic. I'm switching my theory to alien possession. This has gone too far for spiked drinks."

I tried to smack him, but he dodged past me and we raced up the steps, leaving Antonio in the exercise room.

CHAPTER 9

ELEПA

As I walked through the doors of Sidney Smith Hall, I quickened my pace and surveyed the rapidly filling corridor. The chances of running into Clayton out here were next to nil, but I looked anyway. More significantly, I let myself look.

Part of me still rebelled, urged my legs to slow down, not to get to class early. But I wasn't giving in to that. Not today.

I spent too much of my life worrying about how things look, how they might be interpreted, never wanting to seem too enthusiastic, to let anyone know I gave a damn. It was hard work maintaining those defenses, and some days I wanted to tear them down, act as I pleased, and not care what anyone thought.

I'd begun to feel that maybe, with Clayton, I could. When it came to acting strangely, I was pretty sure I couldn't outdo him. He didn't care what anyone thought of him, so he wasn't likely to judge me. And, even if he did, he was leaving in another month or so, and I'd probably never see him again.

Was it only another month? Alarm raced through me, but I chased it back. I had other things to worry about.

At least the weekend was over. Any holiday that revolved around family saw me sitting in my dorm room alone, keenly aware of the empty halls, afraid to even turn on the television, knowing I'd be confronted with images of the holiday, even the commercials leaping out to remind me that normal people were home with their families.

I hated dwelling on this, but never seemed to be able to get past it. My one bit of "family" contact that weekend had been a former foster mother phoning, not to invite me to Thanksgiving dinner but to accuse me, yet again, of ruining her son's life. As if it was my fault—

"Elena!"

A dark-haired young woman pushed past a group loitering outside an open classroom door.

"Hey, Jody," I said, stopping.

"Hey, yourself. You didn't call when you got in last night. I was hoping we could grab coffee. So how was your weekend?"

"Good. And yours?"

"I survived." She stepped closer, moving out of the lane of foot traffic. "So, what'd you do? Visit lots of relatives? Eat lots of turkey? Pray you don't have to see either again until Christmas?"

I forced a smile. "Something like that. You joining us for dinner?"

"Of course. Share some holiday war stories before my night class. Get your best one ready, 'cause I think I've got everyone beat this time."

We chatted for another couple of minutes. I hated lying to my friends, but the alternative was worse. Admit you have no place to go for the holiday, and they'll do what any good friend would do—invite you to share their family celebrations. While I appreciated the gesture, the only thing worse than sitting alone in my dorm was sitting with strangers who were all trying very hard to make me feel like family, and only reminding me all the more that I wasn't.

After talking to Jody, I was no longer early for class. By the time I swung through the door, the room was nearly full. Clayton was at the front, sorting papers. I paused, expecting him to look up. He always did, with that weird sixth sense of his, seeming to know when someone was heading to the office even before I heard footsteps. He kept working, though. I swung past the desk. He lifted his head, but he didn't meet my gaze, let alone sneak me a smile.

I climbed to my seat, disappointment mingling with reproach. So he didn't notice me. Big deal. I was his TA. What did I expect? A hug?

As I took my seat, he began the lecture. He didn't look my way, and I tried not to worry about that. Of course, I *did* worry. Had he talked to someone at home who'd convinced him that a friendship with a female student wasn't such a good idea? Or, worse, convinced him that I might interpret his interest as more than friendship?

He began passing out papers, handing them down the rows. He gave me one, then passed the rest to the person beside me, his gaze never dropping within a foot of my head. Okay, something *had* happened.

I took my sheet. Instructions for an assignment . . . with a handwritten line, dark against the faded copy.

How was your weekend?

I looked up just as he was heading back down the middle row. As he passed me, he glanced over, brows lifting. I grinned, and his smile broke through before he turned away.

A second page followed the first, this one a list of possible topics. Again, mine came with an extra note.

Run tonight?

I laughed, startling my neighbor, then stuffed the pages into my binder. As Clayton stepped up to the lectern, his gaze shot my way, brows arched, expecting an answer. I bit back a smile and pretended not to notice . . . just as I pretended not to notice the glower that followed when he realized I wasn't going to respond.

When class ended, I took a few minutes to tidy my notes, waiting for the room to empty. By now students rarely lingered to ask more than a quick question, having learned that anything else only earned them a scowl.

As the last students filed out, I slipped from my seat. Clayton had his back to me, gathering his papers from the table.

"So?" he said, without turning.

"Passing notes in class? Isn't that a no-no?"

"Only for students."

"Still, you'd better be careful. Hand that to the wrong person and you'll get yourself in trouble."

"Which is why I passed it directly to you." He leaned against the lectern. "So? Can you run tonight?"

"Hmm, no. Sorry. But I could pencil you in for three weeks from Thursday."

"Watch it or you'll find yourself joining the ranks of the unemployed."

"There are laws against that."

"So?"

I swung my knapsack onto my shoulder. "Tonight is fine. I'm meeting friends for dinner, but I should be done by seven-thirty. How about I meet you in front of the ROM at eight?"

He agreed, and I left.

It was a cold night for October, single-digit temperatures with a wicked north wind blowing in, reminding the unwary that it wasn't too soon for a blast of early snow. With daylight saving time over, the sun was long gone by eight, taking any hope of heat with it. When I arrived at the museum, I was ready to head back to my dorm and dig up my winter coat, but once we started the long walk, talking as we went, I forgot the cold.

"Change facilities are a problem," I said as we entered the park. "The washrooms are locked, so I usually slip into the woods. Hardly decorous but—"

"Whatever works. I never see what the big deal is anyway. Someone sees a flash of bare skin, what are they going to do, run away screaming?"

I laughed. "I'd hope not. But if the flashing involves certain sections of skin, they'll run screaming to the nearest cop. On a night like tonight, though, I'd be more worried about frostbite than unintentional flashing."

"You want me to break into a bathroom for you?"

I glanced over, wondering whether he was joking, but pretty sure he wasn't. When he just looked back at me expectantly, I shook my head.

"Thanks but no. I run year-round, so I've learned the art of speed-changing. If we head around that pavilion, we should be out of the wind."

So we did, each finding a place in the woods to change into our running clothes. Had I been with anyone else, this is the point where I would have gotten nervous, undressing in the forest a few feet from a near-stranger. But one advantage to being with a guy as good-looking as Clayton is that I was sure he didn't need to lure girls into the forest to get them out of their clothes.

When I stepped out of the woods, he was already there, and I quickly realized one *disadvantage* to being with a guy as good-looking as Clayton. The gape factor. In the last few weeks, I'd become less aware of his looks. As Shaw said, "Beauty is all very well at first sight; but whoever looks at it when it has been in the house three days?"

So far I'd only seen him in his professorial clothes—usually a jersey or pullover and loose-fitting casual pants. As he stepped out in a tank top and shorts, I became keenly aware that, as nice as the picture had been with those baggy clothes, I'd been missing half of it. It was obvious Clayton wasn't the kind of guy whose only exercise was the occasional jog around the block. I tried not to look. Failing that, I tried not to stare.

As much as I like the solitude of running alone, there's something to be said for having company of the right sort. Preferably someone who can keep up a light chatter and keep up the pace. Clayton managed both easily, and we were back where we started before I knew it.

"—hadn't seen it, so we ended up watching *Die Hard* again," he said as we slowed to a walk.

"Is that the kind of movie you like?" I asked.

"Pretty much. Action and adventure flicks, mostly, though comedy's fine, sometimes horror. A few months ago, we went to see the new *Crocodile Dundee* one, but it was sold out, so we saw . . . now what was it? Something about a baby. *We're Having a Baby*, I think. Now, that *wasn't* my kind of movie."

"A chick flick."

"Huh?"

"A film aimed at the female portion of the moviegoing public."

"Oh." He peered over at me. "You like those kind of movies?"

"No, I'm saying that's who they're *made* for. Not that every woman likes them, no more than every guy likes movies where stuff blows up."

"What kind do you like?"

I grinned. "The ones where stuff blows up."

"We should go to a movie, then."

I glanced over at him, but already knew what I'd see. No hint that this was anything other than a friendly suggestion. Like the invitation to run together, he blurted out such things with a guileless innocence that couldn't help but put me at ease.

"Sure," I said. "We should do that someday."

"How about Friday?"

I laughed. "I said *someday*." A pause, then I glanced over at him. "Maybe Saturday."

"Saturday, then. Any idea what's play—"

He stopped. As I took another step, his fingertips brushed my arm, and I looked back to see him still standing there. He motioned for me to stop and scanned the grassy hill leading to the pavilion.

"Someone's here," he murmured.

"Oh?" I squinted into the darkness. "Where?"

"Over by the parking lot. You go get changed. I'll wait."

When I came out, he was standing by the pavilion, watching the distant parking lot.

"Still there?" I asked.

"There *again*. He left a couple times, but keeps coming back. Like he's waiting for someone."

"Probably is. Get dressed, then. I'll stay here."

After about a minute of squinting at the parking lot, I saw a figure. Male, it looked like. A cold night for a tryst, but I suppose that never stops anyone who's determined enough. I ducked behind the pavilion wall. No need to advertise my presence.

A moment later, a man appeared, walking along the path beside the pavilion. He didn't see me, and I only caught a glimpse of his back as he passed. Something in his stride made my heart jump into my throat, but I shook it off. Couldn't be. Not out here.

He reached the end of the path, then headed back. As he turned, I stiffened. No one knew I was here . . . no one except my roommate. Damn it! I quickstepped back into the shadows, but not before he saw me.

"Elena!" he called, grinning as he broke into a jog. "There you are. You're a hard girl to find."

Apparently not hard enough.

CHAPTER 10

ELENA

"What are you doing here, Jason?" I asked, shooting a quick look over my shoulder and praying Clayton didn't pick that moment to step from the shadows.

"I should be asking you that." He walked over to me. "What are you thinking? Jogging in a park at night? When your roommate told me where you were, I thought she was putting me on. Who the hell does crazy stuff like this? It's not—"

"Normal?" I said.

"I didn't mean it like that." He stepped forward, hand rising to brush a stray wisp of hair off my cheek. "You know I didn't."

I backpedaled out of his reach. His gaze dropped in that wounded look, as if he was the victim here, the poor besotted guy under the spell of the evil ice bitch.

"I'm not canceling the restraining order," I said. "So you can tell your mother to stop calling me."

"Ah, shit. Is she—?" He smacked his palm against the pavilion wall. "Goddamn her! Why does she always do this to me? You were right to get that."

"Don't."

"No, I deserved it. I got carried away. I couldn't help myself. You weren't returning my calls. You wouldn't see me. I got confused—"

"Confused?" I said, nails biting into my palms. "What the hell is confusing about the word *no*?"

The wounded look again. "You don't have to swear, baby."

"I am not your *baby*." I dug my nails in harder. "I have never been your *baby*. I have never been your *anything*. No, wait . . . I was your something. Your foster sister."

"I know that. But I couldn't help it. You were so—"

"Available? Trapped? I couldn't slam the door in your face and walk away, because there was no place for me to walk to. You were there, all the time, and there wasn't a damn thing I could do about it. Complain to your mother, and she tells me I'm overreacting. You're a seventeen-year-old boy; I'm a seventeen-year-old girl. What do I expect? I should be flattered. Well, I'm not seventeen anymore. I wasn't flattered then. I'm not flattered now. And I want you to get the hell out of my life before I do something that is really *not normal*."

"You're upset, baby. I understand that. My mother pisses me off, too, so I don't blame you one bit."

At that moment, I wanted nothing more than to haul off and deck him.

But it wouldn't help. I could knock Jason off his feet and he'd just look up at me with those hurt eyes and say, "I understand why you did that, baby."

I spun on my heel and strode away. Got about ten feet before his hand closed on my shoulder.

"Let me go," I said, voice low, back still to him.

"No, Elena. Not until you've calmed down."

I jerked forward, but his grip only tightened, fingers digging into my shoulder. I flung his hand off. His jaw set. I stood my ground. He stepped forward, closing the gap between us.

"You don't want to do that," drawled a voice to our left.

I looked to see Clayton in the shadow of a pine tree, arms crossed, as if he'd been there for a while.

"I can handle this," I said.

My words came out sharper than I intended. I glanced over at him and lifted a finger. He nodded, and stayed where he was.

"Go home, Jason," I said, "or I'm walking to the nearest phone booth, dialing 911, and seeing how well that restraining order works."

The perfect threat—calm yet clear—and I'd have been very proud of myself . . . had Jason heard a single word of it. Before I was half finished, he was striding toward Clayton.

"Who the hell are you?" Jason said.

"An interested party."

"Interested in what?" Jason swung to face me. "Is this guy with you, Elena?"

"Could be," Clayton answered before I could. "Or I could be just a fellow jogger, heard the ruckus, and came over to see if I could help. Or maybe I'm not a jogger at all. Maybe I just like hanging out in empty parks, see what kind of sludge crawls out of the pond after dark—" He grinned, teeth flashing. "See what kind of trouble I can get into."

"What the hell is that supposed to mean?"

"Not a damn thing. Now, I think Elena was talking to you, and I think you'd better start listening."

Jason stalked over to Clayton and pulled himself up, eye to eye. "Or what?"

Clayton only shrugged. "You'd have to ask her that."

Jason looked from Clayton to me, face scrunched up in confusion. "Who is this guy?"

"An interested party," Clayton said.

Jason's finger shot up, pointing in Clayton's face. "Don't you start—"

Clayton grabbed his finger. I tensed, but he only held Jason's finger, then pushed it slowly down.

"Lift that hand to me again, and you'd better be prepared to use it. Now go on back to Elena. This is her fight, and I'm not making it mine unless you insist."

Jason looked from me to Clayton. He paused, then stalked off, calling over his shoulder a promise that he'd talk to me later. I wanted to run after him, grab him by the shoulder, the way he'd done to me, swing him around, and set him straight—tell him he *wasn't* going to talk to me later, and why. But I was just happy to see him go. Happy and relieved, and dead-set against doing anything that might interfere with his leaving.

"You want to go get something?"

I wheeled to see Clayton at my shoulder. I hadn't seen him move from his place by the trees.

"Hmm?" I said.

"You want to go get something? I'm sure I can find a place on the way back."

I shook my head. "No. Thanks, but I'm really not . . ." I shrugged.

"Not hungry?"

"Eat? Oh. I thought you meant a drink."

I should have known he didn't mean the obvious. He never did.

"We could get a drink, if that's what you'd like," he said.

"Definitely not. Doesn't do a thing for me except put me to sleep. But something to eat would be good." I forced a smile. "Vent my frustration on a hapless burger."

"Good. Grab your knapsack and we'll go."

We walked down out of the park in silence. Comfortable silence, not that deadweight quiet that comes from waiting for me to talk about what had happened. He didn't mention it, and I appreciated that. Like I appreciated the invitation to a late-night snack—something, anything, to keep my mind off Jason and to give me an excuse not to head back to my dorm room, where he could be lying in wait.

Clayton found an all-night diner. We couldn't see it from Bloor Street—not even the sign—so I assumed he'd been there before, but when we got inside, he looked around, orienting himself the same as I did.

He started toward a table in the back corner, then glanced over his shoulder.

"There okay?" he said, jerking his chin toward the table.

"Perfect."

We settled into our seats.

"Burgers page three," he said after a glance through the menu.

"On second thought, I may change my mind. They serve all-day breakfast." I skimmed through the grease-spattered menu. "I think I might go for pancakes. Weird, I know, but—"

"Have what you like."

"Comfort food. Does the trick better than alcohol."

He started to say something, but the server arrived, coffee pot in hand.

"No, thanks," I said, covering my cup. "Too late for caffeine. I think I'll have . . ." I flipped to the back of the menu, then smiled. "Root beer floats. Haven't had those in years. I'll take one. And the pancakes and ham steak."

The server peered over her half-glasses. "With a root beer float?"

I hesitated. Kicked myself for letting a server make me rethink the "appropriateness" of my order, but I did it nonetheless.

"Same here," Clayton said, smacking down his menu. "Pancakes, ham, and a root beer float."

The server rolled her eyes and left mumbling about college kids.

"You like root beer floats?" I asked.

"Never had one."

I stifled a laugh. "Well, I'm not sure how well it'll go with maple syrup, but we're about to find out." I glanced around the diner. The few other customers were all across the room. "I should have said it earlier, but thanks for trying to help back there. At the park. I didn't mean to snap at you."

"You wanted to handle it yourself. Nothing wrong with that."

"Hmm, well, as you saw, handling it myself doesn't seem to be—" I bit off the sentence and looked away. "Anyway, thanks." I glanced back at him. "You confused him, and that's probably the best way to get rid of Jason."

"Not too bright, is he?"

I laughed and eased back in the booth. "No, not too bright, though I'm pretty sure he can't be as dense as he acts. It's just an excuse: Pretend he honestly misinterpreted our relationship—or lack of one."

"So you and he never . . ."

"Absolutely not. When you're a foster kid, you can't get into that."

I paused, realizing I'd let slip something I preferred to keep to myself. But if he'd overheard any of my conversation with Jason, he already knew I'd been in foster care. So I continued.

"Any relationship Jason thinks we had took place only in his head."

"But he keeps following you? What's it been now? Three, four years?"

"Three. And two since I turned eighteen and got the hell away from him and his screwed-up family. As for Jason, I don't know what his problem is. He doesn't have a problem getting dates with willing girls. So why me?"

"Because you're not willing. Buddy of mine is like that. Not like *that*—stalking and shit. But if you put him at a party with ten girls, and nine of them are falling over him, he'll make a beeline for number ten, spend the night trying to charm her."

"The thrill of the hunt."

"I guess so. He likes the challenge. 'Course, if she tells him to get lost, he does."

"Most guys do. A chase is fine, but if she fights when cornered, they back off."

Our floats arrived. Clayton waited until the server left.

"Has he ever hurt you?" he asked.

I shrugged. "Not really. He sometimes grabs me, like he did in the park. Leaves bruises, but not the 'fear for my life' kind of hurting."

Clayton's jaw worked, and he dropped his gaze, but not before I saw a flash of rage there, so intense it startled me. It should have scared me—I know that. But it didn't.

"That's bad enough," he said. "You can't let him do that or it'll only get worse."

My head jerked up. "You think I'm *letting* him—"

"No." He reached out and, for a second, I thought he was going to put his hand on mine. At the last moment, he plucked a napkin from the dispenser. "I didn't mean it like that. The problem is, the harder you fight, the harder he's going to pursue. You can't give in, and you can't fight back, so you're stuck."

"So I've noticed."

He crumpled the napkin. Then he looked at me. "I could fix this for you. Make sure he doesn't come back. Not kill him—if he isn't threatening *your* life, then that isn't necessary. But I could make damn sure he never wants to see your face again."

Again, I should have been shocked. Again, I wasn't. I knew he wasn't just offering to give Jason a stern talking-to. And the casual mention of killing him, as if this was an option I should keep in mind? That should have sent me bolting for the door.

Instead, I only shook my head. "Thanks, but I still want to try handling it on my own."

"If you change your mind, you let me know."

"I will."

Clayton walked me back to my dorm. Luckily Jason wasn't there. Nor did he make good on his "promise" to talk to me later. Maybe he was still trying to figure out what Clayton had been threatening in the park. Or maybe he'd seen something in Clayton's eyes, the same thing I'd seen later at the restaurant, and decided he didn't want to find out what he'd been threatening. Either way, I was glad for the respite.

Clayton and I did go to see a movie that weekend. Had a good time, too, though by now I'd come to expect that. Over the next few weeks, we saw a couple more movies, went out for a few meals, and jogged together almost every other day. I knew I should have been concerned about getting him in trouble—socializing with a student—but he was careful and I was careful, and the selfish truth was that I didn't want to worry about it, didn't want *him* worrying about it, not if it meant we'd spend less time together.

After that night in the diner, I started opening up. Not that I poured out my guts at his feet; I just didn't change the topic when conversation turned personal.

He gave as good as he got. Before that night in the diner ended, I'd found out that Clayton understood my situation better than I could have imagined, having been orphaned himself when he was only a couple of years older than I'd been.

Like me, Clayton had no biological family . . . or none that he knew of. Unlike me, though, he'd found a home, with a guardian that sounded like everything I'd ever dreamed a foster parent could be, plus a close extended family. I suppose I could have felt jealous about that, but instead it reaffirmed my own hopes that just because you didn't have blood relatives didn't mean you couldn't, someday, have a normal life with a family of your own.

As October drew to a close, I became increasingly aware of Clayton's imminent return to New York. We hadn't discussed that. Maybe there was nothing to discuss. His term would come to an end, he'd hand me my final paycheck with a "Nice to know you," and that'd be it. Maybe if I expected otherwise, that was my mistake.

I held out as long as I could, until exactly two weeks before he was due to leave. Then I asked whether I could use his office computer to rework my résumé. He mumbled something, but when I tried to get an intelligible answer, he changed the topic.

Two days later, I showed up at work to find the office empty. With no note. For a few seconds, I stood by the desk in shock, wondering if he was already gone. Silly, I know, but he was always there when I arrived for my shift. If he couldn't be, he left a note, telling me he was gone—as if I couldn't see that for myself—and telling me to wait—as if I might take his absence as an opportunity to snag a day off.

So when there was no note, I kind of panicked. Then I saw that his books were still on the shelf. He might leave papers and old journals scattered all over the office when he finally did vacate it, but he'd never abandon his books.

I sat down and started to work. Less than ten minutes later, the door banged open.

"I hope that's not your résumé you're typing," he said as he tossed a file folder onto the desk.

"Not without your permission."

"Good, 'cause I don't give it. You may not revise your résumé."

"I meant I'd need your permission to use your computer and printer, not to write the résumé. That I don't need."

"And you need it to use my printer? Why? I might complain about you using up the ribbon? Hell, I have a box of them." He dropped into his chair and spun it to face me. "But, back to the original subject, you do not have my permission to revise your résumé. I expressly forbid it."

"Uh-huh. Well, that's great, but I do need a job—"

"You have one."

"*After* you leave."

"Not leaving."

"What?"

"Is that disappointment I hear?" He bounced off the chair and scooted his rear onto the desk, looming over me. "Too bad, 'cause I'm not leaving. The university likes the research paper we're working on, and they want me to finish it here, so they can slap their name on it. Plus Dr. Fromme wants me to keep teaching his fourth-year class. Meaning you're stuck with me until the end of the term."

"Damn."

"Damn?"

"Well, see, there's this other job. Better working conditions. Less demanding boss—"

"You'd better be kidding, because I just went through a helluva lot of work to make sure you kept your job."

"Oh, so you did it for *me*."

"Of course. You need a job." He jumped off the desk and headed for the door. "So get back to work and earn your keep. I have to meet with Fromme. It might take a while, but I'll be back by lunch, so wait for me." He threw a grin over his shoulder. "You're buying, too. A token of appreciation for your continued employment."

He zipped out the door before I could answer. I sat there, smiling, then turned back to the keyboard.

At ten, I decided to go grab a coffee. I was pushing the office door when it flew open, nearly sending me into the wall.

"Thanks a helluva—" I began, then stopped, cheeks heating.

In the doorway stood not Clay, but one of his students. A guy about my age with short dreadlocks and an easy grin.

"Sorry about that," he said. "Is Clay—Professor Danvers here? This is his office, right?" A glance over at the paper-littered desk and the grin returned. "Oh, yeah. This is definitely his office."

"You must be in his fourth-year class," I said. "I'm Elena, his TA."

His brows arched. "TA?"

"Well, TA, receptionist, typist, research assistant. All-round girl Friday, pretty much." I waved at the office. "Housekeeping not included."

As he laughed, I unearthed a pen.

"Professor Danvers has office hours tomorrow, but you can leave a note for him, or I can pencil you in for an appointment."

"Sure, you can pencil me in for an appointment, but will he *keep* the appointment? That is the question."

I smiled. "Yes, he *does* keep them. I make sure of that. So can I schedule—?"

"Actually, I'm not a student. I'm a friend of his."

"Oh?"

"Yes, Clayton has friends. Shocking, isn't it?"

"I didn't mean—"

"No?" He met my gaze, grinning. "Oh, come on. Admit it. *Friends* and *Clay* are not words that go together."

"Okay, I was a little surprised. Not that I didn't know he had friends. I just haven't met any of them. And, now that you mention it, I'm going to hazard a guess that you're Logan."

The grin fell away. "Uh, yeah. He's mentioned me?"

"Now you're the one who sounds surprised."

"I am. Not that I'm not perfectly mentionable, but Clay doesn't usually talk about his personal life. Huh. Well—" He looked around. "So what kind of— Oh, wait, you were going somewhere when I rudely barged in, weren't you?"

"Just to grab a coffee."

"Perfect. I could use one . . . and I have no clue where to find it here. Mind if I tag along?"

"Sure. Or I could bring you back one—"

"I've just spent six hours in the car. Please don't ask me to sit and wait."

I smiled. "I won't, then. Come on."

After we got our coffees, Logan persuaded me to sit in the cafeteria. Normally, I would have pulled the "Gee, I'd love to, but I really have to get back to work" routine. I'm not antisocial, but neither do I go out of my way to have coffee with strangers. Yet Logan was one of those people with the gift for making you feel, almost from the first word, that you've known him for years. So we sat and talked, mostly about school. He was also in his third year, at Northwestern, which gave us plenty of common ground.

"You live on campus or off?" he asked halfway through our coffees.

"On. Though I'm hoping to change that next term."

"Same here. And I bet I know the reason. DMFH, right?"

"Hmm?"

"DMFH. Dorm mate from hell. There's gotta be a better acronym, but that's the best I could come up with on the fly. So how bad's yours?"

"Not too bad . . ."

"She has to be bad," he said, "because that's the rule."

"The rule?"

"You're a serious student, right? Obviously, if you're a TA. You work your ass off because that's what college is for—learning and getting a job, not an all-expenses-paid party tour."

"Sometimes I wish it was."

"But it isn't. Especially if you're paying your own way. You are, I'll bet. Otherwise, you sure as hell wouldn't take a job with Clay."

I smiled. "Yes, I'm paying my way."

"Me, too. Well, someone's helping me, but I have every intention of paying him back. Point is that we've paid for this education, and we're damned well going to get the most out of it. So we're guaranteed to get dorm mates who don't give a shit, who stay up all night, expect us to get up quietly in the morning, blast music while we're trying to study, give their friends the room key . . . Happens to me every year."

"Same here."

"It can't be by accident. I think it's a baby-boomer conspiracy."

I sputtered a laugh. "Baby boomers?"

"We're studying to take their jobs, right? What better way to keep us out of the workforce than to make sure we have a rough time at college? They pair us up with the worst party animals and hope we fold."

A flash of motion across the cafeteria caught my eye. I looked to see Clayton barreling toward us, eyes blazing, mouth set in a grim line.

"Looks like Clay got my note," I said. "But I don't think his meeting went very well."

Logan glanced over and grimaced. "No, I do believe that scowl is intended for me." He looked around. "Think it's too late for a speedy escape?"

"'Fraid so."

"Damn. Hold on, then. I'm about to get blasted."

CHAPTER 11

CLAYTON

I stood at the back of the cafeteria and watched Logan with Elena. He'd pulled his chair as close to the table as it could get, and was leaning forward. My hands clenched. There was a rule about Pack brothers visiting me when I was here. A rule *against* it. Jeremy's rule. It was bad enough that Logan didn't respect my authority. But to disobey Jeremy? That went too far.

Elena laughed at something Logan said and replied, hands moving. Her back was to me, but I could imagine her face, eyes sparkling with animation, her full attention on him. How long had it taken for me to see that spark, to get her to look me in the face every time? She'd known Logan for an hour. Probably less.

I started toward them, looping around the cafeteria. The moment I passed into Elena's field of vision, she looked up, almost instinctively. I braced myself, expecting to see consternation. Instead, she grinned and lifted her hand in a wave.

My stride caught. I tried to smile back, but my lips didn't move fast enough, and she saw my scowl. Her smile faded, eyes clouding. She turned and said something to Logan. He glanced up at me, eyes widening in feigned horror. My fury returned. It was bad enough he was here; I was damned if he was going to mock me, too.

I strode to the table.

"Clayton," Logan said, smiling up at me. "About time you—"

"I want to talk to you."

"Well, then, you're in luck, because that's what we were doing. Talking." With his foot, he pushed out a chair—the one on the far side of the table. "Elena and I were just about to swap roommate horror stories. Did you ever get a bad one?"

Elena grinned up at me. "Or were you the bad one?"

My anger started to fizzle under the blaze of that smile. A glance at Logan, and I rallied it back.

"I want to talk to you," I said. "In private."

Elena pushed her chair back. "You guys don't need me hanging around. I should get back to work—"

"No," I said, touching her elbow as she started standing. "You stay. Finish your coffee. I just want to talk to Logan for a minute."

She hesitated. Logan shot me a "don't be a jerk" look—one I'd seen often enough to recognize. As much as I wanted to snarl something back at him, I couldn't help noticing Elena's discomfort.

"Stay," I said. "I can talk to Logan later."

She hesitated another moment, studying my face, then sat down, and pulled out the chair beside hers. I took it.

We spent the next hour talking. Logan did most of it. Typical. More than once, I got the impression he was steering the discussion in directions he hoped I couldn't follow. Yet Elena always managed to bring it back to a three-way conversation.

When Elena talked to Logan, I watched her expression. She seemed less guarded than she was with strangers, but not nearly as open as I'd envisioned, and I was pretty sure there was extra wattage in the smiles she tossed my way.

As for Logan, I knew him well enough to pick up his signs of interest. When Nick, Logan, and I went out, Nick never made the return trip home with me. Put him in a bar with more than one woman, and he could always find someone suitable. It took a lot more looking for Logan to find someone he liked, but when he did, it was obvious—and sitting at that table, watching him with Elena, I saw all the signs. I told myself it was just Logan being Logan, always finding a way under my skin, always challenging me. But I wasn't sure that was it.

After the first half hour, I started watching the clock. At 11:45, I cut Logan short.

"Elena? We have to get lunch or you'll be late for your next class. Logan? There's food here, food out on Bloor Street just north of campus, and food back in my apartment. I'll meet up with you at my office later." I took my keys from my pocket. "You want these?"

Elena looked at me, brows knitting, and I knew I'd committed some social misdemeanor. I glanced at Logan for a clue, but he rubbed at a smile and avoided my gaze.

"I'm sure you want to eat with Logan," Elena said.

"Not really."

Logan choked on a laugh. "And you wonder why you've never met any of his friends before?"

I glared over at him. "If you'd called or otherwise told me you were coming, I'd have left lunch free. But I have plans. I'm buying Elena lunch to celebrate her continued employment."

"I thought I had to buy lunch," she said.

"I was kidding."

"Good," Logan said. "'Cause you'd put the poor girl in hock. Have you seen how much he eats?"

"I have," she said. "Which is why I'd planned to take him to McDonald's."

"Well, consider yourself saved from that fate, 'cause I'm buying," Logan said. "You're the townie, Elena, so you pick the place. My mom sent me a check this week, which is how I could afford the gas money to get up here. Every few months she remembers she has a son and sends guilt money, some of which I promptly blow on the most frivolous, unnecessary expenses I can find. That way, neither of us feels guilty about it."

Elena laughed. I shook my head. I never knew how Logan did that, tossing out the most private tidbits of his life as if they were nothing more intimate than his name.

"Shall we go?" he said, grabbing Elena's empty coffee cup. "What time's your class?"

"One-thirty."

"Lots of time, then. Is it journalism?"

She nodded. "Advanced interviewing techniques."

"Oooh, could use some of those in my prelaw course. I'll sit in on it with you."

"You can't do that," I said. "It's against the rules."

"Words we never thought we'd hear Clayton Danvers say," Logan said. "Profs don't care if you sit in—not if you ask them first and ask nicely. If I get in shit, I promise not to mention your name. Now come on. I have fifty bucks burning a hole in my pocket, and I intend to have it gone by one-thirty."

After her class, Elena returned to finish her shift. Not that she got much work done, between answering Logan's endless questions about our project and arguing with me over the interpretation of data. This was an ongoing debate—a spirited disagreement over two ways to interpret our research findings. Her interpretation was wrong, of course, but I liked challenging her about it, if only to see her temper flash.

I had no interest in renewing a personal debate in front of Logan, yet when she got to that part of the explanation, there was no way around mentioning our disagreement, if only in passing. Logan jumped on it and had to hear both our arguments. Then he promptly declared that Elena's interpretation made more sense. This from a guy who has never taken an anthropology course in his life, has never read any of the articles we cited, and hadn't even heard 10 percent of the facts.

I told myself he was only baiting me, but I couldn't shake the suspicion he was trying to impress her. It didn't work . . . or at least I didn't think it did.

At five-thirty, Elena left for dinner. Logan tried to persuade her to join us, but she insisted she had enough homework to last her into the night, and besides, we must want time alone together. From the look on Logan's face, this was the last thing he wanted.

He closed the door behind her, then slowly turned to me.

"Okay," he said. "Blast away."

I leaned back against my desk, crossed my arms, and said nothing.

After a minute, he sighed. "Okay, I know I shouldn't be here. Jeremy—"

"Jeremy forbade it. This is a direct violation of his authority."

Logan lifted a finger. "Uh-uh. He said he doesn't think we should visit while you're here. He never said we couldn't."

"You knew what he meant."

"But it's what he actually *says* that counts as Law, not our interpretation of it."

"Who the hell told you that?"

"You."

I pushed off the desk. "I never said—"

"Not in words, maybe, but certainly by example."

I growled and leaned back again. "The point is—"

"The point is that I came because I was concerned. Obviously something was up, and I wanted to know what it was. One Pack brother looking out for another."

I met his gaze and held it. After a moment, he sighed again.

"Okay, more curiosity than concern, but only because I know you're capable of looking after yourself. As a friend, I wanted to know what was going on. Now I do."

"And what are you going to do about it?"

"Do?" He laughed. "You like a girl. Hardly cause for emergency intervention. If you don't want to tell the Pack, that's your choice and, frankly, I don't blame you. That 'no long-term relationships' rule?" He shook his head. "Most Laws I can understand, but that one goes way overboard. Couples keep secrets from one another all the time. What's the big deal? Hell, there's no reason a werewolf couldn't *marry* if he was careful."

I stared at him.

"What?" he said.

"How could you keep a secret that—?" I bit the words off, turned, and grabbed my jacket. "I'm hungry."

"After that lunch? Shit, I couldn't even look at food."

"Well, I'm going to, so if you want to come, get your coat."

He slid a look my way. "I was right then?"

"About what?"

He rolled his eyes.

"If you mean the Pack Law, no, you're not right."

"I didn't mean that."

"Well, what then?"

He searched my face, then shook his head. "If you didn't dispute it that must mean there's nothing to dispute. You like her."

I threw him his jacket.

"More than like, I suppose," he continued. "If Nick's right and you haven't shown a passing interest in a woman since puberty, you're not going to start now with just a passing interest. You're serious."

"I'm hungry."

"Oh, so you're not interested? Good, then you won't mind me asking her out—"

I turned on him.

"Down, boy," he said, lifting his hands. "I was kidding. Well, not that I wouldn't mind asking her out, but I know I'd get turned down. Doesn't matter how many other guys are in the room; that girl only sees you."

I grabbed my keys from the desk. "Elena isn't like that. I don't even think she notices what I look like. She sure as hell doesn't care about it."

"I don't mean that. I mean you're the only guy she's—" He caught my blank look and waved his hand. "Never mind. You'll figure it out eventually."

Logan left after dinner the next night. He accompanied Elena to both her classes, including mine. I tried not to read anything into it, but couldn't help being relieved when he finally left.

That night, Elena and I went for a run. Afterward, we found a grassy spot overlooking the water and ate the subs and sodas we'd brought along.

"So you like Logan?" I asked finally.

"Sure. He's a nice guy." She smiled. "Easy to get along with, you know? I envy that in people."

"So you like him."

"Didn't I just say—?" She caught my expression and choked on a mouthful of sandwich. "Not like *that*. Is that what it seemed like? I hope he didn't think—"

"He didn't."

"Good." She leaned back against a tree trunk. "That's the problem sometimes. You meet a guy, and think he's nice, but you need to worry about how that will be interpreted. Sometimes I'm interested because I'm, well, interested. Most times, though, it's just because I think he's nice."

I looked across the water, then over at her. "And what about me?"

I heard the thought coming from my mouth, and tried to bite back the words, but it was too late.

"Do I think *you're* nice?" she said.

Her lips twitched, then her gaze met mine. She blushed and, in her eyes, I saw what Logan had been talking about.

"Yes," she said softly. "In your own way, I think you're pretty nice."

I leaned over, and my mouth found hers before I even realized what I was doing. The moment our lips touched, I finally got it, and even if my brain still didn't quite understand what "it" was, my body did. My lips parted hers. I shivered at the feel of her, the smell and taste of her, and my hormones kicked into overdrive, like when I'd been sixteen, finally hitting puberty, feeling everything and not having a damned clue what to do about it. Now I knew. I'd found—

Shit. Was she kissing me back? I could feel her lips moving. Or was I moving them with mine? An image shot into my brain: Elena's face, frozen in horror, too shocked to push me away.

What if she wasn't kissing me? It was Logan's fault. Damn him! He'd tricked—

Was I still kissing her?

I pulled back. "Shit, I'm sorry."

She blinked, eyes sleepy, as if waking up. "S—sorry?"

"I didn't mean— If this isn't what you want—"

She leaned over and kissed me, her arms going around my neck. For a second, I just sat there, stunned. Then I kissed her back.

A few minutes later, she eased out of my arms and smiled. "And that, I hope, clears up any confusion."

"It does."

Another smile. "It does, doesn't it? I wasn't sure myself, but—" She looked up at me. "I think I've figured it out."

Someone laughed and we both jumped. I inhaled and caught the scents of perfume and booze.

"Kids coming," I said. "You wanna go head back to my apartment?"

Panic darted behind her eyes. Why? She'd come to my apartment before, to eat or study. As I replayed my words, I heard an interpretation that wouldn't have been there ten minutes ago.

"No, not for sex. I just want—" I shrugged. "You know, to spend more time with you."

"Me, too. I mean with you, not with me. I like spending time—I'd like to spend more time—" She pulled a face. "Blah. I think my tongue's gone on vacation."

"Is that a yes, then? Head back to my apartment and hang out there awhile? No strings attached. I'd tell you if there were."

"Like 'Hey, do you want to go back to my apartment for sex?'"

"Exactly."

She laughed. "You probably would, too."

For a moment, she just looked at me, then she broke my gaze, her face reddening. She pushed to her feet and brushed herself off. I followed her to the path.

CHAPTER 12

ELENA

And again our relationship changed—a sudden veer that didn't seem sudden at all, as if we'd been curving in this direction from the start, but only saw the signposts when they were upon us. From teacher to employer to friend to boyfriend, the signs drifted past, evoking no more reaction than a raised eyebrow and a halfhearted "Hmm, wonder how that happened?"

Eventually there might be another sign: lover—but I wasn't going to crane my neck over the horizon trying to see it. Like the others, it would come when it was time. Or it wouldn't. I'd never reached that stage with a guy. One could say, I suppose, that technically I'm not a virgin, but I don't— won't—see it like that. I've never made love, so when it does happen, it'll be my first time.

I do date, but sporadically, never letting it amount to much. I wasn't ready for that. Not after what I went through as a foster kid. I'm not afraid of an intimate relationship—it'll just take a lot of trust building to get me there and so far no guy had made it. Whether Clay would remained to be seen.

The next month spun past like a carousel ride. New emotions, new sensations, new thoughts, everything so blindingly new, a merry-go-round of first love, all bright colors and laughter and music and, occasionally, a slightly queasy feeling, as if it was all just a little too much to take.

It wasn't perfect, but the flaws kept it real. Of course, that didn't keep me from worrying about them.

First, Clay was possessive. Maybe that's not the right word. More like he was jealous of my time. He liked being together. A lot. If I wasn't in class or in my dorm sleeping, he wanted to be with me. Not that he clung to me or demanded my attention. He was content to be in the same room, each doing our own thing, sometimes a whole afternoon passing with scarcely a word exchanged.

There was a sense of comfort in having him there, reading across the room as I did my homework. But I felt like I *should* mind. Such behavior was one of the four danger signs of an unhealthy relationship—a list that had been drilled into my head in a twelfth-grade health class.

Another sign was not wanting you to spend time with your friends. While Clay didn't complain about me hanging around with others, I could tell he was biting his tongue. But I suspected that was just part of his desire to spend time together, so that would make it only one danger sign, not two. One quarter of the list, not half. Or maybe I was rationalizing away something I didn't want to see.

Equally troubling was that Clay kept our relationship a secret from his family and friends. Again, maybe I'm overstating the matter, but that was the impression I got. He called his guardian, Jeremy, daily and yet, no matter how much time we spent together, I was never around when he made that call. I couldn't help feeling that was deliberate.

At least once a week, I was at Clay's apartment when his friend Nick called, and Clay would always make a quick promise to call back. When I'd tell him to go ahead, take the call, he always refused, saying he had plenty of time to talk to Nick later, that this was his time with me.

And yet . . . well, it was almost enough to make me wonder whether he had a girlfriend at home. My gut told me it was unlikely to the point of impossible, yet the only thing that kept my brain from overruling it on this was Logan. He'd come up to Toronto again a few weeks after his first visit, and whenever he called Clay, and I was around, he and I did more talking than him and Clay.

From Logan, I knew there was no other girl. He'd laughed when I'd tiptoed past the subject. Laughed his head off, and assured me there was no one else in Clay's life—no girlfriend, no boyfriend, no past lover he was still pining for, absolutely no cause for concern on that front.

So why the secrecy? When I broached that subject with Logan, he brushed it off with a crack about Clay's eccentricities, and a quick change of subject. So the answer, I assumed, was no. So what, right? Clay was a grown man, not a boy who needed his parent's approval. Maybe he just didn't think this was a "meet the parent" kind of relationship yet.

It didn't help matters that our first rough spot hit right after his next trip home. He'd called me five times that weekend. The first time, from the airport in Syracuse, he'd sounded fine, bitching about the flight, normal Clay stuff. The next two calls had been furtive and short. I could picture him in some back room, whispering for fear of being overheard, and I'd started getting angry, wondering why he'd bothered calling at all.

The next call was clipped, almost angry, as if I'd done something to piss him off. I'd blasted him for that. I told him he was under no obligation to call me when he was away and if this was how he was going to act when he did call, I'd rather he didn't. Then I hung up.

Two hours later he'd called back—from a pay phone, judging by the background street noise. He'd talked then, talked and talked, as if desperate to keep me on the line.

None of it made any sense and by the time he returned, my gut was twisting, my brain feeding me all those little warnings I tried so hard not to hear, telling me something was wrong, wrong with us and wrong with him, and why the hell wasn't I taking the hint?

I didn't sleep much Sunday night, and barely heard a word the prof said in my first class Monday. I spent the whole period glancing at my watch. When class ended, I was the first one out the door.

I zipped over to Clay's office. Only when I could see his door did I slow down. It was cracked open, as it always was when he was expecting me. See? Nothing had changed. A bad weekend, that was all. Everyone has them. Going home can be stressful . . . or so my friends always told me.

Everything would be back to normal now. He'd hear me coming, as he always did, and he'd be there, sitting on the edge of the desk or lurking behind the door waiting to pounce. He'd grab me and kiss me, one of his deep, hungry kisses that would drive away every worry—

I stepped inside and he was across the room, leaning over the printer, fiddling with the buttons. Even when I closed the door with a loud click, he didn't turn.

"Jamming on you again?" I said, forcing the disappointment from my voice. "Here, let me—"

"I got in last night," he said, still bent over the machine.

I stopped. "Well, that's good. That's when you were supposed to get in, wasn't it?"

"I thought you'd come to see me."

"When? Your flight didn't arrive until two."

He said nothing, just kept playing with the printer. I gripped my knapsack, knuckles whitening as the trepidation in my gut hardened into anger.

"I had an eight o'clock class," I said. "You expected me to meet your plane at two A.M.?"

He turned and rubbed his mouth. "Yeah, I guess not. I'm sor—"

"And even if I didn't have an early class, how the hell would I get to the airport? Pay twenty bucks for a cab? I can't afford—"

"I wasn't thinking. I'm sorry."

He stepped toward me, but I backpedaled, lifting my knapsack to my chest. He looked down at it, then up at me.

"I didn't expect you to meet me at the airport," he said. "I just— I wanted to see you. If I didn't make plans, like meeting you for breakfast, then that's my fault."

I let the knapsack slide down. He crossed the few feet between us, arms going around me.

"I missed you," he said.

I lifted my mouth to his. The moment our lips touched, it was like a dam breaking and he grabbed me, kissing me hard, pushing me back against the bookcase. When I tensed, he pulled back, breathing ragged, gaze searching mine.

"I missed you, too," I said.

I lifted my hands to the back of his head and kissed him. This time when he grabbed me, I let his kiss shove back all my doubts. There was an air of desperation in his passion, like when he'd talked to me on the phone the day before. After a minute or two, that frenzy ebbed and, after another couple of minutes, we pulled back to catch our breath.

"I'm sorry," he said. "This weekend. It was just . . . I don't know."

"Did something happen?" I asked.

"No. It's . . . I had a rough time. I wanted to be there, but I wanted to be here, too."

I took his hand and walked to the desk, and backed my rear onto it. He did the same, then shifted against me, forearm resting on my leg, hand on my knee.

"You've never been away this long, have you?" I said. "From home, I mean."

"I guess that's part of it. I'm happy here, but when I go back, I'm reminded that I miss being there, and at the same time I miss you." He shook his head. "It'll work out. I'm doing okay. Better than usual. When I was away at college, I hated it. Loved the education part, the classes and all that, but once my day was over, I'd just pace in my dorm room, going nuts, wishing I was home."

I smiled. "See? You *were* the dorm mate from hell."

"Nah, I never had roommates. Not for very long, anyway."

I laughed and leaned against his shoulder. "Did you go home every weekend? Or is that a stupid question?"

"Left the minute my last class ended and didn't come back until my first one. It was better in my undergrad years, when I was still living at home and I could pick my optional courses according to scheduling. I could usually wrangle an extra day or two at home each week if I did it right."

"So you took whatever courses gave you days off? No matter what they were?"

"Well, within reason. Usually I could get something I wanted. In my last year, though, the only thing I could find to fit my schedule was a course in women's studies."

I sputtered a laugh. "So what'd you do?"

"Took it. Nothing wrong with women's studies. I think I got off on the wrong foot with the prof the first day, though, when I asked why there weren't any men's studies courses."

"What'd she say?"

"Nothing. Just gave me a look, like I shouldn't even be asking. But we got along okay after that. She even mailed me a congratulations card when I got my doctorate, said I was still the only guy who'd ever earned an A in her course and she hoped that I'd live by the lessons I learned there."

"What lessons were those?"

"I have no idea."

I laughed, and hopped off the desk. "We should get to work. Mind if I go grab something to eat first? I skipped breakfast."

"I'll go with you." He glanced over at me. "So we're okay, then?"

I smiled. "We're fine."

We were "fine" for another couple of weeks. Then we hit our next rough patch and, again, it blindsided me. Everything was great, and then, things just started getting . . . strange.

Clay had to make a presentation to the department on his paper, and he was stressed. I'd never imagined he *could* be stressed, but he was, working at it relentlessly and driving me almost as hard, snapping over details, getting frustrated over every setback.

When the printer jammed for the umpteenth time, he threw it against the wall. Smashed it to pieces. I could only stand there and stare. He snapped out of it right away, and apologized for losing his temper, but still . . . well, it knocked me off balance. When you're trying very hard to pretend you don't see things in someone, it never helps to have them thrown in your face . . . or at the wall near your face.

I could understand a young academic worrying about the initial presentation of his first big paper. Or I would if that young academic was anyone but Clay. His attitude toward his career was laissez-faire at best, that arrogant, casual air of someone who knows he's brilliant and doesn't give a shit if anyone else agrees. To see him flipping out over this made no sense.

The presentation seemed to go fine. So I wanted to surprise him with a celebratory night. I made reservations for dinner in the theater district. Then I'd try to scoop half-priced last-minute tickets to a show. And then . . . well, I wasn't sure about the rest of the night, but if things went well, maybe, just maybe, we'd be passing that next sign on the road. I didn't quite feel ready to take that step yet, but I really wanted this to be a big night, to shift our relationship back on track.

I bought a new outfit. A black wool dress. I never wore dresses, or even skirts, and I wasn't sure whether Clay would like me in one, but I was willing to give it a shot.

So I left a note on his desk telling him I'd come around to his apartment with dinner. Then I hurried to my dorm, showered, dressed, put on makeup, fussed with my hair, strapped on a new pair of heels, and walked the two blocks to his apartment, trying hard not to fall in the heels.

I used my key, went up to his apartment, and knocked. Then I waited. Knocked again. Waited some more. I had a key for this door, too, but I wanted that moment when he opened it and saw me dressed up for the first time.

Finally, after five minutes of waiting, I let myself in.

"Clay?"

"Here."

I went into the bedroom, where he was pulling on a sweatshirt. I waited. He straightened and ran his hands through his curls, his back to me.

"I gotta go," he said, grabbing his motorcycle keys from the nightstand. "Wait here for me."

"Clay?"

"What?"

He snapped the word, his back still to me. I stood there, teetering on my heels, my stomach lurching and twisting. He snatched his motorcycle helmet from beside the bed and brushed past me without even looking.

"I gotta go," he mumbled. "Wait here. I'll be back in an hour."

Three long strides, and he was out the door. I stood there for at least five minutes, too stunned and hurt to think. Then I brushed back the first prick of tears, whipped his keys across the room, and marched out the door.

❧

I lay on my dorm bed, staring up at the dirt-speckled ceiling. I wasn't the perfect girlfriend. I had my moods, too. But I'd been nothing but cheerful and supportive these last few days—nauseatingly cheerful and supportive, which was undeserved considering how he'd been acting. He should have been the one taking me out for a special night, a reward for putting up with him.

The roar of a motorcycle sounded outside my window. My heart skipped. I rolled over, trying hard not to listen for the next sign, but straining just the same, then exhaling a small puff of relief when it came: the tinkle of stones at my second-floor window.

I forced myself to wait for the third pebble shower before I deigned to respond. Even then I just walked to my window, not opening it. He was probably just here to give me shit for not "waiting" like he commanded. At the thought, I clenched my fists. I shouldn't have thrown away his keys. I should have kept them, so I could throw them at him now, see his reaction.

I stood at the window and looked down. He was there, between the back hedge and the wall, blond hair pale in the moonlight. He lifted something white. A Styrofoam box. He opened it and pointed inside, mouthing something. I shaded my eyes to see better. It was a takeout box stuffed full of pancakes. He mouthed something again. This time I could make it out: "Please." I hesitated, then lifted a finger and pulled the curtains to dress.

CHAPTER 13

CLAYTON

When I was younger, I often tried to figure out the thought processes of animals—both predator and prey—convinced that if I knew what was going on in their heads, I'd be a better hunter and a better fighter. Same with humans. If I knew how their brains worked, I could alter my behavior just enough to fit in, and not one iota more.

What eluded me most was the mental lives of prey animals. They consistently fell for the same tricks that wolves had been using for eons. At first, I thought that this was because they never got the opportunity to learn from their mistakes or to pass that knowledge on to the next generation.

I'd tested this theory. I persuaded Jeremy to chase a young deer into my ambush position, then I pounced, and let it escape with only a torn flank. A few weeks later, we found the same yearling, and did the same thing. Again he fell for it—and this time paid with his life.

So I asked myself, what was going through that deer's head when he saw the same scenario playing out? He couldn't have forgotten the first time; his wound had barely healed. Did he think, "What stupid wolves, trying this again." Or did he see what was happening, and not know how to stop it? When Jeremy jumped out behind him, and he started to run, did his heart start thumping with blind panic, knowing what was coming but seeing no way to avoid his fate?

Now I was that deer. I was racing headlong into danger with both Elena and the Pack. I saw it. And I seemed unable to do anything about it.

I was breaking Pack Law. Having an affair was fine, having a casual girlfriend was fine, but long-term relationships were forbidden. Six weeks was hardly long-term, but I knew there wasn't anything casual about what I felt for Elena.

When I'd hit puberty, my wolf brain had made itself very clear: I needed a mate. A lifelong mate. Now that part of my brain was finally at rest, having found what it wanted . . . and abandoning the rest of me to flounder about trying to figure out how to make it happen.

Logan had said he saw no reason why we couldn't have wives, and just never tell them our secret. The thought of that—well, it baffled me. Of course, Elena eventually needed to know I was a werewolf. Even now I felt sick every time I had to lie or misdirect her.

I saw no reason why any human mate couldn't know. Sure, there was a risk that if the relationship broke down, she might betray him. But what sane woman would reveal such a thing, knowing that the Pack would be forced to kill her to protect itself?

Yet none of that applied to Elena. No matter how angry she might get with me, betrayal wasn't in her nature. With Elena, the true danger was that she would hear what I was and run the other way, never to return. What I had to do, then, was bide my time. Wait until she loved me enough, and trusted me enough, to hear the words and stay.

Now if I could only get that far before I scared her off for good. That was proving increasingly difficult. Like the deer, I was already hurtling toward peril, sealing my fate with every stride.

First, the catastrophic trip to Stonehaven. Talking to Jeremy by phone was one thing. Having him there, delighted by my happiness and clueless about the cause, made me miserable. Then there was Nick. He knew something was up, and he'd be hurt when he learned the truth, especially when he discovered that Logan had known.

Even just being at Stonehaven, out for runs and hunts, had been painful, reminding me that this double life was betraying two more people: Elena, by not telling her that this was what I was, and myself, by pretending that this wasn't what I was. For the first time in my life, there were moments when I wished I was human. They didn't last long, but the fact of them shamed me.

In Toronto, runs were no longer the highlight of my week—they were a chore to be squeezed in quickly so I could get back to Elena. I was Changing only as often as I had to, pushing it off as much as possible. Then, in the last week, I'd pushed too hard.

I needed to stay in Toronto. That was a given; our relationship wasn't strong enough yet for me to head back to Stonehaven after Christmas. To stay, I needed an excuse. As I'd been scrambling to create one, a fresh opportunity landed in my lap. A new professor who was supposed to start in the winter term had accepted a job offer from a more prestigious American college, and the department had to find someone to take over his classes next term. This time there was another interested party, a semiretired prof, and the department had made it clear that there was only one way I was getting the job: with my research paper. They wanted a presentation . . . in four days.

For those four days I worked my ass off, and worked Elena's off, too. I couldn't tell her why this was so important. My need to be with her was already making her nervous.

So we'd worked on the paper, and I'd put off Changing. By that time, I was already due for one, but I thought I was strong enough to hold out. I wasn't. My temper frayed, and by the end of it, I could feel my skin pulsing, the wolf clawing at my insides.

When Elena told me she was bringing dinner over that night, I should have said no. But I needed to make up for all the crap I'd put her through that week. So I told myself I'd leave her a note, hurry out to the ravine, Change, and get back to her. Then she showed up before I could get away.

I hadn't dared look at her, fearing she'd see something, a twitch of my skin, a look in my eye. Better to get the hell out of there, hurry back, and make it up to her then. Only when I got back, pancakes in hand, I found my apartment empty, the keys thrown across the room, and I knew I'd gone too far.

When Elena came out from the dorm that night, I'd planned to take her back to my apartment, where we could eat and talk in private, out of the bitter November wind. But the moment I saw her face, I knew I'd be lucky if I could get her out of the parking lot. I settled for a secluded spot behind a wall that blocked the worst of the wind.

She let me lead her there without a word. I snuck looks at her, trying to read her body language, but she kept her gaze down and her body still.

As she looked around for a place to sit, I tugged off my jacket, but she sat on the grass before I could offer it. When I tried to hand it to her anyway, she fussed with her own coat, adjusting the zipper and pretending not to see me holding out mine for her.

"I found your shoes," I said.

She stopped fidgeting. "My shoes?"

"The ones you left in the parking lot at my building. Beside the trash bin."

"How'd you know they were mine?"

"They aren't? I thought— They weren't there when I left, and they were there when I got back, and I just figured . . . Well, if they aren't yours, I'll put them back."

"They're mine. New shoes. They were pinching my feet, so I took them off by the bin. I guess I was distracted and just left them there."

Her gaze shifted from mine, confirming what I already knew, that she'd thrown them away, probably as hard as she could, like she'd whipped the keys across my apartment.

If I hadn't smelled her scent on the shoes, I'd never have guessed they were hers. They didn't look like anything Elena wore, which had made my mind flip back to the scent lingering in my apartment, the one I'd been too busy to notice when she'd first come in: the smell of soap and shampoo, with the faintest touch of perfume. There was no reason for Elena to shower before coming over with a takeout dinner, and certainly no reason to wear new perfume and new dress shoes . . . which told me I'd made a bigger mistake than I'd thought.

"You had something planned," I said. "For tonight. Something special."

A shrug. "I knew you were worried about the presentation and, now that it's over, I wanted to . . . I don't know, celebrate, kick back and relax, something. But when you plan a surprise, you take a risk. The other person might have different plans. I accept that." She looked up, her gaze meeting mine. "What I don't accept is how you reacted."

"I—"

"I asked if I could bring over dinner, and you said yes, so you knew I was coming. I didn't barge into your apartment without warning. I knocked. You've told me a hundred times just to use my keys and come in. I didn't ask for keys. I wasn't even sure I wanted them. But you insisted so I could use the apartment to study when you're not there. It was your idea, not mine."

Logan had exploded when he'd found out I'd given Elena keys to my apartment, but I knew what I was doing. There was nothing in there that Elena couldn't see. I had to keep one secret from her, but the rest of my life was open for her inspection, and I needed her to know that.

"And that still stands, right?" she said. "You didn't change the key-ownership rules in the last twenty-four hours and neglect to inform me?"

"Of course not."

"Well, you sure as hell acted like you had. I put up with your shit all week, Clay, your moods, your temper, your demands. And when it was over, I felt like I should treat you to an evening out, 'cause God knows, you deserved it. I told you I was coming over, I knocked, I let myself in. You snarled and stalked out without a word of explanation."

"It wasn't your fault."

"I know."

Her eyes bore into mine. Fury blazed just below the surface. Her face was taut as she struggled to keep it under control. A tendril of that heat licked through me, sharp and white-hot, and my hands gripped the cold ground as I fought the urge to reach for her. I wanted to kiss her, to taste that anger, feel it release as she—

"I owe you an explanation," I said quickly.

"No, you don't. You never owe me an explanation for anything you do, Clay. If I haven't made that clear already, let me state it, for the record, right now. I only demand two things of you. One, that you treat me with respect. Two, that you're honest with me—that you be yourself. If you're doing that, then I don't need to know what you're doing, where you're going, where you've been, and I'll never demand to know."

"Like me, you mean. Like I do."

She blinked. "That wasn't a jab."

"I don't demand those things from you, Elena. I ask because I like to know what happened in your day. If I can't be there, I want to hear about it. If you don't want to tell me, you can just say so."

"And sound like I have something to hide." She opened her mouth to continue then, again, shook it off. She picked up the box of pancakes and opened it. "They're cold, but I can pop them in the toaster oven. Just hold on and I'll—"

I grabbed her arm as she jumped up. When she stiffened, I let go fast.

"Just a sec, okay?" I said. "I *do* want to explain."

She hesitated, then lowered herself back to the grass.

Of course, I couldn't explain; not really. Maybe it would have been better to keep my mouth shut. But, like giving her the keys to my apartment, I needed for her to know as much as I could tell her.

"You're right, about the presentation. I kept thinking, when it was over I'd be fine, but then it ended, and I still wasn't sure how well it had gone. I came back to the apartment, and I was just . . . frustrated. Restless. More than restless. Ready to jump out of my skin. I wanted to work it off before you came over. I didn't want you seeing me like that."

I shifted, stretching my legs, but careful not to get closer to her, knowing I hadn't earned that right back yet. "I already screwed things up this week. And I knew that if I even stopped to give a proper explanation, I'd snap. I shouldn't have let things build up that way in the first place."

She glanced up at me, eyes hooded. "And now you're going to tell me that it was a mistake and it'll never happen again."

I wished, really wished, I could tell her that. But my conscience wouldn't let my lips form the words.

"I can tell you that I'll *try* not to let it build up like that," I said finally. "I can tell you that I'll warn you if it does. I can ask you to tell me if you see it starting. But I can't promise that it'll never happen again."

She pushed up onto her knees and I knew I'd blown it, that she was leaving. Why hadn't I just told her what she wanted to hear and—?

She leaned over and kissed me.

"Thank you," she said. "For being honest. That's all I ask."

Her lips went to mine again. For a moment, I sat there and let her kiss me, knowing I didn't deserve this. I wanted to be honest with her.

And so you will, whispered a voice in the back of my brain. *When she's ready, you'll tell her, and everything will be fine. You can't rush it or you'll lose her.*

My arms went around her and I kissed her hard enough to make a laugh ripple through her. I eased down onto my back and pulled her along with me. In the beginning, she'd tensed every time I moved her into any position approaching horizontal, but she'd soon learned it meant nothing.

I'd told her from the start that I'd let her set the pace, and I'd meant that. Patience was never one of my virtues, but in this case, it wasn't an issue. I'd waited more than ten years to find a lover, and there was no rush to get to the finish line.

As Elena stretched out on top of me, her hands slid under my shirt, fingers tugging it out of my jeans, palms running over my stomach, skin hot against the rising chill of the night air. She pulled back, kissing me more lightly as her fingers tickled over my sides, pushing my shirt up. Then she paused.

"Too cold?" she whispered.

"Never."

I pushed my shirt off over my head and tossed it into a nearby bush. Elena laughed. As I lifted my head to kiss her, I unzipped her coat. Then I pulled her shirt out from her waistband and unbuttoned it. She wasn't wearing a bra. My hands slid up to her breasts, covering them, nipples squeezed between my thumbs and forefingers.

"Too cold?" I asked.

She grinned. "Never."

Her tongue peeked between her lips as my mouth moved to her breast. She wriggled up to meet me, her bare stomach pressed against mine. Her knees slid down over my thighs, and she straddled me. She wriggled again, up then down, sliding until she found just the right spot, then she moaned softly as she pressed into me. I moved my hips up, rubbing against her, and felt her heart race as her fingers dug into my sides.

I teased her nipple with my teeth, then moved my hands down to her waistband, undid her jeans, eased one hand inside, and squeezed it between us. I slid my middle finger into her. She gasped, head arching back. As my finger moved in her, the back of my hand rubbed over my crotch and I pushed against it, swallowing a growl.

I could feel the wet heat of her, smell it, and the scent permeated my brain, scattering every other thought. I moved my mouth up to hers and kissed her hard. She returned the kiss full force, arms going around my neck. I ground against my hand and imagined that I was inside her.

When I thrust up, she nipped my lip, just hard enough to draw blood. I felt her tense as she tasted the damage, but I only kissed her harder, tongue flicking against hers. She started to relax, then tensed again, this time the muscles around my finger tensing with them.

I pushed into her, thrusting my hips against her, and her breathing accelerated, my own racing to meet it. Her fingers dug into my shoulders and I pulled back from the kiss to watch her as she climaxed. Her lips parted, eyes rolling up. A soft growl rolled up from her throat, and I lost it, thrusting against her, barely able to see her through the haze of my own climax.

A few moments later, her grip on my shoulders relaxed, and she pulled back, exhaling in a long sigh. Then she paused and wiped something from my shoulder. I caught the scent of blood on her fingers.

"Sorry," she murmured. "I didn't mean to—"

"Hear me complaining?"

A soft laugh. "No."

"Then don't apologize."

She rolled off me, shivered, then slid her hands to my waistband. "Now, your turn."

"I'm good."

"Hmm?" She looked into my eyes, then blushed. "Ah, okay, then." Another chuckle. "I'll get you next time."

I reached up and pulled her onto me again. She started to lie down with me, then stopped and looked around.

"What's wrong?" I asked through a yawn.

"Uh, just realizing that we're lying on the ground, half naked, about twenty feet from my dorm building."

"See anyone around?"

"No."

"Then don't worry about it. If I sm—see anyone, I'll tell you." I yawned, gulping fresh air to wake my brain before I slipped again. "And you're not half naked. Just me." I straightened her coat over her shoulders. "There. Lie down on me again, and no one will see anything."

"Except me lying on the ground in the middle of November, on top of a professor."

"Stop worrying. I won't let anyone see you."

She grinned down at me. "You'll protect me?"

"Always."

As she looked into my eyes, her cheeks reddened slightly, and she ducked her gaze, almost shyly. Then she kissed my chin, snuggled up, and relaxed against me.

November turned to December before the university told me I had the teaching position. By then, though, I'd already come up with an alternate plan. I'd stay and work on that second proposed paper, whether the university chose to support me in it or not.

Two days before my monthly trip home, when I'd planned to tell Jeremy I was staying, the department gave me the news. If my decision to accept surprised Jeremy, he gave no sign of it, just told me he was proud of me. That made me feel just about as good as when Elena had thanked me for my honesty. I reminded myself that I was on the road to truth. I'd just have to earn forgiveness once I got there.

The next week, as Elena and I headed to High Park for a run, a light snow started to fall and we decided to forgo jogging and enjoy the mild winter night. We'd been out for about an hour when we passed a huge evergreen on a corner. As we walked by, the tree suddenly lit up in a blaze of colored lights.

Elena jumped back, then shook her head. "Must be on a timer."

I walked a couple more steps before I realized she was no longer beside me. I looked back to see her still in front of the evergreen, looking up at it. When she glanced my way, her eyes shone brighter than the tree lights.

"Do you like Christmas?" she asked.

I blinked. "Um, sure. I guess."

She laughed. "Not big on the holidays, huh?" She caught up with me and resumed walking. "Christmas can be stressful. All that pressure—buy the right gifts, spend too much money, hang out with relatives . . . not that I ever—well, I've *heard* it can be stressful."

"It isn't. Not for me, anyway. We're pretty laid back about the holidays. And I do like Christmas, I just never considered it before. How about you?"

I asked on reflex, then wished I hadn't. From the look she'd given the tree, I knew Christmas meant something special to her. Yet I also knew that if it brought back any happy memories, they'd be bittersweet, the vague remembrances of those few years before her parents had died. Since then she'd have spent the holidays alone, maybe with foster families, but still alone in every way that counted.

She turned to look out at the street and let the shadows swallow her expression. Before I could say anything, she looked back at me, eyes bright again.

"When do you go home?" she asked.

"Go—?"

"For the holidays. I was just thinking, maybe we could do a little Christmas of our own, before you leave. Nothing big, maybe presents and a nice dinner. Just . . . something. If that's okay with you."

I looked at her, then made a decision. "I'm not going home."

"But—"

"I need to have that paper done by the end of the year, remember? So I'll stay here, have Christmas with you, and go home for the first week of the new year."

"You're almost done with the paper. You should spend Christmas with—"

"They'll wait. Everyone usually comes down for a couple of weeks anyway, and they don't care exactly when we celebrate it. If someone can't make it, everyone else waits."

Her smile turned wistful. "That must be nice." She looked at me. "If it's really okay—"

"It is."

I put my arm around her waist and we started walking again.

I'd call Jeremy tomorrow. We'd rescheduled Christmas for others before, and the holidays weren't really a big deal for the Pack, just another excuse to get together. For Elena, though, Christmas obviously *was* a big deal. Or it would be this year. I'd make sure of that.

CHAPTER 14

CLAYTON

What I knew about Christmas could be summed up in three words: holiday, presents, and food. For the Pack, that's what it was—an excuse to take two weeks off work, hang out together, and eat. The gift exchange was the only thing that differentiated it from an extended summer Meet.

As for the customs, traditions, and spiritual significance of Christmas, I understood the last best, having studied the religious aspects of Christmas in relation to non-Christian midwinter celebrations. Yet I doubted that Elena's idea of a perfect Christmas meant listening to me expound on Christianity's adaptations of Mithraic and winter solstice celebrations . . . though I could always fall back on that if things went wrong.

What Elena wanted was something closer to the Pack's interpretation of the holiday: a celebration of family. To her, though, that meant more than food and gifts and time together. As I'd seen in her face when she'd looked at that tree, she wanted trappings, all the things that meant Christmas. And I'd give them to her. As soon as I figured out what they all were.

"First we need a tree," I said.

Elena stopped drying a plate and looked at me, nose scrunching. We were in my tiny apartment kitchen, doing the dinner dishes.

"A tree . . ." she said slowly.

"That's where I thought we'd start."

"With a . . . tree . . . ?"

"Right. Or should we buy the decorations first?"

"Decor—" She laughed. "Oh, you mean a *Christmas* tree. Context, Clay. You must learn the fine art of conversational context." She slid the plate onto the shelf. "A tree would be nice. Is it too soon?" She leaned over the counter to squint at the dining-room calendar. Her lips moved as she counted. "Just over three weeks—it should last that long. When do you want to get it?"

"Tomorrow. We'll stop by the hardware store for an axe, then head out to the ravines."

"The ravines?"

"Right. That's where the trees are."

"So we'll just go chop one down." Her cheeks twitched as she bit back a laugh. "Highly illegal, but perfectly sensible, and that's what matters in Clay's world."

Before I could answer, she leaned toward me, chest brushing mine, thumbs hooking my belt loops. Her lips moved to my ear.

"Did you notice the trees in the grocery store lot? Hint: They didn't grow there overnight. That's where we get Christmas trees from in our world."

"Yeah, half-dead ones, cut down in October. Damn things would be naked by Christmas."

"True."

She started to move away, but I put my hand against the small of her back, keeping her close.

"I suppose that's what you do at home, isn't it?" she said. "Grab an axe, walk out to the back forty, and chop down a tree. That'd be nice."

A wistful look, then she brightened. "Oh, wait a sec. There are tree farms, outside the city, where you can cut your own—"

She stopped, gaze skipping to the side. "On second thought, maybe not. They'll be packed with people—crying kids, crowded wagons— definitely not your idea of a good time."

"I'd survive."

"No, we can—"

"Find a place and we'll go tomorrow."

The tree-cutting trip did hit an obstacle, but it wasn't the one Elena had anticipated. Yes, the farm was packed, and the hay wagon trip from the parking lot to the bush was hellish—crammed onto a trailer full of grumpy adults, overtired kids, straw that smelled like it'd been recycled from a horse barn, and two lapdogs dressed in knitted pink sweaters, which spent the whole trip yapping at me.

But I survived. Better than that—aside from the wagon ride—I had a great time. We stayed on the trailer until the last stop, when everyone else had impatiently tumbled out right at the start. So we found ourselves alone in the bush, tramping along the rows of trees as dusk turned to moonlight, our footsteps crackling across the frozen ground, the silence broken only by the distant shouts and laughs of children and Elena's equally excited chirps of "Oh, this one . . . No, wait, there's one over there."

We were in no rush, so we wandered, bickered, and teased, all the while pretending to search for the perfect tree, but really just enjoying the clear winter night. When we did choose one, I chopped it down. Then we celebrated the victorious hunt with powdered doughnuts and a thermos of hot chocolate, and when that didn't warm Elena up enough, I moved on to other heat-producing activities.

We caught the last wagon back, paid for our tree . . . and hit the road-block. You can't strap a Christmas tree to a motorcycle. We had debated taking the bike, but only because we knew how cold it would get when we left the insulation of the city. We'd decided that with no fresh snow on the road in days, riding the motorcycle would be cold, but better than the hassle of taking a cab. The motorcycle's limitations as a method of tree transport had somehow failed to occur to either of us.

So we had to arrange delivery after explaining our oversight to the tree farmer who, on hearing my accent, took twenty minutes to kindly explain to the young southerner that Canada really didn't have a winter climate suitable for motorcycles, and to recommend places where I could pick up a cheap winter beater. Then Elena's stifled wheezes of laughter got the farmer's wife scrambling for cough drops and we spent another ten minutes waiting while Elena dutifully copied down her herbal cold-remedy recipes. Finally, we escaped, and headed home, with our tree to follow.

The next day we put up the tree and decorated it. Only one thing was missing: the presents to go underneath. At home, I did most of my shopping by catalogue, as did Jeremy. We suffered through an annual New York gift-buying excursion with Nick and Antonio, but always scheduled it for early November, to beat that Thanksgiving-to-Christmas rush.

Just picking out decorations at the department store had been enough seasonal shopping for me, but it was getting late for catalogue ordering, so I resigned myself to a Saturday in shopping mall hell. And if I was going to put myself through that torture, I might as well get a second duty over with, and please Elena by inviting Logan to join us.

For a few weeks now, Logan had been making noises about paying a visit. Had it been just me, I'd have welcomed the company. But I knew I wasn't the one he wanted to see.

His growing friendship with Elena baffled me. It worried me, too.

I couldn't help but think he had an ulterior motive. The most obvious answer was that he didn't want me to forget that he knew my secret. A blackmail card he could use against me at any time. Yet I didn't get the impression that's what he was doing.

Logan's interest in Elena seemed genuine. Too genuine for my liking. I pictured him circling over our relationship like a vulture, waiting for it to die so he could swoop in and take my leavings.

Only Elena, and my concern for her happiness, kept me from thwarting their relationship. That and the knowledge that she saw him only as a friend. So, as much as his attentions rankled, I bit my tongue and invited him up for a Christmas shopping weekend.

I stood in a store corner, wedged behind a rack of clothes, the only place I could stand without being jostled and bumped. I breathed through my mouth. I could still smell the mall, though, and my brain spun, trying to sort out and categorize all the scents despite my best efforts to ignore them.

My breath came in short, shallow gasps, almost hyperventilating. My heart raced, gaze darting about the store, trying to map escape routes as my brain kept trying to organize the scents, sorting them into predator and prey, threats and food.

I squeezed my eyes shut and choked back a growl of frustration. I should be able to control my instincts better than this. Most times I could, but when the stimuli became overwhelming, my brain dropped into survival mode, knowing only that I was trapped in an enclosed space with potential enemies at every turn.

Logan shifted the rack to slide in beside me. "Really don't like humans, do you?"

I said nothing. My feelings about humans, like my feelings about other werewolves, could never be summed up under the simplistic umbrella emotion of like versus dislike. Yet I'd rather my Pack brothers interpreted my hatred of crowds as a dislike of humans than as the panicked fear of a trapped animal.

Elena walked around a corner. My gaze followed her, grateful for something to cling to, something comforting and distracting.

"Have you asked her what she wants?" Logan asked.

"Don't need to."

She caught my eye, smiled, and started searching for an open path through the crowd. Partway to me, she stopped, gaze snagged on a rack of sweaters.

"Word of advice, Clayton," Logan murmured. "Save yourself a world of grief and ask for a list."

Elena's fingers flipped through the jewel-bright colors, frown deepening, then lightening. She paused on a dark burgundy, then shook her head. As she looked away, she stopped, and tugged out the arm of a deep royal-blue sweater. A smile. A glance at the price tag. The smile faded and she dropped it fast then resumed her course to me. I glanced around at the store, committing it and the location of the sweater rack to memory, along with the other items that had caught her eye.

"You want me to ask her what she wants?" Logan said. "Then at least she won't be expecting them from you. I'll make up a list—"

"Don't need it."

He sighed. "You'll pay the price, my friend. Don't say I didn't warn you." He turned to Elena as she approached. "I don't know about you, but I'm ready for lunch. How about that food court we passed on the first level?"

Elena's gaze darted my way, then back again too fast for Logan to follow.

"One more stop and my list is done," she said. "Maybe we can grab a muffin or something, finish up, then swing through Chinatown on the way back, find someplace less crowded. And more appetizing."

"Works for me," Logan said.

"So who do you guys have left?" she asked.

"Jeremy." Logan looked at me. "And, I'm guessing, Jeremy."

I nodded.

Elena laughed. "There's always one, isn't there?"

"Is there an art store here?" Logan said. "That's the usual standby for Jeremy."

Elena pulled a face. "And I'm sure when he picks up a gift from his pile, he's going, 'Hmm, paintbrush or paper?' Let's show some originality this year, guys. There's a huge sports store in here. We'll head there."

Logan looked my way. "Uh, Jeremy's not really the sports type . . ."

"Clay said he likes marksmanship, right?"

"Uh, sure. But—"

"Come on, then."

On the way to the sports store, Logan kept shooting looks my way, clearly worried about what Elena had in mind, but not wanting to denigrate her efforts. I was trying just as hard to think up a way out of this potential minefield. Jeremy . . . well, it was tough enough for us to pick something for him. I couldn't imagine someone who had never met him being able to do it.

Elena led us to a row of locked glass cabinets near the back of the sports store. Inside were tournament bows, BB guns, camping knives, and all the other sports paraphernalia that couldn't be put out on the shelves.

Logan pretended to survey the cabinets. "Umm, you know, this would be a great idea . . . if Clay or I knew a damned thing about what kind of equipment Jeremy uses. I know, we should pay attention, but, well, it's Jeremy's thing." He shrugged. "Bullets, sights, arrows, they all look the same to me."

"Which is why I'm not suggesting that," she said. "Bullets and arrows are as bad as paintbrushes and paper. Supplies, not presents. A gift should be something different, something he doesn't already own." She moved down the row and stopped at a bow display. "Does he have a crossbow?"

I shook my head.

"Has he ever said he *doesn't* want one? Tried one and didn't like it?"

"Nope." I bent to look at the crossbows. "That's what I'll get him, then."

"You don't have to. It's just a thought—"

"It's a great thought. He likes trying new stuff. Thanks."

Her lips curved in a shy half-smile. "You're welcome. Oh, but make sure you save the receipt. And pick out something not too expensive, so he won't feel bad if he doesn't use it."

Logan bent beside me. "You know, that *is* a good idea." He slanted a look my way. "Clay must have told you a lot about Jeremy, huh?"

Elena shrugged. "This and that. He sounds . . . well, I look forward to meeting him." She blinked fast. "Assuming, I mean, that I will meet him. I'd like to, of course . . ."

"You will," I murmured.

"Someday, right?" She hesitated, as if considering something, then said quickly, "Maybe you can set it up when you're home for the holidays."

"I . . . sure, I could . . ." I glanced at Logan for help, but he'd busied himself with a racquetball display.

"Not a weekend visit or anything big like that," Elena hurried on. "We could meet halfway, like in Buffalo for dinner."

"That would be a good idea." I turned. "Hey, Logan. Help me pick out one of these, will you? I'll buy the bow, you can pitch in with the arrows and stuff. Make it a joint gift, then get the hell out of here and track down lunch."

Logan looked over at Elena, then nodded and walked back to help me.

That night, when I returned after walking Elena to her dorm, Logan was in the living room, flipping television channels. I stopped in the doorway.

"I gotta get one of these," he said without turning.

"A TV?"

He gave an exasperated sigh and waved the remote over his head. "This. Mine is still one of those old 'get off your ass and do it yourself' jobs."

"Speaking of getting off your ass, you can do that right now. Time for a run."

He still didn't turn. "You have to tell Jeremy."

I wanted to say "About what?" but I knew.

"I will," I said. "As soon—"

"I know, all along I've been telling you there's no rush. No need to worry Jeremy over a fling. But obviously that's not what this is."

"I told you—"

"That you were serious. I know. But what the hell do you know? It's your first time, and it always seems serious the first time. Then there's Elena. She might not—" He paused, lifted the remote again. "But she does. So that's that."

He turned to another channel. Canned laughter filled the room. A quick flip and the evening news came on.

Logan continued, "Jeremy was right. All that stuff about how your moods were about searching for a mate. It sounded like bullshit to me— Jeremy taking the wolf stuff too seriously again. You're a man, not a wolf. A little fucked-up sometimes, but still a man."

Another channel change. A cooking host exhorted her audience to use only whole peppercorns, freshly ground. Logan turned the television off. Then he looked over at me.

"I'm getting worried," he said.

"I'm fine."

"It's not you I'm worried about."

I flexed my hands against the door frame. "I'd never hurt her."

"Are you sure?"

I met his eyes. "Absolutely."

He locked gazes with me. "Good, because if you ever . . ." His eyes sparked with anger, then he jerked his gaze away and got to his feet. "You have to tell him. Soon."

"I will."

CHAPTER 15

ELENA

A rms loaded with wrapped gifts, I twisted sideways to push open my dorm-room door. I held the door with my foot, then managed to swing around and get out of the way before it hit me. Penny sat on my desk and watched me struggle.

I lowered my load to the bed. The stack looked impressive, until you realized this was every gift I was giving this year. They were all for friends, stored and wrapped at Clay's apartment because I knew if I'd kept them here, one or two would be missing by wrapping time.

Not that Penny would covet any of my friends' presents—they weren't her style and certainly not her quality—but she'd likely have scooped a couple and passed them along as duty gifts, to cousins, aunts, and the like, because, God knows, Christmas shopping can really take a toll on your social life.

I'd hoped she'd be gone by now; she'd said she was leaving for home this morning, but for Penny, I guess morning was anytime before dark. I could only hope she wasn't desperate enough to snag a prewrapped gift, in hopes it contained something suitable for Aunt Milly.

"He called five times," she said. "I'm not your freaking answering service, Elena."

Normally, "he" meant Clay, but even he wouldn't have called five times in the twenty minutes it would take me to walk from his apartment.

"*Who* called?" I said, unwrapping my purse from my arm.

"Your ex."

I swore under my breath. "Jason, you mean. He's not my ex."

"Whatever. Just tell him to stop phoning. Other people have to use this line, too, you know."

"If he calls back, you have my permission to hang up on him."

She was about to answer when the phone rang. I busied myself rearranging the parcels. Penny grabbed the receiver and passed it out to me without answering.

"Hello?" I said.

"Hey, gorgeous," slurred a male voice. "Why'd ya take off so early this mornin'? I wasn't done—"

I held the phone out to Penny. "It's for you."

So Jason was back. Not unexpected timing, considering that for the past three years, he'd used the holidays as an excuse to get in touch. He'd say he had a present for me. No strings attached. He just wanted to give it to me and say hello, maybe have a coffee. The first year I'd fallen for it.

I'd ended up getting groped in a dark parking lot behind the coffee shop, until he'd ended up with a knee to the crotch. I should have kicked harder. As it was, that little jab wasn't enough to deter him from trying again.

I didn't return Jason's call. Even phoning to tell him off only encouraged him. In a few hours, I'd be lunching with friends before they went home. From there I'd head straight to Clay's for Christmas Eve. If I could make it through the next few days without a Jason encounter, his "Christmas gift" excuse would expire.

I wrapped the gift I'd bought for Clay. One gift. Not even a very big one. I turned it over in my hands, wondering whether there was still time to race out and buy something else.

I did have another present for Clay. Something I couldn't wrap in a box. But the more I thought about it, the more I was convinced it wasn't just the lamest gift idea ever, but inappropriate.

A gift implies something you selflessly give to another person, with no expectation of deriving anything from it yourself. To apply that concept to the gift I had in mind was hideously old-fashioned. And just plain wrong. But couples gave each other mutual gifts all the time, things they could both use, like a new stereo or a romantic getaway. So I was giving him this in that spirit, and could only pray he didn't say, "Hmm, thanks, but I was really hoping for a new pair of socks."

"Just one," Clay said, sliding his foot under the tree and nudging the stack of gifts. "Look, lots there. Opening one early won't hurt."

We were stretched out on his living-room carpet, surrounded by short-bread and gingerbread cookie crumbs, two mugs of hot chocolate leaning precariously on the deep carpet pile. I'd made the drink from scratch, with baking chocolate and milk, spiked with a dollop of crème de cacao and topped with real whipped cream. I'd even grated extra chocolate on the whipped cream. Turned out pretty good, which was more than I could say for the gingerbread men. They tasted fine but looked like circus freaks—one drawback to having two non-artistically-inclined people fashion cookie men without cutters.

Clay waved his cookie toward the tree, scattering more crumbs. "Go on. Open one. You've been eyeing them all night."

"Have not."

"Have too." He hooked one with his foot and punted it out. "There. It fell off the pile. Don't make me put it back. Open it."

"But if I open one, then you should open one, and I only brought—"

"I don't need gifts. I already told you that. And I'm *far* more patient than you."

I snorted a laugh. "Who burned his tongue on the hot chocolate after I told him it was still too hot?"

"That's different. That was food."

He twisted and stretched over to the end table, reached up, and grabbed a tissue. Then he took two cookies from the plate and wrapped them.

"There, a gift for me," he said.

"But you already know what it is."

"Doesn't matter. If it's edible, I'm not complaining." He unwrapped the tissue. "Oh, look, a hunchback cookie. Thank you."

He bit off the head.

"There," he mumbled around the mouthful of cookie. "I've opened and accepted my gift. Now your turn."

I laughed. He grabbed me around the waist and pulled me to him. He kissed me and I tasted gingerbread. The kiss deepened and I pressed against him, feeling the first lick of heat. My mind tripped to what I had in mind for tonight, and the heat spread, confirming what I already knew—that I was ready to pass that last signpost, and had been for a while. I was glad I'd slipped into the bathroom a few minutes ago to pre-pare. I only hoped I'd put the damned thing in right.

After a few minutes of kissing, Clay pulled back and twisted as he reached behind him.

"Now for your gift," he said.

"You mean *that* wasn't it?"

"Nah, I don't reserve that for special occasions, darling, or I'd have to make up a whole lot of them. Two-month anniversary; two-month-and-one-hour anniversary; two-month, one-hour, and twenty-three-minute anniversary . . ."

He lifted the gift and rolled back to see me staring down at him.

"What did you say?" I said.

"I said I don't reserve that for special occasions, or I'd—"

"No, what did you call me?"

"Call you?"

"Maybe I misheard. I hope so, because if you have to call me something—" I shook my head. "Never mind. Just give me the gift."

"So we've gone from 'Oh no, I don't really want one early' to 'Hand it over'?"

I sighed and snatched the gift from his hand. It was rectangular, about half the size of a shoe box, with something inside that jangled.

"It's a present, not a psychic test," he said. "Just open it already."

I ripped off the paper, opened the box, reached inside, and pulled out a key. Two keys, actually, looking remarkably similar to the set I had in my purse.

"They're for the apartment," Clay said.

"That's what I thought." I lifted them from the box. "Oh, wait, it's a new keychain. No, that's the free one they give you at the key-cutting place."

"The keys are the gift, not the chain."

"A set of keys to match the set I already have?"

"Right."

I looked at him.

"Backup keys," he said. "If I piss you off, and you get the urge to throw my keys away, go ahead. You now have replacements."

"Doesn't that defeat the purpose?"

"Only if the purpose is really to break up with me. If you just want to tell me I'm being a jerk and I'd better shape up, then this works fine. Symbolic key whipping without the risk of keyless inconvenience."

"Uh-huh."

"I could get you a nicer keychain."

I laughed and flicked cookie crumbs off the carpet at him. As I took another swig of hot chocolate, I glanced at the tree again.

"What, eyeing the pile, hoping there's something better in there?"

"No, I was just—" I leaned toward the presents. "What happened to that one? Looks like you used a whole roll of tape on it."

"I ran out of paper, so I covered the hole with tape."

I inched toward the tree. "Meaning, if I look closely, I can probably see right through it?"

"Don't you dare."

As I lunged for the present, Clay scissored his legs around my waist. I squirmed, and almost got free before he grabbed my arm. I knew better than to struggle. Clay had a vise grip—once he got hold of me, I wasn't getting away.

I let him tug me away from the tree. When he let go of my arm, I shot back toward the gift pile. My foot accidentally struck his jaw. He let out an oath and I turned to see him wincing as he ran a finger along his front teeth.

"Shit," he muttered. "It's loose."

I scrambled back to him. "I'm so sorry. Which one—"

He grabbed me around the waist and yanked me off my feet. His hold slipped as my shirt pulled from my jeans, and I managed to twist almost out of his grip, but he moved fast, tugging me down as he rolled on top of me.

We tussled for a few minutes, laughing and cursing, depending on who had the upper hand. Soon his mouth found mine and he pinned me, arms over my head, grip slack, letting me know I could get away anytime.

I caught his lip between my teeth. He growled, the sound sending shivers through me. I slid the tip of my tongue between his teeth and he let go of my hands, his fingers sliding to the back of my head to kiss me deeper.

I counted to three, then pushed out from under him, scuttling to my feet. He grabbed for me, but I danced out of the way. He rose up on one knee, then crouched there, body tight, tensing for the pounce.

His gaze lifted to mine and his lips curved in a tiny smile. The look in his eyes sent my pulse racing, and I could hear my breath coming in pants. I took a slow step backward, smiling a challenge. His eyes sparked and he let out a rough chuckle, almost a growl.

He pushed to his feet. I stepped back again. He matched me, step for step, keeping a small gap between us. When I feinted to the left, he quick-stepped right, gaze locked with mine. Another feint left. He started to match it with a step right, then lunged left and wheeled around me so fast he was behind me before I knew it.

I twisted and leapt out of his way. He followed. I backed up . . . and hit the wall. He gave another chuckling growl and took a slow step forward, stopping close enough for me to smell the cookies and chocolate on his breath.

"Clay . . ."

"Hmm?"

"I want to stay the night."

He tilted his head. Then his lips curved in a slow grin that licked fresh heat through me.

"You sure?" he murmured.

"Very."

A flash of a grin, then he leapt, grabbing me around the waist and whirling me around. His mouth went to mine and we crashed over the ottoman, hitting the floor hard, still kissing. I seized the sides of his shirt and yanked. He lifted his hands and wriggled out as I pulled. Then he grabbed the back of my shirt. When it caught, twisted around my torso, he wrenched, and the fabric ripped. He froze.

"I'll slow down."

My fingers slid to his waistband and I popped the button on his jeans. "I don't want you to slow down."

A sharp intake of breath. He grabbed for my shirt again, then stopped, tensed, as if holding himself back. "I'll be careful."

I looked him in the eyes. "I don't want you to be careful."

When he hesitated, I lifted my mouth to his. Only a split-second pause, then with a growl, he pulled me to him in a crushing kiss, mouth hard and insistent, hands ripping away the rest of my shirt. Our pants followed, off so fast I didn't even notice until I felt his bare legs against mine. Underwear followed, just as quickly.

I felt him between my legs and my brain fogged. I wriggled into position, felt the tip of him brush me, closed my eyes, held my breath, and—

"Are you sure?"

My eyes flew open. His face was over mine, so close I could see only his eyes.

"Are you sure?" he said again, words coming in raspy gasps.

I pressed my lips to his and arched my hips up, pushing against him, feeling him slide into me. A moment's . . . something, maybe pain, though my brain refused to interpret it as such. He threw back his head and inhaled sharply.

Then his head whipped forward, lips slamming into mine, kissing me hard. Only a few thrusts, and my nails were digging into his shoulders as the waves of climax rocked through me. I heard him growl deep in his throat, the sound hard and dangerous, and I gasped as he shuddered, arms tightening around me.

A moment later, he looked down at me. "It's supposed to last longer than that, isn't it?"

"How would I know?"

We collapsed into a fit of laughter, limbs still entwined. Then he rolled over, pulling me on top of him.

"So was that my gift?" he asked.

My cheeks heated. "Uh, no. Of course not. I just thought . . ."

He grinned. "It *was* my gift, wasn't it?"

"Yes," I said. "And you only get it on special occasions. Valentine's Day is next. Maybe Groundhog Day, but I'm not making any promises."

He laughed and tugged me down in a kiss. Then, lips still close enough to feel them tickle mine, he said, "You know this is it for me, right? *You're* it. First and last."

I looked up and met his gaze. "Same for me. First and last."

CHAPTER 16

CLAYTON

I arrived at Stonehaven early on the twenty-seventh. I sailed through those first few days, riding the high from my Christmas with Elena, finally reassured that we were heading in the same direction. Christmas Eve had proven that. Sex might mean little to Nick and the rest of the Pack, but to me it signified a life commitment, and I knew it was the same for Elena. One lover, one partner, one mate for life; that's how we were made.

For three days, I coasted on that high, enjoying my visit, playing with Nick, hanging out with Jeremy, hunting with the Pack, calling Elena when I could, for once feeling no guilt, no warring loyalties. Whatever came, we'd work through it.

Not having Logan at Stonehaven helped with the guilt. Since I'd planned to come home late, he'd decided to spend Christmas at his half-sister's place. They weren't a tight-knit family—never had been—but they liked to maintain the illusion of closeness at Christmas, and if he skipped out, he'd feel the cold front all year.

While I was in a great mood, Nick seemed off, one minute bouncing along on whatever adventure I suggested, talking nonstop, the next minute reflective and quiet. I'd catch him studying me with an odd look on his face, or turn and see him hovering in the doorway, as if waiting for me to acknowledge him before he'd enter. I asked him if anything was wrong— trouble with his human friends, problems with women, tension with his father—but he'd just give me that piercing look, then mutter something and walk away.

On the second night, as I waited for Nick in the sunroom, I watched the snow falling outside the window. It reminded me of Christmas night, when Elena and I had gone out after dinner. We'd hoped the long trek to

High Park would give time for our turkey dinner to settle so we could run, but when we got there, Elena was still stuffed, so we'd walked through the ravine instead.

When it had started to snow, I'd pulled her to the side for a warm-up. As we'd kissed, I'd slid my hand under her shirt and she'd jumped, laughing at my cold fingers. When I'd asked if I should stop, she'd smiled, unzipped her jacket, unbuttoned her shirt, and let it fall open, braless underneath. I'd grabbed her under the armpits and lifted her up, mouth going to her breast, her nipple cold and hard against the heat of my tongue—

"There you are!"

I jumped as Nick swung through the sunroom doorway.

"Ready for that run?" he said.

"In a minute," I said, brushing past him.

"What?" He followed me into the hall. "Where are you going now?"

"Shower."

"Shower? It's ten o'clock at night. What the hell do you need—?"

I bounded up the stairs to my room, cutting him short as I closed the door behind me.

When I came out, I found Nick in the guest room, snappish, almost sullen, declaring he didn't want to go for a run anymore. After ten minutes of teasing and cajoling, he gave in, but grudgingly, as if he was doing me a favor. As I ushered him from the room, I decided I'd talk to Antonio in the morning, see if anything was wrong at home.

We finished our run in the early hours of the morning. Still in wolf form, we stretched out in the snow and dozed. Jeremy, Antonio, and Peter weren't back from their evening in Syracuse, and probably wouldn't be for an hour or more.

When the car sounded in the drive, we roused ourselves to Change. The rousing part came harder for me—I'd been in the midst of a sleepy daydream about Elena, and was reluctant to leave it. So by the time I was pulling on my pants, Nick was already done. I was buttoning up when I noticed him standing, uncharacteristically silent, behind me.

"Trying to sneak up?" I said without turning. "Thought you knew better by now."

"What's on your back, Clay?"

"Huh?"

I reached over my shoulder, and found healing nail-tracks from Elena. I grabbed my shirt and twisted around.

"Did I lie in the mud again?" I said. "Never fails. Spring, summer, winter, fall, if there's mud back here, I'll find it."

"There are scratches on your back, Clay."

"Yeah? Figures. The ravines up in Toronto? They're in the middle of the damned city. Only safe way to run is through forest so thick I get covered in scratches."

He said nothing as I pulled on my shirt. Then he looked at me.

"You aren't going to tell me, are you?" he said quietly.

"I'll tell you I'm starving—if you can't hear my stomach growling already." I headed for the path. "Jeremy better not have forgotten the takeout this time. And it better not be curry. Last time he brought curry . . ."

I kept talking, filling the space as fast as I could. I was almost at the house before I realized Nick wasn't behind me.

The next day, Nick and I picked Logan up at the airport, and the pressure started almost the moment he got off the plane. We went to collect his luggage, and as soon as Nick got separated from us by the crowd, Logan glanced around, then asked, "Have you told them yet?"

I shook my head.

"Are you going to tell them? And I don't mean someday. You have to tell at least Jeremy, before he figures it out." He grabbed his suitcase from the conveyor belt. "Christ, I can't believe they haven't *all* figured it out by now. Every time they start floating theories about your good mood, it's all I can do to keep from groaning. Guess when it's the last thing you expect, it's the last thing you see, no matter how obvious it is."

I snagged his other bag and hefted it onto my shoulder.

"They're going to figure it out, Clay. Remember what Plato said: 'Once you eliminate the impossible, whatever remains, no matter how improbable, must be the truth.'" He pulled a face. "Or was that Sherlock Holmes? Damn, I need a break. Two weeks after my last exam and I'm still reeling. But the point is—"

"Nick!" I called, lifting my hand.

A dark head in the crowd turned. Nick threw up his hands and hurried over to us.

I'd been hoping that once Logan arrived, it would be easier to phone Elena. Nick didn't follow at my heels all day, but at any given moment he was liable to drop whatever he was doing and seek me out for a change of activity. If I announced I was going into town, he'd want to join me. And if I didn't announce it, he'd know something was up—I never left Stonehaven without asking whether he wanted to come along. So I'd been getting by on short, furtive calls when he was busy.

With Logan around, Nick would have someone else to hang out with. Or so I thought. Yet I'd wait for the two of them to get talking, then sneak from the room . . . only to hear Nick's footsteps in the hall before I could even finish dialing Elena's number.

"You want some help?" Logan asked, after my third attempt of the day was thwarted.

"In return for what?"

His eyes widened in feigned outrage. "Geez, maybe a thank-you, if it wouldn't be too much to ask."

"Yeah, okay. I'd appreciate it. Thanks."

"Good. After dinner, then, I'll tell Nick I'm calling a friend. Let me talk to Elena for a bit—"

"A bit?"

He shrugged. "Fifteen, twenty minutes . . ."

"And it's *me* you're helping by making this call, right?"

"So I'll chat, make it look good, then you slip in and take over, and I'll keep Nick occupied for a few minutes."

"A *few* minutes?"

"Hey, I'm doing my best here. You in?"

I paused. "You have to call collect. Then I pay Elena back."

"Will do." He paused, expectantly, then looked at me. " . . . and where's the 'Gee, thank you, Logan, you're such a pal'?"

I snorted and headed for the kitchen to start dinner.

After we ate, Logan told us he was going to call a friend, and left us in the weight room. I gave him fifteen minutes with Elena, then headed upstairs. When I got there, though, he took another ten minutes "saying good-bye," meaning I got to talk to her for exactly sixty-five seconds before I heard a creak in the hall.

Logan stalled Nick while I signed off. When I got in the hall, Nick was standing there with a look on his face that I hadn't seen since we were teens, and I'd gotten into a scrap at his friend's party.

"I want to talk to you, Clayton," he said, barely unlocking his jaw enough to get the words out.

"Sure," Logan said. "Let's all talk. Better yet, let's go into town, get a drink—"

"I want to talk to Clay."

Logan laughed. "Why the hell would you want to do that? *I* am, by far, the more engaging conversationalist. Come on, let's grab our coats. Hey, did I tell you about my Christmas Eve? Had all-star wrestling, right in my sister's living room. Her husband and my brother were absolutely wasted, started bickering about—"

"Who's Elena?" Nick cut in.

"The girl I just called," Logan said. "Friend of mine from school. We went out a few times, didn't really go anywhere, you know how it is. Stayed friends, though, which is—"

"It's okay," I said. "I've got this."

Logan shot me a "You sure?" look. I nodded and waved Nick to my room.

"Why didn't you tell me?" Nick said before I could start.

"I was going to, but—"

"Twenty years, Clay. We've been pals for twenty years and I have never—*never*—kept anything from you."

"Yeah, I know, but—"

"For fifteen years, I've been trying to get you a girl. Fifteen years of worrying about why you didn't want one, feeling bad for you, wondering what I could do. 'Cause I'm your friend, and I feel like I should do something about it. I give you advice. I set you up. I take you to gay bars. Hell, I even bought you a hooker for your birthday. But nope, you aren't interested. And when you finally are, I have to find out about it by listening at the door."

I pulled the chair over from my desk. "It just happened."

"And you 'just happened' to tell Logan about it first?"

"I didn't tell Logan anything. He showed up in Toronto and found out for himself. Otherwise, I sure as hell wouldn't have told him. Anyway, I wasn't looking. I met someone and it just . . . happened."

He struggled to keep his scowl, but a tiny smile broke through. "About time."

"Guess it took the right girl. Even then, it was a while before I figured it out, but we've been going out for a while, so—"

"Going out?"

"Yeah."

"How long?"

I shrugged. "Couple months now."

"Couple—" Nick groaned and thumped backward onto my bed. "Damn it, Clay, *this* is why you should have talked to me. I always said, you get interested in a girl, talk to me."

"I'm doing fine."

He lifted his head. "You've been seeing the same girl for months. You don't have to do that. Yeah, sure, that's what they might like. And sometimes, it's what they expect. That's why you have to be careful. You have to let them know, right up front, what you're looking for—a little fun, no strings attached. Be honest, that's what my dad always said. Don't ever let them think it's going to turn into something else, and if they do, apologize for the misunderstanding and cut out. Be nice, be respectful, but most of all, be honest."

This was why I hadn't been looking forward to telling Nick about Elena. "This is what I want. Elena and I— It's not—"

"You're in love," he said.

"What?"

"You're in love. She's the most amazing girl you've ever met and you want to spend the rest of your life with her."

"Uh, yeah."

"And that's why you didn't tell me. Because of the whole 'no long-term relationships' rule. You didn't want to tell me something that could get me into trouble with the Pack."

"Yeah . . ."

He leaned forward and thumped me on the back. "I'm still pissed, but I understand."

"You do . . . ?"

"Your secret is safe with me. No need for the others to find out. So when does your term end?"

"April."

A small, almost superior smile. "Should be just about right. For now, though, it's my turn to educate you. I've been waiting a long time for this. Make up for all those days you left me in the woods to help me get better at tracking. I know tricks you wouldn't believe—make your girlfriend so happy she'll never let you out of bed."

"Thanks, but I think I'm doing pretty good—"

"Sure you are." That smile again. "Now, the first thing you need to remember is that girls aren't like us. They need foreplay—the more the better. It's like exercise. If you want to get the most out of it, you can't skip the warm-up. Takes time and it can be frustrating, but it's worth the effort . . ."

I considered telling him that Elena didn't seem to need much warming up, but he looked so happy at finally having the chance to advise me that I couldn't bring myself to interrupt.

My last night at Stonehaven I had a dream. I don't have them often, and when I do, it's usually a mishmash of images. This one came as clear as a daydream.

I was at Stonehaven with Elena. We were out back. Running—only I'd Changed to wolf form and was play-chasing her, the sound of her laughter leading me. Finally, I saw her hiding in the bushes, naked, peering out and trying not to laugh. I snuck up behind her and dropped into a crouch. When I pounced, I was careful, making sure I hit her only with my body weight, keeping my fangs and claws clear of her bare skin. When I pinned her, I resisted the urge to put my mouth around her throat, even in play.

She laughed and crawled out from under me, and I Changed back right there beside her as she waited, patient and unperturbed. When I finished catching my breath, she jumped up and ran again, and I chased her, catching her easily this time. We fell, laughing and rolling, then kissing and groping, working each other to a fever pitch before I slid inside her.

We started rolling again, mock wrestling as we made love. Her teeth nipped at my upper arm, her nails dug into my back, each dart of pain only adding to the pleasure. My mouth went to her shoulder. I felt her skin there, under my teeth, but held back, knowing I couldn't. One last thrust and I came, and as I did, my teeth closed on her shoulder, chomping down in a hard bite. I pulled back, but it was too late.

I wiped the blood from her shoulder.

"I'm sorry," I murmured.

Only I didn't feel sorry. I felt relieved.

I woke up streaming sweat. I pressed my palms to my eyes and tried to push back the images. But it wasn't the images that were making my heart pound—it was that overwhelming sense of relief.

As I gulped air, my door eased open. Jeremy looked around the edge.

"You cried out," he said.

"Me?" I took a deep breath and shoved the covers off me. They were soaked with sweat. "Nightmare, I think. Can't remember." A pause, heart thudding, then I forced myself to look up at him. "Did I . . . say anything?"

He shook his head. "Just a shout."

I mopped my face on the sheet, then kicked it off the bed and lay down, hoping he'd leave. All went quiet, but I could still hear his breathing.

After another couple of minutes, he said, "If you ever want to move out, Clayton, you can. Things change. I know that. Most kids grow up saying they never want to leave home." A small laugh. "You were never *most* kids, but I still didn't expect you to stay forever. If you're staying because you think I need you—the company, the protection—then, as much as I appreciate that, it isn't necessary. I'd be fine."

"I'm not leaving. Not until you kick me out."

Another soft laugh. "I'd never do that, no matter how badly you tempt me sometimes. This is your home and you can stay as long as you like. But . . ." A pause. "Being away these last few months, it obviously—well, you certainly don't seem to be suffering. Maybe that means something, even if you don't want it to."

I mumbled something and feigned a yawn. I doubt Jeremy bought it, but he took the hint and, with a quiet good-night, closed my door.

I stayed awake, thinking about the dream. That initial rush of emotion past, I could analyze it logically. Did I want Elena to become a werewolf? Sure I did. Had I thought about it? Of course I had. Did I plan to give her that option when I told her the truth about myself? Absolutely.

The process would be difficult, but not dangerous. Yes, most people didn't survive a werewolf's bite, but that was because they were bitten and abandoned, as I'd been, left to deal with the physical changes unaided and unprepared. Elena wouldn't have that problem. She was young, physically fit, and strong willed, and she'd have Jeremy to guide her through it, as he had for Nick and Logan. Like them, she'd know what was happening, and what to expect, which is why it had to be her choice, an informed, unequivocal personal choice. Anything else . . . well, nothing else would do.

CHAPTER 17

ELENA

The day Clay left, Jason called. He'd probably been phoning since Christmas Eve, but I hadn't been back to my dorm since then. Had I been thinking, avoiding Jason would have been the perfect excuse to take Clay up on his offer to spend the week in his apartment. Instead, I was stuck in my crappy little dorm room, answering the phone every time it rang in case it was Clay. Half the time it was Jason.

For two days, I fielded his calls with excuses, demurrals, and, when that failed, hang-ups. Then, on my way to the gym, I walked out the side door and saw Jason heading in the front.

My first thought was "Whew, I missed him." Then, on the verge of making a run for it, I turned around and strode to the front of the building.

"Jason!" I called.

He stopped and squinted my way, shielding his eyes against the sun. As I drew closer, confusion passed behind his eyes, but he flashed a wide smile.

"Merry Christmas, baby." He lifted a garish metallic bag. "Thought I'd better deliver this in person, or you'd never get it."

"Thanks."

When I reached for it, he didn't move, just clutched the bag and stared at my outstretched hand. Then, almost reluctantly, he passed it over.

"I—uh—hope you'll like it." As he regrouped, his gaze shifted past me and fixed on the path leading into the bushes. "How about we grab a coffee? We can cut right through there and head up to Bloor."

"That doesn't lead to Bloor. Or to any coffee shops. But I'm sure we could find a nice shadowy parking lot somewhere."

His gaze went blank.

"I'm sorry, Jason, but I don't have time for coffee. I was just heading out to meet my boyfriend. So thank you for the gift, and please, give my regards to your mother—"

"Boyfriend?"

"Right. You've met him, remember? A few months ago? In the park?"

A flash of recognition with a chaser of fear. "Is that a threat, Elena?"

"No, it's a hint. I'm with someone else and never was, or will be, with you."

The hurt look fell again. "Aww, baby, I know we've had some problems—"

"But if you choose not to take that hint, then yes, it will become a threat. Not that I'll sic my boyfriend on you. He has nothing to do with you and me. I'm talking about the restraining order. I'm tired of doing this the nice way, Jason. If you phone me again or visit me again, I will go to the police. Is that clear?"

"You don't need to get mad, baby—"

I stepped toward him and lowered my voice. "It had better be clear, Jason, because I'm serious, and a hundred nasty phone calls from your mommy won't change my mind. Understood?"

I gave him a moment to answer. When he didn't, I walked away.

Jason didn't call again or stop by again or "accidentally" bump into me again. With any luck, my outburst had solved the problem. And if it hadn't? Well, it had felt damned good, so I didn't regret it.

Clay came home in as good a mood as he'd left, proof that things were finally hitting an even stride. Better yet, those strides were advancing in the direction I wanted, because almost the first words out of his mouth were "When do you want to meet Nick?"

Nick's visit didn't happen as soon as either of us hoped. Clay kept inviting him, but Nick was always busy. Work commitments, he said, which made sense to me, but only seemed to infuriate Clay. I didn't care. The point was that Clay wanted me to meet his best friend. It was only a matter of time before he introduced me to everyone else in his life. Then I could stop worrying.

Clay's next big relationship move was quite possibly the last I would have expected. The night before Valentine's Day, we went to a movie, and Clay insisted on cutting through the mall instead of heading out the theater's rear exit, which was the first sign that something was afoot.

When he steered me into a jewelry store, my heart sank. I knew what was coming: He'd want me to pick out a gift for myself. Very sweet, but

I'd been hoping he'd follow up on hints about my fraying knapsack instead.

Clay had never been the roses, candy, and jewelry kind of boyfriend, and I liked it that way. But I guess Valentine's Day brings out a certain set of expectations in even the least conventionally romantic lover. So I slapped on a smile and let him lead me to the jewelry counter.

A salesperson flitted over, her smile as wide and fake as my own.

"Can I help you, sir?" she trilled.

Clay waved her away. She didn't leave, but he acted as if she had, turning sideways to face me.

"How about one of these?" he said, tapping his fingers on the glass.

Inside the case were rings. Diamond engagement rings.

I bit back a laugh. "Uh, wrong type. I think what you want is over there." I pointed at the regular ring display on the other side. "Offer me one of these and you'll find yourself forced to make good on that first and last thing."

"That's the idea, isn't it?"

My heart skipped. For a minute, I stared, certain I'd misheard. When I finally opened my mouth, Clay's gaze slid to the hovering clerk. He tugged me aside and lowered his voice.

"That is what you want, isn't it?" he said. "Marriage? Doesn't matter to me. I said first and last, and I don't need a piece of paper to hold me to it. But it's important to you, right?"

"I, uh, well—" *Oh God, were we really having this discussion in a shopping mall?* "I don't *need* it. Not now, that's for sure. I'm only twenty. But someday, of course, well, that *is* where I'd like to end up . . ."

"It's important, then. Getting married."

I nodded. "Yes, it's important to me."

"Then that's what we'll do. Whenever you want it. But even if you don't want that"—he jerked his thumb at a bridal photo—"just yet, you should have *that*." He nodded at the ring display case. "Make things clear."

"You mean, if we're engaged maybe I'll stop being so damned stubborn and move in with you?"

"Makes sense. That roommate of yours—"

I lifted my hand. "I've heard all the arguments, and I'm not going to promise that an engagement ring would change my mind. I'm funny about that, I guess. Old-fashioned."

"You want to do it right. So do I." He nudged me back toward the counter. "If I'm going to do it right, I want to make sure I get something you like." He pointed at the biggest rock in the display. "How about that?"

I laughed. "You can't afford that."

"Don't be so sure."

The clerk sidled back again.

"Even if you could, I wouldn't want it," I said. "Definitely not my style."

"So pick your style. Anything you'd like."

I surveyed the selection. "I don't know. Something simpler, I guess. Any ring can be an engagement ring, right?"

The clerk cleared her throat. "The diamond ring is the traditional choice, and you have lovely long fingers, perfect for showing off a large solitaire—" At a look from Clay she swallowed the rest of the sentence. "Or, if you'd like something nontraditional, it is, of course, your choice."

I moved to the standard rings, frowning as I looked them over.

"I want something simple," I said. "But . . . I don't know. It should still *look* like an engagement ring, I suppose."

"How about this?"

Clay pulled a box from his pocket. Now it was the clerk's turn to glare, arms crossing over her chest. Clay opened the box. Inside was what looked like two rings, one crossed over the other. When I looked closer, I could see that the thin bands were fused in the middle. The outside one was white gold with diamond chips across the front. The other was yellow gold, inscribed with a delicate pattern. Very simple . . . and yet not simple at all.

"Wow," I said.

"You like that?"

"It's— Wow." I stared at the ring, speechless, then blinked hard. "Can I try it on?"

"Nope." He snapped the box shut and shoved it back into his pocket. "Haven't proposed yet."

"What—? Didn't you just ask—?"

"No. I was just checking. Even I know better than to propose in a shopping mall."

"So when are you—?"

"Eventually. No rush, remember?"

"I didn't mean—"

He headed out of the store, leaving me sputtering. The clerk rolled her eyes. I ignored her, laughed to myself, and hurried after Clay.

I woke up early the next morning to make a surprise Valentine's Day breakfast for Clay. The night before, I'd cracked open the blind so the sunlight would wake me. From the way Clay was snoring, though, I could have set the alarm without disturbing him.

I rolled over. Strange, seeing someone lying beside me. Not that I'd never awoken to find someone in my bed, but when it had happened, it hadn't been by invitation. Those first few times with Clay—well, waking to the sight of a person beside me had brought back a rush of memories, and I'd scrambled back so fast I'd fallen out of bed. Now the neural pathways of my brain were changing course, coming to accept that this wasn't a cause for panic.

Clay was sleeping on his stomach, his head half buried under the pillow. I reached out to run my finger down a thin scar on his back. When I closed my eyes, I could trace it by memory. I loved that—the sense of knowing someone's body so well that you could close your eyes and still see every freckle, every mole, every scar. Someday, when I was feeling brave, I'd learn the story behind each of those scars. I'd memorized the map; now I wanted to know what it meant.

When I reached the end of the scar, I opened my eyes. And I blinked, seeing something on my finger. The engagement ring.

"Fits?" he said, voice muffled by the pillow.

"When did—?"

"Last night while you were sleeping. Happy Valentine's Day, darling."

I said nothing. He flipped onto his back, face clouding.

"What's wrong?" he said.

I took the ring off. "I can't wear this."

"What?"

"I didn't accept."

"Wha—? Sure you did. In the jewelry store."

"But that wasn't a real proposal, remember? Therefore my answer couldn't have been real either." Struggling to keep a straight face, I dropped the ring on his chest. "Sorry. Maybe next time."

He growled and grabbed for me. I tried to scramble off the bed, but he caught me and pulled me down, then showed me—once again—the best part about not waking up alone.

Afterward, I curled up against him, drowsy again, thoughts of my special breakfast giving way to plans for a special brunch instead. His arms tightened around me, and his mouth moved to my ear.

"Marry me, Elena," he whispered.

I put my hand out, and he slid the ring on.

By late March, those two nights a week at Clay's apartment had increased to five, sometimes six. I still refused to formalize the move, but I kept so much of my stuff there that the point was moot.

Late one afternoon, when I swung by Clay's office to grab my jacket, I found a note.

Got a surprise for you.
Wait here.
Be back soon.
C.

I waited for forty minutes. By then, I'd run out of homework, and really needed to start working on the essay I'd left at the apartment. So I wrote an addendum on Clay's note, telling him I'd meet him there.

When I got to the apartment, I found the door unlocked.

"Hey," I said as I stepped inside. "I thought you wanted me to wait at the office."

I tossed my knapsack into the hall closet and followed the sounds of movement from the bedroom.

"If you're hiding that surprise you mentioned, you'd better hurry," I said.

When I stepped into the bedroom, the first thing I saw was a sweater in a man's hands, and I was about to backpedal and give Clay time to hide it. But then I recognized the sweater as the blue one he'd bought me for Christmas. My gaze traveled up to the man's face . . . and I didn't recognize *that*.

Before I could hightail it out of the room, I realized I *did* recognize the guy staring at me. I saw a teenage version of him every day, in a small watercolor Clay had pinned on his bedroom wall.

Something about the face was different, but all the pieces added up—dark, wavy hair, olive skin, and heart-stopping big brown eyes in a classically handsome face. I realized what was missing. The smile. In the picture, he had a wide, easy grin that lit up his face. There was no trace of that on the man holding my sweater by the edges, as if he'd picked it out of the trash.

"You must be Nick," I said. "I'm Elena."

I smiled and stepped forward, hand extended. He didn't take it. Didn't return the smile. Just stared at me with a look not unlike the one he'd given my sweater.

My gut clenched and I stood there, feeling like an idiot, hand still out, smile still pasted on. His gaze dropped to my other hand.

"You have keys," he said.

"Uh, yeah." I lifted my hand and tried to smile brighter. "Two sets, actually. Long story."

He blinked, shock darting across his face. I followed his gaze, not to the keys, but to the ring on my finger. He opened his mouth, but before he could say anything, Clay barreled through the bedroom door and grabbed me from behind.

"Hey, darling. Didn't I say wait?" He swung me off the floor, then kissed me before plunking me back on my feet.

"Yes, and you also said you'd be back soon."

"Yeah, I know. I got tied up in the dean's office. So I see you've found your surprise."

He turned to Nick, who was staring at us with that same look of shock he'd given my ring.

Clay walked over and slapped his back. "About time he showed up, huh?" He bared his teeth in something that could be passed off as a smile. "For a guy who doesn't believe in working, you've been doing an awful lot of it lately, buddy."

Nick didn't seem to hear him.

"What?" Clay said, smile turning brittle. "At a loss for words? That'll be the day. Come on. I bought some steaks—"

"I need to talk to you," Nick said. A glance my way, one that didn't even bother to meet my eyes. "Alone."

"Anything you have to say to me, you can say in front of Elena."

"No, that's okay," I said. "You guys obviously have a lot of catching up to do."

Clay grabbed my elbow as I backed up. I hesitated. Then I looked at Nick, saw that gut-twisting expression on his face, the one I'd feared seeing when I finally did meet Clay's friends and family, that look of bewilderment that said "What the hell are you doing with *her*?"

So this was why Clay had taken so long to start introducing me. Because he knew I'd be a disappointment. Exactly what I'd felt every time a new foster family had taken me in. That I didn't measure up.

Dimly, I heard Clay say something, but the blood pounding in my ears drowned it out. I tugged free of Clay's grasp, and hurried out the door.

Chapter 18

Clayton

I followed Elena into the hall and tried to talk to her. The moment someone stepped off the elevator and looked our way, though, she brushed me off with assurances that everything was okay. I wanted to pursue it, but I was seething at Nick and knew that every sharp word I said, Elena would take personally. She promised to meet me for breakfast, and I watched her leave, then stormed back into my apartment.

Nick was in the living room.

"What the hell were you doing?" I said as I strode toward him.

He stood his ground. "What the hell are *you* doing? There's a ring—an engagement ring—on that girl's finger. If you're screwing around with some guy's fiancée—"

"That's my ring."

He winced, as if that was the answer he'd been dreading. He slumped into the nearest chair. "How could you—?"

"I told you I was in love."

"With the first girl you've slept with. Of course you think you're in love! Do you have any idea how many Pack rules you're breaking?" A harsh laugh. "Sure you do. You're the rule expert. And you make damned sure that *we* follow each and every one of them."

"This is different."

"Right. Because you're different and the rules don't apply to you."

"Yes, they do. I know I'm disobeying—"

"*Betraying*, Clay. Not disobeying. Jeremy trusted you up here. You lied to him and you lied to me and to everyone in the Pack. The only person you told the truth to was Logan, and only because he found out your secret."

"I never lied—"

"Bullshit! You lied every time we asked you what was going on and you said 'Nothing.'"

"I was waiting for the right—"

"And what about this girl? She's in love with you, and she thinks you're going to marry her."

"I am."

"You—" He stared at me, unblinking, then leaned back into the chair and shook his head. "You can't keep this a secret, Clay. My father tried it."

When I looked over sharply, he continued, "Yes, I know about that. I pretend I don't because he doesn't want me to know, and bringing it up would only hurt him. That's important to me—not hurting people."

"And you think it isn't important to *me*? Since when have I—"

"Lied to everyone you're supposed to care about?" He shook it off. "It doesn't matter. It won't work. It didn't with my father and it won't for you. This isn't a secret you can keep from someone you're supposed to love."

"I'm not going to. I plan to tell her."

"Tell—?" His mouth worked, but nothing more came out. After a moment, he rubbed his hand over his lips. "Jeremy won't let you. He can't. It would break Pack Law and he cannot do it, even for you. You know that."

"He'll understand."

Nick threw up his hands and stood. "Oh, right. Stupid me. He'll understand. And I suppose she'll understand, too. Whoops, did I forget to mention I'm a werewolf? Hey, you understand, don't you?"

"She will."

"In what universe—?" He stared at me, then gave a slow shake of his head. "Yesterday, if someone had asked me who I know better than anyone in the world, I'd have said you. But now?" He met my gaze, then dropped his. "I don't know who you are. Maybe I never did."

He walked to the door, then stopped, his back still to me. "You have to tell Jeremy."

"I will. Just as soon as—"

"You're going home next week for Easter, right?"

"Yes, but—"

"You'll tell him then," he said, his voice taking on a tone I'd never heard from him before. "And if you don't, I will."

"Nick, you—"

"I won't let you fuck up your life, Clay, and I won't let you fuck up that girl's. When my father did this, he was just a kid. He didn't know better. You do."

He opened the door and walked out.

I stood in the middle of the room, blood roaring in my ears. I hadn't betrayed anyone. I would never do that. Never.

Nick didn't understand. Jeremy would. He'd know I never intended to hurt anyone, that I would never hurt anyone I loved. I couldn't. If my best friend didn't know that—

I don't know who you are. Maybe I never did.

My hands clenched and my skin started to pulse. Change— I had to— No, I couldn't. Elena could come back at any moment. I couldn't let her see me like this.

Can't let her see you like what? *Like you really are? Can't let her see the truth? Can't let her see that everything you've told her is a lie?*

"It's not a lie!" I said aloud. "She knows me."

Like Nick knows you? Like Jeremy knows you? What is she going to say? What is Jeremy going to say?

"He'll understand," I muttered. "They both will."

The voice started again, but I clenched my teeth and willed it to silence. I had to Change—no, I had to see Elena. Yes, Elena. When I saw her, everything would make sense, as it always did. I'd see her, and I'd see a solution, a way to make it right.

I took deep breaths and watched the hairs retract from my arms. Then I straightened, grabbed my coat, and walked out.

As I left the parking lot, I saw Elena at the side door. At first I blinked, sure I was mistaken. Then I caught the unmistakable sound of her voice.

"—test my threat, Jason, you've made a very big mistake. I said I'd go to the police, and that's what I'm doing. Right now."

She took three steps, then the figure beside her shot forward and grabbed her arm.

"Let go of me or—"

He twisted her arm. She yelped. I charged.

I got to them just as Elena kicked Jason's shins. As he stumbled, I grabbed him by the collar. Through the blood pounding in my ears, I heard her shout for me to stop, that she had things under control. But it wasn't under control. Nothing in my life was under control. I'd broken Pack Law. I'd lied to my Pack brothers, my Alpha, my mate. I hadn't even been able to protect Elena from this bastard.

I slammed Jason into the wall. His head crunched against the brick, eyes going wide, the irises sliding up as he lost consciousness.

"Clay!" Elena ran up behind him. "Don't—!"

I loosened my hold and Jason slumped forward.

"Oh, my God," she whispered. "You—you killed him."

"Not yet."

I drove my fist into his jaw. Bone crunched. Elena screamed, her voice filled with panic and rage as she shouted at me to let him go. I heard footsteps coming toward the corner. I grabbed Jason, dragged him behind the building, and was about to throw him to the ground when a hand clamped around my arm. I wheeled, fist in flight, saw Elena and checked my swing, blowing past her face so close my knuckles grazed her cheek. Her eyes went wide. For a second, we just stared at each other. Then she turned and ran.

It took me a moment to recover enough to go after her. I tracked her to the subway station, but she'd already boarded the train, so I went back to her dorm to wait. There was an ambulance there. I ignored it. Yes, maybe someone had seen me earlier. Maybe they'd recognize me now and point the police in my direction. I couldn't have cared less. I plunked myself onto a bench behind the dorm. I waited all night, and she didn't come back.

I split the rest of the weekend between waiting outside her dorm and checking places she might take refuge—the library, the museum, the student lounges. When Monday came, I waited outside her first class, and both other classes she had that day. She didn't show up.

On Wednesday, I walked into my office to find her sitting there, face pale, dark circles under reddened eyes.

"I can't do this, Clay," she said as I walked in.

She put her hand out over the desk and let the ring drop. It rolled, hit a pile of papers, and fell still. I stared at it.

"I've tried," she said quietly. "I kept telling myself—I kept *lying* to myself, saying everything was okay, but it isn't, and I can't do this."

She stood and stepped toward the door. I jumped into her path. Panic flashed behind her eyes. I quickly moved aside.

"I can explain," I said.

"Explain *what*?"

"Everything. Everything that worries you about me—scares you."

"I don't think any explanation could—"

"Come home with me."

A slow shake of her head. "If you have something to say, say it here. I'm not going back to your apartment again."

"Not the apartment. Home. Stonehaven. Come with me to Stonehaven this weekend, and you'll understand everything."

She met my gaze. "Understanding doesn't always mean accepting, Clay."

The knot in my stomach tightened, but I pushed on. "I know. But just—just come with me, and then you can make up your mind."

A hesitation that seemed to go on forever. Then she nodded.

CHAPTER 19

ELEΠA

"This way." Clay took my hand and led me off the driveway onto the lawn.

It was past ten at night and the yard was dark, with a half-moon lighting the way. Clay's eyes glowed, like a boy returning home after his first summer camp. Still holding my hand, he ducked through the evergreens, following a faint path. I could picture him as a child taking this same route, his secret trail home.

Home. *His* home. I swore I could feel him, embedded in this place like the well-trodden pathway etched on the lawn.

We turned a corner and he swung behind me, grabbed me around the waist, and held me still. I could feel his breath against my hair, the pound of his heart. Then he eased us to the left, past the trees . . . and there it was. Stonehaven.

A house with a name. I'd only ever heard of such things in books. An ancestral home. A place you grew up in and died in, as had your family before you and as would your family to come. A place so important, such an integral part of your family, that it needed its own name.

If anyone had asked me to picture a house called Stonehaven, the one before me would have been exactly what I would have imagined. A stone house over two stories tall, as plain and sturdy as the material it was made of. A haven of stone, like some residential fortress tucked away from the world, surrounded by its cushion of lawn and trees.

"You like it?"

When I looked at him, I saw how important it was that I liked it. This was where he wanted us to live after we were married. Here, with Jeremy. As much as I loved the concept of a family home, when it came to the reality . . . well, I hadn't been so sure. I knew how close Clay was to his guardian, but to set up married life in your father's home . . . ? As I looked up at this house, though, and looked over at Clay, my gut ached with longing.

782

"I love it," I said.

He smiled, a smile so wide that it cast my doubts into exile. I smiled back, and he grabbed my hand and led me to the front door.

Those doubts resurfaced as we stood on the front step, doorbell rung, awaiting a response. Clay's reason for ringing the bell was the same he'd given for taking a cab on the long and expensive ride from the airport.

"I want to surprise him," he'd said.

"He doesn't know we're coming?"

"It's Easter. Of course he knows I'm coming home. It's *when* that's the question."

Of course, he knows *I'm* coming home. I hadn't missed that. Yet Clay was the one who'd be expected each Easter, not Clay and his fiancée, so the phrasing wasn't inappropriate.

I could have squelched my doubts with a single question: Does Jeremy know you're bringing me? But I told myself that was ridiculous. Clay wouldn't bring me home without telling Jeremy. This visit was so important that he'd never risk screwing it up like that.

Clay was lifting his hand to knock again when the door swung open. I braced myself, then relaxed. This wasn't Jeremy. I hadn't seen pictures of Clay's guardian—Clay kept only sketches Jeremy had done of their friends, and there were no self-portraits. Yet I knew this wasn't him.

As Clay's surrogate father, Jeremy had to be at least in his late forties and this man, without a wrinkle on his lean, angular face, or a strand of gray in his black hair, couldn't have been more than thirty. I mentally flipped through the portraits on Clay's wall. Jorge? The friend who'd moved to Europe a few years ago? The coloring was right, but the face—

"Hey, Jer," Clay said, his voice tight with strain. "Aren't you going to let us in?"

I blinked and looked at the man again. It couldn't be . . . But as I saw the look on his face, his shock double my own, I knew the truth. This *was* Jeremy. And not only hadn't he known I was coming . . . he hadn't known I existed.

Those next few minutes were a blur. Jeremy backed up to let us in and Clay performed introductions, both Jeremy and me struggling to overcome our shock and give some appropriately polite response. Then Clay grabbed our bags, mumbled something about seeing Jeremy in the morning, and rushed us up the stairs.

He ushered me into the first bedroom on the left. I'd often wondered what his room here would look like—he kept his apartment and office so utilitarian—but now that I was there, the room could have been empty for all I noticed. The moment the door closed, I turned on him.

"How could you?" I whispered.

He reached for me, but I backed away.

"How could you?" I said again, rage turning the whisper to a hiss. "To bring me here—show up on his doorstep—without a word of warning to him—to *me* . . ."

Clay said nothing. In his eyes, I saw desperation and shame. And fear— fear that he was losing me. He looked so lost that I had an overwhelming urge to hug him and tell him everything would be okay. He loved me. Sincerely and deeply, and I so desperately wanted that to be enough.

How many times had I seen women in destructive relationships? Friends, classmates, foster mothers. I'd seen women battered by abuse— physical, sexual, and psychological—and when asked why they stayed, so often their only defense was "I know he loves me." Until now, I'd never understood how you could cling to those words, that belief, and use it to wash away every misgiving.

I had other talismans, too. He doesn't drink. Doesn't use drugs. Doesn't gamble. Doesn't even smoke. He's never cheated on me. Never even looks at other women. He's never insulted me, degraded me, pushed me to do something I didn't want to do. He's never hit me. Never threatened to . . . except for last weekend, when he'd turned on me, hand raised, eyes blind with rage, knuckles brushing my cheek. But that had been a mistake. A mistake . . .

So many excuses. Talismans to ward off the fear and doubt.

"So . . ." I said. "We're here. You said you'd give me something when we got here."

"Hmm?"

"An explanation."

"Right. I will. Just as soon as—" Doubt flickered over his face. Then he shook his head. "No, I'll do it now. We'll—"

A rap at the door. Clay tensed. His gaze cut to me. A pause, then another knock, louder. I motioned for him to answer it. He paused, then called, "Come in."

Jeremy eased the door partly open, but stayed in the hall. He nodded my way, before turning to Clay.

"I'd like to speak to you."

"We were just—"

"It's getting late and I'm sure Elena is tired from the trip. I'll keep it short."

Clay hesitated for at least thirty seconds. Then he swallowed, murmured something to me, and left, closing the door behind him.

CHAPTER 20

CLAYTON

Jeremy led me into the study. Then he sat in his recliner and stared at the fire.

"I'm sorry," I said after a few minutes.

"Sorry?" The word came slow, hesitant, as if spoken in a language he didn't recognize. "I don't even know what to say, Clay."

Neither did I, so we sat in silence for at least ten minutes.

"I should have seen this coming," he said finally. "I knew what you were looking for and when you came home, excited and happy, the obvious reason should have been that you'd found it. But the thought never crossed my mind because I thought you could never find what you wanted, because there were no female werewolves. A human mate? That never occurred to me. The way you feel about humans—"

"Elena's different."

"Different?" Again, that careful, confused enunciation. "How long have you—? No, I guess I already know that. Since fall. But all those months . . . And you never . . . Not a word. I can't—" He let the sentence fall away.

"I knew I had to be sure—to be able to prove to you that I was sure."

"Sure of what?"

"Of us. Elena and me. That we could make it work."

"Make it work?" Enunciated even slower this time. He paused. Then his gaze swung to mine. "And how do you intend to make it work, Clay? By turning that poor girl into a werewolf?"

"No. Never. Not unless she—" I saw his look and backpedaled. "*Never.* I meant that we could be together without that."

"With that secret between you?"

"There wouldn't be any secrets."

Jeremy's hands clenched the chair arms so tight his knuckles went white. "You haven't told—"

"Not yet. I'm telling her tonight."

"No, you will not." His gaze locked on mine. "You will not tell her, Clayton. That is an order."

"You don't understand. She—"

"No, *you* don't understand. Maybe that's my fault. All your life I've made allowances for you. Yes, maybe you need a mate, but do you think none of us ever feels that urge? If I've led you to believe that this is another concession to your nature that I'll make, then that is my fault. But the misunderstanding is about to be corrected."

He met my gaze, held it, and said, "The girl must go."

"*Never.*"

The word came out as a snarl. Jeremy blinked, genuine fear flashing behind his eyes. Then he pulled himself up straight, face going as hard as his eyes.

"Don't you ever challenge my word, Clayton." His voice was low and sharp. "You have a choice to make and, as Alpha, it is my duty to insist that you make it. Either you end it with this girl or you take her and walk out that door—for good."

I jerked back as if punched. I stared at him, unable to think, let alone speak.

Jeremy blinked, and in that tiny reaction, I knew that he hadn't understood at all. He'd thought that if he put it that way, I'd capitulate. I might rage, throw a tantrum, break furniture, but there would be no question about which I would choose.

"Don't make me. It would—" I swallowed hard. "*Please* don't make me."

An awkward moment of silence. I could feel his gaze on me, confused. Finally, he sighed, head falling forward, exhaustion etched on his face.

"Let me . . ." he began. "Give me some time to think about it. I'll look after this for you."

With that, he pushed to his feet and left the study.

As I climbed the stairs to my room, one refrain looped through my head: Jeremy will help. I repeated it over and over, not because I believed it, but because I so desperately needed to believe it.

Jeremy was more than my Alpha, more than my father. He was my savior. He'd rescued me from the bayou and he'd rescued me from every pitfall I'd stumbled into in the twenty years since. There had been nothing he wouldn't do for me, no battle he wouldn't fight for my sake, no obstacle he wouldn't find a way to overcome. And so he would again.

Yet I knew I had found the one battle he couldn't fight on my behalf. I'd broken Pack Law. The only way he could avoid punishing me, by death or exile, was to eliminate the threat. To clean up the mess I'd made.

He wouldn't kill Elena. As long as there was another way, he wouldn't take that step. But if I pushed him into a corner—

No, he still wouldn't do it. Never.

As much as I told myself that he'd find some convoluted way around the Law, I knew that wouldn't be it. He would solve my problem by making the choice for me. He'd convince Elena to leave me. And, as I walked into the bedroom and saw her in bed, gaze shuttered and cool, I knew he wouldn't have to work very hard to do it.

For a long minute, we just stared at each other. Then she crossed her arms, fighting to keep her expression hard, to hide the tremble of her lips.

"You aren't going to tell me, are you?" she said.

Goddamn it, why *hadn't* I told her? Told her yesterday, in the office, when I'd promised an explanation. Told her tonight, on the front yard, her eyes bright as she stared at the house.

I gritted my teeth and tried to force my brain past Jeremy's command, but it wouldn't budge. He'd expressly forbidden me to tell her, and I could find no loophole to slip through.

"I—I can't."

She lifted her hands to her face, shoulders crumpling. I hurried to the bed and sat beside her.

"I can't tell you tonight, Elena. But I will tell you before this weekend is over. I swear it. If I don't . . ." I took a deep breath. "I'll lose you if I don't. I know that. Believe me, I know it."

She nodded, gaze down, her face as exhausted as Jeremy's had been. Exhausted from worry and doubt and disappointment. Nick was right. I'd let everyone down. Betrayed them all.

My gut clenched and I reached for her, but she shook her head and moved to the other side of the bed and curled up with her back to me. A moment later, I heard a muffled sob. When I touched her shoulder, she shrank from my fingers, and all I could do was lie beside her, listening to her struggling not to cry.

More than once that endless night, I thought of waking her, begging her to pack her things and come away with me. To leave here. Get someplace safe, where we could sort all this out. But each time I reached to wake her, Jeremy's words stopped my hand.

If I left, would he think I'd chosen exile? If he did, could I ever come back? Banishment would destroy me, just as sure as losing Elena would. My Pack and my mate—two equal commitments, an impossible choice. I had to find another way.

The next morning, when I woke, Elena was gone. I jumped up so fast I tumbled out of bed. Then I saw her coming out of the bathroom, showered and dressed.

"Wait," I said, scrambling up. "I'll be ready in a second, and I'll make you breakfast."

She nodded and, without a word, sat down to wait.

Jeremy had already eaten. When we finished, he took me aside as Elena cleared the table.

"Last night you said you wanted me to understand," he murmured, too low for her to hear from the kitchen. "You're right. I need to understand, and the only way I can do that is to spend some time with this girl, talk to her, get to know her."

A day ago, I'd have jumped at those words. But now I knew the truth. Jeremy would never understand. Like the rest of the Pack, he obeyed the Law by avoiding temptation and drawing a firm line between sex and emotional involvement.

While others had a string of casual girlfriends, Jeremy never even did that. He had no idea what I felt for Elena, and I'd been deluded to ever think otherwise. As he stood there, telling me he wanted to get to know her better, I knew he only wanted to learn more about her so he could figure out the best way to get rid of her. Still, I held out hope—

"I can't talk to her with you hovering. I want to speak to her alone."

"I'll keep quiet—"

"No, you won't. You can't. I'm going to speak to her, and you will stay away while I do. Then I'll figure out a solution for your problem."

My gut dropped. I opened my mouth to argue, but knew it would do no good. I had to find another way. So I nodded, and went to tell Elena.

I left them in the study. Then I went into the kitchen and filled the sink, as if I was going to wash dishes. There was only one thing I could do to stop Jeremy from sending Elena away—something that would make sure he couldn't let her go. She had to know what I was. Then she would understand and Jeremy would see that she wasn't a threat, that she loved me too much to ever betray us.

I'd found the loophole to Jeremy's command. He'd forbidden me to tell her what I was. So I wouldn't tell her. I'd show her.

I eased open the back door, slid into the sunroom, undressed, and began my Change.

As I padded down the hall, I heard Jeremy talking. I concentrated to understand the words, still clinging to the hope that he really was just trying to get to know her better and all this could be avoided. He was talking about Elena's schooling, and how she expected to continue after we were married, and did she understand what she'd be giving up. Searching for the weakness, the way to make her leave me.

I eased open the door with my muzzle and slipped in, head low. Jeremy had his back to the window. As I crept forward, Elena saw me and gasped. I paused in midstep. Then she smiled. Smiled right at me and in that second I was sure she recognized me. After all those months of worrying about how she'd react, now she finally knew, and she wasn't angry, wasn't even surprised. Maybe she'd known all along—

"She's . . . gorgeous," Elena said. "Or is it a he?"

She kept smiling, fingers out, coaxing me forward, and I knew she didn't see me at all. She saw a dog.

As she spoke, Jeremy turned and saw me for the first time. He said my name and again, for that brief second, I thought I'd succeeded—surely now she'd make the connection. But she only said something about me letting the dog out, and I knew then that she would never see—that it was too far outside her realm of possibility.

I crept forward, drawn by her smile and her dangling fingers, calling me closer. Jeremy tensed, as if not knowing what to do. But I knew, and even as my brain screamed for me to stop, instinct took control and I grabbed her hand, my teeth sinking in, breaking the skin. As she let out a yelp of surprise, I ran my tongue over the wound, working in the saliva.

And it was done.

CLAYTON

E lena passed out after I bit her. Hours later, she was still unconscious, fevered and delirious. That wasn't what I expected. I don't know what I did expect. Even when I realized what I'd done, I told myself she'd be fine. I'd been bitten and I was fine.

Elena was not fine.

Elena would not be fine for a very long time.

Would I have done things differently if I'd known how much she'd suffer? Yes. Without question.

I can try to justify what happened. I panicked. I was in wolf form, not thinking rationally. Excuses that can never excuse what I did.

I was the only person Elena had ever allowed herself to trust, and I'd broken that trust. When Jeremy banished me that night, I left determined to make it up to her . . . and knowing I never could.

Bitten

ACKNOWLEDGEMENTS

This being a first novel, I have a lot of acknowledging to do, not just for help with this book, but for help with every short story, poem, and literary rambling that came before it. Thanks to my family, friends, instructors, fellow writers, everyone who ever offered a word of praise or criticism. Special thanks to my old writing group (Anonymous Writers of London). This novel was born at that group and, without their encouragement, it would have died there.

Now, for those who helped this book from concept to publication. To Brian Henry, writing instructor, who saw the promise in the story and recommended it to my amazing agent. To Helen Heller, aforesaid "amazing agent," who worked nothing short of miracles. To Sarah Manges and Carol DeSanti at Viking for their enthusiasm and dead-on editorial suggestions. Finally, to my husband, Jeff, for knowing that a closed study door meant it was his turn to make dinner, and to my daughter Julia, who grew up knowing that a closed study door meant she could help herself to all the snacks she could eat.

Stolen

ACKNOWLEDGEMENTS

With thanks,

To my agent, Helen Heller, my miracle worker.

To Sarah Manges at Viking US, for always going the extra mile.

To Anne Collins at Random House Canada, for all her wonderful advice.

To Antonia Hodgson at Little, Brown and Co., UK, for her early and ongoing support.

To Bev Irwin for her professional advice on the medical segments.

Finally, to my family, for usually letting me retreat undisturbed to my writing dungeon and for forgiving the snarling that erupts when they trespass.

KELLEY ARMSTRONG is the bestselling author of the Women of the Otherworld series. She is also the author of the *New York Times* #1 bestselling young adult trilogy Darkest Powers, and is about to publish the second book in Darkness Rising, her next YA trilogy. She lives in rural Ontario.

www.kelleyarmstrong.com